IN THE SHADOW
OF LIGHTNING

IN THE
SHADOW
OF
LIGHTNING

BOOK ONE OF
THE GLASS IMMORTALS

BRIAN McCLELLAN

A TOM DOHERTY ASSOCIATES BOOK · TOR · NEW YORK

This is a work of fiction. All of the characters, organizations, and events portrayed in
this novel are either products of the author's imagination
or are used fictitiously.

IN THE SHADOW OF LIGHTNING

Copyright © 2022 by Brian McClellan

All rights reserved.

Maps and interior illustrations by Ben McSweeney

A Tor Book
Published by Tom Doherty Associates
120 Broadway
New York, NY 10271

www.tor-forge.com

Tor® is a registered trademark of Macmillan Publishing Group, LLC.

Library of Congress Cataloging-in-Publication Data

Names: McClellan, Brian, 1986– author.
Title: In the shadow of lightning / Brian McClellan.
Description: First edition. | New York : Tor, 2022. | Series: Glass immortals ; 1 |
"A Tom Doherty Associates book."
Identifiers: LCCN 2022008029 (print) | LCCN 2022008030 (ebook) |
ISBN 9781250755698 (hardcover) | ISBN 9781250755704 (ebook)
Subjects: LCGFT: Fantasy fiction. | Novels.
Classification: LCC PS3613.C35785 I52 2022 (print) | LCC PS3613.C35785 (ebook) |
DDC 813/.6—dc23/eng/20220225
LC record available at https://lccn.loc.gov/2022008029
LC ebook record available at https://lccn.loc.gov/2022008030

Our books may be purchased in bulk for promotional, educational, or business use.
Please contact your local bookseller or the Macmillan Corporate and Premium Sales
Department at 1-800-221-7945, extension 5442, or by email at
MacmillanSpecialMarkets@macmillan.com.

First Edition: 2022

Printed in the United States of America

0 9 8 7 6 5 4 3 2 1

To the CA. You know who you are.

$$N_B = (B^T \cdot B)^{-1} \cdot B^T \cdot B^N$$

FORGEGLASS

WITGLASS

SIGHTGLASS

SKYGLASS

CUREGLASS

MILKGLASS
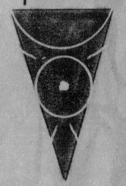

Se (221°)
Ti (1668°)
CdS (1750°)
MnO_2 (535°)
Mn (1246°)
Cr (1907°)
$AgNO_3$ (210°)
Ni (1455°)
PbO (888°)
Cu (1085°)
S (115°)

- Enforcer earrings
  - M wit
  - M forge (80 hrs)
  - L sight

- Assemblyman's bracelet
  - M aura (120 hrs)
  - L wit
  - silver frame

- Medic's bit
  - M cure (100 hrs)
  - L milk

- Mistress's ring (210 hrs)
  - M sightglass

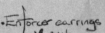

$$Na_2CO_3 + SiO_2 \ -1500° - \ Na_2SiO_3 + CO_2$$

A Brief Glossary of Common Godglass

ACTIVE GODGLASS

Auraglass: augments charisma
Cureglass: augments healing
Dazeglass: augments euphoria
Fearglass: augments fear
Forgeglass: augments physical strength and speed
Milkglass: augments pain tolerance
Museglass: augments artistic creativity
Shackleglass: augments obedience
Sightglass: augments sensory perception
Skyglass: augments tranquility
Witglass: augments mental acuity

PASSIVE GODGLASS

Omniglass: increases the resonance of nearby godglass

INERT GODGLASS

Hammerglass: extremely durable, most often used for armor
Razorglass: can be given an edge that can cut through almost
    anything

A MAP of
THE GRENT DELTA
AND
WESTERN OSSA
HARBORTOWN AND THE COPPER HILLS

N

Raggard Bay

Glass Isles

HARBORTOWN

The Copper Hills

THE
DUCHY
OF
GRENT

THE
CITY
OF
OSSA

Eastern Ossa

The Grent–Ossa Highway

The Great Cliffs of Grent

Ossan Imperial Highway

Notable Locations

1. The Forge
2. Grent Royal Glassworks
3. Ducal Palace
4. Kirkovik Rock
5. Castle Hill District
6. The Slag
7. Glasstown
8. Assembly District
9. Hyacinth Hotel
10. Family District
11. Ivory Forest Glassworks
12. Wagonside Glassworks
13. Bingham
14. Waterside Park

Distance in Miles

IN THE SHADOW
OF LIGHTNING

PROLOGUE

Demir Grappo picked his way through the aftermath of a battle as the sun began to set over the mountains. The sky was a brilliant hue of red, wispy clouds looking like the flames of an eternal forge, a scene worthy of a painting if not for the carnage spread out across the plain in every direction. Demir let his eyes linger on that sunset, trying to block out the screams and moans of the dying. He wondered if his army had an official artist. Most armies did, didn't they? If not, he should get one.

He held up his fingers to make a rectangle like that of a landscape painting. It *was* an incredible view. Slowly, he lowered his fingers so that they took in the rapidly darkening battlefield. This . . . less so.

Demir had grown up on stories of wartime glory—of heroism and last stands and outnumbered cavalry charges; of unstoppable breachers in their brightly colored sorcerous armor cutting a swath through infantry while glassdancers rained shards of glittering silica across the battlefield.

Those painted words had always been so much cleaner than reality. They hadn't talked about the clouds of powder smoke, or the putrid slurry of mud and blood underfoot. None of his tutors had ever mentioned the screams of grown men and women—weeping for fear, for wounds, or for their dead friends. They *certainly* hadn't mentioned the smell.

And the blood. Oh, so much blood. There always was when glassdancers were involved.

Demir had managed three victories in seven days, and he could not deny that watching a battle unfold to his specifications had made his heart pound in a way he'd never before experienced. Seeing the enemy routed; listening to his soldiers cheer—those things certainly felt glorious. But this? There was no glory for the medics, surgeons, and priests wandering the aftermath.

Demir contemplated the swampy morass of blood left in the wake of a company of soldiers who'd fallen beneath a glassdancer's attack. The bodies were eviscerated, sliced apart by millions of shards of glass. Those that survived looked like horror-house dummies, screaming in agony until a medic could reach them with various types of godglass to distract the mind, lessen the pain, and speed recovery.

Was that *his* handiwork, he wondered? They were rebel soldiers, after all, and it was easy to lose track of these sorts of things during the chaos of a battle. His eyes fell on one of the wounded, a young woman sitting up with precious pain-deadening milkglass clenched between her teeth. She was staring at Demir with a mixture of horror and fear so intense that Demir found himself covering the overlapping triangle tattoo on his left hand that marked his sorcery.

His glassdancer tutor had once told him that it was good and right for their kind to stand above others. It was a gift, she had claimed, and beyond the sorcerous power to manipulate common glass it would also give him a psychological edge over others. They would always fear him, because they knew he could kill with a thought.

The evidence was before him. Hundreds of men and women, cut to ribbons. They were right to fear him. He had never witnessed his own destructive power with such acuity as he had on the battlefield these last seven days, and deep down, it terrified him. Would he get used to this over time? He was only twenty years old, after all, and this was his first campaign. Would he harden? Or would it always leave him sickened?

Demir looked around for something—anything—with which to ground himself. His staff of officers hadn't yet noticed his disappearance, and he was alone but for the dead, the wounded, and the healers and priests who tended to both. The living gave him a wide berth the moment they connected his decorated black uniform with the silic sigil marking him as a glassdancer. They might not actually recognize him, but they could do the math. General Grappo, the glassdancer commander.

He hated that so much. Why couldn't they see the victories he'd given them, instead of the deadly sorcery he never wanted?

His eyes finally fell on a familiar figure and he turned his aimless wandering in that direction. He passed a medic handing a piece of white godglass the size and shape of a horseshoe nail to a wounded soldier. "Clutch it between your teeth until the pain passes," the medic instructed, glancing at Demir as if it were his doing. Half the soldier's guts were hanging out. She would be dead in a few hours, but the sorcery of the milkglass would ease her passing. On a whim, Demir tried to feel the little piece of milkglass with his sorcery, but the spot it occupied was cold and dead to his senses. Godglass was the only glass a glassdancer could not manipulate.

Putting the medic and his dying patient from his mind, Demir approached the man he'd seen kneeling in a small clearing in the field of dead. Demir knew him just well enough to guess that he was not praying. Clearing his head, he called it, before and after every battle. Demir wished more soldiers attended to their own minds as carefully.

Idrian Sepulki was big, over six feet tall, with skin as dark as coal, broad shoulders, and legs strong as tree trunks. He wore the armor of a breacher: halfplate of interlocking steel worked with a myriad of high-resonance godglass; accents of milkglass to suppress pain; bands of yellow forgeglass to increase his strength and speed; pinpricks of purple witglass to invigorate the mind. Most predominant of all was the dark blue hammerglass that was harder than steel, making the armor itself almost indestructible. Idrian's kite shield and immense bastard sword, both also inlaid with godglass, lay on the ground beside him, crusted in blood from the battle. His helmet had two hammerglass ram's horns curled tightly against the steel. Among the soldiers, Idrian was known simply as the Ram.

The sorcery of so much godglass in one place would sicken a normal person in a few minutes and kill them in mere hours, but Idrian was a glazalier—one of those rare individuals resistant to glassrot. All breachers were, by necessity. Demir glanced down at the back of his own hand where a purple, scaly shimmer had appeared on his skin. It was the first sign of glassrot, caused by using witglass to plan and command the battle. Without care, the patch would harden into something akin to fish scales and become permanently fixed to his skin. He would need to be judicious with his exposure to sorcery for a few days.

"Breacher Sepulki," Demir greeted Idrian. The soldier cracked open one eye, saw that it was Demir, and made to get to his feet. Demir stopped him with a wave. "Don't let me interrupt."

"There is nothing to interrupt, sir," Idrian replied, his voice a deep, vibrant bass. "I am simply emptying my mind of violence." He opened both his eyes, revealing that the right had been replaced long ago with a false eye made of purple witglass. Demir had asked around a couple of weeks ago, but no one seemed to know when he'd gotten that glass eye, or why it hadn't killed him yet. Taking godglass into one's own body wasn't unheard of, but it was very dangerous, even to a glazalier.

"Sounds healthy," Demir responded. "I was enjoying the sunset, myself."

Idrian fixed Demir with that unsettling, one-purple-eyed gaze. There was no fear in that gaze, and for that Demir was grateful. At least *someone* in this army viewed him as more than a monster. But then again, breachers were little more than state-sponsored killing machines. Power understood power. "It is quite striking, sir. Congratulations on the victory."

Demir gave Idrian a cool nod and wondered if it irked the breacher to call someone less than half his age "sir." "It does seem to be a victory, doesn't it?"

"The enemy has been crushed. Whatever strength they have left has fled to the mountains. Holikan lies defenseless before us." Idrian nodded to himself. "At least, that is the intelligence I have received. You may have more current information."

"No, that's about the sum of it."

Idrian snorted. "Thank you, sir. Do you happen to know where my battalion is?"

Demir considered this for a moment, going through a catalog of the thousands of commands he'd sent out over the last twenty-four hours. He wouldn't usually keep tabs on a single battalion, but Idrian belonged to the Ironhorn Rams—they were commanded by Demir's uncle Tadeas and they were the best combat engineers in the Ossan Empire. Idrian would normally be with them, but Demir's plans for this battle had required an extra breacher.

"Haven't caught up to us yet," he answered. "I imagine they're still blowing up bridges along the Tien." He frowned. "That reminds me, let's send a fast horse to let them know the war has been won. No need to destroy infrastructure that doesn't need to be destroyed."

"Of course, sir. Should I carry the message myself?"

"Eager to join back up with them?"

"They're my friends, sir. I don't like them being without their breacher."

"Ah. No, stay with me a while yet, at least until I'm completely certain of the enemy's surrender. We'll send a horse, and I'll make sure you rejoin them soon."

"Thank you, sir." Idrian paused. "If I may?"

"Yes?"

"The soldiers are calling you the Lightning Prince. I thought you might want to know."

"I hadn't heard that." Demir took the name on his tongue and rolled it around. "Is it meant to be a diminutive for my age, or a celebration for the speed of my campaign?"

Idrian hesitated just a moment too long.

"Come now, be honest."

"Both, I think."

Demir chuckled. "I like it." *The Lightning Prince.* Most great men were middle-aged before they'd earned an honorific like that. He hummed to himself, enjoying the way the nickname sounded in his head. It almost made him forget the blood soaking his boots. Maybe he would get used to this. Maybe he would harden to killing, and to ordering others to kill.

He shuddered. No. More importantly than being a glassdancer or a general, he was a politician. He was in charge of this campaign by circumstance only, and within a few days he planned on heading right back to his province, where he could put the bloodshed behind him and focus on helping his people.

Idrian climbed to his feet, towering over Demir by eight inches. "Sir, I believe that your staff is looking for you."

Demir glanced the way Idrian nodded to see a small group approaching on horseback. They were an odd mix of Ossan political liaisons—here to oversee negotiations with the enemy—and grizzled officers sent along to make sure this young upstart governor didn't make a complete disaster of his first campaign. The lot of them grinned at him like asylum fools. He could see in their eyes that they expected to gain prestige, land, and merits on the coattails of his victory. Demir didn't mind. Sharing credit meant they would be beholden to him in the future; a card to keep in reserve for if he ever needed it.

He let his eyes wander across the group for several moments, making mental notes of who he could use in the future, who might be trouble, and who he could forget. Tavrish Magna was a great potbellied jokester with few ambitions. Helenna Dorlani whispered behind Demir's back constantly, undermining him with the subtlety of a company of cuirassiers. Her cousin Jevri gladly took Demir's bribes to report on her. Three members of the small Forlio guild-family had managed to finagle their way onto his staff, and they stood to gain the most from this campaign, while Jakeb Stavri had made deals in the Assembly that bet strongly against Demir's success. He would lose hundreds of thousands, and based on the look on his face, he knew it.

It was a complex group, both personally and politically—untrustworthy adders slithering about his feet, any one of which might bite at any time. Even in victory he needed to be cautious, lest one of them turn on him for their own gain.

The man out front was named Capric Vorcien, and he was a personal friend that Demir had brought on campaign to cover his back against all the rest. Capric was a tall, thin man in his early twenties with the black hair and olive skin of an Ossan native. Tattooed on his right hand was an inverted triangle crossed with the wavy lines of a sun setting over the desert—the silic symbol of the Vorcien guild-family. He saluted Demir grandly and swung down from his horse.

"Hail, Victorious Grappo!" Capric called. The others echoed the words with various levels of enthusiasm. Demir gazed back at the group, still evaluating each person, noting the secrets hidden in the eyes of each. Behind their pleasure at a battle won, there was fear there, just like the soldiers'. How many glassdancers were there in the officer corps, after all? Not many. Capric was the only one who didn't seem to walk on eggshells. "That was an incredible battle," he complimented Demir.

"Satisfactory," Demir demurred. "That countercharge from their dragoons surprised me."

"But you shattered it anyway. Glassdamn you, man, take some credit!" Capric clasped his hand, pulling him into a congratulatory hug during which he whispered, "Look over my left shoulder. If you want to go ahead with your next plan, now is the time."

Demir's eyes found an unfamiliar trio among his staff: a middle-aged woman with the blond hair of an eastern provincial, accompanied by two bodyguards, all three of them looking haggard and defeated. He pulled back from Capric and gestured at the group. "What is this?" he asked loudly, though he knew exactly who they were.

"The mayor of Holikan has come to surrender." At Capric's gesture, the woman approached Demir, hands held out in supplication. She fell on her knees, pressing her face to the ground.

"I surrender the city of Holikan," she intoned. "I do not ask for terms—but I offer my life in exchange for the lives of my subjects. They do not deserve the wrath of the Empire."

Demir blinked down at her. He had discussed this moment with Capric at length. It was the crux of the next step in his political career, and yet it still managed to surprise him. Beside the prostrating mayor, Helenna Dorlani produced a short silver lance and now held it, pommel-first, toward

Demir. *Tradition* dictated that he accept the surrender and then pierce the mayor's neck with the ceremonial weapon, executing her on the spot. She *was* a rebel, after all; an insurrectionist and traitor to the Ossan Empire. Demir glanced toward Idrian, his confidence wavering at the idea of such immediate, formalized bloodshed, but the breacher had taken two long steps back as if to say that a soldier had no business in this kind of thing.

Demir took the lance from the liaison and turned toward Capric. Capric himself just shrugged. He knew Demir's mind. He knew Demir had no intention of following outdated traditions just to please the Assembly. Demir gave the lance a little twirl, then slapped the haft thoughtfully against his left palm. "Stand up," he said.

The mayor glanced up at Demir, then at the gathered officers. She seemed confused by the fact that she wasn't being speared at this moment. Demir thrust the lance into the ground, point-first, then leaned on it while he took the mayor under one arm and pulled her to her feet. He offered her his hand.

"Good evening. I'm Demir Grappo."

The mayor stared at his *other* hand for several moments—or rather at the glassdancer sigil on it. Finally she answered the handshake. "I am Myria Forl, mayor of Holikan." She hesitated for another few moments, then added, "I've heard of you, Demir Grappo."

"Good things, I hope."

She nodded. "What are you doing here? You're a governor two provinces over; a politician, not a warrior."

"Warrior?" Demir laughed and jerked his thumb at Idrian. "*He's* a warrior. I'm just a bit clever. Tell me, Myria, what do you want?"

"I . . . Excuse me?"

"Seven months ago, you declared your independence from the Ossan Empire. You've defeated two armies, gathered support from your province, and from what I can tell were doing a damned good job of this whole rebellion before I showed up. And yet . . . you're still calling yourself a mayor."

"Because that's what I am," she said incredulously.

"So this wasn't a personal power grab? You haven't made yourself Monarch of Holikan?"

"No," she said emphatically. "I declared independence because Ossa has only ever treated us as provincials. We are not, and will never be, equals. We want fair taxes and local magistrates, and—"

Demir cut her off gently. "I know. I read your declarations, all eighty-seven of them. I just wanted to ask you in person."

A throat cleared, and Demir turned to find that Helenna Dorlani had retrieved the silver lance, wiped the blade, and now held it toward him once again. "General Grappo, it is tradition that you spill the blood of the rebel leader, then decimate the city." She seemed confused, her eyes darting toward the sigil on Demir's left hand as if wondering why a glassdancer wasn't ready to kill at a moment's notice.

Demir ignored her and took a long look toward the city, where lanterns were being lit in the windows as night fell. He could imagine the fear of all those people, having just witnessed their army scattered, knowing the traditions of the Ossan Empire. "Decimate," Demir muttered. "To force the entire city to draw lots, and then make them murder one out of every ten of their own number. No quarter for children or the infirm. That sounds unpleasant."

"It's meant to be," Helenna insisted. "It's a punishment."

"For what? The crime of wanting to be treated as citizens in their own country?" Demir snorted. "I don't believe the punishment fits the crime, and I will not allow it."

"But . . ." Helenna stuttered, "you must!" She turned to Capric. "Tell him that he must follow tradition."

Demir didn't let his friend answer for him. "What law requires it?" he asked lightly. "None. I may be young, but I was the governor of my own province when I was fourteen. There is a difference between law and tradition—and I know the laws like my own silic symbol." He held up his right hand to show the tattoo of an upside-down triangle with cracked lightning spreading from the center. It was the sigil of the Grappo guild-family, a complement to the glassdancer sigil on his left—the two tattoos of true power within the Empire. He took a deep breath. "Madame Mayor, do you surrender Holikan into the care of Demir Grappo of the Ossan Empire?"

Myria Forl stared at him warily. "I do."

"Wonderful."

As the words were said, Capric was already removing something from his saddlebags. He produced and unfurled a black and crimson cloak with solemnity. Demir felt the twinge of a smile on his lips, his heart skipping a beat. The victor's cloak was another tradition, one of pomp and foolery, meant for nothing but flattery.

But he'd damn well earned it, and he savored the moments that it took Capric to lay the heavy fabric across his shoulders and then clasp the golden chain. Capric finished the ceremony by placing a single kiss on Demir's left cheek and giving him a small bow. "Well done, Lightning Prince."

The hairs on the back of Demir's neck stood on end at the formal statement of his new honorific. He kept his face expressionless, nodding to Capric and then declaring, "The city of Holikan is now under my protection. They are not rebels, they are our cousins, and we will treat them accordingly!" The officers stared back at him in vague surprise. None of them would argue, of course, not with their general and certainly not with a glassdancer—but he knew they were all furiously penning letters to the capital in the backs of their heads.

"What the piss are you doing?" Myria whispered.

He replied in a low voice, "I may be an Ossan citizen, but I'm also the governor of a province. My people have the same complaints as yours, and I will take them to the Assembly."

"They won't be happy."

"The Assembly is made up of a bunch of rich, self-fellating fools. I know, because I am one. We're never happy."

"You're mad to defy them."

"Madness and greatness are separated only by the degree of success. Besides . . ." Demir glanced at the battlefield around them. His stomach turned at the sight, and he found himself struck with a longing to return to his province. This last week had proved he was good at war, but he much preferred peaceful administration, where he could spend all day greasing the cogs of government and then climb into bed with his mistress. He thought briefly about how most citizens his age were busy going to university, getting laid, and looking for the next drink. He wondered what it would be like to be idle for once. The option had never been given to him. "I find that I prefer the living to the dead; and having friends to making enemies."

Demir glanced over his shoulder to find Idrian still there, the big breacher wearing a thoughtful expression, gazing past Demir's head and into the distance. He rubbed at his godglass eye. Demir wondered if he disapproved. Perhaps he would ask him on another day.

"Breacher Sepulki," Demir said, "I'm placing the mayor under your protection. Keep her safe until we can sort out the rest of this mess, hmm?"

Idrian nodded silently.

"Good." Demir slipped one hand into a special cork-lined pocket in his uniform. He produced an inch-long, spoon-shaped piece of witglass. The handle end of the spoon was worked into a flared hook that he pushed through one of the piercings on his right earlobe. Witglass was fairly common—it augmented natural mental faculties, making it a favorite among shopkeepers, officers, politicians, and more. But high-resonance witglass, the very best quality, had a habit of driving its wearers mad. Demir was the only person he knew of with a strong enough mind to make use of it.

The sorcery took effect immediately, the barely perceptible hum and vibration creeping into his brain to speed his mind, allowing him to visualize the branching possibilities of the near future. He made calculations at an inhuman speed, processing decisions weeks ahead of time, preparing himself for his next hundred moves as if he were playing a complicated game.

But this wasn't a game. It was his career, and the lives of all these people, and perhaps even the future of the Empire. He would use his victory to bolster his guild-family name the same as any good Ossan, but he would also use it to better the lives of millions. Ambitions, he had decided when he was barely twelve, did not have to be just for oneself. He had ambitions for *everyone*.

One day the world would see that he was more than his innate sorcery. The masses would smile at him without fear.

Satisfied with his plans and remembering his own encroaching glassrot, he slid the witglass off his ear and back into his pocket, where the velvet and cork lining protected him from the godglass sorcery when he didn't need it. He let his fingers remain there for a moment, running them over the various godglass baubles. Each was shaped differently so as to be picked out by feel; a comforting assortment of sorcerous crutches for his weak, mortal body.

He was deep in thought from his brief meditation when one of the staff, still on horseback, called out. "Sir, there's something going on back in camp."

Demir felt the tug of his own thoughts, and it took a force of will to pull himself out of them. He let go of Myria's arm, giving it one last reassuring pat as if they were old friends, before lifting his eyes in the direction of the camp. The plain here had only a slight incline, and it wasn't until he had found his horse and gotten into the saddle that he was able to tell what the staffer had been talking about.

There was, indeed, something going on in camp. Hundreds—no, thousands—of torches had been lit, and a large procession was breaking away from the encampment and heading across the plain directly toward Holikan. The torches glittered as the last vestiges of sunlight disappeared over the horizon. Despite all of his mental faculties, Demir found himself completely flummoxed. After the battle, select regiments had been sent out to treat the wounded, hunt the fleeing enemy, and secure outposts, but the bulk of the soldiers had been ordered to return to their tents, where casualties could be counted and control could be asserted over an army with their blood up.

So what the piss were they doing marching toward the city?

"Capric," he called, "find out what's going on over there."

Capric scowled in the direction of the city for a few moments before throwing himself into the saddle. Demir watched him ride away, transfixed, something in his brain refusing to click over, *knowing* that something was wrong but unable to find an explanation. This was not in his calculations. Unwilling to show himself in a panic, but unable to remain completely idle, Demir began to ride slowly toward the south, a fear of the unknown growing in his belly. He took the fabric of his victor's cloak between two fingers of his left hand, rubbing it anxiously.

It wasn't until Capric returned, breathless, that the fear really took hold.

"Demir," Capric barked, "there's been some kind of communication error. The Eighth seems to think they have orders to sack the city."

"Sack the . . ." Demir whispered. "What glassdamned century is this? We don't sack cities! Get back there and tell them to return to camp! Spread the order to all the colonels. Go!" Capric galloped off, and Demir glanced over his shoulder at his staff. He eyeballed Helenna Dorlani first, then Jakeb Stavri and the oldest of the Forlio brothers. Everyone wore the same expression of vague confusion and surprise that he imagined on his own face. "Who gave orders to sack the city?" he demanded.

They all looked at each other and shook their heads. "No one would give an order like that," Jakeb said. "Decimation, yes. But nobody has sacked a city in a hundred years!"

Demir swore and turned back, watching until the realization finally settled in that the soldiers would reach the outskirts of the city before Capric even made it back. Once they'd actually started their pillaging, it would be impossible to get them to stop. He dug in his own heels, forcing his horse into a gallop, barely hearing the startled swearing of his staff. The darkness quickly forced him to rein in lest his mount break a leg crossing the uneven plain, and it was almost ten minutes before he reached the column.

He was greeted by a harried Capric. "The colonels say they all have orders to sack the city!" Capric reported.

"Who gave the order?"

Capric winced. "*You* did!"

"*What?*"

"They all have orders with your personal seal telling them to conduct the sacking."

"No, no, no," Demir breathed, watching the stream of soldiers flow past him, torches and bayoneted muskets in hand. Some were somber. Some cheered the dark promise of a night spent slaking a bloody thirst. All of them were heading out to follow orders. *His* orders, apparently. He fumbled for his witglass, fixing it to his ear long enough to churn through his memories, looking for some kind of mistake.

Had he sent out a poorly worded missive? Had he said something offhand to one of his secretaries? Nothing immediately came to mind, and that terrified him. Mistakes could be made along the best lines of communication, but this was beyond anything he'd encountered in his studies.

He needed to find out what had happened, but first he had to curtail this impending ruin. He pointed at an officer among the group. "You there, Captain, hold your men!" The captain either didn't hear him, or ignored him. The soldiers themselves were so engrossed in the prospects of their new mission that they didn't even notice his presence. Demir urged his horse closer, wishing he had a pistol to fire in the air. "Stop!" he shouted. "Hold! Get yourselves in order, damn it!"

Anger warred with the growing panic in himself. He reached out, grasping for scattered bits of glass left over from the battle and plucking them up with his mind. Hundreds of shards rose into the air, hovering in place like frozen raindrops as they awaited his mental command. His eye twitched, his thoughts stayed by indecision. Could he kill his own men to avert this disaster? How many would he need to massacre to get their attention? After several moments he let go. The pieces fell, sprinkling to the ground, unnoticed by the marching soldiers.

He heard a gunshot, then another. Screams came from the direction of the city, followed by the sounds of whooping. Demir could feel control slipping from his fingers, eliciting a panic deep in his chest like one he'd never felt in his life. He turned and galloped toward the outskirts of the city, where the gunshots, screams, and shouting grew louder and more chaotic. He soon passed a woman's body lying by the wayside, bayoneted several times. The sight of it made him want to vomit. He saw another corpse, then another—obvious civilians, all of them.

A stronger man—a more experienced glassdancer—would have ended this with a quick, brutal show of discipline. Demir knew he could still do it, but he couldn't bring himself to take the action. His mind was spinning now, frayed at the edges and threatening to snap. What madness was this? How could any of his officers have thought *he* would give such an order? He had marched them across the mountains with uncanny speed and won them three great victories but he'd never been cruel in triumph.

He reached the outskirts of the city and found that thousands of his soldiers had already plunged into the interior. They rushed from building to building, snatching anything of value, throwing children into the street, killing men and women where they stood, all in the flickering of torchlight while the smoke of burning buildings began to thicken.

Demir continued to ride, searching for officers, trying to find *someone* to help him get this under control. He was half blinded by smoke, confused and disoriented, when his horse stumbled over a tipped cart. He barely threw himself free of the animal, landing on his left hand, pain lancing up his arm. His horse rolled over, making a murderous racket, then got upright and galloped off into the night.

Clutching his wrist, unable to think through the pain and the cacophony, Demir rushed from building to building, ordering his soldiers to stop. He berated them, lambasted them, and finally begged them. A few of them frowned at his mud-covered uniform. No one recognized him. Why would they? Few had ever seen his face up close, and he couldn't get the glove off his broken left hand to show them his glassdancer sigil.

"Who is this?" one would ask.

"Some madman," another would say.

"He has an officer's uniform and an expensive cloak."

"The officers are all getting drunk in Grappo's tent. We have orders to follow. If we don't do it quick, someone else will get the good loot. Three cheers for the Lightning Prince!"

They would laugh, and ignore him. Someone finally grabbed him by his victory cloak and threw him into a ditch, where he barely caught himself before going facedown in the filth.

He lay partially submerged in the muddy, shit-filled water, staring into the street. His whole body shook with fury and terror. Not a half hour ago he had pledged that Holikan was under his protection, and now there were orders under his seal to sack the city. With trembling fingers he reached into his pocket, searching for skyglass to help him calm his nerves. He pulled out a handful of baubles that immediately slipped from his fingers, falling into the mud. He plunged in after them desperately, but came up with nothing.

Across the street, the cry of a child caught his attention. He looked up to see a little girl—probably no more than four or five, screaming into the air. Demir pushed himself to his feet and struggled out of the ditch. If he could not save the many, he would save the one.

The sound of galloping hooves filled his ears, and his path was suddenly blocked by several dozen of his dragoons. He'd never been so close to them before, and the thunder of their passing would have made him piss his pants if he hadn't already done it in the ditch. He searched his pocket for godglass, remembered that he'd dropped it all, and then gathered his courage. The dragoons were soon gone, and he took several more steps before his eyes fell on the spot where the child had been.

The child had been trampled. Her little body was silent and still, broken and bloody. He staggered toward her, tearing off his victor's cloak and using it to scoop her up before sprinting to the other side of the road just ahead of another group of dragoons. He clutched the body to his chest, every fiber of him shaking, and dropped onto the front step of an abandoned shop.

The nightmare had only just begun.

➤   ➤   ➤

By the time his staff found him, Demir had not moved. He had not slept, or eaten, or had a coherent thought in more than twelve hours. He sat on the step, cradling the corpse of the child in his victor's cloak, having spent a night watching every atrocity that a victorious army could inflict upon a city. His head lay against the cool stone of the shop's threshold, his eyes burning from the acrid smoke of a hundred fires, his tongue parched and his wrist swollen.

It was Idrian who discovered him and called for the others. The breacher had discarded his armor, wearing an officer's uniform stitched with the ram's horns that gave him his moniker. He came and knelt before Demir, examining his face. Demir flinched away from that purple godglass eye.

"Sir, are you all right?"

Demir could not find the words to reply. He felt hollow, stripped. He knew that his legs still worked, but the very *idea* of standing felt impossible. He licked his cracked lips, tried to summon words, and failed. He felt tears in his eyes and tried to look away; to hide them from the breacher.

"It wasn't supposed to happen this way," he finally managed. "I didn't give those orders."

"I know, sir," Idrian replied gently. "Communication went awry. We'll find out what happened, I promise."

Slowly, the rest of Demir's staff gathered behind Idrian, staring down at Demir. In the place of those victorious grins of yesterday were looks of horror and disgust. Capric came close enough to pry into what Demir had wrapped in his cloak, only to stumble away and retch in the ditch. Idrian's one eye darted toward the dead child, but he did not flinch from it. Demir could feel the stares of his staff—he could see the calculation in their eyes, each one wondering how this development would affect their career or their guild-family. He could see that each of them was trying to figure out how to detach their name from this disaster.

It was one thing to punish a rebelling city with defeat and decimation. It was another entirely to put it to the torch.

Demir tried to think. He attempted to gather all his faculties, to calculate the possibilities of the future. He had given his word, before more than a dozen people, that Holikan was under his protection—and then *his* army had sacked it. They'd murdered and burned and plundered on *his* apparent orders. He needed to start an investigation; to pin this disaster on someone else, either real or invented.

"Witglass," he croaked.

Capric returned to his side, pressing a piece into his hand. Demir fixed it to a piercing, trying to *think*. His mind was blank, and the witglass caused a sharp pain behind his eyes until he removed it and gave it back. He could no longer calculate. The future was dark and silent.

His mind had broken.

"Myria Forl?" he asked, raising his head to look for the mayor.

"She is safe," Idrian assured him. "Your uncle arrived in the middle of the night and I left her with our battalion. No one will harm her."

Demir's gaze went to the black column of smoke that rose above them. "I wish she were not safe. I wish she could not see what I have done."

"You didn't do this," Idrian said firmly. "It was an accident. A crossing of orders."

Demir looked across the faces of his staff. They all avoided his gaze. Not from fear this time, but from shame. He had not done this, certainly, but it was *his responsibility*.

Slowly, every muscle hurting, Demir managed to climb to his feet without dropping the body of the child. He found the door to the shop open, and the inside ransacked, though he had no memory of soldiers forcing themselves past him. He deposited the body, still wrapped in his victory cloak, on the shop counter.

He touched the child's hair briefly, searching for a prayer from his childhood, wishing he believed in a god to pray to. He tried to gather his thoughts. How could he face another person after this? How could he return to his guild-family, or his lovers, or the people of his province? How could he ever look another soul in the eye? He returned to the front step. For the first time in years he felt his youth; helpless, inexperienced, and wondering when a real adult would come along and fix all of this.

Idrian produced a milkglass bauble and pressed it into Demir's hand. The godglass was not as high quality as his own, but the sorcerous effect was immediate—the ache began to bleed from his bones. "We should see to that wrist," Idrian said. "It looks like it might be broken."

Even with Idrian's milkglass, Demir's wrist hurt so bad that he no longer felt it. Like his soul, it was numb. "Who is my second-in-command?" No one answered. He peered at the faces of his staff. "I don't even know." A mad-sounding laugh slipped through his lips. "In my arrogance, I never thought I'd need them. Well. Whoever they are, congratulate them on their promotion."

"Sir?" Idrian asked.

"I resign."

"You can't resign!" someone said. "This is your moment of triumph!"

Demir looked for Capric, hoping for an ounce of reassurance. His friend was staring slack-jawed at the dozens of dead in the street, all civilians. A triumph. He still might be able to salvage this. His mother, political genius that she was, would certainly try. But if he marched back into Ossa at the front of a triumphal parade after this, he would never be able to live with himself.

He avoided Idrian's gaze. "Apologize to Myria Forl for me. Tell my uncle that I'm sorry for not finishing the campaign. Capric, write up my resignation. Forge my signature." His mother would be disappointed. *So promising,* she would say. *Such a fool. We could have fixed this.* Demir stumbled off the step, regained his balance, and began to walk. "Tell them not to come looking for me," he said over his shoulder. "The Lightning Prince is dead."

1

NINE YEARS AFTER THE SACK OF HOLIKAN

Demir Grappo stood in the back row of an amphitheater, a small cudgeling arena in the provincial city of Ereptia. Even by provincial standards Ereptia was a backwater; a little city in the heart of wine-making country with less than ten thousand people, most of them employed as laborers on the vast vineyards owned by distant wealthy Ossan guild-families. The only arena in Ereptia sat a few hundred people, and just a third of the seats were full for an afternoon exhibition match.

Cudgeling was the national sport of the Empire—bigger and more popular than horse racing, cockfighting, hunting, and boxing combined. The two contestants in the arena wore powerful forgeglass earrings to make them stronger and faster, and then beat the shit out of each other with weighted sticks until one of them forfeited.

Or died.

It was a visceral sport, and Demir felt that it defined the entire Ossan experience wonderfully—the way contestants broke their bodies for the chance at glory while everyone else cheered them on. Someday he would write a philosophical treatise on the subject.

He clutched a bookie's receipt in one hand, watching the two fighters go back and forth across the arena as the sparse crowd shouted curses and encouragement. The woman was named Slatina. She had the milk-white complexion of a Purnian with short blond hair, and was six feet of solid muscle. The man's name was Overin, and he was shorter but faster, with a bald head, bushy black beard, and the light olive skin of an eastern provincial.

They were well-matched—brawn versus speed—and the crowd was absolutely loving it as strikes fell, skin cracked, and blood spattered the sandy floor of the arena. Demir himself was paying close attention to *how* they fought, rather than who was actually winning. It needed to be a good match, with little doubt that the two fighters wanted nothing more than to kill each other.

By the time Overin fell to the ground beneath Slatina's cudgel, weakly raising a hand to forfeit before she could administer a final blow, Demir knew that everyone had bought it: neither the judges, the audience, nor the book-ies had any idea that the pair were well-paid for the inevitable conclusion.

Demir loitered until the last of the audience trickled out of the arena and the cudgelists themselves had long since been given cureglass and escorted away. He watched and listened, making sure that no one so much as sus-pected that the fight was fixed. When he was certain that their performance had been accepted, he sauntered down the steps, out the front of the arena, and across the street, where a slummy little cantina held one of Ereptia's many bookies. Demir slid onto a stool at the bar, set down his betting re-ceipt, and gave it a tap with one finger.

"I need a new piece of skyglass," Demir said, adjusting the gloves that hid his dual silic sigils.

The bartender and bookie was a middle-aged man named Morlius. He had a harried look in his eyes but moved slowly as he rinsed out mugs in a barrel of water underneath the bar. Demir wouldn't normally order god-glass at a bar, but this far out in the provinces it was the only place a stranger could get their hands on a luxury commodity.

Morlius barely glanced at him. "Can't get skyglass at all right now," he said.

"Not even the cheap stuff?"

"Not even the cheap stuff. No idea why. Supply just isn't coming in from Ossa and what little I could get last month was bought up by the vineyard managers."

"Shit." The calming sorcery of skyglass wasn't going to save Demir's life, but it certainly would make it easier. His last piece had run out of reso-nance three nights ago, and he'd had a hard time sleeping without it since Holikan. He rubbed at his temples. "Dazeglass?"

Morlius shook his head.

"Fine. Give me a half pint of Ereptia's best, and put it on this tab." He tapped the bookie's receipt once more.

"You won, huh?" Morlius asked, gazing at him sullenly.

"Sure did." Demir gave him his most charming smile. "Lucky afternoon." He pushed the receipt across the bar. "Drink?"

Morlius did not reach for a wineglass. "You won yesterday, too. And the day before that."

"And I lost the three days prior," Demir replied, keeping that smile fixed on his face. "Good luck follows bad, I suppose."

"I don't think there's any luck in it."

Demir let his smile fade into faux confusion, cursing himself silently. He was very careful about losing *almost* as much as he won. Had he made a mistake? Or was Morlius tipped off? "I'm not sure what you're implying," Demir said, huffing loudly. Morlius did not have a pleasant reputation. Rumor had it he was in the business of drugging cudgelists before fights to get the result he wanted. He didn't do it often—not enough to attract official attention—but the reputation was well-earned enough that cudgelists in the know avoided his cantina.

Demir didn't begrudge the foul play. That would be hypocritical, after all. He *did* begrudge the treatment of the cudgelists. *His* fighters always got a cut. That was the rule.

One of Morlius's goons appeared from the cellar carrying a new wine cask. Morlius not-so-subtly jerked his head at Demir. The goon set down the cask and closed the cantina door, then moved to stand behind Demir. Morlius reached under the bar and produced a cudgel of his own. "Heard a story about a man of your description over in Wallach. Got caught fixing fights and then skipped town before they could string him up. Ripped off my cousin for thousands."

Demir sighed and glanced over his shoulder. The goon behind him was well over six feet tall, thick and powerful and with the oft-broken fingers and battered face of a retired cudgelist. The goon drew a long knife from his belt.

"You're pulling a knife on a patron because of a vague description of a grifter from three towns over?" Demir scoffed. He wasn't quite ready to move on from Ereptia yet. Slatina, other than being a talented cudgelist and quite a good actress, had invited him to meet her parents next weekend. Demir loved meeting people's parents. It was like looking into the future to see what they'd be like in thirty years. "Don't be dumb, Morlius. It's not even a big bet. If you can't pay out today, I'll take it against my future tab."

If Morlius were smart, he would pleasantly drug Demir, rob him blind, and leave him in an alley on the other side of town. But Morlius was not smart. He didn't know when to rein in his greed. Demir turned on his stool so that one shoulder was pointed at Morlius and the bar, and the other at the goon. He glanced over the goon's shoulder, out a window into the street, where he saw something that hadn't been there before: a *very* nice carriage with sky-blue curtains, six bodyguards on the running boards, and the silic symbol of the Vorcien guild-family etched on the door.

Demir's thoughts were instantly knocked awry. What was a Vorcien doing way out here in the provinces?

Morlius suddenly lurched forward, grabbing Demir's wrist and raising his cudgel. "I think you match the description too well."

Demir's heart fell. No getting that payout, then. Or meeting Slatina for dinner tonight. He would have to move on to the next town, interrupting his life and abandoning his friends and lovers like he'd done dozens of times over the last nine years. The very thought of it made him tired, but it also made him *mad*. He cast his mental net outward, using his glassdancer sorcery to make note of every windowpane and wine bottle in the cantina.

"Let go of my hand," Demir said flatly.

"Or?" Morlius grinned at him.

Demir applied a small amount of sorcerous pressure. A wine bottle behind Morlius shattered, causing him to jump. A second shattered, then a third. Morlius whirled toward the rack of wine bottles, yelling wordlessly, reaching toward the bottles without touching them. Demir shattered two more before slowly and deliberately removing his left glove and laying his hand flat on the bar. When Morlius turned back toward him, the glassdancer sigil was on full display.

Morlius's eyes widened, filling with that familiar look of terror that had gazed back at Demir from so many sets of eyes since he got his tattoo at the age of eighteen. It made his stomach twist into knots, but he kept that from his own expression. Morlius was not a friend. Morlius had just unwittingly destroyed Demir's life in Ereptia, and he could damn well rot in his fear.

"I'm . . . I'm . . . I'm . . ." Morlius stuttered.

Demir leaned on the bar, channeling his disgust. "Take your time," he said. The goon behind him fled back into the cellar, slamming the thick wooden door behind him. Smart man. "I have all day." Demir burst another wine bottle, enjoying the way Morlius flinched. Demir knew that Morlius would do nothing. Who would, with a glassdancer right in front of them? If he so desired, Demir could get away with *anything* at this moment.

Demir drew in a deep, ragged breath. He was being petulant now. He'd made his point, but it still took a force of will to keep himself from destroying every piece of glass in the bar and then throwing it all into Morlius's face. That wasn't who he was. Demir touched the bookie's receipt with one finger and pushed it toward Morlius again. The bookie stared at it for several moments before realization dawned in his eyes. He pulled the purse from his belt and set it on the bar.

"Take it. Please." He was begging now. What a damned reversal.

"I'm not robbing you," Demir said softly, "I'm just a customer getting a payout."

Somehow, this seemed even more painful for the bookie. His hands trembled fiercely as he opened the purse and began to count out heavy imperial coins. He scattered the stack twice with those trembling hands, checking the receipt three times, before nodding at Demir.

Most of the glassdancers Demir had ever met lived up to their reputations, in some way or another. They enjoyed using the threat of their power to lord over others. They stole and they threatened and they seduced without thought of consequence. Such displays had never brought Demir pleasure. Occasional satisfaction, like putting Morlius in his place? Sure. But never pleasure.

He swept the coins into his hand and deposited them in his pocket. "I'll have you know that I left Wallach on very good terms. All the judges and fighters got rich with my fixed fights. The only person who didn't like me was the bookie stupid enough to make bets with his clients' money—I'm guessing he's your cousin. Be smarter than your cousin, Morlius. I left him alive, but I also left him very poor."

"R . . . r . . . right."

"If you say one word about this, or if I find out you've drugged any of my fighters . . ." Demir nodded at the shelf of destroyed wine bottles. "I'll actually do something with all that glass." He slapped the bar. "Have a good day, Morlius."

Demir turned away before his frustration could truly start to show. Another lost life, another town he had to leave before anyone figured out who he *really* was. Another crack in his identity's facade, held back by nothing more than a threat. Should he say goodbye to Slatina? She would—rightfully—want an explanation. She didn't even know his real name. Best to just disappear. He was suddenly exhausted by it all, wishing he had *some* semblance of normalcy in his life.

He'd forgotten all about the Vorcien carriage out front, so it came as quite a shock when he opened the door to the bar and found a familiar face staring back at him. It had been nine years since Demir had last seen Capric Vorcien. Capric was thinner, more statesman-like, with features that had grown almost hawkish as he crept into his thirties. He was wearing a very expensive jacket and tunic, clutching a black cane with one hand. A pair of bodyguards stood in the street behind him.

"Demir?" he asked in surprise.

Demir peered hard at Capric for several moments, shook his head in confusion, then peered again. Sure enough, this was Capric Vorcien in the flesh. "Glassdamn. Capric? What the piss are you doing here?"

"Looking for you. Are you okay? You look miserable. Did you already hear the news?"

Demir felt his blood run cold. He'd gone to great lengths to make himself hard to find. If Capric was here with bad news, it must be *very* bad. He offered his hand, which Capric shook. "I haven't. What brings you out to my corner of the provinces?"

"You have a corner? Talking with Breenen, you haven't lived in the same spot for more than six months since you fled Holikan." Demir felt his eye twitch at the mention of Holikan, and Capric immediately hurried on. "Forgive me, I just . . . It sounds like you've been moving around a lot."

"I have," Demir confirmed. "Stay too long in one place and people start to wonder why you wear gloves all the time. What's Breenen doing blabbing about my movements? Did Mother send you out here to try and fetch me back?"

Capric looked around and said, "Can we speak in private? My carriage is just outside."

Under normal circumstances, Demir would refuse. Speaking in a private carriage stamped with a guild-family silic symbol would bring up a *lot* of questions for Demir's friends in this little provincial town, but that run-in with Morlius just now had already ended Demir's stint. Besides, it was best to find out bad news quickly. "Lead on."

He followed Capric out to the carriage. Local kids were running around it, alternately shouting barbs at and begging from the bodyguards. The bodyguards shooed them off as Demir and Capric approached, and they were soon inside, where Capric immediately pulled out a bottle of sherry and poured them each a glass on a fold-down side table. Demir was studying his old friend closely now, trying to get a read on this entire visit. He took a sip, set the glass back on the side table, and said, "What's going on, Capric? How did you find me and what are you here for?"

Capric gulped his glass, poured himself a second, and sipped half of it before answering. "I'm sorry, Demir."

"For?"

"Your mother is dead."

Demir felt the blood drain from his face. "Is this a joke?"

"I wish it was. Breenen told me where to find you, and I rushed out here at speed to reach you before you had to read it in the newspapers."

Demir examined Capric's tired, earnest expression for several moments to see the truth of things, then opened the door and vomited out his breakfast on the cobbles. He felt a gentle hand on his back while he spat out bile, then wiped his mouth on an offered handkerchief.

A million thoughts flashed through his mind: regrets, plans, recriminations. He might have seen his mother only a few times in the last decade, but she'd always been a reassuring candle burning in a distant window. Now that she'd been snuffed out he cursed himself for not visiting more—and for failing to live up to her expectations for a child prodigy. He searched his pockets for skyglass before remembering that he didn't have any left. When he next looked up, Capric was holding out a light blue piece for him.

Demir took it gratefully and threaded the hooked end through one of his piercings. His racing heart and mind immediately began to slow, giving him time to take a deep breath and compose himself.

"What happened?" he asked.

"It's unpleasant," Capric warned.

"Death always is," Demir replied, steeling himself.

"She was beaten to death on the steps of the Assembly."

Demir let out an involuntary sound that was halfway between a laugh and a sob. Adriana Grappo was a reformer: one of the few Assembly members who dedicated their lives to helping the masses, rather than enriching themselves. Reformers in Ossa had a long and glorious tradition of dying publicly, killed by their peers for pushing societal reforms too strongly.

"Who did it?"

Capric shook his head. "We don't know yet. There were six masked figures that descended on her quickly, finished the job, and fled in all directions before guards could be called. And before you reply, I know what you're thinking: she wasn't killed because of her reforms. Sure, her proposed taxes annoyed the elite, but everyone loved your mother. The Assembly is furious and I will be shocked if they haven't caught the culprits by the time I return."

Demir pulled himself out of a spiral of suspicions and tried to focus on the calming hum of the skyglass in his ear. Capric was right. Adriana had always walked a cool line between radical reformer and harmless politician. She always knew when to push and when to back off. "So it wasn't her fellow Assemblymen?"

"I can't imagine," Capric said.

Demir leaned his head against the wall of the carriage. Who did it, then? What enemies had she made in the years that Demir had been gone? "An investigation has been launched?"

"A very serious one."

"Has Uncle Tadeas been told?"

"I'm not sure. The Assembly is covering up the murder until they have more information. Adriana was very popular with the common people. Announcing her death before they have a solid lead could result in riots."

Covering up a public murder might sound ridiculous to some people, but the Assembly was very good at that sort of thing. They had a lot of practice. "Smart," Demir agreed. "Baby Montego should also be informed."

Capric paled. Most people did when Montego was mentioned. As the cudgeling champion of the world he was one of the few normal people who could command the same sort of fear as a glassdancer. He was also Demir's best friend and adopted brother. "I have sent word already," Capric promised, "but last I heard he was on his yacht in the Glass Isles. It might be months before he returns."

Demir sucked on his teeth loudly, using the calming sorcery of the skyglass to shove aside his personal feelings and tick through the list of things he needed to do now that he was the head of the small Grappo guild-family.

As if anticipating his thoughts, Capric said softly, "I have brought with me an offer from my father."

Demir lifted an eyebrow. "Yes?"

"He would take the Grappo on as a client guild-family. You'd have the protection of our patronage. We'd pay off any debts Adriana might have had, take care of the hotel, look after your own clients. You won't even have to return home if you don't want . . ." He trailed off, looking as if he might have shown his hand too early.

Demir ignored the impropriety. This was Ossa, after all. Everything was business: even the death of a family member. It was a generous offer. The Vorcien were one of the most powerful guild-families in Ossa. Slipping underneath their protection *could* benefit Demir greatly. But it would also end the Grappo guild-family, and severely curtail Demir's freedom. Patronage came with stipulations and responsibilities. He shook his head. "Thank you, no. I need to return home and put Mother's affairs in order before I even consider anything like that."

"The offer is there."

"Tell Father Vorcien that I'm most grateful."

"Of course. Are you returning to Ossa immediately?"

Demir examined Capric carefully, trying to weigh any hidden meaning in the question. The Grappo might be a tiny guild-family, but Adriana Grappo had been a colossus of Ossan politics. The return of her failed prodigy son might cause havoc in various corners of the capital. Did Capric—or the Vorcien family at large—have a stake in Demir's possible return? He swallowed a bit of bile and removed the skyglass from his ear, bathing in the return of his anger and uncertainty. It helped him feel human.

"What talk is there of Demir Grappo?" he asked.

Capric looked somehow more uncomfortable than before.

"Am I hated?" Demir pressed.

"Forgotten," Capric said slowly. "Adriana did a wonderful job of cleaning up after Holikan. It was all but covered up. Demir Grappo and the Lightning Prince are distant memories, and no one talks about Holikan at all."

Demir chewed on this information. He removed his right glove and rubbed at the silic sigil of the Grappo guild-family. With his mother dead and his uncle abdicating responsibility in favor of a life in the military, Demir was the last full-blood Grappo left. Could a failed politician without progeny of his own possibly hope to keep the line afloat? "That's about the best I could have hoped for."

"Really? For a few years there you were the greatest politician in the Empire. You were everything: a guild-family heir, a general, a politician, a glassdancer. All that prestige, all that work . . . lost."

"I'm not reentering politics," Demir told him.

"Then why return at all? Why not become a client to the Vorcien?"

Demir considered this for a few moments before deciding not to answer. He patted Capric's arm. "Thank you for coming all the way out here to tell me. That is a kindness that I will repay. It'll take me a couple of days to put my affairs in order. I'll see you at Mother's—at *my*—hotel in a week?"

"Of course."

Demir stepped out of the carriage and off to one side, ignoring the curious stares from the townsfolk and the open hands of the street children crowding around him. Capric gave him a wave from the carriage window, and then it pulled away and trundled down the street.

He reached into his pocket, searching out a piece of witglass. It was a small hoop, no bigger than the end of his finger, with a hook on one end. The sorcery still had a small effect when clutched in the fingers—not nearly as much as when worn on the ear or held between the teeth, but enough to speed his thoughts. It had, he realized, been a gift from his mother. They'd last spoken three months ago, when she tracked him down in one of the southern provinces and begged him to return to Ossa and restart his career.

If he had done as she asked, would she still be alive? It was a question that he knew would haunt him for the rest of his life.

So why return at all? Why not take Capric's offer and become a client to the Vorcien?

A hundred different answers swirled around in his head. His mother's death changed things, and the responsibilities he'd avoided for nine years were suddenly multiplied tenfold by virtue of inheritance. "Because," Demir said softly to himself, "she deserved better than to die like that. I wasn't there to protect her, so I can at least protect her legacy—and destroy the people who did this."

There was a time when Demir would have entered Ossa only with great pomp and circumstance; dancers, jugglers, wild animals, provincial exotics, bread for the masses. It was the prerogative of a popular politician when visiting the capital, and Demir had used it to build up massive amounts of goodwill with the Ossan people.

That was before Holikan. Before he ran away from his own damned failure.

Entering the city on a private coach service was . . . something else. For nine years he'd lived among poor provincials, experiencing the dirty, depraved depths of the human condition. In all that time nothing had compared to Ossa: the noise of millions of people packed together; the smell of Glasstown glassworks burning through whole forests every day to produce valuable godglass; the taste of soot and human suffering on the tip of his tongue. Returning to that was not a welcome experience, but it did feel a bit like home.

He went directly to the Hyacinth Hotel, where he stood in the street, looking up at the building where he'd spent much of his childhood. The Hyacinth was a magnificent structure, four vaulted stories of granite with golden gargoyles, immense windows, and a location in the Assembly District that would make an emperor jealous. Purple drapes hung from each window, stamped with the lightning-cracked silic sigil of the Grappo.

Incredible as it might be, it was a painful reminder that the Grappo had once been one of the most powerful guild-families in Ossa. Generations ago, to be sure, but the Hyacinth was all that remained of that wealth and prestige.

And Demir was practically all that remained of the Grappo.

All around him, the streets were full of people celebrating the coming winter solstice. Masked revelers, dressed scantily despite the cold, carried tin flagons of winter beer, throwing paper streamers back and forth across the street, following the bread wagons distributing free meals for the poor. On another day, Demir might have enjoyed the levity of it all. He would have admired the women, laughed at the clowns, and helped distribute winter beer from the front step of the hotel. Not today. Not with the hotel steps draped in a black mourning carpet.

Demir jogged up the massive marble stairs and through the big double doors of the Hyacinth, slipping a few banknotes into the hand of a surprised porter as he passed. During his journey he had made a transformation, changing out his provincial workman's tunic for a scarlet jacket with purple and gold trim. He rolled his shoulders, feeling the fine clothes hanging uncomfortably, trying to take himself out of the role of Demir the provincial grifter, and back into Demir Grappo, dignified glassdancer and new patriarch of the Grappo guild-family.

Like the sights and sounds of the city, it was a change that felt regrettably natural.

He did not recognize most of the porters, bellboys, or waiters moving through the foyer, but he knew the rhythm with which they walked. He skirted the main floor, heading up the large double staircase to the second floor, where he was stopped by a Grappo enforcer dressed as a porter. She was a young woman, pretty face marred by a soldier's scar across one cheek, a sword and pistol hanging from her belt along with a cork pouch filled with godglass. The pinkie nail of her left hand was marked with purple client paint to show her allegiance to the Grappo.

"Are you visiting someone, sir?" she said as she maneuvered herself between him and the hallway. To his surprise, she did not look at his hands before interfering, instead meeting his gaze without submissiveness.

Demir lifted his right hand, palm flat against his chest to display the silic sigil. "Adriana is dead already," he said. "I think Breenen might be overdoing it by posting a guard *now*."

A look of confusion crossed the young woman's face, and then her eyes widened. "Master Demir?"

"In the flesh."

She inhaled sharply. "Master Vorcien said you weren't supposed to be here until tomorrow!" She looked around, seemed at a loss, and snapped a salute. "My name is Tirana Kirkovik. I'm the hotel master-at-arms."

"We have one of those now?" Demir asked in surprise. His mother had always been light on security, insisting on treating the hotel as such, rather than as a guild-family mansion.

"Yes, sir. I've been with the hotel for four years."

Demir searched her eyes. Still no fear, nor submission. She did not care that he was a glassdancer, and was only mildly embarrassed to realize that he was her new boss. Good. "You're a Kirkovik."

"Indeed. Hammish Kirkovik is my grandfather."

"I like Hammish. Still with the Foreign Legion?"

"Retired last year, sir. He's said a lot of good things about you."

"That's because he has very poor judgment of character." Demir glanced Tirana up and down. She had a soldier's stance, confident and erect, one hand resting comfortably on the pommel of her sword. At first impression, his mother had chosen her master-at-arms well. "Pleasure to meet you, Tirana. Could you let Breenen know that I'm examining my mother's suite?"

"Of course, sir!" Tirana turned and hurried down the stairs back to the foyer.

Demir continued on his course, walking down the long, crimson-carpeted hallways of the hotel until he found a little side hall with a sign hung on a string to block the way. It declared this hallway HOTEL PERSONNEL ONLY.

He ducked under the string and walked down to the only door. It was locked, but pressing a catch beneath the gold leaf three inches to the right of the latch caused the door to click and spring open. He stepped inside.

His mother's quarters occupied a pair of rooms that had once been a servants' galley and recovery room. It was much as it was the last time he'd seen it: white walls with purple accents, a massive fireplace between two blue hammerglass windows that looked out over the park, fragrant cedar desk and bookshelves, with massive wingback chairs for entertaining guests. To the left was the closed door of the bedroom, next to a door that connected to the secret servants' hallways that wound through the hotel.

The only thing missing was his mother's papers. They were gone—all of them, including all the notebooks that had once filled dozens of shelves. There was no clutter, no encyclopedias at hand. It was like she'd just . . . moved out.

The appearance of the room shocked Demir almost as much as news of his mother's death had. He checked the drawers only to find them empty, then the cabinets on the right and left. Personal effects remained: crystal drink holder, silver candlesticks, a small ivory carving of a Purnian elephant.

But all her letters, notes, and personal correspondence were gone. Demir threw himself into one of the wingback chairs in frustration, resting his chin despondently on one hand.

He was staring at the empty bookshelf when he could have sworn he saw something out of the corner of his eye. It was a face, looking at him through the hammerglass window of his mother's study.

It was there for only a moment, elongated and dark-skinned, with delicate features and an unnaturally long neck. Black beady eyes stared back at him over a deformed jaw with a severe underbite and jagged teeth. When he turned to look straight at the window, the face was gone. A cold sweat broke out across the back of his neck. The face was burned into his memory, like a face from a child's illustration of something that walks the night. Except it was broad daylight in the Assembly District.

He reacted by instinct, using his sorcery to seize a water glass from across the room. It shattered into a dozen shards, each poised at chest height, ready to be thrown at an assailant with the effort of a thought. Demir got up slowly, his throat tight as he crossed the room. He slid the hammerglass windowpane open, sticking his head out to look up, down, and to the sides. Nothing there. Entirely his imagination. Could it be the stress of returning to the capital? Could it be a warping in the glass itself? He touched the hammerglass with his sorcerous senses. Like all godglass, it did not respond to his sorcerous touch. It was completely normal.

"Demir!"

Demir brought himself back in and shut and locked the window, to find Breenen standing in the doorway. The Grappo guild-family majordomo looked like he'd aged twenty years in the last ten. He was a small man with a mouse-like, scholarly face and a pair of spectacles perched on the end of his nose and light skin that betrayed his Purnian ancestry. He was in his mid-fifties, with short hair that had long since gone prematurely gray. He'd served Adriana since Demir's childhood, and had been her circumspect lover for much of that time.

Breenen had been a military surgeon with the Foreign Legion in his youth—a hard man to crack during the best of times. Hiding beneath the clear exhaustion, Demir thought he could see hints of worry, grief, and anger in his eyes.

In the few moments that they looked at each other, Demir felt a thousand unsaid things lash at the air between them. Breenen likely wanted to ask him why he hadn't been here to protect his mother. Demir wanted to ask why she'd gone to the Assembly without bodyguards. Reproach, recriminations, anger, and grief. It would all continue to go unsaid. The Ossan way.

Demir cleared his throat, using the sound to cover for himself as his sorcery placed the shards of drinking glass on the table on the other side of the room. "Thank you for taking care of everything," he said quietly. "Has she been buried?"

"Next to your father in the mausoleum. It was a small ceremony, but a dozen guild-family heads insisted on coming."

"Good. I'll visit her as soon as I can."

"I'll make sure you're given time to be alone."

There was a long, awkward pause that Demir broke by sitting down. He still felt slightly unnerved by whatever he thought he had seen in the window. It must have just been the stress on his mind.

"This master-at-arms?" he asked pointedly.

"Captain Kirkovik is a trusted member of the guild-family," Breenen said. "Adriana vetted her. Tirana has renounced her allegiance to the Kirkovik and is a Grappo client."

"I like her. Where are my mother's papers? Her notes? Her spy reports and documents?"

Breenen grimaced, finally walking into the room and sinking into the wingback chair opposite Demir. In that moment his age really showed, and he looked like a frail old man whom life had stabbed in the back by taking away his employer and lover all in the same blow. "The Assembly confiscated everything," Breenen said. "Sent around the Cinders and packed up anything that had her handwriting or an official seal. She was a powerful member of the Assembly, privy to state secrets and government machinations. They didn't want anything left behind."

Demir swore. The Cinders were the elite imperial guard, beholden only to the small group of senior Assembly members that controlled the government. "I'd hoped to get my hands on those secrets and find out what got her killed. Do *you* have any idea?"

In response, Breenen reached into his tunic and withdrew a small, string-tied book.

"What is that?" Demir asked.

"It's Adriana's death journal. She started it years ago, and it was the one thing she instructed me to hide from the Cinders in the event of her untimely demise. I was told that giving this to you was the most important thing I could do to honor her memory."

Demir took it, running his hands across the calfskin cover. His chest suddenly tightened painfully. Was this what grief felt like? "Do you know what's in it?" he asked.

"I have a general idea, but she asked me to keep it secret from everyone. I assumed that included myself, and I respected her wishes."

Demir undid the string and opened to the first page. There was a note scrawled in his mother's perfect handwriting. It said:

> *Demir,*
>
> *If you are reading this, I am dead. I do not know how much of my life's work the Assembly will confiscate upon my death, so this journal contains the most important things you need to know to take over as patriarch of the Grappo and owner of the Hyacinth Hotel. There are calling cards, ledgers, Fulgurist Society introductions, journal entries, spy reports. Study them carefully, and remember that you can depend upon Breenen for the rest.*
>
> *—Your Mother*

Demir pursed his lips. "Fulgurist Societies" was simply the name given collectively to Ossan social clubs. There were at least a thousand in the capital alone, and *everyone* belonged to at least one. He still paid dues to three, though he hadn't kept in touch with any of his old friends and contacts from any of them. His mother belonged to dozens. Her Societies might prove useful, but only if they allowed him entrance. He put that thought aside for the time being. There, at the bottom of the page, was an addendum. It was written in smaller letters in the same handwriting, dated eighteen months ago.

> *Demir, I have begun a partnership with Master Kastora of the Grent Royal Glassworks. If our work has succeeded then you already know of it. If, however, I die before we finish, then you must contact Kastora immediately. Do not mention this partnership to anyone. Secrecy may be the only thing that saves us.*

Demir read the addendum several times, a feeling of disquiet creeping into his belly. He opened his mouth to ask Breenen what he knew about Master Kastora, but the wording of the addendum stopped him. *Secrecy may be the only thing that saves us.* What a strange thing to write. She was not normally one for hyperbole. How serious must it be to be included in the very front of her death journal?

Demir glanced toward the window where he thought he had seen that otherworldly face. It wasn't there, of course. It never had been. Just a figment of his stressed imagination. He cleared his throat, read the letter again, and then closed the death journal before carefully retying the string.

He knew the name. Master Kastora was one of the most highly regarded sorcerous engineers in the world; a genius of a siliceer, admired even by his critics. What might Mother have been working on with him? She wasn't a siliceer, she was a politician.

His thoughts were interrupted by a knock at the door. A porter stuck her head inside. "Master Capric Vorcien is here," she informed them.

Demir exchanged a glance with Breenen. "He'll have news. You can stay if you'd like."

"It's best if I get back to the hotel," Breenen said reluctantly. "Shall I have a suite made up for you?"

"Please. Go ahead and send Capric in."

Breenen made his way out of the office, only to be replaced by Capric a moment later. Demir's friend walked in with a cane under one arm, dueling sword at his belt, his stride purposeful. "Ah, Demir! I didn't expect you back until tomorrow. I just came by to leave an update with Breenen. Are you feeling all right?"

"Just suffering from a quick, sad journey," Demir said, waving off the question. He felt terrible, and that strange addendum had made him feel worse. He needed time to gather his wits. Chasing down a side project of his mother's shouldn't be his top priority, yet the tug of her postmortem instructions was suddenly very powerful indeed. He forced himself to focus. "What news about the killers?"

"As a matter of fact, they've caught one." Capric held his gloves in one hand, shaking them emphatically at the air. "Two days ago, they tracked him down trying to take a coach service into Grent."

Demir scowled, trying not to jump to conclusions. "Only one?"

"It's the only one they could identify from all the witnesses. He's a former Grent soldier, and he confessed under shackleglass that he was sent—along with the rest—by the Duke of Grent. He doesn't know *why* he was sent, but the duke wanted Adriana killed publicly."

Grent was Ossa's twin city, located just a few miles down the river, their suburbs practically bleeding into each other. On a clear day Demir could see Grent buildings from the roof of the hotel. While Ossa was the head of an empire, Grent was a small but powerful city-state with a massive merchant fleet, independent of the larger nations around it. Grent and Ossa had a history of contention, but mostly small trading disputes. Nothing to get a guild-family matriarch killed.

Except . . . Kastora was a Grent siliceer master. That couldn't be a coincidence. "Glassdamn," Demir muttered. "And the Assembly?"

"The Assembly has voted for war."

Demir inhaled sharply. The Assembly rarely acted this quickly. "So soon? On the murder of a single politician? Grent is our neighbor!" Even with no small amount of bloodlust in his heart, Demir could not imagine his mother's death reason enough for an entire war.

"It's . . . more complicated than that," Capric admitted. "I'm not a senior member of the Assembly so I'm not privy to everything, but I can give you the gist. The duke has been meddling in Ossan affairs for decades and he's grown increasingly bold over the last few years. He's stolen trade contracts, bribed Ossan magistrates, and even had Ossan officers assassinated out in the distant provinces. He's been warned repeatedly to back off. Your mother's murder is the last straw. The Foreign Legion has already been activated. We invade tonight."

"To what ends?" Demir asked.

Capric spread his hands. "An international slap on the wrist. We kill some soldiers, occupy the ducal palace and the senate buildings, and then the duke surrenders with a formal apology and a massive restitution payment. You might even see some of that money."

The idea of some government payout for his mother's death felt more insulting than vindicating. Demir scowled. War. The word made his insides twist. And not some distant foreign war, fought through proxies on another continent. War right on their doorstep, mere miles away. Cannons and armies and fires. He tried to remember the last time the Ossan capital had seen actual military combat. Not in his lifetime, nor in those of his immediate predecessors.

It all felt so sudden, but if what Capric said about the Duke of Grent was true, it made sense. The Assembly moved so quickly only when they felt personally threatened, and one of their number murdered by a foreign assassin was awfully damned personal.

Demir said, "I'd like to question the killer."

"Impossible, I'm afraid," Capric said with a grimace. "The high-resonance shackleglass drove him mad. He's a raving lunatic now."

"Convenient."

"Convenient or not, it happens with such powerful shackleglass." Capric's grimace turned into a scowl. "I know what you're thinking. I don't sense any foul play, at least not in the assassin's madness."

"There were five other killers," Demir pointed out.

"And the Cinders are searching for them." Capric shook his head sadly. "I suggest you let them do their jobs. We're invading, Demir. Justice will be done for your mother and a hundred other slights, insults, and attacks."

Demir bit hard on his tongue. It was not unheard of for shackleglass to drive a man mad, but it *did* seem awfully convenient. He would have to resort to unconventional means for his answers, if he was to get any. He glanced down at the death journal in his hands. He desperately wanted to show it to Capric and ask him what he thought it meant. *Secrecy may be the only thing that saves us.* Again, those words stopped him from acting. Mother was working with a Grent siliceer master, only to be killed by the Duke of Grent. Had she been betrayed? Was the work close to completion? What *was* the work?

Something was wrong about all of this. Demir's hand itched to reach for his witglass, to churn through the possibilities. But witglass had done nothing but give him headaches since his breakdown at Holikan.

"Thank you for letting me know," Demir said quietly.

"Of course. I know they . . ." Capric glanced around the office. ". . . ransacked things to preserve state secrets. I'm sorry that you have to stay so much in the dark. I'll pass on whatever I can without getting into trouble." He slapped his cane against his palm. "I should go, and I know you have a lot to catch up with. If you need anything, just call on me."

Demir walked Capric out to the top of the stairs in the hotel foyer. He said goodbye, and then went and found Breenen in the concierge's office. He stood in the doorway, watching Breenen write tiny, neat numbers into his ledgers for a few moments before asking, "Is my uncle's battalion posted near Ossa?"

"It is."

"Where are they?"

"Garrisoned just to the southwest of the city, I believe."

Demir chewed on the inside of his cheek. On a normal day, he might have jumped in a carriage and headed into Grent directly to confront this Master Kastora and find out what he knew. If he did that now, he wouldn't be able to return before the invasion began tonight and would be stuck behind enemy lines—a bad idea, even for a glassdancer.

"Find out exactly where they are. I might need their help with something."

"Right away." Breenen nodded.

"Wait!" He paused, wrestling with the question on the tip of his tongue before forcing it out. "This may seem like an odd question, but has the hotel become haunted in the last nine years?"

Breenen scowled. "Are you being serious?"

"Only slightly." Demir decided not to follow that line of questioning. The staff would already be on edge with Adriana's death and the return of the glassdancer prodigal son. It would complicate things if they thought his mental breakdown had caused him to go insane. Besides, Demir was a modern man. He didn't believe in hauntings.

Demir watched Breenen hurry off across the foyer, his brow furrowed, trying to find his way through the confusion clouding his mind. He was tempted to disappear: to flee back into the provinces, where he could live out the rest of his life as a friendly grifter. Why bother himself with his mother's puzzles and the Assembly's new war? He could go somewhere far away where he might—someday—have the chance to be happy.

Happiness had no place in the Ossan guild-families. Only wealth, prestige, power, and progeny. Demir had little of those things, but he *did* have people that depended on him now. Abandoning his duties meant abandoning the hotel and everyone who worked in it. Many of them were new, but some he'd known since he was a child. He could not discard them.

Besides, there was enough of the old Demir to be intrigued by that addendum in the death journal. He could always disappear into the provinces later. For now, he needed to find out what got his mother killed.

"You left me a real shitshow, didn't you, Mother?" he muttered to himself. "I think I will need some help."

3

Thessa Foleer awoke with a start, sitting bolt upright in her tiny room in the dormitory of the Grent Royal Glassworks. She had dreamed of men dying; women weeping; and a city burning. It was a common nightmare, one she'd had for nine years, though it had grown more frequent as the newspapers ran story after story of the wars in the east. Sweat caused the sheets to cling to her body. She looked out the open window, unable to decide whether she'd been awoken by the nightmare or some sort of noise outside.

"I don't wanna get up," the figure sleeping next to her mumbled.

"Go back to sleep," Thessa said, gently touching the head of golden hair lying on the pillow. The girl's name was Palua. She was an apprentice at the glassworks and at nineteen just a couple of years younger than Thessa herself. Thessa grimaced. She wasn't supposed to sleep with anyone of a lower rank. Kastora was going to give her an earful when he found out. *If* he found out. This would, she promised herself, be a one-time thing. No more bottles of wine and shared cigarettes late at night.

It wasn't even a serious thing with Palua. But this was what Thessa did around the holidays, every damn time; find some way to avoid the loneliness of not having a family to visit. Last year it was that muscular guard, a real asshole of a man who turned out to be married. The year before that she'd eaten until she threw up. "I've got to stop doing this to myself," she muttered, trying to work the ashy taste of cigarettes out of her mouth.

Thessa craned her head toward the sound of thunder in the distance, then forced herself to lie back down. It was just the Forge—a storm-prone series of cliffs a dozen miles to the north. The Forge could often be heard late at night, thunder rumbling distantly even when the air was calm in Grent itself.

Just below her window was a small racket, a series of feathery thumps and a high-pitched repeating screech. Thessa snorted irritably and finally swung her feet off the bed, padding across her cell to open the door with a creak, peering into the darkness of the dormitory. Most of the bunks were empty, siliceer apprentices sent home to celebrate the winter solstice. Thessa herself was the only journeyman left in the building, having volunteered to oversee the furnaces and the small handful of remaining apprentices. It seemed silly to take a holiday when she had no family to visit and her few friends were gone to see their own.

She pulled on a tunic, then hurried down the stairs, following the sound of angry screeching. Just outside the main floor was a large mews—a room-sized falcon cage with a thatch roof and iron bars. A large falcon, just a few inches shy of two feet tall, was hopping from perch to perch, fluttering his wings in agitation. "Ekhi," she hissed, "shut the piss up! People are trying to sleep."

The falcon hopped to the closest perch, cocking his head forward through the bars and staring at her until she reached out to stroke the top of his head. He nipped gently at her fingers and ruffled his feathers.

"What's wrong, Ekhi?" she asked. "I didn't forget to feed you yesterday, did I? No, I definitely fed you. Is the Forge bothering you? It never has before." She sighed. He seemed calm enough with her right here. He must have just had a bad night. "I know I haven't taken you hunting for a while, but I've been in charge of the glassworks. Once Kastora returns I'll take an afternoon off and we'll head into the countryside. Does that sound good?"

Ekhi nipped at her fingers again and she smiled. No matter how annoying the little asshole could be, she still loved him. "Breakfast is in two hours. Here, hold on." She found a little crate nearby containing his anklets and jesses, then reached through the bars to put them on his legs. That always calmed him down—an implicit promise he was going to get to fly soon. "There, now settle down and don't wake everyone up."

Thessa ran her fingers through her hair, pulling out the tangles. Might as well do a round of the building. One of the apprentices should be up by now, lighting the furnace for the day's work. *Keep them on their toes,* Master Kastora always said, *or they won't respect you.* Thessa needed the respect. At just twenty-two in a profession that so often valued age over talent, she found herself too experienced to chum with the apprentices but too young to be properly respected by her peers.

She stilled her anxious thoughts and slipped on her thick-soled boots and heavy apron, then headed across the dark dormitory and down into the courtyard. Navigating the glassworks grounds in the dark was second nature, and she soon entered the main workshop. The furnace still burned hot; a permanent flame that took days to get up to temperature for working godglass. The reheating chamber, however, had not yet been lit and the workshop was empty. Thessa let out an irritated sigh. She found and read through the furnace schedule until she landed on today's date. Axio. That flirty little shit.

She returned to the dormitory, where she found the third bed on the east wall and poked the snoring lump on the top bunk. "Axio."

Axio snorted and rolled over.

"Axio!" She slapped him hard across the stomach.

"Ow! Son of a bitch, I . . . Thessa, what the piss was that for?" Axio sat up in bed, peering at Thessa. He was only two years younger than her, with scraggly blond hair and the kind of pretty face that would have looked more at home on either side of the transaction in a Grent whorehouse than in the glassworks. He was one of the many assistants who worked for the glassworks hauling firewood and keeping the workshops clean. Thessa held up the furnace schedule so he could see it in the moonlight. He ran a hand over his unshaven face and gave her a lopsided smile. "Oh, come on. It's a holiday."

"And you're on the schedule," Thessa said, tossing him the clipboard. "You were supposed to be up an hour ago tending the furnace and prepping the reheating chamber." She turned and headed toward the stairs, listening to him swear as he pulled on his boots and apron. His footsteps followed her, and soon they were in the main workroom. Thessa lit the lanterns while Axio fumbled loudly with an armload of kindling.

"Hey," he said as he loaded wood into the reheating chamber, "you never answered me about going into town for the solstice festival." He shot her a coy smile. "We could even slip into Ossa. Their winter beer is *so much* better than ours."

Ah. Damn, she'd completely forgotten about that. Thessa rolled her eyes as she lit the last lantern. Axio had been flirting with her ever since he arrived at the glassworks six months ago. Other than his looks, he had very little going on. He wasn't from a rich family, or terribly ambitious or bright. He wasn't even all that funny. Besides, she had already tangled herself up with Palua. She needed to make sure that wouldn't blow up in her face before she went looking for more fun.

Court for love, money, or political gain, Master Kastora always said. *Preferably two of the three. Anything else just sullies your reputation.* Fun was never on that list, and Kastora had stopped turning a blind eye to her romps since her promotion to journeyman.

"I'll think about it," Thessa told Axio, before leaving him alone to finish lighting the reheating chamber.

She was on her way back to the dormitory when she was surprised to see a light on in Master Kastora's office. The master had been gone for weeks, off working on one of his secret projects out in the countryside. He wasn't supposed to be back until after the solstice.

Thessa changed directions and paused just outside his office to listen to the far-off thunder. Something was odd about that thunder, but she couldn't quite place it.

She put it out of her mind and knocked.

"Come," a soft male voice said.

Master Kastora's office was an impeccably clean room containing a large drafting table, a single formal desk flanked by wingback chairs for visiting politicians, and two large iron safes stuffed to the brim with his formulas and technical drawings. Kastora himself was a widower in his sixties, "remarried to his furnace" as he liked to say. He was a thin man of medium height, with a bald patch taking over the center of his head of gray hair. His hands and arms were a patchwork of burn scars and permanent glassrot scales from a lifetime of godglassworking. He had a distracted but gentle face, giving her a smile as he looked up from his desk.

"My dear Thessa," he said, "what on earth are you doing up at this hour?"

"Thunder woke me up," Thessa replied.

"The Forge does seem to be unusually loud tonight. I heard Ekhi out of sorts. Did you check on him?"

"Of course. He's just being a brat."

Kastora chuckled. "How has the glassworks been in my absence?"

"Everything has gone smoothly. The shipment for the Atria went out two days early. A military contract came back with signatures—it's on the corner of your desk there."

"Wonderful, wonderful."

"Your work in the countryside?" she asked. Kastora could be capricious and secretive with what he shared. He was one of the best siliceers in the world, and often had secret projects for the duke, foreign clients, and even Ossan guild-families. She did not expect him to give her a straight answer, and was surprised when he leaned back in his chair, a smile flickering across his face.

"Oh, Thessa. You have no idea."

"That's why I asked," she reminded him gently.

He chuckled again, gesturing for her to come close. She leaned in, bemused by his conspiratorial expression. "I," Kastora said victoriously, "have created a phoenix channel."

Thessa blinked back at him. A phoenix channel was a hypothetical mechanism used to turn energy into sorcery. In short, it could recharge spent pieces of godglass, allowing them to be reused indefinitely. A phoenix channel wasn't exactly mythical, but it was close to it. Every master in the world had tried to make one at some point in their career and they'd all failed.

"No you didn't" popped from her mouth before she could stop herself. It was wildly disrespectful, but Master Kastora didn't seem to notice.

"No joking," he said with a grin. "I made a working phoenix channel. Just a prototype, mind you. The energy transfer was far from perfect—I had to burn six cartloads of hardwood just to charge a single piece of forge-glass." He pulled something from his pocket and handed it solemnly to her.

It was a yellow piece of forgeglass—her own work, actually, a tiny stud with a flared tail that amplified the natural strength of most people who wore it. The sorcery didn't affect her the way it affected others. She could hear the slight hum godglass gave off, and feel the resonant vibration on the tips of her fingers, but Thessa was sorcery-aphasic: she could not benefit from godglass, nor did she suffer from the effects of glassrot. It helped make her an especially good siliceer, for she could work longer hours with no cost.

The piece of forgeglass hummed powerfully in her hand. It felt like godglass. It sounded like godglass.

"It was spent when I started," Kastora promised.

If he'd made a working phoenix channel—and Kastora had never been a liar or prankster—this could change the world. Recharging godglass would become a whole new industry, and help undercut the rising prices of cindersand. She looked closer at Kastora, seeing the exhaustion in his eyes and how his hands shook slightly. He was like a schoolboy having miraculously passed his tests after a weeklong bender.

"That's incredible! What will you do next?"

"Well, the reason I'm telling you is because I'm going to move the phoenix channel here to the glassworks. I'll put it in one of the furnaces, and once the solstice is over I'll get a few of the journeymen to help me refine it. Like I said: it's just a prototype. It needs a lot of work."

Thessa looked at Kastora hopefully. Like any siliceer, she'd learned about the phoenix channel early in her apprenticeship and had daydreamed about making one. "Have you already chosen your assistants?"

"Of course!" he exclaimed. "You'll be my number two on this project. The concept is sound, we just need to make it better!"

Thessa inhaled sharply, any last vestiges of sleep fleeing her thoughts. She'd been Kastora's protégé for years and this would be by far the most important project he'd undertaken. His asking her to assist him directly, instead of calling in someone more experienced, was a massive honor. "You're sure?"

"You are—and I will deny this if you ever repeat it—the second-best siliceer in Grent. Behind myself only, of course." He continued to grin at her. "I wouldn't want anyone else helping me. Now, you need to get more sleep. I've already taken the phoenix channel back to my rooms. We'll unpack it after lunch and get working on ideas. If there's rain, it'll be a good day to brainstorm, I . . ." He trailed off, his head cocked slightly to one side. "Are you sure that's thunder from the Forge?"

"I think so," Thessa answered. She opened the door and listened to the distant sound. Several moments passed, and she heard Kastora get up and come over to stand behind her. She said, "Maybe you're right. It's too regular to be thunder. But what else could it be?"

Kastora shoved past her, and she was about to say something but caught a glance at the side of his face. A scowl had taken over his normally cheerful demeanor. "Come with me," he called, striding off across the compound.

Thessa ran to catch up, her boots thumping across the hard-packed dirt. They walked past the dormitory, then down a slight incline toward the small gatehouse that oversaw the main entry into the glassworks. Thessa felt her heart racing, and couldn't help but glance at Kastora every few steps. Kastora kept his eyes on the horizon even after they dipped beneath the curve of the hill and could no longer see the lights of Grent. She could see the outline of Master Kastora putting bits of godglass into his piercings. She couldn't benefit from them herself, of course, but she knew the glassworks enough to follow him without tripping in the near darkness.

They reached the gatehouse, where Kastora poked his head inside the tiny room. "Get me Captain Jero," he told the guard on duty. "Yes, I know the hour. Get her immediately." Within the minute, a dark-skinned, middle-aged woman stumbled out of the door pulling on her white-and-orange royal infantry jacket.

"Master Kastora?" Jero asked.

"I want you to wake everyone up."

"Excuse me?" she yawned.

Kastora reached out and grabbed her by one of the braided epaulets on her jacket. "You hear that? That's cannon fire. It's coming from eastern Grent. Wake everyone up, put them on alert, and send someone to the palace immediately."

"I can't . . . I . . ." It was clear that Captain Jero was still shaking the sleep from her mind. "It's probably just part of the solstice celebrations."

"At four in the morning? I don't give a damn what it might be. Send a messenger to find out. Until we're notified differently, I want you to assume that we're under attack."

"By who?" Jero asked incredulously.

"Does it matter?" Kastora whirled on his heel and marched back up the hill.

Thessa struggled to keep up. She had never seen Kastora like this before and it frightened her. "You really think we're under attack? We're a neutral city-state! Who would attack us?"

"Cannon fire in the east? It has to be the Ossans."

Thessa laughed nervously. "We're at peace with Ossa. We're trading partners! Why would they attack us?"

"Because all of the rules are about to change. We're running out, Thessa."

"Of what?" Thessa's fear grew deeper. Why did he not seem surprised at the prospect of an Ossan attack? What did he know that she did not?

Kastora ignored her question. "If it is an attack, it means things are worse than I suspected. Ossa will want our cindersand reserves, our research, even our siliceers. She warned me about this. I thought she was wrong. I thought we had more time. I . . ."

"Master!" Thessa snapped her fingers. It was the only way to get Kastora out of his own head sometimes. "What is running out? Who warned you about an Ossan attack? I can't help if you don't tell me anything."

He finally seemed to focus on her. "Adriana Grappo warned me," he said. "The woman who hired me to make the phoenix channel. She told me that Ossa's lust for cindersand was going to push it toward war. All we can do is . . ." He turned his head sharply and glared down the hillside back toward the gate, where Thessa was surprised to see that a trio of soldiers had appeared, standing just outside in the torchlight. They all wore the uniforms of Grent royal infantry, and it seemed that Captain Jero was about to let them in. "Keep that gate barred!" Kastora bellowed.

Jero turned in surprise. "They say they're from the capital with a message from the duke," she called up the hill at them.

"And what do they say is going on there?" Kastora shouted back.

There was a brief discussion. "Just the festivities. Should I let them in?"

Kastora stared warily toward the gatehouse like a dog sizing up a stranger at the dinner table. Quietly, he said, "I want you to go to my office. Open both the safes. The key to the left one is hidden under the floorboard beneath the front left foot of my desk. The key to the second is in the first."

Thessa's breath caught in her throat. "What's going on?"

"Keep that gate locked!" Kastora shouted to Jero. "No one in or out except for the messenger you send to Grent." Aside to her, he continued without answering her question, "I want you to gather every paper in both safes. You take them to the furnace, and if I give the signal I want you to burn them."

Thessa fought a wave of nausea. Those safes contained the cumulative research, discoveries, and technical drawings of the entire Grent Glassworks—even some of her own. Burning all that would be burning generations of silic advances. And, she realized, all the Grent state secrets pertaining to godglass. "Should I wake the apprentices?"

"Only after the notes have been burned. Those are more important than any of our lives."

She gave him a nod, hoping she didn't look too frightened, and began to jog toward his office. A gunshot suddenly rang out, and she whirled to look back down the hill just in time to see Captain Jero stumble back and fall. One of the "Grent" soldiers held a smoking pistol. "Tear down the gate! Company One-Forty-Two, grapple those walls!" The orders were barked in a soldier's authoritative voice, with an Ossan accent.

Fear seized Thessa so powerfully that she almost tripped and fell in the dust. Only momentum kept her going.

"You two, stop!" the soldier's voice shouted.

Thessa looked over her shoulder as she rounded the dormitory. Kastora was on her heels, waving her forward with one hand and pushing godglass through his ear piercings with the other. "Go, go!" he shouted.

"Get that gate down!" Thessa heard a voice call in Ossan. "Secure the siliceers!"

Thessa reached the office just a step ahead of Kastora. He tore through the door behind her, barely winded, and aided by his forgeglass threw aside his desk with the strength of three men. He snatched up a loose floorboard, then opened the left safe, then the right, and began piling stacks of papers into Thessa's arms. When it became clear she could carry no more, he slapped her on the shoulder. "The furnace!"

Thessa sprinted back across the courtyard, tears streaming down her face. She burst into the workshop, barely avoiding a collision with Axio. "What's going on?" the apprentice asked in a panic. "Did I hear pistol shots?"

Thessa ignored him until she could get the furnace door open, throwing her armload of notes straight into the glowing fire, her eyes drying instantly from the intense heat and stung by smoke.

"What . . ." Axio tried to ask again as she ran back past him.

She stopped only long enough to bark instructions. "Wake up the apprentices and then the stable boys. No, stable boys first. We need horses saddled. Foreign soldiers are trying to capture the glassworks. We have to get everyone out. Go!" She tried to inject Master Kastora's sense of urgency and authority into her voice. It sounded frantic to her ears. "And make sure Palua gets out. She's in my bed."

She sprinted back to Kastora's office and was surprised to find him standing outside, leaning on the long, engraved blowtube that he used when he worked on bigger projects. Smoke billowed from the open door and windows of his office. Thessa skidded to a halt. "You . . . you set the building on fire!" Fire was one of the great fears of a glassworks. A mismanaged furnace could destroy a workhouse. A deliberately set fire would put an end to the whole complex.

Kastora's face was ashen, expression grim but determined. "This way is faster," he said, "and more efficient. I'm not letting my work fall into Ossan hands."

"I told Axio to wake the stable boys," Thessa said, trying not to think of all that silic knowledge going up in a blaze. "They'll saddle the horses."

"Good, we should flee as quickly as possible." Kastora jerked, as if pulling himself out of a reverie. "The prototype . . ." He paused. "No, it's too heavy for you, and there's no time." He turned one way, then another, seemingly frozen with indecision.

Thessa grabbed him by the arm, pulling him along toward the stables. "We can make another one," she told him. "Leave it to the fires."

"Yes, of course. You're right."

Soon they were running side by side, around the mess hall, skirting the compound walls. They rounded the dormitory, and Thessa paused only long enough to stop at Ekhi's mews. The pistol shots had set him off and he was screeching terribly as he banged around inside the cage. Thessa didn't have time to think about her decision—she simply threw open the door to the mews, unable to stomach the idea of him being trapped in a raging fire. "Go on, Ekhi! Go!" He stared at her for half a moment, hopped to a closer perch, and then leapt over her head. With a beating of his wings, he was off into the night.

Thessa stared painfully after him until she felt Kastora's tug on her arm. "He'll be fine," Kastora promised, and she allowed herself to be pulled after him. They hurried past the next dormitory and around the corner just as the rear gate of the compound suddenly burst open, a squad of soldiers wearing Grent uniforms pouring inside with bayonets fixed on their muskets. Thessa barely stopped herself from calling for help before realizing that these, too, might be impostors.

Master Kastora pulled her back around the corner, a scowl on his face. Back in the direction they'd come, Thessa could hear shouting and gunshots. The garrison, it seemed, had not been taken completely unawares.

"We're fighting back!" she whispered to Kastora.

"Indeed." Kastora seemed to make a decision and, from a satchel at his waist, produced a sheaf of vellum that he thrust into her hands. "We're going to split up."

"What?"

"It doubles our chances of getting away. Flee the compound. I'll rally our garrison and try to save as many of them as I can."

"Where am I supposed to go?" Thessa asked desperately.

"Take these schematics to Adriana Grappo at the Hyacinth Hotel in Ossa."

"It's the Ossans who are attacking us!" Thessa protested.

"Not all Ossans are alike," Kastora replied sharply. "Adriana helped me with the design. Tell her that the prototype was lost, but that these are the schematics." He snatched her by the front of her shirt, pulling her close. "If something happens to me, I want *you* to rebuild the prototype."

"But . . ."

"Don't give these schematics to anyone else. No two-bit Ossan siliceer is going to finish my work. You will. Understand?"

Thessa was trembling all over now, but she tried to get ahold of herself, rallying her courage to meet the determination in Kastora's eyes. "I do."

"Don't worry. I don't think it'll come to that. I'll rally the garrison long enough for you to escape and then we'll retreat into the city. If all goes well, I'll meet you at Adriana's hotel by the end of the week. Go!"

Before Thessa could protest further, Kastora was off, running along the base of the compound wall, his figure periodically outlined by the occasional gas lamp. Thessa waited for a few moments, part of her hoping that Kastora would return and come with her. When it became apparent he would not, she steeled herself with a series of deep breaths. She could do this. She'd been to Ossa many times. It wasn't hard to blend in. All she had to do was escape Grent during a foreign invasion.

Right.

She rounded the back of the stables, pausing for another calming breath. She smoothed the stack of vellum on the ground and then rolled it into a tight scroll before stuffing it into her boot. Making sure it was hidden, she crept to the stable door.

"Axio," she hissed into the darkness. "Axio, are the horses saddled?" No answer. She swore to herself, not sure of her ability to saddle a horse in the dark. The moment of indecision cost her as a sharp voice suddenly barked from her left.

"Stop there, missy! Show your hands and no sudden moves."

A shiver of fear went up Thessa's spine as she turned to see the middle-aged man in an ill-fitting Grent uniform. He held a musket across his chest, bayonet fixed, and looked like he'd use it without hesitation. His accent was most assuredly Ossan.

Thessa was still struggling for a reply when a shape suddenly swooped down from the morning darkness, hitting the soldier directly in the face. A flurry of screeches and swearing followed until the soldier managed to fend Ekhi off. Ekhi hopped twice across the ground and leapt into the air, disappearing from Thessa's vision. The soldier raised his musket, aimed, and shot.

The crack of the musket was followed immediately by a single, agonizing screech. Thessa's heart leapt into her throat, breath snatched away, terror for her own life giving way to immediate fury and grief. She would have thrown herself at the damned soldier if she hadn't been grabbed from behind.

"Go!" Axio hissed in her ear. "I'll buy you time, just run!" Without waiting for an answer, Axio hefted a heavy wood-splitting ax and squared off with the swearing soldier.

Thessa found herself fleeing at a sprint, tears streaming down her face. Cutting through the stables and out the back, she unlocked a small service door in the compound wall and slipped through. Within moments she was hurrying as fast as she dared along the paths that led into the woods out-side of the glassworks, her way lit by the brightening glow of Kastora's burning office.

Tired, shocked, her adrenaline still pumping, Thessa stifled her guilt over leaving Axio alone with that soldier. She had one mission in mind: she had to get out of Grent and then into Ossa, where she could wait for Master Kas-tora in the house of an enemy.

4

Kizzie Vorcien, enforcer for the Vorcien guild-family, stood on a stoop on the edge of the Castle District in Ossa and watched the passing revelers and street performers as they took part in the solstice celebration. It was just after nine in the morning, and distant cannon fire could be heard above the sounds of the street fair.

She wondered how many people actually knew that a war had broken out on their doorstep. It was in all the newspapers this morning, of course. The Foreign Legion had invaded Grent less than six hours ago to avenge the death of Adriana Grappo. But newspaper articles didn't necessarily mean the residents of Ossa *understood* it. Bad things, after all, happened to other people. Holiday celebrations weren't going to stop until cannonballs starting knocking over tenements, and even then maybe not.

One of the street performers had attracted Kizzie's eye. It was an old woman wearing a brightly colored minstrel's tunic and carrying a ratty violin case slung over one shoulder. She seemed to be known in these parts, for a small crowd had gathered, and the old woman was making the rounds, talking and laughing with the onlookers, shaking a can for people to give her coins and banknotes. When no more donations were forthcoming, she walked to the center of the street and set down her violin case. She opened it, removed the instrument, and struck a pose.

A frown spread across the old woman's face as she began to tune the instrument. Her head was cocked to one side, her expression surpassing normal frustration until it became comical. She winked at one of the children. Kizzie snorted at the little display. Despite herself, she was intrigued, and she watched with growing bemusement as this went on for far too long.

A tingling sensation began at the base of Kizzie's neck and traveled down her arms and into her fingertips; the sensation she felt when another glass-dancer had begun to use their sorcery nearby. She looked at the old woman busker more closely just as *something* leapt from the violin case at her feet.

It was a bird. Or rather, the semblance of one made of multicolored glass. It hopped from the violin case to the cobbles, dancing about on two spindly feet as the old woman finished tuning her violin. She drew the bow across the strings to produce a single long note while the bird looked up at her. It flapped its wings experimentally, then shot into the sky as the busker began to play.

Children laughed. Adults oohed and aahed, clapping to themselves. Onlookers shoved each other aside to throw money into the busker's violin case, and the bird moved perfectly with the ups and downs of the music.

"Oh, now that is good," Kizzie found herself saying out loud. She considered herself a cynic on the best of days, but even she was impressed by this display. There were two types of glassdancers: major talents and minor talents. The latter were relatively common and included among their number Kizzie herself. She could sense glass and other glassdancers, and with great concentration she could manipulate small amounts of glass.

Major talents were much more rare, and they almost always joined the military, where they could distinguish themselves quickly on the field of battle and then get themselves adopted into a guild-family. Major talents were respected and feared, and they took themselves and their power *very* seriously. But this woman? Somehow she'd slipped through the norms and was entertaining people on the street—and she seemed to love it.

"If only we could all defy expectations," Kizzie muttered under her breath. She watched the performance for several minutes before her joy disappeared, and she forced herself to look away from the busker and focus on the job at hand. The *job* was a small warehouse located across the street and half a block down from the glassdancer busker. It was a nondescript little place right next door to a major stable. Most people wouldn't give it a second glance. Kizzie, on the other hand, had spent the last two weeks tracking a stolen shipment of cindersand to this very place.

There was a young woman lounging outside the warehouse, wearing a laborer's heavy winter tunic, a blunderbuss slung casually over one shoulder. The woman's head was craned to watch the glassdancer busker; she was yawning occasionally, her mind clearly elsewhere.

The problem with gangs, Kizzie had long ago decided, was that they attracted the stupid, the talentless, and the lazy. If someone wasn't skilled enough to make it as a guild-family enforcer or to join the National Guard, what business did they have as a lookout for ill-gotten goods?

Kizzie pushed away from her stoop and wandered slowly down the street, passing the warehouse and its lookout before stepping inside the stable next door to find a pair of middle-aged men loitering near the door, both with their pinkies marked by light blue client paint that showed that they served—and were protected by—the Vorcien.

"You the teamsters I asked for?" Kizzie showed them her silic sigil: the Vorcien inverted triangle with the setting sun over the desert. Her sigil was much smaller than a proper guild-family member's—she was only a bastard, after all—but it tended to elicit the proper amount of respect.

One of them nodded, glancing into the street nervously. "I hope this job is going to be fast. I heard the Castle Hill Garroters are dangerous." His companion nodded eagerly.

"The Castle Hill Garroters are a wannabe guild-family that can't figure out how to safely sell the cindersand they stole from a Vorcien riverboat," Kizzie replied. She tried to keep the irritation out of her voice. It didn't used to be like this. She used to have status and regard. She used to be in charge of an entire National Guard watchhouse, wining and dining powerful Vorcien clients. Now she was relegated to tracking down thieves.

"Shouldn't we come back when things aren't as crowded?" the other asked.

"It's Castle Hill. It's always crowded. Besides, they'd expect us to hit them at night. Now bring your cart and horse around."

Without waiting for an answer, Kizzie emerged from the stable. She hugged the wall, walking slowly and casually, approaching the lookout from the left. The poor woman didn't even know she was there until Kizzie had a stiletto pressed against her side. The lookout inhaled sharply.

"You have a choice," Kizzie said pleasantly. "Scream, and I will perforate your lungs. Or you can answer my questions and continue to breathe. Nod if you choose the second one."

The lookout swallowed hard and nodded. "Who are you?"

Kizzie lifted her right hand to show the silic sigil, while keeping her left, along with the stiletto, firmly pressed against the lookout.

"Glassdamn," the woman swore. "Iasmos said the Vorcien couldn't track us."

Iasmos was a petty crook, the self-styled head of the Castle Hill Garroters. "Iasmos is an idiot," Kizzie said. "How many are inside?"

"Just Iasmos and the girls."

"Define 'girls'?" When the lookout didn't respond quickly enough, Kizzie gave her a little poke with the stiletto.

"Ah! His sisters, Dorry and Figgis."

"And that's it?"

"Yes!"

"What kind of godglass do they have?"

"All three have forgeglass. Iasmos wears witglass, but I think it's been spent for months."

"All right. Slide that blunderbuss off your shoulder. Good, now tell me what you learned from this little lesson?"

The lookout gave an "eep" sound as Kizzie poked with the stiletto again. "Not to steal from the Vorcien!"

"Wow. I'm surprised you actually picked up on that. Now get the piss out of here. I'm going to pretend like I never saw your face."

The lookout did as instructed, hurrying down the street without looking back. Kizzie waited long enough to be sure she hadn't doubled back before heading around to the narrow alley next to the warehouse. She tossed the blunderbuss in the mud and removed a pair of godglass earrings from her pocket. The earrings were expertly braided, three wire-thin godglasses—witglass, forgeglass, and sightglass—wound together into one powerful piece. They were by far the most expensive items she owned, and she held them up to the light to see just how much sorcery they had left in them. The color had leaked out of perhaps half of the intertwined glass, like a partially filled cup of wine. If she rationed herself, she would get another five months of use out of them. She slid the hooked ends into a piercing on either ear, listening to the hum of the sorcery and feeling more alive from it.

Kizzie was not, by nature, a violent person. Even discounting her minor talent as a glassdancer, she could be dangerous. That was a prerequisite to being a guild-family enforcer, after all. But violence always seemed like the first resort of morons. A bit of careful planning, some bribery and blackmail, maybe some good old-fashioned investigation. Those were her usual tools.

Unfortunately for her, cleaning out an upstart gang did not require a lot of subtlety.

She walked down to the warehouse's side door at the end of the alley and pounded on it hard. Putting her back to the wall, she shifted her stiletto to her right hand and drew the blackjack from her pocket. The door opened and a woman's voice asked, "Who's there?"

Kizzie brought her blackjack down hard across the woman's thigh, eliciting a pained yell and giving her enough time to check the woman's face. Yup, it was one of Iasmos's sisters, Figgis. Kizzie slit her throat and kicked her backward into the warehouse, following her falling body in at a run. The forgeglass pushed Kizzie beyond normal limits, giving her supernatural strength and speed while the witglass allowed her to process her surroundings as if the world were standing still.

The light in the warehouse was dim, and it might have hampered Kizzie's abilities if not for the sightglass in her earrings. She spotted Iasmos to her left; a man in his mid-twenties, wearing a soiled but expensive jacket he probably took off someone he murdered. Dorry, the other sister, was just behind him. Both stared at Figgis with mouths agape.

Kizzie threw her blackjack overhand, striking Iasmos right between the eyes. He stumbled back, distracted long enough for Kizzie to close the distance. Her stiletto found the space between his ribs. Kizzie caught a glimpse of Dorry raising a pistol. She jerked up on her stiletto, lifting Iasmos slightly, using him as a shield as the pistol went off.

The sound, amplified by her sightglass, deafened Kizzie in the enclosed space. She ignored the ringing in her ears, tossed aside Iasmos, and buried her stiletto in Dorry's eye.

Kizzie checked the small warehouse for any other gang members before returning to make sure all three of her targets were dead. She wiped her stiletto on Iasmos's jacket. Her heart was pounding, there was blood on the sleeves of her tunic, and she couldn't hear damned much of anything. Otherwise the operation had been a success.

She paused that thought and did another sweep of the warehouse. It was a typical thieves' hideout, with stolen goods scattered on the floor and stacked haphazardly on shelves. Mostly stuff that had "fallen off" a riverboat or been pickpocketed. Kizzie still didn't know who their connection down at the riverboat docks was, but that wasn't part of her job. What mattered was the crate of cindersand, just a couple of feet square, tucked into a corner, stamped with the Vorcien silic symbol. It was still full of the fine grayish-colored sand, and for that she breathed a sigh of relief. She didn't need any other perceived failures in her life right now.

She switched out her braided earrings for a piece of cureglass, and the ringing in her ears went away within moments. She poked her head out the side door of the warehouse. Revelers *must* have heard the gunshot, but no one seemed to care, so she walked back to the front door and slid it open.

Her teamsters were just outside with their horse and cart.

"You bring the canvas I asked for?"

"Yes, ma'am."

"Good. Put the cindersand in the cart, then wrap up those three bodies and toss them on top."

The teamsters looked at the blood on Kizzie's jacket but didn't comment. They knew better than to question a Vorcien enforcer. As they got to work, Kizzie helped herself to some of the stolen goods: three gold watches, six pocketbooks, a couple of pieces of low-quality godglass, and a bottle of twelve-year Ereptian wine.

"Deliver the cindersand first, then take the bodies to Cannery Six on Butcher Street," she instructed. She waved at the hideout. "Any godglass you find goes to the guild-family. The rest of this shit is yours."

"Really?" one of them asked in surprise.

"Kizzie Vorcien takes care of her people," she told them.

"Much obliged, Kizzie!" the teamsters replied in unison.

She returned to the street, where she tossed one of the gold watches in the glassdancer busker's violin case and made her way across town to the Assembly District. By eleven she'd reached her favorite café, where she rolled up her sleeves to hide the blood on them. She sank into a wrought iron chair in the outdoor seating area, putting her head in her hands, still burning off the fumes of her adrenaline.

She knew plenty of enforcers who liked killing people. They considered it a perk of the job. Not her. It wasn't going to ruin her life, but it would take her a few weeks until she slept properly again. Tracking down stolen shipments, wiping out petty thieves who'd made a misstep: that was all low-ranking enforcer work. She hadn't had to do this kind of shit for over a decade. Yet here she was, biting her tongue, doing the dirty jobs. The price of failure, she supposed.

"Kissandra Vorcien."

Kizzie looked up sharply at the person who pulled out the chair across from her and dropped into it. There was a word of rebuke on her tongue, but she let it die as her sorcerous senses picked up *something* that told her that this man was a major talent. In front of her was someone whom she vaguely recognized. He was an inch or two shorter than her, with swept-back black hair, a fine scarlet jacket over a gray tunic, and the dark olive skin of an Ossan native. She could see a piece of high-quality skyglass threaded through a piercing on his right ear.

"Glassdamnit," she found herself saying aloud. Her frustration was instantly forgotten, her fatigue evaporating. "Demir Grappo!"

Demir grinned at her. "You recognize me?"

"Barely!" Kizzie was a seasoned enforcer, someone used to surprises, but seeing Demir Grappo was a damned shock. Gone was the rotund, soft-skinned political genius who'd managed to charm himself into the beds of half the guild-family daughters in Ossa. He'd lost at least three stone, and his face and hands were covered in old scars. Demir looked *hard*, like he'd worked two lifetimes as an enforcer. She found her mouth hanging open. "Glassdamnit," she said again.

"You haven't changed a bit," he said with a cheeky grin. "I mean, you didn't have blood all over you last time we saw each other, but I have to say, you look good."

"Is that a come-on or a genuine compliment?" Kizzie asked dubiously.

Demir placed his hand on his heart, feigning shock. "I have never flirted with you even once."

"Yeah, and we both know why." Kizzie's snort cracked into a laugh and she found herself grinning. She'd been short on friends as of late. Seeing Demir was a genuine, if unexpected, pleasure. "What happened to you? I mean, I know the rumors, but . . . you . . ." She found herself trailing off, her pleasure turning to awkwardness as she tried to figure out what to say to someone who'd sacked a city and then disappeared after a mental breakdown. She mentally checked herself, remembering that she was just an enforcer and he was high above her station in several ways. Would he forgive the impropriety of a childhood friend?

To her relief, his grin remained. "Moved to Marn," Demir said. "Married a princess, fought pirates on the high seas, and founded a new religion. Now I'm back in Ossa looking for followers."

Kizzie squinted at Demir, wondering how much of that was actually true. With him, it damn well might be. "Glassdamn, your mother! I'm so sorry. You know how much I looked up to her."

Demir's smile wavered, but did not disappear. "Thank you. Tea? Coffee?"

"Coffee."

Demir gestured over a waiter and ordered. "I'm going to apologize in advance and skip any more pleasantries. I've got a very busy day ahead of me. I want to offer you a job."

"I . . . have a job," Kizzie said, blinking at Demir in confusion. She had a thousand questions she wanted to ask. Last time they spoke, Demir was still the very popular governor of an Ossan province. So much had changed.

"You're out of favor, Kizzie."

Kizzie felt herself suddenly on the back foot, surprised that he was talking about her instead of himself. "You don't have to tell me that."

"And I have asked your brother to lend me your services. He agreed."

"Which brother?"

"Capric."

Kizzie rolled her eyes. Capric wasn't the worst of her half siblings, but he wasn't the best, either. Their relationship had always been pure business. Lending out one of their enforcers to a family friend—without actually asking the enforcer in question—was typical of his behavior. "So this is one of those things where I don't have a choice?"

Demir shrugged. "I'm not like that. I'll tell you the job. If you don't want it, I'll tell Capric that I changed my mind. If you do want it . . . I pay well and I'm a good friend to have."

Kizzie chewed on the inside of her cheek as the waiter set their coffees in front of them. *Was* he a good friend to have? Adriana dead, Demir gone for these past nine years. Being lent out to the Grappo wasn't exactly high-society stuff. On the other hand, he *was* a guild-family patriarch now, and even if he weren't he still commanded the respect that any major-talent glassdancer did. Of course she would hear him out.

"I didn't even know you were back in town."

"I've been home for less than twenty-four hours." He tapped his fingers on the table impatiently. "Well?"

"Lay it out," she said.

"What do you know about my mother's death?"

Kizzie shook her head. "Only what I read in the papers. There have been rumors for the last two weeks, but the news only broke this morning. Assassinated on the steps of the Assembly by Grent agents."

"Six people killed my mother. Only one was caught. I want you to find the other five."

"Oh." Kizzie leaned back in her seat, setting down the coffee she'd been about to sip. "I thought all six were from Grent." Though, now that she thought about it, the newspapers hadn't actually made that claim.

"I don't know. The apprehended killer seemed to think so, but that's the thing about shackleglass: it only provides the truth as the wearer knows it. Public murders are messages, Kizzie. I want to know what message was being sent. *Who* killed my mother is not as important as *why* they killed her."

"You're not going to deal with this yourself?" Glassdancers were not known to shy away from blood. Demir had never been a violent man, but Kizzie would have thought the murder of his mother would bring that violence out.

Demir flinched and shook his head. "I'm going to approach it from a different angle," he said thoughtfully. "My mother . . ." He trailed off, then repeated, "A different angle."

"Am I just finding and questioning them? Or am I supposed to mete out justice?"

Demir drummed his fingers on the table, looking off into the street. This was clearly not something he'd actually decided on himself. Finally he said, "As you see fit."

"Seriously?"

"Seriously. As I said, the *who* is not important. I want to know the *why*."

"That makes it a lot harder."

Demir removed his coffee cup from the saucer and dropped something on the dish, pushing it across the table to her. It was a piece of horseshoe-shaped light green godglass about the size of Kizzie's pinkie finger, with one end of the horseshoe tapered and hooked to go in a piercing.

"Shackleglass?" she said in surprise. Shackleglass was illegal for use by civilians, but you could get it if you were rich or connected enough. She hadn't seen a piece in person for years.

"I want confessions."

Kizzie looked carefully into Demir's eyes. There was an edge to him that hadn't been there in his youth, a hardness that mirrored the changes to his appearance. Perhaps he had already become a violent man. He was a glassdancer, after all. Was he going after something bigger than the killers themselves? Perhaps the hands that swung the cudgels were merely a loose end. "Does Capric know what you're 'borrowing' me for?"

"He does not." Demir sipped his coffee, studying her right back over the lip of the cup. "I told him I needed some extra security around the hotel."

"Why me?"

Demir raised an eyebrow as if the answer should be obvious. "Because you have a hard-earned reputation for being the only honest enforcer in Ossa. You put personal integrity above your loyalty to the Vorcien."

"I'm out of favor for exactly that reason," Kizzie snorted.

"And I like that. We were also childhood friends. I could use a friend right now. So? Will you take the job?"

That phrase echoed something that had gone through Kizzie's head just minutes ago, lowering her guard. She *should* say no. A murdered Assembly-woman was something for the Cinders to deal with, not a lone enforcer. But it sounded like the Cinders had already moved on. The Grent were the fall guys, and Demir didn't accept that explanation.

"You might not like the answers I dig up," she offered.

"I'm prepared for that eventuality."

"One last question."

"Ask anything."

"Is Montego going to be involved in this?"

Demir hesitated just a moment too long. "He has been summoned. I have no idea when he will arrive. Are the two of you still . . . estranged?"

"Interesting choice of words," Kizzie replied with a tired chuckle. "We also haven't spoken in fifteen years." Just thinking about Montego was vaguely unpleasant, for a number of reasons. Their personal past was one. Another was the reason that Montego made *everyone* nervous: he killed for sport.

"I won't ask you to work with him, but you might see him around," Demir said.

In a self-abusive way, Kizzie realized that this sealed the deal. The chance to see Montego again, with Demir acting as a buffer between them, was too good to pass up. Fifteen years without so much as a letter passed between them, after the way it ended last time; the sudden yearning for closure was a powerful motivator.

She snatched up the piece of shackleglass and stuffed it into her cork-lined pocket, the momentary contact causing her to feel a little tired and giddy.

"Fine," she said, "I'll do it."

Something seemed to pass across Demir's expression. Relief, perhaps? "The Assembly won't tell you any more details. They covered things up pretty well, and they'll probably be irritated if they find out that you're meddling around their investigation."

"I have circumvented official investigations before," Kizzie replied. Most experienced enforcers had. It was, after all, their job to maneuver the space between the National Guard, the guild-families, and the law.

Demir suddenly downed his coffee in one go and stood up, tossing enough coins onto the table to pay for them both. "Find me at my hotel if you need me. Breenen will arrange for expenses and payment. Thank you, Kizzie. This takes a weight off my shoulders."

Kizzie raised her cup to Demir, then watched as he walked away. "And," she said quietly, "puts that weight onto mine." Despite her misgivings, Kizzie was intrigued. She had never been given permission to stick her nose into a proper conspiracy before. It *might* be simple. She might track five killers to the Grent border and then tell Demir that it was exactly as it seemed.

She had a feeling, however, that this job would be anything *but* simple.

5

Thessa used the cover of the early-morning darkness to cross the river, commandeering one of the many public canoes that could be found tied to docks throughout the Grent delta. She was no strategist or soldier, but as far as she could tell the invasion of Grent seemed focused on the east many miles away. The attack on the Grent Royal Glassworks appeared to be an isolated contingency. She almost turned back a hundred times, reasoning with herself that Kastora might have rallied their small garrison and turned away the Ossan invaders. But she'd been given a task and she *would* deliver the schematics to Adriana Grappo. If Kastora wanted them with the Grappo, despite the breakout of war, then she would follow his instructions.

By dawn, just a couple of hours after the attack on the glassworks, she had reached the northern boroughs of Grent. Church bells rang, people crowding the streets, rumors spreading faster than wildfire. The duke was already dead, one man claimed. The Ossan surprise attack had failed entirely, another shouted. Some people screamed and panicked, while others stood on their doorsteps and stared toward the smoke rising to the east, loudly positing that this was all some sort of mistake.

Thessa stopped only long enough to ask for news from passersby. None of it was helpful, and yet she kept moving. She'd been given a mission. She intended on carrying it out. She found herself staring at the sky, looking for Ekhi's familiar silhouette circling above the glassworks far behind her. His absence felt like a hole in her gut. He was, she realized, the last thing she had from home, given to her as a chick when she apprenticed with Kastora ten years ago. He'd been her companion ever since.

By noon she had reached the suburbs. Roads turned into dirt tracks, tenements giving way to houses, which gave way to farmsteads. She walked for miles, her feet hurting in her heavy siliceer's boots, her apron discarded so as not to so candidly give away her profession. She had no money, no godglass, and no papers. She was exhausted and scared, but she forced herself to keep her eyes up and her shoulders squared. If she walked with purpose, she would be less likely to be questioned.

She couldn't cry for Ekhi. Not yet. Her plan was simple: follow the cobbled highway all the way around Ossa and enter the city from the north, where she was less likely to be questioned. She might have to sleep under a hedge for a night or two, but it *should* be safe.

It was getting into the late afternoon when she came over a hill to see a small group blocking the road just below her. It was a large family, perhaps twenty people all told—mostly children and the elderly. They had three wagons, all piled with what looked to be their worldly possessions. The last of these wagons was stuck in the ditch at the bottom of the hill, one wheel sunken deep into the mud. The four healthy adults and their ox couldn't get the cart unstuck.

The children and elderly stared back toward the smoke rising from Grent, wringing their hands nervously. Refugees then, fleeing the city at the outbreak of the fighting.

"Ma'am!" one of the men called. He was perhaps in his forties, covered in mud from trying to get the wagon unstuck. "Ma'am, please help us!"

Thessa had already moved to give them a wide berth, and it took her a moment to realize they were talking to her. She hesitated. Slowing down meant that more fleeing refugees might overtake her on the road. These poor folks seemed worried about the same thing. Could she risk stopping to help?

"Please, ma'am," the man called again. "Just one more to help push should do it. We're all about spent and we still have miles to go."

Thessa weighed her options for half a moment. "Where are you headed?" she asked.

"Vlorstad," the man replied. "I've got an Ossan cousin up there who'll take us in until whatever is happening blows over."

Thessa's route would pass Vlorstad later this evening. It was still many miles away, over the border. Traveling with a group like this might actually be safer. "Give me a ride to Vlorstad?" she asked.

"Absolutely!"

Thessa rolled up her sleeves and hurried down to the bottom of the ditch. She was no ox, but years of working the furnaces had given her a strong back and arms. She set her heavy boots against the slippery sides of the ditch, and threw her shoulder against the back of the wagon with the other four. True to the stranger's word, they managed to rock it back and forth until the wheel popped out of the rut. Within minutes, they had freed the wagon entirely and helped push it up the next hill.

The group caught their breath there, where they were joined by the others. Thessa quickly found herself swamped by children hugging her legs and elderly men and women shaking her hand enthusiastically. The leader— the man who'd called to her—shooed them all away. "My name is Serres, by the way." He offered his hand.

"Teala," Thessa replied, giving the fake name she'd thought up a few miles back.

"Mighty obliged, Teala. Had half a dozen others pass right by us without so much as a glance. You said you're going to Vlorstad?"

"Past it, actually. But a ride would save my feet."

"No problem at all, if you're willing to help us out of any more pickles like that one."

The agreement was made, and Thessa was soon riding on the back lip of the wagon she'd helped rescue, sitting beside a sleeping child and listening to Serres's wife sing softly to pass the time. It was a massive relief to be off her feet, but it also gave her empty time to think about Ekhi. She could still hear his pained screech after that musket shot and, though she had not witnessed it, she could imagine the plume of feathers and blood as he tumbled to the earth.

Her dark reverie was interrupted by Serres. "Teala, do you know what's happening in Grent?" he asked over his shoulder. "Nobody seems to know why Ossa attacked."

"I don't either," Thessa admitted. That wasn't strictly true. If Kastora was correct, then the Ossans had decided to seize cindersand and research from the smaller city-state.

He nodded as if that was what he expected. "Where are you heading?" he asked.

Thessa sought an easy lie. "I have a friend in Havshire. As soon as I heard the cannons, I thought it was a good idea to get out of town."

"You're a wise woman," Serres responded, patting a trunk lashed in place just behind him. "We did the same thing. The missus had us up at five o'clock this morning, packing everything we could fit. If Ossa has finally decided Grent's time has come it's best to get somewhere we can pretend we've been Ossan all along, right? I doubt anyone will even notice." He paused. "Havshire is forty miles. Are you really going to walk all that way in those boots, without a jacket?"

"I panicked," Thessa said, hoping she sounded passably sheepish. "My family was at Holikan when I was a kid. I spook pretty easily at the sound of cannon fire."

Serres shuddered. "My sympathies, young lady. I've heard the rumors about that place. Glassdamned Ossans. If you'd like to stay with us in Vlorstad tonight, I can't offer you a bed but might be able to rustle up a spare blanket and let you huddle under the wagons."

It was better than sleeping in a bush. "That's very kind of you," Thessa said. She would prefer to make it into Ossa tonight, even if she had to walk past midnight, but this gave her an extra option. She could make the decision once they reached Vlorstad.

She looked down at her boots dangling off the back lip of the wagon, covered in mud. She wasn't supposed to wear them outside the compound—they were heavy and expensive, and the less wear on them the better. The thought of Kastora scolding her for tramping through a ditch in them almost made her smile. Surely that was exactly what would happen when he caught up to her at the Hyacinth Hotel. She could hear the lecture tumbling out of him as he distractedly examined the schematics she'd smuggled into Ossa.

Checking to be sure no one was watching, Thessa drew the vellum schematics out of her boot and unrolled them on her knee. It felt a little like opening someone's personal journal. She pushed past that thought, reminding herself that Kastora was going to bring her into the project anyway. She might as well know what it was.

Each piece of vellum was dominated by technical drawings of the phoenix channel and the compartment in which it was housed, viewed from several different angles. It looked like a weapon of war—a cannon in which energy was loaded in one end and sorcery came out the other. The margins of the vellum were crammed with tiny notes.

She was mostly left to her own devices there at the back of the wagon, and it gave her plenty of time to study the schematics. Within a couple of hours she had a good grasp of Kastora's working theories and the materials he had used. Had anyone ever thought to use cinderite as the core of a phoenix channel before? Cinderite had its own sorcerous resonance but in a thousand years of research no one had ever found a use for it. She slid the schematics back into her boot, her mind turning as she considered ways to improve upon his design.

The sleeping child beside her soon woke, and Thessa was bemused to find him watching her. The little boy was perhaps eight or nine, curled up in a large tunic. Thessa looked toward Serres, wondering if she should alert him that his child was awake. She was, she was the first to admit, not good with kids. Plenty of the apprentices at the glassworks were as young as twelve, but she didn't have experience with anyone younger than that since her own little sister died at Holikan.

"Hi," she ventured.

The child remained silent.

"I'm Teala. It's good to meet you."

Still no response. Thessa side-eyed the child for a few minutes, waiting for some kind of reaction, but he seemed content to watch her. She eventually let her gaze drift back to the south, where the plumes of smoke stood out in the golden rays of the setting sun.

She felt a tug on her sleeve and looked down to find that the boy had produced a number of little wooden toys and laid them out on his lap. There were perhaps a dozen of them, all different animals. He displayed them without expression, as if waiting to gauge her response.

"Are those yours?"

A solemn nod.

Thessa pointed to one of the animals, a little bird with wings spread. "I have a bird. Had." She flinched, feeling her smile slip. "His name was Ekhi, and he was a falcon. He had gorgeous brown feathers, tipped with red, and a speckled white and brown breast."

The boy handed her the bird, placing it in her palm. Taking it between two fingers, she mimicked it flying around his head, then used it to pounce on one of the other animals in his lap. He finally cracked, a shy smile darting across his face so quickly she might have imagined it.

"Leone," Serres called, "leave our guest alone."

"He's fine," Thessa assured him.

"If he's bothering you, just ignore him." Serres stretched and yawned. "Just a few more hours to go. I'll be glad to be off the road, let me tell you. I don't like traveling with all the old folks." He gestured to the two wagons in front of them, where the oldest of the group were riding in the back like Thessa, while most of the other children were walking alongside. "Last thing we need is one of them catching sick. I—"

They came over a hill, the other wagons momentarily leaving their vision over the crest, and then Serres yanked at the reins, swearing loudly. The sudden jerking of the wagon nearly dumped Thessa off the back of the cart. Thessa steadied herself and craned her neck to look for the problem, half expecting to see a tree across the road.

What she *did* see made her blood run cold. There, less than twenty paces in front of the lead wagon, was a handful of Ossan legionaries. Four men, three women, all wearing their black uniforms with gold trim, muskets held with bayonets fixed. The soldiers blocked the road.

There was no hailing, no conversation. The soldiers approached, two of them coming out front while the others hung back just a little ways.

"What's going on?" Serres demanded.

The soldier in charge, a woman with a crimson-and-silver braided collar, ignored him. "This is good," she told her closest companion. "Told you it would pay off."

"Ma'am," Serres said firmly, "I have papers showing Ossan relations. We're simply trying to get to our family."

The soldier didn't even seem to notice she was being spoken to. "That one," she said, pointing at Serres. "That one, that one, that one. Oh, definitely that one." She pointed directly at Thessa. The other soldier came over and grabbed Thessa by the arm. She tried to struggle but found his grip like iron as he yanked her down from the wagon. She twisted, landing hard on one knee, looking up to see a forgeglass stud in one of his ears.

No point in fighting him at all.

The other five soldiers finally approached. They grabbed family members, yanking them out of wagons, pushing them to either side of the road, emptying each cart of people before guiding the horses to a clearing just to one side of the highway.

Serres's objections grew louder and more violent, until one of the soldiers flipped around his musket and bashed the stock across Serres's head. Thessa stifled a gasp as he was dragged over to Thessa's side of the road and dumped beside her.

It was all so sudden that Thessa barely had time to react. She stared at the soldiers, dumbfounded, then across the road to where all the children and older members of the group had been herded. The boy, Leone, stared at his father with mouth agape, clutching his wooden toys. Thessa wrestled with her fear and confusion, realizing she should have made a plan for this eventuality, not knowing what she could even do. Should she escape? Abandon the family that had given her a ride? It wasn't like she could actually help them.

Children cried, adults wailed, and with growing horror Thessa realized that all the able-bodied adults had been deposited over with her. She looked around for some sort of leadership among the group but they seemed even more shocked than she was. She knelt down beside Serres, splashing him with a little bit of water from his own canteen, pressing the hem of her tunic against the split in his brow until he came around.

The sorting finished. The soldier in charge looked bored, yawning toward a weeping child while one of her subordinates pointed across the street. "What do we do with them, Sergeant?"

"Run 'em off. We got no use for 'em."

Serres sat up, casting a grateful look toward Thessa. "What are you going to do with us?" he demanded. "I have Ossan family, I . . ."

The sergeant drew her pistol with the casual confidence of someone who was always prepared to kill. Serres fell silent and a smile flickered across her face. "You're trespassers," she said with a shrug. "Spies, coming across the border to spread chaos and dissension."

"We are no such thing!" Serres objected.

Another yawn from the sergeant. "Does it look like I give a shit? We're confiscating your goods. The Ossan navy needs sailors. I need a country home." One of the other soldiers laughed at this. She continued, "If you survive a few voyages, I'm sure they'll let you find your family when the war is over."

Thessa barely listened. She was watching carefully, looking for the chance to escape. Sprinting off into the trees might be her best chance. There were only seven soldiers and they had over twenty prisoners to corral. If even one tried to come after her, they would risk losing the rest of the family. Thessa had just planned out her escape route when a young man whom she had not met suddenly made a break for it, sprinting toward the very trees she'd been eyeballing.

Without batting an eye, the sergeant took a musket from one of her subordinates, sighted, and put a bullet between the young man's shoulder blades.

The crack of the musket felt like a physical blow. Thessa stared at the fallen body, listening to the gasps around her. A middle-aged woman—probably the young man's mother—tried to run toward him but was restrained by her family.

"Got no patience for your shit!" the sergeant proclaimed. "Friend of mine will be by in an hour and then you'll all start your careers in the Ossan navy. Get used to being on your knees, because there's a lot of decks that need scrubbing!"

To this point, Thessa had managed to keep some veneer of calm. Her glassworks had been attacked, she'd been forced to abandon her master—they'd killed her glassdamned bird—and now she was being *sold like a dog*? Her panic finally broke through. She couldn't help the family, but maybe she could help herself. She could *not* fail Kastora. She leapt to her feet, facing the sergeant, squaring her shoulders.

"I'm not being sold to the navy," she snapped.

"Nobody's selling anyone," the sergeant replied with a chuckle, as if amused by Thessa's outburst. "Slavery is illegal in the Ossan Empire. You're merely being . . . impressed into service for an indeterminate amount of time."

"I won't do it."

Whatever humor the sergeant found in this situation seemed to fade away. "Reload your musket," she ordered her subordinate.

Thessa sought desperately for something that could save her without revealing who she was. Kastora's orders echoed through her mind: Trust no one. Get to Adriana Grappo. "I'm more valuable to you here in Ossa than I am on some ship."

"Do tell," the sergeant said flatly.

"I'm a siliceer."

The sergeant's eyes narrowed. Everyone was staring at Thessa now, from the soldiers to Serres to the rest of the kind people who'd allowed her to share their company for the last few hours. The sergeant stepped over and grabbed Thessa by the arms, pulling up her sleeves to examine the scars on them. She looked at Thessa's tunic, then at her boots.

"Well glassdamn," she said, "I guess you are. What rank?"

Thessa hesitated. She shouldn't expose herself too much. "Senior apprentice."

"Impressive."

Thessa felt a wave of relief flood through her. "I can arrange a payment for my freedom. I promise, you'll get more from me that way."

The sergeant seemed to mull this over, a thoughtful frown on her face. "From who?"

Trust no one. But Thessa had to take a chance here, otherwise she wouldn't deliver anything. "From Adriana Grappo at the Hyacinth Hotel. She's a family friend."

The sergeant stepped away, conferring with two of her subordinates while the others kept a strict watch on the refugees. Thessa's heart pounded in her chest. She could feel her brief companions staring at her with a mix of fear, anger, and jealousy. She hated to abandon them, but forced herself to keep her thoughts on her mission. Maybe she'd gotten through this.

The conference stretched on for several minutes. Sweat began to trickle down the back of Thessa's neck, and the soldiers on guard duty shifted nervously.

Finally, the sergeant returned looking irritable. "Tempting offer," she said shortly, "but I'm turning it down."

Thessa's breath caught in her throat. Was she being literally shipped off into the Ossan navy? Was there *any* way to escape? "Why?" she demanded, putting every ounce of imperiousness into her voice that she could manage.

The sergeant seemed unimpressed. "Because we have strict instructions to deliver captured Grent siliceers to the Ivory Forest Glassworks. And"— she shrugged—"Adriana Grappo is dead. It's the whole reason for the war. I doubt we're going to get a good ransom out of her failure of a son."

Thessa barely heard anything after the word "dead." She stared back at the sergeant, her mouth hanging open, feeling numb. "I . . . What happened . . . I don't . . ." She tried to form a coherent sentence.

"No more questions," the sergeant sighed. Her demeanor had changed noticeably. Perhaps not respectful, but not as severe as she was behaving toward the other prisoners. Thessa tried to take solace in that and failed. She'd had *one* ally within Ossa, and a corpse wasn't going to provide the protection Thessa needed to get through this war. How was she going to meet back up with Master Kastora? Where would she go?

Assuming, of course, she could get out of this mess.

6

Grent was a city-state built daringly across the length and breadth of a massive river delta. Countless channels and canals divided the city into hundreds of island districts of various sizes, and incredible levies and dikes controlled the flow of the delta in a feat of engineering that had never been matched. It was a city long used to battling the inevitable, which was one of the reasons it had survived so long mere miles from the capital of the aggressive Ossan Empire.

Ossan soldiers often joked about invading Grent. It was a joke because it was so outlandish: Grent was not a threat to the Empire, and there was far more to lose than gain when invading such a headache of a city.

That joke, Idrian Sepulki reflected, was funny right up until the moment the order came for the invasion.

Idrian returned from the front line bruised, sore, and exhausted after nearly fourteen hours of savage street fighting through the eastern suburbs of Grent. In that time he had killed eighteen people, watched three friends die, and taken one wound that would leave a nasty scar. Killing was part of the job of a soldier, and the wound was already mostly healed thanks to the powerful cureglass sorcery in his breacher armor, but losing friends had never grown easier over his decades in the Foreign Legion.

As was his habit, he would bury his feelings until the end of the conflict, at which time he could properly grieve.

He paused at the top of a hill, leaning on his massive breacher shield, looking across the suburbs where his battalion—the Ironhorn Rams—trudged behind him carrying their dead and wounded. The sun was starting to set, shining gold off the placid river and half blinding Idrian's view of the delta. Smoke rose from several places along the front lines, where the Ossan Foreign Legion had pushed miles into the Grent suburbs, while the report of artillery duels had been going for almost as long as the Ironhorns had been fighting.

This sudden war was, Idrian didn't mind admitting to himself, disconcerting and frightening. He was used to shipping overseas, where he'd have weeks or even months to prepare himself for a coming conflict against a distant enemy. This time was different. Just two days ago he was playing cards with Tadeas, enjoying their cushy ceremonial posting in the Ossan suburbs. Now they were on the offensive against their closest neighbor.

"Almost back to camp," Idrian said encouragingly to a flagging engineer. "Keep your head up."

"Thanks, Idrian," came the weary reply.

Idrian was just about to continue on himself when the distant plume of cannon smoke drew his attention. It was followed mere moments later by the hair-raising whoosh of a cannonball flying overhead. He ducked behind his shield by pure instinct, though he knew a direct hit would cut him in half with or without his hammerglass armor. The street, which had been so peaceful moments before, was suddenly chaos. When Idrian raised his head it was to screams of alarm and panic accompanied by choking dust and a terrible rumbling series of crashes.

It did not take him long to realize what had happened—the building just at the top of the hill, a massive five-story tenement, had taken a direct hit and collapsed entirely. Idrian found himself sprinting toward the rubble. An officer wearing the silver braided collar of a major came stumbling out of the dust, eyes wide, mouth gaping like a fish out of water. "They're shooting at us! They're shooting at us!" he screamed.

"You idiot," Idrian snapped, grabbing the officer by the jacket and giving him a shake. "We've invaded their glassdamned country. Of course they're shooting at us."

"But we're supposed to be the ones who win!"

Idrian had to restrain himself from throwing the man to the ground. Another Ossan guild-family officer without combat experience, baffled that their enemies bothered to fight back. Damned fools. "Was there anyone in that tenement? Listen to me, man! Was there anyone in there?"

"Half my battalion," the major finally managed.

Idrian's stomach lurched. "Glassdamnit, those are your people! Get ahold of yourself and start digging! Every moment you waste is a life lost!"

"Me? Dig?"

Idrian finally did throw the idiot to the ground. He raised his sword in the air, the massive pink razorglass blade catching the light from the sunset. He bellowed, "We've got trapped soldiers! All hands to me! Move that rubble!"

He felt a tug on his shoulder and looked down to see Fenny, a soldier in his own battalion. She was a slight woman, little more than a waif whose black flatcap always looked too big on her. Her eyes were wide, her white skin especially pale. "Idrian," she whispered loudly, "Squeaks was in there."

Idrian's head whipped back around to the rubble. "What? How? We just got back!"

"She ran in to buy a bottle of wine from one of the Forty-Second quartermasters. We were gonna share it tonight."

"Piss and shit. Where was she?"

"Right there." Fenny coughed, pointing to a no-longer-existing tenement. "I saw her in the first-floor window half a second before the ball hit. She waved at me." Fenny began to tremble fiercely.

Idrian turned and grasped her gently by the side of the face. "Look at me. Look at me! Your woman is going to be fine. I'll find her myself. You run back down the hill and find Mika. Tell her to bring all her engineers up here to take charge of the digging." Idrian gave her a shove to propel her along, then tossed his sword aside and sprinted to the spot that Fenny had indicated. The tenement was little more than a massive pile of shattered bricks, with dust-covered limbs sticking out at odd angles. Screams and shocked moans issued from the pile, sending a shiver down his spine. Idrian shucked his own exhaustion and soaked in the forgeglass sorcery of his armor to give him strength and speed.

He used his shield as a shovel, piling bricks on it until he could barely lift it, then taking it out of the wreckage to dump off to the side. The first body he found belonged to a young man he vaguely recognized from the Forty-Second. The poor bastard was already dead. Idrian was soon surrounded by his own battalion, dozens of men and women bending their backs to move brick and timber, pulling people—both alive and dead—out of the wreckage. Sweat poured down Idrian's brow and neck, soaking the uniform under his armor.

At some point the sun had set completely, and the site was lit by hundreds of torches and lanterns. Idrian kept digging, periodically calling out Squeaks's name. Slowly, he became aware he was being watched. A young man stood somewhat back from the edge of the wreckage. He had white Purnian skin, and was wearing an Ossan uniform though he couldn't have been more than seventeen with that fresh face of his. A large pack rested on his shoulder. He was staring at Idrian strangely.

"Are you going to help?" Idrian demanded.

"I . . . I wouldn't know where to start."

"Move bricks."

"You shouldn't use your shield like that."

Idrian paused and shot a glare at the young man, who shrank beneath the gaze. There were few people who didn't find Idrian's purple godglass eye disconcerting. This young man was not one of them. "This shield is a tool used to protect my battalion," Idrian grunted as he lifted it onto his shoulder, heavy with rubble. "One of my battalion is trapped under there. The tool does the job." He staggered through the rubble until he found a safe place to dump it off to one side, then returned. "Well?" he demanded. "Help or get out of my way. Squeaks! Squeaks, are you in there?"

The young man finally moved, depositing his pack off to one side and joining in with the calls of the Ironhorns.

The digging continued for some time, and Idrian's stomach twisted whenever he caught sight of Fenny carefully moving across the rubble, tears streaming down her face as she called out the name of her wife. He'd completely lost track of the hour when he heard a muffled sound somewhere off to his left.

"Sir," the young interloper called, "over here, sir! We've got a few live ones trapped under a support beam!"

"Mika!" Idrian shouted. "Mika, come help me!"

Idrian was soon surrounded by a dozen engineers, who carefully helped clear rubble until Idrian could get his shoulder underneath the support beam.

"Wait!" one of them called. "Wait! Hold on! Okay, lift!"

Idrian slowly leveraged the beam up from its resting place. The weight was impossible, probably over a thousand pounds, and despite the forge-glass sorcery enhancing his strength he felt like every sinew was about to pop. He listened to the engineers as they scrambled around him until one slapped him on the back of his helmet. "All clear!"

Idrian dropped the beam and staggered backward, tripping and stumbling until someone caught him and helped him right himself. Relief surged through him as he turned to find Squeaks lying in a clear spot with several others. She was a young woman, just a year or two older than Fenny, and a skilled engineer. One arm was mangled, but she was alive and alert, wrapped in Fenny's embrace. Idrian breathed a sigh as his adrenaline finally crashed, leaving him hard of breathing and barely able to stand. He made his way out of the rubble, looking for his sword, only to find it lying on the boardwalk next to a nearby tenement. The young man who'd accosted him about his shield earlier was standing over it as if he were on guard.

To Idrian's surprise, the young man had a yellow ram stitched to the front of his uniform jacket. "Why are you wearing an Ironhorn uniform?" Idrian asked, setting his shield on the boardwalk beside his sword and sinking down to lie next to them. He pulled off his helmet, sweat dripping off his face, and tossed it aside.

"I'm your new armorer, sir."

Idrian lifted his head and stared at the young man. "I've been asking for a new armorer for six months, and *now* I get one? What's your name?"

"Braileer, sir. Braileer Holdest."

"How old are you?"

"Eighteen."

"They really must be short of armorers if they sent you."

Braileer flinched and tried to stand up straighter. "I'm trained in working steel and godglass. I can make all necessary field repairs. Give me a forge and a glass furnace and I can do anything but a total rebuild. Your armor, sword, and shield will be in good hands with me, sir."

Idrian had his doubts. Most breacher armorers were experienced professionals in their thirties or forties. "What about my back?"

"Sir?"

"Armorers are also soldiers, kid. I see that little hammerglass buckler strapped to your back and the smallsword on your belt, but do you know how to use them? My job is to keep the Ironhorns alive. I am the sword of their vanguard and the shield of their flank. *Your* job is to keep *me* alive. Understand? You care for my armor but you also go into combat zones with me."

Braileer's confidence seemed to wane. "I have a few weeks' combat training, sir."

"Piss," Idrian sighed. If he hadn't done such a number on his shield moving that rubble, he might have sent the young man straight back to the Ministry of the Legion. But he was in a war now, and he needed his armor cared for. "Piss and shit. All right, follow me." Idrian got to his feet and gestured for Braileer to carry his sword, shield, and helmet. The young man did so without complaint, though he was carrying his own pack as well. They walked around the ruined tenement and headed over the next hill, where they descended into a makeshift camp that took up two streets and three more captured Grent tenements. A fire burned in the middle of it all, next to a banner stitched with a yellow ramshead that matched the sigil on Idrian's armor and Braileer's uniform.

"How much do you know about the Foreign Legion?" Idrian asked.

"Um . . . sorry sir, but I'm trained as a craftsman. They conscripted me less than a month ago and they've been teaching me to shoot and stab and not much else."

Idrian stripped off his gauntlets and ran his sweaty hands across his face. "Glassdamned Ministry just can't get their training right. Fine. You've been assigned to the Ironhorns. We're a battalion of combat engineers. We repair bridges, put up barricades, level ground for artillery batteries—whatever dirty work needs to be done, we do it and often under fire. We've got three hundred proper soldiers, two hundred engineers, and one breacher—that's me. It's not a brag to say we're the most famous battalion in the Foreign Legion, and for good reason. We have a high success rate and a low casualty rate. Veterans think twice before engaging with us directly." Idrian turned to Braileer. "Our motto is 'Horns ready, hooves steady.' Keep your weapon on hand, your feet planted, your eyes sharp, and you might just live through the war."

Braileer was very clearly trying to keep his eyes from bugging out of his head. "Yes, sir."

"You okay?"

"It's a lot to take in, sir."

"There's a lot more. I won't dump it on you now. What do you do for fun, Braileer?"

"I play cards. Play a little fiddle. I . . . train rats."

Idrian glanced at him curiously. "Rats?"

"To do tricks. Steal coins. Little fun things."

"Huh. Good way to catch the plague. Fiddle will make you popular. You're a corporal, so Tadeas will let you play cards with the officers. He's our commanding officer. He cheats, though you'd never know it. Mika and Valient are the captains of our little outfit, in charge of the engineers and soldiers, respectively. They've been married for longer than I've known either of them, and both will try to sleep with you. My advice is to tread carefully on those grounds." Idrian scratched at the back of his neck. He was absolutely spent, ready to hang up his armor and get a good night's sleep. He'd need it, too. The Ironhorns would be rotated back to the front before first light. "Help me get my armor off. Repair it and polish it before you hit your bunk. I took that room right there—" Idrian pointed at a tenement window on his left. "I prefer privacy when I can get it. You can sleep in the hallway outside my door."

Despite his youth and inexperience, Braileer clearly knew his way around a set of breacher armor. Idrian was stripped down to his under-uniform in less than a minute, and Braileer hauled off his armor, leaving him alone next to the fire, where he let his sweat-soaked clothes dry. Despite his exhaustion, he found himself remaining there for some time, meditating as he stared into the flames, letting his body and mind recover from the day's fighting.

He was soon joined by Mika. She was a short Marnish woman with cropped black hair, skin darker than his own, and wearing an ill-fitting Foreign Legion uniform that made her look like a sack of potatoes in bad light. She carried a massive pack, heavy with tools. Dozens of ram's horns hung from the back, clacking together as she walked. She swung the pack from her shoulder and sank down on the ground beside the fire, looking up at Idrian. "You know," she said, "I'm going to miss you when you turn in your debt marker."

Idrian touched the little silver tag that hung around his neck by instinct. It represented the amount of his life that the Foreign Legion still owned—a debt he owed them until the time was done. "You'll get another breacher," he told her.

"Not one who'll spend hours digging in rubble for a single infantryman. Fenny and Squeaks have always liked you. I think they're going to worship the ground you walk on now."

Idrian chuckled and shook his head. "They'll repay the effort someday."

"Or they won't."

"Or they won't," Idrian acknowledged. It didn't really matter. As he'd told Braileer, his job was to protect the Ironhorns. Idrian took that job very seriously. It didn't just mean when they were in active combat. "How's she doing?"

"Squeaks busted up her arm pretty good, but a few days with quality cureglass should have her back on duty. Glory is tending to her now. That cannonball was a fluke. Managed to hit the main support beam of a poorly built tenement. We'll know the casualty counts in the morning, but I'm guessing we saved two-thirds of that battalion."

"Now that," Idrian said, grinning at Mika, "is a debt we'll collect."

She grinned back, producing a couple of bottles of wine from her pack. "Already started. These are courtesy of the Forty-Second." She handed one bottle to him and popped the cork on the other. They clinked the bottles together. "Have you seen Tadeas?" she asked.

"I was just about to ask you the same thing," Idrian replied, setting his bottle aside for later. "Last I saw him he was called back to headquarters."

"Did you hear the rumors about his sister and nephew?"

Idrian frowned and shook his head. "Demir?"

"Yeah. Rumor has it that this whole war is because of Adriana's murder a couple weeks ago. They traced the killers back to the Duke of Grent."

"Sounds like a pretty flimsy excuse for a war," Idrian snorted. He'd always liked Adriana, and her death had come as a shock to all of them. She was their sponsor, after all. But he wasn't going to happily get killed because of a political assassination. "There's always another reason."

"From what I heard there's a lot of reasons," Mika replied with a yawn. "The duke's covert operations have grown more and more aggressive over the last few years. Adriana's death is just the last straw. He poked the sleeping giant one too many times and now we're at his door."

It was not an uncommon story, and this would not be the first war Idrian fought purely as a show of force. Peace made the Empire rich, but war reminded everyone else who ruled half the world. "Lucky him. What about Demir?"

Mika shrugged. "He's back, supposedly. He's already taken control of the Grappo."

"Wonder what Tadeas thinks of that," Idrian grunted, hiding his own surprise. He hadn't thought that he'd ever see Demir again, much less that the wayward Grappo would ever return to Ossa. "Last time I saw him, I would have bet pretty good money he was going to put a bullet in his own head before long."

"Returning to guild-family politics might push him over that edge." Mika waggled her eyebrows comically. It was half a dark joke and half a truth. For Tadeas's sake, Idrian hoped it would remain a joke. Demir was the only other Grappo left now. Idrian looked around and stretched, watching as the rest of Mika's engineers stumbled into camp. A few threw themselves onto bedrolls under the open stars, while others headed into the tenements where they'd staked a temporary claim earlier in the day. The conversation was muted, the jokes few. Despite their taking few casualties, it had been a hard day. Everyone was just too damned exhausted and it was only the very beginning of the war.

"I'm going to bed," Idrian said. "If you see Tadeas, tell him to only wake me if it's important, I—" He was cut off by the arrival of Valient. Mika's husband was a light-skinned Purnian, tall and willowy, with a clean-shaved head and a musket slung over one shoulder.

"Hey Idrian," he interrupted, yawning. "There's a guy just over there claiming to be a guild-family member. Wants to talk to you."

Idrian blinked back at him, then turned to stare into the darkness in the direction Valient had indicated. There was a tiny bit of sightglass in his false eye, giving a very slight boost to his senses and allowing him to see in the dark better than most. He could see a hooded figure lurking just beyond the light of the fire. None of the other Ironhorns paid the figure any mind. "You didn't get a name?"

"Didn't give one." Valient yawned again, sitting down beside his wife and putting his head on her shoulder.

Idrian glanced around, fighting a feeling of frustration. Some soldiers took on a client role with guild-families, but he'd always been very careful to avoid that entanglement. The closest he ever got was the Grappo sponsorship paying a portion of his wages, and that was more about their public prestige than anything else. It didn't leave him beholden to them. So who the piss was lurking around in a war zone wanting to talk?

"You want me to get rid of him?" Mika asked.

"Nah. I'll do it myself." Idrian walked over to where the figure stood out of earshot of the others, peering hard to try and get a look under that hood. He could make out embroidered cuffs and fine cloth. Whoever it was had money for sure, but was also wearing gloves to hide his guild-family sigil. "I'm Idrian Sepulki," he said, drawing himself up.

"Hello, Idrian. Been a long time."

Idrian's senses all perked up at once and he peered harder. He recognized that shadowy jawline and the clever glint of the firelight off those eyes. They looked exactly like a younger version of Tadeas. "Demir?"

Demir made a shushing gesture. "I'd prefer people not know that I'm hanging out in a war zone," he replied quietly.

Idrian lowered his voice and tried to hide his shock. Had Demir been loitering here long? Did he hear Idrian and Mika gossiping about him? "Does Tadeas know you're here?"

"Not yet. I tried to catch him earlier but he got pulled into a meeting with General Stavri." Demir grimaced. "Like I said, I'd rather people not know I'm here. I need a favor. Shouldn't take more than a few hours."

"Now?" Idrian looked around, bewildered. It wasn't even nine o'clock yet and soldiers were already snoring. He wanted to do the same.

"Unfortunately, yes. I need an escort behind enemy lines."

Idrian snorted. "I need direct orders for something like that."

"Not from your new sponsor, you don't. I have some prerogative over your assignments."

Idrian was still reeling from Demir's presence. This was the Lightning Prince; the provincial governor who squashed a major rebellion and made it look easy while doing it. Even though Holikan was ultimately remembered as a disaster, soldiers still whispered about just how good a commander Demir was on that campaign. The heights he'd fallen from were truly dizzying. "Escorting you behind enemy lines is stretching that a bit, don't you think?"

"Maybe. But I understand you have some interest in my mission."

"Which is?"

"I need to extract Master Kastora from the Grent Royal Glassworks."

Idrian had to resist the urge to reach up and touch his godglass eye. "Is he in danger?"

"I believe he is. I've been meeting up with my mother's old spies all afternoon. The Grent Glassworks was hit early this morning in an attempt to capture their designs, stockpiles, and siliceers. They repelled one of our regiments, but Kastora was wounded badly. Fighting in the area has tapered off and soldiers from both sides have moved east. The two of us should be able to slip in and slip out without being noticed."

Idrian's mouth was dry. If something had happened to Kastora, he didn't know what he'd do with himself. This time, he did touch his eye, thinking of the master siliceer who made it. "You're absolutely sure about that intelligence?"

"There shouldn't be any obstacle that a breacher and a glassdancer can't handle," Demir assured him.

Idrian warred with himself briefly. He was still reeling from Demir's sudden appearance and would be well within his rights to rebuff the demand. Demir had been gone for nine years, after all. Could he even be trusted? But this was Tadeas's nephew, and if Master Kastora was in danger . . . "I'll get my armor," he said.

7

Demir was surprised that Idrian came along so readily, especially looking as worn-out as he did, but he wasn't going to look that gift horse in the mouth. The big breacher returned in his armor ten minutes later, sword and shield slung over his shoulders, a massive cloak draped over his armor to keep the moonlight from glinting off the steel.

No one questioned him as he moved past his sleeping companions, and he simply nodded to Demir to lead the way.

Demir remained for a few moments, watching Mika and Valient sitting quietly by the fire. He desperately wanted to say hello. Back during the Holikan campaign he'd spent only a few days with the Ironhorns but they'd all treated him more like family than a commanding officer. He'd loved it then, and he craved it now. At a grunt from Idrian he shook off the thought. The Ironhorns were not his family—none of them but Tadeas, anyway—and he had his own responsibilities now.

It was the same with Idrian. The big breacher had aged in the last nine years; a little gray at the temples of his short black hair, a little more weathered and scarred; but he was the same man whose company Demir had enjoyed on the Holikan campaign. It was so damn good to see him that it hurt, and Demir wanted nothing more than to give him a hug. That would be wildly inappropriate, of course, and he doubted that Idrian felt the same. Once they were out in the darkness, Demir matched his stride with Idrian's, glancing sidelong at the breacher. "I did the best I could to find us a safe route, but you know better than I do that things change quickly in a war zone. Stay close, keep your eyes open."

"Horns ready, hooves steady," Idrian replied, lowering an eye patch down to conceal his purple godglass eye.

Demir felt a flicker of a smile cross his face. His uncle had been saying that since he was just a kid. Anyone who'd ever served in the Foreign Legion, officer or soldier, knew that motto and who it belonged to. Demir nodded his thanks, and the two set off into the night.

Demir navigated the city partly from memory—he'd spent plenty of time in Grent in his youth—and partly from a memorized map provided by one of his mother's spies inside the Ministry of the Legion. They crossed a dozen bridges, went through six checkpoints manned by Ossan soldiers where Idrian was waved through by recognition alone. They finally crossed into the northwestern districts of Grent, where the combat lines were hazy and whole communities seemed untouched by the war going on less than a mile away. They were behind enemy lines for sure, but Grent military presence was light, focused as it was on Ossa's primary attack.

Demir removed a glass egg from his pocket, holding it up in front of him and grasping it with his sorcery. He cracked it into half a dozen bullet-sized shards, letting them float just over his shoulder. If this action unnerved Idrian, the breacher didn't show it. Why would he? Demir had some idea how many glassdancers Idrian had fought and killed over the years, and it was not a single-digit number.

The night was relatively silent, broken only by the artillery duels going on to their south. The normal evening traffic was practically nonexistent, and the few Grent civilians they passed stared at Idrian's sword warily before hurrying on, no doubt mistaking Idrian for one of their own breachers.

"We're getting close," Idrian told him, gesturing toward a wooded hill looming less than half a mile from them. Smoke rose in the moonlit night, and the hillside flickered with building fires. It did not bode well for their journey. Demir swallowed bile, wishing he'd arrived in Ossa just two days earlier. He could have gone in and gotten back out, questioning Kastora without having to travel into a war zone.

It was, Demir realized, the first time Idrian had spoken in over an hour. The silence was comfortable, between two men with a job to do, but it still made the small of Demir's back clammy. What was going on in Idrian's head? No doubt he'd come along because of his own ties to Kastora, rather than as a favor to Demir. But what was he thinking about? Nine years since they last saw each other, and it was at the lowest point in Demir's life.

Idrian was not the kind of man Demir could *catch up* with, not like Kizzie. It made him very difficult to read. Were his commanding officers just as infuriated by his quiet dependability? Or did they take it for granted? If there was one thing a guild-family member hated, it was not knowing how to get inside the heads of their underlings.

Demir discarded his musings as they began to ascend the hill to the wrecked glassworks. The area was deathly silent and appeared to be abandoned. He stretched out his senses, looking for glassdancers. No one. He turned to meet Idrian's eye and gave a shake of his head as they hurried up to take position just outside the wall of the compound. "No glassdancers," he told Idrian. "In fact I don't hear anyone." He tried to keep the frustration out of his voice. If Kastora was dead, or had withdrawn farther into the city, he was equally out of Demir's grasp, and his mother's mystery would remain unsolved.

"Two soldiers in that doorway there," Idrian said, nodding around a corner, "a young man and a middle-aged woman. They're both half asleep." He put up his sword, sliding it into the strap across his back and hanging his shield from the hook on his left pauldron. "Looks like you didn't need me after all."

Demir glanced around the compound, his stomach falling. Not just for Kastora, but for the place itself. The main office had gone up in flames, possibly taking decades of silic knowledge with it. Furnaces had been destroyed by the flames, and one of the two dormitories. The destruction made him sick. He rounded the corner, keeping his senses taut, and approached the pair of Grent soldiers in their orange-and-white uniforms sleeping in the doorway to the only remaining furnace room.

Neither noticed him until he was practically on top of them. The young man started awake, leaping to his feet and leveling his musket at Demir while hissing at his companion. "Show us your hands, stranger! Looters will be shot on sight!"

Demir carefully removed his left glove and showed his glassdancer sigil. "I'd suggest lowering your weapons." He subtly altered his accent, giving himself the slightest Grent drawl.

Both soldiers were up and alert now, and they paled visibly in the firelight before lowering their weapons. The woman, nervous and haggard, swallowed hard. "Apologies, sir. We didn't know . . ."

Demir waved it off. "I'm looking for Kastora. I haven't been able to find him, nor get news of his health."

The soldiers glanced at each other, seemingly about to answer, when the woman gasped. "Holy shit. It's the Ram."

Idrian moved up to stand beside Demir. Demir shot him a glance, wondering if it would be easier or harder with him out in the open. "At ease, soldiers," Idrian said.

"You're . . . you're not supposed to be here," the young man said. If they'd balked at seeing a glassdancer, they were practically shitting themselves now. "You're an Ossan."

"Ossan or not," Idrian replied, "Kastora is my friend." He peered at the woman. "Tinny, right? And . . . Geb? You're part of the glassworks garrison. We met last time I visited to have my eye worked on."

"The Ram remembered my name," Tinny whispered loudly to Geb, her mouth hanging open.

Demir put his hand over his mouth to hide a smile. No pretending to be a Grent glassdancer then. But this might be easier. "Kastora?" he prompted gently.

The pair seemed to deflate. Geb said, "I'm sorry, Ram. He's hurt. Hurt real bad. The garrison was ordered out and even with all the best godglass at hand we couldn't stabilize him enough to move him. He's not going to last the night. Tinny and I volunteered to stay with him until the end. It's the least we could do after he's been so good to us over the years."

Demir's gaze fell on the open door behind them. By the flickering light of the burning buildings he could just make out a makeshift cot, piles of bloody bandages and blankets, and a person lying in that heap. He shoved his way between the soldiers and approached quickly, falling on his knees. He'd met Kastora, long ago, but had no memory of the kindly, pained face that stared back up at him through half-closed eyes. Demir examined the face for a few moments, then glanced down at the bloody coverings. He was no surgeon, but an aggressive bayoneting was the only thing he could think of that would put a man in such a state.

"Kastora?" he asked.

The old man opened his lips to reveal that he was clutching several pieces of milkglass and cureglass between his teeth. He used his tongue to move them off to one side. "Who are you?" he muttered.

"I'm Demir Grappo. Adriana's son."

"She sent help, did she?" His words were slow, but surprisingly coherent for someone at death's door. He'd probably made that milkglass himself. "Could have come sooner, Lightning Prince."

Demir flinched at the nickname, surprised someone like Kastora even knew about it. He turned and gestured for Idrian to join him. The breacher said something quietly to the two soldiers, then joined Demir at Kastora's bedside.

"Idrian? Piss, I could have used the two of you this morning."

"I'm sorry, Master," Idrian said softly. "I would have come if I'd known."

"Of course, of course." Kastora's eyes returned to Demir. "What's *your* excuse?"

"My excuse?" Demir felt his eyes narrow, and tried to remind himself that he was talking to a dying man. "My excuse is that I only just returned from the provinces yesterday. My mother has been murdered, her death used as pretext for this war, and all I have from her is a note telling me to talk to you immediately."

Kastora stared back at him in silence for some time. "That's a good excuse," he finally admitted. "What happened to Adriana?"

Demir could see the death in the old man's eyes. It would be here soon, no helping it, but he bit back his questions and recounted the details of his mother's death—and the subsequent outbreak of war—as best he could in a brief few moments. He had barely finished when he realized Kastora was muttering to himself. He leaned forward to listen.

"They couldn't have known what we were up to, could they? No. It's impossible. No one knew. It must have been unrelated. But the confession, the war. It is too convenient. It is . . ." He stopped, his eyes once again focusing on Demir. "The prototype. It was . . ." He tried to gesture. ". . . destroyed in the fire."

"What prototype?" Demir asked, feeling his breath catch in his throat. Here it was—the reason his mother had partnered with Kastora. Some kind of silic advance? A new godglass? He grasped Kastora by the shoulder, hoping the physical touch would help the old man focus.

"Adriana didn't tell you?"

Demir felt a pang of conscience. If he'd been here, he would already know what was going on. If he'd been here, his mother might still be alive. "She didn't get the chance."

"Of course. The prodigal son. Do you know *anything*?" The final word dripped with despair and derision.

"You'll have to be more specific," Demir replied, trying to keep the sarcasm out of his voice.

Kastora let out another shuddering sigh. "There is so much to explain and not enough time. Where to begin?" He raised his voice. "Tinny, Geb. Leave us in private, please."

The two soldiers, still standing in the doorway, withdrew without protest, leaving Demir and Idrian alone with Kastora. Despite how well-acquainted he must be with dying men, Demir was surprised to see Idrian looking very uncomfortable. Idrian said, "I should go too. Whatever you two have to discuss is silic business. I'm just a soldier."

"No!" Kastora objected. "This is my deathbed confession. I will not give it before just one man that I do not know. You will stay, Idrian, if only to repay the kindness I've shown to you."

Idrian's apparent discomfort grew, but he remained, pressing gently on his godglass eye with two fingers. Demir reached out to take Kastora by the hand. Blood smeared between their fingers. "Tell us what you need to say." Kastora stared at the ceiling in silence for some time, and Demir worried that he was slipping away. He gave him a shake, his patience waning. "Come on, man! You have to tell me!"

"There is too much," Kastora said again in barely a whisper. Stronger, he continued, "The cindersand is running out."

Demir scoffed. He couldn't help it. It was a simple statement, at once true—cindersand was a finite resource, after all—and ridiculous. "That can't be possible. There are thousands of mines and quarries all over the world. They produce so much . . ." He trailed off at the serious stare from the old master. "Explain."

"Those mines," Kastora said, "are empty, or close to it. Governments all over the world are already tapping into their stockpiles. Production is down, prices are up. At the current rate, it will take less than six months before the general public will find it impossible to buy godglass. In a few years, only guild-families and kings will be able to acquire it."

Demir glanced at Idrian. The breacher's facade was close to unreadable, but there was a glint in his one eye. Fear, perhaps. Demir didn't blame him. Without cindersand you couldn't make godglass. *Everything* depended on godglass. What Kastora was intimating wasn't just the loss of a lesser material, but of sorcery itself. Civilization would collapse just as surely as it would with the disappearance of gunpowder or printing presses or waterwheels.

It couldn't be true. Demir's mind warred against the idea, and yet here was one of the greatest silic masters stating it as his deathbed confession. Demir thought back to his last day in the provinces, unable to buy a piece of cheap skyglass. Before that, he'd struggled to find witglass, and before that, forgeglass had been more expensive than he expected. At the time he'd just ascribed it to the breakdown of supply in the poorer regions of the Empire, but now he wasn't so sure.

"What do I do with this information?" Demir asked, not bothering to hide the edge of desperation in his voice. He felt as if a massive burden had been placed upon his shoulders. "What did my mother have to do with it? What is the prototype?"

Kastora took a deep breath, as if summoning some reserve of inner strength just to get the words out. He seized Demir by the arm. The master's hand was surprisingly strong. "Do you know what a phoenix channel is?"

It sounded familiar, like something Demir's studies had brushed upon long ago. He glanced at Idrian, who just shook his head.

"It is the great goal of the silic sciences," Kastora explained, "a mechanism by which energy is turned into sorcery, effectively allowing us to recharge spent pieces of godglass."

Demir scowled. Memories of long-forgotten studies leapt forward. What had his tutor called the phoenix channel? *Simple. Elegant. Unobtainable.* "A phoenix channel would allow us to avert the disaster of sorcery running out," Demir replied slowly. He could feel his eyes widen at the implication. "You made one, didn't you?"

"I did! Your mother and I designed it together. It was her idea to use cinderite, rather than just regular godglass. It was destroyed in the fire. You can find what remains . . ." Kastora shuddered again, closing his eyes briefly. ". . . in the corner over there. It can be rebuilt, but you will need the schematics and someone talented enough to follow them. I sent both away."

Demir searched his pockets for a small notebook and a pencil. He wrote down the word "cinderite." It was a rare material, formed naturally when lightning struck deposits of cindersand. "Where did you send them?"

"To your hotel. Her name is Thessa Foleer." Kastora took a deep breath. "She is a twenty-two-year-old journeyman, and my protégé. She is the only one I'd trust to finish my work. I have not seen more raw silic talent in my lifetime. If she does not make it to the hotel, you *must* find her."

Demir stared over Kastora's head, mind churning, trying to form some kind of a plan. Thessa could be anywhere—captured, dead, on the run. She might be at the hotel by the time he returned, or she might have already boarded a ship for Purnia to escape the fighting. "What does she look like?" Kastora stared back at him with the eyes of a dying man who'd just been asked for a laundry list, but Demir did not retract the question. "I need to know," he pressed.

Finally Kastora said, "A little taller than you. Dirty-blond hair. Soft features. Light skin." He seemed to push the words out with great effort, and Demir wondered if he had more than moments left. Kastora continued, "She has the scars of a siliceer but . . . she is also an experienced falconer. You'll see those scars as well."

Demir scribbled more notes—Thessa's name, her description. He let Kastora talk, giving him additional details about both the siliceer and the phoenix channel. He could sense the life slipping out of Kastora, each word growing more pained, each breath more labored. When he finished, his whole body seemed to sag in exhaustion.

"The soldiers who attacked you this morning," Demir asked, "did they know about the phoenix channel?"

"I'm not sure," Kastora gasped painfully. "They didn't seem to be looking for anything in particular. They just wanted to capture the glassworks. Good strategic sense at the start of a war." He chuckled, though Demir wasn't sure what was funny about it. Perhaps the giddiness of so much pain-killing milkglass. Kastora's head lolled to one side, his skin pale, the light in his eyes growing dim. Demir squeezed his hand, silently wishing the old man more life so that he could get more information.

Kastora gave another shuddering sigh, and this one felt more final than the others. His face relaxed, his body sagging against his makeshift bed. His grip on Demir's hand loosened. "I can't fight it anymore, Demir."

"Is there anything else?" Demir begged, shaking Kastora's shoulder once more.

"It's time to let him go," Idrian said.

Demir swore under his breath. So many questions. No time. This wasn't Kastora's responsibility anymore. It was now Demir's. "It's all right," Demir relented, "I'll make sure your work is finished."

"You must find Thessa," Kastora ordered. "Enough of this. Let me die." He spat the cureglass out of the corner of his mouth, and though he still held the milkglass between his teeth, he began to convulse. It took him several minutes to die, and he did not go quietly.

Demir clutched the master's hand until long after he was dead, thinking. There was so much to consider, more than he could fathom in a single day. Finding out that the cindersand was running out was enough to stagger anyone. The possibility of a phoenix channel—of recycling pieces of godglass—was a light at the end of a very dark tunnel. He was brought out of his reverie by the appearance of Idrian, who he did not even realize had left. The breacher carried a piece of canvas, which he laid gently over Kastora's body. Demir got to his feet and took a step back to stand next to Idrian, wondering what was going through the breacher's mind.

"You understand what you just heard must remain a secret?" Demir asked.

Idrian nodded solemnly.

If it were anyone else, Demir would have already killed them with a shard of glass through the back of their neck. There was enough lying around to make it easy and this was too big to be trusted to flapping mouths. But he knew Idrian's character. He trusted him, just as Kastora had trusted him. Demir forced himself to walk away from the body and found, resting in the opposite corner of the furnace room, the remains of what had once been Kastora's prototype. It was an odd contraption, mostly destroyed by the flames, but what remained was a box containing a broken tube, several large pieces of godglass, and half-melted sheets of tin.

Kastora had said that the design was Demir's mother's idea; another gift she'd left behind, but one that had been destroyed by idiot soldiers trying to capture the glassworks. Demir ran a hand through his hair. "I have no idea how I'm going to do this. I don't have the knowledge to make a new one of these. I don't even have the connections with people who could try."

Idrian snorted. "Find Thessa. I know her, and she's just as skilled as Kastora claimed."

"And if I can't find her?"

"You're the Lightning Prince. You'll think of something."

"The Lightning Prince has been dead for nine years," Demir snapped. "He lived a short and horrible life." He pinched the bridge of his nose, trying to get his temper under control. This was too much for one man and he could feel the very concept of it threatening to break him. He pushed back. He could not afford to break again. There was too much at stake. In mere minutes everything in his life had become an afterthought. Hiring Kizzie to pursue those killers on his behalf suddenly seemed like the smartest thing he'd done in years. "I apologize."

He turned to find Idrian staring at him. The normally stoic breacher had a desperate, almost crazed look in his eye. For half a moment, Demir thought that he was going to be attacked.

Idrian said, "This phoenix channel: It can recharge spent godglass?"

"That's what Kastora said."

"So if you rebuild that, you could recharge the godglass in my eye?"

Demir was taken aback. "I suppose I could."

Idrian nodded to himself as if making a decision. "If you need anything—*anything at all*—I will exchange my services for use of the phoenix channel."

"Oh." Demir raised both eyebrows. Clearly that eye was even more important than he'd suspected. One would be a fool to take such a promise from a breacher lightly, and from the Ram in particular. Demir had just been offered a very valuable piece of credit. He sucked on his teeth, thinking of a way he could use it, but stopped himself. "I won't make any promises," he said. "I don't even know if I can rebuild the damned thing."

"I suggest that you make every effort possible to do so," Idrian said quietly. "And I'm not just saying that on my own behalf. I'm only a soldier, but I know what will happen if the cindersand runs out. This phoenix channel could save the Empire; the world."

Demir looked back to the other side of the furnace room, where Kastora's body was still warm. The pressure of this sudden new burden weighed on his shoulders like an anvil. Despite this, his thoughts were starting to focus better, his ideas feeling more concrete than they had in years. Purpose—not just pursuit of wealth or fame or sex or revenge but *real* purpose—had been thrust upon him. It did not resurrect that old part of him entirely, but it did wake it up.

"Anything at all?" he asked.

"Anything within my power," Idrian responded. "This is more important to me than you realize."

"For now, help me get the prototype back to the Ironhorns' camp. I'll have Tadeas deliver it from there." Demir stepped outside, glancing sidelong at the two Grent soldiers sharing a cigarette some ways down the road. He felt a pang of guilt that he hadn't thought to summon them over for Kastora's final moments. They had earned it, after all. He walked over to join them, offering them each a piece of fine-quality godglass. "Kastora has passed," he told them. "Thank you for what you did for him."

Tinny cleared her throat. "I don't know who you are—I don't even really know why this war broke out—but I'm glad you and Idrian were here for his final moments. We'll be going, if that's all right." She said the last words with trepidation, as if still waiting to be murdered at any moment.

Demir gestured for them to withdraw and turned back to the glassworks. He frowned at something that caught his eye. There, sitting up in the branches of a large tree that stretched over the compound walls, was a falcon. He couldn't name the species in the darkness, but it was a big, beautiful bird. It was wearing anklets and jesses, the little leather straps dangling from its legs. A trained bird for certain. Was it Thessa's?

"Idrian," Demir called, "lend me your gauntlet."

8

Enforcers for the guild-families of Ossa fulfilled many different roles. Most were mere thugs: foot soldiers who could wield a cudgel and didn't mind breaking legs or skulls or property. Some were bodyguards or security. The most trusted of enforcers worked as personal couriers, taking contracts and correspondence between guild-family matriarchs and patriarchs.

Kizzie had always been good at two things. Her favorite was making Vorcien clients feel comfortable. Did a warehouse get burned down? Kizzie would hold the client's hand, commiserate, and liaise with the National Guard investigators. In her hands, an otherwise unimportant client would think the Vorcien had their best interests at heart at all times. Sometimes they really did, and sometimes Kizzie put on a good show. It helped that she had the Vorcien name and silic symbol, even if she wasn't a "real" member of the family.

Her other skill set—the one she'd had to rely on more since falling out of favor—was finding people.

She started her work for Demir immediately, and spent the first day discovering everything she could about the one man who'd already confessed to having a hand in Adriana Grappo's death. He was a Grent national named Espenzi Darfoor; a well-known blaggard from a family of medium importance within the Grent government. He was a gambler and womanizer with a dozen successful duels under his belt. He had no public connection to anyone in Ossa.

So why, Kizzie wondered, did he come to Ossa to kill Adriana?

The official explanation—the one that the Cinders had torn out of him using powerful enough shackleglass to drive him mad—was that he'd been paid a hefty sum by the Duke of Grent to participate in the killing. Was that true? Could Kizzie trust the Cinders, or the Inner Assembly, to actually tell the truth? Or was it all a convenient lie for a convenient war? The thought was a discomforting one, but Kizzie tried to focus on the facts as she knew them rather than jump to conclusions.

Six people, all meeting in Assembly Square, wearing masks to kill a well-liked reformer. As Demir had intimated, that was a conspiracy. Why a conspiracy, rather than just a good old-fashioned knife-in-the-dark assassination? With Espenzi in Cinder custody, insane from shackleglass, Kizzie would have to find his co-conspirators in order to get her answers.

Kizzie started at the beginning, looking for any clues that might lead down an untrodden path. She found the coach service that brought Espenzi into Ossa. She spoke with the waiter at the restaurant he ate at the night before, and then the concierge at the hotel he stayed at. She even tracked down the café he ordered tea from the following morning. She followed his footsteps perfectly all the way up until an hour before Adriana's death.

He had no clandestine meetings with hooded figures. Not at the restaurant, café, or hotel. To everyone that had met him, he was simply a middle-aged man slipping into Ossa for a brief change of scenery. He wasn't even armed.

It was frustratingly mundane. Not a single clue that Kizzie could use to find one of the other killers.

The following morning she changed her tactics, heading down to Assembly Square in person. The square was a busy place, filled with politicians, clerks, loitering bodyguards, and beggars. Winter solstice celebrations were still going on, causing impromptu parades of masked revelers, following the bread wagons as free food and drink were passed out to all who wanted it. Kizzie used gossip columns and newspaper reports to rebuild Adriana's murder in her mind's eye, trying to figure out in which directions the killers would have scattered to escape a passing National Guardsman.

She crossed the square, looking for a little nook underneath the towering statue of one of the founders of Ossa. The nook was barely two feet square and maybe six deep, and it was the home of a beggar who called herself Madame-under-Magna.

"Hey Courina," Kizzie said, squatting down next to the nook and peering inside. It was hard to tell in the bright morning sunlight reflecting off the marble, but the nook was crammed with blankets, newspapers, and the odds and ends a beggar might collect to survive the mild Ossan winter.

A pair of beady little eyes stared back at Kizzie, and a tiny, wizened hand was thrust out of the nook. "You will address me as Madame-under-Magna!"

Kizzie glanced up at the statue rising above them. It was, she realized, quite anatomically correct, despite wearing a long tunic. "Sorry. How are you, Madame-under-Magna?" She placed a heavy coin in that wizened little hand.

The hand and coin disappeared immediately. "Well enough, Kissandra. I heard you cleaned out the Castle Hill Garroters."

"You hear a lot of things."

"Poor Iasmos. What a nice little boy. Dorry was the cruel one, the real leader. But they're all gone now!" There was a strange little giggle. "I hear and I see, Kissandra. You want my services? I can tell you about a Stavri mistress or a corrupt Foreign Legion secretary." The eyes seemed to grow a little closer. "There are things that walk in the night. I have seen them, but to tell would be a king's ransom!" Madame-under-Magna cackled loudly. Kizzie had never actually been able to tell if Madame-under-Magna was insane, or just a good actress.

"I'm hoping you can tell me about Adriana Grappo's death. Who was behind it? Spies? Revolutionaries? A Fulgurist Society?"

Madame-under-Magna made a clicking sound with her tongue. "Oh, that I cannot do."

"You didn't see the killing?"

"I did, in fact! I saw her stop to check her pocket watch, as was her habit at the bottom of the stairs over there. I saw the killers flock, and I was the first to scream for help as the cudgels fell."

"If you saw it all, then why can't you tell me about it? I can pay."

"Because the Cinders have already bought my silence. I have a reputation to uphold, after all."

Kizzie settled back on her haunches, watching the afternoon light reflect off those beady little eyes. Madame-under-Magna was one of the most reliable sources of information in the city; a truly neutral figure who actually followed her codes of silence. Once someone paid her to *withhold* information, there was no getting it out of her short of shackleglass. Kizzie *did* have that piece that Demir gave her, but was not about to inflict it upon Madame-under-Magna, and certainly not in public.

Kizzie asked, "Can you at least tell me whether the facts presented to the public are true?"

"Ah. Hmm." Madame-under-Magna stared at her for a few moments before answering. "I would not break my contract with the Cinders to tell you that the facts are, indeed, true."

That was a surprise. "Six killers?" Kizzie asked. "And Espenzi hired by the Duke of Grent?"

"All true."

Kizzie thought she saw a fiendish little smile in the dark nook. Her informant was leaving something out. Kizzie considered the possibilities for a few minutes, crouching in silence beside the statue, before asking, "Was Espenzi caught on purpose? Offered to the Cinders to let the others get away?"

"You're a clever girl, Kissandra. I'm sad you didn't come to me before the Cinders."

Kizzie snorted in frustration and considered her options. The Cinders swept through right after Adriana's murder. Kizzie would get a similar response from every beggar, busker, food vendor, and loiterer. Any possible witness had already been threatened or paid into silence. Espenzi was a dead end, and so was Madame-under-Magna. Although . . . perhaps Kizzie was just asking the wrong question.

"If I can't ask you about Adriana's murder, then who *should* I ask?" Kizzie held out two more heavy coins.

"*Very* clever girl," Madame-under-Magna said again. She sniffed. "I have a cold."

Kizzie fished in her pocket until she found a good-quality piece of cure-glass and added it to the two coins. The hand snatched all three from her palm, and Madame-under-Magna cackled again. "You should ask Torlani the Breadman." A wizened little hand thrust into the sun to make a *go away* gesture. "No more questions."

Kizzie found Torlani the Breadman in one of the dozens of alleys that separated the various government buildings of Assembly Square. It was a narrow track, crammed with vendors, with barely enough space for two people to pass each other. The Breadman had a small cart at the far end. He was an old man, bent from years of reaching into ovens, his cart constantly being loaded by boys who rushed back and forth between him and his bakery on the other side of the district. He wore a tiny nose piercing; a little piece of low-quality auraglass, no doubt in the hope that it made him seem more enticing than his competition.

Torlani eyeballed Kizzie as she approached, taking in the stiletto at her belt and the silic sigil on her right hand. "You're Kissandra Vorcien," he said as she glanced over the various loaves. She found a small loaf, particularly crusty with burnt edges, and plucked it up, handing him a banknote.

"I am," she replied.

"I heard there was a gang over in Castle Hill stealing from you folks."

Glassdamn, word sure got around quick these days. "Not anymore." She bit into the bread, chewed, and grinned at him over it. "This is really good," she said between bites.

"Thank you." He looked down at her silic sigil again. "I'm not looking for protection."

Kizzie snorted. "And I'm not here to shake you down."

"Ah," the old man replied, visibly relaxing. "My mistake."

She made a magnanimous gesture. "No offense taken." She glanced around to make sure the other vendors were far enough away not to overhear her and said, "I was told you might know something about Adriana Grappo's murder."

Torlani went *white*. It was impressive, really. His whole face went slack, his eyes filling with fright, hands shaking slightly. "This . . . this is my little alley here. I was here when she was killed. Couldn't possibly know anything about it." He paused, seemed to gather himself. "Who told you that I did?" he demanded.

"Who do you think?" Kizzie snorted.

"Madame-under-Magna. That bitch! That . . ." Torlani made a frustrated sound. "I've already told the Cinders everything I know. I have nothing to add, and certainly not to a Vorcien."

Kizzie took a step back to examine the alley as a whole, then glanced toward the center of Assembly Square. If six people murdered Adriana and then scattered, it was almost guaranteed that one of them would run down this alley. Kizzie scoffed to herself and looked Torlani in the eye. "You saw one of the killers."

"I . . . have nothing to say!"

"I'm not asking on behalf of the Vorcien," she said.

Torlani frowned in a moment of confusion. "Then who?"

"Demir Grappo hired me."

At the very least, this information seemed to catch Torlani off guard. A dozen different emotions crossed his face in the space of a few moments, from surprise to consternation. "Why you?"

"Because we were childhood friends, and I have a reputation for personal integrity." It wasn't a boast. Everyone knew she'd fallen out of favor for exactly that reason. She pulled a calling card out of the pocket of her jacket, putting on an air that made it seem as if he were just one of dozens of leads. "You can ask around if you like. If there's something you'd like to get off your chest, just find me at this address."

Torlani didn't reach out for the card. He licked his lips. She could see immediately that he *wanted* to tell her something. It was on the tip of his tongue, straining to get out. All Kizzie needed to do was coax. He said, "The Cinders paid me well not to make a fuss."

"I'm not asking you to make a fuss," Kizzie replied gently. "Just tell me what you know."

"Adriana . . . was a secret patron of mine."

It was Kizzie's turn to be caught off guard. Secret patrons were not common. The whole point of the client-patron relationship was to publicly display prestige, clout, and allegiance. A secret patron might get a cut of the profits from, say, a bakery, but they couldn't tell their friends that they had ownership in the best bakery in town. The client, on the other hand, couldn't take advantage of their patron's name to prevent shakedowns or get better service from their suppliers.

"Why secret?" Kizzie asked.

"Independence is important to me," Torlani replied with a sniff. "Adriana financially supported my bakery on six different occasions, and sent her enforcers around anonymously when the Dorlani got pushy. I owe . . . I *owed* her my livelihood."

Kizzie picked her next words carefully. "Is there anything you want to tell her son about the way she died?"

She could see Torlani wrestling with himself. He picked up one of his own loaves of bread and bit into it, chewing savagely, muttering to himself. He swallowed and said, "If this comes back to me, I will deny everything."

"I'm not doing this for a magistrate," Kizzie said bluntly. "Nobody is going to know *who* it came from."

He hesitated for several more long moments before he spoke quietly. "Fine. I was standing just here at the moment of her murder. I heard yelling from the square, and when I looked"—he glanced toward the other end of the alley—"a man wearing a plain white mask came sprinting from that way. He tripped right in front of my cart and his mask came off for just a few seconds. I pretended not to see, but he didn't even look at me. He put his mask back on and took off."

"And you recognized him?"

"Of course I did. He's bought bread from me before."

Kizzie felt her heartbeat quicken. "And?"

"It was Churian Dorlani."

Kizzie felt her knees go just a little bit weak. Churian Dorlani was not, as these things went, a very important person. He was a mid-ranking cousin in the Dorlani guild-family. The fact that he had the Dorlani name at all was what caused a sweat to break out in the small of Kizzie's back. They were one of the five most powerful guild-families in Ossa, and their matriarch sat on the Inner Assembly.

This was supposed to be a Grent conspiracy. Why was a guild-family member involved?

"Did you tell the Cinders?" she asked.

Torlani shook his head. "Of course not. Outing one of the Dorlani to the Cinders would be a death sentence."

"But you told me. Even if you owed Adriana your livelihood . . ." Kizzie stopped herself. Was she so surprised by this she was questioning the intelligence of her own witness?

Instead of being annoyed, Torlani simply shook his head. "I sold a lot of bread to Adriana *and* to Demir. People have tried to forget him, but I remember when he was the most important person in Ossa. I remember how hard he tried to get people to see him as a politician instead of a glassdancer. There aren't many people who pass by my cart who want to change the world for the better, and I make note of those that do. If Demir wants to avenge his mother I will aid him in what small way I can."

"Thanks for the tip." Kizzie pulled a wad of banknotes out of her pocket—Demir could afford to be generous—and slipped them onto Torlani's tray, taking another loaf of bread with her. She walked back out into the square again, pondering her predicament. She'd half expected *some* guild-family to be involved. But the Dorlani . . .

This job had suddenly gotten a lot more complicated and a lot more dangerous. Part of her wanted to go back to Demir, return his money, and tell him to deal with it himself. She buried that inclination. She was not a coward. She'd taken on a job and she would damn well see it through.

She would have to be careful from here on out.

9

Demir returned to the Hyacinth in the early morning. He'd been up all night trying to piece together the rest of his mother's spy network within the Foreign Legion—dozens of contacts, of which only seven proved viable—and he'd done it all while lugging around an injured, frightened falcon. It wasn't his best work, and by the time he slipped through the back door of his hotel he was exhausted and frustrated. He went directly up the back stairwell to the roof, where there was a flat section set back from the vision of the street below.

The mews here was a large one, nearly as big as a stateroom—a massive cage divided into sections for multiple birds, and with its own equipment closet. It was long-abandoned, seemingly untouched since his own falcon died when he was twelve. He took the injured bird with him into the biggest of the cages and gently let it find a perch before removing the makeshift hood. It shuddered, looking around and giving a loud, piercing screech.

The falcon leapt from one perch to another, favoring its left wing, trembling slightly. It shied away from the sound from the street below, and Demir wondered if he should erect a baffle along that side of the roof to stop some of the racket. It was a project for another day—or one of the hotel staff.

Demir sank down to the floor of the mews, watching the falcon adjust to its new surroundings, and took a deep breath. He'd pored over the morning newspapers on his ride back to the hotel. Every piece of news he came across seemed to read in a completely different light—a minor increase in the price of cindersand made his heart skip a beat; the closing of a major quarry in Purnia caused his jaw to clench; a Stavri cindersand warehouse burning down, all contents ruined, left him feeling genuinely ill.

Yesterday all of those things would have been discarded as unrelated incidents—nothing major to worry about. Today they were obvious symptoms of a greater disease. The world was running out of cindersand. Without intervention, common sorcery would die out.

Just to settle himself down he'd spent the final leg of his journey reading a page 3 story about monsters being spotted in the provinces. That kind of lunatic rubbish usually put him in a better mood, but it had only caused his thoughts to grow darker. How could he solve the world's problems when the average person believed in ghosts and swamp crawlers and tree men? The effort required to face the road ahead seemed insurmountable.

"Best I can do for you right now," Demir said to the falcon, looking around at the mews. "I'll send someone up to tend to that bloody wing, and I bet the kitchen has a hare or two. For now, though, I have something of my own I need to deal with."

He left the poor animal in the mews and headed down to the hotel garden, purposefully avoiding his own staff—and the problems they'd present him with. He could let Breenen take care of all those, at least for the moment.

The hotel garden was a massive enclosed area the size of a regular city block, lined on all sides by hallways on the main floor and hotel rooms above those. It was a peaceful spot, keeping out the worst of the city noise, filled with trees, the beds layered with winter flowers. On the far side of the garden was an old glassworks—a small furnace room left over from when the hotel used to keep a siliceer on staff, well before Demir was born. He made a mental note to have it fixed, just in case he managed to find Thessa.

The old glassworks was not his destination, however. The only other building in the garden was a mausoleum. It was a beautiful construction of rare white Purnian marble with thick veins of purple running through it, decorated with the likenesses of the founders of the Grappo dynasty, their carved faces looking severe in the stone. On the surface the mausoleum was not very big—just a decorative obelisk with a heavy, worn wooden door. Most hotel visitors walked right past it, more interested in the rest of the massive garden.

The heavy door opened on oiled hinges, revealing a dark pit that Demir lit by turning a screw beneath a gas lantern just inside. White-and-purple marble stairs descended sharply into the ground. Demir proceeded slowly, lighting every lantern, as if dispelling the darkness within the crypt would dispel the same within his mind. The narrow stairway opened into a larger, vaulted room deep beneath the garden; a long chamber bigger than a hotel suite and lined with the marble busts of every guild-family matriarch and patriarch going back thirty generations.

Adriana Grappo's ashes were contained in an urn near the far end of the crypt. The pedestal above the ashes was empty, as her bust had not yet been completed. Demir gazed at that empty spot with a frown, wrestling with something deeply unsatisfying about seeing her remains without her likeness to gaze upon. Of course, the likeness would not be the mother he remembered—the sculptor would produce a likeness of a young Adriana, taken from a portrait of her in her early twenties. He knew he would struggle with that too.

"Hi, Mother," he said to the empty room. To his surprise, it felt good to say it. But there was no answer. There never would be, and he felt a pain deep within his chest. "You really screwed me over, didn't you? I could have handled the hotel and the clients and sponsoring the Ironhorns—but a phoenix channel? The weight of saving the Empire on my shoulders? You should have said something earlier. You should have prepared me. We saw each other just a few months ago. You could have told me then."

He wrestled with his thoughts, feeling them pulled this way and that. He was being unfair and he knew it. "I'm sorry I wasn't here to protect you. I was selfish, and a fool, and I've spent a third of my life hiding from the person you raised me to be." He turned away abruptly, walking back to the stairs and pausing there for several minutes before he was able to return to her urn.

"I hated you so much after Holikan," he said, hearing the anger in his own words. "I hated the way you had raised me; the tutors and the schedules and the expectations. I hated that my childhood was years shorter than those of my friends because you saw my potential and sought to cultivate it. I was a prodigy at what I did, but the pressure you put on me made me brittle. I wasn't prepared for a disaster like Holikan. It was *my* fault—my responsibility—but you were culpable.

"I don't think I can blame you any longer, though. You just did what you thought was best. I know how much you loved me. Love is in short supply among the guild-families, and I wish I had told you that I loved you back while you were still alive. I wish I'd forgiven you." He paused, staring at the empty pedestal. "I forgive you, Mother. You made mistakes, but you also put a lot of good in me. You made sure that I cared about people and ideals, and not just godglass and money. You made sure I was the type of person who would save a glassdamned bird from a war zone, even though it was a waste of my time. You made me different from the rest of these guild-families, and if there's anything that redeems me it'll be that. I can't promise I'll make you proud. But I will try."

He knelt and touched the urn briefly before turning his gaze toward the marble bust immediately to the right of the empty pedestal. It was of a young man with a strong jaw, high forehead, and flat ears. He looked nothing like Demir, oddly enough, until you peered into the eyes. Even in marble they were clever, and the cocky smile on the man's lips looked like the sculptor had taken it from Demir's mirror.

Demir ran his hand over the familiar contours of the man's face, like he'd done hundreds of times as a child. "Take care of her, Dad," he said, and turned and left the crypt.

He emerged into the afternoon sun and took a moment to stare up into the sky, composing himself until the pain in his chest began to recede and he could breathe deeply without difficulty. He felt . . . a little more complete. Like he'd taken a step he didn't know he needed to take. He shook it out of his head, forcing himself to return to the greater world.

There was a lump caught in his throat, and no matter how hard he tried he couldn't get it down. How was he possibly going to do this? To find Thessa? To make a phoenix channel? To protect all his new responsibilities? His mother's note had said not to trust even Breenen with knowledge of the phoenix channel. Did he really have to do all this alone?

A sound suddenly reached him, echoing from inside the hotel. He tilted his head, listening carefully until it repeated again, then again. It was his name, and he recognized the voice that was shouting it. He was sprinting for the garden door before he could stop himself, flying down the hallways.

"Demir!" the voice demanded. "Where is Demir?"

He reached the top of the stairs to find the biggest man he'd ever seen standing just inside the front door. He was six and a half feet tall and half as wide, with the light skin of a northern provincial and the thick accent to match. He wore a fine embroidered jacket of crimson and purple that made Demir's whole wardrobe look drab. His face was enormous, as big around as a barrel, small eyes and mouth buried in flesh like a bucketful of bread dough. His brown hair was pulled back in a ponytail that went down below his shoulders.

Demir could pick out the newest members of the hotel staff by which ones were staring with absolute awe and fear. Baby Montego, world champion cudgelist, one of the few people who could make a glassdancer piss themselves in fear.

"Baby!" Demir yelled. He took the stairs two at a time and sprinted across the lobby.

"Demir, what are you . . . Do not do that!"

Demir leapt into the giant's embrace, wrapping his arms around the thick neck and squeezing as hard as humanly possible. Montego gave a long-suffering sigh and Demir felt a hesitant pat on the back.

He dropped to the floor, took a step back, and gave his best friend a long and thoughtful look. "Baby, you have gotten really glassdamned fat."

"I have broken stronger men for smaller insults," Montego grumbled.

"Then you should stop looking like a milk-fat, overgrown toddler," Demir shot back. He turned to call toward the concierge's office, "Breenen, have the suite next to mine made up for Montego. Make sure he gets every service and comfort."

"I am here on the matter of your mother's death," Montego replied, shaking a newspaper at Demir. "I will not be babied."

"Then I shall not have our carpenter construct an enormous crib. Tell me how you got here so quickly."

"My yacht had just returned to port when Capric's message arrived. I bought every spare horse and carriage between here and Yavlli so I could travel without interruption. Speak, Demir! Tell me what has happened."

"In private." Demir grabbed Montego by the sleeve, dragging him toward the stairs. They were soon inside his office, where he closed the door and allowed himself to collapse onto one of the sofas. For the first time in two days, he felt all of the public masks he wore fall away and he was able to be himself—raw and unguarded—around another person. At that moment he made the conscious decision to tell Montego everything. To piss with Mother's warning. If he couldn't trust Montego with the world, he might as well hang himself now.

The giant cudgelist remained near the door, staring at Demir. "You look awful."

"Thanks."

"I'm not joking, Demir. I haven't seen you look this out of sorts since Holikan. This isn't just your mother's death. Something has happened. You will tell me now."

"Mother is dead. I have returned. I now have to save a young woman so that she can help me save the world."

"I think I'd like the longer version."

Demir took a deep breath, resisting the urge to reach for a glass of whiskey or a piece of mind-numbing dazeglass. "Then you shall have it." He recounted the events of the last two days in detail, leaving nothing out, talking until his throat was dry and his head pounded. Montego sat on the sofa opposite of him, leaning on a silver-headed cane, a look of focus on his comically broad face. When people saw Montego they rarely looked past his size or his cudgeling record, but Demir knew that beneath that heavy brow was a mind not unlike his own. Montego was sometimes quiet, sometimes gregarious, but always brilliant.

Demir finished his tale with a sigh, throwing his arms wide. "It's too much, Baby. I can't do it."

"Slow down," Montego responded, holding up a massive hand. "You do not trust the Assembly's investigation?"

"Of course not."

"Kizzie was a good choice. I'm glad you brought her in."

"Will that be awkward for you?"

"Your mother is dead," Montego replied seriously. "She funded my first fight. She *adopted* me. I want Kizzie to continue the hunt for her killers. Awkwardness has no place in whatever happens next."

"Well said."

Montego made a few thoughtful sounds. "We shall let her work that angle. You do believe Kastora about the cindersand?"

"No reason not to."

"I haven't worn godglass for years," Montego snorted. "Makes the glassrot scales on my legs itch. I suppose I would miss it, at least for those around me." He grimaced. "The consequences of its absence would be . . . drastic."

Demir chuckled. "Your talent for understatement will never cease to amaze me."

"And your talent for despair will never cease to amaze *me*. Don't try to hide it, I can see it in your face. You're wearing the same expression you wore that month you'd convinced yourself you were in love with that Nasuud princess."

"You don't think I should despair? Kastora was clear on one thing: we need this Thessa woman if we're going to remake his phoenix channel, and she's disappeared." Demir finally did cross the room and pour them each a finger of whiskey. He brought one glass to Montego, then lifted his own, noting that it was the glass he'd destroyed the other day when he thought he saw someone outside his window. A glassdancer could force glass back together again, but he'd done a sloppy job of it, leaving the cup warped and ruined.

Montego sipped his whiskey and shook his head. "No, I don't think you should despair. Clearly there are enemies to be rooted out. Clearly there is an economic disaster on the horizon. Clearly . . . Look at me. Demir, look at me!"

Demir forced himself to meet Montego's beady eyes.

"Clearly," Montego continued, "this will be a difficult road. But you are Demir Grappo. I am Baby Montego. I have returned and I will not leave again until the world is set right. I swear it."

Demir swallowed hard, only to realize that the lump in the back of his throat was gone. He felt lighter, almost giddy, the darkness that had covered him retreating before Montego's unflinching gaze. "Your optimism," he said, his voice cracking, "is foolhardy."

"And your despair is pointless. We have work to do, Demir. You are a glassdancer and the finest mind of our generation. You were a provincial governor at fourteen! You negotiated a massive trade agreement between the Nasuud and the Balkani, ending centuries of enmity, and your province got rich on the deal!"

Demir felt the corner of his mouth twitch upward at the memory. "I *was* the finest mind of our generation."

"I believe you still are. You're just out of practice."

Demir wanted to fight him. Every fiber of his being protested against his own abilities, convinced that he could not possibly accomplish this task in front of him. His whole psyche felt on wobbly ground, waiting to crack and crumble like it had at Holikan. But Montego hadn't been with him that horrible day. The cudgelist was a firm foundation upon which to get his mental footing, his confident optimism battering down Demir's most powerful doubts.

He took a shaky breath, pulling himself together, restoring his public masks so that the hotel staff wouldn't see how he truly felt. "Fine. We'll do it your way, you big, dumb optimist. But when I fail, I'm going to blame it on you."

Montego slapped his thigh and bellowed out a laugh. "Hah! I knew I'd bring you around. Remember, Demir, you can't conquer your enemies until you conquer yourself."

"One of Mother's sayings," Demir said, cocking an eyebrow. That specter he felt last night—the niggling, hesitant memory of his old self—seemed to pace around in the back of his head, coaxed out by Montego's presence. Perhaps he really could do this. He closed his eyes, forcing out all the chaos until he could focus on what was immediately before him. "Fine. We can do this. Breenen is taking care of the hotel. Capric is helping me set up a number of business deals to buoy the Grappo coffers. I still have the responsibilities of the patriarch, but you and I must cast our net wide if we're to find Thessa."

"Where do we look first?"

Demir had been asking himself the same question all night. "She would have gone either north or south from Grent, giving the fighting a wide berth to enter the city."

"I'll go looking in person," Montego offered.

"You're not tired from your journey?"

"Bah! My friend needs me. What is sleep before such an obligation? I shall leave immediately to begin my search for Thessa."

"And I'll find out if one of the guild-families snatched her up." Demir could feel his confidence growing, the strength returning to his mind and body. "Thank you for coming, Montego."

Montego cracked a smile at Demir's use of his given name. "I wouldn't be your friend if I didn't. But you're hesitating again. Do not hesitate, Demir. Act!" He leapt to his feet and threw open the office door. "Breenen!" he bellowed. "I need new horses for my carriage. I must fly!" With that, he disappeared.

Demir did not allow himself the time for doubt—he began to write letters immediately, preparing queries for his mother's spies, his own contacts, and old acquaintances that might be able to help. He was careful in his wording, never inquiring directly after Thessa, making sure not to tip his hand to anyone who might prove untrustworthy.

He'd been at it for some time when a porter appeared in the doorway. "Sir, you have a delivery from Idrian Sepulki. The soldiers guarding it said you wanted to receive the delivery yourself."

Demir sealed several of his letters and gave them to a bellhop. He followed the porter down to one of the rear delivery doors of the hotel, where he shooed everyone out of the room before prying open what looked like a standard military musket crate. Inside were the burnt-out remains of Kastora's phoenix channel.

It was Demir's first good look at the prototype, and he circled it for several minutes as he tried to work out what it had looked like before the fire. The outer shell—a chamber with thin tin walls, stuffed with cork insulation— was mostly burned away. Inside that, cracked and broken, was a two-foot-long piece of cinderite decorated with omniglass rings.

Demir had rarely seen a piece of cinderite this big, and the clear omniglass with which it was encircled was almost as uncommon. Omniglass was an expensive, finicky sorcerous material that enhanced other god-glasses, probably used in this case to accentuate the energy-conversion process Kastora hoped to capture.

To re-create the prototype, Demir would need both the materials and someone skilled enough to put them all together without ruining it. His and Montego's energy would go toward the latter, but that didn't mean he couldn't acquire the former while they worked. He found a porter waiting for him outside. "Have this taken up to my rooms," he told the young man, "and then take Breenen a message. I want him to locate every large piece of cinderite—in both private and public collections—within fifty miles."

Idrian sat in one corner of his temporary tenement room with the palm of one hand pressed against his godglass eye. Sunlight streamed in through the narrow window, slashing rays through the dusty air, and he could hear the organized chaos of his battalion preparing themselves for the day just outside. Sleep had not come easy for him, not after watching Kastora die and then making sure that the phoenix channel was delivered to the Hyacinth. He felt beaten down, imagining mud on his knees and welts across the back of his neck, though it had been decades since his father had dared to raise a hand to him.

Somewhere in the tenement, a child laughed.

Idrian forced himself up, leaving his bedroll and crossing to the other side of the room, where Braileer had set out his armor. He ran his fingers across a few small mendings, feeling the deep notches in the steel frame of the shield and the heavy scratches across the hammerglass of his left pauldron. It was apparent that repairs *had* been done, though it would be a stretch to say they'd been done well. Idrian grimaced. Was an inexperienced armorer better than no armorer at all? Braileer hadn't made the damage worse, at least.

Idrian looked in his pack for a pencil and paper, half minded to write a message back to the Ministry. When he could find neither, he began to compose it in his head: Braileer needed a few more years of training before he saw active duty; his presence was a disservice to them both; Idrian needed an experienced armorer. Returning to his armor, Idrian did a more thorough examination. One of the broken straps was mended, and quite well. The polish on the metal was properly done. There were, he admitted to himself, a few competent points.

A child laughed again somewhere in the tenement and Idrian shook his head. Glassdamned civilians needed to get out of here. He could be sympathetic that many of them had no place to go, but fleeing into the countryside or deeper into either Grent or Ossa was a better alternative than staying in an active war zone. He stepped into the hallway, following the sound of the laughter to the end of the building, where he found a tenement door opened a crack. The child's giggle issued from within.

"Listen," he said loudly, knocking on the door and pushing it open, "you need to move . . ." He trailed off, staring at the room for several moments. It was abandoned, just as threadbare and empty as his own, with a bedroll and pack belonging to one of the Ironhorns' sergeants sitting in the corner but nothing else. Certainly no children. Idrian swallowed hard and pressed on his godglass eye. "Shit," he whispered.

He gripped the eye carefully and pulled it out of the socket, lifting it to peer into the purple, cloudy depths with his one good eye. The color was a little duller than the last time he'd checked, but not so much as to reduce the effectiveness of the sorcery it emanated.

"Sir," called a voice.

Idrian pushed the eye back into its socket and whirled around to see Braileer standing just outside the door.

"Everything all right, sir?"

Idrian glanced into the empty room and closed the door, forcing himself to ignore the child's laughter that came from within instantaneously. "It is."

"Your breakfast is ready, sir."

Idrian joined Braileer back in his own room, sitting down on his bedroll as the young man set a tin plate in front of him. Idrian was deep in his own thoughts, trying not to think about that child's laughter while coming up with a way to let Braileer down easy. Would the young man be ashamed of being immediately removed from his position? Or secretly relieved not to have to go into combat? Or both?

He tapped his knife against the tin plate a few times thoughtfully before using it to shovel food into his mouth. He was immediately jolted back to the present, his palate hit by several powerful flavors. He looked down. "This isn't Laurent's gruel," he said.

Braileer was watching him keenly. "I'm sorry if it's a bit substandard, sir. The quartermaster—"

"Laurent."

"Laurent wouldn't believe that I was your new armorer, so I had to swipe a few things from the castoffs at his prep station. It's just potatoes fried in lard, with onion leaves, some old garlic, and a bit of cheese."

Idrian took another bite and chewed slowly, tilting his head to one side to listen for more distant laughter. Nothing. His phantoms were silent for the moment. Pleasure of any kind tended to quiet them. "This is better than anything Laurent has ever made us. And you whipped it up from his extras?"

"Yes, sir."

"You always light-fingered?"

Braileer seemed to sense the trap in that question and ducked his head. "I'm not a thief, sir. I'm the youngest in a big, poor family. If I wanted to eat I needed to swipe from my brothers' plates without getting caught."

"Then how do you know how to cook?"

"I apprenticed with an armorer's chef for three years. One day the armorer's regular assistant got ill, so I filled in. The poor girl died, and I learn quick, so I became an armorer's apprentice."

Idrian finished his meal, enjoying every bite, taking solace in the warmth and richness of the food. When he finished he leaned back against the wall and set aside his plate, watching Braileer right back. "The work you did last night is . . . well, it's not bad, but it's not good either."

"I understand, sir. I won't lie—my master argued with the recruiter for over an hour when they came around and conscripted me. Said I wasn't ready, and he was right. I can't do a perfect job, but I guarantee I'll be better than nothing."

Idrian already liked this kid. Quick, self-aware, attentive. "A Foreign Legion armorer pays a lot better than an armorer's apprentice," he observed.

"That it does, sir."

Idrian licked clean his knife, wiped it on his uniform pants, and returned it to his belt. "How much?"

"A thousand a month, sir." Braileer hesitated for a moment. "Are you going to dismiss me from your service, sir?"

"Hm." Idrian looked at his plate and seriously considered licking that clean as well. "Not yet. We'll see how you fit in," he said. "Where is Tadeas?"

"Major Grappo is just outside, sir."

Idrian left Braileer to roll up his bedroll and headed outside, where various Ironhorn squads all headed off in different directions. It was clear that orders had already been handed out, but Idrian himself hadn't been included. His commanding officer and longtime friend stood in the center of the makeshift camp, hands on his hips, his eyes raised to the sky as if deep in thought.

Tadeas Grappo looked like an older version of his more famous nephew. He was in his late forties, with black hair, a scarred and weathered face, and thoughtful brown eyes. Despite having renounced his Assembly seat long ago to Demir, he still held himself like a guild-family member. His shoulders were squared, head up, a hint of regality in his presence despite his sweat-stained, dusty uniform.

"Finally joining us, our illustrious breacher?" he called as his eyes fell on Idrian.

"You didn't send anyone to wake me up," Idrian replied. "They aren't ordering us to the front today?"

Tadeas shook his head. "They've split us up to babysit a bunch of artillery as they move them up. It's drudge work, but better than what we went through yesterday."

"Agreed." Idrian came to stand next to Tadeas, pressing gently on his godglass eye as he made sure they were alone. "It's happening again," he said softly.

"Already?" Tadeas's gaze snapped to him, his expression immediately growing worried. "I thought you had a couple years left until the eye started to degrade."

"I thought I did too, but . . . Demir was here last night. At his request I accompanied him to the Grent Royal Glassworks to extract Master Kastora. We found Kastora mortally wounded, and he died within minutes of our arrival." Idrian spoke as if giving a report to a fastidious general, trying to keep all emotion out of his words lest that dam burst.

Tadeas didn't even twitch an eye at the mention of his nephew. Either he already knew he'd been here, or he just wasn't surprised by it. He put a hand on Idrian's shoulder. "I'm sorry. Your agreement with the Ministry—they know the eye holds your madness at bay. They'll have to find you a siliceer to make a new one, correct?"

"Per our agreement, but I despair that no one out there can replicate Kastora's work. He was the best."

"We'll find you someone."

The words were hollow in Idrian's ears, but still offered a margin of comfort coming from a friend. "I have a policy of never grieving for someone until after the war, but it was hard last night. Kastora saved my sanity. He was a good man, and our own stupid, glassdamned soldiers bayoneted him to death. He should not be dead right now. Captured, maybe, but not dead."

"I know he meant a lot to you," Tadeas said softly. "Both as a friend and,

I suppose, a doctor of sorts. What form has the madness taken?" Tadeas leaned forward to examine Idrian's godglass eye like a surgeon.

"Child's laughter."

"I don't remember that one."

"It's new."

"I should report this to the Ministry," Tadeas said unhappily. "For your safety."

Idrian snatched Tadeas by the arm. "Don't." The last thing he needed was to be dragged off by Ministry doctors, taken away from his friends and observed like an asylum lunatic for all hours of the day. "I'll be fine."

"The madness will not impair your ability to fight?" The question was asked carefully and Idrian snorted in response. Tadeas already knew the answer.

"No, of course not," Idrian replied.

"You'd tell me if it did?"

"Yes."

Tadeas gave him a doubtful look. "Perhaps your mind was just reacting to Kastora's death, and it'll settle back down. Your eye is still full of color. You should have a couple years to find another master siliceer before it runs out of resonance."

Idrian swallowed, holding back a thousand worries and insecurities. He found no shame in voicing them, but it was unnecessary. Tadeas knew them all. Instead, he said, "I can only hope." He did have to bite back the urge to tell Tadeas about the phoenix channel. He trusted Tadeas with any secret, of course, but he took his promise to Demir seriously. It would not leave his lips again, nor would he let it cloud his thoughts. If godglass disappeared, Idrian's fate would be sealed. No sense in dwelling on it more than that.

Tadeas shook his head, touching Idrian gently on the shoulder. "I'm sorry. When this war is over, I'll help you deal with the Ministry and finding a new master siliceer."

"That's kind of you to offer," Idrian replied. It definitely helped to have a friend who cared at his side. Breachers were important, but a guild-family member could get results easier than Idrian. "Sometimes I wonder if I'd have gone mad if I'd never lost this eye."

"And I wonder if I'll be able to resist killing your father if I ever meet him," Tadeas snorted. "I don't know how you do it."

"Patricide doesn't look good in front of a Ministry tribunal."

"Only if they can find the body." Tadeas checked his pocket watch. "Shit,

I have to get to a staff meeting with General Stavri. Nothing for you to do today, so get some rest. Mika will be through here any time with one of those artillery regiments. Stay out of sight or one of those puffed-up guild-family pricks will try to bully you into guard duty."

Idrian bid his friend farewell with a raised hand, watching Tadeas jog down the street. He touched his godglass eye briefly. Most people assumed he'd lost his eye in battle. He let them think that. Only Tadeas knew about the paternal cruelty—of the screaming and the beatings. He tried to cast it all out of his mind. He needed the rest after yesterday's events, but he wished there were *something* for him to do, if only to keep his thoughts off of his own encroaching madness. He paced nervously, ignoring the looks from the Ironhorns' support staff as they cleaned the camp and washed and mended uniforms.

Braileer came out on a nearby stoop, laying out Idrian's armor, sword, and shield. Idrian paused his pacing long enough to watch. Perhaps the young armorer would do a better job at his repairs in the light of day. Even if he was just coming out to give them another polish, it was good that he was staying busy.

Idrian joined him, sinking down onto the stoop and staring up into the sky. "Do you think a lot about death, Braileer?" he asked.

"No, sir."

"You will, if you stay with the Foreign Legion long." Idrian bit his own tongue immediately after the words slipped out. It wasn't like him to maintain such a dark mood around someone he barely knew, and a fresh recruit at that. Braileer didn't deserve it. "You'll see the best of life as well," he added.

"Yes, sir," Braileer said, ducking his head to his work. Idrian wondered if he'd scared him.

A movement caught Idrian's eye, and he turned to see a small girl watching him from the window of a tenement down the street. Most Grent civilians had fled ahead of the fighting, trying to stay well clear, but thousands were left hunkering in their homes with nowhere to go. Idrian waved. The girl waved back. A young woman suddenly appeared behind the girl and pulled her inside, closing the shutters with a quick, angry glare at Idrian.

He didn't blame her. Nobody wanted this: not the civilians, not the soldiers. If not for the orders coming down from on high, he might be on holiday on this very street right now, enjoying the solstice and Grent's darker, higher-quality winter ale.

The sound of a small explosion reached him, and Idrian's head came up.

Another followed, far too close for comfort. "Braileer," he hissed. "Those are Mika's grenades." He was on his feet in half a moment, pinpointing the sound. "Arm yourself and come with me," he ordered, snatching his helmet from Braileer's hands and slamming it onto his head. He grabbed his sword and shield and set off at a run, not bothering to make sure the armorer had followed.

As he drew closer to the source of the explosions he could hear screaming. "Grent breacher!" someone shouted. "We have an incoming breacher!"

Idrian emerged from an alleyway to see a full-fledged battle taking place in front of him. A dozen artillery pieces were stretched out down the street, their crews huddled around them protectively, trying to keep the horses from panicking, while a mix of soldiers and engineers with the Ironhorn crest on their uniforms formed a perimeter.

That perimeter had already collapsed at the head of the column. A Grent breacher wearing full-plate armor chopped a brutal path up the line of artillery. Two horses were already dead, their artillery pieces cleaved into useless pieces, the bodies of crew and Ironhorns alike scattered around them. As Idrian watched, an artillery officer lost his head. In moments that breacher had killed the next horse, sliced off the wheel of a six-pound gun, and cleaved through half the crew. The rest fled, while the Ironhorns peppered the breacher's armor with musket shot.

"You can't go out there without your armor," Braileer gasped as he caught up. He carried his smallsword and hammerglass buckler, and looked absolutely terrified.

"Try and stop me," Idrian snapped. A wave of Grent soldiers—probably a small company's worth—followed in the wake of their breacher, bayoneting the wounded and returning fire to drive the Ironhorns back. Idrian searched his comrades until he found Mika standing with her engineers, right in the path of the enemy breacher. She held a sling, loading it with a small grenade before whipping it over her head to send the explosive soaring into the enemy. The explosion drew their attention, and Idrian used that to his advantage.

He broke cover at a full sprint, praying that the sorcery in his helmet would be enough to get him through this. He hit the Grent soldiers from the side, sword-first, sweeping through them just as easily as their own breacher was slicing up the Ironhorns. Their organized shouts became screams and within moments he was covered in gore.

A grenade soared over Idrian's shoulder, clattering across the cobbles and exploding right at the feet of the Grent breacher. She was too busy turning herself to face Idrian to notice the grenade, and the resulting explosion knocked her off her feet.

Idrian blocked a bayonet thrust with his shield, felt another slice across his calf, and cut through an entire squad of Grent infantry with the razorglass blade of his sword. A bullet whizzed past his ear and, conscious of the fact that he wasn't actually wearing his armor, he whirled toward the enemy breacher as she regained her feet.

She closed on him in moments, and he caught her opening thrust on his shield, batted it aside, and slammed the dull edge of his sword against her hammerglass armor so as not to break his razorglass. The blow staggered her but she recovered quickly. She tossed aside her own shield, caught Idrian's riposte with the flat of her sword, and then came at him swinging with all her might.

The blunt edges of their swords slammed off each other, enormous slabs of metal and godglass crashing together with the speed of a fencer's smallsword and the force of a miner's pickax. Idrian felt each reverberating blow all the way to his toes, and it became quickly clear that, while he might be the more skilled of the two, the forgeglass in her armor made her just too strong and too fast. He fell back, trying to figure out a way to disengage without being cut in half, praying that the damned fools behind him had retreated to safety.

They hadn't, of course. Even within Idrian's singular focus he could sense the continued battle raging around him. His sword arm was growing heavy, his legs sluggish, trying to wield sword and shield without the extra forgeglass. He caught a blow at the base of his sword that numbed his fingers and rattled his knees. He grunted, shoving the breacher back, staring into her victorious smile.

A ball suddenly flew through the air, bonking the Grent breacher in the side of the helmet. She barely seemed to notice, a brief frown crossing her face. Idrian might have laughed if he didn't recognize that ball as one of Mika's grenades.

There was his exit strategy.

He threw himself backward, putting his shield between himself and the grenade just as the explosion threw him and his opponent in opposite directions. He felt his ears pop. A great pressure passed through his chest. He allowed himself to continue falling backward, knocked from his feet, rolling across the cobbles and then coming back up with his sword at the ready. The Grent breacher had done the same, her armor protecting her from the blast, and she turned to sprint away. Idrian blinked sweat out of his eyes, hearing the Grent bugle call that signaled a retreat. The rest of the Grent infantry fell into an organized flight, waiting until their breacher was safely among them before turning tail completely.

A loud whistle cut through the air, followed by two short bursts. Idrian felt a wave of relief wash over him. That would be Tadeas, and with him Valient's reinforcements. Musket shots ceased, leaving an eerie silence over the smoke-filled street filled only by the tramp of boots and the cries of the wounded. Idrian was soon surrounded by Ironhorn soldiers.

"You all right, sir?" one asked.

"Where is my armorer?" Idrian asked, casting about. To his surprise he found Braileer standing just behind him. The young man's sword was still clean but his shield was scratched, and a rivulet of blood ran down his brow from a close cut. His eyes were wide but he seemed otherwise unhurt. "Were you with me that entire time?" Idrian asked.

Braileer's whole body trembled, but he managed a nod.

"Good lad." Idrian slapped him on the shoulder and knew in that moment that he would not dismiss him. He let himself sag, feeling suddenly sapped of all energy, his arms almost too weak to hold his sword and shield. He set them down where he stood and removed his helmet to wipe away the sweat. He turned around just in time to see Tadeas running toward him.

"If you ever," Tadeas shouted, "*ever* rush into battle without your glass-damned armor again, I will have you pissing court-martialed!"

Idrian gazed back at his friend flatly. Tadeas's face was red, and his eyes were full of worry, searching Idrian for wounds. "Whatever you say, boss."

"Don't 'boss' me, damn it!"

"Tad!" Mika said, right on Tadeas's heels. "If he hadn't intervened we would have lost a whole battalion's worth of artillery, their crews, and the engineers that were helping them!"

"Nothing compared to losing a breacher," Tadeas spat.

Idrian held up both hands, palms out. There was no arguing with Tadeas when he was in a rage like that. He was right, of course. That was damned stupid of Idrian. "I'd do it again," he told Tadeas, hoping that his calm voice would help bring down Tadeas's blood. "You think I'm gonna take the time to put on my armor when people are dying? You've met me before, right?"

"You . . ." Tadeas shook his finger at Idrian. "Damn it!"

"How about you find out who let a Grent strike force slip through our sentries," Mika said, grabbing hold of Tadeas's arm. Tadeas shook her off, his face contorting through a dozen different expressions before settling on dismay. At a glance, Idrian estimated they'd lost several engineers and twenty or thirty soldiers from the Ironhorns, not to mention a handful of artillery crews and their commanding officer. It was a testament to just how much damage a good breacher strike force could do in minutes.

"Valient!" Tadeas called. "Find out who glassdamned let that strike force through our sentries and bring them to me so I can cut them into little pieces!"

"You got it!" was shouted back from the other end of the artillery column.

"You." Tadeas whirled back on Idrian. "See a medic for stitches and cureglass."

"I'm fine." Idrian's blood had finally cooled and he could feel the sharp pain of the cut across his calf. He bent to examine it, happy to find that it was superficial. "Did we get new orders?" he asked.

"We did, and they're damned strange. Did you even notice she cut off your earlobe?"

Idrian touched his left ear. It stung badly, and his fingers came back covered in blood. "That was my favorite ear," he said to Mika as Tadeas stormed off.

Mika raised both eyebrows and said in a low voice, "I appreciate it. You just saved a shitload of my people."

"That's my job," Idrian said, waving off the thanks. "That grenade at the end there saved my life."

"You looked like your arms were about to fall off, and your armorer was about to get skewered by a Grent bayonet."

"Thanks. Another thirty seconds and she would have had me. That sword is blasted heavy with only the forgeglass in its grip and my helmet." He nodded Mika off, letting her go check on her wounded engineers, and found a piece of cureglass to slow the bleeding until one of their medics came to check on him. By the end of the hour he had stitches up a long gash on his right arm, as well as around what was left of his earlobe. It hurt like piss, but he forwent his milkglass. The pain reminded him not to be so stupid next time.

He probably would, but a reminder couldn't hurt.

At some point, he could hear Tadeas screaming at someone around the corner. Probably the poor bastard in charge of their sentries—some middling officer from the regular infantry. Fighting soon broke out close by as Ossan infantry struck back at the Grent lines. Idrian waited for word for him and the Ironhorns to join that fighting, but it never came.

The dead were all but cleaned up, the wounded taken care of, when Idrian saw Tadeas heading back toward him from across the street. Idrian went to intercept his friend. "What happened?"

Tadeas sighed and sat down on one of the destroyed artillery pieces, staring at the flies buzzing around the dead horse in front of it. "A good strike force," he replied. "Damned good. Took out our sentries and killed seven squads of regular infantry without even raising an alarm. Nobody's fault. Wish it was. Then I could have them shot."

"We gonna hit them back?" Idrian asked.

Tadeas shook his head. "The Fourth will deal with that. We just got new orders." He scowled as he said this. "The Seventh is making a go at the ducal palace. General Stavri figures if we can capture that, we can force the duke to consider an early surrender. It'll satisfy the bloodlust of the masses angry over Adriana's death, and we'll have suitably slapped Grent on the wrist for their political meddling."

"Over bloody and quick." Idrian nodded. "That's what I like to hear. Are we helping the Seventh go after the palace?"

"That we are. From what I heard, the fighting is even hotter than what we saw yesterday."

Idrian groaned. He liked the strategy; he just didn't like the idea of spearheading it. But that was, he reminded himself, their job. To his surprise, Tadeas shoved something into his hand. It was a letter, still sealed with purple wax stamped with the Grappo silic sigil. "What's this?" he asked.

"Letter from my nephew."

Idrian broke the seal. It said:

The Duke of Grent has a large piece of cinderite in his art collection at his palace. I've arranged for the Ironhorns to be moved closer to the fighting there. Fetch me this piece of cinderite undamaged, and you have yourself a deal.

"What does it say?" Tadeas asked.

Idrian shook his head, reminding himself that he'd promised Demir not to say a word about the phoenix channel to anyone. His heart was beating hard now, a pleasant tingle between his shoulders. Not only had Demir accepted his offer, but he'd done so quickly. With a working phoenix chan-nel, Idrian could restore the sorcerous resonance in his eye. He wouldn't *need* another master siliceer. Idrian might actually be able to save his sanity. He thought hard, back to a meeting at the duke's palace some months ago where he'd gone along as a ceremonial guard, and realized that he'd actually seen this piece of cinderite. It was on display in the foyer of the palace.

He needed to be the first person through the front doors of the palace, and since he was a breacher that wasn't completely unlikely. Never mind the brutal fighting. He'd do what needed to be done if it meant saving civilization—and his own damned sanity.

11

Thessa was loaded unceremoniously into a cart and bundled off north by her Ossan captors, taking the exact highway around Ossa that she had intended to use in the first place. She watched forlornly while they passed by the road she would have followed down into the city.

She couldn't stop thinking of Serres and his family. The adults and teens impressed into naval service; the elderly and the children chucked off to one side, robbed of all their possessions. Would they even survive the cold winter night? Would they find help or succor? All she could do was hope that they managed to reach their relations and scrape together enough of a bribe to get their family back from the navy. If she wasn't thinking of them, she was thinking of Ekhi. She tried to reason to herself that he'd gotten away, but she'd heard that pained screech. Even if he survived the shot, an injured falcon was as good as dead in the wild.

She did not have much hope for Ekhi, but perhaps Kastora had gotten through unharmed. Palua too, and all the other apprentices.

Thessa's captors handed her off to a pair of Magna enforcers—a man and a woman in their mid-forties, heavily armed and silent, with pinkie nails painted red to show their guild-family allegiance. They did not mistreat her, but they made it very clear that an escape attempt would result in broken bones. All three of them slept crowded together in the back of the cart that night. Thessa dreamed of fires and screaming once more, but this time she saw the solemn little figure of Leone standing in the muddy streets, holding his toys, staring at her unblinking.

In the morning they continued their journey. Thessa wrestled with her despair, trying her best not to give in to the abject terror swirling in the back of her head. This was just a hiccup, she told herself; a side trip on the way to her ultimate goal. She would escape. She *had* to escape. The future of silic science was stuffed in her boot.

It was mid-afternoon when they trundled into a smoky, downtrodden town on the edge of a dark forest. Thessa was pulled from the back of the cart and marched through the front gate in a high wall. She instantly recognized the type of place: it was a large glassmaking compound, much bigger than the Grent Royal Glassworks, with proper streets and dozens of buildings spewing black smoke into the air. Everything was coated with soot, and the streets were packed with hundreds of people—laborers, siliceers, assistants—all heading in different directions.

There were also enforcers carrying bayoneted muskets, and they watched the crowded streets in a way that made it clear that they weren't a normal garrison. These were prison guards.

Thessa's escort pushed her into a small room just inside the gate and closed the door behind her before she could ask any questions. She found herself staring at the door in frustration, a thousand questions on the tip of her tongue, worry, anger, and fear causing a maelstrom of emotions that made her want to cry or punch someone.

"Thessa?"

She whirled, reaching for a belt knife that had been taken away from her, but her hand immediately fell away from the empty spot. Sitting on a little wooden bench in the corner of the room was Axio. The young assistant looked exhausted, his face streaked with tears, expression wide-eyed. He leapt to his feet and ran to her, catching her up in a hug before she could respond.

Thessa hugged back, a wave of relief rushing through her. A familiar face, even in a place like this, was as refreshing as a sip of cold beer. Her raging thoughts calmed instantly and she took a deep breath.

"Axio, what are you doing here?" She broke the hug, pushing him out at arm's length and looking him over. His left eye and right cheek were both blackened from a beating but he seemed otherwise unhurt. She wasn't sure if it was some kind of motherly instinct, or just her position as an authority figure at the Grent Royal Glassworks, but she felt instantly protective. She wanted to know who had done that to him and then make them *hurt*. As she had with the thoughts of that family who helped her yesterday, she forced herself to let go of her fury as pointless.

Axio shook his head. "That soldier gave me a bit of a beating, but they were soon calling for a retreat. I tried to get away, but they dragged me with them when they withdrew."

"And Master Kastora?" Thessa couldn't imagine the sweet old master fighting enemy soldiers, but it seemed he *had* rallied the garrison. She wished she'd listened to her instincts and returned.

"I didn't see."

Thessa pulled him back into a hug. "You did well. Thank you for distracting that soldier. Master Kastora sent me . . ." She paused, considering her story. Best not to mention the schematics in her boot to anyone, even Axio. "He told me to flee to some Ossan allies of his, but there were soldiers guarding the border."

Axio sniffed and wiped a grimy sleeve across his nose. Like her, he was still wearing the same clothes from the previous morning. She paused at that thought, shocked. That was only yesterday morning? It felt like weeks had passed. She laughed out of horror more than anything else.

"It's okay," she reassured Axio again. She looked back at the door, then around at the featureless little room. She was a journeyman, a proud siliceer, and she now had the extra responsibility of protecting someone beneath her. That felt far more concrete than simply delivering important schematics. Another deep breath. She could do both. "I don't know how long we have alone," she said in a low voice. "Tell me what you know."

Axio seemed to also take some courage in her presence. "Not much," he said, his voice growing more steady. "Just that we're at the Ivory Forest Glassworks."

"I see." She recognized the name and tried to remember what she knew of this place, though it wasn't much. "It's a big glassworks," she told Axio. "They specialize in mass-produced low-resonance godglass. Based on what I saw just now, this is a labor camp. Explains a lot, I suppose. The quality coming out of here has never been good." She paused to think for a moment. "If it's a labor camp, they're going to put us to work. They'll give me daily quotas and a set schedule. They'll give you . . . What's wrong?"

At the mention of quotas, Axio looked like Thessa had just kicked him between the legs. "I, uh . . . told them I was a siliceer apprentice."

"You're shitting me." It didn't take half a second for Thessa to realize what that entailed. A siliceer, even an apprentice, was a first-rate commodity. Skilled labor. A siliceer's *assistant,* however, was only a step above a common laborer. Axio had claimed to be an apprentice for better treatment, not thinking ahead to when someone asked for work out of him.

He looked ill. "Sorry, Thessa."

"Piss and shit. Fine. We can deal with this. I'll . . . I'll think of something." She could hear people talking just outside the door and lowered her voice even further. "If anyone asks, my name is Teala. We're both apprentices at the Grent Royal Glassworks. You can claim to be new, maybe that will help keep your quota low."

"You won't use your real name?"

"No. Don't tell them who I am or my rank. It's very important! Follow my lead, and we'll both get through this."

As she finished speaking, the door opened to reveal a small, squirrel-faced man. The man's apron was stitched with an inverted triangle covered in wavy lines emanating from a single point. Within a glassworks it was the symbol for cureglass, but in Ossan society it was the sigil of the Magna guild-family. The man had a small matching sigil tattooed on the back of his right hand. He looked to be in his mid-fifties, with long black hair, a pointed face, and sharp, nervous eyes.

He had a tiny piece of auraglass in his ear—a common godglass that enhanced the wearer's natural charisma. Auraglass, in Thessa's experience, was worn only by those who lacked confidence. His arms bore no scars, reminding Thessa of one of Kastora's sayings: *Scars are the true reflection of a siliceer. Too many and she is an oaf. Too few and she's never truly worked the furnaces.* None of this boded well.

The man stared at Thessa and Axio for a few moments, his expression bored. "These are the new arrivals from Grent?" he asked the enforcer standing just behind his right shoulder.

"Yes, sir."

"Do we have a file on them?"

"No, sir."

The man sniffed and looked from Axio to Thessa. Thessa met his eye, hoping that some confidence would divert his attention to her. It worked. He settled his gaze on her and said, "I am Craftsman Filur Magna. You may call me Sir, or Craftsman, or Craftsman Magna. I am the overseer of this compound."

"Is this a labor camp, sir?" Thessa asked.

A flash of annoyance crossed his face. "This is a workshop for undesirable siliceers; convicts, hostages, debtors. Enemies of the state. You are both prisoners of war, and this will be your home until your ransom is paid or the war has ended."

"Sir," Thessa said, trying her best to conceal this sudden avenue of hope, "what is our ransom?"

He glared back at her, and Thessa got the distinct feeling that Craftsman

Magna wasn't accustomed to being questioned by his wards. He removed a board from under his arm, to which were clipped several pieces of paper. He flipped through them, and his eyes settled on one. "Ah. No ransom being allowed. Too early in the war, you see. We need you working for *our* war effort. Not the enemy's." A cruel little smile cracked his face. "No one knows you're here. You will be allowed no visitors or contact with the outside world." He turned to the enforcer behind him. "Search them."

The enforcer stepped into the room. Before Thessa could react, she found herself shoved face-forward against the wall. Thick fingers probed her in places they shouldn't, running up under her tunic, through her hair, touching her everywhere, making her stomach flip. It was blessedly brief and about as professional as she could have hoped. She closed her eyes and tried to relax, though her heart was beating hard as she could tell what was coming.

"Boots off," the enforcer commanded.

Thessa tried to come up with an excuse not to follow his instructions, but nothing came to hand. Reluctantly, she pulled her boots off. The enforcer picked them up one at a time, shoving his hand inside. He came away with the rolled-up schematics, which he handed over to the overseer without comment.

The overseer unrolled the vellum sheets, frowning as he flipped through them. "Well, well, what have we here? This looks interesting." He peered at Thessa. "Where did you get these?"

Thessa stared at the ground, speaking the first good lie that came to mind. "I . . . took them when I fled the glassworks, sir."

"A thief, eh?"

"I didn't know—"

"Don't try to explain yourself!" he cut her off. "I'm not going to listen to excuses. What are they?"

"I'm not really sure, sir. I just snatched them from the furnace room. I thought maybe I could sell them." Better to be thought a thief than Kastora's protégé. She let her gaze flick to the overseer's face. He was looking at the schematics again, turning them this way and that with a frown on his face. Finally, he rolled them back up and put them in his pocket. He did not seem bothered by her explanation.

Thessa glanced at Axio, hoping that her message to keep quiet had gotten through to him. *He* knew she'd never steal from Master Kastora. At a nod from the overseer, the enforcer grabbed Axio and submitted him to the same quick, thorough search. It came up with nothing. Thessa forced herself to watch. Seeing Axio's hands tremble and the look of fear on his face gave her strength. She was his superior. She needed to be confident for both of them. With no ransom being allowed, she was glad she'd decided on a fake name. She and Axio might have to be here a long time. Without knowing who she was, the overseer would expect less of her. She might even be able to get away with sabotaging their operations in some way. Grit in the molten cindersand? Impurities in the fires of the furnace?

She forced herself to focus, formulating a quick plan. First, learn to navigate this place. Second, plan an escape. Third, get the schematics back. Fourth—if escape was impossible—figure out how to fight back.

The overseer studied his papers again. He produced a nub of pencil from behind his ear and looked directly at her. "Name?"

"Teala." His eyes narrowed, so Thessa added, "Sir."

"Last name?"

"None, sir. I was an orphan."

"Rank?"

"Senior apprentice, sir."

He nodded along with her answers, firing off a number of basic questions about who she was, her role under Master Kastora, and what kind of work she did at the Grent Royal Glassworks. She replied with half-truths and a few outright lies, presenting herself as a lowly cog at her old glassworks, someone who barely saw Master Kastora and rarely spoke to him. By the time Craftsman Magna finished, Thessa felt like she had learned more about him than he had her. She knew his type precisely: an administrator who played at silic knowledge; half competent in an office, uncomfortable in front of the furnace. He was small-minded, probably petty, more concerned about his ledgers than about any of the people under him. She would have to figure out a way to use that.

He turned to Axio. "Name?"

"Axio Darnasus, sir." Axio's voice was unsteady.

"Rank?"

Thessa cut in, "Junior apprentice, sir."

"I did not ask you," Craftsman Magna snapped. The overseer's patience with her had clearly worn thin.

"I'm sorry, sir. He's just very new."

"If you speak out of turn again, I will have you flogged before the entire compound."

Thessa heard her own teeth click shut. She nodded sharply, looking at her feet in what she hoped was a subservient gesture and hoping that Axio didn't give himself away. Much to her relief, he went through the rest of the questions without arousing the overseer's suspicions.

Craftsman Magna finished the questions and put the papers and board back under one arm. "Follow me," he said sharply, turning on his heel. They followed close, their enforcer escort hovering ominously just behind them as they were marched down the street. Thessa remained alert, counting the buildings, examining the walls, trying to gauge the people they passed.

The compound appeared entirely secure. There was one main entrance, but there were several service hatches through which laborers brought firewood, cindersand, and other necessities. Every exit was heavily guarded by armed enforcers. While the siliceers were all wearing drab, matching tunics and aprons in a sort of prison uniform, it appeared that support staff was all hired—they wore their own clothes, talked freely. Some wore forgeglass to help them carry loads. Perhaps Thessa could get a message out through one of them.

But to whom? Adriana was dead. Kastora was besieged. The former would have been the better option, since they were already in Ossa, but the latter might be able to smuggle them out or arrange the proper bribes. Of course, anyone she might contact might very well be unable to help them. Thessa needed to assume that, for the moment, she and Axio were on their own.

As they were escorted across the compound courtyard, Thessa's gaze turned to a young man being dragged in the opposite direction. He wept violently, held under each arm by an enforcer, and Thessa found herself following his journey with morbid fascination. The back of the young man's tunic was ripped and bloody from a horrible flogging.

"Ah," Craftsman Magna explained, "a failure. He didn't meet his quotas, and I'm afraid I have very little patience for laziness."

Thessa risked speaking out of turn to ask, "What will happen to him?"

"He's going to the lumber camps. If he can't make godglass, then we'll put him to work in some other way. This way, please." Thessa was careful to keep her expression neutral, but she caught Axio's worried eye. She shook her head, hoping the gesture gave him some reassurance.

The young man's weeping echoed in the back of her head as they were escorted to a door marked clearly as FURNACE NUMBER THREE, where the room inside was instantly recognizable. An immense furnace took up the center of the room, workstations radiating from it like spokes on a wheel. There was space for fourteen siliceers—far larger than any workshop in Grent. Most of the workstations were occupied, with a variety of men and women of all ages sweating badly as they navigated the heat. A few glanced up, eyeballing Thessa and Axio as the overseer led them around to the other side of the room to a pair of empty workstations. Each station was neatly prepared: tools set out, blowtubes and bit irons on an overhead rack, and a bedraggled, plain apron hanging from a hook.

Thessa breathed a sigh of relief when Craftsman Magna directed them to the two workstations. Working immediately next to Axio meant she could look out for him, instruct him—perhaps even cover for him. Craftsman Magna paused, glancing at them both, his eyes lingering briefly on Axio. Thessa hoped he could not see just how uncomfortable Axio looked standing in front of the workstation. He was, after all, accustomed to running and fetching. Not to making godglass.

"Are these our workstations, sir?" Thessa asked to bring the overseer's attention back to her once more.

"Indeed. Get to know them well, for you will be at them six days a week until the war is over."

Craftsman Magna went on, droning through dozens of small rules and telling them where to find their mess hall and dormitory. Thessa half listened as she examined the rest of the furnace room, trying to get a feel for the people here. Their body language spoke of exhaustion and fear. No wonder. How far could they fall behind before they could expect a flogging? Or being sent to the camps? Lumber camps were notoriously dangerous places. An accident in the glassworks might end your career, but an accident at a lumber camp would take a limb or kill you outright.

No one met her gaze. Shoulders remained hunched, eyes downcast. No one wanted to attract Craftsman Magna's ire.

She brought her full attention back to the overseer as he said, "Your daily quotas *will* be enforced. Finish them quickly and you will be allowed to rest. Fail, and you will work all night. Fail continuously, and you will be sent to the lumber camps." As he said this last part, he looked directly at Axio.

Thessa swore silently to herself. Sweat poured from Axio's brow, and probably wasn't just from the heat.

"I'm sure we'll keep up, sir," she said.

That cruel little smile flickered across his face again. "See that you do."

He inhaled sharply and checked one of the papers under his arm. Without another word, he turned on his heel once more and marched out of the furnace, leaving Thessa and Axio at their workstations, staring after him.

She forced herself to focus, glancing surreptitiously around the room. Several of the siliceers seemed to have relaxed the moment the overseer was gone. A few glanced in her direction with varying amounts of interest. Most kept themselves bent to their work. Aside from the shuffle of feet, the creak of furnace doors, and the roar of the flames, there was very little sound. Only a handful of the siliceers spoke to each other. The usual furnace banter, it seemed, did not exist.

This place was a stifling, heartless labor camp, and was clearly meant to be. Thessa bent to scratch at her ankle. The schematics in her boot had been chafing her skin for the last day and a half, but now that they were gone she felt the emptiness acutely.

"Thessa," Axio hissed. "What do I do?"

Thessa took a deep breath and turned her attention on her workstation. Her tools were cheap and well-worn, but everything was here. Each workstation had clear access to the furnace, including a reheating chamber and a godfunnel, used to direct heat at tiny pieces of godglass. There was already molten cindersand in a crucible in the furnace, and on the workstation was a piece of paper with the day's date and her quota. She showed it to Axio, and he showed her his. They were the same.

So much for getting him a lighter quota.

"I'm going to teach you to make godglass," she told him.

"How?"

"The same I teach any apprentice. We can do this. Forgeglass is the easiest thing to make. You've seen it done hundreds of times."

"I've never actually paid attention," Axio replied. His eyes were a little wild, his face pale.

"Then pay attention now!" Thessa kept her tone calm, quiet, but firm. She took down bit iron—a four-foot rod—and set the end into the reheating chamber. "Always heat the iron first," she told Axio, "then dip like this." Once the iron was cherry red, she used it to gather molten cindersand from the crucible inside the furnace. It was just a tiny dab, and she brought it to the steel plate on her workbench, where she began to manipulate it with a pair of heavy tweezers.

Her movements were easy and fluid. These circumstances might be terrible, the equipment subpar and the workstation unfamiliar, but Thessa could do this kind of work blindfolded. Axio's nerves, on the other hand, seemed entirely shot. He was trembling, sweating, his eyes looking everywhere at once. If Thessa couldn't get him to focus, this wasn't going to work. "Watch closely," she instructed.

Axio shuddered deeply. He snatched down his bit iron, clutching it with both hands, still facing away from his own workstation. Thessa continued the task in front of her, rolling the small gather of godglass across the steel plate, adjusting it with her tweezers. She stopped once to hold the molten glass in front of the godglass funnel, operating a foot pedal to blow hot air up through the furnace and keep the godglass glowing.

Back on her workbench she bent over the tiny piece of molten cinder-sand, listening for the soft resonance of sorcery. "You do it like this. It might take you a few days, but you'll get the hang of it. Twirl, crimp, shape. Move the molten cindersand around until you start to hear the hum of the sorcery, then slowly try and make that hum louder. If it goes away, undo the last thing you just did. If it fails, have no shame in giving up and starting over. You can reheat the piece at the funnel here, or discard it for a new one."

Looking up to make sure Axio was paying attention, she saw silent tears streaming down his face. "I can't do it," he whispered.

"You *can*," she shot back quietly. "You're strong, Axio. You were strong enough to fight an Ossan soldier to give me time to escape." Lowering her voice even further, she reached deep down, steeling herself, digging around in the anger and indignation she felt at her treatment. "They attacked our home. They killed Ekhi. They shot Captain Jero. Now they're going to steal our labor and I will *not* stand for that. Understand? We're going to survive this place and escape. We're going to get through this *together*."

Axio took a shaky breath. "You really think we can?"

"I know we can. But I need your help. I need you to be the strong man I know you are."

Axio hesitated for a few moments and then gave her an uncertain nod.

It would have to be good enough.

"Practice," she ordered him. "You need to look like you're working. I'll try to cover for you until you can do these on your own." That meant twice as much work for her, and then sneaking finished pieces onto his tray. It wasn't going to be easy, and she had no idea how terrible the consequences would be if she was caught.

She tried to keep all her uncertainties off her face. Escape *did* seem impossible. With Adriana Grappo dead, they had nowhere to go even if they did manage to flee the prison walls. She stopped herself. She couldn't afford to despair. She had to figure out how to get those schematics back from the overseer, and now she had the extra burden of Axio. She couldn't abandon either of these duties, nor would she. One step at a time.

12

It was Montego who picked up Thessa's trail, following scant rumors of a young woman walking north out of Grent alone. He explained his method and findings in brief, and though Demir couldn't be entirely confident that they had the right person, he knew all he could do was follow that thread until it either broke or proved fruitful.

Within four hours of Montego's report, Demir stared across the café table at a diminutive woman sitting across from him. She wore a demure gray coat over her tunic, embroidered richly but not ostentatiously. She had light Purnian skin, an easy smile, and an affected calm manner that made her, at times, infuriating to deal with. Her name was Duala Jaass, and she was one of the thousands of independent brokers who made their living setting up deals between guild-families.

It was just after dark in the Assembly District, a humid chill seizing the night air and cutting through Demir's light jacket. The café courtyard was lit by gas lamps, casting shadows across Duala's face.

"I think it's your girl," Duala said.

"Thessa Foleer?" Demir confirmed, leaning back in his chair, trying not to look too eager. Duala had served as his spymaster while he was governor all those years ago. She might be a broker now, but she was damned good at moving around information. He'd been half tempted to send her after his mother's killers, but violence was where she ended her services. "You're sure?"

"As sure as I can be with the trail Montego was following," Duala said, spreading her hands. "A woman matching Thessa's description was filed into the Ivory Forest Glassworks this afternoon at three o'clock."

Demir checked his pocket watch. It wasn't that far after six. "How the piss did you find out already?"

"Because the Ivory Forest Glassworks is a labor camp for siliceers and the Foreign Legion has a standing order to send any Grent siliceers they capture directly there." She gave him a tight, self-satisfied smile. "Thessa gave them a fake name—calling herself Teala—but I cross-checked with the records I had on hand and there was no Teala at the Grent Royal Glassworks. It's either your girl, or a damned big coincidence."

Demir let out a relieved sigh. So he'd located her. That was step one. Step two . . .

"Does the labor camp know who they have?"

"I doubt it. Ivory Forest is not a prestigious position, and it's not run by clever people. All they care about is turning a profit off the back of prisoners of the state."

"So how do I get her out before they realize they've got a genuine talent on their hands?"

"That's more complicated," Duala replied. "The Ivory Forest Glassworks is a government contract. It has exclusive rights for siliceer prisoners within the Empire, her provinces, and overseas colonies. They have very strict rules for how the prisoners are treated and how ransoms and prison sentences are dealt with. They are *not* going to let Thessa out of there until the war is over."

"Then I need to gain access. Who owns it?"

"The Magna."

"Will they sell any shares?"

"Absolutely not. Supi Magna likes to keep it completely within the family."

Demir drummed his fingers on the table next to his teacup saucer, considering his options. The easiest way to retrieve Thessa would be to buy up shares in the glassworks, get access to their books, and figure out the right people to bribe on both the Magna and the government sides of things. But that didn't seem to be an option. So how else could he gain access? "Do you have a list of names of the people who oversee the glassworks?"

Duala's self-satisfied smile faded. "That's harder to get with the Magna owners. They keep a pretty tight lid on things. I have the names of a few government secretaries involved, but that's it." She pulled a piece of paper out of her pocket and slid it across to him. Demir ran his eyes across the names, feeling irritated and glum, worried he'd hit another dead end, when his eyes fell on the name at the bottom of the page. It was a name he knew well. "All right," he told her, "I think that'll give me a good start."

"I'm sorry I can't help you more with that," Duala said. "Is there anything else?"

"The Stavri deal is going through?" Demir asked, switching over from spy work to Duala's basic brokerage services.

"Yes. That lumber mill is yours."

"And the Prosotsi steelworks?"

"Also yours."

"Good." Demir mentally filed through the dozens of deals he'd made in the forty-eight hours since returning to Ossa, putting the cash he'd made fixing fights in the provinces into tangible, moneymaking ventures that would enrich the Grappo. His new investments avoided glassworks—the whole industry was about to fall apart, after all.

Making all these deals made him realize something that he'd never really stopped to take stock of out in the provinces: He was rich. Not just as a guild-family patriarch, but independently wealthy in a way that few people unsupported by dynastic wealth could claim. He'd gone out into the provinces with a handful of coins and a few cheap pieces of godglass, and he'd turned it into a fortune over nine years. Even with everything else, he could be proud of that, and he could use it in the trials to come.

He mulled over this thought for a moment before moving on. "I have a strange question: Are the major guild-families acting . . . out of character in their silic dealings?"

The cool look that Duala returned was almost answer enough. It was not, it seemed, a strange question at all. She leaned across the table. "There are rumors."

"What kind?"

"That all the major players are conducting a secret silic war. Nothing formal, mind you, but serious. They're buying up cindersand, tripling their espionage efforts, even sabotage—though none that can be proved. They're trying to be the first to develop something, but what it is only the silic masters and the guild-family heads know."

They were all trying to make a phoenix channel. It was the only logical leap that Demir could make. Those masters and matriarchs and patriarchs would have access to the same sorts of information that Kastora and Demir's mother had. They knew the cindersand was running out, and they were scrambling to come up with a solution. Demir clicked his tongue and pulled out a few banknotes, weighing them down with his teacup. "Fine.

Let me know if anything changes. See if you can dig up something else on the Ivory Forest Glassworks. Quietly."

"Of course."

"Thanks, Duala. I'll be in touch."

"My pleasure," she answered. Before he could stand up, she reached across the table and touched the back of his hand. "It's good to work with you again, Demir."

"Is it?"

"You always pay on time and you're never boring. I have few clients who can claim both of those things."

"It's good to see you too," Demir told her. "Say hello to your adorable husband for me. The three of us should have dinner soon." He got up, kissing her on the forehead as he left.

He walked out into the middle of the street, where he could see up and down the well-lit avenues of the Assembly District. The streets were packed with dinnertime traffic: businessmen making last-minute deals before the year's end; Assembly members chatting quietly about their next votes; young guild-family scions flaunting their wealth at respectable establishments.

Despite the deals he had put in motion to secure the future of his tiny guild-family, he couldn't help but feel as if it would all be for nothing unless he could rescue Thessa from the Ivory Forest Glassworks. He needed the schematics she was carrying *and* her expertise. If he got those, and if she was able to re-create the phoenix channel before anyone else finished theirs . . . well, the Grappo wouldn't be a tiny guild-family anymore. He could save the Empire and get mind-blowingly rich at the same time. There were a lot of ifs in there, and that made him nervous.

He still had to figure out how his mother's murder connected to all of this. Was it really the Grent? Was it a conspiracy? Did it have to do with the phoenix channel, or her reforms, or some deal gone bad? So many questions. With any luck, Kizzie would start answering them. In the meantime, he needed to be careful that no one got wind of Kastora's phoenix channel. The moment they did, the Hyacinth would be crawling with guild-families' spies, saboteurs, and assassins. Montego's presence might keep them at bay for a while, but not indefinitely.

Demir reached into his pocket for the list of secretaries Duala had given him, then raised his hand for a hackney cab.

The Slag was often said to be the largest slum in all the world. Demir had seen bigger, but he'd never seen more miserable. Just downriver and downwind of Glasstown, he could taste the smoke from the glassworks on his tongue as he exited his cab. He'd gone less than two miles from the Assembly District but the world had changed completely: the streets here were trenches of mud, haunted by gangs, the darkness deep and impenetrable without those neat rows of gas lanterns. Beggars wallowed in the mud or fought over the few slices of dry sidewalk, and every surface was covered in a thick, tar-like film.

"You make a wrong turn?" a voice asked as Demir gathered his bearings. It belonged to a rough young man, leaning against a wall with three others about his age, crimson painted across the middles of their faces in a gang marking that Demir did not recognize.

Demir glanced sidelong at them, his senses finding the closest glass window by pure instinct, and laid his left hand flat against his chest to display the glassdancer sigil there. The young man who spoke gave out a slight gasp, his face turning an amusing shade of green.

"I'm sorry, sir," he said quickly, tripping over his own words. The other three took a long step back, as if to disassociate themselves from their friend. "I just meant to offer you directions."

"Sure you did." Demir did not let him linger. "Where's Harlen's place? The cab dropped me off too early."

After a whispered conference, the four all pointed down the street in unison. Demir fished around in his pocket, found a piece of low-resonance forgeglass, and tossed it to their leader. He could hear them fighting over it as he headed down the street, striding through the mud, pasting a look on his face that he hoped would discourage any more interruptions.

He found Harlen's two blocks down on the left, tucked between a pair of factories. It was a small door at the end of an alley, lit by a single gas lantern, the name of the establishment written in chalk across the alley wall.

Demir stepped through the open door into one large, low-ceilinged room that reeked of cigarette and cigar smoke. It was poorly lit but comfortable in a low-class sort of way. Demir flashed his guild-family sigil to the hulking enforcers standing just inside the door. They let him pass without comment. A handful of men and women lounged on cushions in the middle of the room, enjoying the mind-numbing effects of the little maroon pieces of dazeglass in their earlobes.

Demir found a short, fat goblin of a man wearing expensive clothes and with a tooth capped by low-resonance sightglass. He grinned at Demir, throwing his arms wide. "Demir!"

"Harlen. Been a long time."

"I got your note yesterday. Placed all those bets for you." A thick wad of banknotes appeared in his hand as if by magic, and he tossed it to Demir. "You keep winning like that and people will get mad."

"Ah, it was just a lucky day," Demir replied, grinning back at Harlen. They'd known each other since Demir placed his first bet at the age of eleven. Harlen might not be upper-class material, but he never got greedy over the percentage Demir paid him. He did, Demir noticed, eyeball his glassdancer tattoo with some trepidation. Demir fought down his annoyance. An old business associate should know better, but he supposed that was the price of being a glassdancer. One more person just a little too nervous to be around him. "I need a favor," he told Harlen.

"Anything for my friend."

"Does Lechauri Pergos still place his bets with you?"

"Of course."

"Does he still lose way more than he wins?"

Harlen smirked.

Excellent. "How much does he owe?"

"A hundred and fifty-three thousand."

Demir swore under his breath. Glassdamn, Lechauri. That gambling habit had gotten bad. "Good. Call in the debt."

"Oh?" Harlen said, raising his eyebrows. "Right now?"

"At this very moment." Demir could see in Harlen's eyes that he was curious about this little development, but the bookie knew better than to ask too many questions. As much as Demir resented his status as a glassdancer, it did come in handy.

"I can do that. Oi! Jeely! Grab a piece of forgeglass and run this note to the Assembly offices right damned quick." As he spoke, Harlen scrawled out a note, which he then handed to one of his thuggish young guards. The woman took off, and Demir listened to her sprint down the muddy alley. He borrowed a piece of low-resonance dazeglass from Harlen and threw himself onto one of the dirty cushions in the corner, enjoying the way the sorcery made him feel pleasant and tingly.

He was there for less than half an hour when the thug returned, and ten minutes after her a familiar face rushed through the door. Lechauri Pergos was a tall, thin man with the striking combination of olive skin and long, fire-red hair. He wore the colorful robes of an Assembly clerk and his pinkie nails were painted crimson to show his allegiance to the Magna. He was shouting as he entered. "Harlen! I still have two weeks, damn it! I have my receipt right here! What kind of a business do you think you're running? Two. More. Weeks."

Harlen turned to face him with the long-suffering expression of someone used to such tirades. "I'm running *my* business. Debts get called in all the time, and I'm calling in yours."

Demir removed his dazeglass, immediately missing the pleasant feeling that came with it, and sauntered toward the pair. He leaned against a support column and removed the wad of banknotes from his pocket, holding it conspicuously in one hand.

Lechauri continued to rail at Harlen. "You can't call in my debts two weeks early. This is criminal! This is . . ." He trailed off, slowly turning his head toward Demir as if finally registering his presence.

"Hi Lech," Demir said with a grin.

Lechauri stared at Demir for several moments, his face pale, looking like he'd seen a ghost. "Demir? I heard you were back in town."

"Fancy us meeting in a place like this." Demir tossed the roll of banknotes into the air and caught it. "Having trouble with something?"

Lechauri's eyes followed the roll of banknotes. He licked his lips, and Demir could see the thoughts turning behind his eyes. "Yeah," he said slowly. "Crazy meeting here." His eyes narrowed. "You son of a bitch. You called in my debts, didn't you?"

"I would never. But it sounds like you need some cash. I thought maybe we could help each other."

Lechauri eyed Demir's banknotes greedily. "And what do you want?"

"Step into my office," Demir said, gesturing for Lechauri to follow him into the alley. Once they were alone, Demir slapped Lechauri on the shoulder. "How are you? I heard you married a Magna and got a cushy job as an Assembly clerk."

"Yeah," Lechauri answered flatly.

Demir searched his old friend's face, looking for all the telltale signs of a down-on-his-luck gambler: the worry lines, the exhaustion, the shifty eyes. Of course, Demir knew just how much Lechauri owed to Harlen, and if Lechauri's Magna in-laws found out about his gambling problem things wouldn't go well for him.

"Remember that play we wrote?" Demir asked, allowing himself a moment of nostalgia. "We were what, thirteen? Visited every whorehouse on Glory Street trying to get actresses. They didn't take our genius seriously."

"Those were good days," Lechauri agreed half-heartedly. "What do you want, Demir?"

Demir feigned a surprised look. "Well, now that you mention it . . ."

"Just get it out," Lechauri said impatiently.

"I understand that one of your duties includes clerical oversight work for the Ivory Forest Glassworks."

"And how did you find that out?"

"That's not important. Is it true?"

Lechauri kicked at a clod of mud underfoot. "Yeah, it's true."

"I need information," Demir said. "Lots of it. Every little scrap you can get me on the Ivory Forest Glassworks and, piss, let's say the entire Magna guild-family. I want bank records, prison records, enforcer rosters, family member dossiers."

Lechauri scoffed. "You're joking, right?"

"Not even slightly."

"I can't do that. If Supi found out, shit even if my wife finds out, I'm a dead man. They'll never find the body."

"Is that preferable to the pieces left behind by Harlen's goons? You're not going to pay off a hundred and fifty thousand ozzo tonight, are you?"

"You can't know that," Lechauri said defensively. Demir just stared at him until he began to fidget and said, "Okay, so maybe I won't. I still have two weeks left. Harlen *has* to give me that much time. It's in our agreement."

"Can you get that much money in two weeks?"

". . . No."

"Didn't think so." Demir threw the roll of banknotes into the air and caught it again. "Get me everything I just asked for, delivered to my hotel before breakfast tomorrow morning, and I'll pay off sixty grand."

Lechauri's eyes bugged out. "How the piss do you have access to that kind of cash?"

Demir held up the banknotes. "There's fifty right here." The money meant nothing to him. It never really had. Greed had never been his vice, a fact that had separated him from the rest of the guild-family scions at an early age.

"Glassdamn," Lechauri muttered. He eyeballed those banknotes greedily. Demir almost had him, but he could see the hesitance in his eyes. "I can't make copies of anything that quick. I'd have to give you originals."

"I don't care about the details. Do we have a deal or not?"

Lechauri's face contorted in faux pain. "I . . . I just can't. I'd still owe Harlen a lot of money and . . ."

"Seventy grand," Demir offered, cutting him off, "and I'll ask Harlen to extend you a courtesy of four months on the rest of your debt."

". . . and I suppose no one will notice a few records going missing. The Magna family is huge, after all."

Demir grinned at Lechauri. "It's so good to see you, Lech."

Lechauri made a noncommittal noise, which turned upward into a squeak as Demir tossed him the roll of banknotes. He juggled the roll, finally got it in his grasp, and made it disappear into his pocket as deftly as a street magician. He was bought and paid for now. With any luck he'd be able to get Demir the information he needed to mount a proper rescue attempt.

Demir said, "I'll pay the other twenty—and get you that extension—the moment I get those files. I'll be waiting at my hotel."

13

Kizzie had never met Churian Dorlani, but she'd seen him from a distance on several occasions. As a first cousin in the Dorlani guild-family he'd fallen into an overseer's job at a large lumber mill just outside of Ossa, where he collected an immense salary letting his more competent underlings do the entirety of his job for him. He was not smart enough to truly excel, not dumb enough to truly fail. He was, Kizzie reflected, a man who had gone far in life by being entirely average.

It was a common story among the Ossan elite. Kizzie tried not to think of the injustice of it all.

It cost her two hours and a pittance of Demir's money to find out everything she could possibly need to know about Churian—his hobbies, lovers, social groups. Kizzie then spent the rest of her evening waiting down the street from his Fulgurist Society on Glory Street. Glory Street was a tiny little borough between the Assembly District and the Slag, dividing the richest of the rich from the poorest of the poor and giving them a place to meet. Kizzie watched the second-rate Ossan elite come and go, entertaining herself with fantasies of one day joining their lazy, hedonistic lifestyle.

It *was* a fantasy. Her father, one of the most powerful men in Ossa, had publicly denounced the whole concept of legitimizing bastards. Without legitimization, she would never be anything but a favored enforcer, allowed to wear a smaller version of the Vorcien silic sigil as a birthright but having only a fraction of the other privileges that came with it. If she were to ever have children, they would have no silic sigil of their own.

Right now, she wasn't even favored. Her oldest half brother, Sibrial, hated her more than usual because she refused to lie to that magistrate. Father Vorcien was irritated at her. The chances of her surviving Father Vorcien's death and the ensuing power transfer had gone from slim to none.

Kizzie spotted one of her own cousins—a nineteen-year-old layabout wearing next to nothing despite the cold and hanging on the arm of a powerful glassdancer—go into the cockfighting arena that housed Churian's Fulgurist Society. Kizzie swallowed her irritation and checked her pocket watch. It was almost eight o'clock. The mild winter night was cool and dark, the street filled with the sound of chatting passersby and clattering carriages.

She blew on her hands to warm them. Few people so much as glanced in her direction. Bodyguards and low-level enforcers hung around, waiting for their wards to emerge from whatever whorehouse, gambling den, or dazeglass hotel they were enjoying. She nodded at an enforcer who raised his hand in greeting, then pulled the brim of her felt hat down closer to hide her face.

It was just after nine when Churian Dorlani emerged from the cockfighting arena. He was a middle-aged man; tall, balding, and awkward with one hand crudely shoved up the back of the short tunic of the young woman next to him. She leaned into him, giggling in that obviously fake manner of a mistress who puts up with a lot because she has bills to pay.

Kizzie waited for them to reach the end of the street and then detached herself from the shadows to follow.

It was not a long walk; just five blocks to one of the nicer tenement buildings on the edge of the Assembly District. Churian had two mistresses and a mister, and he brought them all to the same apartment. It was, as far as these things went, rather tasteless, but it made Kizzie's job a lot easier.

She watched them go inside, waited five minutes, and then approached the doorman. "Excuse me," she said, raising one hand, "the side door of the building is wide open. I can't imagine anyone will be happy for the cold."

The doorman swore quietly. "Every damned day. I even put up a sign," he complained.

"Sorry," she replied with a sympathetic smile. "I figured you'd want to know. My own doorman was dismissed for such a breach. I thought it was unfair, but a Magna owns my building and you can't argue with them."

"Thanks," he replied. He glanced in both directions, seemed to decide no one needed his help for the moment, and then hurried around the corner. Kizzie slipped inside the tenement the moment his back was turned.

Kizzie walked with purpose, chin raised and eyes confident, an excuse on her tongue in case anyone questioned her presence. She found Churian's apartment and stopped outside to check that she was prepared. Her stiletto was hidden underneath her jacket, along with a pistol just in case, and Demir's shackleglass was still in her cork-lined pocket.

Putting one ear to the door, she listened until she was certain that the pair inside were "occupied."

She often wondered what other pathways she might have followed. What if she *hadn't* tried to blackmail that professor her first year at university? She might be off in the provinces, running a winery, with her choice of provincial misters and mistresses. She sighed to herself and removed three small, square regular glass beads from her pocket. No point in ruminating over past mistakes. At least she was listening to idiots have sex instead of slitting the throats of gang members. She could thank Demir for that tiny step up for the moment.

She knelt beside the door, holding the three beads in her palm and focusing. A minor talent in glassdancing was not considered valuable—certainly not one worth adoption into a great guild-family, and the respect, fear, and authority that came with it. Still, she found it had its uses. The beads rose up into the air, moving forward as a clump into the lock. A drop of sweat sprang to her forehead as she maneuvered the beads around inside the lock's mechanism, putting three different amounts of pressure on the tumblers until they finally clicked.

Within the minute she was inside the apartment, closing the door gently behind her and walking softly across the wooden floor. She ignored the sounds of the liaison in the bedroom and did a quick sweep. It was a simple place, with vaulted ceilings, a few cheap pieces of art on the walls, and gas lanterns. She turned all but one of the lanterns down and found a chair that looked at the bedroom.

This wait felt longer than the one outside the club, though in reality it couldn't have been more than forty-five minutes. Kizzie held her stiletto in one hand, resting her head against the chair, lounging in the dim light until the mistress emerged from the bedroom.

The young woman paused briefly at the sight of her, then closed the bedroom door behind her. She had her clothes clutched to her chest, and her makeup was smeared.

"Is he asleep?" Kizzie asked quietly.

The mistress nodded. "Is everything as we agreed? You won't kill him? He's not evil. Just . . ." She trailed off, as if even she wasn't sure why she cared about Churian's survival.

"I won't kill him," Kizzie promised, removing a wad of banknotes from her pocket and placing it on the table next to her. It was enough money to pay several months' rent on an apartment like this, or several years on a place in the Slag. The young woman plucked it up, regarding Kizzie warily, then crouched in the corner of the sitting room to pull on her tunic and jacket. She was soon gone, leaving Kizzie alone in the apartment with the soft sound of snoring.

Kizzie entered the bedroom, looking down at the slovenly guild-family asshole sleeping nude under a sheet that left little to the imagination. His breathing was heavy, indicative of a deep sleep, and she very carefully slid the shackleglass through one of Churian's piercings. Shackleglass was not a violent sorcery, and his body didn't so much as twitch at the feel of it.

Sure that everything was prepared, she shoved Churian's own under-garments into his open mouth. *That* woke him up, and she stood above him and watched him flail and grunt for several moments before giving him very specific instructions: "You are to remain still. Do not speak unless to an-swer a question. Do you understand?" Kizzie turned up the gas lantern above the bed. She could see in Churian's eyes that his panic was warring with the sorcery of the shackleglass. Eventually the sorcery won out. His expression became one of frightened acceptance, and he nodded in response to her question.

Low-resonance shackleglass was known to make people suggestible and truthful. It was commonly given to convicts and prisoners, and sometimes to the house staff of particularly paranoid or cruel guild-families. High-resonance shackleglass forced the wearer to tell any truth and obey any com-mand. The piece that Demir had given Kizzie was medium-resonance, and it would be perfect for her needs.

She removed the undergarments from Churian's mouth, sitting on the bed next to him. "What is your name?"

"Churian Dorlani," he answered fearfully.

"What is your most embarrassing secret?"

His eyes widened, but he answered immediately. "I once let out a fart at a fancy dinner party. Poo came out with it. I blamed the dog."

Kizzie rubbed at her nose to cover her smile. Well, the shackleglass defi-nitely worked. She tugged on the gloves hiding her silic sigil. "Do you rec-ognize me?" she asked.

"No," he answered.

"Good. Did you participate in the murder of Adriana Grappo?"

Churian's eyes grew wide. He began to tremble, struggling as if against invisible ropes, his body unwilling to disobey Kizzie's direct command. His mouth opened, closed, then opened again as he fought the sorcery. He chewed on his tongue—not enough to bite it off, but enough to draw blood. Kizzie lost patience and pulled out her stiletto, pressing it against his throat for added incentive.

"Did you participate in the murder of Adriana Grappo?" she asked again, more forcefully.

"Y-y-yes," Churian answered.

Kizzie gazed down at him, frowning. "Well. Damn." She had expected this answer—the Breadman seemed like a reliable witness—but she still didn't like it. "Why did you do it?"

Churian licked his lips, glancing over Kizzie's shoulder as if to search the room for help. Sweat poured off his brow. Finally he said, "I was ordered to by my grandmother, Aelia Dorlani."

"That's it?" Kizzie asked. "You were ordered to?"

"You don't say no to Aelia."

Aelia was the matriarch of the Dorlani guild-family and widely considered a sadist. Saying no to her was akin to saying no to Father Vorcien—except she would kill you herself, rather than have an underling do it. Kizzie's uneasiness grew. If the Dorlani were behind the killing and word got out, it could start a guild-family war. They had enough enemies, and the tiny Grappo guild-family was well-liked enough, that it wouldn't take but hours before enforcers were gunning each other down in the streets. "Do you know why she wanted Adriana dead?"

"I don't. I . . ." Churian hesitated, then spat out, "I didn't want to! I didn't even know Adriana. Why would I kill her? But Grandmother said to."

"So you followed orders." Kizzie sighed. That was not nearly as good a lead as she'd hoped. It wasn't like she could slip into the Dorlani estate and do something similar to Aelia. Piss, even asking to see Aelia would raise suspicions, among both the Dorlani and her own family. "The other killers. Were they also ordered there by your grandmother?"

"I don't know."

"Guess."

Churian's eyes twitched. The blanket beneath him was soaked with sweat now. "I don't think so."

"Why not?"

"We met anonymously, just before the killing. Everyone was wearing masks. I . . . recognized one of them. My grandmother would not have sent a Magna for a public killing."

A cold finger seemed to creep up Kizzie's spine. A Grent agent, a Dorlani, *and* a Magna. Glassdamn, this *was* a conspiracy! Conjectures began flying around inside her head, and it took all her willpower to silence them so that she could properly work. "Who was it?"

Churian had stopped trembling. He was nothing but resignation now, his whole body looking slack and exhausted from trying to fight the shackle-glass. "Glissandi Magna."

Another guild-family cousin. Kizzie chewed on her lip, considering. "Don't move," she ordered Churian, withdrawing to the sitting room, where she could pace and think.

Was this a real conspiracy? Were the guild-families and the Duke of Grent somehow working together? Had Capric lied to Demir about that captured Grent agent? It all seemed so impossible, but so did the idea that agents from three major powers had come together for the murder.

Kizzie vacillated on what to do next. While Churian was considered little more than a bureaucratic nobody within his own family, Glissandi had actual power within the Magna. She was as close to the main family as was possible without being an actual daughter. Fiercely independent, quite rich, and with connections all over Ossa, Glissandi would be a difficult target.

But it was also Kizzie's best lead.

She walked to the door. "You definitely didn't recognize anyone else?" she asked.

"I didn't, I swear!" came the answer.

This was becoming more dangerous by the minute. Once again, Kizzie found herself wondering if she should just return Demir's money and swear off the job. Just a day and a half had passed. She could probably back out. If she did, the question of what had actually happened would haunt her for the rest of her life. What's more, she would miss her chance at reconnecting with Montego.

Something else about this whole thing was bothering her. Assuming Capric was telling the truth about the Grent agent, then at least two of the six killers were patsies. They were killers but *not* conspirators. Neither of them knew *why* Adriana Grappo needed to die.

Glissandi might.

Kizzie tossed her stiletto up into the air and caught it deftly by the blade between two fingers. Glissandi Magna. She would be difficult to corner alone, but not impossible. Certainly easier than Aelia Dorlani.

She forced herself to stop worrying. The politics wasn't part of her job. All she had to do was get the facts back to Demir. If *he* wanted to start a guild-family war, that was his problem. Kizzie would have to hide her involvement in all this from her family, but if they somehow found out then she would have plausible deniability. They were, after all, the ones who loaned her out to the Grappo.

She returned to the bedroom once more and tapped Churian's bare chest with the flat of her stiletto blade. "I'll give you two choices," she said. "You can either sell all your worldly possessions by noon tomorrow and board the next ship to Marn, or I can tell Baby Montego that you took part in the killing of his adopted mother. Which do you choose?"

The trembling returned, and Kizzie quickly caught a whiff of the scent of piss. "I'll leave!" Churian said. "I'll be gone. I . . . I . . . I won't talk to another soul. I won't even sell anything. You'll never see me again."

Satisfied with the answer, Kizzie leaned over and plucked the shackle-glass from Churian's ear. "If you try to follow me, I'll kill you. If you try to find out who I am, I'll kill you. I'd lay there for a few minutes after I'm gone, if I were you. I promise that if you haven't disappeared by noon tomorrow, Baby Montego will be visiting you by dinner."

She left that threat, letting herself out of the apartment and then leaving by the same side door that she'd tricked the doorman with earlier. It was around ten o'clock. Perfect time to get a drink. She would need it if she was going to figure out how to fit the next piece of this puzzle without getting murdered by Glissandi Magna's bodyguards.

14

Lechauri was true to his word, and by morning Demir's office was filled with files on the Ivory Forest Glassworks. He enlisted Breenen, Montego, and even the hotel's master-at-arms, Tirana Kirkovik, to comb through everything. He did not tell them *why* they had to extract Thessa, just that it needed to be done. He could afford little time, and he himself focused on the owners of the Ivory Forest Glassworks.

"I don't mean to complain," Tirana said quietly after several hours of reading, comparing notes, and discarding useless information, "but do you do this sort of thing a lot?"

Demir flipped through the documents in front of him—what looked like internal Magna spymaster reports on their own family members—and was amazed that Lechauri had even gotten his hands on them, let alone handed them over. He must have been *terrified* of Harlen. "When needed," he answered.

Out of the corner of his eye he could see Tirana grimace down at yet another ledger outlining the glassworks' financial records.

"Oh. That's, uh . . ."

"A waste of time?" Demir guessed.

"I was trying to come up with a more polite way of saying it."

"When I was young," Demir explained, "I had a very particular method—I would gather every single piece of information I could get my hands on, then use high-resonance witglass to analyze it. I could fully understand this much content in about ninety minutes, taking into account the fact that I'd have to remove the witglass periodically for my own safety."

Tirana's eyes widened, though it hadn't been Demir's intention to show off. "You did all this *by yourself*?" she asked.

"That's what happens when you get a genius who isn't driven mad by high-resonance witglass," Montego rumbled. His own stack of missives and reports had been set aside so he could read the morning newspaper. He held a large glass of wine in one hand, his fourth of the morning, though he showed no effect of intoxication.

Demir allowed himself a demure smile. "That was before I . . . broke at Holikan," he said, tapping the side of his head. "I still like to use the same method, but it takes much, much longer."

"And this is really useful?" Tirana asked.

Demir said, "The more you know, the better you can plan. Primary plans, secondary plans, tertiary plans. Plans for failed plans. Plans for the failed plans of failed plans. Information is not just useful, it is everything." He glanced at Tirana. "You think I didn't look into you within hours of our meeting? I memorized your military record and everything I could find about your personal life."

Tirana glanced sidelong at Breenen, but the majordomo just shook his head. Demir could read that silent message—*Get used to it, he's in charge now.* She said, "You couldn't have possibly memorized everything about me."

"Everything I could find," Demir answered, flipping to the next document and running his eyes over it.

"Oh yeah? How could—"

"You were engaged to Sandri Vorcien for six months. You both seemed happy with the match, but Johanna Vorcien canceled the marriage at the last minute because she didn't want Sandri marrying a woman, despite how well that would have worked out for two non-inheriting granddaughters. Some bullshit about wanting proper great-grandchildren and not adoptees."

Tirana gasped and half stood, her hand going to her sword. "That is *not* public information!"

Demir immediately felt a stab of guilt. That time he *was* showing off. He rubbed his eyes and gestured for her to sit. "I apologize, I took that too far." He glanced at Tirana and saw that her shoulders had slumped as she fell back into her chair.

"I joined the army because of that," Tirana said quietly.

Demir's guilt grew deeper. He tried to stave it off. He did, after all, have more important things to worry about than hurt feelings. "Again, I apologize. Information is very important to me. The world is a great big calculation. I did not keep you on when I returned because my mother hired you, or because your grandfather and I are friends. I kept you on because everything about your history showed an independent but loyal woman I could depend on to guard my hotel."

Tirana glanced up at him shyly. "You're not just saying that?"

"No. Now read that glassdamned ledger to look for more information we can use to rescue Thessa." Demir rubbed his eyes again. "I think I may have something. Breenen, how long will it take you to find Ulina Magna?"

"Thirty minutes?"

"Do it."

Breenen left the room with a nod, stepping carefully through the stacks of documents. Demir continued his studies until the majordomo returned. "She's at the Castle Hill Arena," Breenen reported, "enjoying the afternoon fights in her private box."

Demir selected a few pages from the spymaster reports and stuffed them in his tunic pocket for further study. He plucked up a newspaper, found the arena schedule, and grabbed his jacket. "I used to be very good at layered plans," he told Tirana. "I may have lost that skill, but let us hope I'm still good at primary plans. Now I must go introduce myself to a Magna. Baby, I will need your help."

Montego folded his newspaper and joined Demir without a word, and they left Breenen and Tirana in the office, hurrying down to the lobby, where a carriage was prepared for them in minutes. They were soon trundling down the road at speed.

It was Montego who broke the silence. "Why are we confronting Ulina Magna at the Castle Hill Arena?" he asked. He didn't seem particularly bothered by the prospect of meeting a Magna—Montego was hard to ruffle at the worst of times—but he leaned forward curiously.

Demir showed Montego what he'd been studying back in his office. "This," he explained, "is a spymaster report on Ulina Magna. She's one of forty-seven Magna grandchildren. She's twenty-eight, by all reports quite pretty and charming, and she owns a sixteen percent share in the Ivory Forest Glassworks."

Montego took the document from Demir and studied it, his beady eyes darting across the page rapidly, his expression growing thoughtful. He handed it back. "Looks like a lot of funds enter and leave her personal bank account every month. Hundreds of thousands at a time."

"Exactly. Could be debts. Could be corruption. Could be gambling. We need to find out what, and then use it." Demir tapped the paper against his cheek. "I think Ulina is exactly what we need to save Thessa."

"Do you have a plan?"

"Sort of. I might have to wing it."

Montego rolled his eyes. "The old Demir always had five plans."

"I'm not the old Demir," Demir answered. Montego waved his hand as if to concede the point.

Their carriage rumbled across the Assembly District and up Castle Hill, soon depositing them at the base of the old castle that had long been gutted and converted into a cudgeling arena. A massive sign hung over the gate, declaring that the arena was sponsored by the Glasstop Cudgelists, a popular Fulgurist Society for retired athletes. Demir loosened his jacket collar, tousled his hair, and prepared a thick wad of banknotes. He needed to look like someone who attended early-afternoon cudgeling matches on a regular basis.

"I'm sorry, sir," a porter said as Demir exited the carriage, "but the arena is full for the afternoon. No more entry."

Demir had never wanted to use the phrase "Do you know who I am?" so much in his life. Instead, he peeled several banknotes off his wad and pushed them into the front pocket of the porter's tunic. "You're sure?"

The porter gave Demir a regretful smile. "I'm sure, I . . ." His eyes widened as Montego exited the carriage, nearly tipping it over onto himself as he stepped on the running board. Montego put one hand on the porter's shoulder and tripled the amount Demir had tipped him.

"Baby Montego and Demir Grappo," Montego rumbled. "Surely you can find some room for a retired world champion and his friend?"

"Oh . . . oh! Of course, sir. Let me see what I can do." He scurried off without another word, leaving Demir to gaze after him ruefully.

"Did I undertip?" Demir asked.

"No. You're not a dues-paying member." Montego nodded to the sign over the front gate. "You may have the run of the provincial cudgeling arenas, but there's a different language spoken in Ossa."

"Do I have to eat you to gain your powers?" Demir asked flippantly.

"You'd have to eat me to get this big. There he is, come on."

Demir fell back, allowing Montego to cut a path through the crowd. Those that didn't move out of the way were gently but forcibly pushed to one side, and Demir could hear a trail of whispers in their wake as they passed.

"Holy shit," one woman said, "is that Baby Montego?"

"I had no idea he was back in town!" a man replied.

"Do you think he'd sign an autograph?"

"Piss on an autograph," another woman cut in, "what hotel is he in? I've heard he's an absolute monster in . . ."

Demir chuckled to himself as they met up with the porter, who led them down a narrow hallway, leaving the whispers behind them. Montego had a point. Demir was famous in his own right, but in a cudgeling arena, Montego was a god.

"You found a place for us?" Montego asked the porter.

"Yes, sir! It's not a perfect view but if you make arrangements for next time we will absolutely clear a box for you."

They emerged from the hallway into the back of a packed crowd in the courtyard of the old castle. The actual cudgeling ring was on a raised platform in the center of the courtyard, with some tiered seating on the east side, boxes built haphazardly into the north and west walls, and more people watching from a handful of windows and lining the tops of the castle walls.

The porter led them to a spot about halfway between the walls and the ring. As he'd said, it was not a good position to see the actual match, but Demir barely glanced toward the ring. He scanned the walls, windows, and boxes, searching for a woman in her late twenties. He found one, but she was a Nasuud blonde. He kept looking until he spotted an eager-looking woman staring down toward the ring from the window of the corner tower.

The porter shoved people aside until there was room for Montego and Demir, then stationed himself at Montego's shoulder with the clear intent of someone who's ready to serve and plans to make some very good tips doing it. Demir hadn't been to a proper Ossan cudgeling match for over a decade, but Montego acted as if this was all to be expected. Even when people began edging away from him, staring in wonder, he didn't really seem to notice.

"Why is it so crowded?" Montego asked.

"Special exhibition match," the porter shouted above the noise of the crowd. "Do you know Fidori Glostovika?"

"The Balkani champion?" Demir asked. "I didn't see his name on the schedule."

"Oh, he's the very last match," the porter said. "Everyone packed in here will watch the whole afternoon just to get a glimpse of him. Very exciting! He might have even been a match for you in your heyday, Master Montego."

Montego grunted noncommittally, but Demir could see the way his eyes narrowed. Perfect. Demir didn't like going into these things on so little information, but he could use this. "Who's his sponsor?" Demir asked.

"That would be the Magna."

"Oh? I haven't spoken to any of them since I returned to town. Is anyone here to watch the match?"

"Lady Ulina Magna," the porter answered, pointing up at the tower Demir had already suspected was Ulina's private box. "She's here almost every day."

Demir turned toward Montego, feigning surprise. "Weren't you just saying you wanted to meet Ulina?"

"That I was!" Montego replied, playing along.

The porter made a tutting sound. "I'm afraid Lady Ulina doesn't like being disturbed during the matches, I . . ."

Montego leaned over suddenly, putting his arm around the porter's shoulder as if to take him into his confidence. He said, "I have heard Ulina is very pretty. My friend and I would very much like to meet her. If you could arrange it? As a personal favor to me?"

The porter's face went red. "Of . . . of course," he stuttered, "Master Montego, I'll do what I can!" Once again he hurried off, and Montego turned to Demir with that same smirk.

"I've still got it."

"Of course you've still got it, you big oaf," Demir responded, "you're glass-damned Baby Montego. Can you see a damned thing?"

"Enough to see that both the men fighting right now will never get further than regional exhibition bouts. Bah, is the quality in the capital slipping so much?"

Demir stood on his tiptoes, trying to get a view of the arena. He could see the fighters' heads moving back and forth, the occasional raised cudgel, and nothing else. He gave up and waited for the porter to return. The young man was back soon, looking very pleased with himself, and shouted to be heard, "Lady Ulina has graciously offered to share her box with you today. This way, please!"

Demir allowed himself a flicker of a smile. Perfect.

Once again Montego plowed through the crowd, cutting a path that Demir followed gladly. They were taken back the way they came, through a series of narrow passages, and then up an original stone spiral staircase that Montego barely fit through. They arrived at the box to find what looked like Ulina's entourage standing outside, pushed out to make room for Montego and Demir. The small group wore unhappy glares that were immediately replaced with surprise.

"It *is* him!"

"Montego, I saw your last fight! I can't believe it's you!"

Hands reached out, touching Montego as he passed. One of the young women actually swooned, while the men stared in awe and fear. None of them objected as Montego entered the box. Demir gave them a smile as he shut the door to the box behind them.

Ulina Magna was a statuesque woman, well over six feet tall, with long, curly black hair that cascaded over a crimson-and-white tunic. She spun away from her view as Demir and Montego entered, somehow managing to sweep across the narrow box. "My dear Master Montego, what a pleasure it is to meet you! I cannot believe my luck!"

"Lady Ulina," Montego responded, grasping Ulina's hand in his and kissing it gently. "My friend, Demir Grappo."

"Ah! The new patriarch of the Grappo guild-family. A double pleasure indeed!" Ulina's tone cooled noticeably upon greeting Demir, her eyes giving him a quick up-and-down and a silent judgment that indicated she did not think much of either him or his minor guild-family. Her gaze dipped toward his glassdancer sigil, the corner of her eye twitching. Demir pretended not to notice. Her smile remained warm through it all, and she quickly turned back to Montego.

Demir did not mind. He didn't need attention right now. He needed to observe. The box was small, with just six seats all crammed in together. Ulina deposited herself between them, leaning against Montego's arm, pointing down to the cudgeling ring below them. The last fight had just finished and Demir could see the two new fighters preparing themselves while blood was mopped up. He settled in to watch, glancing through the newspapers available in the box as well as a pamphlet printed up by the arena for the day's fights.

He'd heard the names of several of the fighters. No one of particular skill or fame, but men and women who put on a good enough show to get fans into seats. Fidori Glostovika was clearly the draw for most of the crowd.

Ulina talked nonstop, seemingly without bothering to take a breath, a constant stream of anecdotes that was interrupted only by demands for food or drink from the attending porter. Montego danced through the conversation skillfully, interjecting witticisms and occasionally challenging her knowledge of the sport. This was clearly not the first wealthy young fan that he'd watched a cudgeling match with.

Only one thing broke up the conversation, and that was when Ulina ordered a second porter to run to the bookie in the arena foyer to make bets on her behalf. The bets were rapid-fire, sometimes contradicting a previous bet with even more money as the fight wore on. She discussed each decision with Montego in detail, occasionally changing her bet upon his advice.

Demir remained silent, studying and thinking, and it was by the fourth match that Ulina excused herself for a moment, stepping just outside the door to the box to berate one of her porters.

"You seem to be getting along well," Demir commented.

Montego shrugged. "She's quite knowledgeable, but too arrogant for my tastes. Do you have a plan yet?"

"I believe I do," Demir replied. "Do you remember that little con we used to do when we were kids?"

Montego snorted. "Of course."

"How do you feel about resurrecting it?"

"Here? Are you serious?"

"If I can make it work, yes."

"I am not properly dressed."

"If you were, the con wouldn't work."

Montego considered this for a moment. "The last time we did it, we were chased out of the Blacktree Arena by six angry bookies and their enforcers."

"We gave fake names. This was before you were famous."

"We're *both* famous now. If we get caught . . ."

Demir nodded in understanding. If they were caught he would lose what little standing he had with the other guild-families. The cudgeling league would begin to tail him, and his whole operation throughout the provinces could be at risk. Considering that that operation was funding his above-board purchases for the Grappo, it was a dire risk indeed. But he needed access to the Ivory Forest Glassworks immediately. "Let's do it," he finally said.

"Fine."

Ulina reappeared a moment later, another drink in her hand. "The porter was being too slow," she explained sweetly, "so I sent her to be flogged. Are we about to start yet?"

"Ulina," Demir said, raising a hand.

"Hmm?" She turned to him as if only just remembering that he was here. "Yes, Demir?"

"I'm getting the gambling itch."

"Hah! Of course you are. Please, feel free to make use of my runner."

"I don't want to get involved with bookies so soon after returning to the capital. How about a friendly wager between you and me?"

Ulina regarded him for a moment, looking at him closely for the first time in the last hour. "What did you have in mind?"

"I don't know the next fighters, but I'm feeling lucky. Who do you favor?"

"It'll be close, but I think Blago."

"Then I'll take Wasti. A thousand ozzo?"

Ulina's face split in a grin. If she feared his glassdancer tattoo, she had now forgotten all about it. "You're on!"

The fight went much as Demir expected. He did, in fact, know both of the fighters. Blago had been indirectly on his payroll several years ago, and though Blago was older and losing energy, it was an easy win for him. Demir pulled out his wad of banknotes and peeled off ten of them as the match ended with Wasti's forfeit.

"Good fight, good fight," he said to Ulina. When she reached for the money, he pulled it back slightly. "Give me the chance to win it back?"

Ulina's attention had shifted from Montego now. She smiled slyly at Demir. "Double or nothing? I'll give you the choice of fighter."

He had her now.

Demir won the next match, and then lost the following three, then won another. Ulina sent one of her entourage to the closest bank and a hefty stack of banknotes began to build on one of the empty seats in the box. Montego looked on in bemusement, refusing to participate in the betting despite Ulina's repeated invitations.

By the eighth fight, Demir's blood was pumping and his mouth was dry. Over two hundred thousand ozzo had bounced between them, and even he had not guessed that it would escalate so quickly. He looked at the schedule. Just one more fight: the exhibition match between Fidori and a local champion that Demir did not know. Demir reached for the pile of money.

"Uh-uh!" Ulina said, slapping his hand playfully. "What do you think you're doing?"

"Collecting my winnings?"

"There's still one more match."

Demir laughed and shook his head. "Fidori is on the Magna payroll and for good reason. I've been having fun but I'm not going to bet against him."

"Oh, please?" Ulina pouted.

Demir pretended to consider, then shook his head again. "Not a chance."

"I'll give you good odds."

Again, he hesitated. "No. I'd be a fool."

Ulina glanced down at the pile of money. From her personal ledgers,

Demir knew that she won and lost piles like this on a monthly basis, but it *was* still a lot of money. A very tempting pot for anyone, no matter how rich. "Suit yourself, I suppose," she sighed. She managed to maintain her composure, but Demir could see the frustration in her eyes.

Preparations were made for the last match. The crowd was noticeably excited, pointing and waving, screaming Fidori's name as he strolled out among them and entered the ring. He was truly a specimen: almost as tall as Montego, light skin sun-bronzed, muscles oiled. He held a cudgel in one hand and a bouquet of flowers in the other, which he threw to the audience as he gained the ring.

Demir glanced sidelong at Montego, who rolled his eyes. "He stole that from me," Montego grumbled.

Ulina was noticeably muted, though still a gracious host. She leaned forward, putting in an extra-large bet with the arena bookie, no doubt hoping to recoup some of the losses she'd made to Demir. Instead of putting his winnings in his pockets, Demir left them on the chair beside him. Ulina glanced in their direction every so often.

The fight was, he had to admit, very good. Fidori and the local champion sparred back and forth across the ring with astonishing speed and strength, blows connecting that would have felled normal fighters.

"You're sure you won't bet?" Ulina asked Demir. "The local chap is doing quite well."

Demir waved her off, and it was a good thing too. The local fighter was soon bashed across the shoulder, staggering to one side and failing to protect himself as Fidori whaled on his useless arm. He fell to one knee, clearly trying to signal the referee for a forfeit.

"Come now!" Montego roared, leaping to his feet. "End the fight!" It was his first display of real investment the whole afternoon.

The referee scrambled into the ring, pushing Fidori back, while the local fighter was quickly carried away. Montego turned to Demir red-faced. "That was not a good fight."

"Oh, don't be like that," Ulina said dismissively, "you've killed dozens of fighters in the ring."

"I never swing once the forfeit signal is given."

"He didn't signal."

"He was trying to. Always give a fighter the chance to back out. That's good sportsmanship."

"Fidori only does that with fighters he considers worthy," Ulina laughed.

Demir pushed his way between them. "Hey, hey. It was a good fight. Sit down, Baby, that fighter will be good to go after a week on cureglass."

Montego rumbled angrily to himself as he sat down, and Demir could tell it was not an act. "I'm sorry," Demir said to Ulina, "he feels very strongly about these things."

"Hm. Fidori is at the top running for champion next year. Unofficially, of course. The season hasn't begun."

"He's not *that* good," Montego snapped.

"Hah! He's incredible. Don't be sore. Fidori has a long career ahead of him. I bet he could have even beaten you in your heyday!"

It was the second time someone had said that, and was the moment Demir had been waiting for. "You really think so?" He turned to Ulina curiously.

"Yes, most certainly."

Demir pretended to think hard about this, letting a grin sneak its way onto his face. "All right. I'll give you the chance to win your money back. Another match here and now, Montego against Fidori."

Ulina gasped. "You're kidding!"

"Not at all. Baby, how are you for a fight?"

"I don't have my cudgels," Montego complained. He drew out the words like a petulant child, though Demir could practically *feel* how badly Montego wanted to put the younger fighter in his place.

Ulina practically leapt at him. "We can get you cudgels. Oh, this will be the most glorious match of the century! And all for just us! We'll clear the arena, pay off the manager. Old champion against future champion!" She actually squealed, an ecstatic sound that made Demir's ears hurt.

"Let the audience stay," Montego rumbled. "Give them a show."

"Of course! Whatever you want to make this happen!"

"What will you bet?" Demir asked.

"Cash. Just tell me the amount."

"Come now, let's make it interesting. I have a new lumber mill I just purchased the other day. Put down some property." Demir spoke casually, but every inflection was purposeful and chosen with care. He wanted to pull her in like a master fisherman, not scare her away. From her file he knew exactly what properties she had.

"I could put down a mine in Fortshire," she said.

"What kind?"

"Copper."

"Done. How will we validate?"

Ulina gestured dismissively as if she'd done this many times. "The manager and porters will be our witnesses. And Montego, of course."

The arrangements were made in a secret whirlwind. The arena manager was paid off, a new referee summoned, and the porters cleared a large area immediately in front of the ring so that Demir and Ulina could watch from the very best seats. There was an announcement about the surprise fight and Demir could *feel* the excitement ripple through the crowd. People who'd grown tired from standing all afternoon were back on their feet, cheering and laughing at the prospect of seeing Baby Montego step into the ring once more.

Demir consulted with Montego while Ulina did the same with Fidori. Montego did not, Demir had to admit, look great. In a cudgeling girdle he seemed even more obese, his arms flabby, his stomach drooping. Montego reached down and touched his toes while Demir eyeballed Fidori.

"You are," Demir asked quietly, his words almost drowned out by the roar of a reenergized crowd, "sure you can win?"

"Eh," Montego responded.

"What the piss is that supposed to mean?"

"He is actually quite skilled," Montego admitted. "It will be a good fight."

"Even if you lose?"

"Even if I lose."

Demir groaned. "Please don't. Aside from the money, this is our best chance to rescue Thessa."

Montego didn't answer him, pulling himself up onto the raised ring and taking a few experimental swings with his cudgel. Fidori watched him skeptically—and so did Demir. Montego was not a young cudgelist anymore, many years retired, and Demir wondered if he'd made a mistake.

Forgeglass was handed to both men. Montego examined his distastefully before fixing it to his ear, and the match began slowly, the pair circling each other. There was no time limit and the crowd did not seem to care. It was clear both fighters wanted this to happen in its own time. Demir took up a spot beside Ulina and glanced at the arena manager, who held a promissory note for both properties and the pile of cash from earlier.

"You really think Fidori could beat Baby Montego in his prime?" Demir asked Ulina.

"Well," Ulina said, watching intently as the first blows were exchanged. "Perhaps not in his prime, if I'm being honest. But now? Look at Montego. Your friend can barely move his cudgel without wheezing."

Demir resisted the urge to defend Montego. It wasn't *that* bad. On the other hand, he couldn't actually tell whether Montego was acting as he barely blocked a flurry of blows from Fidori. The Balkani champion pressed the attack, putting Montego on the back foot, hammering at his thighs and shoulders mercilessly.

Montego took the beating without so much as a groan of pain. His own ripostes were slower, stronger. When they landed they certainly staggered the younger Fidori, but they did not put him down.

"Up the bet?" Ulina asked slyly.

Demir responded with a negative gesture.

"Two-to-one odds," Ulina said.

Demir let her hang herself on that rope. "How could you possibly back up a bet like that?" he asked. Fidori was practically chasing Montego around the ring now. On any other day it would be a good fight—it was always fun when an outmatched fighter refused to back down—but for a world champion it was comically pathetic.

"I have a sixteen percent stake in the Ivory Forest Glassworks. It's a big complex just outside of Ossa. I'll put down my whole stake."

"And what would I have to answer that with?"

"Let's say four hundred thousand."

"Fine. A coal mine in the Glass Isles." He glanced at the manager and the accompanying porters, who nodded that they'd heard the bet.

Montego stumbled and fell heavily to one knee. The crowd screamed—some in jubilation, some in anger. A group of women just behind Demir shouted for Montego to get back up. He managed to get his cudgel up between his face and Fidori's, but the barrage of blows was so withering it looked like he might drop it.

"Forfeit, Montego," Fidori shouted between blows. "There's no shame in it. I don't want to kill you in an exhibition match."

Montego's arm drooped, but he did not go down.

Fidori backed away a step and glanced at Ulina. "He won't forfeit."

"Then finish him!"

In that moment, Montego's eyes met Demir's. Demir gave the slightest of nods, and Montego took a deep breath. Fidori turned back toward him and raised his cudgel. "Last chance, old man!" He waited half a second, then swung with all his might.

Montego surged to his feet, catching the haft of the cudgel in his left hand. With his right, he swung low, the weighted bulb of his cudgel catching

Fidori on the side of the knee. It did not *look* like a powerful swing, but it was impossibly precise. Fidori's knee shattered sideways, collapsing unnaturally in a way that almost made Demir throw up. Fidori fell, screaming loudly. Those screams were immediately swallowed up by the crowd, who went absolutely wild at the reversal.

Demir glanced sidelong at Ulina, doing his best to keep the smile off his face. He climbed up into the arena, ignoring Fidori as the referee, the arena manager, and Ulina hurried to help him. Demir clasped Montego by the hand. "Very good fight."

Montego stifled a yawn. "Amateur," he muttered, glancing at one of the welts on his arm as if it bored him. The exhaustion had left his eyes, and his breathing was no longer heavy. Glassdamned showman. "How did I do?"

"I am now the proud owner of sixteen percent of the Ivory Forest Glassworks."

15

Idrian's sword rang like a bell as it clashed with that of his opponent, each blow reverberating through his hand, up his arm, and spreading through his body with terrifying force. He caught a swing, shunting it to one side, keeping his shield tight against his left shoulder as a ferocious patter of bullets cracked against it like hail on glass.

He did not recognize the Grent breacher, but he'd heard of the feathered sigil on his shield. The Hawk was a young man, probably no more than twenty-five, with a goateed face and a wicked grin. All Idrian knew was that the Hawk was ambitious, and it showed in the way he pressed hard, with little consideration for the company of infantry backing him up. His entire focus was on Idrian.

It would, Idrian knew as he fell back several steps, be the Hawk's undoing.

He caught the Hawk's sword against his shield, looking for an opening that he did not find, and instead rebounded off his back leg. The push took the Hawk off guard, and Idrian forced both of their shields down enough that he could lean out over them with a head butt. The tightly curled horns on his helmet connected with the Hawk's left cheek, and the Hawk stumbled back, spitting blood, blinded momentarily.

Idrian pulled his shield up to protect himself from another volley from the Hawk's infantry. The Hawk was not so aware, and Tadeas's soldiers took the opportunity to pepper him with musketfire. At least two bullets found chinks in the Hawk's armor. The Hawk jerked twice, stumbled again, and Idrian had only to spin the grip on his sword and thrust once at the neck with the broad razorglass tip, neatly removing the Hawk's head.

Cries of dismay went up among the Grent soldiers. Unlike their now-deceased breacher, they seemed well-trained, and they immediately fell into an organized retreat. Idrian could sense the Ironhorns moving behind him, bringing themselves up to capture this next street.

The fighting had gone like this for hours, a ferocious back-and-forth between Grent and Ossan infantry through the rows of magnificent townhouses of the evacuated Grent elite. Idrian's armor was coated with blood and dust and the air choked with powder smoke. Directly ahead of him, less than a mile away, he could see the rising slope of Grent Hill, topped by the ducal palace, its white stone shining bright in the afternoon sun.

Idrian stared at the palace for a few moments, wrestling with his uncertainties. Would they even be able to capture it against the fierce Grent defenses? Would it really give them a shot at ending this war quickly if they did? More important, would that cinderite still be on display in the foyer for Idrian to steal?

The rest of the Ironhorns had reached him by now, securing the intersection. Mika and her engineers tore up the cobbles to create low barricades to protect against a counteroffensive. A medic paused in front of Idrian, glancing him over to make sure most of the blood on his armor belonged to someone else, then moved on to serve the soldiers wounded in the skirmish.

Idrian was lifting his shield, ready to move forward to the next street, when a whistle cut through the air—a long note followed by two short notes.

Cease the advance.

He ground his teeth, looking over his shoulder, then back again at the ducal palace. If they were to capture it today they couldn't waste another minute. On the other hand, three clashes with the Hawk throughout the afternoon had left him exhausted. A few moments of rest would do him good.

"Are you all right, sir?" Braileer asked. He had barely left Idrian's side all day. As before, his sword was still unblooded—the young armorer could not seem to bring himself to kill—but his hammerglass buckler was bashed to piss. Despite his obvious terror, the kid had enough of a spine to remain in the thick of things, defending Idrian's flank with enthusiasm alone.

"I'm fine," Idrian answered, taking an offered wineskin and having a swig. He removed his helmet and pressed the cool wineskin against his forehead, then handed it back. "You're doing well," he said, "but hold back another ten paces or so. The enemy will focus their fire on me, but if you make yourself an easy target they'll take advantage of it."

"Yes, sir!"

The two of them withdrew from the front line, looking for the reason for the order to cease advancing. They found Tadeas back a couple of hundred yards, hunkered down in a restaurant that had been gutted by Mika's grenades less than an hour before. Most of the pieces of Grent infantry had been carted away, but Idrian spotted a powder-stained finger underneath Tadeas's planning table as he entered.

"Why are we halting the advance?" Idrian demanded.

"Because we've pushed too far ahead of everyone else," Tadeas responded. He stood over a table covered with notes, correspondence, and a hastily drawn map of the surrounding area. He appeared to be using beans—one pile of black, one pile of orange—to represent troop placements. He took a note from a messenger, dismissed the young woman, and then moved three orange beans from one end of the map to the other.

Valient, Mika's husband, stood beside Tadeas and gave Idrian a grin. "You're pushing damned hard today, big man. You got a fire beetle biting your ass?"

Idrian set his sword and shield against a wall and ran a hand through his sweat-slick hair. Without the extra forgeglass in his helmet to prop up his sore muscles, his legs felt wobbly and uncertain. He bit his thumb at Valient, eliciting a laugh. "Braileer, go find us some lunch."

"It's almost five o'clock, sir."

"Have we eaten lunch?"

"No, sir."

"Then find us some lunch." Idrian waited until the armorer had gone before continuing. "I thought General Stavri wanted the palace captured by day's end."

"Not if it gets everyone killed," Tadeas responded, frowning down at his bean map.

Idrian joined him. He'd spent enough years staring at Tadeas's makeshift maps to understand it at a glance, and could see that the Ironhorns had, indeed, pushed several blocks past their allies. The operation included eight battalions—roughly four thousand infantry—and it seemed that the Grent *really* didn't want to lose the ducal palace. He found a pile of orange beans just a few blocks to their west. "What's going on here?"

"Grent roadblock," Valient answered with a grimace. "I was just over there. The Green Jackets are getting the absolute shit kicked out of them trying to take that intersection. I sent a few squads over with Mika's grenades, but it doesn't seem to have made a difference. They've got a pretty powerful glassdancer with them. Anybody that shows their face gets eviscerated immediately. We've called for our own, but it could be hours before they arrive."

"That's what's holding us up?" Idrian could see that the Ossan advance was contracting on that spot.

Tadeas sighed. "Sure is. Look here—the Grent are pulling back, trying to get the Ironhorns to overextend. Our spies say they've got reserves somewhere over here"—he gestured vaguely off the side of the map—"so if we do, we'll get clobbered without backup."

"But," Valient pointed out, "if we transfer everything to reinforce the Green Jackets, those same reserves can move forward and hit us in the flank."

Idrian walked back outside, looking down the street to where Mika and her engineers were securing the position under the watchful eye of Valient's soldiers. For the moment, their little slice of the neighborhood was quiet. That could change at any time. Beyond their front line, the ducal palace sat up on that hill, taunting him. Should he tell Tadeas about his secret mission? He certainly couldn't tell him the *reason* for the mission. "Yes, Tad," Idrian muttered under his breath, "I've promised to help your nephew save civilization in order to protect my own sanity. I'm going to need you to endanger our battalion on that dubious premise."

He thought he heard a child's laughter, echoing as if from the other end of a deep cave. Decades ago, when the madness first manifested itself, he had initially just learned to live with it. He could, if he was paying attention, tell the difference between what was real and what was not. But it had grown apparent that it got worse over time, and doubly so during times of stress. It wasn't until he had attacked a glassdancer that wasn't there that he had reported his madness to a friend at the Ministry of the Legion.

The Ministry had been more than willing to add twenty years onto his debt marker in exchange for funding Master Kastora's efforts to control the madness.

Idrian did not mind the debt. That was life, after all. But he could remember the terror he felt after realizing that he'd swung his sword at the empty air, when he thought he saw a rebel glassdancer standing right in front of him. That was a mistake he couldn't make again. It could get him killed—or worse, his friends. Fear of doing so had gone away once Kastora perfected his eye. Now the fear was back, nestled in the pit of his stomach like a lead weight.

He turned back to Tadeas and Valient. "Is that map any good?" he asked.

"My maps are always good," Tadeas replied, looking hurt.

Idrian rolled his eye. "These buildings here. Townhomes just like these ones outside?"

"Correct."

"*Just* like them?" Idrian demanded.

Valient nodded. "Like I said, I was just over there."

"Then I should be able to come along here," Idrian said, pointing, "and drop down into here. If I can catch the glassdancer by surprise, we should be in a good position to take the intersection."

A light seemed to go on in Tadeas's eyes. "Like that time in Folia?"

"It was Stagro, but yes," Idrian corrected.

"Ah, right. Stagro." Tadeas stared at the map, lips pursed. "You remember that redhead in Stagro? Haven't thought about her in years." He seemed far away for a moment, then nodded. "All right, I like that. In and out quick before the Grent reserves even know we've moved. Valient, take a hundred infantry over to here. I'll send word to the Green Jackets that we're moving in."

"Done." Idrian slammed his helmet onto his head, fastening the leather strap and then snatching up his sword and shield. The forgeglass in the helmet reinvigorated him immediately. He found Braileer outside, looking dismayed at the meager army rations in his hands. The armorer seemed surprised to see Idrian wearing his helmet again. Idrian said, "Stay here. I've got a quick one-man mission. I'll expect lunch *and* dinner when I'm finished." With that, he took off at a run while Valient shouted for his sergeants behind him.

Like so much street fighting, the violence was so close as to be claustrophobic, with enemies within a stone's throw in seemingly every direction. It was a deadly labyrinth, even here in the wealthy district of Grent where the streets were broad and the townhouses had front and back gardens.

Idrian hurried farther behind his own lines, cutting down side streets and following the picture he held in his head of Tadeas's bean map. He passed through a contested neighborhood, shield held overhead to block shots from marksmen in the high windows, and reached a narrow alley that cut between the back gardens of a row of townhouses. Here he hunkered down for a moment, looking carefully, until he spotted what he needed next: a chimney sweep's access ladder, little more than heavy nails bolted into the side of a massive townhouse chimney.

Taking one last look around for the enemy, Idrian sprinted across the garden and threw himself up the ladder.

Within moments he was four stories up, crouched in the shadow of a chimney with a view across the whole neighborhood. He could see the ducal palace, Grent soldiers scurrying back and forth across the lawn. Sandbag barricades provided cover for a garrison that knew the exact purpose of the Ossan mission in this borough.

But they didn't know *his* mission. He tore his eyes away from that distant view and focused on the present, where all across his vantage point he could see hundreds of marksmen in both Ossan black and Grent orange waging their own miniature war across the rooftops. Individual shots rang out, spouting plumes of black smoke as figures ducked beneath rooflines and hurried from vantage to vantage, worrying just as much about each other as they did about the soldiers down in the street below.

None seemed to have noticed his presence, so Idrian kept low behind the chimney. His vantage allowed him to look down into two intersections. At one, he could see the Green Jackets forming up for another charge, the bright green stars on their jackets glittering in the sunlight. At the other, hidden back to the point where he could barely spot them, were a hundred Ironhorns.

Valient raised his hand in Idrian's direction, waving in the affirmative. The charge was ready. Idrian returned the wave.

The blast of a ram's horn suddenly cut through the air, reverberating off the townhouses, and the Ironhorns advanced at a steady march. Their bayonets were fixed, six lines of soldiers backed up by engineers with slings and grenades. A few beats later, the Green Jackets began their advance.

Idrian counted to ten, then burst from his cover and began to sprint along the rooftops parallel to the charge. He ran hard, feet slipping on the tiled roof as he went up the crown of one, down the other side, then leapt the six-foot gap between townhouses. His forgeglass spurred him on, sorcery humming through him.

One house. Two. Four. By the time he reached the fifth one he was firmly in Grent territory. He came over the crown of one roof and spotted a marksman taking aim at the Ironhorns below. The marksman whirled, trying to bring her rifle up to bear. Idrian was on her in half a second, his sword slicing through musket, arm, and chest in a single stroke that didn't even slow him down.

He was past, leaping a gap, his sword streaming a ribbon of entrails behind him as he landed on the next roof. Two more marksmen saw what he did to their companion. One took aim, firing a shot that Idrian easily blocked with his shield. Idrian skewered him while the other leapt from the roof, clearly more interested in fighting gravity than a breacher. Up ahead, Idrian heard the tight Grent defenses fire off their first volley. He was almost to the end of the row of townhouses. One more gap to jump, and he landed on a flat-roofed maintenance building swarming with Grent marksmen.

Not one of them saw him coming, and it did not go well for them.

Mere moments had passed since Idrian had begun his run. He was now four stories directly above the Grent defensive position, and he could see why they'd been so hard to unseat: two whole companies lay in wait behind high barricades, firing in rotation, a glassdancer hiding just behind the second barricade with several thick shards of glass hovering just over his shoulder, ready to be hurled at the oncoming infantry.

Idrian waited for a few moments, watching down the street until the Ironhorns paused their advance. He could hear Valient screaming orders. The first line knelt and, along with the second line, released a volley at the Grent defenders. The shots had barely been fired when another blast from a ram's horn sounded. Grenades were flung from slings, arching over the barricades, exploding with enough force to shake the building Idrian was hiding on.

The Ironhorns charged with bayonets fixed, and it was exactly the signal Idrian had been waiting for. He looked down, found the glassdancer again, and saw that the man was ready to hurl death at the Ironhorns. Idrian leapt, sword and shield spread to either side like wings. Four stories of empty air whistled past his ears, barely audible over the adrenaline fueling his blasting heartbeat. Time seemed to slow to nothing, and the glassdancer glanced up half a second before Idrian landed on his shoulders.

Idrian's used the glassdancer's body to absorb much of the shock of his landing, but even still he felt the impact through his entire frame. Without the forgeglass to strengthen him, he would have broken both legs.

He felt the glassdancer crumple, rolled across his shield, and came up quickly with a horizontal slice that vivisected an entire squad. He shattered an officer's skull with his shield, sliced again, and then began to sprint at the next group of infantry. The Grent defense collapsed around him as soldiers turned to face the breacher in their midst mere moments before the Ironhorns flooded over their barricade. The Green Jackets appeared next, hungry for vengeance.

It was a glassdamned massacre. A few pockets of grenadiers—the duke's own bodyguard—held out for as long as it took Idrian to locate and clear their position. The rest of the Grent infantry either were chewed up by Ossan bayonets, were blasted to bits by Mika's grenades, or fled.

Less than ten minutes passed before Idrian stood panting among the bodies, his ears barely hearing the screams of the wounded and the occasional cry for mercy from a downed Grent infantryman. The Green Jackets now commanded the intersection, their entire battalion flooding in to shift the barricades and prepare for a counterattack.

If it came, that was their business. Idrian found Valient, who was already organizing his soldiers to double-time it back to their own position.

"Five dead, eighteen wounded," Valient reported.

Idrian nodded. Not bad, all things considered.

"That was quite the leap. Tash says you landed on their glassdancer. Is that true?"

Idrian grinned. He couldn't resist. He was, he had to admit, a little impressed with himself for aiming that jump so well. "Last thing the poor bastard saw was my boots." He raised his head, looking once more to the south, where he could see the palace at the top of the hill. The Green Jackets had a good position now, which meant the entire push could continue.

Valient slapped him on the shoulder, then made a face as his hand came away slick with Grent blood.

"Let's get back," Idrian told him. "We're not going to take the palace today, but we can push them out of the townhouses entirely." He was close enough to taste it. He was going to lead the charge up that hill, and with any luck he'd be the first one through the front door of the ducal palace. He could secure the cinderite, and if they were lucky, capturing the palace might even lead to the end of this little war. "Oh, and do me a favor."

"After that jump? Hah! Name it."

"Find me a sheepskin. I need to wrap up something fragile."

16

The first twenty-four hours in the Ivory Forest Glassworks left Thessa an exhausted husk. She plowed through it, working late into the night, catching a few hours of sleep in the dormitory she shared with twenty other prisoners, and then got up early enough to watch the assistants light the reheating chambers in the morning. She worked through the midday meal to catch up on the previous day's quota, finishing both her own work *and* Axio's, only to immediately start on the current day.

She daydreamed about the phoenix channel as she worked. Her time in the back of that wagon had allowed her to grasp the project pretty well, and she bounced ideas off herself to keep her mind occupied. That cannon-like sorcery converter floated in her head, turning this way and that, allowing her to imagine every aspect—and the small changes she'd need to make to improve it.

If the other prisoners noticed that she was covering for Axio, they said nothing. In fact, Thessa was left almost completely unsupervised. The quotas were given, the prisoners worked to fill them, and that was it. No interference by the guards or the other prisoners. Barely anything but a nod from the hired assistants and laborers. It was as if Thessa—and the other siliceers working the furnaces—was nothing but a machine to be occasionally greased and otherwise ignored.

It was dehumanizing. Humiliating. Thessa let those two words repeat over and over again in the back of her head, fueling her work with her fury. They wouldn't break her. She wouldn't allow it. She would use their dehumanizing tactics against them to plan her escape and, if there was any chance at all, she would find justice for both herself and the others forced to work here.

Axio did not learn quickly—nobody became a practicing siliceer overnight—but he helped her gather information. He was a second pair of eyes and ears, making mental notes of guard positions, work rotations, sympathetic laborers, and even the other prisoners. They spoke in hushed tones, exchanging information, and Thessa cast it all to memory as she worked to fill both their trays with godglass.

Heat, pinch, snip, shape, listen, repeat.

Heat, pinch, snip, shape, listen, repeat.

She fell into a trance, transferring tools between hands and the workbench with speed and efficiency. Heat, pinch, snip, shape, listen, repeat. She was deep in her own thoughts when they were interrupted by an older woman with gray-black hair and a limp standing immediately next to Thessa's workstation. Thessa jumped, catching her breath. "I'm sorry, I didn't see you there."

The woman was one of the other prisoners. None seemed interested in sharing their names, so Thessa had labeled them with the numbers of their workstations. She herself was Nine. This older woman was Three. Three didn't meet her eye, instead staring straight at the floor as she mumbled apologetically, "You're working too much."

"Excuse me?"

"If you continue to work as much as you do, you'll get glassrot. Take breaks when everyone else does."

Thessa inhaled sharply, realized the mistake she'd made. One of her greatest advantages in a glassworks was her sorcery aphasia. Most siliceers needed to be judicious about the time they spent working, but not her, and she'd used it to her advantage to catch up on the quotas. It hadn't even occurred to her that other people would notice.

She pretended to scratch at some nonexistent glassrot on her forearm, trying to be nonchalant. "You're right, I should. Thanks for the warning."

The woman shuffled back to her workstation without another word. If anyone else had taken note of their conversation, Thessa could not tell. She glanced back at Axio, who continued to go through the motions, making forgeglass pieces that had no resonance. Periodically Thessa would remove them from his tray, replace them with her own, then melt his down in her own crucible to be worked again. It was inefficient and wasteful, but the ruse seemed to be working.

A whistle was blown, signaling the top of the hour. The other prisoners immediately began to rack their tools. Some knuckled their backs, others bent over their workstations to weep quietly. Most just trudged outside. Thessa's nerves had tightened with Three's warning, and she knew she had to take that advice before someone else noticed her lack of glassrot. It would slow her down but it couldn't be helped.

She and Axio left their stations and stepped out into the courtyard, where dozens of prisoners from several different furnace rooms were taking their break. The air was thick with smoke from the belching furnaces, the light dim from the setting sun, but it did feel nice to be out of the heat.

Thessa sank to the ground just outside, rolling her shoulders, swearing to herself softly. Axio came to sit next to her, his head raised, looking at the guards up on the walls. She should be doing the same, she knew, but she needed this breather. Let him do the reconnaissance. Had it been only a day in this place? It felt like weeks. She couldn't help but wonder how long some of these prisoners had been here. Months? Years? How did they keep going every day?

Muted conversations filled the courtyard, and some of the woodsmoke was mixed with the scent of cigarettes begged from guards or laborers. Only two people had books, and they held them protectively whenever someone walked by. There were no newspapers or entertainment. She thought she heard someone mention a weekend cudgeling match between guards.

Dehumanizing. The word rolled on her tongue as if she were about to spit it at a tribunal. Was this what all prisons were like? Did anyone deserve this? Thessa didn't even know if her fellow siliceers were thieves or murderers, or if they'd just had the same bad luck to be on the wrong end of an Ossan war.

"That side door over there," Axio whispered, "only has one guard. They use it to bring in firewood. Might make a good exit."

Thessa glanced in that direction but could immediately see that the double doors were in plain view of everything else in the courtyard. All the guards would have to be blind or distracted—and if that was the case, they might as well use the front gate. "Good eye," she told him. "Keep watching it—but don't be obvious." She gave him a quick, reassuring smile. He nodded back, holding his chin up. Since his breakdown upon their arrival he'd been putting on a good face. Whether it was for her benefit or his own she did not know.

Thessa watched one of the laborers—a young woman, tall and sinewy, probably no more than a few years older than herself, with short-cropped brown hair and light Purnian skin—pushing one of the massive carts of firewood across the uneven cobbles. No one seemed to pay her any mind as she struggled with the load. The left wheel hit a rut between two of the cobbles, and the laborer gave a resigned grunt. She pulled, frowned, then pushed. The cart would not budge.

Minutes passed. The laborer looked at the cart from all angles, tried to rock it out of the rut once more, then walked away. She returned moments later, red-faced, muttering under her breath. By now her predicament had been noticed, and the prisoners watched her struggles surreptitiously. Three of the guards on the walls above gazed down, chuckling to themselves. No one came to help.

The laborer tried to get underneath the stuck wheel, shoving and grunting. Thessa watched with everyone else, bemused at the efforts until the wheel suddenly slipped forward. Thessa had a clear view, wincing in sympathetic pain as the wheel rolled across the next cobble and dropped squarely into another rut, trapping the laborer's hand underneath it. The laborer inhaled sharply, eyes going wide, her face twisting. She didn't make a sound but threw her shoulder desperately against the cart, trying to lift it.

Thessa looked around. Everyone had seen what happened. Dozens of prisoners, five or six guards. Many of them laughed openly. Thessa scoffed and got to her feet. "It's not funny when people get hurt in a glassworks," she snapped at a nearby chuckling old man, then hurried over to the wood cart. "Axio, help me!" Together, they got beneath the cart and managed to get the wheel out from between the cobbles.

The laborer gasped in pain, clutching her hand to her stomach. She made a low keening noise and turned away when Thessa approached.

"Someone needs to look at that hand now," Thessa said firmly. "Show it to me." She ignored the shake of the woman's head and pulled her arm out so that the injured hand was flat in front of her. It didn't *look* bad—some redness around her pointer finger and several deep scuffs. The woman tried to pull away, but Thessa could see the shock still in her eyes. Thessa gently touched the pad at the base of each finger, watching carefully for reactions.

"I'm going to lose my hand," the laborer whispered.

"What's your name?" Thessa asked.

"Pari."

"Pari, you're not going to lose your hand. It only landed on one finger. It's broken, but a day with cureglass and it'll be good as new."

"I can't afford a day at a healinghouse." The laborer trembled in pain, but was clearly trying not to show it. Thessa had met plenty of laborers and assistants like her—people from the types of backgrounds where showing weakness would cost them.

"This is a glassworks. They have cureglass on hand. They'd be fools not to."

"Not for us laborers, they don't."

Thessa searched Pari's eyes, realizing with surprise that she was telling the truth. There was pain there, but there was also fear and shame. Thessa swore softly. She broke a piece of kindling from the wood cart, then tore the hem of Pari's tunic into a long strip. "This is a splint," she said. "It's rudimentary, and you'll want to see a doctor for something better, but it'll get you through the rest of the day. If you keep the finger splinted properly, it should heal in around eight weeks."

The laborer did not object as Thessa bound the finger. Up on the walls the guards had gotten bored, wandering back to their posts, while the prisoners actively ignored the situation. Thessa sent Axio running to the mess hall for watered wine—one of the few luxuries the prisoners were allowed— and finished the splint.

"Why didn't you ask for help?" Thessa asked.

"I did," Pari responded petulantly. "Everyone here is an asshole."

"I meant once the cart fell on your finger."

Pari snorted. "You're new. Haven't seen your face around."

"I was brought in yesterday."

"Grent?"

Thessa nodded, glad to finally get the woman to engage with her.

Pari just snorted again. "Then you should know about the Magna."

"I've heard *they're* assholes."

"You don't show weakness in front of a Magna," Pari replied.

Just as Thessa had suspected. "You're not a client?"

The laborer lifted her other hand to show the nail of her pinkie finger. It was unpainted. "I'm not going to sell my soul to the Magna, but I will work for them when money's tight." The moment Thessa let go of her hand, she pulled it back as if she'd been burned.

"You're welcome," Thessa said.

Pari said nothing. She got behind her wood cart, studying the cobbles carefully before awkwardly leveraging it up on her shoulder and pushing it recklessly across the courtyard. The gamble succeeded, and the last Thessa saw was her disappearing around the corner.

Thessa sighed and looked around. Axio had yet to return—probably arguing with a cook over taking wine out of the mess hall—and the rest of the prisoners seemed to want even less to do with her now. She walked back into the furnace room and around to workstation nine, looking across the subpar tools and the low-quality molten cindersand crucible. She swore again. She didn't deserve this. She'd put in her licks—lost her family, spent years as an apprentice, worked herself to the bone. She was not a damned criminal.

"Hey, blue eyes," a voice said.

Thessa turned to find that one of the other prisoners had followed her in. He was about her height, probably in his early thirties, with broad shoulders and plenty of scars from working the furnaces. She'd already dubbed him Six based on his station number. "What do you want, brown eyes?" she asked.

"You're a soft one, aren't you?" he asked, sidling over beside her. "Helping one of the hired pricks. Sneaking godglass in to fill out your friend's quota."

Thessa felt her eyes narrow. She wasn't even surprised or afraid. She didn't have those qualities left anymore, and all that fury and indignation that drove her had reached a peak. "Walk away and forget what you're about to say," she told him.

"No, no. You're going to fill in for me, too. I've earned a break and you're going to give it to me, or I'll tell Craftsman Magna that your friend can't make godglass. He'll get sent straight to the lumber camps, and I bet he'll get chewed up like a two-penny—"

Master Kastora always said that a siliceer could show their authority by earning respect, or earning fear. The latter had no place in his glassworks, but Thessa had spent the last twenty-four hours seeing firsthand how effective it could be. She didn't let Six finish his sentence. The fool had pushed her past her limits. She grabbed the heavy shears off her workbench and slammed them across his cheek, then readjusted her grip to press the sharp end against his collarbone.

He grunted at the blow, swore twice, then gave out a squeal at the feel of the steel on his skin. She forced him back against the next workbench. "Do not mistake my compassion for weakness," she hissed. "If you whisper a word to Craftsman Magna—if my friend gets flogged or pushed around or sent away because of your loose lips—you *will* have an accident. You might lose an eye, or a hand, or get locked in a furnace when no one can hear your screams." She could barely believe the words coming out of her own mouth. They didn't *sound* like her, but she continued. "Test me, and you will lose bits of you. That's a promise. Get it?"

Six nodded carefully, his eyes wide. Thessa jerked her head and stepped back, letting him flee. The moment he was out of the furnace room she felt her knees buckle and had to lean on her workbench for support. Was this going to get worse? Was this what she had to become to survive in here? In Ossa? She leaned forward, pressing her forehead against the cool steel plate on the workbench.

"Well that was unexpected."

Thessa jerked around, the shears still in her hand coming up like a weapon. Pari, the laborer she'd just helped with the wood cart, stood just inside a service entrance. Thessa lowered the shears. "What do you want?" she demanded. The stress inside her was starting to wear through, and for the first time in her life she seriously considered whether she could kill someone in a rage.

The laborer raised her hands, palms out, wincing at the gesture. "I came to say thank you. Had to calm down a little before I did. I'm not going to owe a prisoner a favor, so I'm putting it out once: if there's anything you need, tell me right now."

Thessa blinked back at her in surprise. "What do you mean?"

"Something smuggled inside," Pari explained impatiently. "Some cigars, some spending cash. I can't do much, but I can get you a little luxury. Then we're square, right? But you have to tell me now. No favors in the future."

Thessa glanced around in bewilderment, her mind spinning. "Can you get a message out for me? To someone who might pay my ransom?"

"That's not going to work," Pari said, shaking her head. "Too risky for me, and even if I did, no ransoms will be allowed until after the war ends. That's policy all the way from the top of the government, and even Crafts-man Magna won't break that rule."

"Then . . ." Thessa tried to think of something—anything—that would help her escape. It was clear this favor had pretty strict limits. Pari wasn't going to risk getting killed by Magna enforcers just to help someone who lifted a cart off her. Thessa grimaced. Could she take a greater risk? Did she have a choice? "Craftsman Magna took something important from me. Where would he keep it?"

The laborer raised both eyebrows. "You really are a daring one. I guess it's cheap information." She considered this for a moment before nodding to herself. "If it's a personal effect, one of the guards already pawned it. If it was something more valuable, then it's in his office somewhere."

"Really?" Thessa asked. Could it be that close by?

"Yeah. He keeps anything he values here in the compound so his addict brothers don't steal it."

"Is his office guarded?"

Pari just shook her head. "I do *not* suggest doing whatever it is you're thinking about. The moment they catch you . . . well, the lumber camps will look pleasant. Don't try to seduce him either. It's been tried before and it just annoys him."

Thessa pulled a face that elicited a laugh from the laborer. "I will *not* try that."

"Then we're square here, right?" Pari said, turning toward the service entrance. "No favors, no nuthin'."

Thessa took half a step toward her. "Is there anything else you can tell me about the prison offices?"

The laborer hesitated. "Look, I shouldn't have even . . ." She sighed. "Piss, I guess I'm heading back into Ossa tonight anyway. Can't haul wood with this. Need a new job." She held up her splinted finger, wincing at the motion. "Fine. The offices are rarely locked. The two enforcers on normal guard duty are always there, but they're sleeping together and I can't think of the last time they paid attention to anything." She tilted her head thoughtfully. "One other thing: Craftsman Magna is religious. He's a vehement Rennite. Good luck with whatever it is you're doing." Gesturing goodbye, Pari slipped out the service entrance.

Thessa barely noticed her leaving. She was thinking now, planning. That bit about Craftsman Magna being religious might be the key to this whole thing. She knew where the schematics were now. She had to get them out. Maybe even cause the distraction she needed in the process.

17

The High Vorcien Club, on the edge of the Family District, was a sprawling single-story building covering two whole city blocks with gambling, daze-glass, whores, food, cigars, private cudgeling matches, and more; all without the stain of lower-class revelry at Glory Street. It was the premier place to be for the elite of the elite within Ossan society.

It was also owned by Kizzie's oldest half brother, Sibrial.

Kizzie slipped through the back entrance, dodging porters as they carried in crates of expensive wine and nodding to the madams smoking cigarettes outside the delivery bays. There were a handful of enforcers hanging around, rolling dice on the floor or reading books in forgotten corners. A few raised their eyebrows at her, but no one stopped her as she made her way through the labyrinth of kitchens and service passages and up to the raised gallery behind a massive one-way mirror that overlooked the main floor of the club.

She clung to the wall, allowing waiters to come and go without interruption, watching the chaotic dance that kept the club running. Standing by the mirror, snapping orders like a general on a battlefield, was a statuesque, dark-skinned woman in her late fifties wearing a translucent black tunic cut to be a more professional version of the club uniform.

Veterixi Jorn, the concierge, had been with the family since well before Kizzie was born—a High Vorcien Club porter back before Father Vorcien had passed it on to Sibrial. She was the ultimate authority in this place, almost akin to a guild-family majordomo in her own right. She could be trusted with pretty much anything, and refused to play at family politics, including the spat between Kizzie and Sibrial.

"You know that your brother will kill you if he sees you here," Veterixi said suddenly, filling a brief lull in the constant stream of reports. She did not look away from her view of the club.

"It's still the family club," Kizzie said, holding up her hand to show the silic sigil, "and I still have a few privileges."

"Oh yeah? Sibrial's playing cards at his usual table," Veterixi shot back. "You want to go join him?"

"I'm brash, not stupid," Kizzie snorted. "I just came to ask a favor."

Veterixi held up one hand as a young man—one of the scantily clad servers—rushed into the gallery weeping. She touched him gently on the shoulder, conducting a quick exchange that was too quiet for Kizzie to hear, and then sent him on his way. "Get rid of Needor Plagni," she ordered one of the porters standing at attention. "And ban her from the club for a full month. I don't give a shit if she is a glassdancer, if she lays a hand on another one of my employees against their will, she will be banned permanently."

Kizzie coughed in her hand once the porter had gone. "I heard one of the Plagni's glassworks was vandalized last night. Hundreds of thousands of ozzo's worth of godglass smashed and the guards blaming it on everything from foreign nationals to giant birds. I bet they're on edge."

"And I," Veterixi said, "heard that you've been relegated to hotel security for Demir Grappo." Veterixi's tone made it clear what she thought of *that*. A step down, even after falling out of favor.

"It's a very nice hotel and I'm not going to have to launder blood out of my tunics for a while."

"Breenen is a colleague," Veterixi admitted, "and I admire him. I hope the hotel doesn't go to shit now that Demir is back." She sighed, ordering one of the porters to send a bottle of wine to the table of Marnish merchants who were losing a *lot* of money. "What favors do you need of me, Kissandra?"

Kizzie resisted the urge to defend Demir and stepped up to the one-way mirror to search the club. She spotted Sibrial immediately—wide shoulders, light skin, and long blond hair that favored his mother. He was thick without being fat, big-boned and broad-shouldered, laughing like a braying donkey at something one of his mistresses said. Just the sight of him turned Kizzie's stomach. At a nearby table was Capric, his eyes closed, a piece of dazeglass in his ear, snoozing while conversation continued around him. There were nine full-blood Vorcien children, and it wasn't uncommon to find most of them here on any given night. Sibrial and Capric were the only two she could spot.

But they weren't her target. Kizzie moved on, searching the crowd until her eyes landed on the prize. Glissandi Magna was middle-aged with short hair, wearing a fine, dark blue tunic, lounging in a booth not far from the mirror. She smoked a thick cigar while she watched one of her cousins— third in line among the Magna heirs—play cards with several other guild-family scions.

"I want to know about Glissandi Magna."

Veterixi snapped her fingers, and the remaining few porters standing at attention in the gallery vacated the area. Within moments they were alone, interrupted only by the muted sounds of the club from the other side of the mirror. "Now why would you want to know about Glissandi Magna?"

"She's messing with some of Demir's hotel suppliers. Demir has asked me to look into it." One of the benefits of having a reputation for personal integrity was that most people assumed she never lied. It was a stupid assumption, of course, doubly so because it was held by otherwise intelligent people. Kizzie's personal code was quite specific: she always kept her word, and she rarely lied to public authorities. White lies that were unlikely to be verified were a common part of her enforcer's toolbox.

Veterixi took her gaze away from the club to glance sidelong at Kizzie. Kizzie pretended not to notice. Finally, Veterixi said, "She's a firebrand. Opinionated, intelligent, ruthless. If she's made a decision there's no swaying her. If I were you, I'd go back to Demir and tell him to find new suppliers."

"You think a Grappo glassdancer is intimidated by a Magna cousin?"

Veterixi shrugged. "I don't really know *what* intimidates Demir. No one knows a damned thing about him, other than the fact he broke at Holikan. Even so, Glissandi is not one to cross."

"The suppliers are clients," Kizzie lied.

"Ah. Certainly makes it more complicated."

"I'd like to talk to her alone."

"Can't help you with that," Veterixi said. "She's got a couple of hulking Purnian bodyguards that go everywhere with her. Outside of this club or her own home, you won't have the chance to chat in private."

"You think she'd take an appointment?" Kizzie asked. It wasn't really an option anyway—Kizzie didn't want any record that the two of them had ever spoken—but she might as well ask.

"Maybe if you're willing to wait six months. More likely, she'll have her bodyguards beat you within an inch of your life just for the audacity of asking."

Kizzie watched Glissandi smoke her cigar, trying to get inside that head of hers. "Any vices? Peace offerings that might put me in her good graces?" A sordid vice made for either bribery or blackmail material.

"Nothing," Veterixi said with a sympathetic frown. "She loves money and herself. She's not scared of anyone, even glassdancers, and Demir isn't rich enough to bribe her."

It seemed, at least on the surface, that Glissandi was impenetrable. Kizzie went through her list of options. Demir wanted this done in a timely manner, and digging around Glissandi's businesses, family, and friends for something Kizzie could use would take time. It would also be dangerous. If the Magna found out what Kizzie was up to, she could expect a visit from more than just a pair of Purnian bodyguards.

An idea occurred to her. Perhaps, she considered, it didn't have to be that difficult. "How's her reputation?" she asked.

"Impeccable. I hear a lot of secrets in this place, and absolutely nothing juicy has come to my ears."

"Is she that clean?"

"More like she's that fastidious about cleaning up after herself."

That might work. Kizzie chewed on her lip, her new idea slowly taking form in the back of her head. "If you think of anything else," she said, "let me know."

Veterixi pretended to tip a hat toward her. "My pleasure. Was that it?"

Kizzie nodded to the corner booth at the far end of the club, where Sibrial was still playing cards. "If you can think of anything to get me on his good side, let me know."

"I'm a club concierge, not an omnipotent being," Veterixi replied.

"Is it that bad? I didn't know it would matter so much. The fines were a pittance for him."

Veterixi made a sound in the back of her throat. "It wasn't about the fines he had to pay, it's about the fact he had to pay them at all. You humiliated him when all you had to do was give the magistrate an alibi."

"He ran over a little boy with his damned carriage. Broke the kid's leg and could have killed him."

"And even if he *did* kill the kid, Sibrial is the Vorcien heir. You still should have lied to the magistrate."

Veterixi was right, of course. Guild-family heirs were almost entirely above the law—if not in theory, then in practice. Having the most honest Vorcien enforcer give an alibi was meant to get Sibrial off completely. Instead,

Kizzie had told the truth just so she could watch the magistrate yell at her idiot half brother. It was, in retrospect, a moment of vindictive foolishness she should never have indulged. She'd expected Sibrial's ire over the whole affair. She had *not* expected to lose favor with Father Vorcien.

"Well, I'd still like to make it up to him."

"Good luck with that." Veterixi sounded sincere, but not hopeful. Her eyes suddenly narrowed, and Kizzie followed her gaze back to Sibrial's table, where one of the porters was leaning over and whispering in Sibrial's ear. Sibrial's head came around and he glared directly at the one-way mirror Kizzie was standing behind. Veterixi swore. "That little prick just sold you out to your brother. Glassdamnit, I don't want to deal with this tonight. I'll slow him down, you get out of here."

Kizzie didn't have to be told twice. Sibrial was already getting up from his table as she bolted for the exit, hurrying as quickly as she could down the winding back passages, past the private rooms, and through the kitchens. She'd almost reached the rear exit when her flight was arrested by a familiar voice barking her name.

"Kizzie!"

Kizzie froze. She fixed a demure look on her face and turned to find Sibrial standing in the hallway behind her. Sibrial was said to look much like their father had at that age, aside from his hair color: barrel-chested with thick arms; a clean-shaven square jaw. He had a cane in one hand and his face was flushed from drink.

"Brother," Kizzie acknowledged with a slight bow. He must have left instructions with the staff to let him know if she arrived. She swore silently. This was the *last* thing she needed.

"What the piss are you doing in my club?" he demanded.

"I have—"

"If you say one thing about your privileges I will have you shot."

Kizzie bit down on her tongue, hard. Sibrial might just do that, consequences be damned. He certainly was unhinged enough. No need to antagonize him. "I came to ask Veterixi if there was anything I could do to make things up to you," she said, holding out both hands in a gesture of peace.

"Make it up to me? You glassdamned bitch. I was in every paper in Ossa for a week because of you, and you have the nerve to think you could possibly make it up to me? Don't you bloody move!" He turned in mid-tirade, screaming at a serving girl trying to slip past with a bottle of brandy. The hallway was suddenly silent, including the kitchens at one end and the club at the other. Kizzie could see faces poking around that far corner as curious club members came to see the commotion.

"I'm sorry, Sibrial. I really am. I didn't know what would happen." It was a lie that played on Sibrial's low opinion of her.

"Ignorance is no excuse for betraying me."

"Betrayal" seemed a strong word for something that had so few real consequences. Kizzie slowly backed her way down the hall, her stomach tying itself in knots. She needed to deescalate things as quickly as possible, or this confrontation would get back to Father Vorcien. She didn't need that kind of attention right now. "I'm sorry," she said again. "Let's talk again when you're sober." At that, she hurried around the corner, through the kitchens, and out into the alley behind the club. With any luck, Sibrial was drunk enough that he would have no recollection of this in the morning—or at least lose interest in continuing the confrontation.

Kizzie's luck was absolutely shot through. She was barely halfway down the alley when Sibrial burst out through one of the delivery bays shouting her name. Porters, servants, and enforcers scattered before his fury. Kizzie was ready to abandon her pride completely and hide behind a whiskey barrel, but Sibrial had already spotted her.

"You scummy piece of shit," he bellowed, advancing quickly. "You aren't fit to wear the Vorcien sigil. I'll cut it off you myself!" He searched his belt for a knife but, to Kizzie's relief, came up with nothing. Instead he brandished his cane. Several more steps and he was upon her.

Sibrial was a noted duelist and boxer, and if he'd had his sword on him he might have killed Kizzie then and there, even if she defended herself. She could not, however, defend herself. Raising her hand to the Vorcien heir was the greatest sin she could commit in the eyes of her father, so she allowed the first blow to strike her unimpeded. The cane cracked against her left arm, hard enough that it went numb immediately. She staggered to one side.

"Sibrial," she hissed, "don't do this." It took all her willpower not to reach for her stiletto, but she reacted in another way—using her sorcery to seize one of her little glass lockpicking beads. It shot from her pocket, so small she could barely see it, and she held it just beside Sibrial's neck. If he *did* kill her, the last thing she intended to do before she went was push the damned thing through his neck.

He struck again, hitting the exact same spot. Kizzie hardly felt the blow but it staggered her once more. She caught herself on the wall of the club, swearing quietly, hoping that *someone* would come out and stop Sibrial before he killed her. Capric would do it, if he wasn't deep in the dazeglass. Maybe Veterixi, one of his friends, another guild-family heir. *Anyone.*

She dodged the next blow, and then the next. The hammerglass tip of his cane cracked loudly against the brick, and she held her concentration on the bead floating unnoticed over his shoulder.

"Hold still, damn it! I'm going to give you the beating I should have given you . . ."

Kizzie lost all patience. She wasn't going to kill him with that bead, no matter how much she wanted to, but she also wasn't going to let him kill her. As a lowly enforcer there was nothing she could do in the face of Sibrial's fury. But as his half sister, she had one option. She ducked the next swing, barreling up against him and grabbing him by his tunic with one hand. "Montego is back in town," she hissed in his ear. "Do you want my death in the newspapers right now?"

Sibrial jerked himself out of her grip, and for half a moment she thought he would continue his attack. Instead he stared at her, wide-eyed, his cane half raised. His fury was gone, like a candle blown out by a strong wind. He visibly gathered himself. "You're not worth the beating," he spat. Whirling, he strode back toward the club service bay.

Kizzie was left alone, holding her left arm, dozens of porters and servants watching her warily. It took the last of her energy to direct the glass bead back into her pocket. Once Sibrial was gone, one of the porters called out to her asking if she needed cureglass. She waved him off and staggered down the alley and out into the street.

She fished a piece of pain-numbing milkglass out of her pocket. It wasn't very high-resonance, but it took the edge off the pain as feeling came back to her arm. Putting on her gloves and covering her face with a handkerchief, she found a nearby courier office. She pounded on the door until a boy of about thirteen unlocked it.

"Paper," she instructed. Veterixi had given her one good piece of information: that Glissandi guarded her reputation closely. Kizzie could use that.

The courier boy provided her with a paper and pencil, and she scrawled out a quick note. It said, *I know who you killed eighteen days ago. Meet me in front of the Palmora Pub on the Lampshade Boardwalk tomorrow night at ten. Come alone, or your name will be in the papers.*

She thrust the note and a handful of coins into the boy's hands. "Deliver this to Glissandi Magna at the High Vorcien Club," she ordered.

The boy stared at her. "Are you okay, ma'am?"

"Perfectly fine. Go on!" She waited long enough for him to apply the courier's wax seal, then went back into the street and watched him take off toward the club.

It was not a perfect plan. More than likely, Glissandi would have her Purnian bodyguards try to jump her. But unlike that confrontation with her brother, Kizzie had no qualms about fighting back against some hired muscle. She was in pain, angry, and not a little bit humiliated.

She also had a job to do. One way or another, Glissandi was going to tell her why Adriana Grappo died.

18

Demir's first destination the next morning was a visit to the hotel carpenter. The old man was in the large workshop and carriage house across the street, greasing axles when Demir arrived and dismissed all of the assistants. He found the carpenter's workbench and laid out a pair of technical drawings he'd spent half the night on. The carpenter finished his work and joined him.

"I need you to modify a carriage," Demir said. "Give me a cubby hidden underneath the seat like this, with a false top."

"That looks big enough to hide a person in," the carpenter observed.

"Sure does, doesn't it? Can you do it?"

"Easy enough. Might have to shave a couple inches off to hide the cubby. Perhaps put decorative wings inside the wheels here and here."

"Excellent. How long?"

"A week."

"Make it five days." Demir was about to elaborate when a porter appeared holding a calling card. He rolled his eyes, remembering why he'd always found life in the capital annoying. There was just so damned much to be done. "Who is it?" he demanded.

"Sir," the porter said, handing him the card, "Master Supi Magna is here to see you."

"Huh." Demir took the calling card. He'd half expected this visit, but not so quick. He'd only just taken possession of the paperwork guaranteeing his share of the Ivory Forest Glassworks at midnight last night. He tapped the card against his cheek. "I'll receive him in my office. No! Wait, in the restaurant, thank you." It wouldn't do to have Supi Magna walk into Demir's office to find it filled with spymaster reports on the Magna.

Demir took his time crossing the street back to the hotel and went to the restaurant, where he arrived just as the porter showed Supi into a corner booth. Demir slid in across from him, shaking his hand with a warm smile. "Supi, what a surprise."

The patriarch of the Magna guild-family was a tall, willowy, hawk-faced man whose tunic hung from him like from a scarecrow. He was in his late sixties though looked to be in his fifties, and rumors had circulated for years that his personal siliceer masters had created godglass that would keep him from aging. Demir suspected he simply took a lot of care in his appearance. Supi, along with the four other members of the Inner Assembly, was one of the most powerful men in Ossa. He was worth hundreds of millions, belonged to dozens of Fulgurist Societies, commanded an army of enforcers, and had a quarter of the Assembly in his pocket.

Supi did not return Demir's smile. "Condolences on your mother's death," he said. "Adriana was a friend. But congratulations, of course, on taking her place at the head of the family."

"Thank you. Breakfast?" Demir asked, raising his hand toward a waiter.

"I'm afraid I don't have time for a meal. It's come to my attention that Ulina, my foolish granddaughter, gambled away her share in the Ivory Forest Glassworks."

Demir leaned back, raising his eyebrows. "Well, yes. We had a rather lovely afternoon together. The betting might have gotten a little heated. Do you often take such close interest in the family holdings?"

"When it comes to glassworks I do." Supi produced a small satchel from within his jacket. Demir recognized it as the type banks would give to their rich clients when they wanted to carry a particularly large amount of money on their person. "I would prefer to keep one hundred percent of the ownership of the glassworks in Magna hands. You understand, I hope?"

"Of course."

"I'm willing to pay one hundred and fifteen percent value for the immediate return of the shares my granddaughter lost."

Demir gave Supi a quizzical look. One hundred and fifteen percent for part ownership in a glassworks with a government contract? Cheap bastard. "I'm afraid I will have to pass."

"One hundred and thirty percent."

"Pass," Demir said again, meeting Supi's eyes coolly. He could see some anger there now, but it was well-bottled.

"You'd pass up a thirty percent profit on something you've owned only since last night?"

Demir drew invisible pictures on the table with his finger. "I don't need cash right now, Supi. I need investments. The mere fact that you are willing to buy at such a price means it's more valuable than even I expected. I won't let it go."

Supi's nostrils flared. "A hundred and fifty."

"You're notoriously cheap, Supi. You're only reinforcing my decision."

"You . . ." Supi growled, his eyes widening.

"Oh, come now. Don't be so agitated. I really did have a lovely time with Ulina. Maybe in a year or two you'll get it back in the family!"

"As if a Magna would stoop to marrying a Grappo," Supi said quietly.

"As if," Demir replied. He did not let the smile leave his face, but he was sure his eyes told a different story. The greater guild-families had tried to push him around when he was a young politician. They hadn't succeeded then because he could outthink them. They wouldn't succeed now because he had proper steel in his spine. "You sure you won't stay for breakfast?"

Supi stood up suddenly and stared down that hawkish nose at Demir. "Your mother was my friend. I had hoped you'd be more reasonable."

"My mother was everyone's friend, Supi. That didn't mean she was a fool."

"Be careful, young Grappo. You might have once been a commanding politician, but Ossa has changed since you left. If you forget your place, you will be ground underfoot."

Demir placed both hands flat on the table in front of him, presenting Supi with the dual sigils of glassdancer and Grappo. Inner Assembly or not, Supi needed to be reminded who Demir was. "Where is my place, Supi? Under your chair like a good pet? We may be a small guild-family, but be sure to remember my mother's legacy: the Grappo sit at the table with the rest of you. You can be my friend or you can be my enemy, but I assure you that the latter will cost you more."

"You're impudent."

"We've met before, Supi. A lot has changed, I know, but that has not."

Supi made an angry sound in the back of his throat and whirled, striding out of the restaurant. Demir waved away the waiter and counted to sixty before he practically ran across the hotel foyer to Breenen's office. "Get Montego and a carriage," he said. "I have decided to visit my new holdings."

⟩   ⟩   ⟩

Demir spent the long ride up to the Ivory Forest Glassworks studying spymaster reports that he'd managed to bully, steal, or bribe from the Dorlani,

Vorcien, and Stavri. Some of it touched upon the Ivory Forest, but most was just generally useful. He was going to need every scrap he could get if he was already making enemies among the Inner Assembly. They were only just approaching the glassworks when he broke the long silence between him and Montego.

"Something else is going on here," he said, gesturing out the window.

Montego looked up from the book he'd been reading. "Oh?"

"Supi was very angry that I wouldn't sell him back Ulina's shares in the glassworks. I've known him a long time and he doesn't often take things personally. Either he thinks that I'll use my sixteen percent share to destroy the place and lose them their government contract, or they are hiding something."

"What could they be hiding?" Montego asked.

Demir shook his head. "The usual: laundering ill-gotten gains, prisoner abuse, selling their wards. It's a glassworks so maybe they have their prisoners working on illegal godglass. We won't know until we dig around, but my focus is going to be on finding Thessa. You remember her description?"

"Early twenties, a couple inches taller than you, dirty-blond hair."

"Keep your eyes open. I'll work the people." Demir fixed a smile on his face as their carriage rumbled over the uneven streets of the dirty little glassworking town. Outside the left window he could see a twenty-foot wall meandering along the roadside, with a couple of guard towers occupied by armed Magna enforcers. "This really is a serious operation," he commented to Montego as they turned into the gatehouse.

The carriage jerked to a sudden stop, nearly throwing him into Montego's lap. He stuck his head out the window to see a dozen enforcers crowding the gate, all of them shouting angrily at Demir's driver. Demir put a glove on his left hand to cover his glassdancer sigil but left his right hand naked. He was here to make friends, not threaten people. He opened the door, hopped down, and gave them all a grin. "Is something the matter?"

A man wearing a flatcap, differentiated from the other enforcers by a Magna silic sigil stitched on his jacket, pushed his way to the front and pointed at Demir, then at the carriage. "Tell your driver to back up. This is a restricted compound and we *will* shoot if he tries to push through."

"You will shoot?" Demir asked, laying his right hand flat against his chest. The captain's eyes fell to Demir's silic sigil and his shoulders slumped.

"Oh. I'm sorry, I didn't realize you were a guild-family member."

"Demir Grappo, at your service. Summon the overseer, let him know that

I am now sixteen percent owner in the glassworks. I'd like to take an immediate tour."

The captain's mouth hung open for several moments. "Uh . . . that's . . . not possible."

"My ownership? Or a tour?"

"The tour. Either. I mean . . ."

Demir knew that look in the captain's eyes—a low-level functionary just trying to do his job, confronted with something he hadn't expected. Was he allowed to tell Demir to piss off? Or would he bring shame on the entire guild-family if he did? He was flustered. Exactly where Demir wanted him.

Finally the captain said, "I'll summon the overseer."

"I'll come with you. Baby, bring the carriage!" Demir threw an arm around the captain's shoulders, pulling him through the gate and pretending to ignore the desperate way he motioned to one of the other enforcers to run on ahead. Once inside, Demir ran his eyes across the general layout of the place: halfway between a prison and a labor camp, it appeared to have one main road going through the center of the compound and another wrapping around just inside the wall. It was probably twenty acres, with dozens of buildings, each of them labeled with its function in large black letters.

Demir cast everything to memory. He never knew what information he might have need of, from how readily the enforcers carried their weapons to the width of the roads.

"Incredible," he said. "I've only seen a few glassworks bigger, and I had no idea we had a forced labor camp just for siliceers. Amazing world!" He strolled to the nearest workshop, yanked open the door, and shoved his head inside. The workshop was hot, well-lit by high windows, and showed a row of men and women in heavy siliceer aprons and boots toiling at spartan-looking workbenches. A few glanced in his direction. The rest ignored him.

"Stop it! You can't . . ." The captain clearly struggled to get control of himself as he tugged at Demir's sleeve. "You shouldn't do that. You need permission. Please, sir, wait until you've met the overseer."

Demir remained long enough to make sure that Thessa was not one of the siliceers in the workshop before allowing himself to be dragged away from the door. He turned to the captain, grinning ear to ear. "You have no idea how exciting this is! I've owned small glassworks before but this is really something else." He leaned in conspiratorially. "How do you keep them in line? Is that a problem? What if one gets violent?"

"Sir, please save your questions for the overseer."

"Come now, I am part owner in this place and you will get to see me quite often from now on."

The captain stifled a groan. "Sir . . ."

"Don't worry about the overseer," Demir said in a low voice, turning away from the other enforcers and slipping a thick stack of banknotes into the captain's hand. "I'm generous to the people under my employ."

The captain worked his jaw, staring down at the banknotes for a moment before hurriedly stuffing them in his pocket. He cleared his throat. "Ahem, um, no we really don't have any problems with the prisoners. Most violent siliceers are treated like common criminals and punished in their own provinces. These are mostly debtors, thieves, foreigners. That sort of thing."

"Is being a foreigner a crime these days?" Demir asked.

"Well, no. Depends on where they came from. We've got a couple of Grent siliceers that were caught trying to cross into Ossa when the war started. Then there's the Balkani who got caught up in the revolution. You know, it's—"

He was interrupted by shouting from across the complex. Demir turned to find a short, wiry man in a clean siliceer's apron rushing toward him, waving his arms. "Get them out of here! What do you think you're doing! This is a government site, restricted to the highest levels! The Assembly will hear about this!"

Demir met the shout with a grin and thrust out a hand. "Demir Grappo. The large man trying to extricate himself from the carriage is Baby Montego." The overseer's eyes grew wide at Demir's name, then wider at Montego's. Demir continued, "I am now sixteen percent owner of the glassworks and am here for my inaugural tour."

The overseer reached him finally, staring warily at Demir's outstretched hand. "I wasn't notified of any of this."

"That's because I only took ownership at midnight last night."

"I will have to check with the proper authorities," the overseer huffed. "I can't have just anyone traipsing about the complex!"

Demir sought to remember his name from the files Lechauri had sent him. "Filur, was it? Excellent name, by the way. I had a great-great-uncle by the name of Filur. Strong name. Manly name." Demir clenched a fist and thrust it in front of him in pantomime of the flexing cudgelists sometimes did in front of the audience. "Baby! The paperwork!"

Montego came to Demir's side and handed him a bundle of papers, which

Demir then handed to Filur. He gave the overseer a full minute to read over them.

"As you can see, it all checks out," Demir said proudly.

"This certainly seems official," Filur said slowly, looking slightly ill.

"Filur, my friend, I have a really glassdamned busy life. I drove all the way up here for a tour. I'm a sixth of your owners and I have it on good authority that Ulina was one of the few owners who actually liked you. You want to make me happy, Filur." It was all a fiction, of course, but in Demir's experience most marginalized guild-family members were in constant terror of someone younger, more charming, better looking, or simply more convenient taking their spot.

Filur swallowed hard. "I see."

"Here's a thousand ozzo," Demir said, thrusting the money into the pocket of Filur's apron. "If for some reason my paperwork doesn't check out, then you'll have shown around a couple of famous tourists. If the paperwork *does* check out, you'll have pleased one of your new overlords. Do you have wine?"

"I . . . uh, up in my office."

"No need, I brought plenty. Baby, a bottle of wine for the overseer and the captain and then . . . a dozen bottles to the enforcers. Did we bring that wheel of stiarti? I've never met an enforcer who didn't love cheese. Take it to their barracks." He looked over the overseer's shoulders, cementing his memories of this place. "Oh, and a few bottles of wine for the hired help. Laborers get thirsty too! Now then, my tour!"

Demir began walking, forcing the overseer to choose between restoring order as his enforcers mobbed Montego, or following him. The overseer followed him.

"How many furnaces?" he asked as Filur caught up.

"Uh," Filur responded, clearly still quite out of sorts, "eleven. Well, twelve."

"Twelve? Wonderful, I'd like to see them all."

Filur blanched. "I can . . . show you nine of them, I suppose. They all look the same, I assure you."

"What about the other three? I want to see what I've bought, Filur. I want to make sure this place isn't going to burn down, fall down, or fall victim to the accidents and malfeasance that other glassworks have suffered recently."

At the mention of malfeasance, Filur perked up. "Oh, that won't happen here. We have thirty enforcers on the premises at all times! No one can get through that gate without my say-so. As for the other three furnaces, they are restricted. I really will have to get permission to show you those."

Demir was a little disappointed. Not enough creativity to come up with a good excuse. Restricted, even within a restricted compound? Those furnaces were almost certainly being used to produce illegal godglass. But which ones? Rageglass? Fearglass? Ailingglass? He strolled to the next furnace room and opened the door to stick his head inside. It looked exactly like the last workshop, all the way down to the dejected, tired expressions on the faces of the siliceer prisoners. No one matched Thessa's description.

"Are they overworked?" he asked, whirling on Filur, who seemed to have finally resigned himself to showing Demir around.

The overseer gave him a wan smile. "Well, they would certainly say so. It's part of how we maintain order: we give them big enough quotas that they're always on the edge of dropping from exhaustion."

"Can't get good-quality godglass out of siliceers like that." Demir frowned.

"It's a trade-off for sure, but one we're very happy with. We've refined the process over decades, you see."

"Hmm." Demir continued walking down the main road through the center of the compound. He opened doors, looked in closets, showed himself around two dormitories and a mess hall, all while Filur tagged at his heels like an unwilling hound. Demir was certain to keep up a barrage of questions, punctuated by nonsense anecdotes. As intended, the overseer seemed completely overwhelmed by it all, rocking back frequently on his heels and managing to successfully deflect only a handful of questions.

Demir simply reworded them and asked them a few minutes later.

It was in the fifth workshop that he spotted someone who matched Thessa's description. It was a young woman, dirty-blond hair pulled back in a ponytail, leaning over her workbench with one ear just inches from a piece of godglass. Demir looked up the line until he found another siliceer—probably in her mid-twenties, with dark skin and a shaved head. She was quite attractive.

Demir fixed a leer on her and bent in toward Filur. "Tell me," he said quietly, "do you ever . . . you know?"

"Excuse me?"

"The young women."

"Oh. Oh! Of course not. No, the government oversight of this compound is much too strict to afford a scandal like that."

"Just thought I'd ask," Demir said, feigning disappointment. He kept his eyes on the Marnish siliceer, then looked toward Thessa. It was far better to be thought a degenerate than to give up his real purpose here. He strolled around the circular furnace, examining each workstation. When he reached the blond young woman he suspected was Thessa, he turned toward her. "What's your name, girl?"

"Ah, ah!" Filur interjected. "I really don't think you should talk to the prisoners, sir."

Demir folded his hands across his stomach, careful that his silic sigil was pointed toward her. "Come now, I have a new ownership stake in this place. I'm not going to completely ignore the gears of industry! Girl, tell me your name." He adopted the tone he'd heard so often throughout the Empire: that of a man who believes his underlings are little better than animals.

The woman barely seemed able to keep a look of disgust off her face. "Teala, sir."

Demir's heart soared. Found her—the exact woman Duala had told him was being held, and she definitely matched the description. Glassdamn. Now he just needed to get her out of here. That would probably take a lot longer. "Teala, what are you working on?"

"Forgeglass earrings, sir."

Demir drummed his thumbs against his stomach, trying to draw her attention to his hands. It worked. She looked up at his face sharply, then back at his silic sigil. Once he was certain she'd gotten the message, he reached into his pocket and palmed a small piece of razorglass, then dropped it into the tray that held her finished products. He picked one up, put it to his ear, then did another. When he finished, he ran his fingers along the earrings so they covered the razorglass.

"Adequate work," he said with a yawn. "Filur, I do hope some of the other prisoners have more talent."

Thessa didn't hide her glare. When he was certain no one else could see, Demir winked, then looked pointedly at the tray. She stared at him suspiciously until he whirled away from her, leading Filur back to the street.

"Of course," Filur said, "she's just a senior apprentice from Grent. No one special."

"I certainly hope not!"

Demir finished his tour, making sure not to alter his behavior in any way. He talked to a few more of the prisoners, checked the godglass, split a bottle of wine with the overseer, and then retired to his carriage, with Filur and the captain standing nearby to see him off. "It's a good operation," he told Filur through the window. The overseer nodded eagerly. Demir had him on the hook. "See that you keep up this good work, and I'll make sure you're well-rewarded. And of course, feel free to check back with Ossa about my credentials so there is no confusion on my next visit. If you need anything from me, I'll be at the Hyacinth Hotel. Baby, let us be off!"

They were moments out of the compound when Demir turned to Montego. "Found her," he said. "She seems unhurt. As long as she can remain that way for a couple of weeks, we'll just have to make frequent visits and watch for our chance to slip her out. I've already got the hotel carpenter refitting one of our carriages with a hidden compartment."

"Did you make contact?" Montego asked.

"Not in so many words, but I think she knows who I am. I left her a piece of razorglass just in case she needs to defend herself. I don't think the guards are allowed to get handsy, but she'll not be unarmed on my watch."

"What excuse will we use to return?"

Demir grimaced. "Anything we can think of. If I have to pretend to be friends with that rat of an overseer, I'll do it. Let's come back first thing in the morning. The quicker the guards, laborers, and overseer get used to my presence, the less suspicious I'll seem. I might even get the chance to talk to Thessa alone."

19

Thessa stared after the man as he left the workshop, his arm thrown around Craftsman Magna's shoulders like they had been friends for years. A part of her was offended and deeply confused. "Girl"? *"Adequate"*? Thessa was a glassdamned woman and the work in her tray was stellar even with the corners she was cutting to get it done so fast.

But that wink and the silic sigil. Her heart hammered away at the inside of her chest with optimistic excitement. That *was* the Grappo silic sigil, wasn't it? It wasn't a common sigil, what with them being a small guild-family, but she'd seen it on several occasions. That man must have been a Grappo. A relative of Adriana's? A brother? A cousin? The soldiers who'd captured her at the border had mentioned Adriana's "failure" of a son. If he'd managed to track Thessa down in just a couple of days, he didn't seem so much like a failure to her.

"Thessa, are you okay?" Axio whispered.

Thessa pulled her gaze away from the closed door to the furnace room. A couple of the other prisoners glanced in her direction but no one said anything. Behind her, Axio leaned over her workbench.

"He's a piece of shit," Axio said. "Don't let it get to you."

"I'm fine, thanks," she replied, turning back to her work. She put her bit iron back in the furnace to reheat the glass for a few moments, then brought it to the metal plate on her workbench and began work on a new piece. She moved slowly, trying to think.

There were other possibilities, of course. Perhaps he was just an asshole? Maybe she misremembered the silic sigil and that man was simply one of the overseer's friends and was flirting with her. If that was the case she would have to be careful around him. She did not know for certain and it drove her mad as she worked through the rest of the morning.

Of all the possibilities that haunted her, one stood out. If that was really a Grappo, and he was here to get her out, she had to find the phoenix channel schematics *immediately.* There was no telling when a rescue might take place. But could she manage to steal them back? The laborer had given her good information about the overseer's office, but Thessa was no sleight-of-hand artist; a thief or a trickster. Did she really dare to sneak in there alone? And what if they were locked up?

The midday meal finally arrived, and the other prisoners filed out while Thessa remained behind to fill both her own and Axio's trays. She touched Axio on the shoulder as he left.

"I'll join you in a minute," she told him, "and do me a favor: ask some of the hired help who that man was. Surely someone knows."

Axio gave her a determined nod and left her alone in the furnace. She reveled in the moment of silence and solitude, bending to work the knot out of the small of her back and giving herself a minute of sitting on the floor with her boots off to rub her feet. She could hear one of the hired laborers clunking around at the back of the furnace, tossing more firewood into the flames.

Still on the floor, Thessa reached up and pulled down her tray, setting it in her lap to count the earrings. Something about the weight was slightly off. She frowned, searching around in the earrings until she found what appeared to be a piece of paper. No, something *wrapped* in paper. It was about six inches long, an inch wide, quite thin. She opened the paper, letting the object fall into her hand.

Her breath caught in her throat. It was a piece of razorglass. The blade was only about two inches of it, secured in a thin handle, the type of tool used by high-level craftsmen for delicate cutting work. Good razorglass was incredibly difficult to make and could slice through just about anything. She looked at the paper to find a message written inside.

For emergencies only! Hold tight. Escape in the planning.

Glassdamn, she was right. He was a Grappo, and he was here to help. The leering and arrogance had been an act—or at least she hoped it was—for the benefit of the overseer.

Thessa's throat was dry as she looked over her shoulder, clutching both paper and razorglass to her chest. When she was triply sure she was alone, she threw the paper into the furnace. Using the razorglass, she cut a ribbon of heavy canvas off a spare siliceer's apron hanging by the door, wrapped the razorglass in it, and stuffed it in her pocket.

She returned to her work and had only just managed to calm herself by the time Axio and the other prisoners came back from lunch. She snatched a hard biscuit from Axio, choking it down as he whispered, "His name is Demir Grappo. Everyone's talking about him. I guess he won a share of the glassworks ownership from one of the Magna while gambling, and insisted on an inspection. The overseer is pretty shook up over the whole thing and so are all the guards and hired help. Glassworks ownership hasn't left the Magna family for years."

A shiver of anticipation went down Thessa's back. Relief flooded through her, and the excited tightness in her chest felt less uncertain. She touched her pocket to be sure the razorglass was still there. For emergencies only.

She knew exactly what emergency she could use it for.

⋆　　⋆　　⋆

Idrian wasn't often required to attend intelligence briefings, but when an order came down that breachers had been summoned along with the regular officers it never boded well. It was just past noon and the world was surprisingly still for midday. He'd heard nothing but distant shots for over an hour—it was almost like both sides of the war had agreed upon a little break while they independently figured out what the piss they were up to.

For all he knew, that was exactly what had happened.

He trudged back far behind the lines with Tadeas and Mika, wearing his officer's uniform, his boots and godglass eye both freshly polished. Valient was in charge of the Ironhorns in their absence. Idrian felt torn about the brief respite—on the one hand, he'd get to spend a few hours without getting shot at. On the other, he needed the Ironhorns to continue their push toward the palace. They could take it today, and when they did he'd come away with that cinderite for Demir. He could *feel* it.

They arrived at a repurposed Grent dance hall that had remained undamaged during the fighting, shuffling inside with the rest of the weary officers, exchanging nods and a few words of greeting. Idrian spotted at least a dozen other breachers, their monikers stitched into their uniforms like his own—the Steel Horse, the Falcon, the Trebuchet, the Black Pit, the Glass Pisser. There would be more breachers in their midst, ones that hadn't earned a nickname, but without their uniforms they were impossible to tell from the other officers. There were several dozen glassdancers too, their uniforms covered in brightly colored embroidery to show off their status and flout military regulation. While breachers mingled, glassdancers were most often alone.

Tadeas elbowed his way to a position along the side of the community hall, near an exit, and Idrian was happy to follow. He recognized some of the senior staff already on the stage at one end of the hall, and this position gave him a view of both the order givers and the order receivers. It was a good place to be to read the room.

"I hate these meetings," Mika whispered to him, "makes me feel so exposed. A well-placed barrel of powder beneath the floorboards and an enterprising engineer could wipe out the cream of the Ossan officer corps for three brigades."

"Four armed breachers," Idrian answered.

"Eh?"

"That's what it would take to kill everyone in this room and escape before a response could be mustered."

"Even with the glassdancers?"

Idrian considered his assessment. "They'd still have a good chance at succeeding in full armor."

A couple of nearby officers glanced worriedly toward Idrian and Mika. Idrian grinned back at them, noting the way their mouths opened—probably a rebuke—before their eyes fell to the ram stitched on the breast of his jacket. Once they saw that, they kept their thoughts to themselves.

Mika noticed it too, chuckling, and whispered, "I have two grenades in my pocket."

"I thought you were walking funny," Idrian said, still looking across the room for people he recognized. He noted a few absences. Otherwise occupied, or dead? He'd have to check up on friends later. "Didn't Tadeas tell you to leave the explosives behind?"

"What? Regular officers can wear a sword or a pistol, but I can't have a grenade handy? Pissing unfair and I won't stand for it."

"You two are making our compatriots nervous," Tadeas said. He seemed to be doing the same thing as Idrian; scanning the room, occasionally exchanging a nod. "Glad to know you're carrying, Mika. If something happens I'll have Idrian light you on fire and throw you at the enemy."

Mika narrowed her eyes at Idrian, as if gauging whether he could throw her far enough to be effective.

"Hey," he responded to that glare, "I didn't say it."

"Shut your yappers," Tadeas said, "General Stavri has arrived."

A murmur rose through the hall as a number of senior officers took the stage. General Stavri was a robust man in his mid-fifties, with broad shoulders, a potbelly, and strong arms. He had short brown hair and a complexion that favored his father. He was the third in line for leadership of the Stavri guild-family and had made his bones all around the world in the Ossan Foreign Legion.

He had, in Idrian's experience, no personality whatsoever. The military was his life, but he was only an officer of middling competence, and his command of the Grent campaign had left Idrian feeling neither confidence nor terror. Wariness, perhaps. Grent would need a tougher nut to crack it than Stavri. How long would the street fighting continue before he was replaced? General Stavri whispered with his aides for almost a full minute before walking to the front of the stage and clearing his throat. He was all business, his face expressionless, a sheaf of reports carried under one arm.

"Officers of the Third, Seventh, and Twelfth," he said with the voice of a natural drill sergeant, "there has been a change in the winds of war today. Some of you may know that Kerite's Drakes, the mercenary company, overwinters in the Glass Isles. Our government has been in negotiations for their services ever since Adriana Grappo's murder."

A pleased murmur swept through the assembled officers, but Idrian found himself frowning. General Stavri certainly didn't sound happy about it. At the mention of Adriana, a few nearby officers glanced at Tadeas. Tadeas, for his part, kept his expression neutral.

Stavri continued, chewing on his next words in an obvious effort to keep his temper in check. "I've been informed that negotiations broke down, and the Grent government hired Kerite's Drakes. They are landing just south of Harbortown as we speak, and plan to march on Ossa immediately."

All around Idrian the pleased murmurs turned into angry muttering. "Oh, glassdamn," a captain said. "We have to fight Kerite now too?"

"Pissing mercenaries!" someone shouted.

"Ach!" Another made a disgusted sound. "We'll clear them from the field!"

Idrian exchanged a glance with Tadeas and could see his own worry reflected in Tadeas's eyes. Devia Kerite, the Purnian Dragon, was widely considered the greatest battlefield commander in the world. Her career had spanned thirty-five years, mostly fighting in Marn and Purnia. She'd fought both for and against Ossa in proxy wars. To Idrian's knowledge, she'd never lost a battle.

He quietly asked Tadeas, "How many soldiers do the Drakes have?"

"Last I heard?" Tadeas chewed on his bottom lip. "Around ten thousand. She's got breachers, glassdancers, and artillery."

"Quiet! Quiet!" Stavri shouted, raising his hands until he could command silence. "Pissing mercenaries is right, and we *will* sweep them from the field. But Kerite should be taken seriously. To that end the Assembly has summoned every available brigade from the provinces; ten whole divisions are coming to our aid."

"Yeah, but when will they be here?" someone shouted from the back.

Stavri glared toward the voice, clearly trying to figure out who had spoken out of turn. Finally he said, "Weeks until the first of them arrive. Our orders have changed!" he shouted over a rising wave of discontent. "We are pulling everything out of Grent and focusing on the north bank of the delta. Our orders are to stall Kerite's forces until our troops arrive from the provinces."

A stunned silence quelled the group in a way that Stavri's glares couldn't. Idrian could hear his own heartbeat. His mouth was suddenly dry, his thoughts jumbled.

"Holy piss," Mika whispered. She stood on her tiptoes and shouted, "All that glassdamned street fighting and we're *pulling out*?"

Idrian choked on his own words, but managed to get out, "We're half a mile from the ducal palace! We've conquered half the city!" A well of emotions seemed to spout from within him, lending an angry edge to his voice. It wasn't just the losses they'd already suffered; the fighting for a city they didn't care to conquer, on the orders of an Assembly that wasn't here to fight the war themselves. If they pulled out today, he wouldn't get a crack at the palace. He wouldn't retrieve that cinderite for Demir.

He and Mika weren't the only ones shouting. Curses flew across the hall, people shouting questions and demands, lamenting the soldiers they'd lost in the last few days for, apparently, nothing. Others questioned this new arrival, demanding to know how the Assembly could be so stupid as to let the Grent outbid them for such a large and famous mercenary company.

Beside Idrian, Tadeas was notably silent. He glanced sidelong at Idrian and shook his head.

"What?" Idrian demanded. He felt hot under the collar now, his left eye twitching. From somewhere in the back of the hall he heard a child's laughter.

It took a full five minutes before order was restored again, and General Stavri stood red-faced in front of them all. When he could finally be heard, he said, "We must protect Ossa at all costs! We will oppose Kerite in the Copper Hills. The Grent forces in the city will surely dog our withdrawal, so extraction orders will be given carefully to each battalion and they are to be followed to the letter. Wait outside until you get your orders. Dismissed!"

The hall vomited out its contents—a hundred furious officers, swearing quietly, some of them still shouting at Stavri long after the general had left through a back door.

Idrian followed Tadeas and Mika through the crowd and across the street, to a quiet spot in a hillside park where Tadeas paused to produce his pipe and tobacco pouch. He packed the pipe in silence, his calm almost as infuriating as General Stavri's announcement. Idrian looked around for something to punch. When he didn't find it, he sat down on the hillside and gripped the grass with both hands like he might fall off the world at any moment.

Mika plopped beside him, and Tadeas came around in front of them both as he puffed his pipe to life. "They're doing the right thing," he said.

Idrian scowled at his friend. "Don't," he said, raising a finger in warning. He was in no mood for this.

"They are," Tadeas insisted, plowing on. "I'm not happy about the soldiers and engineers we've lost over the last few days. Feels damned meaningless to give up all the territory we gained through sweat and blood, but if Kerite and the Drakes are attacking, we need to pull everything back and face her head-on. If we don't, she'll just go around us and burn Ossa to the ground. We are the Foreign Legion, after all."

"Let her attack," Mika snorted. "She'll bounce off our defensive lines."

"You mean the ring of star forts around Ossa?" Tadeas shook his head. "I used to play cards with one of their commanders. They haven't been updated in a hundred years. They are undermanned, underarmed, and dilapidated."

It made sense. Of course it made sense. Idrian wasn't even thinking about giving up the gains they'd made in the city anymore. He was furiously casting about for some other way to get a piece of cinderite for Demir. He'd made a promise to do anything Demir needed in exchange for use of the phoenix channel, and if Idrian didn't fulfill it, he would slowly, painfully, descend into madness.

If, of course, he lived through the war.

As Idrian fumed, he slowly became aware that both Tadeas and Mika were staring at him. He scowled back. "What is it?"

"Something is going on with you," Mika answered, and Tadeas nodded in agreement.

"Don't know what you mean," Idrian responded. Even to his own ears it sounded half-hearted. His fury seemed to whistle out of him like air from an inflated pig's bladder, replaced with cold uncertainty. He had no idea what to do next, and that was more terrifying than charging an artillery battery alone.

"She means," Tadeas said between puffs on his pipe, "you've been like a man possessed since we shifted over to the palace assault yesterday morning. The engineers could barely keep up. I haven't seen you like that since our second tour in Marn."

Idrian regarded them both warily. What excuse could he give? Both of them had been with him for twenty years. They knew his tics. They knew why his eye was so important to him.

"You gonna explain what's going on?" Tadeas asked. "Or why you've been acting like this ever since you got that note from my nephew?"

Idrian chewed on the inside of his cheek. He couldn't betray Demir's confidence, even if he wanted to. That secret—the cindersand running out—was too dire to let roll from his tongue. He was given a brief respite by the arrival of one of General Stavri's messengers.

"Major Grappo?" the messenger asked, offering a note to Tadeas.

Tadeas took the note and broke the general's seal, reading the message within. He said, "We're pulling out first thing in the morning. The Green Jackets will cover our withdrawal, and we're to report to the Copper Hills to help prepare for the confrontation with Kerite."

Idrian pulled back into his own thoughts, forcing himself to calm down and *think*. Eighteen hours until their withdrawal. Could he work with that? Perhaps, but it would be risky. He would need help. Could he say anything without breaking his promise to Demir? Did he have a choice?

"Demir gave me a secret mission," he said quietly.

If he'd lost his companions' attention, he had it back immediately. Mika actually laughed, while Tadeas groaned. "Glassdamn," Tadeas said, "of course he did. Were you going to tell me?"

"Not if I could avoid it."

"So why now?"

Mika laughed again. "It's the palace, isn't it? You barked about capturing it all day yesterday and all this morning."

"Yeah," Tadeas said slowly, "you did. This isn't just about cutting off the Grent from their seat of power and forcing them to surrender. What does Demir want with the glassdamn Grent ducal palace?"

Idrian glared back at the two, feeling like he was being ganged up upon.

IN THE SHADOW OF LIGHTNING · 201

It wasn't especially pleasant, but he used the moment of defensiveness to gather his wits. "I've promised to steal a piece of cinderite from the duke's personal collection," he told them.

There was a long silence, broken by Mika. "You gonna give us any more details than that?"

"I've already betrayed too much of Demir's trust. No more."

Tadeas waved Mika off, his forehead creased in a considering frown. Idrian could see him putting pieces together in his head. He might not be Demir, but he was still a Grappo. Too clever for his own good but, thankfully, smart enough not to guess out loud.

"Fine," Tadeas finally said, "so why tell us now?"

"Because tonight is my last chance to retrieve it. You're going to notice my absence anyway, so I might as well get some help."

"Your absence?" Mika echoed. Realization dawned on her face. "Oh shit, you're going in there alone?"

Idrian nodded. It was the only option available to him. The fact that their orders were to withdraw tomorrow instead of today was a damned gift. If he didn't take advantage of that, he would never forgive himself.

"That," Tadeas said with a chuckle, "is why you told Valient to find you a sheepskin."

"Correct."

Tadeas paced back and forth, chewing violently on the stem of his pipe. Idrian waited for the rebuke; the chastisement; perhaps even a direct order to stand down. He wondered if he'd be able to disobey. In their long friendship, they'd truly butted heads only a few times and Tadeas had won all those contests through sheer willpower.

Tadeas suddenly stopped his pacing and spun to face Idrian. "What do you want from us?"

The plan in Idrian's head was less than half formed, considered only these last two minutes since the arrival of their orders. He raised his hand for Tadeas to give him a moment to think, then said, "I'll have to go in without my armor. Too noisy. So I'll need a shitload of forgeglass. A sack of grenades. Architectural drawings of the ducal palace, and spy reports about the enemy lines."

"Mika?" Tadeas asked.

"I can do the grenades easy, and I think Valient has some medium-resonance forgeglass squirreled away."

"I think I can take care of the rest once we return to the front," Tadeas said. "The Green Jackets owe us from that maneuver you pulled yesterday, and their commander is the sister to Stavri's spymaster. They'll ask questions. What do I tell them?"

"To mind their own glassdamned business," Idrian snorted.

"I think I'll say it nicer than that."

Idrian let out a shaky breath. They did not know just how important this was. Without that cinderite, he didn't have a deal with Demir. Without a deal with Demir, he would continue to slide into madness without hope of reprieve. He could practically see himself swinging his sword at imaginary enemies on the battlefield. He opened his mouth to voice his thanks but Tadeas stopped him with the shake of his head.

"Don't say a glassdamned word," Tadeas said. "If Stavri's staff finds out about this, both of us could be court-martialed. You better believe I'm having words with my nephew when all of this is over."

20

The Lampshade Boardwalk was a mighty wooden structure that thrust itself out onto the Tien River in the northeast corner of Ossa. Much like Glory Street, it was a place where the castes of Ossa mixed easily; poor fishmongers hawked their wares mere feet from high-end jewelry stores, or a sailors' bar might rent space from an expensive hotel for passing merchants. The Lampshade had a carnival-like air, but unlike Glory Street it was a family-friendly place, mostly closed down by dark during the summer, or nine o'clock during the winter.

Kizzie arrived to her meeting two hours early, strolling around the area while shops closed down and restaurants snuffed the gas lanterns above their patio seating. She eyeballed everyone and everything; looking for hiding spots, watching for ambushers. She wanted to be ready for any trickery that Glissandi might attempt. She cast a mental net with her sorcery, looking for nearby glassdancers just in case Glissandi was that well-connected. There were none.

It was nearing ten when she turned her jacket inside out, switching the brightly colored embroidering for drab gray. She took the crimson feather out of her felt hat, cocking up one side, then pulled a handkerchief up over her mouth.

The Palmora Pub was one of the few places that stayed open after dark; a place for all the laborers, cooks, buskers, and salesmen to go drinking after their clientele had gone home. Kizzie walked up to the second story of the boardwalk half a block away, positioning herself next to the top of a thick wooden pylon and watching the pub.

Much to her surprise, Glissandi arrived at exactly ten. The scarlet jacket she wore over a black tunic was clearly meant to be subdued, but she still looked extremely wealthy, like someone who'd lost her way leaving a jeweler's kiosk. She wore a deep frown, glancing this way and that, clutching at something heavy she was concealing beneath her jacket.

A pistol, perhaps? Too big. A pair of pistols?

Kizzie produced her braided earrings, threading one into each ear. The witglass quickened her thoughts, and her muscles responded to the forge-glass, but it was the sightglass she needed. The whole world came a little more alive. Sights and sounds grew sharper. The fishy scent of the river became almost overpowering. She let herself grow used to the difference and then used her vantage point to investigate the area. No sign of Glissandi's bodyguards or any kind of a trap. Were they well-concealed? Had Kizzie spooked her into honesty?

Kizzie stuck her hands into her pockets, gripping her blackjack with her left, and strolled in a circular path around and then down so that she approached the Palmora Pub from the opposite direction. She came up alongside Glissandi.

"Walk with me," she said, keeping her voice low.

Glissandi's nostrils flared. "You sent the note?" she demanded.

"In private," Kizzie told her, jerking her head down the darkened boardwalk. She half expected Glissandi to refuse. Instead, the Magna sighed and fell into step beside Kizzie. Once they were a little farther from the hubbub of the Palmora, Glissandi cleared her throat.

"Who are you?"

"No one of consequence."

"You certainly won't be if this goes further than tonight."

Kizzie stopped and turned toward Glissandi. They were out of earshot of the closest boardwalk patrons. "What's that supposed to mean?" she asked.

Up close, Glissandi looked older and more severe. She had crow's-feet in the corners of her eyes and several blemishes covered by makeup. "I mean," she said, her voice dripping with the arrogance of someone who'd done this many times, "that this sack has forty thousand ozzo in it." Slowly, she drew a leather satchel from beneath her jacket and tossed it on the ground between them. "Accept it, and then take whatever secrets you might think you know to your grave. I don't want to see you or hear from you again."

Kizzie was a little amused. She glanced over Glissandi's shoulder toward the Palmora, where a fistfight had broken out between two keelboatmen. "I think you read this wrong," she said.

Glissandi's jaw tightened. "I made you an offer. This is nonnegotiable. Pick up the bag and be grateful that I don't snuff you out where you stand."

Kizzie glanced toward the closest rooftops. Marksmen on the boardwalk? Not even Glissandi would dare something so brash. The minute a rifle blast went off this place would be swarming with National Guardsmen. Kizzie was far safer armed with a knife in the dark than anyone carrying a firearm. "I don't want your money," she said. "I want to know why you killed Adriana Grappo."

"I see." Glissandi's demeanor grew somehow more cold. There was a glint in her eye now, something that hadn't been there a moment ago. Anger? Fear? Kizzie could see she had taken her off guard, and it took her a moment to gather herself. She suddenly rubbed furiously at her nose. "I don't know what you're talking about."

"You do, and you're going to hold a piece of shackleglass and tell me *why*," Kizzie said.

"Who are you with?" Glissandi demanded. "The Cinders? The National Guard? A private investigation firm? Who?" Her voice cracked. "The matter was dropped. *Dropped!*"

"Private investigation firm," Kizzie lied. "Why did you kill Adriana Grappo?" She reached into her pocket to palm the shackleglass, intent on forcing it into one of Glissandi's piercings. As she did, she noticed that Glissandi was rubbing at her nose again furiously while her eyes grew a little bit more wild. Glissandi glanced to her left and right.

That wasn't an itch, Kizzie realized. It was a signal.

She heard the feet pounding along the boardwalk with moments to spare. Kizzie whirled just as two massive shapes sprang out of the darkness. She grabbed Glissandi, jerking the Magna woman between her and the assailants. A cudgel swing was abruptly aborted. A man swore, trying to stop his forward momentum but slamming into Glissandi and—right behind her—Kizzie.

Kizzie stumbled back, barely keeping her feet as the other two went down. Her sightglass allowed her to see just well enough to ascertain that the attackers were a pair of big Purnians, no doubt the bodyguards that Veterixi warned her about. The second bodyguard leapt the heap of his boss and companion with surprising dexterity. He came at Kizzie hard, swinging a short cudgel. She ducked one swing, sidestepped the next, backpedaling toward the Palmora.

Kizzie's opponent was easily six inches taller and outweighed her by four stone. He was in his late thirties. He had a forgeglass stud in his left ear and a broad, smashed face like he'd headbutted an anvil in his youth. Godglass was not always a great equalizer. It merely augmented existing traits, so even if Kizzie's forgeglass was better, that big brute was probably a lot stronger than her. She couldn't let him catch her. Lucky for her, she didn't need strength. A sharp knife would equalize things well enough.

She didn't even bother with her sorcery, as she wasn't good enough to manipulate glass in a quick-moving situation like this. Instead she drew her stiletto, still bobbing and weaving, looking for an opening that she could exploit before the other bodyguard joined the fight. She had mere moments to do it, so when her opponent swung just a little too hard, Kizzie sidestepped the blow and brought her blackjack down across his elbow.

He gave a pained grunt. Kizzie stepped in, felt his offhand catch her by the lapel of her jacket, and buried her knife between his ribs. She jerked it out, stabbed again, and then shoved him away as he gasped for breath while his lungs filled with blood.

Glissandi was up. She'd recovered the leather money satchel and was sprinting down the boardwalk, away from Kizzie and toward the crowded Palmora Pub. Kizzie checked her face to make sure her handkerchief was still covering it. The move turned out to be a mistake, as the second bodyguard had also gained his feet and was already closing the distance between them.

She barely managed to get her knife up between herself and his cudgel. The exchange was badly mismatched, her hand going instantly numb from the force of his strike. She threw herself to the side, tripped, and rolled away from another blow. She sprang back to her feet, but too slowly. The bodyguard grabbed her roughly by her knife wrist. He raised his cudgel to brain her in the side of the head.

Before the blow could fall, Kizzie tapped him between the eyes with her blackjack. He staggered back, sudden tears pouring from his eyes. She tried to shake the grip he had on her knife hand, didn't succeed, so smacked him twice more with her blackjack—once on the temple, and then on the throat.

He stumbled, gagging, dropping his cudgel to clutch at his throat with both hands. Her knife finally free, Kizzie buried it in the spot where his throat met his shoulder.

She was already sprinting after Glissandi before the bodyguard hit the ground.

"Hey!" one of the sailors outside the Palmora shouted as she approached. "Slow down there!"

Kizzie looked down at the bloody stiletto in her hand, looked in both directions for Glissandi, and responded, "That bitch and her friends jumped me! She stole my bag!"

In broad daylight that excuse would never have worked, but the sailors outside seemed just drunk enough to accept it at face value—at least for long enough that one pointed to his left. Kizzie didn't give them a chance to second-guess themselves. She followed his direction at a sprint, heading up the stairs to the second level of the boardwalk.

It was dark here, very few gas lanterns still lit, the lights of Ossa glittering across the river. Kizzie paused long enough to take a deep breath and hold it in. She could hear the blood pounding in her ears, but she could also hear the sound of someone running across the planks of the boardwalk just on the other side of the darkened windows of the closest restaurant. Kizzie's witglass helped her calculate speed and distance, and she rushed to cut Glissandi off. She ran lightly, sacrificing a little speed for as much stealth as she could manage. She passed one narrow alley, then another, and turned right at the next.

She emerged just behind a dark figure clutching a bag. Kizzie saw the glint of city lights reflected off Glissandi's eyes as she looked over her shoulder, and then Glissandi tripped and fell right on her face. Kizzie had to grab on to a pylon to keep herself from running over the damned woman. Stiletto in one hand, Kizzie pocketed her blackjack and grabbed Glissandi by the back of her jacket. She hauled her to her feet and shoved her up against the wall.

Discarding the satchel full of money, Kizzie used Glissandi's confusion as a distraction while she patted her down. No knife. No pistol. Damned arrogant guild-family member thought that she could buy her way out of a murder, and that her two bodyguards would take care of things if that didn't work.

"Move and I'll give you a red smile," Kizzie said, raising her stiletto to Glissandi's throat.

Glissandi's composure and arrogance were gone. She stared back at Kizzie in fear, breathing heavily. Kizzie brushed her free hand across Glissandi's ears. A tiny stud of forgeglass and another of sightglass, both of them low-resonance by their feel.

"What do you want?" Glissandi demanded between breaths.

"We already established that. I want answers."

"No. I'll give you money. I'll double what's in the bag. That's all I can offer."

"You can offer a lot more than that." Kizzie felt in her pocket for the shackleglass. With one quick movement, she forced it into one of the piercings in Glissandi's right ear. Glissandi's shoulders immediately slumped, her whole body relaxing. Her expression became resigned, but fear still remained in her eyes.

"Don't do this," Glissandi hissed quietly.

Kizzie had no compassion. She'd just been forced to kill a pair of bodyguards over a question. She'd not demanded money or evidence, just answers. She was damned well going to get them. "Tell me the truth," she said. "Did you help kill Adriana Grappo?"

Glissandi began to tremble violently, much like Churian Dorlani. Her mouth opened. A tiny noise issued forth, but it was barely more than a squeak. "I did," she finally managed.

"Why?"

Glissandi's right eye twitched. For half a moment, Kizzie thought she was going to have a full-blown seizure, but the Magna spat out one word: "Orders."

"From who?" Kizzie waited a moment and gave Glissandi a shake. "From who?" she demanded again. "Who wanted Adriana dead? Who were the other killers? Why kill Adriana?"

Glissandi gave a high-pitched whine. Her jaw moved strangely, and it took Kizzie a few moments to realize that there was something leaking from the corner of Glissandi's mouth. Kizzie took a half step back in horror. Glissandi smiled at her, dark liquid pouring out of her mouth, and mumbled something victoriously.

She had bitten off her own tongue.

"What the pissing . . ." Kizzie began. She didn't get the chance to finish. Glissandi suddenly lurched forward, falling on Kizzie's knife with surprising force, ramming the weapon into her own chest. Glissandi gave a gurgling laugh as she tumbled to the ground. It was a sound Kizzie knew she would remember forever.

Kizzie stared down at the body at her feet, mouth hanging agape, unable to comprehend what had just happened. She felt suddenly very cold. What kind of a person *killed* themselves rather than sell out their employer? Kizzie's mouth was dry, her thoughts muddled. She pulled herself together enough to kneel down next to the body, checking Glissandi for more godglass and a pocketbook. She grabbed the leather satchel. She had no way of getting rid of the body. Best make it look like a robbery gone bad.

She swore quietly to herself through the entire process, her hand hurting, her blood pounding. She needed to leave as quickly as possible.

She'd just fetched back the shackleglass when she noticed that there was still life in Glissandi's eyes. They were moving very slightly, staring past Kizzie with powerful intent. Slowly, Kizzie turned around.

There, out in the darkness, just beyond the help granted to her senses by the sightglass, was a figure. It looked like a man, bald and impossibly tall and thin, nearly seven feet tall. She could see the glint of light off his eyes as he stared at her, but he did not move or speak. Kizzie's pulse quickened further. Snatching everything she had gathered to herself, she hurried away from Glissandi's body.

She paused at the next alley to look back. The figure remained where he was, staring directly at Kizzie. He didn't even look down at Glissandi's body. Who was he? A night watchman? Another bodyguard? A damned boardwalk madman? Kizzie did not want to know. She'd had enough of confrontation for one night. She hurried down to the Palmora Pub, where she ducked inside and then let herself out through a service hatch underneath the bar. Creeping along beneath the boardwalk, she heard heavy footsteps above her.

The footsteps paused, and between the cracks she could see a light-skinned man staring toward the Palmora. It was definitely the tall man. He did not go any closer, but gave a heavy sigh and then turned and walked back the way he came—up toward Glissandi's body. Kizzie waited until she could no longer hear his footsteps before she found a ladder and made her way back up to the boardwalk.

She had never once before in her life run home out of fear. She wasn't about to do it now, but she'd be damned if she didn't find herself moving much faster than usual until she'd sought out a hackney cab and had paid the driver to take her to her apartment. A powerful guild-family member had just *killed herself* rather than admit who gave the orders to kill Adriana Grappo. With her dying gaze, she had looked at that tall man in the shadows.

Something was rotten in Ossa—far more rotten than usual.

21

Idrian left the relative safety of the Ossan front line at around two o'clock in the morning. He wore a cloak that covered his civilian's clothes, and a strip of cloth that acted as an impromptu eye patch to cover his godglass eye. A sack of Mika's grenades hung from his belt, precariously close to his nethers—not that it would matter if one went off accidentally. He wore sightglass to let him see well in the dark, and enough forgeglass that his body was practically humming with sorcery. Every step felt light, as if he weighed practically nothing.

The night was as cold as any he'd ever experienced in Ossa, and he could see the fogging breath of the Ossan sentries as he slipped past them in the darkness. His footsteps made barely a sound. No one so much as twitched in his direction, and for that he was grateful.

Thanks in large part to the Ironhorns, the Ossan Foreign Legion controlled almost the entire wealthy district of townhouses that lay at the bottom of the palace hill. Beyond that was a wooded park—a no-man's-land between the two armies—and then a series of barricades and entrenchments that worked their way up nearly a half mile of open hillside. Some two thousand troops camped on that lawn, many of them on guard against a possible night attack. There were at least six artillery batteries as well, but so far the Grent had not stooped to blasting away at their own upper-class townhouses.

Idrian could see those defenses, lit at regular intervals by torchlight, from his position beneath a tree in the park. Up ahead was the first row of sandbags, and he could see the eyes of the sentries at their watch. It was a daunting display that would have given him pause with a whole brigade at his back. On his own, it was downright terrifying. The one piece of good news was that Tadeas had gotten his hands on spymaster reports indicating that the palace itself had been abandoned by the ducal family—sent off to safety in the Glass Isles—and that it was now being used as a barracks for the Grent officers. He would face soldiers, but not the dozen breachers that made up the duke's closest bodyguards.

Crouching, moving from tree to tree at a careful run, Idrian worked his way along the park parallel to the Grent defenses until he reached a babbling little brook. He took his turn there, following the brook into a narrow crevasse that wound up the hillside, all the way to a small spring just beneath the palace. It was the one piece of real topography on the hill, and it ran directly through the center of the Grent defenses.

Idrian gave himself a fifty-fifty chance of a guard being posted at the bottom of the gully against exactly this sort of thing. Why wouldn't they? But, on the other hand, who would be insane enough to try to sneak into a Grent garrison alone?

He took the gamble, proceeding slowly up the gully, stepping lightly so as not to dislodge even the smallest stone. Each movement seemed painstaking and the forgeglass he wore caused his muscles to scream in protest that they weren't being used to their full potential. He took deep breaths as he went, reminding himself he used to do this all the time hunting crag cats as a kid in the highlands of Marn.

Of course, that was thirty years ago.

Ten yards. Then fifty. Then a hundred. The gully got deeper and wider as he proceeded, and he watched the edges continuously for any sign of a sentry. He could hear talking; smell the waft of a late-night cigarette. Despite the forgeglass he wore, he felt naked without his armor—deeply exposed to the point where discovery was almost certainly a death sentence. Thankfully the gully proved empty.

He was almost to the palace itself, less than a stone's throw away, when the sound of laughter stopped him in his tracks. He crouched and froze, looking up, watching for movement. Two shadows appeared just ahead of him. Six more feet and he could have reached up and yanked them down by their ankles. They were backlit by nearby torches, paused on the very edge of the gully.

"Glassdamn, man," one said, "I swear I'm never drinking that stuff again. Barely gives me a buzz but I have to piss all the damn time." As if to accentuate his statement, the sound of a stream of urine pattered on the stones just in front of Idrian. Idrian swallowed his disgust and didn't move.

"Your choice," the other chuckled, "I can't get enough of it. Hey, did you hear that rumor that the Ossans are pulling out?" Another stream of urine joined the first.

"No. What's going on?"

"Supposedly a few battalions withdrew just after dark, and more are going to retreat tomorrow."

"Cease-fire?"

"Nah. They're shifting troops to oppose Kerite's Drakes."

"Thank piss for the Drakes. Duke must have spent a fortune to hire her." He made a disgusted sound. "We'll have to go on the offensive tomorrow. Last thing I want to do with the Ironhorns sitting front and center."

"No kidding. Did you hear what they did to the Two-Seventy-First? Absolutely cut them to ribbons. The Ram leapt off a four-story building and landed on their glassdancer!"

"I don't believe that."

"My cousin is in the battalion that was supporting them. Said it was the scariest thing she's ever seen, and one of those damned grenades blew off her hand."

The other snorted. By now both streams of urine had finished, and the two men left the gully, continuing their conversation as they went. Idrian let out a sigh of relief when he was finally alone. Even knowing that a single sound might get him killed right then he'd nearly laughed at them talking about him. What a damned way to go out that would have been.

He proceeded to the genesis of the gully and pulled himself up over the lip, checking carefully before rolling across the ground and sprinting to the dubious cover of one of the big, decorative square columns that marched down the face of the palace. He remained there for as long as he dared, listening carefully for any sign of more sentries. There would be fewer here by the palace proper, but they'd also be more likely to catch him in torchlight.

Idrian tried to assess the situation within the palace itself. An officers' garrison could mean anything: well-ordered and quiet from sundown to sunup, or a damned festival with bottomless drinks and whores dancing on the duke's billiards tables. It seemed, much to Idrian's relief, that it was the former. Other than the occasional officer going for a piss, the palace was relatively quiet.

Somewhere in the distance he could hear a child's laughter. He ignored it petulantly.

Idrian found a servants' entrance and slipped inside, treading carefully down the darkened hallway. Everything was still. No sign of the officers or the servants. Could it really be this damned easy?

He answered that question himself after winding his way through the servants' passages, getting lost twice, before finally entering the main foyer. This room was well-lit by gas lamps, causing him to double his speed lest a stray messenger find him here. He hurried to the middle of the room, looked up, and had to choke down a shout of frustration at the sight above him.

The case that had held that cinderite upon his visit just a few months ago was empty.

Idrian hurried back to the dark servants' halls and swore quietly in every language he knew. The cinderite wasn't the only piece missing. The walls were conspicuously bare of art and tapestries, the display tables bereft of vases. They must have moved all the valuable art as soon as the Foreign Legion got close. Maybe even at the beginning of the war. It made sense.

A fool's errand. He would have to return to Demir empty-handed, and hope that Demir gave him another shot. He leaned against the wall for a quick breath, pressing on his godglass eye to get rid of the headache creeping across the front-center of his skull. The child's laughter was getting closer, as if it were coming from the next room. Time to go back the way he'd come.

Or . . .

Idrian could hear the soft, steady footsteps of someone patrolling the marble hallways just around the corner. Should he risk it? Was it worth his damned life? He crept forward, head cocked to follow the source of the sound, until he reached an open door into one of the main hallways. It was darker than the foyer, but he could see a tall woman in orange-and-white ducal livery walking slowly down the center of the hall.

She faced away from him, hands clasped behind her back, and she didn't seem to be listening for anything in particular. One of the duke's staff? A chaperon for the officers borrowing his palace? The woman stopped at the bottom of a staircase, half toward Idrian, looked around once, and sank to sit on the bottom stair. She looked exhausted, her hair mussed though her uniform was spotless. She gave a yawn and set her head against the banister.

A few minutes later, her eyes were closed.

It was the opportunity Idrian needed, though quite risky. He crept out of his hiding spot and hurried across the hall. He was on her before her eyes could even open, and he yanked her up into his grip with one hand on her neck and the other on her mouth. She tried to scream, but the sound was muffled into his hand.

"Your silence or your life," Idrian hissed.

To her credit, she kept trying to scream. Nerves of glassdamned steel, and it called Idrian's bluff. He wasn't going to kill a servant just for a piece of information. He *would* give her a good shake, and he did exactly that.

"Tell me where everything is," he whispered. "The tapestries, the art. Did they move it to a warehouse? Is it in the city, or secreted to the country-side?" The woman glared back at Idrian over his hand. She'd stopped trying to scream, and it was clear she was readjusting her line of thinking—an assassin might be worth losing her life over. But a thief? He slowly took his hand off her throat to encourage thinking of him as the latter. "Tell me and you'll live through the night."

She looked down at his hand. Slowly, ready to clap it right back into place, he pulled it away from her mouth. In a low voice, disgust dripping from her tone, she said, "It's all downstairs, moved to the undercroft in case of Ossan shelling." Idrian held in a sigh of relief. Right under his damned feet. She stared at the strip of cloth covering his eye, and he hoped she didn't make the connection between a large Marnish man without an eye and the Os-sans' most famous breacher.

"Show me," he told her.

The woman's glare did not go away, but she did not struggle or try to flee as she led him back to the servants' passages and wound them most of the way back to where he'd entered. She indicated a door, paneled to look like the wall around it. Idrian gave it a shove, and it creaked open to reveal a dark, narrow staircase going down.

"How many exits?" he asked.

"From the undercroft? Just two—this one, and another into the stables on the west end of the palace."

Idrian considered his options. Going down into the undercroft might well seal his fate. Up here, if an alarm was raised, he could make a break for it and hope the darkness fouled the aim of the guards. If he was cornered un-derground he wouldn't have that luxury. He reached into the stairwell and found a gas lantern by the tiny flicker of its pilot light, and turned it up to illuminate the stone walls.

He was still considering it when a light suddenly illuminated the other end of the passage some thirty feet from him. It bobbed into sight, showing another figure in the duke's livery, who held his lantern up over his head and peered hard in their direction. Idrian didn't even have time to say a word before a voice was raised. "Intruder! Intruder! Raise the alarm, for the enemy is upon us!"

"Son of a . . . !" Idrian swore. He shoved his captive in the direction of her compatriot. He had moments to decide on his next course of action. With another curse, he leapt into the stairway of the undercroft and slammed the door shut behind him. It didn't have so much as a latch, so he reached into Mika's sack of grenades and pulled out one she'd painted black. It was about the size of his fist with the gauntlet on, and had a little chain and hook coming out of one end. Carefully, he hung it from the inner doorframe so that the chain would be pulled from the grenade if someone hastily opened the door.

Trap set, he hurried down the stairwell.

The undercroft was a massive basement, a single room twenty feet tall, broken up by the even march of columns from one end to the other, that took up the entirety of the palace floor plan. Even lighting several gas lanterns around the base of the stairwell, he could not see very far into the dark.

But he didn't need that much light to see the treasure hoard before him. As the woman had promised, the valuables of the palace had been brought down here. Crate after crate were stacked head-high, rolled-up tapestries shoved between the stacks. Paintings were wrapped in linen. As a young man he'd taken a job in the Ossan Museum and had spent a summer moving around displays. This looked much like the basement of the museum.

Idrian moved quickly, no longer caring for stealth. Even down here he could hear that a commotion was being made up in the palace. He could not afford to let them barricade him in here. He estimated the size of the cinderite, ruling out everything smaller, and began attacking the stacks of crates. He found a crowbar quickly, and used it to pry lids off as fast as he could move. He found a sculpture of some philosopher. Old pottery. Gold and silver knickknacks. He ignored the treasures before him, knowing that none stacked up to the price of his sanity, and that slowing even for a moment could cost him his life.

A massive set of expensive porcelain dinnerware. Silver goblets. Crystal goblets. Platinum goblets. Godglass goblets. Glassdamn, someone in the ducal family loved goblets.

He could hear boots thumping up above. Soldiers were probably flooding the corridors upstairs at this very moment, demanding answers from the poor servant who'd raised the alarm and trying to figure out how stupid someone had to be to attempt to rob the ducal palace while it was being used as a barracks. He'd wasted valuable minutes already. How long did he have until they got over their confusion and came after him?

An explosion split the air, causing him to flinch and reach for the shield he wasn't carrying. He placed the size and sound—Mika's trap grenade. The soldiers were coming. With any luck, that had taken away their courage for a while longer.

He continued his search, kicking over crates, cracking the lids off them, bashing through wood with the crowbar. He wondered just how loudly his old overseer from the Ossan Museum would scream if she saw him now. Very, he imagined, but he had no time left. He knocked a box of crates over with his shoulder, grabbed the top one to tear off the lid, and froze. It had cracked when it fell, and through the crack he could see a familiar bit of stone-like texture. He slowed immediately and, taking great care, removed the lid the rest of the way.

The cinderite was about three feet long, four inches thick, with branching protrusions at irregular intervals. It looked like the trunk of a young tree turned to stone. He held his breath as he pulled it from the box and lifted it up to the light. No damage that he could see.

Setting the crowbar to one side, he laid his sheepskin out flat. He could hear shouting now, as officers at the top of the stairs argued loudly over whether to proceed further. Someone was screaming in pain somewhere in the palace—probably whoever had tripped the grenade trap. Idrian set the cinderite on the sheepskin, put a few long scraps of wooden crate on either side of it for stability, and then wrapped the whole package up and tied it with twine.

Using a leather strap, he slung it across his back, then ran to the base of the stairs. The arguing among the soldiers upstairs was fierce. They no longer thought he was a mere thief, and were wondering if he was a saboteur. He had moments until someone braved it again. Producing another of Mika's grenades—this one painted orange—he set it down very obviously on the bottom step.

Just the doubt would slow them down.

What had the servant woman said? An exit into the stables on the west end? Idrian sprinted into the darkness, the sightglass hanging from his ears helping him stretch the light of the lanterns behind him just enough that he didn't trip or run into anything as he went. He could hear his boots splashing in puddles on the stone floor, his breath coming out ragged. Even his hands were trembling.

Any moment now he was going to have a fight on his hands, and it wouldn't be pretty. He was armed only with grenades. He reached the west wall and followed it, looking at the ceiling so hard that he almost missed the door just to his left. He threw it open only to find himself bathed in lamplight, blinking into the sudden brightness.

The blast of a carbine was deafening, a bullet ricocheting off the door-frame inches from his head. He threw himself backward into the undercroft with only a glimpse at his surroundings, and paused to catch his breath. The door let out into the back of the stables. He'd caught sight of two rows of stalls, stacks of hay bales, and the room filling with armed Grent soldiers.

So much for that way out.

There was shouting behind him now, back on the other side of the un-dercroft. Shouting ahead of him in the stables, too. Idrian growled softly, cursing himself for a fool. Trapped, just like he knew he'd be. What kind of a pissing idiot would do this to themselves? Searching through Mika's sack of grenades, he found another orange one and pulled hard on the string coming out one end. Counting to three, he opened the door just enough to roll it into the pile of straw farther from him.

"Grenade!" someone shouted, and he could hear soldiers leaping for cover. A few moments passed, followed by a distinct cracking sound, and then someone else shouted in a far more frantic voice, "Fire!"

"Deal with that, assholes," Idrian spat. He'd spotted another door now, farther along in the undercroft. He needed something; a crawlspace, a window—anything that would let him get out of here. He could see torches and lamps back by the treasure hoard, and he pulled a grenade out of his sack at random, yanked the string, and hurled it in that direction. It clattered along the stone, making it only about half the way toward those torches before it exploded.

Blinking the flash from his vision, Idrian reached that other door and wrenched it open. Even with his sightglass he could only really see vague shapes: tools hanging from the walls, a massive hopper of some kind, a great furnace. He stuck his hand in the hopper, running his fingers through what felt like chunks of coal before it dawned on him: this was the palace fur-nace room. It smelled dusty, perhaps completely disused. He found the coal chute, but the latch was chained securely.

He felt his way to the furnace, with a door big enough he barely had to duck through it.

And looked up at a chimney. It was narrow and dark, ascending for a very long time but there, at the very top, he could see stars.

He could imagine the newspapers back home: BREACHER IDIOT DIES AFTER GETTING STUCK IN A DUKE'S CHIMNEY. There would be crude jokes. The Ironhorns would never live down the shame. Demir would pretend to have never known him. Piss on all of them, he thought. He lifted himself to a lip immediately above the firebox and was struck by sudden claustrophobia. He forced himself to push through it.

Here went nothing.

Bracing arms and legs carefully, Idrian began to climb his way upward. The chimney walls were dusty rather than properly dirty, lending credence to his idea that the whole thing was disused. Soon he could smell smoke. Had someone lit a fire under him? He stopped long enough to look. No flame. It was probably from the stables. The chimney narrowed very slightly as he climbed, causing his claustrophobia to grow. He was forced to pull in his arms and legs but still exert enough strength to keep himself from falling. Despite all his forgeglass his whole body trembled with the effort. Muscles burned like they hadn't in years.

Idrian's head bumped into something. He paused, breath held, and carefully looked up. He was at the top, and he only had to push past a narrow lip to squeeze his way out through the opening. The roll of sheepskin caught on the lip and for half a moment he thought he would lose the cinderite—and then he was free.

He pulled himself into a sitting position on top of the smokestack and appraised the situation: he was on top of one of the palace turrets, balanced precariously some sixty feet in the air. He could see what felt like forever in every direction with the lights of Grent and Ossa to his east and the rest of the delta spreading out to his south and west. There was a fleet way out there where the delta met the ocean. Probably Kerite's mercenaries. If Idrian survived this, he would be fighting them in a couple of days. A shadow passed beneath the moon; a speck of an animal soaring through the night.

"That," he whispered to himself, "is a big bat."

Sound beneath him brought Idrian back to the present. There were voices, and then the flash of lights. They'd found his exit. Idrian fished into the sack of grenades and pulled one out at random.

Green for big boom, as Mika liked to say. Perfect. He pulled the string and dropped it.

The explosion caused the entire building to shudder violently. Idrian's stomach lurched into his throat. He clung to the stone until he was certain he hadn't just blown up the entire tower, then let out a long shaky breath and wasted no more time. He dropped to the roof, slid down the copper shingles, and then leapt across a gap to a windowsill one floor below.

How his arms and legs managed to carry him down without failing, dropping one floor at a time until he reached the ground, Idrian did not know. When he did hit the ground, he might have fallen to his knees to kiss the solid earth if not for a nearby shout.

"There he is! Rouse the troops!"

Muscles feeling like they'd been run through a washerwoman's wringer, Idrian began to sprint downhill. A musket blast went off, then another, then another. Bullets whizzed overhead and thumped into the dirt around him as he silently prayed that the darkness would continue to foul their aim. He ran straight through the center of the camp on the ducal hillside, and could see soldiers climbing out of their tents to respond to the call of alarm, looks of surprise as Idrian passed them. One ill-advised young soldier tried to leap into Idrian's way. Idrian lowered his shoulder and plowed over the poor bastard.

Idrian leapt a row of sandbags, crossed an artillery battery filled with small cannons, and then threw himself off a twenty-foot drop. He hit the ground hard enough to stagger, his legs buckling and finally giving out. He tripped, fell off another smaller drop, and twisted his body so as not to land on the cinderite. The landing knocked the wind out of him, only his forge-glass protecting him from a broken ankle or worse.

He had not yet caught his breath when he heard the sound of hoofbeats.

Would these pissing Grent not let up? He looked to see that he was nearly at the bottom of the ducal hill, probably less than fifty feet from the ring of trees that marked the no-man's-land between armies. It was an easy jog, except that several squads of dragoons were riding toward him hard from the side. They would be on him in moments.

Idrian reached for his sword, remembered that he didn't actually have it, and then fled toward the trees as fast as his tired legs could carry him. He was completely spent, and despite all his forgeglass would not beat the dragoons in a contest of speed. Without slowing, the dragoons drew their carbines. They would pepper him with bullets and then run him down. Sloppy, but effective.

The tree line of the park suddenly erupted in thunder and flame. Half the dragoons went down among the screaming of men and horses. Idrian stared at them for several moments, confused, before he heard his name shouted from the underbrush. He could see figures there, and then heard a shouted order to fire. Thunder and flame erupted once again, dropping even more of the dragoons. Those that hadn't already fallen turned and fled.

Limping, still wary of any infantry nearby, Idrian made it to the tree line.

He found Tadeas and Valient waiting for him with over a hundred soldiers. They didn't bother waiting for him to catch his breath before the whole group began an immediate withdrawal. Tadeas grabbed Idrian by the arm, pulling him along. They were soon out of the trees and back among the townhouses, where bewildered Ossan sentries watched them breeze their way back to camp. When they arrived, Idrian found Braileer waiting for him with a worried expression.

Idrian waved him off and collapsed in the street, panting.

"Well," Tadeas demanded, "did you get it?"

Idrian gave him a flat look and unslung the sheepskin from his back, shoving it into Tadeas's hands. "As long as it didn't break in my fall back there, yes."

"Did you, uh, light the palace on fire?" Valient asked, staring past Idrian back toward the ducal palace. Idrian glanced that way to see smoke and light. There was a lot of screaming coming from that direction. Part of him felt a little guilty—there was a lot of art in that undercroft—but another part of him realized he couldn't hear children's laughter.

"Mika will be proud," he replied. "I dropped her biggest grenade right down the duke's chimney. Tadeas, start coming up with excuses. I imagine General Stavri's staff will have a lot of questions for us come morning."

22

In an ideal situation, Thessa would have waited for several weeks before attempting to steal back the phoenix channel schematics. She would have gotten to know the guards, the other prisoners, and their habits. She would have a better grasp of Craftsman Magna's personality. She might have even made several casual forays into the administration building just so she knew the layout.

This was not an ideal situation. She wasn't in her early apprenticeship, dared by the other young apprentices to steal sweets from Master Kastora's desk drawer. She did not know how much time she had until Demir actually mounted that rescue—whether it would come in hours, days, or months. She didn't even know if she could rely on him, and so her own plans had to keep moving forward.

Despite her fears, despite a certainty of the consequences if she was caught, Thessa found herself depending on those silly skills learned as an apprentice in a glassworks dormitory. If she could steal low-resonance godglass to sell in town for beer, or sneak older boys and girls into her bunk for some teen fumbling without one of the garrison reporting her late-night movements to Kastora, then she could damn well outsmart some bored Magna enforcers and their small-minded overseer.

And he *was* small-minded. She knew his type, and better yet she had seen how Demir had talked circles around him. Filur Magna could be manipulated. She would take advantage of that.

The first thing she did was work late again. She didn't need to, but after the rest of the prisoners had finished their own quotas and gone back to the dormitory was the perfect time to inspect the furnace room for loose paving stones. She found one just beneath workbench number seven, pried it up with her fingernails, and used her heavy shears to dig out a space large enough to hide the vellum schematics. She tossed the dirt into the fire and deposited Demir's razorglass into the hiding spot before making sure the paving stone fit back in its spot without a wobble. She then left the furnace room, walking casually down the road that ran through the middle of the compound.

It was a short walk, but an important one. It was late, the night lit by a handful of gas lamps. Craftsman Magna's carriage was still parked just inside the compound entrance, and lamplight flickered in the large window that overlooked the courtyard. Thessa couldn't see the man himself from this angle, but she bet he was in there. A driver waited beside the carriage, and the horses stamped.

Thessa passed the administration building and walked around the corner to the end of a little-used alleyway. She was in clear sight of the courtyard, well within the light cast by the nearest lamp, when she knelt down and took three smooth stones out of her pocket. She stacked them one on top of the other, regarding them thoughtfully for several moments before bowing her head.

Religion was a peculiar cultural artifact in this part of the world. It was both meaningless and everywhere; dozens of belief systems and hundreds of sects practiced to some degree by millions of people throughout the Ossan Empire and its neighbors. The Empire itself had no official religion, but it tolerated pretty much anything as long as none of them threatened the unofficial worship of godglass and money. Thessa's mother and father had been omniclerics—priests of a sort, with a thorough knowledge of many of those religions, who could offer advice, ablutions, blessings, or rites to locals and travelers alike. Thessa hadn't revisited her religious upbringing in almost a decade. There was no time for religion in Kastora's glassworks.

But that knowledge was still there, and Thessa had spent her entire day thinking about how she could use it to get back the schematics.

She heard a nearby door slam shut and the call of voices across the courtyard. At the sound of them she leaned forward, rocking back and forth in front of the three smooth stones, pouring her focus into them. For this to succeed, she had to get it *right*. She needed to pass as a worshiper not just to the casual observer, but to another worshiper.

Footsteps echoed across the courtyard. More words were exchanged. The driver of the carriage said something, and there was the click of an opening door. Thessa began to wonder if she'd been overlooked, or if her guess had been wrong, and genuinely began to pray to Renn, the Nasuud goddess of commerce, whose altar was a pyramid. Thessa didn't think she had any actual belief left in her, but it was worth a glassdamned shot.

After a long silence, footsteps slowly approached. Thessa swallowed a lump in her throat and kept rocking back and forth.

"What are you doing?"

Thessa almost choked. It was Craftsman Magna himself. Thessa leaned forward all the way, pressing her forehead to the cobbles in front of the three smooth stones, then looked up. She pretended to do a double take and snatched up the three stones, shoving them in her pocket as she leapt to her feet. "I'm so sorry, sir. I didn't think I'd disturb anyone here!"

Craftsman Magna's eyes narrowed. "What's in your hand? Show me now, quickly!"

Slowly, as if with great hesitance, Thessa removed the stones from her pocket and held them out.

"What is that?"

"It's . . . it's an altar, sir. I was praying."

The overseer's frown deepened. "It doesn't look like an altar."

Thessa stacked the stones one on top of the other, largest on the bottom, in her palm. "It's a pyramid, sir. Not a very good one, but the best I have. For the goddess Renn. She's the Nasuud—"

"I know who she is," he cut her off. In that moment, Thessa could have sworn the overseer's eyes softened. "You're a Rennite?"

"Yes, sir. My parents were Rennite priests, sir, before they died in the accident."

"Why are you praying here?"

"I couldn't find an omnichapel, sir, and this alley seemed quiet. None of the laborers bring their woodcarts through." She kept her eyes fixed on the ground, daring only the occasional glance up at the overseer. He was deep in thought now, his expression turned down in a scowl.

"You insult Renn with such a rudimentary altar. And with nothing to offer!" He sniffed and turned away. "See that you stay out from underfoot."

Thessa cursed silently as he began to walk back toward his carriage. She'd thought the bait would be too much for him to resist. On an impulse she called after him. "Sir!"

He paused and turned back, clearly impatient. "What is it?"

"I understand I'm a prisoner, sir, but is there an omnichapel somewhere nearby I can visit? Even just once? This"—she hefted the little altar—"does not bring me as close to Renn as I'd hoped."

"Hah! What are you praying for, little Rennite?"

"The end of the war, sir. So that commerce may return to normal."

"And your release, I assume."

"If it pleases Renn."

The answer seemed to satisfy Craftsman Magna. "It will be months until you are eligible to earn a town pass," he replied. "You will have to be patient. . . ." Thessa hefted the little rudimentary altar and his eyes darted to it. He flinched. "Bah! Come with me." He whirled and strode back toward the administration building. Thessa shoved the stones back in her pocket and hurried to follow. She had to force herself to breathe evenly, wondering if her luck—or Renn's blessing, whichever it was—would hold.

The overseer led her inside through the front door, past a couple of curious Magna guards and down a long hall. They went up a rickety flight of stairs, doubled back down another hall, and then entered an office that was in surprisingly tidy shape. It didn't look all that different from Master Kastora's office: desk in the middle, chairs for receiving visitors, a heavy Purnian rug, and a pair of drafting tables off to one side.

Thessa did not have time to make a thorough examination. Craftsman Magna thrust his arm out toward a shrine tucked back in the corner of the room. It looked like a small wardrobe, opened at the front, papered over with a glittering sheen. On top was an incense holder—well used and, by the smell of the office, quite recently. Inside the shrine was a gold pyramid just too big to fit in the palm of Thessa's hand.

"Pray," the overseer ordered. His body language screamed of impatience, his expression both long-suffering and fearful. This was not a man who would test his god by rejecting a fellow worshiper.

"Oh, thank you, sir!" Thessa fell on her knees in front of the shrine. "Sir, may I light the incense?"

He made a *get on with it* gesture. Thessa found a match and lit the incense, then bowed to the shrine. She wondered, however briefly, if Renn was real. Was the goddess blessing her right now? Or would this come back later, when a vengeful goddess decided not to countenance a false worshiper? Just in case, Thessa whispered as she bowed.

"Thank you," she said. "Thank you, thank you." Out of the corner of her eye she could see Craftsman Magna making magnanimous gestures, as if the words were directed at him.

She pretended to pray for as long as the incense burned—about ten minutes, she guessed. Long enough to look convincing, but not so long as to test the overseer's patience. In the back of her head she took in the room and analyzed the overseer. Where would he keep the schematics? His desk? His safe? Hidden in some cubby under the rug?

She finished and dusted off her knees. On a whim of daring, she grasped the overseer, kissing him on the hand. His eyes widened momentarily. "You are too kind," she babbled quickly. "I can feel Renn's spirit strongly in this room."

Craftsman Magna pulled his hand out of her grasp and wiped it on his tunic. "Yes, well. Do not think this will happen again."

"Of course. Thank you so much." Thessa waited while the overseer locked his office and let him escort her down and out of the administration building, where the same guards gave her a bemused look. "I'll return to my dormitory now, sir," she said.

"Wait!"

Thessa froze. "Sir?"

Craftsman Magna took on the expression of someone who thought they were being incredibly generous. "If you meet your quotas and keep out of trouble, I may consider allowing you to worship. On the weekends only."

Thessa thanked him profusely and returned to her dormitory, pausing in the darkness of the doorway to watch as he got into his carriage and left through the front gate. Just inside the dormitory she could hear muted voices. It was, she realized, Three—the woman who'd warned her to take more breaks. Thessa waited for a few minutes, listening. Three seemed to have gotten her hands on a newspaper and was reading it out loud to the dormitory. The story detailed a series of gruesome murders in Glasstown; of siliceers found cut groin to chin and left dead in the Tien River. Thessa found herself engrossed in a moment of déjà vu until she realized she'd read the exact same article the night before the Ossan attack.

She wasn't waiting for the end of the story, however. She was waiting to see how the guards reacted once Craftsman Magna was out of the compound. As she predicted, things changed almost immediately. It was not unlike when Kastora went off on one of his trips. The few remaining laborers stopped to have a smoke. Guards congregated on the walls to gossip. Security wasn't exactly lax—the gates were still locked and enforcers posted to exits—but the general air of the place grew significantly less watchful.

Thessa joined the rest of the prisoners, lying in her bunk, listening to Three finish reading from the newspaper. Soon the dormitory was filled with snoring, punctuated only occasionally by someone leaving to use the outhouses in the far corner of the compound. It was a long, exhausting vigil. Thessa stared at the ceiling, trying not to think of all the ways her plan could go wrong.

It was, she decided around midnight, time to act.

Thessa retrieved Demir's razorglass and used it to cut the lock on the administration building. She passed the guard post where, true to her informant's word, the enforcers meant to be on watch were occupied quite graphically with each other. She hurried up to the overseer's office, where she did not waste time. This was meant to look like, as she'd heard a less-savory assistant once describe a robbery, a "smash and grab." She used the razorglass blade to cut carefully into Craftsman Magna's safe, then his desk. She found the schematics in a false bottom of the latter, along with what appeared to be a number of illegitimate ledgers.

She gathered everything she could easily carry and took it with her.

The trip back to her furnace was a harrowing one, and she hid both inside another dormitory and in the compound outhouses to avoid patrols. No sound of alarm went up. No one stopped or questioned her. Thessa slipped in through the service hatch of her own furnace room. She read the ledgers by the light of the furnace flames, scoffing to herself. Illegal godglass shipments. Under-the-table sales. Illegitimate trading. There was enough information here to destroy Craftsman Magna's career, but only if she could actually get it out of the compound.

Wishing she had another choice, she burned everything in her possession but the phoenix channel schematics. It was vitally important that Craftsman Magna believe that the whole lot had been stolen by a rival guild-family spy. If he even suspected that they'd never left the compound, she'd be done.

A sound brought her attention back to the present, and she quickly made sure all the evidence was destroyed before shoving the schematics up the back of her tunic and securing them in place with her belt. Someone had entered the workshop. She kept her head low, peering through from inside the furnace itself to see one of the hired assistants roll himself a cigarette on one of the workbenches. Much to Thessa's chagrin, he turned up a lantern, pulled a book from his pocket, and began to read.

Piss and shit. With him there, Thessa could not reach her new hiding spot.

She waited as long as she dared, but the assistant was going nowhere. Thessa finally snuck out through the service entrance. She still had both the schematics and the razorglass on her person. The discovery of either would damn her, but she had no choice. She would have to wake up early and hope she reached the workshop before anyone else.

Slipping back into the dormitory, Thessa returned to bed. No point in holding her breath any longer. What was done was done. Exhausted, her body hurting from the tension, she let herself get some rest.

She woke from a restless sleep. The compound was quiet save for the early-morning sound of laborers hauling firewood. The faintest tinge of light touched the sky outside the dormitory windows. It was perhaps six o'clock in the morning, and she didn't have much time until the whistle was blown and everyone rolled out of their beds. Some of the other prisoners already stirred.

Thessa quietly sat up and pulled on her tunic and siliceer's apron, then laced up her boots. She had only minutes to spare to go hide her ill-gotten goods, and . . . The thought trailed off. Three beds down, Axio was not in his bunk. The blanket was thrown back, his boots missing but not his apron. Gone to take a shit? Or maybe up to try and practice what she'd been teaching him? She hoped it was the latter.

Thessa tilted her head, listening for the call of an alarm. The overseer would be here soon, no doubt, and when he discovered the robbery heads would roll. She had to move.

She was halfway to the dormitory door when it opened. A word of greeting for Axio died on her tongue at the sight of two Magna enforcers. They were both armed with cudgels, and they looked directly at her.

"Oh good," one said pleasantly, lifting his cudgel, "you're already up. The overseer wants to see you."

⸙ ⸙ ⸙

Demir and Montego arrived at the Ivory Forest Glassworks right at dawn, their carriage laden with more gifts—silver pocket watches for the overseer and captain, heavy winter tunics for the enforcers, tin flasks for the hired help. Their arrival was greeted far more enthusiastically this morning, and Demir was pleased to see them waved through the front gate and directed to the little compound square just inside, where they were mobbed by enforcers.

Demir leapt from the carriage, shaking hands and handing out the tunics, addressing every enforcer by name and giving them a warm smile. "Cold morning," he said, "wrap up tight. My, that looks threadbare. Ostis, you look like you could use new boots. Send your measurements to my hotel. Fedia, I heard you're a big fan of Baby Montego—he brought you a signed cudgel."

He kept his glove on his left hand to cover his glassdancer sigil, and it made all the difference in the world. Surely these enforcers knew he was a glassdancer—it was a rumor hard to quell—but without the reminder, they didn't have that fear in their eyes. They told him jokes and responded to his words with grins. The whole damned garrison was practically eating out of his hand. Demir spotted the captain running toward him, nightcap on his head, pulling on his jacket as he waved a greeting.

"Morning, Captain," Demir greeted him.

"Master Grappo! I thought you weren't going to be able to visit us again any time soon."

"I got to thinking about that," Demir replied with an easy grin, "and I was so impressed with this operation that I thought I'd make sure everyone here is taken care of." He put his arm around the captain's shoulders, pulling him off to one side and saying quietly, "I know that the Magna aren't exactly happy about my new ownership share. I thought maybe I could prove to them that I'm serious and they'd take *me* seriously."

The captain looked over his shoulder before replying in a whisper. "It's true. We validated your credentials last night, but we also got a message from Supi Magna himself. He's . . . well, 'unhappy' undersells it a bit."

"And like I said, I'm going to prove to them—and you and the overseer, of course—that I'm no fool. Now, where is Filur? I have some thoughts I'd like to share with him."

"I'm not actually sure," the captain replied, rubbing his chin. "He normally doesn't arrive for another hour or so, but his carriage is parked just over there. Oi, Fedia! What time did the overseer arrive?"

"He came in about three," came the reply. "He spent half the night in Furnace Number Nine."

"Furnace Number Nine," Demir replied slowly. "That's one of those secret furnaces, isn't it? One of them he wouldn't show me yesterday."

The captain went slightly pale. "It's . . . complicated. I'm sure he'll explain in due time."

"Of course! He's a busy man. Is there an officers' mess in this place? I brought some very lovely caviar and scones for our breakfast."

"Caviar?" the captain coughed in surprise. "Glassdamn. I . . . Yes, let me go make sure it's all cleaned up!"

Demir sent the captain running with a pat on the back, then looked around. The enforcers were clustered around the wagon now as Montego continued handing out loaves of expensive bread, still warm from the bakery from the next town over. A few dozen of the hired laborers hung about on the fringes, clearly hoping for some scraps but boxed out by the enforcers. He wondered if any of them had been treated this well in their lives.

Probably not.

At that moment, something caught his eye. A pair of enforcers emerged from a nearby dormitory. Held between them closely was Thessa Foleer. They walked by quickly, without so much as a glance toward the hubbub at the front gate. Demir swore under his breath. He knew that walk. He'd seen it in prisons and labor camps all over the provinces, both as a governor and as a grifter. It meant the prisoner was in for a bad time.

Demir felt his stomach tighten at the implication. If she'd been discovered, all of his plans would be for naught. Filur Magna would know her mission and her skills. Even worse, what if she was questioned with shackleglass and Demir's involvement came out? This needed to be dealt with, quickly and quietly.

Demir hurried to Montego, pushing through the enforcers and then whispering in his ear, "We might have a problem. I'm going to cause a distraction and slip away. Be ready to back me up."

A curt nod was the only response he got, and Demir plastered that easy smile on his face and found one of the hired help still hoping to receive a gift. The woman was tall and scarred, and she glared at the enforcers with ill-disguised anger as they received all the attention from Montego.

Demir sidled up next to her and produced a stack of banknotes. "How well are you paid?" he asked.

The woman glanced down at his guild-family sigil, then averted her eyes. "Very well, sir. Thank you for asking."

"Tell me truthfully and there's money in it for you."

The woman glanced left, then right, hesitating for a long time. In a quiet voice she said, "The laborers here are not paid or treated well."

"I'll give you a thousand ozzo if you start a fight. But don't look like you're trying to." He palmed the banknotes and flashed them to her.

"Done."

He slipped them in her pocket, took a step back, and watched as she steeled herself with a deep breath and elbowed her way into the enforcers. She stepped on feet, bruised some ribs, and within moments had the attention of several very angry-looking enforcers. Chaos erupted immediately, and Demir slipped away, following Thessa and her guards.

23

Thessa was half carried, half dragged down the center street of the compound. She tried to think, tried to plan, but nothing but panic circled through her thoughts. Someone must have seen her enter the administration office. The schematics would be found on her person and then she would follow the fate of the other poor bastards who crossed Craftsman Magna. At best, flogged and sent to the lumber camps. Or worse . . .

She didn't want to think of the worst, and was more than a little surprised when they escorted her right past the administration building. She craned her head to stare back at it, expecting to be taken directly to Craftsman Magna, when a new thought occurred to her: perhaps this was part of her escape! The enforcers were paid off, Axio already fetched away. She used the thought to calm herself. When her struggles finally ceased, the enforcers let her walk on her own.

There was a small building in the corner of the glassworks, down a narrow alley and isolated from the rest of the compound behind a pair of warehouses, labeled only with small letters calling it Furnace Number Nine. Thessa had seen it once in passing and had given it no thought.

A single enforcer stood outside a reinforced door. He opened it for Thessa and her escorts and then closed it behind them. Thessa heard a heavy lock fall into place. It *was* a workshop, with just a single workbench in front of a single furnace and space to work not much larger than her bedroom back at the Grent Glassworks. There were extra aprons hanging on the wall and a heavy crate slid against one corner. The walls were covered in cork panels, the room lit by gas lanterns. There were no windows.

All her hopes fled the moment she stepped inside. Sitting on the crate against the far wall was Craftsman Magna. He lounged happily, feet up on a smaller box, fingers knitted over his stomach. Axio stood in front of him.

The young man looked like he'd been worked over by a cudgel. His face was battered, his bottom lip bleeding heavily, and his tunic torn in several places. His eyes were downcast, not even lifting to glance at Thessa when she entered. A light green godglass collar had been placed around his neck, the sight of which made Thessa's blood run cold.

Shackleglass.

Thessa's breath caught in her throat, her thoughts screaming in terror. She didn't even think to keep the fear off her face, and when he saw it, Craftsman Magna grinned back at her.

"You almost had me last night," he said pleasantly, shaking his finger like a grandfather might at a rascally child. "A fellow Rennite? A young worshiper, stuck here for as long as the war lasted? It gave me ideas! Maybe I could have an assistant among the prisoners! An informant, even. Someone I could trust. But I don't trust easily, young lady, and so I snatched your friend to ask him a few questions. Imagine my surprise when he spilled it all at the simple application of shackleglass."

That collar Axio was wearing was no simple application. At a glance it looked like good-quality shackleglass, augmenting Axio's compliance, turning him into a slave in both mind and body.

"You didn't have to hurt him," Thessa said.

"Oh, that was just a bit of fun for the guards!" Craftsman Magna hopped up from the crate and slapped Axio on the shoulder. "We had a long talk. Very long, very productive, as you can see."

Thessa tried to summon a response; an excuse, a cry for mercy, anything. Nothing but a croak came out, and the overseer laughed cruelly.

"So!" he said. "You are Thessa Foleer, Master Kastora's own protégé. Thanks to Axio here, I now know everything about you: your wonderful skill, your plans of escape, your sorcery aphasia. You really are a delightful catch, and to think you were right under my nose this whole time!"

Thessa forced herself to focus, holding on to the only crumbs of hope she had left: Axio didn't actually know her plans for escape, only that she'd promised him they would. He didn't know about the schematics, or about Demir.

Axio's gaze lifted slightly, his chin trembling. "I . . . I'm sorry, Thessa," he squeaked.

"Shut up!" the overseer said, turning and backhanding Axio. Axio stumbled back against the wall, his expression barely changing. He didn't so much as make a noise of protest at the abuse. A closer look revealed that light green glassrot scales had begun to form on his neck and arms. Thessa took a half step forward, reaching for him, only to have her arms grabbed by her escort. The two guards held her tight.

The overseer returned his attention to her, a brief frown crossing his face. "Where was I? Oh yes, a delightful catch. This place—the prison compound—holds many different types of siliceer. Most are apprentices. A few journeymen. We seldom get people of *real* talent through here and when we do, we take full advantage of it. I have a craftsman convicted of murder making shackleglass in Furnace Seven, for instance.

"You," he continued, "might be the most raw talent I've had come through here in my tenure. Master Kastora's protégé!" He gave a happy little squeal and did a jump that seemed very out of character. "This furnace is where we make fearglass."

Thessa did not think that her terror could get any deeper, and yet somehow it managed to do just that. Fearglass was just what it sounded like: a type of godglass that augmented fear. It had little practical application beyond torture, and to her knowledge it had been banned in the Empire since the discovery of the "gentler" shackleglass. Master Kastora used to say it had no place in a civilized society. It was notoriously dangerous to make; many siliceers had gone mad just trying to perfect the recipe.

Dangerous to make *unless* you had sorcery aphasia.

"I'm not making fearglass," she whispered.

"Eh?"

Thessa repeated herself louder, putting every ounce of confidence she possessed behind the words. "I am *not* making fearglass!"

"Oh, yes you are," the overseer chuckled. "You're going to do whatever the piss I want you to do, because you are my pet. Don't you get it? You're alone, Thessa. No friends, no family. No one will come looking for you. You're entirely at my mercy and unless you obey my commands I will make what's left of your life *very* miserable." There was a glint in the overseer's eye as he spoke, as if he enjoyed the prospect of her resisting his rule.

"I'm not alone," she replied. Her body shook like a leaf, yet she was proud that her tone was steady. "The war will end eventually and Master Kastora will come looking for me. He's one of the greatest voices in the silic science. You don't think—"

"Hah! Kastora is dead, you stupid girl," Craftsman Magna cut her off. "He was killed the first day of fighting. Bayonet through the gut."

Thessa's mouth hung open, and she stared at the overseer in horror as a cold despair crept through her belly. That wasn't possible, was it? The sweet old master, dead to Ossan bayonets. Thessa tried to speak but choked on her own bile. She swallowed rapidly to keep herself from throwing up.

Craftsman Magna practically danced around the little workshop. "You're going to make me so rich! Glassdamn, this is incredible. I'm not even going to tell Supi about you! Ah!" He paused, turned toward Thessa. "First thing I want to know is what is on those schematics I took from you, you filthy little liar. You didn't steal those. Kastora entrusted them to you, and I want to know exactly what they are."

The schematics she'd already stolen back, that were tucked up her tunic at this very moment. Thessa managed to get herself under control long enough to say, "I don't know."

"Don't lie to me!" The overseer suddenly lunged at her, taking her chin in one hand and squeezing it until tears sprang to her eyes. When she tried to pull away, her escort held her tight. "I may not be able to use shackleglass on you, but I'll find other ways of making you cooperate." He pulled away, his fury turning back to joy in the blink of an eye. "In fact, let me reiterate to you: *you are alone.*"

The overseer strode over to the furnace, where he pulled a bit iron from its spot in the reheating chamber. He dipped the end into the furnace, gave it a twirl, and then pulled it back out. The end of the bit iron was now covered in a fist-sized lump of molten black godglass, glowing cherry red at the center. "You might know this from your studies," he said, "but fearglass has some unique properties. For one: it contains sorcery in its molten form, without any actual work—the only godglass that does. Axio, be a good boy and don't scream."

Before Thessa could react, he turned to Axio and smeared the honey-like molten fearglass across his arm. It made a sizzling sound, filling the room with the smell of burnt flesh. Axio responded immediately, clutching at the molten glass, burning his fingers as he let out a low keening moan. His eyes bugged out, his body trembling like he'd developed the worst kind of rheumatism. Thessa struggled against her escort, trying to pull away, to get to Axio and help him somehow, but they held her strong.

"You piece of . . ." she tried to shout, but a hand was slapped over her mouth. She was held in place, able to do nothing but stare as Axio's state grew worse.

He was tearing at his skin now, strips of it coming off under his fingernails, leaving his arm a bloody mess. He seemed to have gotten most of the molten fearglass off but he continued to get worse. The keening sound grew more desperate, and he looked wildly from Thessa to the overseer, as if begging for permission to scream. "Please," he sobbed, "it hurts so much. Please help me! Thessa, help!"

"No speaking," the overseer said. Axio's teeth clicked together as he continued to dig at himself. He ripped out whole chunks of flesh now, eyes wild, teeth bared in a painful grin. The overseer went on in a pleasant voice, watching Axio with a clinical expression. "Another interesting property of fearglass is that its effects are permanent. We're not sure why—perhaps because, in the process of augmenting one's fear, it also breaks the mind. Really quite remarkable. See, he's gotten it all off now but he's quite insane."

Axio foamed at the mouth, his whole body convulsing in waves. Thessa watched in horror, trying to speak through the hand covering her mouth, wishing she could do anything to soothe the poor boy. Suddenly, as if a candle had been extinguished, his eyes rolled into his head and he collapsed. He did not move.

As if by some signal, Thessa was free. She threw herself to the ground beside Axio. She touched his skin, her fingers coming away all bloody, and then pressed them against his neck. Nothing. He was dead.

"You're a monster," she whispered.

"I'm your monster now," Craftsman Magna said, coming to crouch across from her over Axio's body. He grinned at her wickedly, so damned pleased with himself. "Now, tell me about the schematics."

"Piss off."

She could see the rage building once more behind the overseer's eyes. He still held the bit iron with a large chunk of molten fearglass at the end, and he dipped it toward her dangerously, holding it just inches from her face. She could hear—very quietly—the resonance coming off it and, though the sorcery didn't affect her, she could feel the heat. He said, "I *will* break you. You're going to make me rich, or you're going to die painfully. Choose which."

Thessa felt dizzy, ready to collapse from terror and exhaustion. She looked down at Axio, then up at the overseer, desperately wanting to honor Kastora's and Axio's memories by spitting in the man's face. She couldn't bring herself to do it. The fear for her own life was too strong. She flinched away from the molten fearglass still hovering beside her face.

Something odd happened then. Behind the overseer, behind his two goons, the door to the furnace room slowly opened. A hand slipped inside, pressed briefly against the wall, showing her the double triangles of a glass-dancer sigil. The rest of him followed, and in a few moments Demir Grappo stood with his back to the closed door. He looked like an entirely different person than yesterday: gone was the jovial guild-family idiot. His expression was hard, the many scars on his face standing out against a squared chin. Thessa wondered if she'd snapped. Was she seeing things?

Demir was absolutely silent. He raised a hand slowly to his lips and surveyed the room, his eyes remaining on Axio for several moments. Faintly, Thessa thought she heard a cracking sound.

One of the enforcers suddenly frowned, reaching for the breast pocket of his jacket and removing a pair of spectacles. There was no glass left in the rims. His mouth opened in confusion as a dark, bloody stain began to spread across the front of his jacket. His whole body seemed to deflate and he collapsed to the floor with a thud. The other enforcer turned to her fallen companion just as something tiny seemed to tear itself out of the dead man's throat, shooting between them and punching through the center of her head. She jerked once as if she'd been shot, then fell.

This all happened in mere moments, and Thessa was still processing what she'd seen when the overseer turned to look at his enforcers. He leapt back, staring between Demir and the two dead enforcers. The color drained from his face, the haughtiness destroyed. Thessa would have found it incredibly satisfying if she didn't want to throw up at the sight of three dead bodies.

No one had told her that Demir Grappo was a glassdancer.

The overseer snatched at her, but she leapt away in reflex, throwing herself to the other side of the small room so that Demir was on her left and the overseer was on her right. The overseer swore and readjusted his grip on the bit iron, thrusting the molten fearglass toward Demir as if it were a spear. The room was completely silent. No one moved.

"Well?" Thessa blurted, gesturing at the overseer. She was immediately horrified by her own expectation that Demir should execute him just as he had the other two.

"Killing someone like him is complicated," Demir replied, not taking his eyes from the overseer. He was terrifyingly cold.

"Yeah," the overseer spat. His breathing was heavy, his eyes wild with fear. "Yeah, he can't kill me. I'm a guild-family member." He let go of the bit iron long enough to thrust his silic sigil at both of them. "There will be consequences."

"So now the negotiations start," Demir said.

"There won't be any negotiations," the overseer replied. He pointed at Thessa. "That is my prize. I don't know what you're playing at, but you're too late. She belongs to me." His eyes darted toward Thessa with a cold, hungry look. He really did think of her as a piece of machinery.

"That," Demir said, working his jaw, the fury tangibly emanating from him, "is a person." He took a step forward, then another. "That is a human being with friends and knowledge and hope and you are treating her like a toy. She's walking free of this place one way or another. You have ten seconds to give me an offer that's easier than me killing every enforcer in this compound to make it happen."

"You wouldn't!" Craftsman Magna hissed.

"Baby Montego is just outside. You don't think the two of us could level this place in an hour?"

Thessa had never actually met a glassdancer. She'd heard the stories—the way everyone talked about them as cold-eyed killers—but she'd never really believed them. In this particular moment, her own rage had subsided and she was *afraid*. There was little doubt that the man in front of her would do exactly as he'd just said.

"You're bluffing," the overseer said.

"He's not bluffing," Thessa said, suddenly overwhelmed by the desire not to see another corpse. "Give him an offer!"

Demir said, "Four seconds." The overseer trembled, his eyes darting around the furnace room in a facsimile of what had happened to Axio succumbing to the madness moments ago. "Two. One."

Without warning, the overseer threw the bit iron underhanded at Demir. It was not a hard throw, but the distance between them was slim and the action seemed to take Demir completely off guard. He let out an undignified grunt as the bit iron hit him. He stumbled backward, tripped, and fell. The overseer charged behind the throw, but watching Demir go down seemed to jostle loose that fury within Thessa once again. She put her shoulder down and hit the overseer hard from the side. He tripped over Axio's body, stumbled against the open furnace door. His hands sizzled as he tried to grab ahold of the furnace and he screamed.

Thessa's eyes were on Axio now. The poor, brave kid who'd fought a soldier to help her get away from Grent; who just wanted a trip to Ossa for some winter beer. She snatched up the bit iron, turned the hardening fearglass toward the overseer, and *shoved*. He went through the door of the furnace with another scream, and she leapt forward to slam the door shut. She threw the latch, listening to the thumping of his fists on the inside, accompanied by ever more desperate screams. Thessa tossed the bit iron aside.

"Demir! We have to go quickly, we . . ." She froze, staring as Demir pushed himself to his knees.

His face was pale, his limbs shaking like those of a rheumatic old man. It took Thessa only a moment to see that a jagged piece of fearglass had caught him across the collarbone, burning through his clothes and now jutting from his skin. "Demir?"

Demir's shaking grew more violent, nearly throwing him to the ground. He somehow managed to get to his feet, shoving one hand into his pocket. Thessa understood his purpose immediately and helped him search for a piece of calming skyglass, which she threaded through one of his piercings. He staggered toward the door. "Montego . . . big man . . . outside," he gasped.

Thessa threw herself out the door. The biggest man she'd ever seen stood halfway down the narrow alley, looking away from her, hands clasped behind his back. Of the guard that had been standing here minutes ago, there was no sign. "Are you Montego?" she called. "Demir needs your help!"

The big man turned and was hurrying toward her before she'd finished speaking. She led him back to the furnace room, where he immediately rushed to Demir's side, picking him up with one massive arm. He surveyed the scene for a moment. "This is not good," he rumbled.

"No . . . shit," Demir wheezed.

"What has happened to him?" Montego asked.

She took a deep breath, wincing to herself, meeting Demir's eyes. There was pain there; the kind of horrified deep suffering she'd seen on the faces of people who'd survived terrible wars. Though he had stopped trembling with the application of skyglass, there was froth at his mouth and his skin was deathly pale.

"Molten fearglass," she told Montego, gesturing at the black, glassy spot burned through his jacket and the jagged piece of hot glass sticking out of his skin just above the collarbone. She had never made fearglass, for obvious reasons, but she'd read several books on it during her course of studies. The fact that Demir was still able to speak at all was incredible. "Did you hear the screams?" she asked. She could still hear the subdued sound of movement from within the furnace.

"Faintly," Montego replied. "I doubt anyone else did."

"Good. Give me those pincers," Thessa ordered. She shoved all her fear and anger and disgust into one corner of her mind and slammed the door on it, allowing her analytical brain to take control of her body. There wasn't a moment to lose. "There should be some water in that bucket there under the workbench. Dampen a handkerchief."

Montego obliged, and she had him hold Demir up while she positioned herself in front of him. "I'm sorry," she told Demir, "but this is going to hurt." Not wasting another moment, she used the pincers to pluck the fearglass from his skin, trying to ignore the sharp inhale from Demir. Skin came away with it, white and cooked. She tossed the piece of fearglass aside.

"Handkerchief," she ordered, taking the wet handkerchief from Montego and using it to stanch the blood.

"Is that it?" Montego asked. "Can we give him cureglass and milkglass and let him walk it off? Demir, do you understand me?"

Demir's eyes left Thessa's face long enough to move toward Montego. There was more coherence there now, but only just. "Go. Rot. Yourself."

"Does that mean he's better?" Montego asked, wringing his hands in a way that seemed very un-murder-giant-like.

"Unfortunately no," Thessa said, pressing on the compress gently. "Fearglass is different from most godglass—it's why it's so dangerous. It leaves an imprint on the mind, even after it's gone. It's not nearly as bad as if he were exposed to a completed piece, but it's still bad."

Understanding blossomed into horror on Montego's face. "This is permanent?"

"Unless we undo it." Thessa chewed on the inside of her cheek. Her mind rushed through all the texts that Kastora had made her read years ago, trying to remember all the bits and pieces. "I need a glassworks." She looked around and almost laughed. "But not this one."

Demir made an awful sucking noise, and she looked down to find him clearly attempting to speak. She gently moved his head a little to the right, and he said, "Prosotsi. Wagonside."

"I was thinking the same thing," Montego replied.

Thessa looked between them. "I don't understand. Prosotsi is a guild-family, right?"

"Yes," Montego explained. "Allies of the Grappo. Wagonside is a small but well-stocked glassworks. It belongs to someone we can trust. We're about an hour away, if we go quickly."

"How will we get out of here?" Thessa asked, glancing sidelong at Demir. He was trembling again, so badly that she could barely keep him upright, foam leaking out of the corner of his mouth. To her surprise he seemed to be fighting it, his hands curled tightly into fists, momentary flashes of comprehension entering his eyes. She could not understand why he was still upright. Axio had gotten much less on him and was dead by this time.

Montego remained silent for another moment, then nodded to himself. "Leave that to me, but you must trust me."

"What does that mean?" Thessa asked, recoiling.

Montego threw himself into action without answering. He jerked open the door to the furnace. Smoke billowed out into the room, along with the powerful scent of burnt hair and flesh. Thessa thought she saw a charred hand and turned her face away while Montego plucked out a burning brand. He began to set the flame against everything in the room: the cork baffling, the crate, the clothes of the enforcers. The smoke became overwhelming in moments.

Thessa was just about to ask what she could do to help when he snatched up a canvas tarpaulin from beneath the crate in the corner. He met her eyes, his face solemn. "Absolute silence," he said.

"What . . ." she began, but he threw the tarpaulin over her head. Before she could consider another thing, she felt herself snatched up as if she were light as a babe and tossed across Montego's shoulder. She felt Demir's body draped over her own and stifled a groan at the weight of it.

There was a thump, the rush of cool air, and Montego bellowed, "There's been a terrible accident! Fire, fire!" They pounded along at a blistering speed, not bothering to stop as they passed a startled enforcer captain shouting questions after Montego. Montego simply yelled in return, "One of your damned guards went mad! Filur has been murdered and Demir is badly injured. Get that fire out!"

Thessa felt herself lifted once more and practically hurled through the air, landing hard, still wrapped in the tarpaulin. She recognized the bouncing squeak of carriage springs but dared not move.

"Out of my way if you want to keep your lives, you bloody wretches!" Montego bellowed. The carriage suddenly jerked into motion, and Thessa soon found herself bouncing along violently. She got up the courage to extract herself from the tarpaulin. She was lying on the floor of a carriage next to Demir, Montego on the bench above them, and the walls of the prison compound rapidly disappearing out the window.

She let out a little gasp. She was free of that place, but her relief was short-lived. Demir's eyes rolled up into the back of his head. She adjusted herself into a sitting position on the floor of the carriage and pulled Demir's head into her lap. She did not know if he had any comprehension left. Did he understand where he was, or who held him? She pressed her palms against his cheeks, whispering softly, hoping that it helped to comfort his mind.

She was no longer thinking about the cold killer she'd seen in his eyes, but about what he'd said to the overseer: that she was a person, and she would walk free of that place no matter what. He'd fulfilled that promise.

If they did not hurry, she would lose the only friend she had left in the world.

24

Thessa cradled Demir's head in her lap, whispering a constant stream of re-assurances while she tried to keep him from swallowing his tongue. An extra piece of calming skyglass from Montego seemed to have helped slow the advance of the madness.

An eternity seemed to pass before their carriage stopped. Montego threw open the door and lifted Demir carefully into his arms. They were in a small village on the windswept slope, surrounded by farmland for miles. A workshop, rambling but cozy-looking, with two smokestacks coming off the top, sat directly in the center of the village. Montego kicked open the door, startling a number of siliceers, bellowing at the top of his voice.

"Everyone out! Clear the furnaces! You, make sure there's plenty of wood ready to stoke the fires. You, find me Craftsman Prosotsi!"

Thessa followed on Montego's heels, surprised to see that he was, apparently, known here. Despite the initial confusion, the three siliceers followed his instructions quickly, removing their current projects from the workbenches and pulling crucibles of molten cindersand out of the furnace to make room for new ones. Thessa did not wait for permission, throwing herself into the workshop with a siliceer's eye, noting the layout of the tools and quickly finding the stores of cindersand—accompanied by notes explaining where each bag of sand had been quarried—and locating rows of small jars containing the needed impurities.

She plucked them out, one by one, muttering under her breath. "Gold, copper, selenium. Ah, manganese. Put him someplace comfortable. Wait! We should talk to him while I work. Put a blanket on that workbench there, then lay him down. Keep him focused. It's like . . ." She snapped her fingers, trying to remember bits of her old instruction books. "Like staying awake in the cold, except we risk his mind breaking from the fear."

As quickly as she dared, she mixed cindersand with tiny amounts of each impurity, then used long tongs to set each crucible into the heat of the furnace. Once that was done, she walked around the workshop one more time to make sure she knew where every tool was, and that she would not trip on anything in the unfamiliar space. She then went to Demir's side, where Montego was talking to him in a soothing voice.

"Can you understand us?" Thessa asked, just to make sure he hadn't slipped away since he last spoke to her.

Demir's eyes left Montego and traveled to her. There was a long moment of quiet, the corners of Demir's eyes wrinkling as if he was making an enormous mental effort. "Please tell. Montego. To stop talking. To me like. A child." There was a hint of a smile at the end of this, and Thessa let out a relieved sigh.

"Good, good."

One of the Prosotsi siliceers appeared in the doorway, tiptoeing over to Montego and whispering, though not quietly enough, "Craftsman Prosotsi left for Ossa earlier today. We don't expect him back for several hours. Are you sure we should allow a stranger the run of the glassworks?"

"Do *you* know how to counter the effects of fearglass?" Thessa demanded.

The Prosotsi siliceer glanced at Demir's upper chest, where the now-bloody handkerchief was still lying over the wound. "Ah," he said. "No, I don't. Please continue. Craftsman Prosotsi would put everything at Master Demir and Master Montego's disposal."

"Get clean linens for his wound," Montego ordered. "And the best sample of cureglass you have on hand. Go on!"

Once he'd gone, Thessa turned her attention back to Demir. She leaned over him, looking in one eye, then the other, not entirely sure what she was looking for. He was still wearing both his own and Montego's skyglass. "How do you feel?"

"Like. I am. Drowning."

"Better or worse than before?"

Demir seemed to consider this for several moments, his eyes going in and out of focus. "The water is. Not. As deep? But I fear. Everything. I can hear them screaming. The civilians. I can see that little girl's face." Tears pooled in his eyes, rolling down the side of his face when he blinked.

Thessa didn't know what he was going on about. "You can fight the fear," Thessa told him, taking his hand and squeezing it. To her delight, he had the strength to squeeze back. "Montego is here, and he is your friend. *I'm* your friend. Don't let the fear pull you into madness. I'm working on . . .

244 · BRIAN McCLELLAN

I'm working on a way to bring you out of this. I can't promise it'll work, but—" She flinched, wishing immediately she hadn't said that. "But I'll do my best."

Demir closed his eyes, and did not open them again until Montego gave him a little shake. "It is. Exhausting," he said haltingly. "To be so. Scared. Again."

Again. Had he dealt with fearglass before? Was that how he had survived it for so long? "It's okay," Thessa said, squeezing his hand harder. "That's what fearglass does. It makes you more scared than you've ever been in your life. It makes your body want to flee, but it doesn't know to where. It does all of this until your heart gives out or your mind breaks. If we can prevent both of those things from happening, then . . . What's so funny?"

Demir had begun to tremble, letting out a little wheezing laugh. He looked at Montego for a long minute, then back to Thessa. Once she had his attention, she moved closer. "What's so funny?" she repeated.

"Still not as. Bad. As . . ." He trailed off, not finishing, his eyes growing unfocused once more. He flinched. "Okay. Maybe a little. Worse."

"Don't talk if it hurts. But stay focused on one of us." Thessa left him long enough to check the crucibles in the furnace. They were almost melted. She gave each a stir with a clean rod, then returned to Demir's side. She took another deep breath, trying to maintain her own calm, preparing herself for what was to come. She glanced up to see that Montego was watching her sharply.

"Have you done this before?" he asked quietly.

She shook her head. "I know the theories, but I'm about to attempt a quadruple braiding in a furnace I've never worked before, using firewood and cindersand whose origins I cannot verify myself. This is master-level work and the stake is only the life of the person who just saved me from a fate worse than death. Is he . . . is he laughing again?"

On the workbench between them, Demir was making that rasping, wheezing, chuckling sound.

"He has a very morbid sense of humor," Montego said.

"I hope it keeps him from dying or going insane before we can fix this. If," she added under her breath, "we *can* fix this." A thought occurred to her, and she tilted her head at Montego. "I'm sorry, but this has all gone so damned fast. Are you Baby Montego?"

"You recognize me?"

"I only surmised from the name. I don't follow cudgeling myself, but my master used to talk about you all the time. He was very proud to have seen your last fight."

Montego adjusted the collar of his jacket, looking supremely pleased with himself. "She's heard of me, Demir," he said, slapping his friend none-too-gently on the leg.

Demir let out a pained moan. "Needy. Prick."

Thessa checked the crucibles, then turned back to Montego and Demir. "It's time."

She steeled herself for a few moments, and then leapt into her work. She started with molten cindersand for cureglass, rolling out a curved piece just over an inch long and no thicker than a heavy wire. The resonance eluded her, and she redid it until the tiny piece of glass was too stiff to work. She discarded it and started with another. It took her three tries before she got one she was happy with, and let it harden for several minutes while she began to work with the museglass, curling it around the center cureglass piece. It miraculously worked on the first attempt, but the resonance did not take when she tried to add shackleglass. She discarded it all and started again.

She talked as she worked, explaining each step, letting her mouth run in an attempt to calm her nerves. "I know this has been done before, even if I haven't done it myself," she told them. "You have cureglass for a core—we're trying to heal him after all—and wrapped around that is museglass, witglass, and shackleglass. The museglass and shackleglass are both to make his mind more malleable; to accept the healing that we're trying to get in there. The witglass helps the sorcery target the mind." She winced as she made a mistake, and started over from the beginning.

"This is all theory, of course. We know that it *does* work, but we can only conjecture as to the how or why. There is a division among siliceers. Some claim that what we do is a science. Some claim that it is an art. They are both right. I've seen siliceers without a drop of logic in their minds produce fantastic works of high-resonance godglass using the very worst ingredients. Myself—well, I'm not much of an artist, but if you tell me exactly what I'm working with and exactly what I'm trying to accomplish, I will get there. Eventually."

She worked the bellows for the godglass funnel, reheating her pieces again and again as needed. Her leg eventually grew numb. She switched legs, then ordered one of the apprentices to come and work the bellows for her.

She started over. Then she started over again. She barely noticed the siliceer that brought cureglass for Demir's wounds. The arrival of the owner of the glassworks was similarly ignored. Montego took him aside, and she was not interrupted. Minutes passed, and then hours. She kept her head bent, listening to the resonance of the sorceries as she attempted to mold four pieces of godglass into one. It was, she reflected in a moment of clarity, like a musician trying to put together notes to find the right sound.

Darkness fell, the workshop lit by gas lanterns and the furnace that Prosotsi siliceers continued to stoke without questions. At one point the owner of the glassworks stood and watched her for almost an hour. He did not say anything.

She mixed more cureglass, throwing away her dozens of mistakes.

She did not know what time it was when the resonances finally matched up. At first she thought she had made a mistake; that she had managed only to braid three of the godglasses together without losing their resonance. But holding the curved, still-warm piece of glass at arm's length she could see that it had all four together, and they hummed powerfully in her fingertips. She hurried over to Demir.

Montego rested his head on the workbench by Demir's shoulder, his body slumped with exhaustion, still whispering in Demir's ear in a gentle tone. Demir's eyes were barely open, his breathing rasping and labored. Thessa turned up the lantern above them and moved a recently changed wet compress off Demir's chest. The medium-resonance cureglass supplied by the Prosotsi siliceers had done an incredible job—the burn still looked nasty, but like it had already had a week to heal.

Demir's eyes focused on her briefly as she stood above him. He made a sound that definitely had a question mark at the end.

"High-resonance braided godglass," she told him. "I don't know if it'll work as intended, but . . ." She did not finish, instead pushing the godglass between his lips, using her opposite hand to work his jaw open so that he held the godglass between his teeth. "Keep it in place, but do not bite down. I don't want to have to pick broken godglass out of your mouth."

Demir did as instructed. Thessa searched the workbenches until she found a pocket watch left by one of the siliceers. She checked the time.

It was almost six in the morning. Without rest, food, or drink, she had worked the furnace for twenty hours straight. She shook the thought from her mind and focused on the second hand. One eye on the watch, she looked at Demir's wound. For a moment, she could not tell if anything was happening. Then, slowly but definitely, the burn began to knit itself. Flesh grew where the old had come away with the fearglass. New skin, pinkish and puckered, slowly knit together, closing over the burn.

As the sorcery worked, she could *see* the glassrot scales growing on his chest. They shimmered in the gaslight, becoming more defined with each passing second. She wiped them away with the brush of her hand, but they grew back in moments. A minute passed. A minute and a half. Two minutes.

Once the pocket watch marked that two and a half minutes had passed, Thessa snatched the godglass from between Demir's teeth and found a cork-lined box to put it in. She returned to his side, running her fingers across the pink-and-white scar that had only minutes ago been a terrible burn. Demir's eyes were closed, but his breathing was now steady. She checked his pulse.

It was normal.

His lips moved imperceptibly, and Thessa bent to hear him.

"I am saved," he whispered.

Thessa felt a great tension leave her body. She might have collapsed if she were not already leaning on the workbench. She rested her head against Demir's bare chest for a moment and became aware that every sinew of her body hurt. Not bothering to remove her heavy boots or apron, she rolled onto the workbench next to Demir, closed her eyes, and slept.

25

Idrian received an eight-hour leave of absence—not difficult during the confusion of the entire Foreign Legion pulling out of Grent—to rush into Ossa and deliver the cinderite to the Hyacinth Hotel. The concierge told him that Demir was not available, but allowed him to take the cinderite directly to Demir's office, where he promised that the hotel master-at-arms would keep it under her personal protection. Idrian left disquieted, wishing he could have handed it to Demir directly. It was enough. It had to be. An itch had started right behind his godglass eye that told him a battle was brewing, and sooner than he would have liked.

He returned to the Foreign Legion in late afternoon, far out beyond the western suburbs of Ossa where all three brigades had moved their strength into the Copper Hills. It was rolling farmland, barren for the winter, with plenty of defensible positions and hilltops for artillery batteries.

It was on one such hilltop on the right flank of the army that Idrian found the Ironhorns. Soldiers and engineers alike had out their short military shovels, digging trenches and putting palisades into place to protect seven heavy cannons and four mortars while the artillery crews went through last-minute drills to make sure both they and their weapons were in top order. The entire region was crawling with soldiers and support staff—even backup companies of National Guard from the city. Glassdancers wandered the hillside, getting a feel for the slopes and the winds.

As much as Idrian preferred being in the middle of the action, he could see the relief on the faces of his compatriots. In the city they were on the front line, capturing bridges, erecting barricades, and throwing grenades. Here on the open battlefield, engineers were less useful in combat. Their privilege was manual labor under Mika's expert gaze, and most of them would be glad of it.

Let the regular infantry hold the front line for a change. Idrian and the Ironhorns would protect the artillery.

"How are we looking?" Idrian asked, striding into the camp, where Tadeas and Mika were having a heated discussion underneath a canvas pavilion.

Tadeas looked toward Idrian, giving Mika the chance to flip a rude gesture at his shoulder.

"I saw that," Tadeas snapped. To Idrian he replied, "Most everyone has pulled out of Grent. We've got a solid defensive position here—if Kerite tries to go around us, she'll lose at least a week on the march."

"Stavri doesn't want to go on the offensive?"

"He doesn't see the need to, and for once I agree with him. Let Kerite come to us."

"How long do we have?"

"If she contests us straight on? Two days. If she decides to juke around it could be longer."

"I wager it'll be sooner rather than later."

"Your eye itching again?"

Idrian nodded.

"Shit," Tadeas replied. "It's a weird sixth sense, but it's never steered us wrong before. Better keep your engineers working through the night, Mika."

Mika rolled her eyes. "Glassdamnit. Fine, but I'm going to press-gang some of those National Guard into helping us. Asshole policemen ordered out here to play soldier, they're going to get their hands dirty."

"I'll send a messenger to the nearest regiment," Tadeas told her.

Idrian climbed the hill a few dozen feet to look around, noting the best approaches for enemy soldiers trying to take the artillery battery. Once the fighting began, he'd need to focus his own efforts on those spaces. A breacher was most effective on offense, but that didn't mean he couldn't plug defensive holes when needed.

He returned to Tadeas, who'd resumed his previous argument with Mika.

"I want mines here, here, and here," Tadeas insisted, pointing at the partially finished defenses.

"And I'm telling you they'll be a waste over there," Mika replied hotly. "Focus them right there, and each mine will be worth two more casualties on average, I stake my reputation on it."

"You have a reputation other than the insane explosives woman?" Idrian asked. When Mika whirled on him he waved her off. "Tadeas, you know better than to argue with Mika. Mines are her territory."

Tadeas snorted and turned to one side to spit. "Fine. Go on, make sure the ditches are deep enough." He aimed a kick at Mika's backside as she scurried away, cackling victoriously.

Idrian sank into Tadeas's camp chair and pressed on his godglass eye. Somewhere, as if from over the next hill, he could hear a child's laughter. It was starting to get real old, and the fact that he knew it wasn't real didn't help things. "You think Kerite has a chance of unseating us?"

Tadeas sucked hard on his teeth. "She's never lost a battle. At least that's what the rumors say. She's always been very good at her own publicity." He made a dismissive gesture. "General Stavri is confident that we'll crush any attack she makes."

"What are we facing?"

"Kerite's Drakes—about ten thousand infantry, with breachers and glass-dancers—as well as whatever the Grent lend her for the battle. I think . . . I think we'll be okay."

Idrian had known Tadeas long enough to see through the uncertainty. He also knew better than to press him. Forcing him to talk about his nerves wasn't going to help either of them. As he watched Tadeas continue to pace, Braileer approached from down the hill. The armorer was carrying Idrian's shield, and presented it to him proudly.

"I finally got a chance to work a forge for a few hours, sir," Braileer said. "I popped the godglass plates off and hammered out those deep gouges here and here. The hammerglass is back in place and doesn't have that wobble you've been carrying around."

Idrian inspected the work. It wasn't the best he'd ever seen, but it was a damn sight better than the mending Braileer did a couple of days ago. "That wobble was getting on my nerves. Well done."

Braileer beamed. "I was thinking about getting my fiddle out tonight, sir. Is that allowed?"

"Tad, do we have keep-quiet order in place?"

Tadeas shook his head, and Idrian nodded at Braileer. "It'll help with morale. Go ahead."

"One other thing, sir," Braileer said. "Two women came around earlier. A soldier and an engineer."

"Squeaks and Fenny?" Idrian guessed.

"That's them, sir. They brought you these. A thank-you for saving Squeaks from that rubble."

Idrian reached out and took a pair of calfskin gloves. To his surprise they were of the highest quality, of the kind you might find in the pocket of an officer from a rich guild-family. "I can't take these," he said. "Must have cost them two weeks' wages. Besides, there were others helping dig that night, yourself included." He tried to hand them back.

"The taller one—Squeaks, I think—said you'd say that. No disrespect meant, sir, I'm just quoting her, but she said if you tried to refuse that you could get stuffed. She made them herself."

Idrian rubbed the calfskin between his fingers and noted that the distant laughter had disappeared. The symptoms of his madness always did in moments like these. He slid one onto his hand. It fit like . . . well, like a glove. "Skip my dinner tonight, Braileer, and go get out your fiddle. The Ironhorns could use some fun before a battle."

"Yes, sir!"

Idrian watched Braileer hurry back down the hill and turned to find Tadeas watching him. Idrian said, "Decades in this business of killing, and the people can still surprise you."

"That's why you do it," Tadeas responded.

Idrian looked down at the calfskin gloves. "I do it because I sold my soul to the Foreign Legion to get out of the Marnish highlands. I keep doing it because the Foreign Legion funded Kastora's work on my eye," he answered, touching the eye gently.

"Bah. That might be why you got started, but I still don't believe you're going to walk once you hand in your debt marker. You've got just a few weeks left, right?"

"Nineteen days," Idrian replied. "And you bet your ass I'm going to walk." He could feel the freedom as if it were inches away, just beyond his touch. "I'm going to take my marching bonus and I'm going to move out to the provinces where the land is cheap and the wine is cheaper and I'm going to stare at a vineyard until I grow old and die." That was the plan, anyway. His failing godglass eye certainly complicated things.

"You going to work that vineyard?" Tadeas asked.

Idrian scratched at his cheek. "I seem to remember you offering to fund the labor if I buy the land."

"I was hoping you'd forgotten that."

"Don't want to retire?" Idrian asked.

"Nah, I'm just cheap. Maybe I'll ask my nephew for a loan. I know the kind of bullshit grifting he was up to out in the provinces and he's rich as piss." Tadeas seemed to notice for the first time that Idrian had taken his chair. He let out a sigh. "How are you feeling?"

"Still sore from that run into the palace," Idrian admitted.

"I still can't believe you escaped by climbing up the chimney."

"Me neither. I don't think I've ever used most of those muscles before." Idrian leaned forward to rub his shins. "I should have stopped for a massage while I was in Ossa."

"You delivered the package?"

"Breenen had me leave it in Demir's office. I didn't like it, but I didn't have much of a choice."

"Breenen is a good egg. He'll make sure it's safe. Did you run into the Hyacinth master-at-arms? She's very good-looking."

"You've told me about her. Kirkovik's granddaughter, right?" Idrian shook his head. "Far too young for me." He narrowed his eyes at Tadeas's considering look. "Or you."

"How dare you?" Tadeas replied. "Younger women find me a fantastic companion."

"Yeah, right up until your monthly wages run out. When's the last time you saw someone your own age?"

"The last time Adriana tried to make a match for me," Tadeas said wistfully. "I think that was . . . six years ago? She was a Plagni. Voice like a drill sergeant, legs as big around as tree trunks." His eyes wandered to the clouds above them and he added softly, just loud enough for Idrian to hear, "I'm going to miss Adri trying to get me married."

Idrian shook his head. Tadeas had been married three times during the course of their friendship, and every one of those marriages had ended badly. He'd known plenty of women himself, but never a marriage. Career soldiers weren't meant for it. Their lives were too dangerous, their workplace too distant. The only constant relationship in Tadeas's life during all that time—outside of the military—was Adriana. How would he deal with that now that she was gone?

It was a question for another day. Tadeas was like Idrian, in that he always left his grieving until the end of a campaign. Unhealthy, perhaps, but necessary. Otherwise it would get in the way of him being a good commanding officer.

"Maybe Demir will take over that torch," Idrian suggested. "Start looking to pair you with a good woman."

"Hah! Maybe he will. He's the patriarch now. I'll have to keep my eyes peeled. Adriana always tried to bully me into a marriage. Demir will be tricky about it, mark my words. I'll go to a party and wake up married to a Vorcien." He sighed and turned to Idrian. "Forgot to tell you something," he said, pulling a sour face.

Idrian raised an eyebrow. That was Tadeas's "bad news" expression.

Tadeas went on, "One of General Stavri's staff swung by right after we arrived this afternoon. He asked some very pointed questions about what we were shooting at last night, and where *you* were at the time. Seems one of our spies heard that you were spotted stealing from the ducal palace."

Idrian stiffened. "Did they say what I stole?"

"Nobody knows," Tadeas said with the shake of his head. "Seems that fire you started destroyed a pretty significant swath of the palace, including a lot of the art hidden in the undercroft."

"Oh." Idrian scowled. He felt bad about that, he really did. What was that overseer's name, back at his old job at the Ossan Museum? He couldn't recall, but he could only imagine the fury if she ever found out what he'd done. How many millions' worth of art had he ruined in a single night? "I didn't mean to. Well, I did mean to set the fire. I was in a tight spot. I didn't mean to destroy the art."

"Eh. They'll make new art." Tadeas shrugged. "The fact is, General Stavri knew something was up and at the moment is pretty convinced that you were playing common thief with the duke's art collection. The staff member that came by implied that he wants a cut."

Idrian scoffed. Of course he wanted a cut. Glassdamned corrupt Ossans. "A cut of nothing."

"I don't think they'll buy that."

"What did you tell him?"

"That we have no idea what he's talking about and we didn't shoot at anything and Idrian Sepulki was in fact visiting his father using a two-day pass that I gave him myself. Mika helped me forge the paperwork, and I briefed your new armorer on what to say and do if anyone asked him any questions."

"I hate my father. He is the last person in all of Ossa I would visit on a two-day pass."

"Stavri doesn't need to know that. Regardless, maybe we should have Demir supply a bribe for the good general just to get him off our backs."

Idrian considered this for a moment before shaking his head. "I don't want Demir's name mentioned. If any of that leads back to him, people with more clout than Stavri might start asking questions. Let's stick with your story and deny everything."

"You sure?" Tadeas gave him a look, clearly wanting to know just why a piece of cinderite would cause so much interest.

"I'm sure," Idrian answered. "No need to involve Demir unless absolutely necessary."

"As you say it."

"Thanks. I appreciate you covering for me."

"No problem. Oh, and Mika says you owe her a bottle of twenty-year Fletchling."

Idrian sat up and looked toward where he could see Mika overseeing the placement of her mines. "For what?"

"My silence to Stavri is free. Hers isn't."

"Damned snitch. Next time you see your nephew, tell him he owes me a twenty-year Fletchling. I won't use his name, but I'm not gonna pay his debts either."

"Fair."

Their conversation was interrupted by the sound of galloping hooves. Idrian got to his feet, his legs tightening up instantly, and tried to see where the sound was coming from. When he couldn't he leaned over to rub at his shins again, and by the time he stood there was a messenger riding hard in their direction. The messenger approached the pavilion and snapped a salute from horseback.

"Major Grappo?" he asked.

"That's me," Tadeas replied.

"Word from General Stavri. Kerite's Drakes are already on the move, and they're headed straight toward us, along with Grent reinforcements from the city. You have forty-eight hours at best until contact, but the General wants the hilltop secured in twenty-four."

"Just twenty-four hours?" Idrian exclaimed, his heart falling. That was *not* enough time to prepare for a battle.

"Correct. General Stavri has cut off all requests for extra help. What you have is what you get. Make it work!" The messenger shouted the last sentence over his shoulder, already riding down the hill toward the infantry battalion positioned just a few hundred yards below them.

Idrian watched him go before exchanging a worried look with Tadeas. "Can we be ready for her in time?" he asked.

"We'll do the best we can. Valient! Double rations for dinner, and round up a shitload of torches. We're working through the night!"

A litany of curses was the reply, from Valient, Mika, and several dozen engineers within earshot.

Idrian pressed on his godglass eye. He'd hoped to spend the next two days flat on his back, nose buried in a book, so that his body was in top shape to defend the Ironhorns. No such luck, he supposed. "Get me a shovel," he told Tadeas, "and some good forgeglass. They're gonna need help to finish these fortifications in time."

26

Demir stood in the furnace room of the Wagonside Glassworks, staring into a cork-lined box that lay open before him. The thumb-sized piece of god-glass inside was like nothing he'd ever seen: a core of red cureglass wrapped tightly with peach-colored museglass and then covered with an intricate, knot-like pattern of purple witglass and light green shackleglass. It was a beautiful piece, even aside from the resonance, which was so powerful that he could hear it faintly from almost two feet away.

Craftsman Jona Prosotsi stood next to Demir, a diminutive man in his mid-fifties with a large bald spot in the middle of a head of graying hair and squirrelly little hands clasped perpetually over a potbelly. A distant cousin, he had always been a good friend of the Grappo. Demir would have to think of a way to repay him for the secrecy and use of his glassworks.

Jona cleared his throat and reached out gently to close the box. The distant hum of the sorcery disappeared immediately, and Demir let himself take a deep, cleansing breath.

"It's a master-level piece, isn't it?" Demir asked.

Jona hesitated. "Is there something above master?" Demir glanced at Jona sharply, but the little craftsman just shook his head with a half smile. "I joke. Kind of."

"Is she really that good?"

"You can see the evidence in front of you. She did in twenty hours of trial and error what most masters would take weeks to accomplish. That kind of skill is once-in-a-lifetime. Not sustainable, of course. She would kill herself working like that all the time. But the fact she's even capable is . . . well, no wonder Kastora took her as his protégé."

"I'll be damned," Demir breathed. He reached out to touch the box, thinking to look at that piece again, but let his arm fall away. No need to expose himself to the risk of more severe glassrot.

"You'll be alive, thanks to her," Jona pointed out. "How do you feel?"

Demir shook himself out of his reverie and glanced about the workshop. The furnace burned hot but the reheating chambers had gone out, the assistants given the day off. Montego had gone into Ossa to see if there would be any fallout from what transpired at the Ivory Forest Glassworks. Demir himself had been up for less than an hour, spending most of that time just trying to get his head about him. It was early morning. From the time he was hit with fearglass he'd lost almost two days.

"Did you bring me a mirror?" Demir asked, ignoring Jona's question.

Jona produced a small face-painting mirror from his pocket. Demir took the mirror, pulling down his tunic to look at the scar left by the fearglass. There was a finger-length purple discoloration, looking like little more than a birthmark. Even glancing at the spot caused him mental distress, a jolt of fear stabbing through his gut, but he forced himself to stare at it until the fear had left. His hand, he realized while looking at the mirror, was trembling.

He gave the mirror back.

He was a man who knew scars, both mental and physical. This experience would leave him with both, but . . . he could not fathom how those mental scars would affect him. The last time he'd gone through anything that caused him this much anguish, he'd fled to the provinces for nine years of self-banishment. For the last hour he'd waited for a new crack to form in his mind—for his faculties to crumble and his confidence to shatter. He kept expecting himself to wind up on the floor, weeping and wailing like an injured child.

Instead he felt, dare he even think it, better than before? He turned his thoughts to Thessa and his regrets about everything that had happened. He had wanted to get her out of there without violence. He hadn't wanted her to see him as a glassdancer first, and yet that was exactly what had happened.

"I'm going to check on our guest," he told Jona.

⁊　⁊　⁊

Thessa knelt in the corner of the Wagonside omnichapel, surrounded by shrines dedicated to dozens of different gods, spirits, and ancestors. Omnichapels like this were a common fixture throughout both Ossa and Grent—rather than being affiliated with any of the hundreds of religions practiced by Ossans and provincials, they provided a quiet place for individual worship. Considering her parents' profession, she'd spent a lot of time in places like this.

It seemed like a good spot to remember Axio and Master Kastora, even for just a moment, and Jona Prosotsi had been kind enough to lend her a few pennies for candles.

She watched two of the candles burn down in front of a shrine to Kloor, Purnian god of the dead. He seemed as good a choice as any, and his little shrine was right next to Renn's, before which she placed the third candle. Whether or not Renn was real she did not know, but it seemed like Thessa owed her something. For prayers, she found herself at a loss. Instead she tried to fixate on memories: Kastora showing her how to roll cureglass. Axio trying to steal a kiss during a lesson. Silly things. Happy things.

A sound behind her brought her head up, and she turned to find Demir standing just inside the door, hands clasped behind his back. He was well-dressed, his hair combed and face freshly shaved. The sight of him looking so formal caused her to flinch. He was her rescuer, but she knew nothing about him. During her work on the fearglass countermeasure she had only focused on saving the life of the man who saved hers, but now she couldn't help but wonder who he was. Another guild-family fop; rich, powerful, and arrogant. A glassdancer too, which amplified all three of those traits.

And yet—in the heat of that rescue, he'd denied taking her as some sort of prize. He saw her as a person, rather than a thing, and that seemed important. There was so much hate in her heart right now for Ossa. They'd murdered Kastora, Axio, even Ekhi. They'd killed and stolen and tried to enslave her. Could she bring herself to see *him* as a person too, rather than just an extension of the system that had destroyed her life?

She had to try.

"You're standing," she said, genuinely relieved. "You're walking!" Even after she finished her work yesterday morning she couldn't have been sure if the godglass would restore him completely.

"Thanks to you," he replied softly.

Thessa raised both eyebrows. "Me? Well, I suppose. But you were in that situation because of me. It seemed like the least I could do."

Demir's expression was vaguely bemused, but she could still see exhaustion in his eyes. His skin was pallid, his smile pained. "Are you religious?" he asked.

"Me? No, I . . ." It seemed like a strange question until she remembered where she was. "Right. The candles. Master Kastora wasn't religious but his late wife was. I figured I should light one for him and Axio."

"Axio was the young man the overseer killed?"

Thessa nodded, glancing down at the spent candles. Demir walked over to join her. Thessa had met a lot of guild-family members as Kastora's protégé, and he held himself the same way: a certain rigidity, his chin raised. And yet he didn't look *over* her head, like she was below him, but met her eye. Interesting. There were other differences that she noted immediately. His skin was too cracked from the sun, too many scars on his arms. He'd seen the world, rather than just the insides of estates and comfortable carriages. Did that reflect well on him? She wouldn't know until some time had passed.

A lot reflected well on him, but it all seemed to hide in the shadow of something else: he was a glassdancer. He'd killed without hesitation in order to free her, and he'd been ready to kill more. That was a lot to consider when looking a man in the eyes. Confusing too, for at this exact moment she didn't feel like she was looking at a glassdancer. He was wearing a glove over his left hand to cover the sigil, and his expression was soft.

She did feel her position acutely. Kastora was dead. She couldn't go home to her own country. She was a siliceer without a glassworks, and it brought to mind one of Kastora's lessons: *Always be on the lookout for a patron. Perhaps a friend, perhaps even a lover, but someone you can depend on. They'll need your skills. You'll need their money. Do not let the latter make you forget about the former.*

Why had Demir rescued her, she wondered? Did he need her skills? Did he know about the phoenix channel, whose schematics she'd stuffed back in her boot? Was he planning on offering patronage? She could do worse than a guild-family patriarch, even one as young as he. A guild-family patriarch *and* a glassdancer. Frightening, but damned impressive. "May I?" Thessa lifted a hand to his collarbone.

"Go ahead."

She pulled aside the collar of his tunic and examined his scar clinically, then lifted her gaze to look deep into his eyes. Definitely still some pain there. Was that new? Or had it always been there? He gave her the distinct impression of a man haunted by . . . something. But perhaps she was reading too much into his face.

She tried to think back on her studies, and the checklist one was supposed to go over if one was exposed to fearglass. "You're very pale," Thessa commented. "The scar is small. Your pupils appear normal." She pressed two fingers to his throat. "Your pulse is normal." She let out a little sigh of relief. Probably best not to admit just how little confidence she'd had that the godglass would work. She could certainly be proud of herself, though.

Demir returned her examination, searching her face for something only he knew. He finally said, "Jona and I looked at the piece you made. He said it was master-level work. Far better than he could have done."

Thessa felt her cheeks grow warm. "That's kind of him to say." Thessa knew the piece was master-level. Kastora himself would have been proud of it. "We haven't met properly," she said, extending her hand. "I'm Thessa Foleer."

"Demir Grappo," Demir said. His hand was rough, more like that of a common laborer. Another sign he wasn't quite what she expected. Master Kastora had taught Thessa a lot about navigating royalty and guild-families. Someone like Demir had never come up before. This was new territory, but how to navigate it? This man in front of her was soft-spoken and grateful. It was like she'd met three different Demirs at three different times. A guild-family patriarch, Kastora had told her, always wore masks. She imagined that glassdancers did the same. How many different masks did Demir have, and which one was the real him? It was an important question if she was looking at him as a possible patron.

"Thank you again for coming after me."

"It wasn't entirely selfless," Demir replied, a smile touching the corners of his mouth. "I need your help."

Thessa nodded. As expected, and yet it was best not to tip her hand. "With?"

Demir picked a bit of fluff off his tunic. "I understand that you were entrusted with the schematics for a working phoenix channel designed by Kastora and my late mother. Kastora's prototype was destroyed when his glassworks was attacked. I've retrieved it, but I have no confidence that anyone less than a master-level siliceer is capable of building a new one." He paused for a long moment, frowning at the space above her head. "A working phoenix channel will change the world, and it will change the future of the guild-family that makes one. With the cindersand running out so quickly . . ."

Thessa felt her eyes widen, her pulse quicken. "*What?*" she demanded, the word ripping itself from her throat before she could stop it.

"Oh." Demir looked immediately unhappy, like he'd spilled a family secret inadvertently. "He didn't tell you."

She stared at him, her mouth hanging open slightly. "Did *he* tell you that the cindersand was running out?"

"With his dying breath. I arrived the evening after the invasion and took a breacher in to try to extract him safely. Much to my horror, he was on his deathbed. That's how I know all of this, since my own mother died before I returned to Ossa."

Thessa's mind raced through the implications, first for siliceers and then for all of civilization. She found herself pacing from one end of the omnichapel to the other, no thought left for the candles under her feet. Bits and pieces began to come together in her head that had never corresponded before: Kastora's renewed vigor in bookkeeping the last few years; snippets of conversations with other masters that had stopped when she entered the room; letters that he insisted on posting himself.

A flurry of emotions ran through her, starting with jealousy that Demir had been told this secret before she had. She forced herself to slow down, to *think*. It was a deathbed confession—Kastora's bid to provide Thessa with a protector before he died. He'd kept her interests at heart to the last moment, and that thought alone made the grief throb in her breast.

It was a testament to his trust in her that he'd told her about the phoenix channel at all. And to send her away with the only schematics? She shuddered just remembering how close she'd come to losing them. She looked around for a place to sit, couldn't find one, and thrust her hands in her tunic pockets to keep them from trembling.

All of this had rushed through her head in mere moments. Demir, she noticed, was watching her carefully. "As I was saying," he went on slowly, "the first guild-family that makes a working phoenix channel will find themselves the most powerful in Ossa. The others are all fighting amongst themselves, conducting a secret sorcery war. Under normal circumstances, my guild-family couldn't possibly compete."

"But," Thessa finished, "with me and the schematics, the Grappo could complete a phoenix channel before anyone knew you were involved." She knew enough of the politics of Ossa to take what he was saying at face value, and to extrapolate from there. It was beautiful in its simplicity, and clearly what Kastora and Adriana had been preparing to do. "It seems the two of us have inherited a scheme from our predecessors."

"It does seem that way, doesn't it?" Demir replied. "I think—if you're willing—that we should continue where they left off."

"What kind of a deal do you propose?" she asked. This was a business discussion now, and she adjusted her thoughts accordingly.

Demir shrugged. "The same exact deal my mother had with Kastora. We take on the roles of our respective predecessors, except this time you will be under my direct protection. I have their contract. It is light on details, likely to keep spies from finding out what they were up to, but all the wording is there. You can see it the moment we return to my hotel."

The protection of a glassdancer was nothing to scoff at, no matter how small a guild-family the Grappo were. "And the terms?"

"Fifty-fifty. Equal partners."

Thessa found her breath caught in her throat. The standard contract between guild-families and siliceers was patronage: the lion's share of decision making and profits went to the guild-family. True partnerships were rare, and even if Demir let her walk out of here with the schematics and a "no" there was no great guild-family that would give her such an offer.

As if he'd read her line of thought, Demir tugged on the fingers of his glove and removed it from his left hand. He showed her the glassdancer sigil. "I want to clear something up right now: this is not who I am. I'm not going to threaten or cajole you. I want your help. I have given you an offer to get it. It is *your* choice whether you take that offer, and I guarantee your safety regardless of what you say next."

There was something in the back of Thessa's mind that wanted to disbelieve him. She knew all about guild-families and the tricks of their trade. Besides, she'd seen him back at the prison. She knew what he was capable of. Still . . . she *did* believe him. Was it the naïveté of her youth? Or was he really exactly how he presented himself? Masks wearing masks. What could she trust?

He *had* saved her life, and risked his own to do so. That seemed worthy of a leap of faith.

Thessa looked more closely at Demir. He was handsome, if a little short. Well-mannered. Probably around six or seven years her senior, but that hardly mattered for a partnership. She walked from one end of the omnichapel to the other, stopping to look at the two burnt-out candles in front of Kloor's shrine. Her eyes traveled over to the third candle, and the pyramid-shaped shrine to Renn. The goddess of commerce. What a fitting place to have burned a candle. Thessa turned back to Demir. She realized her mind was attempting to address every possible detail and was getting overwhelmed. These sorts of deals normally took months to hammer out, even years. They didn't have years. If things were so desperate that Kastora had told Demir the cindersand was running out quickly, the phoenix channel had to be made as soon as possible. She needed to decide.

Once again, she looked at him keenly. "Why do you want to do this?" she asked. "I'd like to know your real mind: your exact motivations."

Demir seemed to chew on the question for some time before answering. "I have money. I could disappear into the provinces right now and live a luxurious lifestyle until the end of my days. But that's selfish, and I've already lived a life like that. I'm the patriarch of a guild-family now, and I have hundreds of clients who depend on me, from the lowest of the porters in my hotel, all the way up to businessmen and close friends. The phoenix channel will change *their* world more than it will mine: it will secure their future. But it will also secure the future of sorcery. It'll prevent the world from descending into complete chaos that will claim millions of lives. I thought I'd missed my chance to change the world, and fate has given me another."

Thessa was very tempted to call him a liar, but managed to stop herself. Not only would it be rude, but his tone had been so incredibly earnest; as if he was begging her to help him. She was, as he'd already noted, not talking to Demir the glassdancer right now. Was this earnestness the real him? This wasn't going to be simple.

He suddenly said, "I'll give you some time to think on it," and stepped outside, leaving Thessa alone in the omnichapel. She paced again, her thoughts scattered, wishing Master Kastora were here to help her navigate this. There were nuances present, both in the circumstances and in Demir himself, that she was not prepared for. Another one of Master Kastora's sayings: *Know your shortcomings just as thoroughly as you know your strengths.*

Once again she paused in front of Renn's shrine and wished she had a second candle to burn. "Is this your prodding on some kind of a path?" she asked. "Are you even real?" If someone had asked her to conceptualize Renn just a few days ago she would have laughed at them. Now she wasn't so sure.

Thessa reached down and pulled the schematics out of her boot. She'd memorized them in that cart north of Grent just a few days ago, and spent the last few hours going over them again. In her head, she'd already begun work on improving Kastora's design. All she needed now was a place to practice her theories.

She walked out into chilly late-morning air that caused goose bumps across her bare arms. Demir stood in the middle of the street, face raised to the sun. He'd put the glove back on to cover his glassdancer sigil, and he didn't open his eyes until she was standing next to him.

Demir saw what was in her hands and inhaled sharply. "Are those them?" he asked.

She shook them at him wordlessly, and he took the stack. He looked through the schematics carefully, one page at a time. "Incredible," he finally said. "I've been trying to make sense of the destroyed prototype. Seeing these, it all fits together."

"One other thing," Thessa told him, "before I forget. Craftsman Magna kept ledgers of everything illicit going on at the Ivory Forest. Supi Magna was involved. I was forced to burn them, but no one *knows* I burnt them. That information alone might be valuable."

"It might," he agreed. He held the schematics out in front of him like they were a religious artifact, flipping back and forth through the pages. He finally said, "If anyone finds out what we're up to, we'll be in for a fight. I'm dangerous. Montego is dangerous. But we're only two men, and the greater guild-families have whole armies of enforcers at their disposal. If you decide to do this with me, your life will be in danger."

Thessa found her mouth dry and licked her lips. "Kastora always told me that there was danger in progress. Someone will always try to steal from you, or thwart you, or hurt you. This is no different." With a start, Thessa realized he was giving her one last chance to back out. She shook her head. This was too important. No siliceer of any good conscience or ambition would step away from this project. She considered herself both. "I'll take that risk."

A flicker of a smile crossed Demir's expression, and she wondered if she'd just passed a test of sorts. He turned his attention back to the schematics. "Then we'll begin immediately. Or rather, you will. I'm not going to be much help with the actual siliceering."

"We'll need supplies."

"Omniglass and cinderite, right? We're already working on it."

Thessa raised her eyebrows in surprise. Both ingredients were difficult to get ahold of, especially a specimen of cinderite as big as specified in the schematics. "I'm impressed."

"I made a deal with an old friend," Demir said with a wink. There it was again: something playful, as if he'd just switched masks for a brief second.

How very strange. Thessa glanced down at her borrowed clothes, feeling suddenly self-conscious. She had, she realized, nothing in the world. For the second time in her life, she would start over completely.

No, not completely. She had skills, schematics for an impossible dream, and someone who wanted to fund the use of both. Demir handed her back the schematics. She took them and almost instinctively moved to roll them up and stuff them back in her boot before remembering she didn't have to do that anymore. Instead she clutched them in one hand and, on impulse, thrust out the other. "Partners?"

To her relief, Demir grinned and took her hand again. "Partners."

27

After two days of trying to get in touch with Demir without luck, Kizzie was finally given the nod from Breenen and sent up to Demir's second-floor office at the Hyacinth Hotel. The room was sparsely decorated, the shelves empty, looking like he'd just moved in and hadn't had time to unpack. As she entered she found him staring at one of the hammerglass windows, a scowl on his face. He looked pale, as if he'd just come out the other end of an illness.

There was a young woman in his office with him. Pretty, with dirty-blond hair and light provincial skin, and of medium height. Kizzie might have taken her for Demir's paramour if her arms weren't covered with the old burn scars of a siliceer. Definitely not Demir's type. Or was she? Demir had changed a lot over the years.

"Thessa, could you give us just a moment?" Demir asked the young woman. "Find Breenen at the front desk. He'll get you set up with your own room." He waited until she was gone, then said to Kizzie, "Sorry, we just arrived a few minutes ago."

Kizzie raised an eyebrow at him, with the implicit question, to which Demir just shook his head. "Charming, but no. New business partner. Any progress on those killers?"

"You could say that." Kizzie sat down on a sofa facing Demir, passing her hand across her face. She'd gotten *some* rest over the last two days but she still felt plenty unsettled from the events of the last week. "I've found two of them."

This got his attention. Demir perked up, sitting up straight in his chair with an eager look on his face. "Do I know them? Who were they working for? What did . . ." He paused, seemed to gather his composure, and nodded at her to continue.

Kizzie didn't mince words. "Churian Dorlani was the first. A vendor identified him because his mask fell off while he fled the scene. I cornered and questioned him with the shackleglass."

"And?" Demir's eagerness had gone, as if he'd pulled on a carefully prepared mask.

"And he admitted it. The order came from his grandmother."

"Aelia Dorlani?"

"Correct. He didn't know why she wanted your mother dead, but he was able to give me one of the other killers. Glissandi Magna. She *also* admitted to the killing, but when I tried to force her to tell me *why*, she killed herself on my stiletto."

"Glassdamn," Demir said quietly, covering his mouth with one hand and staring off into the space over Kizzie's head. "Do you have another lead?"

"Not yet, but I'm working on it."

"What did you do with Churian?"

"I told him if he didn't flee the country, I'd tell Montego that he killed Adriana."

"And did he?"

"Without an ozzo to his name."

Demir drummed his fingers on his chin. "Perhaps not harsh enough, but there's a certain poetry in that. What to do about Aelia, though?"

"That," Kizzie replied pointedly, "is beyond me. She's a matriarch on the Inner Assembly. If you want to ask her then you have to do it yourself."

"Noted. For now, she'll be wondering why her grandson abandoned his home and family. I'll let that paranoia fester." A wicked little smile flashed across his face, one that Kizzie returned. She had, she had to admit, become more invested in this thing than she'd expected. There was a deeper mystery going on underneath all of this. Multiple guild-families, Grent, that tall man at the Lampshade Boardwalk. It was a puzzle begging to be solved.

"I think," Kizzie said, "that Glissandi was being followed." Demir cocked an eyebrow at her, so she explained, "The moment before she killed herself, she saw someone on the boardwalk. I didn't get a good look thanks to the dark, but she kept her eyes on him as she died."

"You think he's connected to the plot somehow?"

"Perhaps? I checked back in the morning and he wasn't a regular around the Lampshade Boardwalk. He might be a hired specialist making sure the participants don't talk? I've heard of such people before. He had light skin—probably a Purnian—and was glassdamned near seven feet tall."

"But if he's a specialist, who hired him?"

Kizzie shook her head.

Demir said, "Someone that tall shouldn't be hard to find."

"I've been trying to locate him for two days. No one has so much as seen him before."

"I'll have Breenen do some asking as well," Demir said.

Kizzie nodded. She'd be glad for the help. Her contacts were quite good, but the concierge of the Hyacinth would be able to ask questions more freely and of a higher echelon of society. Demir continued to drum his fingers against his chin. He finally said, "The Magna, the Dorlani, *and* the Grent. Those are strange bedfellows for a conspiracy against a single politician."

"It might have to do with her tax and property reforms?" Kizzie said with a shrug. She'd spent a lot of time thinking about this and still couldn't make sense of things. "There's precedent for the public killing of reformers."

"It's happened a few times," Demir admitted, "but not for a hundred years. I would have liked to think Ossa has grown beyond that. Maybe I'm being too optimistic. It just seems so . . . risky. Why not an assassin in the dark? They could have killed her with poison or a knife to the back or any number of ways. I can't get over why they would do it in public."

"You and me both," Kizzie said.

"Perhaps the Assembly was working together against her," Demir said. "If you're right, and it's because of her reforms . . ."

"But then why the Grent agent?"

"To give them an excuse for war?"

"The duke wouldn't have lent them an agent to start a war against him," Kizzie countered. "There is a chance that Capric lied to you, or was lied to, and the entire Grent agent angle was fabricated."

Demir frowned. "I made contact with my mother's people among the Assembly and the Cinders. The Grent killer wasn't faked."

"Then something else is going on," Kizzie said, wondering if Demir had meant to reveal that little bit of information. It was notoriously hard to get spies among the Cinders unless you belonged to the Inner Assembly. The fact that his mother had contacts there spoke to her skills. Kizzie pushed it out of her mind. "I've spent the last couple of days trying to put the pieces together, drawing every line I could between the three conspirators, and I've only been able to find a single common thread."

"Which is?"

She hesitated. Her information was sketchy—hearsay, rumors, and a tip from Veterixi at the High Vorcien. "Aelia Dorlani, Glissandi Magna, and Favian Grent—the duke's brother—all belong to the same Fulgurist Society."

"Oh," Demir said quietly, "that is interesting. Which one?"

"They call themselves the Glass Knife. They're an exclusive dueling club, but beyond that I can't find out damn well anything about them. They don't publish their membership or their meeting times. They have no pamphlets. I know some Societies like keeping an air of secrecy about them, but the Glass Knife seems particularly closed off to outsiders."

Demir swore quietly. "All right. If that's the only common thread, go ahead and tug on it."

"Of course," Kizzie responded. Among the many things she'd wrestled with over the couple of days since Glissandi killed herself was whether she wanted to keep going on this job. She'd talked herself around several times and ultimately decided to stick with it. She was just too damned curious, and if she was being honest with herself, seeing Demir again had pricked something deep within her—a feeling of childhood kinship that she hadn't felt in years. Demir needed *her* right now. Not just an enforcer or a hired investigator, but a friend he could trust.

It felt good to be that person.

But only to a degree. "If this *does* lead back to other guild-family matriarchs or patriarchs . . ."

"Then I will take over and you will never have been involved," Demir assured her. "This is dangerous and I know you can handle yourself, but if this looks like it's going to get you killed I want you to back off."

Kizzie pursed her lips, wondering if she'd ever had someone care about her personal safety before. Enforcers were expendable, even the valued and experienced ones. Being expendable was a part of their job. She wondered how her life would be different if she'd been born a Grappo. Not even as part of the main family, but as a bastard or a distant cousin.

It was something she'd fantasized about a lot as a child, when she played with Demir and Montego in the park. She sighed. There was no changing who her father was. All she could do was continue being that friend Demir needed. "I'll keep you informed," she told Demir. "By the way, Glissandi Magna tried to bribe me with forty thousand ozzo. I'm keeping it, but I consider it payment against our agreed fee."

"That is more than generous," Demir replied.

Kizzie got to her feet and headed for the door, pausing to look over her shoulder. "How is Montego?" she asked quietly.

"He's well."

"Does he know what I'm working on?"

"He does, and he approves."

That sentence brought up a lot of complicated feelings. If Kizzie had been the blushing type, she might have blushed then. "I'm glad he came back."

"You could say hi," Demir suggested. "I expect him to return in an hour or so. He's meeting with your brother Capric to make sure some recent nastiness with a third party is . . . smoothed over."

Kizzie looked at the floor for a few moments, considering the invitation. Just the thought of seeing Montego again made her both excited and afraid. "Maybe some other time," she said. Before he could try to convince her, she went on, "I hope you'll put a few things on the shelves. I haven't been here for twenty years, but I remember your mom giving me candy from a jar on the shelf there."

To her surprise, Demir crossed the room and opened the left desk drawer. He tossed something to her, which she caught in one hand. It was a piece of toffee wrapped in wax paper, of the very same kind Adriana used to give Demir's friends when they were children. "Keep digging," he told her.

Kizzie rolled the toffee across her fingers as she left the hotel, keeping half an eye out to make sure she didn't run into Montego unawares. Outside the hotel she popped the toffee into her mouth, a thousand tiny memories coming back to her from the taste, and enjoyed it as she walked down the street looking for a hackney cab.

She'd gone less than a block before she became aware of a presence following her.

"Hey Kizzie," a man said as he moved up to walk beside her. He was a short, frog-faced fellow of about forty wearing a tight gray uniform with the pink auraglass buttons of a National Guardsman. His left pinkie was painted sky blue to show his allegiance to the Vorcien. He had a lit cigarette in one hand and touched it to the narrow brim of his bearskin hat in a sort of salute.

"Gorian," Kizzie answered. Gorian was one of her favorite National Guardsmen—a corrupt little bastard with a wonderful sense of humor and a kind family. Unlike most of the guardsmen on a guild-family payroll, he was actually useful and could get her all sorts of gossip, information, or even supplies for the right price. "What are you doing in the Assembly District?"

"Looking for you."

Kizzie's pleasure at seeing her friend seized up immediately. "Oh yeah?" she asked in trepidation. "What for?"

"Your dad wants to see you."

Her mood soured further. "Well, that just puckers my asshole. What does the old man want, and why didn't he send an enforcer?"

"No idea," Gorian answered, spreading his hands, "and he wanted to call you in, uh, circumspect-like."

So she wasn't in trouble. Kizzie found herself grinding her teeth, on edge in a way that had nothing to do with Demir's conspiracy. A summons from the patriarch of the Vorcien could mean any number of things. For a lowly enforcer like her—even if she was his daughter—few of them were good. "Right away?" she asked.

"Right away," Gorian confirmed.

Kizzie didn't press him further. It wasn't like Gorian had a choice about delivering the message. "All right, I'll head over. Hey, I want you to keep an ear out on something for me. Quietly."

"What for?"

"I'm trying to identify someone. Incredibly tall, near seven feet, with light skin. Bald."

"Doesn't sound familiar."

"See if you can find someone who knows him."

"Will do."

"Thanks. Oh, and one other thing." She paused in the street, turning toward Gorian and glancing in both directions to be sure they wouldn't be overheard. "I need the membership list of an exclusive Fulgurist Society. How hard would it be to get that for me?"

"Depends on the Society." Gorian raised his eyebrows. "But yeah, the National Guard keeps tabs on all of them. Easier to root out dissidents when you know who they spend their free time with."

"They're called the Glass Knife."

"Never heard of them."

"Well, see what you can find."

"Fine. Tall man and the Glass Knife." He pretended to write in the air, as if he were making a list. "Got it. Come by the watchhouse when you're finished with your dad."

"I'll do that."

Gorian touched the brim of his bearskin hat again in deference. "And Kizzie, good luck with him. I know things have been rocky."

Kizzie waved Gorian off and hired a hackney cab to take her directly up to the Family District—a walled-off section of the city filled with the guild-family townhomes. The streets here were wide, the townhomes designed like tiny estates with their own decorative walls, expensive gardens, and towering brick manors. While foreigners and commoners might think that the power of the Ossan Empire lay in the Assembly District, those within the guild-families knew that the real power lay here.

Vorcien was among the largest and wealthiest of the guild-families. Their city estate matched their level of power, located nearly at the top of Family Hill, nestled in a grove of trees with a long, winding drive that never lacked for traffic as Vorcien clients, employees, and allies came to pay their weekly respects.

She walked up the drive and entered through the main door, where a handful of merchant clients waited with their hats in hand outside Father Vorcien's immense study. The doors were closed, indicating that the old man was in a meeting. Kizzie checked her pocket watch and paced the foyer, one eye on the office door and another on the clients, all of whom studiously ignored her presence. It wasn't becoming of a guild-family enforcer to hang around in public like this, after all. But Kizzie would cling to her small rights as a bastard until the day she died.

She was far more concerned with what her father actually wanted. Had her altercation with Sibrial gotten back to him? Was she about to be punished further? Would he pull her off Demir's payroll and order her to do something vile?

The door to Father Vorcien's office opened. The family majordomo, Diaguni, held the door open for an old woman to come scurrying out, and she hurried across the foyer without meeting anyone's eyes. Diaguni was tall, thin, and bald, with pale olive skin that marked him as being from the Balk region. He watched the old woman go with a wry look on his face and then raised his chin toward Kizzie.

"Kissandra, your father will see you now."

No appointment? No making her wait until all the important clients were gone? Very strange. Kizzie removed her hat and followed Diaguni into the office. It was a palatial room, all covered in white marble and surprisingly devoid of godglass. Decoration was minimal—some gold trim, two tall windows, and a fireplace big enough to drive a carriage into. A single immense chair sat beside the empty fireplace, turned toward the door, and in it a man in his seventies, bloated and bent, body deformed from years of sitting.

His real name was Stutd, but no one had called him anything but Father Vorcien in years. Supposedly, he'd once been a dashing young man, svelte and athletic, more prone to wearing forgeglass than witglass. Kizzie had no memories of *that* man. Only the fat, old reprobate before her. Still, it was best not to underestimate him. Father Vorcien was the senior member of the Inner Assembly, and one of the smartest and most powerful people in Ossa.

She waited until Diaguni closed the door behind her and walked to her father's side, bending to kiss the large silic symbol tattooed on his hand. He was scaly to the touch, an effect of the glassrot that was a ubiquitous sight on his skin. Godglass sorcery often killed those who abused it. Sometimes, though, it left them twisted lumps of flesh like Father Vorcien.

"Good afternoon, my bastard daughter."

"Father," Kizzie answered, her head still bowed, swallowing the bile elicited by his distinct pronunciation of the word "bastard." She knew that he used it to hurt her. It worked. "You needed to see me?"

"It has come to my attention that Capric loaned you out to Demir Grappo."

No asking after her health. No pleasantries. Just down to business. *That*, Kizzie distinctly appreciated. She did not hate her father, but she didn't want to spend much time in his presence, either. "That's right."

"What are you doing for the Grappo?"

"He's asked me to track down Adriana's killers," Kizzie answered without hesitation. She had no compunctions against lying to or misleading other Vorcien enforcers, employees, and clients—even her half siblings—but she would *not* lie to Father Vorcien. She felt the knot in her jaw grow ever tighter as she waited for some kind of response. Was *he* involved? Would he order her off the job? She risked a glance upward to study his face, but Father Vorcien's lips were pursed, his expression unreadable.

"Capric told me it was about hotel security."

"That's what Demir wanted him to think."

"Clever boy, Demir. Not trusting his own childhood friend. But he trusted you."

"Capric and Demir are friends of circumstance," Kizzie said. "He and I are . . ." She hesitated, hating her choice of words, but said it anyway. ". . . real friends."

"Ah, yes. You and Demir and Montego were quite inseparable for several years. It's still shocking that Adriana allowed her son friends so far below his station. I suppose that wasn't the strangest thing about that family." Father Vorcien gave a careless sigh. "Tell me, what have you found?"

"I'm still working on it." Kizzie dodged the question, hoping that Father Vorcien wouldn't press. She continued to tense, waiting for the ax to fall. She all but expected him to call her off the job and in the process guarantee his own involvement. To her surprise, he simply harrumphed.

"I'll be interested to learn what you discover. I've been wondering myself who was involved, but the rest of the Inner Assembly agreed not to dig further."

Of course they had. At least Aelia Dorlani was involved, maybe other members of the Inner Assembly. Interestingly, it seemed that Father Vorcien wasn't. "You're not . . . going to stop me?"

Father Vorcien chuckled. "Of course not. I told them I wouldn't pry, but Demir Grappo made no such promises. Besides, I have something more important on my mind." He paused for a moment, his mirth subsiding into a little scowl. "Do you know what a phoenix channel is?"

"I don't." Kizzie looked up, cocking an eyebrow at her father.

"It's a theoretical silic device. The details are not important. What's important is that Adriana Grappo, before her death, was working on a phoenix channel."

"She wasn't a siliceer."

"No, but she was partnered with one in secret."

"How do you know?" Kizzie asked, the question coming out somewhat more sharply than she'd intended.

"Because I had my agents steal all the notes the Cinders confiscated from her office." Father Vorcien examined his nails and yawned, as if this weren't low even for him. He continued, "She covered her tracks well, but if you examine her private notes with an eye for what she left out, it was not difficult to ascertain what she was up to. We don't know who her partner was for sure—we have our suspicions—but Demir might try to continue the work that she started."

Kizzie felt her heart fall as she realized what was about to come next. "You want me to spy on Demir," she said flatly.

"I do." Father Vorcien licked his lips and grinned. "He's taken you deep into his confidence. He won't suspect anything."

"I'm not . . . I don't think . . ." Kizzie searched around inside herself for the courage to say no. She was already in trouble for that bullshit with Sibrial and the magistrate. Could she afford to lose even more standing with Father Vorcien? She swore silently. That was not her. She did not spy on her friends. That warm feeling of childhood friendship she'd experienced at Demir's hotel had evaporated, and she found herself suddenly quite scared.

"Before you bore me with your personal integrity," Father Vorcien said, waving dismissively, "I will make you an offer: if Demir succeeds in creating a phoenix channel and *you* inform me of the fact, I will legitimize you."

For half a moment, Kizzie felt like she'd been shot. Her body tightened, all rational thought fleeing her mind. She was frozen in complete disbelief. "You would?" The question came out as a shameful squeak. Father Vorcien's grin widened. The old bastard knew he had her.

"I would, and I will."

"And all I have to do is tell you *if* Demir makes this phoenix channel?"

"Correct. I understand it's a betrayal of sorts, but it's certainly not a big one. I won't have you raise a hand against him."

Father Vorcien was many things, but he always followed through on a promise. Kizzie was trembling now, blown away by the very thought. Moments ago legitimization had been a forbidden fantasy. Now it was a possibility. She wouldn't be just a bastard enforcer with a handful of scant privileges; she'd be a proper family member. She would have money, power, luxuries. Sibrial wouldn't be allowed to touch her, even after he inherited the post of patriarch.

"I won't spend my time rooting through his papers," she said in a shaky voice, trying to cling to some semblance of her integrity.

"You will do what you see fit." Father Vorcien's tone was lazy, confident. He'd just dangled the juiciest of prizes in front of her. He didn't need to say or do anything else. He knew that if Demir Grappo made a phoenix channel and there was any way for Kizzie to discover this fact, she would do it. "Aside from that," he continued, "I *would* like to know if you discover Adriana's killers. That could be very valuable information and even if Demir does not succeed with a phoenix channel . . . well, telling me who killed his mother will return you to my good graces. Adriana and I had our differences, but I liked her. Closure to her death would be both professionally and personally satisfying."

"Understood," Kizzie choked out. Father Vorcien rang the bell sitting on the table beside him and Diaguni opened the doors to his study. Kizzie retreated at the silent dismissal. She found an empty sitting room where she could regain her composure and paced the length of it for some time.

On one hand, she did not want to betray Demir. He was a friend, and even in this short time after his return he'd shown her basic kindnesses that no one in her family ever had. On the other hand, this could solve all of her problems. A single betrayal in return for a guaranteed future? Like Father Vorcien had said, it was a small betrayal. It would never come back to her. She could make that sacrifice to secure her future. She had to.

A thought suddenly occurred to her: Demir had been meeting with a young siliceer that he called his new business partner. Was *she* working on the phoenix channel? She seemed far too young for a project that sounded so important, but it made sense. Kizzie almost returned to the foyer to interrupt her father's next meeting. She stopped herself. No need to jump to conclusions, or slavishly feed Father Vorcien information in the hope of earning his goodwill. The deal was a single piece of information in exchange for her legitimization. She would not give him a scrap more.

Kizzie smoothed back her hair, put the last of her qualms to bed, and returned her thoughts to the matter at hand. It was time to find the next killer.

28

A major component of Thessa's education under Kastora had been contracts. She'd been his chief contract revisionist since she was seventeen, and it was her single most important skill—above even glassmaking itself—that almost guaranteed that she would run her own glassworks someday. She knew how to read them, how to write them, how to understand them. She knew how to watch for underhanded language and how to insert her own. She could spot a bad contract at a glance.

It came as quite a shock to find that the original contract between Kastora and Adriana Grappo had none of that. The language was straightforward, the terms clear-cut. Adriana provided the design and the funding. Kastora provided the silic expertise. They were fifty-fifty partners in the phoenix channel endeavor. The shock did not come from the fact that Kastora had signed a good contract, but rather from the fact that he had not inserted anything to his own advantage over the Grappo. The only conclusion Thessa could reach was that he had respected Adriana too much to try.

Thessa stared at the contract, reading over it for the twentieth time in the last two hours. Demir offered to sign a version of this same contract with no revisions between the two of them. It was, to say the least, generous. A true partnership. She could find nothing to object to in the deal, not even a single piece of punctuation out of place. After reading thousands of contracts over the course of her training and work under Kastora, she'd never seen anything like it. A total anomaly that left Thessa feeling slightly unsettled. It was, Kastora had always told her, in the nature of business partners to jostle for position and advantage.

Could it really be this easy? Could she really trust Demir to hold to this? Then again, why couldn't she? Ossan guild-families took contracts *very* seriously. It was practically a religion.

She finally tossed the contract to one side and rubbed her eyes, looking out the window into the afternoon sun. Three days ago she had been a prisoner with a false name trying to figure out a way to save her own life. Now she was sitting in a corner suite in the finest hotel in Ossa, looking at a contract that—if she succeeded with the phoenix channel—could make her one of the wealthiest siliceers in the world. She had appointments with tailors, cobblers, and a masseuse. Her change in fortunes seemed unreal to the point of fantasy. Where was the catch?

She scoffed, walking to the window to look down into the crowded street and across to the park kitty-corner from the hotel. She already knew the catch. She didn't know if she could truly rebuild and improve upon Kastora's design. Even undertaking such a project made her a player in a wider game that included spies and assassins. The Grappo were barely a guild-family, holding on to a mere fraction of the wealth and prestige of the Magna or Vorcien or Dorlani. She thought about that newspaper article from a couple of weeks ago, and the Ossan siliceers found brutally murdered in the Tien.

The catch was she might end up like that.

Thessa's attention was drawn back to the street, where her narrow line of sight revealed that something beyond the usual traffic was happening on the other side of the park. She frowned, peering in that direction, noting that the pedestrians just below her window were clearing out quickly. She heard someone shout. Another shout followed it, then another. A woman screamed, and began running.

"What the piss . . ." she muttered to herself.

She was three floors up in a hotel and yet the animal instinct deep in her chest wanted her to flee to higher ground. She grabbed the windowsill, watching that movement on the next street over. A young woman dressed like a common laborer dashed into sight, paused to shout behind her, then turned and hurled a brick through the window of a fancy shop. Another laborer followed her, then another. Within moments the street was filled with them—winging stones at shops, chasing down well-dressed pedestrians and knocking them into the ditch.

Thessa ran to the door and out into the hallway, where she found a young woman in the uniform of a hotel porter. Like the other porters', her pinkie finger was painted purple to show her allegiance to the Grappo, but unlike them she wore a belt with a sword and pistol. She must have been in her mid-twenties, with the dark olive skin of a native Ossan and short-cropped black hair. She had hard eyes and a pretty face, her delicate features marred by a scar that ran from her right cheekbone down to her jawline.

After so many days stuck in the prison, watching Magna guards prowl the wall, the mere sight of a guild-family enforcer caused a knot in Thessa's stomach. She pushed through it. "Something is happening outside."

The woman inhaled sharply and scowled. "I know."

"Should I . . . do anything?" Thessa asked, taken off guard by the nonchalance with which the enforcer spoke.

The woman scratched between her eyes and shook her head. "Lady Foleer, I presume?"

"Right."

"I'm Tirana Kirkovik, the Hyacinth's master-at-arms." She gestured for Thessa to follow and walked down to a door, where they stepped out onto a balcony. The shouts and screams were louder out here, and Thessa could hear the sound of shattering glass from down the street. Tirana remained back from the edge of the balcony and craned her head to see. "They've been rioting back and forth through the Assembly District since this morning."

"Who are they?" Thessa asked. Tirana's cool helped take the edge off Thessa's worry, but she still had that urge to flee.

"The price of low-resonance forgeglass tripled last night," Tirana said, "and three of the major teamsters unions went on strike the moment word got around."

"It *tripled*?" Thessa asked, her eyes widening. "That doesn't happen. It's not possible. There are mechanisms in place—laws—to keep the prices consistent."

"You're a siliceer, right? I don't know the particulars, but a few large shipments of cindersand went missing. Combine that with the Ivory Forest Glassworks burning to the ground a few days ago, and speculation has gone through the roof. You'd understand it better than I would."

"It burned to the ground?" Thessa echoed. She felt a pang of guilt. Beyond being grateful for being out of there, she'd done her best not to think of that damned place since escaping. "I didn't know. Did they . . . did the siliceers get out?"

"Only a few casualties," Tirana said. If she had any idea that it was Montego who set the fire, she gave no indication.

Thessa stifled a sigh of relief. She didn't need more death on her conscience. A sound cut through the afternoon—a falcon's distinct cry—and she felt her ears prick up. She turned to the sky for half a moment, searching for the bird, part of her wishing it were Ekhi but knowing that wasn't possible. She brought herself back down to the streets below. "What do we do? Is the hotel protected?" The rioters were getting closer now. A carriage was pushed over half a block away, the occupants dragged out and beaten by the angry mob.

"Master Demir is dealing with it."

Realization was slow to dawn, but when it did Thessa's breath was snatched from her. "Is he going to kill them?" she choked. No answer was forthcoming. Thessa swallowed her bile and left the master-at-arms on the balcony, hurrying through the hotel halls and down into the foyer. Guests and porters alike crowded in the lobby, milling anxiously, and Thessa had to push through a cordon of enforcers that stood between the guests and the front door.

Just outside, lounging on the purple carpet that went down the steps to the street, was Demir. He was alone, a bottle of wine sitting on the step next to him. His jacket was unbuttoned, his tunic unlaced at the neck and both sleeves rolled up. He wasn't wearing his gloves, and the silic sigils on both his hands were hard to miss, as was the assortment of glassdancer eggs sitting on the steps below.

"It's probably best if you stay inside," he said, his gaze on the approaching rioters.

"I don't want you to kill anyone," Thessa told him. Her heart flipped in her chest, and she wondered if it was the first time anyone had ever been brazen enough to say that to a glassdancer.

Demir looked up in surprise. "I don't intend to."

"Then what is this?" Thessa looked pointedly at the glassdancer eggs.

"A warning." As he spoke, the closest of the rioters finally reached the street below them. There were six or seven, carrying massive chisels that they used to tear up cobbles. Three of them ran to a nearby coach and cut the horses loose, then upended the vehicle. When they finished, they turned toward Demir and Thessa and began to approach. They'd halved the distance when one grabbed the other two by the sleeves and said something. They all three stared at Demir for several moments before turning away.

"There is," Demir said, raising his left hand so that the glassdancer sigil pointed toward her, "some advantage to being branded a killer."

The same thing happened again and again. Rioters poured into the street by the dozens, some of them coming as close as the carriage drop-off at the bottom of the hotel stairs before leaving well enough alone. All around the hotel, shop windows were being smashed, guild-family enforcers clashing with the rioters with cudgels and swords, but the violence seemed to stay away from Demir as if he exuded a bubble of calm around him.

"Would you kill them if they ignored the warning?" Thessa asked, sinking to sit on the stair next to Demir. He took a swig of wine, his eyes not leaving the scene. Despite his casual demeanor, up close Thessa could see that his pupils were dilated, his muscles tense.

"I hope we don't have to find out." He sniffed at the air. "Someone has set a fire. Piss and shit, the damned fools. They'll bring out the Cinders that way."

"Tirana said that they're rioting because the price of forgeglass tripled overnight."

Demir gave her a long, significant glance. "That's what I heard too. So glassdamned sudden. Is there any precedent?"

Thessa scowled. "Severe speculation has happened before, of course, but not in the modern world. Not in a city the size of Ossa. Cindersand is too well regulated."

"Glassdamn," Demir breathed.

"This kind of thing is going to keep happening, isn't it?" Thessa asked, though she already knew the answer. "It's going to get worse if we don't finish the phoenix channel."

The street was packed shoulder to shoulder now, with men and women wearing the drab tunics of common laborers. Some of them had the crest of a teamsters union stitched to their jackets, while others seemed like they were just there for the violence and looting. The crowd suddenly parted, and a middle-aged woman strode brazenly to the bottom step of the Hyacinth. Her tunic was a little nicer than those around her, the embroidery fine but demure, the emblem of an ox stitched boldly on the center of her chest. Thessa recognized the shirt—a union boss. The woman pointed a cudgel at Demir.

"You there, Grappo! You're a guild-family patriarch, the only one brave enough to stay in the streets. Why has the price of forgeglass tripled?"

Thessa and Demir exchanged a glance, and Demir answered, "I don't know. I only heard myself when your people started smashing windows."

"How can you not know?" the union boss demanded. "You're on the Assembly!"

"I haven't attended an Assembly meeting in nine years," Demir called back, spreading his hands to indicate the black mourning flags still hanging from the windows above him. "Ask the Magna or the Vorcien. Does it look like I own a glassworks?"

The woman made a disgusted gesture. "We want answers! Your kind expect us to work ourselves like oxen yet you won't provide the forgeglass we need to do it? We can't afford those prices! What good are the guild-family guarantees if prices can leap so readily?"

Thessa looked sharply at Demir. His demeanor had not changed, but she could see he was breathing harder now, sweat rolling down the back of his neck. "What's wrong?" she whispered.

"I've blanked," Demir whispered back. "I used to know what to say; what to do. I used to be able to wrap these kinds of people around my fingers with a few words. They loved me then, and now I can only threaten with my sigil." To Thessa's surprise, his hands trembled. She reached down and took him by the hand, squeezing it hard.

"You don't need to be out here," she told him.

"If it's not me, it'll be my enforcers. People will get hurt. Maybe killed." He cleared his throat and waved dismissively at the union boss. He called, "Take your complaints to the Assembly. You'll get nothing here."

"Bah!" the union boss snapped back with a rude gesture. She withdrew back into the crowd.

Demir let out a long sigh, and Thessa found herself wondering if he *could* actually resort to violence. He ran his hands across his face. "I've seen riots out in the provinces—bread riots, pay riots—I've even been in them. But I've never seen a godglass riot in the Assembly District. If I . . . *Shit.*"

Thessa turned to follow the sharp turn of his head. There, less than a block away, soldiers had emerged out into the street. They looked almost quaint in white, red, and green flowing uniforms, armed with halberds with hammerglass heads and razorglass blades, pistols at their belts, their conical hats looking like something out of an old-timey play. Thessa's breath caught in her throat.

Cinders. The Assembly's trained killers. Even in Grent they had a reputation for being half a step below the arrogance and bloodthirstiness of a glassdancer. There were dozens of them, and many of their halberds were already slick with blood. They rolled out into a line between the rioters and the Assembly Square farther down the street, lowering their weapons. The rioters wavered, but they did not scatter.

"Disperse immediately!" one of the Cinders ordered.

The rioters roared back as one, cudgels and stones raised.

"Get inside," Demir said. He sprang to his feet, running down the steps, his glassdancer eggs shooting from the ground and following him as if they were possessed. "No!" he shouted. "No, no, no!"

Thessa was rooted to the spot, watching as the eggs suddenly cracked and shattered into dozens of pieces that soared over the heads of the crowd and then spread out just in front of the Cinders, driving both soldiers and rioters back in different directions. Demir leapt onto the base of a lamppost and showed his twin silic sigils to both sides.

"He's going to get himself killed." Thessa turned to see that half a dozen enforcers had emerged from the hotel, and with them were Tirana and the hotel concierge, Breenen. "Glassdamnit," Breenen continued, "not even a glassdancer is going to stop this. Tirana, get in there and pull him out."

"Wait!" Thessa knew she had no authority here—these were not her people—but she threw out an arm to stop Tirana just as Demir began to shout.

"Teamsters!" Demir called above the angry shouts. "Builders, haulers, diggers, skinners! Citizens! Look to me and take heed! This"—he pointed at the Cinders—"is only death and despair. You will suffer and they will call you animals and use it against you."

Thessa swallowed hard. The shouting tapered off immediately, hundreds of eyes turning toward Demir. "Breenen," she hissed, "do you have a stockpile of forgeglass? For your porters?"

"Of course," the concierge replied.

"How much?"

"A few hundred pieces, perhaps."

"Go get it. All of it."

The concierge drew himself up. "Young lady, you may be our guest but you do not—"

She turned and grabbed him by the lapels of his tunic. "I'll make more," she whispered desperately. "I can replenish that in a few long days. Go. Get. The forgeglass." At that moment she realized just how close the Grappo enforcers were to forcibly removing her hands from the concierge. She let go, showing him her palms. "Do it."

Finally, he nodded, and two of the enforcers raced inside.

Demir continued, shouting to a now-quiet crowd. His voice wavered at times, but he plowed on, his tone hypnotic. "Let it go! You've shown them your displeasure. Nothing more can be gained."

Someone—the union boss who'd spoken earlier—shouted out from the crowd. "We won't go home until they hear our demands."

"They won't hear your demands at the end of a cudgel!" Demir shouted back. "They'll only answer with blood!"

"That we will!" Several of the Cinders, shoving with the stocks of their hammerglass halberds, had pushed their way within a dozen paces of Demir, and their officer now raised a hand toward him.

Thessa felt something shoved into her arms, and she looked down to find a small box brimming with forgeglass. "Now he's got the Cinders on him!" Breenen growled angrily. "I hope you've got some kind of an idea."

Thessa didn't. "Take this," she said, "and form a cordon at the base of the steps." With that, against all instincts of self-preservation, she shoved her way through the crowd. She reached Demir just as he turned on the Cinders.

"Stand down," he barked at them.

"You don't give orders," the officer replied.

Demir drew himself up. "I am a Grappo patriarch and a glassdancer. I have a seat on the Assembly. Stand down or the blood spilled today will not be theirs!" His voice rose to a roar and Thessa looked up at his back, rethinking her earlier assessment. He was, she decided, quite capable of violence. Glass darted nervously around in the air, hovering dozens of feet above the Cinders, tiny shards that caught the sunlight and glittered like poised knives.

The crowd was completely silent now, not a word spoken, a ripple of tense fear working its way back and forth like the tiny waves on a pond.

"I'll take this to the Assembly myself!" he declared. "We cannot treat people like cattle and then balk when they stampede. These are our friends. Our fellows. They deserve to be heard without the threat of a razorglass blade."

Thessa was right behind Demir now, and though she could not see above the heads of the crowd she could feel a sudden change in the wind. Someone shouted, "The Cinders are backing off!"

"Huzzah! Huzzah!"

Thessa could feel the crowd begin to move again in a rush of adrenaline. She grabbed the lamppost and pulled herself up next to Demir. "What are you doing?" he demanded.

"Helping you end this," she replied. Raising her voice, she said, "The Grappo will share what we have, though it is not much! A single piece to everyone who can hear my voice, and then withdraw and let Demir fulfill his promise!" She tugged on Demir's sleeve. "Quickly, before they can work themselves up again." She half pulled him back to the stairs of the Hyacinth, the rioters parting before her like a wave. The attention of the crowd was now on them, but something had dampened it—within minutes lines had formed, several of the union bosses working their way up to the front and shaking Demir's hand enthusiastically before getting their people in order.

Thessa found herself swept up in the entire thing, kissed on the cheek, showered with blessings as she handed out pieces of forgeglass. She was dizzy and euphoric, and when she felt friendly hands gently pulling her back inside, she did not fight them. She found herself in the lobby, dazed, facing an angry Breenen.

"You could have gotten us all killed," the concierge scolded. "That crowd might have turned on you in an instant."

"Breenen!" a sharp voice rebuked. "Let her be." They were joined by Demir, who removed his jacket and tossed it to one of the porters. Underneath it he was absolutely soaked with sweat. Breenen pulled back, scowling, and Thessa watched him go. "Forgive him," Demir said quietly. "That was brilliant. Risky, but brilliant." His face was flushed, and Thessa knew her own matched it.

"They needed something else," she said. "You halted their momentum, and they needed a victory. Forgeglass is a victory. And it's cheap."

"Not anymore it's not."

"If you have the cindersand, I'll replenish what we've given away," Thessa promised.

"I'll hold you to that." Demir looked uncertain for a moment, eyes traveling around the foyer as if he were seeing it for the first time. He finally focused back on Thessa. "I'll take care of this. Best you not be seen much more in public, or the Magna will come around asking questions."

Thessa nodded her agreement. That was quite enough excitement for a month, let alone ten minutes. Quietly she said, "This is only going to get worse. I have to move quickly. I'll start my work right now." She watched Demir go, then returned to her rooms, where it took some time for the adrenaline to wear off. She watched from the window as slowly, surely, the crowd dispersed. National Guardsmen and enforcers from a dozen different guild-families swept through the streets, driving off stragglers and assessing the damage. The riot was over.

For the moment.

Gathering the schematics, Thessa headed down to the hotel garden, where Demir had already shown her the little workshop where she could rebuild the phoenix channel. The prototype—destroyed by the fires of the Grent Glassworks—was waiting for her. Thessa paced around it, preparing her thoughts, getting ready to bend her neck to the work. She had to do this. For herself. For Kastora. For the stability of the world.

Somewhere above, she heard the cry of a falcon as she got to work.

29

National Guard watchhouses were one of the most ubiquitous sights in the Ossan capital. There were hundreds of them, seemingly one on every corner, and they housed the closest thing that Ossa had to a proper police force. They were all made of a utilitarian red brick with white signs that listed their watchhouse number, and more often than not a pair of National Guardsmen in their sharp gray uniforms with auraglass buttons and bearskin hats patrolling out front. In Kizzie's experience, the National Guard did little actual policing. Their primary role was to enforce the Assembly's will—quell riots, defend the capital, keep the people in line. Their secondary role was to act as unofficial enforcers for whichever guild-family paid their wages.

Kizzie jogged up the stairs to Watchhouse 187, on a narrow street on the edge of the Slag, nodding to the two guardsmen posted outside. It was a small building, jammed between two factories, with a main room, a few holding cells, and a bunkhouse on the second floor.

"Kizzie!" Gorian greeted her as she came through the door. Gorian sat at a card table with three other guardsmen, who all called her name in greeting. Kizzie returned the hellos and set a bottle of Nasuud whiskey on the card table. She might not pay their wages, but keeping 187 in good booze had made her very popular on this street. A chorus of thank-yous followed, and Kizzie jerked her head at Gorian. "Give me a moment," he told his companions, stubbing out a cigarette and joining her as she warmed her hands by the little potbellied stove in the corner.

"What's this I'm hearing about a riot in the Assembly District?" she asked.

"Something about godglass prices riling up the teamsters unions," Gorian responded. "They've got us on standby in case they need us to break some skulls, but I imagine the Cinders will cut down a few hundred of them and that'll be the last of it. How did things go with your dad?" he asked.

So it was true. A riot in the Assembly District felt ominous, but Kizzie couldn't quite place why. "Not terribly," Kizzie responded. She moved on from that quickly, not wishing to dwell on the tiny bit of guilt that had settled in her stomach at the thought of selling out Demir's secret project in exchange for legitimization. "How about you? Did you get me a membership roll for the Glass Knife?"

Gorian glanced over his shoulder at his companions. "We should talk outside."

Kizzie allowed him to move their conversation back out into the cold, just to one side of the front steps of the watchhouse, where they could talk quietly without being overheard. Once they were alone, he spoke in a low voice. "There's a couple of things," he said. "First off, I actually got a nibble about that tall man you described to me. You know those siliceers that have been dropping dead?"

"You mean murdered and thrown in the Tien?" Kizzie asked. "It's been all over the papers for weeks."

"Yeah." Gorian lowered his voice even further. "There's a rumor going around that there's a secret sorcery war going on between the guild-families, and that the killer is working for one of the guild-families."

Kizzie had heard no such thing, which was strange because rumors like that were almost always started by loose-lipped enforcers. She should have been among the first to hear it. Then again, she was out of favor and had been for several months. Nobody told her anything unless she asked. "A secret sorcery war is a very dangerous thing."

"Agreed, but to be honest I can't even confirm that it exists." Gorian made the face he always did when he was about to feed her information that was even less reliable than usual. "I was pulling some of those reports just after we spoke, trying to jog my memory, and I came across three different eye-witnesses that testified to seeing a very tall, bald Purnian near the site of the attacks. There's no conclusive evidence, and the guardsmen assigned to investigate haven't been able to bring him in."

A shiver went down Kizzie's back. That *couldn't* be a coincidence. The man must be a guild-family agent. But which family? Dorlani? Magna? He hadn't moved to help Glissandi. Kizzie's thoughts were suddenly everywhere at once, trying to connect the dots between Adriana's death, this purported sorcery war, and the phoenix channel that her father had told her about just hours ago. That had to be it, right? If Adriana had entered a secret sorcery war that the Grappo weren't actually equipped to fight, it must have gotten her killed. But who, ultimately, gave the order?

"That's more valuable than you realize," she told Gorian. "I'm going to have to get you another bottle of whiskey."

"Hold that thought, because I haven't even gotten to the Glass Knife yet."

"Go on."

Gorian looked around once again. He was normally quite brazen in the way he spoke and acted, and the fact that he was looking over his shoulder caused Kizzie to frown. "Out with it," she said. What could spook him about a Fulgurist Society membership list?

Gorian seemed to choose his words carefully. "You know how you occasionally hear rumors about a Fulgurist Society? Back-page sort of stuff; sensationalism and the like."

"Yeah," Kizzie snorted. "They're never true. It's always some member who kills a mistress on the club grounds, or experiments with high-resonance dazeglass and runs naked into the street. All the really good gossip is hogwash."

"Maybe it is, maybe it isn't."

"What do you mean? What has the Glass Knife done that I haven't heard before?"

"It's the usual rumors, you know?" Gorian said reluctantly. "Pacts with demons; mixing fearglass with shackleglass and eating people; human sacrifice."

Kizzie fixed Gorian with her best expression of doubt. "You expect me to believe any of that is true?" Kizzie didn't think much of the guild-family higher-ups. As much as she wanted to be one of their number, she had first-hand knowledge of how they lived and almost every single one of them was a spoiled, oversexed, overglassed fool. Perhaps Glissandi Magna was a bit mad, but there was no way Kizzie could believe she'd gotten involved in some death cult.

Then again, she did chew off her own tongue and commit suicide to avoid naming her masters.

Gorian threw up his hands. "Of course none of it's true. But rumors usually don't stick around for long. They hit the papers, people talk about them, then the world moves on. The Glass Knife, though . . . the confidential reports attached to their name are full of mysterious disappearances and bizarre accusations. Lots of cover-ups and recurring weirdness. Just gives me the creeps."

"Come on," Kizzie said, finally losing patience. "Hand over the membership list."

There was a little glimmer in Gorian's eye. "It's going to cost you. More than a bottle of whiskey."

Kizzie reached into her pocket for a thick roll of banknotes. Whatever it was, Demir could afford it. "How much?"

"Promise you won't be mad?" Gorian asked.

"Why would I be mad? I know how these things work, and you and I have been friends for a long time." She frowned at Gorian. He was acting pretty strangely about this whole thing and she didn't like it.

"I don't want money," he replied. "I want a story."

"What kind of a story?" Kizzie asked, bemused.

Gorian rubbed his hands together and gave her a long, considering look. "I heard Baby Montego's back in town *and* you're working at the Hyacinth Hotel."

Kizzie's amusement disappeared and she held up a finger warningly. "Careful."

"Look Kizzie, people may have forgotten that you and Montego were sweethearts before he became famous. I haven't. If I'm gonna stick my neck into this Glass Knife business, I want something more personal than cash. I want to know what happened between you and Montego. What was the falling-out? Why are you hunting for killers? Why aren't you Kissandra Vorcien-Montego right now?"

"I'll find the list myself," Kizzie said flatly, turning to go. The very mention of Montego made her hackles go up. She walked briskly to the street and was several dozen paces from the watchhouse when Gorian caught up to her.

"Hey, hey," he said quietly, "I'm sorry, I didn't mean to cross the line. The Montego thing has always driven me crazy. You fell out with someone who went on to become one of the most famous people in the world. That's not just a story, it's a *story*."

"You want me to gossip to you. About myself?" Kizzie turned to Gorian.

"It's not gossip. I just want to know what happened. I won't tell a soul, I swear. Personal curiosity only. Look, the Glass Knife membership list is in my pocket. I'll hand it over right now if you just tell me."

Kizzie considered this for a few moments. Having that list *might* give her suspects for Adriana's murder, or it might just be a massive waste of time. It was all she had right now, and the list would probably save her days of work. Gorian had, she admitted to herself, always been trustworthy. He might be corrupt, but like Madame-under-Magna, his corruption was businesslike. If he said he wouldn't repeat it, he would keep his word.

"Gah!" she exclaimed, and jerked her head to step off to the side of the street. She then stared at the ground, ordering her thoughts, digging up memories that she'd long tried to suppress. "I've never told anyone this," she said quietly.

"It'll never be repeated," Gorian said, placing his hand over his heart.

Kizzie almost kept it to herself, but the idea of saving several days' worth of work was too tempting. Aside from helping Demir himself, Father Vorcien had also promised that she'd get back into his good graces if she found out the killers. It was just a story, right? It was, she realized, also the first time anyone had ever asked.

"Fine. You know the big chatter oak up on Family Hill?"

"Sure."

"Sibrial caught me and Montego down in the roots one day. We were kids, you know, and Sibrial dragged me out of there by my hair screaming about how even his bastard sister defiled herself by lying with a provincial lowborn like Montego." Kizzie hurried on, feeling a rush of adrenaline from saying it out loud for the first time. "Montego came to my defense, and Sibrial hit him with his cane hard enough to stagger a horse." She tapped the bridge of her nose. "Right between the eyes. I'm told you can still see the scar."

Gorian's eyes widened. "What happened?"

"It just made Montego angry. Sibrial—a grown man with a cane sword and decades of boxing and fencing lessons—got the absolute shit beaten out of him by a naked fourteen-year-old."

To her satisfaction, Gorian actually gasped.

Kizzie added, "Montego broke both of Sibrial's arms. Shattered three ribs and cracked four more. I had to beg Montego to spare his life. He didn't want to. This was before he was Baby, right? If anyone found out he'd attacked a guild-family heir he would have been executed. But if he *did* kill Sibrial, we would have been found out." Kizzie played the memory back through her head, still seeing it as vividly as if it had happened yesterday. "I half carried, half dragged Sibrial back home, where we concocted a story about him getting jumped by a street gang in the Slag."

"Glassdamn, I remember that!"

"Keep your voice down," Kizzie told him.

Gorian looked genuinely shocked and Kizzie hoped he would keep his damned word. He whispered, "I remember that. They had the National Guard looking for that gang for weeks."

"Yeah. It wasn't twenty gang members he valiantly held off at sword point. It was Montego. Naked and alone."

"And that's why Sibrial hates you so much," Gorian said softly.

"Yeah. I was the only witness to his greatest humiliation."

"And Sibrial never said a word about Montego."

"If he had," Kizzie explained, "he would have outed himself. The revenge of seeing Montego executed would not have compared to the humiliation of being beaten half to death by a kid. I'm sure if Montego had never made anything out of himself Sibrial might have one day had his revenge. Instead, Montego became Baby Montego, the most accomplished killer in the Ossan Empire. Now hand me that list."

"Glassdamn," Gorian said again, shaking his head. "That is something else. Yeah, of course. Here." He dug in his pocket and removed a piece of paper, which he thrust into her hands. It had a few dozen names on it in Gorian's messy handwriting. She scanned them, shocked at a few, amused by some, and unsurprised by many.

"Is this it?" she asked.

Gorian grimaced. "Maybe. Maybe not. Those lists are rarely complete, since they're made from rumors and surveillance rather than by the Society itself."

"You might have mentioned that," Kizzie grumbled. She felt naked after telling that story, a little worm of regret working its way through her belly. "Remember what I said. You repeat that to anyone . . ."

"Hey, I gave my word. I respect you, Kizzie, and even if I didn't, do you think I'm gonna gossip about Sibrial or Montego? Either of them could eat me for breakfast." His eyes widened slightly. "Montego perhaps literally."

"Keep that in mind," Kizzie said. "Thanks again for the list. I'll be in touch if I need anything else."

30

It was late in the afternoon and Idrian stared out across the Copper Hills west of Ossa, playing a game with himself: Which shadows flitting across the fallow fields were caused by the clouds, and which were caused by the aching madness locked away in the corner of his brain? He could feel the madness pushing at the restraining sorcery of his godglass eye like a prisoner probing at the bars of his cell, and Idrian wondered how much longer he had until the eye just didn't work anymore. Could he handle the madness on his own? Should he tell Tadeas, or the Ministry of the Legion, how quickly his mind seemed to be degrading?

Or was he imagining all of it? The eye still had plenty of resonance. It should last for several more years. Perhaps Tadeas was right and his mind was just coping with the loss of Kastora. If he could push through it—get to the end of this war and turn in his debt marker—he could use Demir's phoenix channel to recharge his godglass.

"Sir?"

Idrian started out of his reverie, turning to find Braileer at his side. "Hmm?"

"You were grimacing, sir. Is something wrong?"

"Just thinking of friends long gone." It was an easy lie. He usually was.

"Oh. Do you dwell on them often?"

"More than I'd like to admit."

Braileer sat down on a rock next to Idrian and the two remained in companionable silence for some time before Braileer spoke again. "Will I dwell on lost friends, sir?"

It was a surprisingly poignant question. Idrian was used to young recruits coming in and thinking they were invincible; that they and their friends would see the end of whatever next war without anything more than

294 · Brian McClellan

a few sexy scars. They were always disabused of that notion violently, and some of them broke for it. "How long have you been with us?"

"Just six days, sir."

"Have you been getting to know the battalion?"

"As much as I can, sir. I think I understand the engineers better than the soldiers. We all work with our hands. We take things apart and make and mend." He paused. "But Mika terrifies me."

"She should," Idrian chuckled. "She's just as insane as the rest of us veterans, but she has access to explosives. Have you fallen in with anyone? People you eat breakfast with, or throw down a bedroll near?"

Braileer looked down at his hands. "Do you know Steph and Halion?"

Steph and Halion were a pair of siblings; engineers underneath Mika, both with the rank of corporal. "Steph take you under her wing, hmm?" Idrian asked, bemused.

"More like Halion," Braileer said slowly, blushing. "I think he likes me. Steph giggles and elbows him every time I'm around."

Idrian breathed out through his nose. It was easy to remember how quickly these things happened when you were young. The terror of the battlefield; the loneliness of being away from home; the need for some respite from blood and suffering. He considered his next words, trying to keep them from coming out too dour. "My best advice for you is that people *will* die. You'll lose friends. Maybe just one. Maybe all of them. But it will happen. You get used to it, kind of, but it always hurts. Have your fun— piss knows we all need it—but guard this well." He leaned over to thump Braileer's chest over his heart.

Braileer swallowed hard. "I'll try, sir."

"Good." Idrian scratched at his godglass eye, feeling that itch in the back of the socket. "Now make sure my armor is polished. We're going to see battle sooner than any of us wants." He got up and headed to the pavilion, where Tadeas had laid out one of his bean maps to represent the defensive array of the Ossan Foreign Legion. Idrian joined Tadeas in staring at that array until his friend finally turned to him.

Tadeas gestured at the bean map. "This whole thing. It's too . . ." He snapped his fingers thoughtfully. ". . . too by-the-book."

"You think Kerite can unseat us?"

"I don't know about that," Tadeas responded, "but from what I know about Kerite, she's read the handbooks and she's found them lacking.

General Stavri thinks he can lure her in and crush her with a straightforward battle. I'll be surprised if it's that easy."

"What's the latest word?" Idrian asked. The itching behind his godglass eye grew in intensity. He'd never truly known if he had a sixth sense, or if he'd just been doing this so long that he had a subconscious feel for the winds of war.

"Last I heard, Kerite is hanging back about four miles to our west. The Drakes have been reinforced by soldiers from Grent. The numbers are about even, if you count our National Guard reinforcements. She's going to give us battle but we don't know when. Tonight? Tomorrow? Kerite has always been unpredictable."

Idrian tore his eyes from the bean map and looked over at his friend. Tadeas was clearly exhausted, his shoulders slumped, a frown fixed on his face for the last forty-eight hours. Like Idrian, he was covered in dirt from helping dig trenches all morning and afternoon.

Despite Mika's insistence that it would take three days to finish the fortifications, they were almost done. A web of dirt barricades and ditches filled with wooden spikes now protected their artillery battery, and that was only some of it. Mika's engineers had carefully laid mines all across the hillside, marked for the soldiers under their command but otherwise hard to spot, as the sod had been taken up and then carefully replaced. If you cared to look closely enough, you'd spot the blasting cord winding through the thick grass, coming up the hill to the "blasting wheel," as Mika liked to call it.

They were by far the most advanced fortifications along the entire defensive line, and Idrian worried that the rest of the army wasn't taking Kerite's threat very seriously.

"Tad!" a voice called. It belonged to a scrawny woman of medium height, well into her forties. Her name was Forsel Pergos, but everyone called her Halfwing. Idrian had no idea why. She wore the black Ossan uniform with a yellow patch on her shoulders shaped like a stack of cannonballs. "Come up here!"

Tadeas sighed. "No rest for the weary, eh?"

"Come on, she looks nervous," Idrian said, tugging Tadeas by the shoulder. The pair walked to the crown of the hill, flattened days ago by the artillery crews and now filled with a number of cannons and mortars. Neat, pyramid-shaped stacks of ammunition stood beside each weapon. The crews were off having an early dinner, but their commanding officer stood alone among the big guns, waving to them eagerly.

Idrian and Tadeas joined her. "Everything okay?" Idrian asked.

Halfwing paced around a stack of cannonballs, a piece of sightglass in her ear and a looking glass in her hand. She paused, turned toward the north, and pointed at a copse of trees on a hilltop about a mile away. "I swear," she said, "I just saw a Grent dragoon in those trees."

Idrian took her offered looking glass and raised it to his one eye, peering through until he found the trees. It was a tight bit of landscape, all thorns and overgrown olive trees forgotten for a hundred years or more. There really wasn't much to see—a man might be able to scramble his way into that mess, but a man *and* a horse?

"We should already have scouts in those trees," Tadeas said. Idrian handed him the looking glass. Tadeas looked in that direction, then did a general sweep of the surrounding hills. "In fact, we should have a lot more scouts than I can see right now."

Idrian looked toward the sun. It was almost six o'clock, with the winter darkness not far off and the evening already growing noticeably colder. He felt a knot form in his stomach. "Is Kerite making her move?"

"Glassdamned hard to tell," Tadeas responded, "and if she is we shouldn't be the ones figuring it out. Stavri should have hundreds of scouts sweeping these hills, keeping us abreast of everything. Kerite shouldn't be able to break camp without us knowing."

"And what was our last report?" Halfwing asked. She wrung her hands, looking nervous. Artillery officers were a strange breed, one that Idrian had never quite gotten used to: completely unfazed by massive explosions and pieces of iron moving at impossible speeds, but ready to flee at the slightest change of plans. Considering how much work it took to prepare a single artillery battery, he didn't blame them for the latter.

"The last report," Tadeas said, still sweeping the distant horizon with Halfwing's looking glass, "was that Kerite had made camp and was conducting practice drills. No communication. No betrayal of her plans. That was around noon."

The itch behind Idrian's godglass eye only grew more severe. *Maybe* Halfwing had imagined the dragoon, or even spotted a single Grent scout hiding out in that copse. *Maybe* Kerite was still several miles distant, running her troops through their paces for a morning battle. That was what any traditional commander would do. But Kerite wasn't a traditional commander.

"Give me that glass," he said, taking the looking glass from Tadeas. He fixed it back on that copse, then slowly moved it down the side of the hill. What he saw then made his blood freeze: there was a woman in black Ossan uniform, mostly hidden by the tall grasses, crawling her way down the side of the hill. Once Idrian had found the soldier he could see the trail of broken grass behind her. The grass was bloody, there was no mistaking it. "Halfwing, get your crews back to their stations."

"What's going on?" Tadeas asked.

Idrian handed him back the looking glass once more. "Look down the hill from that copse. Glassdamned Kerite is killing our scouts." He was running before he'd finished the sentence. "Braileer!" he bellowed. "Prepare my armor! I—" He was cut off by the sight of something out of the corner of his eye. Turning, he watched as a whole company of dragoons suddenly emerged from behind the trees, coming over the hill and thundering directly toward their position.

Tadeas was already screaming at the top of his lungs. "Sound the alarm! Kerite is upon us! Every soldier to their post!"

⸙   ⸙   ⸙

The dragoons swept down the hill and across the valley, and rode hard to flank the artillery battery before Tadeas's troops were in position. Idrian was half in his armor, Braileer fiddling with the buckles, when they heard the first mine go off. Idrian counted four more in quick succession, their blasts mixed with the bone-chilling sound of screaming horses and then followed by an irregular exchange of gunfire. By the time he returned, joining Tadeas in a commander's dugout just below the artillery, the hillside was covered with at least fifty dead or wounded dragoons. The rest had already turned tail, withdrawing beyond the range of the Ironhorns' muskets.

They wore orange-and-white Grent uniforms. Kerite, it seemed, had sent her Grent employers to do her dirty work.

The small victory turned sour in Idrian's mouth as he realized that, without Mika's mines, those dragoons would likely have overrun the hilltop before a proper defense could be mustered. It was a masterful flanking maneuver. He might have pointed out how well Mika's positioning had worked to Tadeas if not for the fact that infantry now poured over the hills to the west. Those directly across from the Ironhorns wore the orange and white of the Grent, while those attacking their opposite flank flew the blue-and-green mercenary flag of Kerite's Drakes.

Idrian searched for Braileer, only to find the young armorer hurrying toward him carrying his hammerglass buckler and smallsword. "You," Idrian told him, "haven't seen open battle yet. Keep your eyes on me at all times, but *don't* follow if I break rank. This isn't street fighting—no hanging on my heels to watch my back. Remain here with Tadeas. Be ready with bandages and extra cureglass if I'm forced to retreat."

"Yes, sir!"

"Good. Don't die. I'm starting to like you." Idrian found a lump of wax in his pocket and handed half of it to Braileer. Below the Ironhorns, the Ossan forces sounded the alarm, soldiers scrambling over each other to reach their positions while cartloads of glass were expedited to a spot just behind the front lines, where glassdancers readied themselves for the battle.

"We should have bloody well known better," Tadeas swore. "Attacking right at twilight. Glassdamned Kerite caught us with our pants down. This is gonna be bloody as piss."

It was the last thing Idrian heard clearly before stuffing wax into his ears, mere moments before the first cannon fired over his head. The blast shook him to the core, making his muscles hurt, and the sorceries mixing in his helmet allowed him the visual dexterity to follow the cannonball as it arced across the valley and slammed into the center of the Grent formation. The ball did not skip as it should, embedding itself into the hillside, and he could hear Halfwing's muffled shouts as she ordered corrections. Within moments the entire artillery battery was thumping away.

The glassdancers began their own attack just moments later. Sheets of glass, squares wider than a man was tall, shot from the hillside, propelled by invisible sorcery like kites high into the air, where they broke into sword-sized shards and began to fall on the Grent infantry. Each sheet could kill a whole platoon if undefended, but when the shards came to within a dozen feet of the infantry's heads they were redirected harmlessly away by Grent's own glassdancers.

The Grent infantry moved at an astonishing pace, barely fazed by either the glassdancers or the artillery attacks. Not even a glassdamned waver, and that alone made Idrian nervous.

The Grent closed to within firing distance of the Ossan line, where they pulled up suddenly and let off a withering barrage at the still-addled Ossan soldiers. Black smoke rose from both sides. A trumpet sounded, and breachers suddenly burst from the Grent formation. Idrian felt his eyes widen in astonishment as he counted—ten, twenty. He lost track at thirty and there might have been four times that many. They crossed the hundred yards between the two armies at a sprint that would make a racehorse jealous. In moments they were among the Ossan infantry, engaging Idrian's fellow breachers at close quarters.

Idrian fought the urge to race down that hill and engage them. They weren't his responsibility.

Someone was shouting at him, and he dug the wax from his ears long enough to hear Halfwing say, "The south battery has gone quiet! There's no communication!"

Idrian swallowed a lump in his throat, exchanged a glance with Tadeas, and then leapt from the commander's dugout. He ran around to a spot on the back of the hill, well behind his own artillery. A thousand National Guardsmen reinforcements waited just down the slope in loose formation, probably praying they wouldn't have to actually see combat today. From here Idrian could see across the four other hilltops that made up the core of the Ossan defense. Each had an artillery battery, and the center hilltop was marked by the large Foreign Legion flag with another, smaller flag showing General Stavri's silic sigil.

It wasn't that that concerned him. The farthest hill, way out on the southern flank of the Ossan defense nearly a mile away, was swarming with cuirassiers and dragoons wearing the blue and green of Kerite's mercenary company. The standards had fallen, the artillery battery overwhelmed even as the battle had only just begun. No doubt they had been hit by the same flanking maneuver as the Ironhorns, and had been less prepared for it.

Idrian's heart was in his throat. He turned to sprint back to Tadeas only to come up short. Around that same copse that had screened the earlier dragoons came Grent cuirassiers, the thunder of their hooves lost beneath the sound of Idrian's own artillery. There were at least six hundred of them and they were coming hard, but not to the position their fellow cavalry had already tested. They were headed straight toward the poorly trained, poorly prepared National Guard reserves. If *they* fled, there would be no one to protect the rear of the hill, where Mika hadn't planted any mines and the earthen fortifications were few.

"Tadeas!" Idrian shouted between cannon blasts. "Look to your rear!"

He didn't wait for orders, acting on pure instinct, knowing that a single moment of hesitation would cost him his courage. He could see the National Guard officers trying to form up their troops to meet a cavalry charge, though half of them didn't even have their bayonets fixed. The National Guard wavered.

Idrian's feet barely touched the ground, eating up the yards, pushing himself harder and harder lest the reserves break before he could even reach them.

"National Guard, with me!" he roared, the words tearing his throat raw. He was close to their position now, and he angled himself to take the cuirassiers head-on. The ground shook from their charge and they seemed to be a wall of horses, men, and glinting breastplates adorned with blue hammerglass and the orange streamers of the Grent ducal house.

What could one breacher do to arrest that charge? But he did not stop. He could not afford to. He was the Ram, and if he relented then good soldiers would die.

He leapt the front line, coming up even with the riders for half a second, his shield clipping a cuirassier on his left and tearing her from her horse while his sword dipped and cut a jagged swath through man and horse on his right. He landed, rolled out of the way of charging hooves, then thrust out his sword like a stick through the spokes of a wagon wheel. It was a chaotic, bloody dance as he darted between the stampeding animals. He dodged horses, ducked swords, and threw himself out of the way of a lance. All the while his own sword dipped and swayed, slicing through anything that came within reach—extended arms, legs in the stirrups, and horse legs. Lots of horse legs, vivisecting themselves on his razorglass with little actual effort on his part.

The screaming of horses would stay with him for weeks. It always did.

As suddenly as the charge had arrived, it was past him, and Idrian found himself standing in the center of a bloody charnel house of the dead and dying. There were dozens of fallen cavalry around him, but was that enough? He swung around to find that the cuirassiers had hit the National Guardsmen as intended. But their charge had hesitated, the heart cut out of it, and despite the guardsmen's disarray they had managed to keep the cuirassiers from cracking them entirely. Even as Idrian watched, the cuirassiers slowed, stopped, and then began to pull back.

They found him waiting for them, and he made them pay for their flanking gambit. By the time they had fully disengaged, less than half of them remained—and those took further losses, as over a hundred of the Ironhorns had come to Idrian's aid. The Ironhorns marched in a tight square, rotating musketmen firing on the retreating cavalry.

Idrian found Valient in the center of the square, but his fellow captain just waved him on. "I'll make sure the National Guardsmen hold!" Valient shouted. "Get back to Tadeas!"

Idrian did as he was told, and it didn't take more than a glance as he joined Tadeas in the commander's dugout to see that everything had gone wrong. The Ossan front lines . . . simply didn't exist anymore. The Grent and their infantry had rolled right over them, and the secondary line, and the tertiary. Ossan soldiers fled openly, running up the hill toward the Ironhorns or across the open valley on their flank, where the fools would be run down by what remained of those cuirassiers. He couldn't even see the brightly embroidered black uniforms of any Ossan glassdancers left down there.

Tadeas stared at Idrian's gore-soaked armor without comment. "Just got signals from General Stavri," he said coolly. "Both southern batteries have fallen and he's being hard-pressed. He's ordered us to hitch up the artillery and withdraw immediately."

"Already?" Idrian breathed, hearing the wondrous despair in his own voice. The Foreign Legion was not some slouching provincial force. They were the best soldiers in the world, and they'd just been absolutely destroyed by a couple of Grent brigades and an equal number of foreign mercenaries. Not even at his most pessimistic had he imagined this going so badly. "If we pull out now," Idrian said, pointing his sword down the hill, "every man and woman of ours down there will be dead by midnight."

"We're to take great pains to save the artillery pieces," Tadeas said.

"Piss on the artillery pieces. What about the glassdamned soldiers?"

"Agreed." Tadeas swung around, barking orders. "Kess, get our standard up to the top of the hill! As high as you can get it, and wave it like your glassdamned life depends on it! Halfwing, switch to grapeshot and put it just over our heads. Just over, hear me? I want our comrades to feel the breeze in their hair. Dristus, tell Valient to get his ass back here and to bring those National Guard reserves with him!"

Idrian watched the soldiers snap to their orders and then turned his gaze on Tadeas. Tadeas squared his jaw, inhaling sharply as he looked down at the swiftly collapsing battlefield. He said, "We form a wedge around the artillery and we get everyone we can inside that wedge, then we withdraw at our leisure. Understand?"

"Understood," Idrian said, taking a shaky breath and looking down at the Grent breachers now coming up the slope, knee-deep in the gore from slaughtering fleeing Ossan infantry. "I'll buy us time."

"Sir," Braileer called, "if you go down there, you might not come back."

"That's my job, armorer," Idrian replied. "Horns ready, hooves steady. Give me some noise."

"Ironhorns!" Tadeas shouted. "We have the Ram!"

"We have the Ram!" Mika repeated from her spot with the engineers.

"We have the Ram!" someone shouted. The call was repeated up and down the line until it became a chant. "Os-sa! Os-sa! Os-sa!"

The artillery fell silent as Halfwing and her crews switched to grapeshot. Idrian leapt onto the front fortification of the commander's dugout and slammed his sword against his shield with the tempo of the chant. Three times, roaring wordlessly into the wind, until he was sure that every soldier within three hundred yards was looking directly at him.

"To us!" he shouted. "To the Ironhorns!"

"To the Ironhorns! Os-sa! To the Ironhorns!" The call washed down the hillside like an avalanche, putting hammerglass into the spines of the fleeing Ossan soldiers. Idrian let himself be seen for a few more moments until he heard Halfwing shout to Tadeas.

"Artillery ready!"

Idrian leapt from the commander's dugout, barreling down the hillside. Ossan soldiers jumped from his path, cheering him on, and he hit the first Grent breacher with the force of a runaway carriage, their shields connecting with a reverberating boom. Idrian plowed over the poor bastard, dipping his sword back to finish the job, only barely slowing his run.

The next was not so easy, dodging Idrian's bulk and forcing him into a duel. It was short and brutal, and Idrian caught the breacher's sword on his own hammerglass, splitting several inches into his shield, before taking her legs out from under her.

Idrian sliced his way through an entire company of Grent infantry who were so intent on bayoneting Ossan soldiers in the back that they didn't even see him coming. Their breacher reacted too slowly, then tried to get the high ground on Idrian, turning his back toward the Ironhorns. He was rewarded with a bullet to the back of the head, no doubt fired by one of Valient's marksmen. Idrian spotted a Grent glassdancer, marked out by the orange epaulets on his uniform. The glassdancer was staring right at him, and Idrian threw himself to the ground.

A shard of glass the size of Idrian's hand sliced through the air where he'd been standing. It stopped in midair, reversing direction, and Idrian lured it to within feet of him before bringing up his shield. The glass hit his shield with surprisingly little force, shattering into a thousand little shards that even the best glassdancer would have a hard time controlling. Idrian ducked and weaved, conscious that a new attack could come from any direction, and charged. The best defense against a glassdancer was not that dissimilar to the defense against a marksman: give them a moving target, get them riled up, and hope their concentration slipped.

It did, and the last thing Idrian saw of the man before he took his head was the nervous sweat pouring down his brow.

The clash continued through the last of the twilight as the Grent advance slowly stalled and then finally retreated, cut down by the score by Halfwing's grapeshot. A lone flare suddenly lit the night, and Idrian could see that he was practically alone. Every soldier who could still run had made it to the Ironhorn lines. The hillside was slick with blood, jumbled with corpses.

Below them, just out of reach of Halfwing's grapeshot, the Grent infantry were re-forming. They would assault the hill once more, and this time there would be nothing between them and the Ironhorns.

Idrian sprinted back up the hill to find Tadeas and Braileer still in the commander's dugout. The artillery had gone silent once again, and though the pieces were still there, the crews were gone. In fact, everyone seemed to have pulled out, or was in the process of doing so, the wounded and harried fleeing down a safe corridor of National Guardsmen. Braileer took Idrian's shield and reached up to fix an extra piece of cureglass to his ear. Idrian let him.

"They're coming, boss," Mika shouted from her blasting wheel.

"We out?" Idrian asked Tadeas.

"We're out. To piss with General Stavri, to piss with the Assembly, and to piss with the Grent. We just saved at least a thousand legionaries and it cost us a few artillery pieces to do, so my conscience is clear."

Over at the blasting wheel, Mika struck a match and touched it to something, which began to burn and crackle furiously. "Slow-burning fuse," she explained to Braileer, shielding her eyes from the light as she peered down into the valley. "If they maintain that march, all my mines will go off right as they reach this dugout."

Idrian looked pointedly to several barrels of powder at Mika's feet. They were connected by blasting cord to her slow-burning fuse. "Those aren't mines."

"Can't leave our artillery pieces for the enemy, now can we?" Tadeas replied. He slapped Idrian on the shoulder. "You did your part. Let's go."

Idrian paused to look back down into the darkness. The hillside seemed to writhe with the wounded, many of whom would not see the morning, and beyond that he could see the newly re-formed rows of Grent infantry marching toward them from the west. Kerite's Drakes moved forward in a pincer movement from the southwest. There were breachers and glass-dancers among them—far too many to fight. The next hill over was almost overrun, the last of that battalion holding on just long enough that the Iron-horns didn't take it in the flank.

Idrian waved his thanks to them, though he knew they could not see it, then followed Tadeas and Mika as they left the artillery battery at a run.

He was so tired he didn't even look back when the entire hilltop exploded behind them.

31

Kizzie spent the rest of the day working through the membership list of the Glass Knife. She created a personal dossier for each name, cross-checking them with easily verified alibis and hyper-loyal potential patsies. There was, she had to admit, a lot of guild-family power in this little Fulgurist Society: a matriarch, two heirs, seven direct children, and five cousins—as well, of course, as the Duke of Grent's brother. The Dorlani, Magna, Kirkovik, and Stavri were all represented. A diverse group by any standards, and one that caused her stomach to tie itself in knots at the thought of them all working together toward a single conspiracy.

Her instinct was to go ask for Capric's help. He was personal friends with one of the Stavri, and he might give her an in. Something stopped her, though. She couldn't help but wonder why there wasn't a Vorcien in the Glass Knife. Was that on purpose? Was this club some kind of secret check on Father Vorcien's power within the Assembly? Perhaps it was a coincidence or perhaps there were other members not listed. A Vorcien might be among those.

Regardless, she needed to be cautious about who she mentioned this to. If the Glass Knife already had blood on their hands from other occasions, they would no doubt move to snuff out an enforcer they found sniffing around in their affairs.

She had to start somewhere, and it wasn't hard to find a somewhat more public link between three of the names on the list: they all belonged to the Bingham Brawlers, a boxing club out in the far western suburbs of Ossa. She knew of the place, though she'd never been to it. It wouldn't be hard to head out in that direction, mingle and ask a few questions, and either stay over-night or take a carriage home. At the very least she could gather alibis for one or more of them. The only problem was that the Foreign Legion was way out there facing a new Grent army, and a battle might take place in the morning.

She took a hackney cab to the edge of Ossa, where the driver insisted on turning back on rumors that a battle had already happened. Kizzie let him go and set off on foot. The walk was long but pleasant, taking Kizzie away from the city as night fell and a chill crept into her bones. She stopped twice for hot coffee at the small cafés that grew farther and farther apart as tenements gave way to tract housing, then to the small, lower-class farms that provided most of the fresh produce for Ossa. Eventually the gas lanterns that lit the highway stopped altogether, and she was left to finish the rest of her journey in the dark.

She was less than a mile away from her destination when she heard the clatter of hooves on the cobbles. It was a horse moving at a trot despite the darkness, and she put her braided godglass earrings in just long enough to make out the approaching silhouette: a military messenger in the black uniform of the Foreign Legion.

Kizzie hailed him with a shout and a wave, holding her hand out flat so he could see her silic sigil. He did not slow until he was almost upon her. When he did, he squinted hard at her hand and then gave her a respectful nod. "Good evening, Lady Vorcien," he said.

She did not correct him. It was always amusing when people mistook her for a cousin rather than a bastard. "Any news from the war?" she asked. "My cabdriver seemed to think a battle had already taken place." Looking closer, she could now see that the messenger was harried, his cloak askew, horse tired, head drooping.

"It'll be in the newspaper in the morning," he answered, his voice exhausted. "We suffered a mighty loss."

Kizzie rocked back on her heels, genuinely shocked by the news. The Foreign Legion didn't suffer losses often, and when they did they were on a distant continent, reported in the newspaper months after the fact. "I'm only going as far as Bingham tonight," she told him. "Am I in danger?"

"You're in no danger tonight, but I wouldn't travel any farther west if I were you. The Grent and their pet mercenary hold the Copper Hills. Is there anything else? I must hurry to take news to the Assembly."

"No, no," Kizzie said, her thoughts suddenly filled with marching armies and roaming soldiers. If the enemy was closing in, the normal rules no longer applied; the region was no longer subject to the complicated alliances of guild-family enforcers and National Guardsmen, but to large groups of infantry. Despite his reassurance, she was tempted to turn back. "Good luck."

"Thank you, Lady Vorcien. Oh, and just a suggestion: avoid the Bingham Brawlers Club."

Kizzie's breath caught in her throat. "Why?"

"I just came from there. General Stavri and his senior officers have stopped to, ahem, gird themselves with a drink before they have to report their loss to the Assembly tonight. The place is packed with angry officers right now."

"Thanks for the warning," Kizzie replied, waving the messenger on his way. She cringed as she listened to the sound of his horse's hooves disappear into the darkness. Losing a battle to Grent this close to the capital was certainly more important than her mission, but it also seemed to have interfered directly. If the Bingham Brawlers Club was filled with officers trying to get very drunk very quickly, it was a *bad* time to go looking for alibis.

And yet . . . General Stavri's little brother, Agrippo Stavri, was one of the names on her list, *and* was attached to General Stavri's staff. That meant four of her fifteen suspects might all be under one roof. It was risky, but a very tempting target.

She decided to continue on, trekking through the cold evening until the street was finally lit once more with gas lamps. She was soon among the tract houses of Bingham, with proper evening traffic out on the streets. She could sense no agitation from the public. Word must have not yet gotten out about the nearby loss. Part of her felt for these people: if the Grent army pressed without opposition, Bingham could be under occupation in days.

The thought hurried her steps, and she wound through Bingham until she reached a side street with an old converted tenement whose entire second floor had been whitewashed, with the words BINGHAM BRAWLERS CLUB lit up by gas lamps. It was a quiet neighborhood, and she was surprised to hear nothing of carousing or angry shouts as she walked up to the front door. There was also no doorman. She paused outside, glancing around. Even quiet clubs had a doorman, often smoking their pipe, chatting with the locals. No doorman, no locals, no guild-family members enjoying a cigar in the crisp night air.

The hairs on the back of Kizzie's neck stood on end. It wasn't that she couldn't hear carousing: she couldn't hear *anything*. It was as silent as if the club were closed. She approached the well-lit doorway, one hand slipping into her jacket for her stiletto, and slowly pushed in the door. It wasn't locked.

"What the piss is going on?" she whispered to herself. The front hall was empty, the club deathly silent. She stopped at the coatroom, glancing inside for an attendant. No one, but the coatroom was absolutely stuffed with uniform jackets and fine cloaks and dusters. She drew out her stiletto, trying to think of an explanation. Was the whole club participating in some kind of lark? Had they rushed out into the street to warn Bingham about approaching Grent soldiers? Had they fled entirely? If that were the case, she would have passed them or at *least* heard them. This didn't make sense.

Perhaps everyone was on the top floor of the club watching a particularly riveting boxing match?

As it turned out, she did not need to go up to the top floor for answers. She didn't need to proceed more than a dozen paces. She rounded the corner to where the narrow entrance hall opened up into a large, formal dining area surrounding a boxing ring only to stop dead in her tracks.

The room was filled with corpses. There were dozens of them, strewn about like confetti; splayed across tables, fallen in the aisle, slumped against walls. At a glance she could not determine what had killed them, but the amount of blood was truly horrific. There was no sound, not even a moan. The entire place was perfectly still, like a sculptor's tableau.

The shock of it numbed her, keeping her from fleeing. She checked the nearest body: a young man in a smart dinner jacket, his throat slit. Still warm. Very warm, *and* the blood was still pooling around the corpses. These people had all been dead for a very short amount of time. A little further inspection showed that every piece of regular glass inside the room had shattered, and was either *in* or near a corpse. The work of a glassdancer. A very, very, *very* good glassdancer.

It didn't seem possible. Kizzie had seen the work of the best glassdancers and it had never looked anything like this. No one had even had time to scream. The neighborhood wasn't roused. Kizzie's blood felt frozen in her veins and for only the second time in her life she realized she was *terrified*. Her feet seemed rooted to the floor and she struggled to make a decision. Shaky-handed, she fished a piece of skyglass from her pocket—almost dropping it in the process—and threaded it through one of her ear piercings.

The sorcery immediately calmed her, settling the tremble in her fingers and letting her *think*. She cocked her head, listening carefully. No sound from the floors above. Her glassdancer sorcery detected no glassdancers in the building. The killer—or killers—must have fled just before she arrived.

This whole thing was terrifying, but it had also given her a unique opportunity.

Kizzie added her braided godglass earrings and, soaking in all four types of sorcery, launched herself into action. She hurried across the room, stepping carefully to keep from leaving footprints in the blood, looking at the face of each corpse. Over half of them were in uniform—the officers from the lost battle—and it was these she focused on.

In her search she recognized two distant Vorcien cousins and a school friend of hers from childhood. She did not give any of them a second glance. General Stavri was easy to identify, lying slumped across a table, the remnants of a shot glass embedded in the back of his skull. She found his little brother at the same table. Colonel Agrippo Stavri was still sitting, staring sightlessly and slack-jawed with a decorative, wind chime–shaped piece of chandelier lodged just above his sternum. Kizzie ransacked Agrippo's uniform pockets. She found a pocket watch, a checkbook, a billfold, and a bundle of letters soaked in blood. She left the pocket watch and checkbook, searched the billfold, and wrapped the letters in a napkin before stuffing them in her pocket.

She resumed her search but found only one of the four suspects she'd originally come to research. Her name was Fioda Jaque, and she'd been walking toward the stairs when a wineglass had decapitated her. Kizzie searched her pockets as well but came up with nothing more than a watch and billfold. She left both.

The search had left Kizzie nauseous and shaky, her nerves a complete mess despite the skyglass. No amount of willpower could force her up the stairs to the next floor, no matter what kind of clues she might find. She took one last glance around and decided she'd stumbled on something military in nature. It couldn't be anything else: the Grent must have sent glassdancer assassins after the losing Ossan officers.

Common sense finally made its way through her shock and the skyglass, and Kizzie realized she was the only living person inside a building full of important corpses. She needed to raise an alarm, and she needed to do it without being recognized.

She was almost to the front hall when a sound caught her ear. She paused, glancing back, wondering if she'd missed a survivor. She was caught in the sudden dilemma of trying to save them or getting out of here quickly. The sound repeated. *Thump. Thump. Thump.* Kizzie's stomach tied itself in knots. Those were footsteps coming down the stairs on the far side of the room.

Kizzie tore her rooted feet from the floor and raced toward the exit, no longer caring to do so silently. As she ran around the corner to the narrow hallway she caught a single glance of someone stepping into the boxing hall: an impossibly tall man with white skin and a bald head. Their gazes met briefly.

Kizzie was not sure if he pursued her. She was practically flying now, summoning every ounce of sorcery that she could get from the forgeglass in her braided earrings. As she raced past the coatroom she snatched up a scarf still sitting on the counter, throwing it around her neck and pulling it up to hide her face. She emerged into the street at a sprint, screaming at the top of her lungs.

"Murder! Call the National Guard! Sound the alarms!" Before she'd even reached the end of the street she could see curious faces poking out the windows of nearby tenements. She found a watchhouse on the next street and banged on the doors until the National Guardsmen emerged, pointing them in the direction of the Bingham Brawlers Club.

As the National Guardsmen rushed past her with their weapons, she caught sight of the Tall Man. He was standing just across the street, a dark splash across the front of his gray tunic. He held no weapons.

He was staring directly at her.

Kizzie stared back, her heart in her throat, a feeling of absolute dread twisting her guts like the knots of a blackwood vine. No one else seemed to note or care about his presence, and she could not bring herself to call the National Guardsmen's attention to the Tall Man. She tried to probe with her sorcerous senses, looking out for any sign of his sorcery, but she came back with nothing. Glassdancers *could not* hide their presence, and she could feel no imminent attack.

The Tall Man took a step toward her. She steeled herself against the dread. *He* wasn't the glassdancer. What had Gorian said? Someone of his description might be connected with the serial murder of siliceers? Perhaps he was a Stavri agent, here to report to his master, and had arrived just moments before her to find the grisly scene. But then, why did he have blood on his tunic? Kizzie had no interest in a confrontation. She forced herself to relax, letting the growing crowd sweep her away. She was pulled along back toward the club, past the screaming and wailing, and then escaped against the growing torrent of onlookers in the opposite direction.

She hired a hackney cab and did not allow herself a sigh of relief until she was back in Ossa, sitting under the bright lights of a late-night café at nearly midnight. It was the second time in three days that she had witnessed that Tall Man near an important body. That couldn't be a coincidence. But the club back there was full of officers, not lone siliceers or a blackmailed Magna. Shaken and exhausted, she ordered coffee and produced the bundle of bloodstained letters from her pocket, hiding them from the waiter with her menu. She did her best to put the Tall Man out of her thoughts.

The first letter was from one of Agrippo's mistresses and it was *very* saucy. Kizzie kept that one. The second was barely legible, perhaps some correspondence with a banker. The third and fourth were too soaked in blood for her to read more than a few words. The fifth, however, was something else. It was a plain white envelope, spattered with Agrippo's blood, and inside was a simple note. It said, *The deed is done. I will tolerate no more blackmail. Deliver your end of the bargain or face my wrath, the newspapers be damned.* Kizzie stared at it for several moments before lifting the envelope. It was postmarked the *day of* Adriana Grappo's murder.

For half a moment, Kizzie forgot all about the Tall Man and his room filled with corpses. This *had* to be something. Agrippo might not have been Adriana's fourth killer, but had he blackmailed that someone into it?

Something about that letter was bothering her, though. She *recognized* that handwriting. But from where? A calling card? A letter? She hid the bundle of letters once more under her menu as the waiter brought her coffee, thanking him and then gathering her wits once more.

The Grent war, Adriana's death, the secret sorcery war, the Glass Knife. This was all connected. But how and why? Agrippo might have been able to tell her, but he was dead. The blackmailed party probably *couldn't* tell her, but at least she would be able to mete out some justice. She just had to find out who it was.

32

Demir remained on his vigil on the front step of the Hyacinth for the rest of the day, though it was clear that the worst of things had passed. Enforcers cleared the streets, the Cinders and National Guard patrolled regularly, and by the late night the district was at peace once more. It was, he decided as he stood out front, looking across at the Hyacinth's stables where the doors had been torn from their hinges, a fragile peace. Godglass prices would continue to increase, and these riots would only get worse.

Would he even be on hand for the next one? Or would Tirana be forced to deploy her enforcers to protect the hotel, escalating the violence until people ended up dead?

The questions haunted him as he went back inside, walking through the empty lobby where only a few gas lamps remained lit and a single porter was on duty at the concierge's office. Demir paused at the desk. "It's Mahren, right?" he asked the porter.

"Yes, sir," Mahren responded with a smile. "What can I do for you, sir?"

"Find out the name of the captain of the Cinders who I defied this afternoon. I want you to send him a case of Ereptian wine."

"Sir?"

"Best not to stay on the bad side of the Cinders," Demir explained. He'd already drawn up an apology in his head, explaining with all earnestness that he'd only been looking out for the safety of the Cinders themselves and he might have overstepped his bounds. It was bullshit, but Cinders weren't known for their grasp of subtlety. A case of wine and some contrition would go a long way.

"I'll send it over first thing in the morning."

"Perfect."

"Good night, sir."

Demir raised a hand in answer as he headed past the stairs, down the hall, and out into the dark, silent garden. Three weeks since his mother's death, and a few candles had still been left in front of the family mausoleum. It was a testament to how much the hotel staff loved her. Demir paused to watch the candles flicker, searching his memories for the last time they'd been together in this very garden. It was probably during a quiet memorial on the anniversary of his father's death thirteen or fourteen years ago. Half his lifetime. It seemed strange that it could be so long.

Lamps were still lit in the small workshop on the far end of the garden, but when Demir reached it he found Thessa missing. She'd been here recently— the workbenches were covered in pages upon pages of notes, and a fire still burned in the furnace. He sat down in her chair and looked over those notes. One page described every single aspect of the workshop itself, from the furnace walls to the tools. *Recent repairs,* it said in quick, flowing handwriting, *keep an eye on crack at the back of furnace.* There was a shopping list beside it. *Better bit iron. Eight ounces of omnisand. Larger water bucket.*

The notes quickly moved beyond the mundane, and he could see that she'd made a thorough examination of both the destroyed phoenix channel prototype and the original schematics. There were a dozen drawings of possible alterations, and extensive ruminations on alternative power sources.

How long was it since the riot? Nine hours? And she'd made this much progress already. Demir flipped through the pages, understanding only half of it, growing more and more impressed. She wasn't just a siliceer with an ear for resonance. She was a proper engineer—someone who understood theory and science at the highest levels. He found a page that contained a small treatise on insulation and how it could be applied to the phoenix channel to increase the energy-to-sorcery return.

He sat back, pushing the papers away from him, lost in thought.

"Demir?"

He craned his neck to see Montego standing in the doorway. "How did it go?" Demir asked.

Montego looked tired, his wide brow creased by a scowl. He'd been gone since sunup, rushing around to make sure that there'd be no further action after the Ivory Forest Glassworks. "I *think* things are quiet," he rumbled. "The Magna want to question both of us but have been distracted all day by the riots. No one followed us to Wagonside, so the Prosotsi are in the clear. Not a single mention of Thessa's name or her pseudonym. They likely think she died in the fire, but that might change once they get a better count of prisoners and the corpses." Montego paused. "I heard you stood up to the Cinders on behalf of rioting teamsters."

Demir grimaced, bracing himself for a lecture. "I didn't want to see people die," he said.

"Good."

Demir raised an eyebrow at Montego. "Good?"

"Yes. That is the Demir I know. The old Demir."

"The old Demir would have never been so stupid."

"Bollocks. The old Demir didn't take shit from anyone. He used his power to help people."

"Did I?" Demir asked faintly, trying to look into his own past. "I don't even remember anymore. My whole past is a foggy tableau of sex, power, and arrogance."

"You were still a child," Montego pointed out gently. "Perhaps you had excesses, but I've always known you to have your heart in the right place. Remember that orphanage out past Bravectia? You seduced a woman three times your age to get those kids indefinite funding."

Demir felt the corner of his mouth twitch upward at the memory. "Did I do it for the kids, or did I do it for the challenge?"

"I met that woman, Demir. You definitely did it for the kids." Montego clapped his hands together. "Bah! I'm exhausted from pretending to care about the Magna all day. I'm going to bed."

Demir turned back to watch the fire in the furnace. Was it the old Demir? Had that shadow of himself escaped the prison in the back of his mind? It didn't feel like it. He still had no confidence. He still feared reprisal from the Cinders, or censure from the other guild-families. Taking the side of a mob so blatantly would surely have consequences.

Sick of his own thoughts, Demir went looking for Thessa. It was with some surprise that he found her on the roof, sitting beside the mews, one hand reaching through the bars to gently stroke the injured falcon inside. He shut the door behind him, sure to make just enough noise that his presence didn't go undetected. The roof was lit only by a sliver of moonlight, and he found a piece of sightglass in his pocket to enhance his vision.

"Is he yours?" he asked.

To his surprise, Thessa sniffed and dabbed at her face with a sleeve before turning toward him. Her eyes were red, her cheeks damp. "You didn't know?"

Demir came over to sit beside her, looking at the falcon through the caging of the mews. Its left wing was bandaged but it seemed to have calmed down since first arriving at the hotel. It bore Thessa's stroking with remarkable patience, huddled close to her. He said, "I couldn't be sure. Kastora told me you were an accomplished falconer, so when I saw an injured falcon outside an empty mews, I made a leap."

"You brought him all the way back from a war zone?"

Demir chuckled. "It was a pain in the ass, really. I had to use a glove as an impromptu hood until I could borrow one from an officer. Your guy was not happy." He paused, tapping the ground with one finger to get the falcon's attention. "I inherited a falcon from my dad when I was a kid. He died right around the time my political career started to pick up, and I just never had the chance to go back to it. I suppose it left me with a soft spot."

"His name is Ekhi," Thessa told him. "He's the last thing I have from my parents. I thought I'd lost him. It twisted my gut into knots, and here he is."

Demir examined the side of Thessa's face, surprised at how raw and vulnerable she looked over a single falcon. "I was going to mention him earlier today, but the riots took my attention."

Thessa lowered her hand from the bird, pulling it back through the narrow bars. She gave a little shudder, and that vulnerability seemed to melt away. "About that . . . look, I'm sorry about the forgeglass. I acted on instinct, and it was completely out of my rights. You had things in hand. I shouldn't have intervened."

"I'm not so sure I did." Every instinct told Demir to give Thessa a dressing-down. That was what a guild-family patriarch did when someone overstepped themselves. It wasn't just his right, it was his duty. He could hear his mother's teachings in the back of his head. He needed to maintain his authority, or no one would respect him. Instead, he just shook his head. "There's no telling what a mob will do. Maybe my dumb speech was enough. Maybe this was enough." He touched his glassdancer sigil. "The mob might have even turned on us in the effort to get free forgeglass. But the fact is they didn't. The Grappo earned a lot of goodwill today, and I have you to thank for it."

"Me?" Thessa scoffed. "You stood up to the Cinders for commoners. When's the last time *that* happened?"

"And I'll probably lose some alliances for it," Demir said thoughtfully. "I suppose I did gain some friends. One of the union bosses came to me this evening asking to become my client. Just him and his family—not the whole union—but it's a powerful message. He's abandoning the Stavri for us."

"May he be the first of many." Thessa wiped her eyes again and smiled at him. It was a sad smile, but pretty, and it caught Demir off guard. The moment suddenly reminded him of his first sweetheart; sitting under the stars on the hotel roof, sharing a bottle of pilfered wine while her father searched the hotel for her. He tried to remember her name and found he could not. What happened to her, he wondered. Her father was a traveling merchant, and Demir had never seen her again after that night.

Demir moved away from the mews, shifting to sit across from Thessa with his back to a chimney. She stretched out, tapping his feet with hers. For the first time he noticed that she was clutching a sheaf of papers. "Did you have a chance to look over the contract?" he asked, guessing at what they were.

"Ah." She lifted the papers, handing them across to him. "I had Breenen draw up a copy. All signed."

"No alterations?"

"None. The contract is perfect. If anything, it favors me by a large margin."

Demir stared at her signature for a few moments, then at the place where his own would go, before he went to bed. They'd already shaken hands on their deal, but he'd nursed a pervasive worry that she would back out at the last minute. "A partner isn't quite the same as a client-patron relationship, but all the same: welcome to the Grappo guild-family."

To his surprise, Thessa gave a happy little shudder. "Oh! So strange. I knew a day like this would come eventually, but I expected it was a decade off."

Demir regarded her for a moment. Perhaps it was the high emotion of facing down a crowd, or the fact that Thessa was finally wearing a sleek tunic that fit her properly, but he felt like he was looking at her with different eyes. She looked so young, but everything about her was old—her poise, confidence, professionalism. She didn't just have the skills of an experienced siliceer, she had the body language of one too. It was, as much as he hated to admit it, deeply attractive.

"I don't mean to pry," she said shyly, "but I saw the mausoleum in the hotel garden. A few of the porters lit candles there while I was working. Is that . . . where your mother is?"

"It's where all the patriarchs and matriarchs of the Grappo get buried," Demir replied. He looked up into the sky, staring at the glittering of the stars, his thoughts turning to that purple-and-white marble. "I think I might be the last one." He looked sharply at Thessa, immediately regretting the words—and the glimpse into his fears that it gave her—but she was also staring into the sky.

"You don't think you'll have children?" she asked.

"I'm twenty-nine. If I had a child next year I'd be ten years too late on creating the brood for a new generation of Grappo. At least according to most guild-families." Demir felt a spike of anger at all the responsibilities and expectations piled on his shoulders, but forced it back down. "You?"

"Hah!" Thessa blurted. "Most female siliceers don't even start thinking about kids until their thirties. The opposite of you guild-family types, I suppose. Until a week ago my plan was to finish my tutelage under Kastora and start my own glassworks. Maybe even inherit his. I'd think about a family after." A half smile formed on her lips. "You know, I've always preferred men, but figured I'd end up with a woman. Easier that way. Cleaner. We'd just adopt, and I'd never have to worry about the rigmarole of pregnancy."

"Smart," Demir commented, watching her carefully. The conversation had turned more personal than he'd intended. Was that by happenstance? Or was she probing? "Does business come into it?"

"Business *always* comes into it," Thessa replied, "as I'm sure you know better than I."

Demir snorted. "It's what's expected." He paused, biting his tongue, knowing he should guard himself. He barely knew Thessa, and she was his new business partner. He needed to remain closed off. "The truth is, I don't want to make a deal with some guild-family for a wife. That's what they all do and it sickens me. I'd take her family prestige, she'd take my money. We'd have misters and mistresses on the side and grow to hate each other over cold dinners in empty dining halls." Demir swallowed a mouthful of bile. "I think I'd leave again before it came to that."

"Even though that's what everyone does?"

"Especially because that's what everyone does." Demir tapped Thessa's boot with his own. "The thing is, I know that there are good people among the guild-families. Interesting people. Intelligent people. If you gave me a week I could probably come up with a dozen women in Ossa who I could live with, and even enjoy. But it's the trappings of it all that I hate. The expectations. The coldness of the contracts."

"I would never have pegged you as a romantic." Thessa was grinning now, and it made Demir laugh.

"Maybe I am. I've always liked the idea of the world being better than it really is. Comes from not being allowed a proper childhood, I suppose. I never got to grow out of childish ideas."

Thessa's grin slowly faded, and Demir wondered if he'd said the wrong thing. After a few moments of silence she said, "Mine was cut short too." Demir waited for her to explain further, but she just stared at her hands. "I don't know where Kastora is buried."

It was an odd non sequitur. "I'm sure we can find out. Might have to wait until after the war."

She seemed relieved by this. She continued, "I'd like that. I still don't know where my parents are buried. I'd already been sent to study under Kastora when they died and I just . . . never returned." Demir peered at her. Not a non sequitur after all. Thessa paused, looking thoughtfully over Demir's shoulder. "I wasn't there, and I blamed myself for that for a long time. It's funny, I have nightmares about their deaths even though I didn't see it. I sometimes wonder if my imagination is worse than the event itself."

"How did they die?" Demir asked, his curiosity getting the better of him. She just shook her head, but Demir got the distinct impression that they'd been killed. He put his hands in his pockets, his attention returned entirely to Thessa. "Why did you blame yourself?"

"Because," she said with a shrug, "I . . . I'm not even sure. I guess I felt like I could have done something. But I was a thirteen-year-old girl. How crazy is that?"

"I *could* have done something to protect my mother," Demir said unhappily. His mirth was gone, and he regretted it. "I'm a glassdancer. Six thugs with cudgels would have been a pile of meat before they could have struck her."

"Only if you'd *been* there," Thessa pointed out.

"But I might have been. If I'd been in the capital at the time, I probably would have walked her home from the Assembly. I used to be on the Assembly myself. I . . . ." He trailed off. "I guess I technically am still. You know, I've been thinking about her death every day since word arrived. What I would have done. The pain I would have inflicted on the people who wanted to hurt her."

"Those people," Thessa said softly, "were not stupid. You're a glassdancer, and they would have made sure to do it when you couldn't defend her."

Demir didn't want her to be right. It was easier to think poorly of himself, to give in to recrimination and anger, than it was to face reality. He knew because it was the same thing he'd done inside his head for years. "You're far too wise for your age," he said.

"And you're far too haunted for yours," she replied. She swallowed hard, her eyes widening slightly, as if realizing that she might have stepped over the line.

Demir knew he should be irritated. She *had* overstepped her bounds, and any other guild-family patriarch would have put her in her place. But as before, he just couldn't quite bring himself to do it. "Oh? What's that supposed to mean?"

Thessa hesitated. "It means I can tell that you think you're some kind of monster, like when you took off your glove in the omnichapel this morning. But it's obvious you're not a monster. I saw the way you protected your hotel, and then those people in the street that you owed nothing." Thessa gave an embarrassed laugh. "I'm so sorry, I'm waxing philosophical about things that I know nothing about. Please forgive me."

Demir stared at her, feeling both touched and bemused. "You are something else," he said.

"I really am sorry."

"Don't apologize. Montego is the only one who's spoken so candidly with me for . . . since I can remember. I'm not sure I agree with you, but I can appreciate your honesty." He snorted, looking down at the contract in his hands. He got the distinct feeling that he'd made out better in this new partnership than she had. "You're a very likable person, Thessa Foleer. Use that to your advantage."

Her eyes narrowed slightly, her chin rising toward him. "Are you tired?" she asked, reaching one hand behind her as if by instinct to pet Ekhi through the mews bars.

"Pardon?"

"I'm just saying . . . we have a new partnership." She pursed her lips in a smile. "Why don't we go back to my suite and split a bottle of wine? You'll have to spring for the wine, though. I seem to have left my wallet in Grent."

Demir felt a warm little pleasant feeling in the pit of his stomach. The darkness that had swirled around inside him just moments ago seemed to have fled. His inner thoughts were quiet, his body relaxed, and he returned her smile. Why not? He pretended to pat his pockets, looking around in mock alarm. "I'm not sure if I can afford it either. Maybe something *very* cheap, I . . . Yes! Of course, let's go raid my glassdamned wine cellar." He got to his feet and reached a hand down to Thessa. She clasped it, and he pulled her up.

She rose to his side and threw her arm around his waist in a half hug. Demir turned them toward the roof access and they walked like that across the darkness. It was quiet and peaceful, and he enjoyed the friendly intimacy.

They reached the main floor and were walking arm in arm toward the stairs to the wine cellar when Breenen came hurrying around the corner. Demir felt all his good feelings evaporate as he saw the look of worry on the majordomo's face.

"Demir!" Breenen called, looking over his shoulder as he approached.

Demir extricated himself from Thessa. "What's wrong?"

"The Cinders," Breenen said in a low voice. "They're in the foyer, and they're demanding your presence. They say they have orders to take you to the Inner Assembly."

"It's after glassdamned midnight," Thessa said. "What could they possibly want?"

Breenen was clearly shaken. Demir kept his own concerns to himself. The Assembly's elite killers weren't known for their patience, and they weren't known for making pleasant calls, either. "Is it an arrest?" he asked. "Did I break some glassdamned obscure law earlier today?"

"They didn't say it was."

Demir swore under his breath, considering his options. "Then don't wake Montego. Best if I go quietly, find out what the Inner Assembly wants. It's probably about the riot."

"Are you sure?" Breenen asked. "They've never summoned anyone from the hotel like this on my watch. People who go with the Cinders tend to disappear."

Demir put his hand on Breenen's shoulder and injected confidence into his voice. "They're taking me to the Inner Assembly. If those assholes want to talk to me, they're going to do it one way or another. Besides, I'm hardly defenseless. Sorry, Thessa. Let's put a cork in that bottle of wine."

She gave him a smile and a nod, but it was clear she was concerned.

Demir adjusted his tunic and strode to the foyer, pausing just once to look back at Breenen and Thessa. "Oh," he called to Breenen, "if I'm not back in a few hours, *then* you can wake up Montego."

33

The Cinders said nothing as they escorted Demir out the front of the Hyacinth. He recognized none of them—they were not the same ones he'd told off at the riot earlier.

Abductions and executions weren't nearly as common as they once were, but they did still happen, and Demir kept his senses keen as they loaded him into a plain carriage and trundled him off across the Assembly District. None of the eight Cinders surrounding his carriage were glassdancers, which was either an oversight on the part of the Inner Assembly, or meant that they really just wanted to talk to him. But why send the Cinders instead of a messenger? What was so damned urgent that it couldn't wait until morning?

He wanted to grab the closest Cinder and give him a shake. *She invited me up to her room for a glass of wine, you assholes.* That wouldn't end well, of course. The summons of the Inner Assembly was more important than getting laid, and the fact that he was, even subconsciously, comparing the two meant that maybe there was more of his old, arrogant self left in him than he thought.

Demir was just beginning to wonder if perhaps he should have woken Montego when their short journey ended abruptly, the door opening, and Demir emerging to find himself in the shadow of the Maerhorn; the squat, central fortress of the Assembly District. The thick, unadorned walls of the Maerhorn stood out among the gorgeous amphitheaters and marble statues like a boil on a courtesan's face. The Cinders quickly surrounded Demir, hurrying him across the covered bridge that connected the second floor of the Maerhorn to the street. Demir allowed himself to be swept along, still trying to ascertain the meaning of this whole affair. A piece of skyglass helped calm his nerves, and none of the Cinders so much as blinked when he slid it into a piercing.

They crossed a massive, foreboding threshold with ancient murder holes and several rows of portcullises, then took an immediate right across a narrow killing room, up some precarious steps, and down one wall where they crossed another bridge to enter the Maerhorn's inner keep. There was no one here but Cinders, lining the walls and halls, backs straight and eyes front. Demir wondered if they'd even need a glassdancer to execute him, or if they had one waiting somewhere. He couldn't sense one.

The whole group stopped so abruptly that he almost ran into the Cinder in front of him. The woman out front turned on her heel, knocked once on a nondescript wooden door, and then pushed it open and gestured for him to enter. Demir eyeballed his escort one last time, throwing out his sorcerous senses in a broad net, before stepping inside.

It was a large, long hall, brightly lit by dozens of gas lanterns that hung down from the ceiling in ornate chandeliers. The cold stone walls were covered in thick tapestries, the floors with battered crimson rugs, and a spread of five wingback chairs faced the door in a semicircle. All five chairs were occupied.

Father Vorcien, elderly, cracked, and frog-like, his chins coated in glassrot scales, sat in the center chair. To his right was Aelia Dorlani, younger than Father Vorcien by two years but trying to hide her age behind gallons of makeup. On that far right side was Gregori Kirkovik, the bearlike northern patriarch. To Father Vorcien's left was Supi Magna, glowering at Demir as he entered, and on the far left sat Sammi Stavri. The Inner Assembly; the five most powerful people in Ossa and, perhaps, the world.

Demir fell into a soldier's at-ease stance and pretended to ignore Supi Magna's glare. Why had they summoned him? Was it about the riots? Or were they going to question him about the Ivory Forest Glassworks? Was this, he thought with the lurch of his stomach, about the phoenix channel?

"This is quite the prestigious gathering," he said.

"Look at him," Supi Magna snapped. "Sun-darkened like a provincial farmer, hands callused. Hardly the Ossan elite material we're looking for."

"We're not asking him to a ball," Gregori rumbled in his thick provincial accent. "Come off it. I don't give a shit about your precious glassworks and side projects. *This* is important."

"As important as a guild-family patriarch threatening the Cinders in front of a mob?" Supi demanded.

"More so," Gregori grunted. "The Cinders need to be put in their place on occasion just like everyone else."

Demir was taken aback by the exchange but tried to keep it off his face. The Inner Assembly was clearly not of one mind regarding . . . whatever it was they wanted him for. "Care to fill me in?" he asked.

"And no respect! Look how flippant he is. Look how—"

"Supi," Aelia said. "Shut up."

Demir glanced at Aelia, meeting her eyes, wondering if she knew that *he* knew that she'd ordered his mother killed. Based on her cool, vaguely distracted gaze, she did not. He then let his eyes settle on Sammi Stavri. She was the youngest of the group, though she was in her mid-sixties, and she sat dejected and despondent in her wingback chair, head lolling like she was either drunk or senile. Last he heard, she was neither. Something was going on here that he did not understand.

Before he could push them further, Father Vorcien finally roused himself and cleared his throat. "It's good to see you again, Demir."

"And you, Father Vee."

Father Vorcien snorted. "I apologize for the Cinders, and the hour." Father Vorcien's eyes wandered momentarily before returning to Demir. On a man who could bluff a gargoyle, that was the greatest tell that he was distressed. "Just a few hours ago, word arrived from the Copper Hills that the Foreign Legion was soundly defeated by a Grent army led by Devia Kerite."

Demir rocked back on his heels, his stomach doing a backflip. No wonder the whole group wasn't lambasting him about the riot. This was far more serious. The Foreign Legion, defeated? That didn't seem possible. "I thought Kerite and her Drakes were in Purnia butchering natives on behalf of the Nasuud."

"She *was* wintering in the Glass Isles," Aelia spoke up. "We negotiated for the use of her mercenaries against the Grent, but the Grent snatched her out from under us. She didn't even give us the courtesy of a counteroffer!"

"And we've been screaming at each other ever since," Gregori rumbled. "Who is to blame for that?" He shot a glance to Sammi Stavri.

"Gregori!" Aelia snapped.

"What?" Gregori frowned at Aelia. "We're talking to Demir Grappo. Even if his mind broke at Holikan he is still Adriana's son! You think he doesn't know we bicker? You think he'd fall for our united public front? Bah!"

"Your sensitivity touches me deeply, Gregori," Demir said. He kept his expression bland, his voice bemused, but inside his thoughts were churning over themselves. There was something deeply comforting about seeing the weakness within this most powerful of cabals, but he did wonder if they had frayed so badly that they were showing it even to him. Of course, an army led by Devia Kerite sitting on their doorstep would fray the nerves of any ruler. Demir had an inkling what this was about now, but . . . could he really be right?

Gregori grinned at him. "My little brother sends his regards, and I understand my grandniece loves your hotel."

"Tirana fits right in."

"I'm glad. She's very pretty, you know."

All four other members of the Inner Assembly rolled their eyes, and Father Vorcien sighed heavily before saying, "Now is not the time to marry off your distant relatives, Gregori. Demir, that is not all that happened. On the heels of this news of our defeat, we learned that the entire senior staff of the Foreign Legion has been assassinated; killed at the very moment they were trying to regroup."

Demir's throat went dry at this news. He didn't quite believe it. He *definitely* knew why they wanted him now, and it was more terrifying than the prospect of the Cinders executing him. "What happened?"

"They were ambushed and murdered by a large team of Grent glass-dancers."

"Shit," Demir replied.

"Shit is right." Sammi Stavri suddenly seemed to come alive, her head whipping around so that she could stare bleary-eyed at Demir. "He hasn't told you the half of it! Two of my little brothers. Two cousins. Two Vorcien cousins, a Magna, and three Dorlani. Of the greatest guild-families, only the Kirkovik came out unscathed." She shot a look at Gregori, as if blaming him for the fact that her brother hadn't kept any of Gregori's family on staff.

That, Demir realized, explained Sammi's current state. Losing two siblings was a personal and professional blow to a family as powerful as the Stavri. Two cousins just added insult to injury. "My condolences," Demir said softly. Sammi seemed to shrink into herself, as if physically repulsed by the sympathy of one as young and powerless as Demir. He turned his attention back to Father Vorcien, noting that Supi Magna had ceased glaring and was gazing unhappily into the darkness outside a nearby window. "Why summon me?" Demir asked, though the answer was now obvious.

"Because the Grent just wiped out all the best officers in the capital," Father Vorcien replied simply. "Everyone else is either stationed in the provinces or gone for the winter holiday. We've spent the last two hours digging around for anyone in the city with experience commanding more than a single battalion of soldiers. There are three of you, and frankly the other two have never won a battle."

"We need the Lightning Prince," Gregori interjected.

Demir puffed out his cheeks and then slowly exhaled. What a name for a man who'd never suffered a loss and still managed to come out of his only campaign looking bad. He glanced around until he saw a stack of wooden chairs in the far corner of the hall. He walked over, took one off the stack, then dragged it back toward the Inner Assembly. The legs screeched across the stone floor, thumped over rugs, then he deposited it exactly where he'd been standing and sank down into it.

"You all must be really glassdamned desperate," he said.

"The safety of the capital is at stake," Aelia replied.

He almost—*almost*—called her out then and there. How sweet it would have been to see the look on her face when he accused her grandson of killing his mother. But that would have accomplished nothing, and she was right: the capital was in real danger. "And you think I can stop Kerite? Don't we have a defensive cordon for that? What's the point of all those massive forts outside the city if not to stop exactly this?"

"Do you know anything about Devia Kerite?" Aelia asked.

"As much as there is to be known," Demir admitted. "I based my tactics in the Holikan campaign on her own lightning war across Purnia. But she's never published her letters or memoirs, or so much as given an interview to a newspaper. She's never disclosed her inner mind to the public in any way—the only career general in modern history to stay so closed off." He considered what he *did* know about Kerite and took a guess as to what they would say next. "You don't think our defensive fortifications will stop her."

"After what she and the Grent did to the Foreign Legion, I don't think they'll even slow her down," Father Vorcien grated. "Our star forts are outdated and in disrepair, not to mention severely understaffed. They're not ready for a regular siege, much less an attack by such a skilled commander."

The news, unfortunately, did not surprise Demir in the slightest. Just another example of Ossan arrogance. "It's too bad no one rich and powerful within the Assembly could have directed funds to their upkeep."

He could *see* Supi Magna's jaw tightening, but none of them responded to his disrespect. He laughed inwardly, a joyless echo in his own mind. Speaking of arrogance, was he even listening to himself? This was how the old Demir had spoken to the Assembly. Had he really not changed?

Gregori spoke up. "The Grent have every advantage at this moment.

Kerite can roll over our fortresses and stab straight to the heart of Ossa, or she can simply rage around the countryside unopposed, destroying our industry, flooding Ossa with refugees, and cutting us off from reinforcement or resupply. She has already cut our line of communication with Harbortown, and her fleet has it under blockade." Harbortown was officially a district of Ossa, though it was some ten miles to the northwest on the coast, connected by canal, so that Ossa didn't need to always go through Grent to reach the ocean.

"We don't need to stop her," Supi Magna said, his tone dripping exasperation, "we just need to slow her down. We've summoned the provincial brigades. If we can buy a month, or even just a few weeks, we'll have enough soldiers to overwhelm her. Surely the Lightning Prince can slow down a single mercenary general?"

"Sarcasm doesn't suit your stately cheekbones, Supi," Demir said. The quip was half-hearted, his thoughts now turning to this impossible task. And it *was* impossible. Slow down Devia Kerite, the greatest strategic mind of any modern military? If he had all the powers of his younger self he could have bought them a single week at best.

"Hah!" Gregori slapped his knee. "I missed you, Demir. Everyone else takes us all too seriously."

"You mean everyone else has respect," Sammi said.

It was clear now which members of the Inner Assembly actually wanted Demir there. Curious that Aelia had voted *for* Demir, considering what she'd done. Demir kept all his doubts inward. They might be so tired and frayed that they showed him their weaknesses, but he'd be damned if he showed them his. This was not, he realized, a choice. It was either accept command of whatever remnants of the Foreign Legion still remained and do his best, or flee the damned country before Kerite could raze Ossa.

"What would I have to work with?" Demir asked, ignoring Sammi.

Father Vorcien resumed the briefing. "The Foreign Legion was badly battered. We won't know just how badly until the morning, but we estimate eight thousand remaining troops. We have a few battalions of cavalry that just arrived tonight, and we can bring up sixty thousand National Guardsmen."

"The National Guardsmen are only slightly above useless in a real battle," Demir said.

"Agreed."

"And Kerite?"

"Ten thousand mercenaries and twenty thousand Grent troops, fresh off their victory with minimal casualties. News has already leaked of both the assassination and the loss, so there will be panic in the streets of Ossa tomorrow. We need you to keep Kerite from sacking Harbortown, or from destroying our forts. If she does either of those things, we won't be able to control the populace."

Demir's fingers itched to pull out his witglass, to churn through the thousands of possibilities in mere minutes, analyzing hypothetical battles like a human thinking machine. He put his hand in his pocket, brushing his fingers across the godglass within. He could feel when he touched the witglass, and shied away from it. "You are sending me to fail," he said.

"Others would fail worse," Father Vorcien stated quietly.

It did not sound like a ringing endorsement, but it did mean something coming from Father Vorcien. The old toad had always seemed bemused by Demir, and though he'd never been a proper mentor, during Demir's political career he'd always thought of himself as Father Vorcien's one-day successor on the Inner Assembly. It was a long-shattered dream now, but knowing that he had Father Vorcien's backing to defend the capital made this . . . well, not exactly possible, but perhaps palatable.

Demir found himself chewing on all this and realized that the knowledge that he was guaranteed to fail made this whole thing a little less terrifying. Leading troops, giving commands; it was all quite scary. But if he cracked like he had at Holikan, what was the consequence? The capital would burn anyway. It was a cynical thought, but comforting in some twisted way.

A smart man would have flipped them all a rude gesture and then gone home to pack up the entire hotel, fleeing the city by morning. Demir wished he *were* that smart. "If I agree, I want assurances that the Assembly isn't plotting behind my back while I'm gone. Dispel any call for censure for what happened with the forgeglass riot earlier today, and publicly call me a hero for dispersing the mob peacefully. Make it a front-page story in all the newspapers tomorrow."

Supi snorted loudly. "Is that all?" he asked sarcastically.

"It's a simple request, all things considered," Demir shot back. "If I don't at least try to slow down Kerite, tens of thousands of Ossan citizens will die. I got a glimpse of the street fighting in Grent, and if I can minimize that happening in Ossa, then I will have succeeded."

"The property damage—" Aelia began.

"Means nothing to me," Demir cut her off gently. "I will do this to save people, not any of your mills or tenements or glassworks. Take that into account when giving me command: I will not accept the meddling of the Assembly. I won't divert resources to save some precious guild-family holding or move a battalion through a neighborhood flying a silic sigil to make one of you look good. Accept that, or be damned."

Gregori and Aelia both frowned, perhaps regretting their votes. Sammi appeared not to be listening. Father Vorcien didn't so much as blink. "Done and done."

"You know my methods," Demir continued. "I want everything."

"That's vague," Aelia drawled.

"I analyze information," Demir said. "To do so I need every single scrap. Every spy report, every copied ledger, every single piece we have on both their forces and ours. I want to know the last time the Grent infantry were issued new boots all the way up to Kerite's favorite breakfast. Not just official reports, mind you, but information gathered by your own personal spymasters."

"That information," Supi Magna said sharply, "is not available."

"Gah!" Father Vorcien retorted. "It is a small price to pay for a chance at victory."

"But our spy reports are guild-family property," Aelia protested.

Father Vorcien thumped his fist on the armrest of his chair. "We will give him everything we have—all of us—and if I suspect anyone has held back I will conduct an audit myself." The other four, even Gregori, grumbled in response, but none seemed willing to stand up to him further.

"Good," Demir said. "I'll take command immediately. I'll need a direct line of communication to those new cavalry battalions that just arrived. I'll deliver the rest of my demands to this room within the hour. Supi, may I speak with you for a moment?"

The Magna patriarch glanced at his colleagues in surprise, then uncoiled his thin body from his chair and followed Demir into the far corner of the hall. His shoulders were stiff, his chin raised as Demir turned toward him.

"I trust you have some news of your investigation into the incident at the Ivory Forest Glassworks?" Demir asked quietly.

The question seemed to take Supi off guard. "Investigation? It's been just two days and one of those was spent dealing with that damned riot. Half the glassworks burned down. There are still prisoners unaccounted for, fled into the forest! I want . . ." Supi glanced back toward his colleagues and lowered his voice. "I want a full shackleglass inquiry and I *will* call you to answer."

Demir knew he couldn't stand up to questions under shackleglass—but the good news was Supi had just handed him a perfect screen for Thessa's disappearance in the form of those escaped prisoners. He also knew about the blackmail material Filur Magna had kept. He didn't *have* it, but knowing about it still gave him a card to play. He took a half step closer to Supi and thrust his finger up under the taller man's chin.

"Look here," he snapped quietly, "I know exactly what you were doing at the Ivory Forest Glassworks—the fearglass, the skimming. I asked questions the moment your granddaughter lost those shares to me. When I confronted Filur, he attacked me and I was forced to defend myself. It was his pissing guards who set the fire. By accident, for sure, but it wasn't me who spread the flames. If you'd like me to repeat all of that under shackleglass, I am more than willing."

There was a glint of something in Supi's eyes—fear, perhaps—and he stiffened noticeably. If the other members of the Inner Assembly found out how baldly he had corrupted a government contract, they would take *all* the government contracts away from the Magna. Demir went on before Supi could answer, knowing that he had to press the advantage to secure this half bluff. "However, if you'd like to keep Filur's secret ledgers a secret, I'm willing to let bygones be bygones. I want nothing to do with fearglass, so I'll sell you back Ulina's shares."

"You're very generous," Supi grated.

"At two hundred percent," Demir finished.

Supi's eyes bugged, his fists clenching and unclenching. Finally, he nodded. "And not a word will be said of the subject?"

"Not a word," Demir promised. "Friends?" He let a small smile play out across his face, but immediately wondered if he'd pushed it too far. Supi ignored his outstretched hand and stormed back to the other guild-family heads. Demir watched him do so, then headed for the door. "You'll have more communication from me within the hour," he promised.

In the hallway, the Cinders had faded away as if they were ghosts. He was grateful for that moment alone and ran a hand across his face, trying to come to terms with his own mortality as he contemplated leading troops into battle once more. It *couldn't* end the same as last time. He wouldn't allow it. He needed to gather all his mental strength and hold it close until after this thing was finished. If he didn't, both soldiers and civilians would die by the thousands.

"I'm going to go stress-shit my brains out," he said to the empty hall. "Then I'm going to take command of the Foreign Legion and pit myself against the world's greatest strategist. This'll be fun."

34

Thessa stared at the dark ceiling of her hotel suite, trying to come to terms with the events of the last week and all the ways her life had changed. The whole thing felt dizzying, from the attack on Grent to becoming partners with the patriarch of an Ossan guild-family. Grief swirling with elation. One moment her stomach would clench up as she replayed Axio's death in her mind, or tried to come to grips with Kastora's sudden absence from her life, and the next she'd quietly laugh to herself at the feel of silk sheets rubbing against her legs.

She tried her best to focus on the latter. She could get used to this: the hotel suite, the fine restaurant downstairs, the tiny but well-equipped glass-works in the garden. Just after Demir left, she'd gone looking for a cup of tea in the kitchen only to be gently turned away by a porter who said he'd have it up to her in fifteen minutes. And he'd done exactly that, setting the table in her sitting room with a porcelain tea set, including sandwiches and cookies, despite the fact that it was past one in the morning.

It was a level of luxury that made her vaguely uncomfortable, but she knew from seeing the way Master Kastora had lived at home that she would quickly get used to it—perhaps even rely on it. Another vaguely unsettling thought. What had Kastora said to her once? *Luxury softens us all, true, but why should I make my own tea when ten minutes of my hands at the furnace could buy a whole shipment of tea leaves?*

Thinking of Kastora brought the tears back to her eyes. She dabbed them away with her sheets and took a deep, unsteady breath. How long would it take the grief to go away? She still had nightmares of her parents' deaths, though she hadn't even been there when it happened. She'd *seen* Axio die violently. Would that haunt her every time she closed her eyes for the rest of her life? Not to mention Demir's execution of the two Magna enforcers, or Craftsman Magna falling into the furnace.

She tried to push it all away, rolling this way and that in bed. What time was it? Two? Three? The hotel was quiet, the city outside peaceful. For a moment she thought to go for a walk, but the lurking specter of the Magna caused her some pause. What if they found out where she'd gone? What if enforcers were lying in wait outside the hotel for the first time she stepped out alone?

Thessa finally sat up and crossed the room, fetching her notes on the schematics from her desk. She turned up the gas lamp above her bed and began to flip through the pages slowly, processing them for the dozenth time.

This project was going to be a tricky one, and not just because of the added pressure of the cindersand running out. She had only one piece of cinderite, which meant one solid try. And not only did she have to remake the prototype, but she had to remake it *better*—to improve upon Kastora and Adriana's design so that it didn't take several cartloads of firewood just to recharge a single spent piece of godglass.

She found a pencil she'd brought up from the glassworks and wrote on a piece of hotel stationery the word "energy," then followed it with "coal," "gas," "wood," "oil." She tapped the end of the pencil against her cheek, flushing her brain of all the chaos and focusing entirely on the task at hand. The source of the energy didn't matter nearly as much as the phoenix channel itself, but it was still a consideration. She stared at those five words for a little longer before setting the paper aside and putting a clean sheet against her knee.

Her thoughts were interrupted by a gentle knock on the door to her suite. Thessa waited for a moment, wondering if she'd imagined it, until another knock followed. She put on a dressing gown and went out, looking through the peephole. To her surprise, it was Demir, still dressed the same as when he'd left with the Cinders a couple of hours ago. He looked sharp-eyed but exhausted.

"Come in, come in," she said, opening the door for him.

He stepped only to the threshold, his thoughts clearly far away, and said, "The contract is signed. Breenen will give you your copy in the morning."

"Oh! Thank you."

They stood in silence for several moments, until Demir said, "This is . . . awkward."

Thessa adjusted her dressing gown so it wasn't showing off too much. "Did I overstep by asking you to share a bottle of wine?" She grimaced. "It didn't mean we were going to sleep together, it just meant . . . I mean . . ." She realized she was babbling and swallowed hard, reminding herself how little sleep she'd gotten in the past week. By the vaguely surprised look on his face, it clearly wasn't *that*.

"Um," he said, his expression turning bemused for just a moment before slipping back to serious and distant. "That's not what I meant. Sex is only awkward if we make it awkward. I was about to tell you what was awkward."

Thessa hugged herself and tried to look casual. "I'll just shut up and let you talk."

He came several paces into the room, seemed to think better of it, and returned to the threshold. "The Grent have reversed the course of the war with a mighty victory just hours ago, and then the subsequent assassination of the senior officers of the Foreign Legion. The Inner Assembly is reeling, and an enormous army is now bearing down on a practically undefended Ossa."

Thessa put her hand over her mouth. It had never even occurred to her that the Empire *could* lose a war against Grent. While the city-state wasn't exactly undefended, with wealth and power and colonies all over the world, they were just a shadow of the Ossan Empire. In that moment she realized that something had happened subconsciously: she'd already made the mental switch from Grent siliceer back to Ossan provincial and was thinking about the war in terms of "us" and "them," with "us" being the Ossans. A wave of shame came across her immediately at the thought that she could abandon her adopted countrymen so easily.

"Will we have to flee?" she asked.

"That's not what's awkward," Demir replied. He was looking at her bare legs now, and she couldn't quite tell whether he was admiring them or was so deep in his own head that he didn't know where his gaze was pointing. "What's awkward is that the Inner Assembly has given me command of what's left of the Foreign Legion. I'm to leave for the front immediately, and slow down the Grent advance at all costs. That means I'm going to be fighting—and killing—your people. I thought that might cause a rift in our new partnership."

Thessa walked to the sitting room table, where hours-old tea was still laid out, the leftover sandwiches gone crusty. She sank into a seat. "You really care?"

"Of course I do," Demir said, clearly taken aback. "I've invited you into my home, signed a business contract with you. Nothing between us, real or implied, included me killing your people."

"I see." Thessa took a cookie off the tea tray and nibbled on it absently. She was relieved that the awkwardness wasn't actually between them in *that* way, but Demir had a point: this brought something ugly to their new partnership. She peered up at him. "Are you really a general?"

Demir inhaled sharply and looked off to one corner of the room with a mile-long stare. "I conducted a very successful campaign a long time ago, back when I was still active in Ossan politics. This puts me in the unfortunate position of being the most qualified person to defend Ossa at this moment."

"If I said that it bothered me?" Thessa asked, more out of curiosity than anything else. It *did* bother her, but not nearly as much as she might have expected.

"I'm not sure yet," Demir replied. "This phoenix channel is part of my mother's legacy, and a way to restore the Grappo to a higher place within the Empire than they've been in a dozen generations. On the other hand, I do have *some* skills to offer my own countrymen. I'm not sure if I can stand aside and let Ossans die."

Thessa searched Demir's face. He so desperately wanted to help people. To protect people. Such a strange thing for a guild-family patriarch and a glassdancer. On an impulse, she said, "I have a confession."

"Oh?"

"I'm not Grent."

This definitely took him off guard, though he covered for it well. "Really?"

"I'm an Ossan provincial. I was orphaned when I was thirteen, and Kastora became my guardian so I did, in a sense, become Grent. But I'm not Grent by birth."

"Huh. Now that you mention it, your accent is quite light."

"That's why." Thessa spread her arms. "It is my adopted country, and knowing that you're going out there to kill those people does bother me, but to me, the phoenix channel *is* more important. I won't let the war get in the way of our partnership."

Demir let out a long sigh. "Good," he said, obviously relieved. "Good good. I'm glad to hear that, I . . . You should close your robe."

Thessa snatched it closed and tied the silk ribbon to keep it that way. "Sorry about that."

"It's only awkward if you make it awkward," he reminded her.

They both started laughing, and Thessa shook her head. "There's been a lot of ups and downs the last few days."

"That's one way of putting it," Demir replied, with a smile. "I'm glad this won't come between us. More seriously, I'm facing the best mercenary general in the world, and I want you to know that you are provided for— Montego is my current heir, and he has instructions to protect you while I'm gone and, if I don't return, make sure you finish work on the phoenix channel."

Thessa felt her mirth slip away. "Oh," she said. "You could die."

"It does happen in war."

"That's a deeply unpleasant thought."

"For me too."

Thessa swallowed. She should be relieved that he had already provided for her future, but Demir was her closest friend in the world at this moment. The idea that this could be the last time she saw him was . . . overwhelming. She wrestled with that thought for a moment, wondering how someone she'd only just met could have had such an effect on her. She was still deep in this consideration when Demir suddenly crossed the room, bent over, and kissed her gently on the lips.

It was soft and very quick, and when he pulled away he said, "For luck."

"For luck?" she echoed. His gaze was steady, but when she glanced away she could see that his hand was trembling. She took it, pulled him back toward her, and kissed him again. She let it linger, and he did not pull away. His lips were still cold from the night air, but his chest felt invitingly warm pressed against her. When they finally separated, she repeated, "For luck. Take care of yourself, Demir. Come back alive and we'll split that bottle of wine."

"Promise?" he asked, giving her a lopsided smile.

"Promise."

Demir returned to the threshold, a pep in his step that Thessa was fairly confident she'd just put there. What a happy thought. "Oh," he said, "if you need to purchase anything for your project, Breenen has funds at your disposal."

"Thank you."

She watched Demir walk into the hallway, then return to close the door for her. He paused there for a moment, a frown crossing his face, and said, "This is a very strange question, but how did your parents die?"

Once again, Thessa felt her good feelings deflate. "Is this important?"

"Perhaps not."

She glanced down at her hands, considering the question before she responded. "I know it was suppressed, so you've probably never heard of it, but almost a decade ago there was a revolt out in the provinces. My parents were in Holikan when it was sacked by the Foreign Legion. They died with most of the city."

Something *changed* in Demir's face. It was not overt, and Thessa thought perhaps she'd imagined it, but all the muscles in his face seemed to go slack at once, his eyes losing life and focus. He nodded sharply. "I must go," he said, and pulled the door shut behind him.

Thessa plucked another cookie from the tea tray, putting that oddness out of her mind as she listened to his footsteps retreat down the hallway. She hummed to herself, trying to stave off a dizzy bit of happiness. Demir was, after all, going to a war that might kill him. But there was something undeniable between them, they both knew it, and if—no, *when*—he returned, she was going to carefully feel this out. *Love, money, or political gain,* Kastora had told her.

What about all three?

She smiled to herself and returned to the notes still laid out on her bed. She was too giddy to sleep now. Best to study, so she was as prepared as she could be when she began work on the phoenix channel in the morning.

35

Idrian leaned heavily on his shield, sword resting on one shoulder as he watched the last of the Ironhorns trudge wearily into town. There was no conversation among the stragglers, just grim-faced determination broken on occasion by a nervous look over a shoulder for the inevitable pursuit. Braileer stood behind him, carrying both their packs, practically asleep on his feet.

The sun was still low on the eastern horizon, and just over fourteen hours had passed since their crushing defeat. The night had been a disaster of communication errors and logistical blunders, with seemingly no chain of command and little coherence among those troops that had managed to escape the Grent onslaught. Dawn had brought no succor—just Grent dragoons and Kerite's mercenary skirmishers, harrying their rearguard and pushing the Ossans out of the Copper Hills and down into the gentle landscape that surrounded the capital.

Their rallying point was Fort Bryce, one of the mighty star fortresses that formed a defensive cordon around Ossa and sat just on the other side of Bingham. Idrian could hear intermittent musket shots on the breeze, a testament to the Grent offensive, and wondered where the reinforcements were from the fort. Why hadn't they sent out the garrison?

Idrian waited until the last of the stragglers entered the town and then looked around for Tadeas. He found Mika first. She was bleary-eyed and quiet, her lips moving as she counted the engineers among the regular infantry. "When's the last time you saw Tad?" he asked her.

"Just a couple hours ago. He should be up ahead with Valient."

Idrian nodded his thanks and fell in beside her. He resisted the urge to put his helmet back on, knowing it would just give him a headache. His body was beginning to weary of all the sorcery resonating through it, and it was showing in the yellow scales forming on the backs of his hands. Even a glazalier couldn't handle so much godglass for so long. He needed to get out of his armor for even just a few hours. He wondered which would do them in: the exhaustion, or the crushed morale. He couldn't think of a worse defeat in his long career. Three brigades of Ossa's best, the vaunted Foreign Legion, routed on an open battlefield in mere hours. Was Kerite really that good? Were her soldiers really that well-trained?

He lifted his head to see Tadeas standing on the next corner, shouting orders in a hoarse voice to dozens of men and women, soldiers and civilians alike. Here, closer to the town center, the streets were packed with Ossan citizens trying to cart all their worldly possessions to somewhere safe. It seemed like everyone was bickering; a fistfight breaking out just to Idrian's left. He ignored it, too tired to so much as cuff sense into the idiots.

Mika shoved her way through the logjam to look for her husband, while Idrian waited on the periphery until Tadeas saw him and waved him over. Tadeas looked just as tired as Idrian felt. A bloodstained tear in his jacket showed a wound received sometime in the night, and the red and white glassrot scales on his cheek were evidence of the godglass that had seen him through it.

"Found out why communication broke down," Tadeas greeted him, bodily shoving an irate local out of his face. The local took a deep breath, ready to scream vitriol at Tadeas, but expelled it with the noise of an ox's fart as he saw Idrian. The man slunk away quickly.

"What happened?" Idrian asked.

Tadeas pointed down the street. "After the defeat, Stavri and his staff, the entire senior administration of the Foreign Legion, retreated to the Bingham Brawlers Club just over there. They figured they were safe while the soldiers trickled in to the rallying point . . ."

"Glassdamned cowards."

". . . and they were all butchered by Grent glassdancer assassins."

Idrian bowed his head and swore under his breath. The headache was back almost immediately, and the shadows darting around in the corners of his vision grew bolder. A child's laughter echoed from the tenement window overhead. "Everyone?" he breathed.

"No survivors. Not even a witness." Tadeas glanced around them. "The whole town is terrified, and we've all been trickling in since last night. The state of us isn't helping things."

"Do they know the Grent are right behind us?" Idrian asked quietly.

"They can probably guess. Those gunshots aren't that far, and skirmishers have been spotted less than a mile away. Every rumor is like wildfire. The only reason it's not worse is that hundreds of people fled in the night when they first learned we'd been routed. This whole disaster might cost Sammi Stavri her place on the Inner Assembly."

"To piss with Sammi Stavri, where's the garrison from Fort Bryce? Why aren't we getting backup?"

"I have no idea. I sent someone ahead to find out."

Idrian looked toward the Bingham Brawlers Club, where a handful of Cinders stood outside eyeballing the packed streets nervously, no doubt wondering how the piss they were going to get out of town before the Grent arrived. His meandering examination fell on a mounted soldier forcing her horse through the chaos, laying about her with the stock of her musket at anyone who got too close.

By the time she reached Idrian and Tadeas, she'd lost her hat and was covered in sweat. Her horse danced nervously, eyes rolling. The soldier dismounted, keeping a firm grip on the bridle and leaning in toward them. "Are you the highest-ranking officer in Bingham?" she asked.

"I think so," Tadeas responded. "I know there are officers scattered to both the north and south of the city, but I think it's just me here. If you want someone higher you'll need to go to Fort Bryce."

"I'm *from* Fort Bryce," the soldier said. "Colonel Wessen has ordered you to retreat into the shadow of the fort, where you'll be protected while we regroup."

"Since when is a garrison colonel giving orders to the Foreign Legion?" Idrian demanded, gesturing at the clogged roads around them. "These people need guidance and if we don't provide it, we'll have thousands of dead on our hands even if all the Grent do is stir their panic."

"Colonel Wessen—" the messenger began.

Idrian cut her off. "This is *your* job. Why isn't the whole garrison out here, keeping this shit organized and providing us some support? Why aren't you—"

Idrian felt himself jerked sideways and looked down to see Tadeas holding him by the breastplate. "Cool down," Tadeas hissed. "We've got no chain of command, we're running low on ammunition, Mika is almost out of grenades. We can't do shit but pull back, or the Grent will just roll over us."

"I'm not leaving these people to get swallowed up."

"Kerite isn't known for brutality."

"Tell that to Purnian revolutionaries," Idrian grunted.

"This isn't Purnia, and we're not some uprising colony. Sure, these people will get all their shit stolen by Grent infantry, but Kerite has more to gain by driving them into Ossa to cause chaos than killing them. If we've orders to pull back, we're pulling back."

Idrian jerked himself out of Tadeas's grip, trying to keep a lid on his own fury. He was exhausted, dizzy, swaying on his feet, and some fort commander was trying to give him *orders*? How dare those clean-booted bastards? He walked away several feet to get his head about him. They *should* be getting orders from the Ministry of the Legion. Who was in charge there? Maj Madoloc was out of the country for the entire month of the solstice holiday. Idrian shook his head again to try and clear it. By the time he returned, Tadeas had chased the messenger off.

"We don't have a choice, Idrian," Tadeas said. He didn't look happy about it either, and Idrian knew that giving that order would pain him deeply. "We can't face Kerite until we've regrouped."

Idrian took a calming breath. Tad was right. He was always right, damn him. When Idrian trusted himself to speak again, he said, "Then we should get out of here before the real panic sets in. Where's Valient?"

"He's just around the corner. I—" Tadeas was cut off by the sound of screams coming from their west, back in the immediate direction that Idrian had come from. A series of musket shots brought Idrian's hackles up, and he could *feel* the panic wash through the packed streets.

"Glassdamned skirmishers are here," Idrian swore, "and they're trying to start a stampede. Now I'm *really* pissed that the garrison isn't out here helping." He slammed his helmet on his head. The musket shots were coming faster and more furious now, and he thought he heard the thunder of cavalry. Dragoons. Even better. "Get everyone out of Bingham," he told Tadeas. "I'll do my best to hold them off and then meet you to the east."

"Piss on you," Tadeas spat, "we'll be right behind you. Valient! Mika!"

Idrian didn't argue. He raised his sword to the hundreds of frightened eyes now looking in his direction and gave his voice all the backbone he could muster. "Out of my way, pissants! The Ram has mercenaries to kill." The cheer that went up was decidedly half-hearted, but a path was made, his coming told ahead of him as he rushed west down the street. He craned his neck, pausing momentarily to try and get a view of what was happening or how many enemies he faced. The musket shots grew more frantic, and then petered out. He could no longer hear hoofbeats.

After several blocks the jammed traffic grew lighter, then disappeared entirely as he reached abandoned carts and discarded luggage from those who had simply fled from the sound of fighting. Though his path was completely clear, Idrian proceeded with caution. If he was going to die facing a company of skirmishers, he wanted to take some of them with him.

To his shock, it was not a Grent or mercenary uniform that he spotted first. It was an Ossan cuirassier bestride a magnificent warhorse, black uniform a little dusty but looking fresh, standing in her stirrups while she peered off in the distance. Idrian joined her quickly and followed her gaze, hardly daring to hope that help had finally arrived when he saw two squads of cuirassiers charge past a crossroads two blocks distant, their silver and hammerglass breastplates glinting in the morning sun.

The woman wore the gold collar of a major. She lowered herself back into her saddle and finally regarded him with a nod. "Fair meeting, Ram."

"More than a fair meeting." Idrian grinned. "You are a sight for sore eyes. How many are you?"

"A battalion. Enough to get these skirmishers off your back. Are the Iron-horns nearby?"

"Not far behind me," Idrian responded. "We thought we were all that was between the Grent and these people."

"You're not," she assured him. "You'll want to check in with my commanding officer."

Idrian blinked at her in surprise. "I thought everyone above major was dead."

She gave him a tight grin. "He took a squad of my cuirassiers on foot into that tenement there," she said, pointing to the next block over, "chasing some of their skirmishers."

"Does he need help?"

"I doubt it."

Idrian scowled at that, proceeding on toward the tenement she'd indicated. It was the first time he noticed that Braileer had followed him, still hauling their packs. Idrian sent the armorer back to find Tadeas.

Just after Braileer retreated a pistol shot went off, and then there was the sound of breaking glass. Idrian looked up to see a second-floor window suddenly fold in on itself, as if sucked into the room by a mysterious force. A glassdancer. Friend, or foe? The answer came a moment later as the body of a mercenary skirmisher was hurled out the empty window and landed on the ground just feet in front of Idrian. The woman's eyes stared sightlessly upward, a piece of glass the length of Idrian's fist rammed through her heart.

Several more shots followed the first, then a scream. Another window shattered and was sucked inward. Then silence. Idrian turned back to the cuirassier major. "Who's the glassdancer?" he called.

She just pointed, and Idrian turned back to the door of the tenement to see a string of young children rushed out through the door, followed by cuirassiers on foot. Seeing the man that emerged behind them might have been a bigger shock than losing that battle yesterday, because Idrian would have bet his life he'd never see Demir Grappo in an Ossan uniform again. The uniform was moth-bitten, hanging off the younger Grappo as if taken in hastily by a poor tailor.

"Idrian," Demir called, "good to see you."

"Demir?"

"That's 'General Grappo' to you, Ram," Demir responded.

Idrian stared back at him, still at a loss for words. It suddenly hit him, and before he could stop himself he said, "Holy shit. You're the most qualified officer left in Ossa, aren't you?"

"Until Hammish Kirkovik or Maj Madoloc get back from the provinces, yes," Demir answered. He gestured to the cuirassiers, who fetched their horses and then escorted the group of children back toward the center of the town. Demir nodded after them. "Makeshift orphanage in that tenement. Their minder fled in the middle of the night, the bloody coward, and then those mercenary skirmishers tried to use the kids as shields."

"I take it that didn't end well."

"Sure didn't." Despite his almost jovial tone, there was a hard anger to Demir's eyes.

Idrian took a step closer to him. It might not be proper etiquette, a breacher acting so familiar with a general, but damn it, Demir was practically his nephew-by-proxy. "Are you all right?"

"No," Demir replied. "No, I am not. Almost died once this week, and now I've got to try and scrape together whatever is left of the Foreign Legion and make a stand against Devia glassdamned Kerite. I'm going to . . ." He paused, his eyes looking up above Idrian's head. Idrian whirled to see a skirmisher in a blue-and-green uniform on the roof of the next tenement over. The skirmisher raised his rifle just as the window on the floor beneath him shattered, coalesced, and then shot upward. The skirmisher jerked once as he was impaled from below by a finger-thick, eight-foot spike of glass. He seemed frozen for a moment before he toppled, shattering the spike with his own weight as he fell.

Idrian turned back to Demir. The vein on the younger Grappo's forehead throbbed violently. Demir touched a finger to that vein before continuing, "I'm going to rally the Foreign Legion at Fort Bryce, and then figure out what the piss to do against Kerite. Find Tadeas for me."

"The Ironhorns were right behind me," Idrian replied. "They should be here any moment."

"Excellent."

"Sir, did you get the package I sent?" Idrian asked, glancing around to make sure they wouldn't be overheard. There had been no communication since he dropped off the cinderite at the Hyacinth.

Demir gave a sharp nod. "I did. Kastora's protégé is already at work using it to re-create Kastora's work."

Idrian let out a sigh of relief. At least *something* had gone right. If he survived this war he might have a future without madness to look forward to. He examined the side of Demir's face, then glanced down to see that the man's fingertips were trembling. Idrian looked closer at his eyes to see his pupils dilated, the whites bloodshot. Demir, he realized, wasn't actually angry. He was terrified, and he was channeling fury to try and cover it up. Would it break him?

Idrian heard Tadeas's voice shouting orders somewhere on the next street and directed Demir's attention in that direction. Demir nodded, his chin tightening, and in that moment a mask seemed to descend upon his face. The terror in his eyes disappeared, his fingers no longer trembling. Idrian reassessed him, trying to understand what was going on in the younger Grappo's head. Was he strong enough to hold together?

Who was in that head? The Demir who'd cracked at Holikan, or the Lightning Prince?

36

Saying that Fort Bryce was a disaster was both unfair and an understatement.

Demir stood in the fort commander's office, looking out the window toward the Copper Hills, where the few roads were jammed with every farmer and townsman from here to the coast desperately trying to get away from the Grent army and their mercenaries and into the protective embrace of Ossa. He wondered what those people would think if he were to tell them that the protective embrace was a lie; that the Foreign Legion was shattered, the forts undermanned and outdated, and the Inner Assembly privately admitting that this weeklong war had been a terrible mistake.

He couldn't tell them. He couldn't so much as mention his doubts to anyone, lest they trickle down through behavior and rumor to affect the common soldiery. Piss knew they were already plagued by enough of their own after having been handed the worst defeat witnessed by the Foreign Legion in centuries. Demir needed to wear a mask of confidence that defied all his doubts about this new command, as well as hid the more private horrors lurking around in his mind. *Thessa was a Holikan orphan.* The savior of his guild-family; his new business partner; someone who had *flirted* with him—was a victim of his failures. The moment she found out, everything would come crashing down.

He thrust it from his mind and turned to Colonel Wessen, the fort's commander. Wessen was a mousy man in his mid-forties, wringing his hands, spectacles constantly sliding down to the end of his nose and having to be readjusted. He was so hunched, his face so drawn, that he appeared to have neither shoulders nor a chin. Despite his appearance he was not a coward. Just . . . ill-prepared.

"Are all the forts like this?" Demir asked.

"Yes, sir," Colonel Wessen replied quietly.

They had just finished a whirlwind half-hour inspection of the massive star fort, and Demir had found that every one of Father Vorcien's statements was true: the walls were crumbling, the weapons were out of date, the garrison was fat and ill-equipped. Even the massive earthen bulwarks that were the first defense against enemy artillery were overgrown and eroding—mostly into moats that hadn't been dredged in decades.

"I'm sorry, sir," Colonel Wessen continued. "My whole tenure here we've had to scrimp and save just to keep the garrison fed. We're technically part of the Foreign Legion but they don't treat us like proper legionaries. Shipments go missing, salaries are delayed, I—"

"Does it take money to dredge the moats?" Demir asked. "Or skilled labor?"

"No, sir."

Demir walked from one end of the office to the other. If Wessen were living the high life—if his office were decorated and perfumed and his home were a big one on a nearby hill—then Demir would assume corruption and have no hesitance in tearing him apart. But the colonel's uniform was even more moth-bitten than Demir's, his office dusty, his liquor cabinet bare. This was not a man living fat on a government payroll like most Ossan senior officers.

"I'm not going to lecture you on fort maintenance," Demir told him, turning back to face the colonel. "You know the situation we're in. I've called in a few favors—Capric Vorcien is arranging for every team of craftsmen and laborers that you might possibly need. The first will arrive tonight, and they will set to work making the necessary repairs to the bastion."

Colonel Wessen blinked back at him. "But sir, some of those repairs will take months. And . . . and . . . shouldn't we retreat, sir? This fort cannot hold against the Grent and their mercenaries."

Demir folded his hands across his stomach to display both of his silic sigils at the same time. The effect was not lost on the colonel, who swallowed hard. Demir said, "What repairs can be made in a short time will be done. You will have supplies and new muskets by the end of the day tomorrow. All of this will happen while I, and what's left of the Foreign Legion, go out there and lay down our lives to slow down Kerite and her Grent masters. We're not retreating, Wessen. There's nowhere to retreat *to*. Understand?"

Another hard swallow, the colonel's Adam's apple bobbing up and down comically. "Yes, sir."

"In the meantime, you and your officers are going to drill your garrison into the ground. Artillery drills, musket drills, bayonet drills. Whip this garrison into shape. I'll make sure you have the double rations and the equipment to do so." Demir dropped his hands from his stomach. He didn't know if any of this would help, but he was damned well going to try. "Now give me the room. Send in Major Grappo, wait ninety seconds, and send in Colonel Jorfax."

At the mention of Jorfax, Wessen's eyes grew wide with terror. "Yes, sir." Colonel Wessen scuttled to the door, took a deep breath, and turned toward Demir. "I wish you'd come along years ago, sir."

Demir answered with a tight smile. "Believe me, I wish you and your garrison were still being pleasantly ignored because no one actually needed you. Go on."

Wessen was gone for moments before Tadeas swept in. His uniform was torn, a piece of milkglass at his ear, though his injuries seemed healed. He looked around the office sharply before kicking the door closed behind him. "I knew the forts were dumps, but this is worse than I'd feared."

"Glassdamned fools, neglecting our last line of defense," Demir answered.

There was a brief pause, which Tadeas acknowledged with a shrug. "I never thought I'd see you in one of those uniforms again."

"Me neither," Demir answered unhappily. He felt his mask slip for a moment, his eyes growing wet, his face warm and his throat tight. "I'm glad you're here with me, Uncle Tad."

"Wouldn't have it any other way."

Demir drew a hand across his face, pulling himself together from the inside out. "When Idrian saw me in this uniform, I thought the big bastard was going to faint."

Tadeas chuckled. "We had a long night. You were a shock to all of us. A welcome shock to be sure."

"At least my cuirassiers were."

"Nah," Tadeas said with a shake of his head. "I don't give a shit what anyone else thinks or says. I'd be a glassdamned fool if I wanted anyone else opposing Kerite. Stavri almost got me and the Ironhorns killed."

"And you don't think I will?"

"At least you'll do it more creatively than Stavri."

Demir searched his uncle's eyes for a lie or omission, but couldn't find it. He really did want Demir here. Poor, misguided idiot. Demir grinned at him, feeling his mask slide back into place. "Straighten your uniform. Colonel Jorfax will be here any moment."

Tadeas cringed at the name. "Why?"

"Because she's in charge of the Foreign Legion's glassdancers, and if I want to get anything done, I'll need their help." A knock sounded at the door. "Come!" he called.

The woman who entered was in every way the opposite of Colonel Wessen. She was tall and beautiful, with short blond hair, an angular, distinct face, and an expression that could hammer an ox to a barn door. Demir had once seen a gossip column refer to her as an ancient beauty chiseled from granite. The columnist had disappeared the next day and the body had never been found. Jorfax fell into a military pose in the middle of the room facing the desk, despite the fact that Demir was at the window. Her hands were clasped in front of her in a way that displayed the silic sigil of a glassdancer on her left hand and the much smaller silic sigil on her right that indicated that she'd been adopted by the Vorcien guild-family.

"You called, sir?" Jorfax asked, speaking to the empty desk.

Demir felt his eyes narrow. He knew glassdancers. He'd trained under them, he'd met hundreds, and they were as dismissive of authority as they were a terror to their underlings. They were, he suddenly realized, all just as arrogant as he was. A shudder went through him at the self-realization. He snapped his fingers. "Over here, Jorfax."

She turned her head in his direction, staring straight into his soul with those piercing blue eyes. He stared right back. "How many glassdancers did you lose in the Copper Hills?" he asked.

"We haven't finished our count yet, sir." She pronounced the word "sir" with something that was just a hair shy of outright disdain.

"How many?"

"I just said—"

"Jorfax," Demir said softly, "if you'd like to have a pissing contest then I'll meet you at dawn with smallswords in eight weeks' time. Right now I have a glassdamned war to win. Now how many glassdancers do you have left?"

Jorfax's expression did not change in the slightest, but she worked her jaw a little before answering. "Thirty-four."

"Out of?"

"Sixty."

"Ouch." Demir glanced toward Uncle Tadeas, who'd taken up a position against the wall with the casual air of a man watching a bear-baiting at the circus. He wasn't scared of the bear, but he was definitely ready to run if the bear got loose.

Jorfax said, "You're not going to win against Kerite."

"Perhaps not," Demir admitted, "but I'm going to do a damned sight better than Stavri, or even you and your glassdancers. In fact, I believe that at least ten of your glassdancers are only alive because Tadeas here provided an avenue for their escape."

"Thank you, Major Grappo," Jorfax said without inflection, her eyes not once leaving Demir. "With all due respect, *sir*, you'll be dead by the end of the week."

"Are you referring to the Grent glassdancer assassins that killed Stavri? I'm slightly better equipped for a threat like that?"

"No. I'm referring to facing her on the field of battle. She will roll right over you no matter what you do."

"Kerite is that good?"

"I fought her on a campaign in Purnia. One of those damned colonial proxy wars. She's the best general in the world, perhaps of all time."

"Everyone knows that."

"But few people have lived to tell the tale," Jorfax said, her voice finally showing some emotion. "Her soldiers always have the best equipment, the best pay, the best training. They're better than the Foreign Legion, and they're loyal to a fault. Stavri was a fool to face both her and the Grent on the open battlefield."

"Did you tell him that?"

Jorfax flinched. "No."

"Good thing you don't fear or respect *me* then, otherwise you wouldn't bother to warn me." Demir eyed the glassdancer carefully. He did not fear her—certainly not one-on-one—but Tadeas was right to regard her as a muzzled bear. One wrong move and she could go berserk. "I have work for you and your glassdancers. Kerite flanked Stavri by blinding his scouts. I'm going to do the same thing to her. Our new scouting policy is squads of twelve light cavalry with a glassdancer attached to each squad."

"Are you insane?" Jorfax replied, finally turning her whole body to face Demir, her professionalism slipping.

Demir continued on as if he'd not been interrupted. "The glassdancers will kill all of Kerite's scouts, and they'll do it silently. The escort will only be there in case there's some sort of a scrape a lone glassdancer can't handle."

"No," Jorfax snapped. "I'm not giving that order. No one would follow it! We're not common scouts, we're glassdancers and—"

"Cowards?" Demir asked lightly.

Jorfax's hand dropped to the smallsword at her belt, her expression somehow growing even more icy. "How dare you?"

"Say the word," Demir replied. "We can even duel with sorcery if you want. Or you can stop being a pampered little artillery supplement and get your glassdancers out into the field. How about that?"

"I—"

Demir talked right over her. "You lost twenty-six glassdancers in a single battle because Stavri thought you could outmuscle a superior army, and you went along with it. I'm not going to play the same game. I'd just lose. Instead, your glassdancers are going to help me put a shard in her eye. Silent killers. The scouts won't see what hit them. Once Kerite is blind, I'll actually be able to maneuver around her."

Jorfax peered hard at Demir, her eyes searching his face for something while her jaw worked like she was chewing a wad of tobacco. Finally she said, "It's completely against custom."

"Correct. That's why it'll work. Not even Kerite can convince her glassdancers to get their delicate hands dirty."

"You of all people should know how hard it is to glassdance from horseback. It's almost as hard as learning to shoot at a full gallop. The skill, the focus, the practice. None of my glassdancers have it."

"Perhaps in a large, chaotic battle. But I'm not sending you out there to fight battalions. I'm sending you to murder individual scouts, maybe small squads at the largest, and I think any military-trained glassdancer should be able to handle that. So are you going to give that order, or am I going to have to strip you of command and work my way through all the remaining glassdancers until I find someone who will?"

If Jorfax had been silently fuming, she was furious now. Demir could see it in the way every sinew on her face was straining as if there were someone inside trying to get out. She said, "You don't have that authority."

"Let's ask Father Vorcien. He's got other glassdancers in his family. He doesn't have other competent generals in Ossa."

"Competent generals?" Jorfax demanded. "Do you want to talk about what happened after—"

"You'll want to shut your mouth right now," Tadeas suddenly spoke up. He added a soft smile and a "ma'am" to the end of the sentence. "Before you speak of things you know nothing about and say something you'll regret later."

Somehow, some way, Tadeas seemed to break through Jorfax's steely exterior in a way that Demir couldn't. She turned her eyes on Tadeas, a frown finally pulling down on the corners of her mouth. "You stand behind him, Major Grappo?"

"Yes."

"For family, or for faith?"

"What do you think?" Tadeas asked.

Something seemed to pass between the two of them, and Jorfax finally gave a sharp nod. "I'll give the order. Have your scout squads ready to go out within the hour. I hope you plan on moving quick, because the moment Kerite figures out what you're doing she'll move to counter it." She turned on her heel and strode out of the room, slamming the door behind her.

Demir took a deep breath and looked down, realizing that he'd been gripping a piece of skyglass tightly the whole time. He didn't even remember pulling it from his pocket. "What happened there?" he asked.

"Last night wasn't the first time I've saved Jorfax's glassdancers," Tadeas answered. "Or the second, or third. We call them glass cannons for a reason. Glassdancers can get disoriented under fire, and once they're even a little bit confused they die as easily as anyone else." He pursed his lips. "Also I think she has a thing for Idrian."

Demir snorted. "I've met Idrian. Every woman and some of the men in the Foreign Legion should have a thing for him."

"Hah! She's right, you know. You have to be ready to move quick. You can't just blind Kerite and not act."

"Come now," Demir replied with more confidence than he felt. "Have you met *me*?"

"So what are we going to do?"

Demir looked out the window, where he could see down into the fort's central courtyard. A lone scout approached at a gallop, crossing the moat, waving at the guards. She reached the courtyard and leapt from her horse. He could hear her shouting to a nearby soldier for directions to the commanding officer.

"I suspect," he said over his shoulder to Tadeas, "that we're about to find out. Before I can act, I need to know where Kerite is going. She can do a million little things at this point, but she only really has seven realistic options for her next big maneuver. The three most likely are that she attacks Harbortown to try and destroy our route to the sea; that she comes straight here to crush Fort Bryce before we can regroup; or that she turns sharply south and attacks Fort Alameda in order to capture the river.

"Kerite is incredibly good," Demir continued, "but she *can* be predicted. When I was a teenager I wore out copies of every one of her unauthorized biographies. I memorized every move she made on a dozen campaigns— not because I thought I'd ever fight her, but to emulate her style. She does not stop, she does not slow down. Her momentum is part of her mastery of the battlefield."

Tadeas laughed. "That's why you risked pissing off Jorfax, isn't it? If you blind Kerite, you either destroy her momentum by forcing her to regroup, or you force her to continue her plans without proper intelligence."

"Exactly."

"That's dangerous, Demir. What happens if she catches us in an open battle without our own glassdancers?"

"Then we're damned," Demir responded, "but we would be anyway, so what's the difference?"

Their conversation was interrupted by a desperate knock on the door, and then the scout that had just arrived pushed her way in without bothering to wait for permission. Her face and uniform were dusty from the road, black hair slick with sweat. She snapped a tired salute. "Sir, just got back from the Grent camp in the Copper Hills."

"They're gone?" Demir guessed.

"Yes, sir. The camp is abandoned."

"Which direction did they go?"

"Southeast, sir."

Demir searched Wessen's office until he could find the standard officer's maps, then rummaged through those until he was able to produce one that covered the environs of the capital. His mind had already abandoned the other six predictions and he was now focusing on Kerite's new target: Fort Alameda and mastery of the Tien River. He gestured for the scout to wait and then showed the map to Tadeas.

"Kerite is going here," he told his uncle, pointing at a spot where a small tributary of the Tien emptied into the main river. It was right at the border between Ossa and Grent, and the point of land between the two rivers was dominated by another massive star fort. "She'll be reinforced by riverboat from the duke's forces still in the city, and she'll throw all her strength at Fort Alameda. Once that falls, she'll be able to work her way up the river, capturing Glasstown and then moving directly into the Assembly District."

Tadeas looked suddenly very tired. "We'll move everyone to the fort side of the tributary here and contest her crossing?" he asked. "The Ironhorns might be able to get there first and blow the bridges if we leave immediately."

It was the obvious countermove, but Demir had his doubts. River crossings had never particularly bothered Kerite. Her troops were too organized and well-trained to get themselves slaughtered doing something stupid. Same with the Grent, whose soldiers would have spent their whole careers training on the delta.

No, Kerite would pincer-attack the fortress, hitting it from landing craft, a northern flanking, bridges, and of course her superior artillery. Demir stuck his hand in his pocket and ran his fingers over the godglass there. The sorcery of each piece resonated softly against his fingertips until he found his witglass. He pulled his fingers back with instinctive fear.

Slowly, he forced himself to find the witglass again. He couldn't put it in his ear. That would be too powerful; too overwhelming. But maybe . . . He pinched it between his fingers hard, feeling the sorcerous vibrations through his skin. A pain immediately began behind his left ear and crawled forward through his mind like it had done every time he tried to use witglass in the last nine years.

He kept his grip firm, forcing himself to think through the mind-numbing headache. Despite the pain, his thoughts *were* moving faster, reacting to the sorcery with something more than *just* pain. He did not let himself dwell on it, instead turning his thoughts to Kerite's upcoming attack on Fort Alameda. Still clutching the witglass between two fingers, he pulled down all of Wessen's maps and tore through them until he found a closer look at the fort. He studied it for several minutes, mind racing, head pounding from the effort of such advanced thought. Finally, he let go of the witglass. It was only when he heard the gasp that escaped his own lips that he realized just how much it had hurt.

He didn't know Fort Alameda, but he *did* know that tributary Kerite would have to cross to make an approach. He knew the land north of it, and most importantly, he knew the topography. "Tadeas," he said, "find a well-rested platoon of infantry for me. There's a Magna warehouse on this side of Glasstown. I need them to march double over there and confiscate a thousand pieces of sightglass."

"You're going to start your command by confiscating godglass from the Magna? That's an . . . interesting choice."

"Supi won't be the last Inner Assembly member I piss off over the next few days. Give the Ironhorns two hours' rest. We'll let Jorfax's glassdancers get ahead of us to eliminate those scouts, and then we're taking as many barrels of powder as we can get our hands on and heading south."

Tadeas gazed back at him doubtfully. "You said the Ironhorns."

"Yes."

"And everyone else, right?"

"I'll bring the fresh cavalry," Demir told him, "but no, I want the rest of the army to have a day to recuperate."

"You want to take three battalions—a thousand cavalry and five hundred combat engineers—to oppose thirty thousand enemy soldiers?"

"We're not going to oppose anything," Demir replied. The plan was mostly formed in his head, daring, dangerous, and perhaps stupid. He could round out the remaining details on the march. "We're going to attack her."

37

Thessa spent the morning prepping her workshop to produce resonance-enhancing omniglass, then the early afternoon in meetings at a corner table in the Hyacinth restaurant. It was a process that felt familiar—not much different from sitting at a café near the Grent Glassworks, processing through all the administration that Kastora didn't have time for, except that instead of buying a cup of tea for local merchants as she reviewed their accounts, she was meeting with Demir's craftsmen.

She had technical drawings for each of them; straightforward pages that she explained in detail, each one outlined with everything she needed from that particular craftsman and nothing more. She ordered a double compartment for the phoenix channel from the tinsmith. From the blacksmith, an internal iron frame to hold the weight. The carpenter would create the external frame, as well as cut thick sheets of cork to her specifications. The mason would provide rolls of asbestos.

The carpenter was the last of her meetings; a middle-aged man who blinked at her drawings and turned them this way and that, clearly trying to figure out what exactly the frame was for. She did not enlighten him. "Two days?" he asked.

"Two days," Thessa confirmed.

"I'll have an apprentice on this," he grumbled.

"Do it yourself," Thessa replied. "I don't want a single delay." She looked up to see Breenen approach from the lobby, his hands clasped behind him. When the carpenter scowled and looked toward him, he only nodded.

"I'll get right on it, ma'am," the carpenter said, excusing himself.

Thessa waited until he was gone to press her fingers against her eyes. "That's the last of my meetings," she told Breenen. "Thank you for setting them up. Every step I don't have to oversee is more attention I can give to the crux of the project."

"My pleasure, Lady Foleer." Breenen bowed his head. "Two days? Is speed such a necessity?"

Thessa looked down at some of the notes she'd been writing between meetings. She shuffled the papers around absently, then turned them all upside down so no passing waiters could read the contents. *Was* speed a necessity? Kastora always told her that rushing a project only led to mistakes, paradoxically causing the project to take longer than it would have otherwise. And yet since the moment she awoke this morning she had felt a burning in her chest—a pressure to see the phoenix channel through with utmost haste.

Part of it was petty—she wanted to impress Demir next time he returned from the war—but the heart of the matter was more immediate. The riot yesterday had spooked her deeply. Every day that passed without a working phoenix channel was another day full of potential violence as godglass grew more difficult to obtain for the common people.

"Yes," she finally answered Breenen. "Speed is necessary. This project has far more variables than normal godglass. Even once it has been built it may require months of testing and experimentation. I can't afford to waste any time."

"Very well. I'll make sure the craftsmen stay on top of their work." Breenen nodded and turned away.

"Do you ever think about your legacy?" she asked, the words coming out impulsively.

The concierge paused, looking over his shoulder at her. After a moment he turned back. "I'm the majordomo for a guild-family and a hotel concierge," he said with half a smile. "Whatever legacy I leave behind will be a small one, quickly forgotten."

Thessa laid her hand flat on her notes. She searched for the right words, digging into that pressure in her chest, knowing there was more to it than wanting to avoid violence. "This *thing* is all that I have left of Kastora. It's his greatest work, and he didn't even get the opportunity to perfect it or to share it with the world. That responsibility now lies on my shoulders. It is exciting and frightening all at once."

Breenen was silent for several moments. "Acting in a master's stead is a daunting task. More so when they are gone for good." He lowered his eyes, and Thessa realized that Breenen's loss of Adriana was only a week or two more removed than her own loss of Kastora. "Yet," he continued, "ensuring a legacy is a legacy in and of itself. One that you or I or anyone who has lived in the shadow of greatness should take pride in. I know that will be my own legacy as a client of the Grappo."

"What specific legacy do you wish to ensure?" Thessa asked.

"This is Ossa, and we are a small guild-family," Breenen replied, cocking an eyebrow. "I only wish to ensure survival."

"Is survival good enough? Shouldn't we want to leave more to the world than that?"

"Sometimes survival is all we can handle. Is there anything else you need today, Lady Foleer?"

Thessa stared at nothing, contemplating Breenen's words for some time before realizing he'd asked her a question. "I need to go shopping. Could I have a carriage in twenty minutes?"

"Of course."

 ⹀   ⹀   ⹀

Thessa arrived at the Lampshade Boardwalk less than an hour later. It was a place she knew well from her forays into Ossa, either on her own or shopping on behalf of Kastora. It was also one of the few places she felt safe— too public for any mischief during the day, and well-patrolled by the Ossan National Guard. She directed her driver to drop her at one end and be prepared to pick her up from the other end in an hour. The war had started only eight days ago and yet she felt a massive sense of freedom—and of recklessness—walking out in the open, bumping shoulders with strangers as she browsed the merchandise of the glassworks suppliers.

She found better tools than those Demir provided almost immediately. Refined cindersand—the ingredient needed for omniglass—was much more difficult. It took her most of her hour to locate just a single pound of the stuff, and when she did the vendor refused to so much as pretend to haggle. Thessa paid what was asked. She knew that the prices were rising quickly, and she knew why.

Her final trip was into a bookstore, where she waited until the clerk had an open moment and came over to her, a salesman's smile fixed on his mousy face. "Good afternoon, ma'am. Can I help you find something?"

"I'm looking for a scientific treatise," she told him.

"Ah, a gentlewoman scholar?"

"Of a sort. A few months ago I read an article from a Marnish engineer on the potentials of petroleum as a heat source. Perhaps you read it?"

"Professor Volos, I believe?" the little clerk asked.

"That's the one. I'd like to see whatever you have along those lines."

"Yes, she's rather brilliant. Especially popular with that new lightning rod of hers."

"I haven't heard of it."

"Oh, you will!" The clerk went behind his counter and rummaged around beneath it. He began stacking books on the counter, speaking as he worked. "She's figured out a very simple device for directing lightning from the top of a building, down through a . . . what did she call it . . . a grounding wire, and into the dirt. Absolutely ingenious. Architects all over the Empire have already started incorporating it into their designs. Her new book sells out as fast as I can stock it, but I think I have a couple copies left in the back. Would you like one?"

Thessa glanced at the titles he'd fetched for her. *The Age of Coal. One Thousand Uses for Whale Oil. Lighting a City: The History of Gas in Ossa.* There were thirteen books. She sifted through them judiciously, setting aside the histories and keeping anything that looked to run on the more technical side. "Sure."

"I'll go fetch you one."

Thessa picked up one of the books she'd chosen and flipped through it. She wasn't entirely certain she knew what she was looking for. Inspiration, perhaps? Hard data? The energy source would be her biggest challenge, and approaching it from several directions seemed like the best place to start. From there she could focus in on the most promising ideas. As she'd already told Breenen, the phoenix channel might require months of experimentation before it worked properly.

"Just the one copy left!" the clerk said, emerging from the back. "You'll have all of these here, then?"

"I will, thank you." Thessa paid the clerk and checked her pocket watch. Ten more minutes until her driver expected her. "Do you mind if I read here for a few minutes? I'm just waiting for my driver."

"Be my guest, ma'am."

Thessa took herself to a corner of the shop and grabbed the top one from her stack of books. *Taming Nature: The Future of Modern Architecture.* It was the book on lightning rods. She flipped it open, half expecting to return it before she left the shop.

The very first page was a technical blueprint of a lightning rod and an explanation for how it worked. It was not, the author claimed, her intention to get rich from her new invention. It was her intent to better civilization. Thessa stared at the device. It was so . . . *simple*. A crown, and a thick cable, and a grounding rod. The device was meant to intercept lightning that would otherwise strike the top of a building, and direct it through the cable and harmlessly into the ground.

Thessa's mouth hung open. She'd witnessed a lightning strike once, when she was a girl. It had blown the entire steeple and a whole wall off a church and set fire to four surrounding buildings. All that power. Could it really be harnessed so simply? It was a thought that begat another: Could *she* harness it? She borrowed a pencil from the clerk and scribbled in the margins, going so far as to balance on one leg and press the book against her thigh as she drew a diagram.

The next time she checked her pocket watch, nearly a half hour had passed. She was late to meet her driver. She shook her thoughts clear, putting them in order for when she returned to the hotel, then thanked the clerk. She had a promising thread working its way through the back of her head now. Her mind raced at the possibilities—the simple elegance—the madness—of directing lightning through the center of her phoenix channel.

She was nearly to the end of the boardwalk, the crowds thinning out, when she felt someone grab her arm. "Ow! What the pissing—"

"Keep walking. If you scream, I stab."

Thessa inhaled sharply, looking down to see a knife held in her assailant's hand, pressed gently against her side just above her hip. Visions of newspaper articles about murdered siliceers floated across her thoughts, and the idea of being slit from crotch to throat almost *did* cause her to scream. Before she had a chance, however, he directed her sharply into an alley.

"What do you want?" she demanded, trying to get a good look at his face. He was a young man—no one she recognized—wearing a laborer's tunic and boots. Probably no more than a common thief. "Is it money? Take it."

"Not from you I don't," he said, continuing to prod her along. They took another turn and Thessa realized to her horror that they were quite alone. The street was close by, and people would hear if she screamed, but nobody could see what was going on in this little alley. Her confidence in the safety of the Lampshade Boardwalk was shattered.

She turned to face him, leaping away, trying to wrench her arm from his grasp.

"Oh no you don't," he said, tightening his grip. He waved the knife underneath her nose until she stopped struggling. She focused on the blade, wondering if her stack of books was heavy enough to knock it out of his hand. Could she risk it? If he tried anything, she damn well would. "I know you," he declared.

"You don't know me," she spat back. Her immediate fear deepened.

"Yes I do. You're the girl from the Ivory Forest Glassworks. The prisoner who went missing—Teala."

"I've never heard that name before in my life." Thessa's mouth went dry. What were the glassdamned chances of being recognized here of all places?

"Oh yeah?" He suddenly jerked up the sleeve of her jacket to reveal her furnace-scarred arms. "A siliceer, eh? One with a light Grent accent, who looks just like a missing prisoner? Was it the Grappo bastard who got you out? Piss! I don't even care. You're going to fetch a good price from Supi Magna." Thessa moved to pull away again, but when she did he thrust the knife up under her throat.

"If it's money you want I can pay," Thessa said quietly.

"Maybe. Maybe not. I'm not going to risk it. I *know* that Supi Magna has money. Now come on, we're going . . ."

Thessa heard a light footstep, then saw a shadow move around the corner of the next alley over. A face appeared over the young man's shoulder, and then a length of cord dropped around his neck and tightened. His eyes widened, and he turned the knife to lash out at the person behind him. Thessa, suddenly free from his grip, grabbed his wrist to keep him from doing so.

The woman behind him, Thessa realized in shock, was Pari—the very same whose hand she'd helped free, and who'd told her about Filur Magna's safe. Thessa tossed her books aside, using both hands to keep the young man from fighting back while slowly, surely, Pari strangled him. He clawed at the air, thumped at her face, trying to pull his knife hand out of her grip. She refused to let go. It felt like ages before his struggles flagged and then ceased altogether. Pari kept her cord around his neck for long after he seemed to be unconscious, then dropped him to the ground.

Thessa stared down at him, her heart pounding, her head light and confused as if in a dream. "Is he dead?"

"Sure is," Pari answered.

"That's the second time in a week someone has had to kill to protect me."

Thessa's gaze snapped back up to Pari. The young woman stared back at her coolly, as if the man she'd just murdered was beneath her in every way. "Why . . . how are you here? Why did you do that?"

"Later," Pari hissed. "We need to go before someone stumbles on us."

Thessa nodded quickly and found her books before hurrying out into the street. Pari followed close behind. The two of them wound through the thinning crowd, heading to the edge of the boardwalk, where Thessa spotted her carriage with its purple drapes stitched with the Grappo silic sigil. The driver greeted her politely, opening the door, and Thessa gestured for him to allow Pari to follow.

The two sat in the cool darkness of the carriage for several minutes of silence. The tension in Thessa's belly was terrible, and she stared across at the laborer.

If Pari understood just how frightened Thessa was at the moment, she did not show it. Pari used one finger to move the drape slightly, watching. "They've found the body already," she said. "They'll summon the National Guard, but no one is gonna look inside a guild-family carriage." She let go of the curtain and leaned back, closing her eyes.

Thessa kept her own eyes on the woman. Tall, lanky, with sun-darkened pale skin covered in the rough scars of someone who worked with their back. She was, in this very moment, the scariest person Thessa had ever seen. "What do you want from me?"

Pari opened her eyes, looking genuinely surprised. "Me? Nothing."

"Then why'd you help me? How'd you even know I was in trouble?"

"The Ivory Forest Glassworks burned down," Pari said, as if that explained everything. When Thessa didn't respond to that, she elaborated, "Every laborer that used to work there is down here now, trying to find a job. The Lampshade is one of the best places to get good work, and you got real damn unlucky. Temmen back there spotted you about the same time I did. Figured I knew what was in his head, so I followed."

Thessa let out a long, shaky breath that she hadn't even realized she'd been holding in. "But you don't want anything?"

"Not me." Pari averted her eyes. "Look, somehow you got out of the prison glassworks. Made friends with the Grappo it seems, and between Glassdancer Demir and Baby Montego, you have some powerful protectors. I know what it's like to be on that side of a labor camp, and glassdamn me if I was going to let Temmen send you back. He was a piece of shit, and you were kind to me. So that's it. I'm not going to shake you down. We're both going to forget this ever happened." With that, she reached for the door latch.

"Wait!" Thessa's eyes fell to Pari's hand. It was still wrapped up with a proper splint, the skin red and swollen. The nails of her pinkies, Thessa noted once more, were not painted with a client's color. Thessa's heart continued to pound but she no longer felt fear. She was safe, and would continue to be so as long as she remained cautious. "You won't let me repay you? You just killed a man for me."

"I grew up in the Slag, my little jailbird. I've done worse for less." She lifted her injured hand. "If you want to pay me back, give me enough money for a day in a healinghouse. Nobody will pissing hire me while I'm like this."

"I'll do more than that," Thessa said on an impulse. It was a wild, perhaps reckless thing to do, but she needed people she could trust. She didn't actually *know* any of the Grappo staff. She didn't know Pari either, but a woman who would kill for her kindness could be useful.

"What do you mean?" Pari asked.

"Hold out your hands." Pari did as she was told, clearly taken aback. Her hands were steady and, despite the injury, callused and strong. Thessa asked, "How long have you worked in glassworks?"

"Since I was old enough to cart firewood, I suppose."

"Have you ever been an assistant?"

"Me?" Pari snorted. "Like I said, I'm from the Slag. Nobody from the Slag ever makes anything of themselves."

"Then be the first," Thessa said. She didn't have time for this. Now that the danger was past, she needed to get back to the hotel with that book. She needed to finish her designs. "You want to make something of yourself? Come work for me. I need an assistant. Someone I can trust, who can keep their mouth shut and work hard."

"I can do that," Pari said hesitantly. "But I don't have any experience."

"Piss on that. I can train an intelligent person to be an assistant in a few hours. Do you want the job or not?"

"I suppose I do."

"Good." Thessa pulled out a wad of banknotes and peeled off several of them. "I don't have time to waste. Take yourself to a healinghouse, then meet me at the Hyacinth Hotel. I'll have errands for you as soon as you are able."

Pari took the money, looking both intrigued and uncomfortable, and

Thessa knew for a certainty that she wouldn't betray her. "I'll be there tomorrow," Pari promised, and got out of the carriage.

Thessa didn't even bother to watch her go. "Back to the hotel!" she shouted at the driver, then flipped open the book on lightning rods and, careful of the jostling of the carriage, began to sketch.

38

The Ironhorns left Fort Bryce on just a couple of hours of rest—bleary-eyed, exhausted, some of them still with half-healed wounds and a piece of cure-glass at their ears. They marched directly south, trailing in the wake of the two battalions of fresh cuirassiers that Demir brought with him from Ossa. The march was brutally fast, double-time down the narrow roads winding through sharp landscape just north of the Tien River. Visibility here was practically nothing, the dark forests of the old imperial hunting grounds now divvied up between the guild-families and used for the same. The forest was broken only by the occasional vineyard stretching across a gentle hillside. Massive estates lurked in the winter gloom if you knew where to look.

At some signal that Idrian was not told, the cuirassiers turned right at a fork in the road, splitting off to head west into what could now be considered enemy territory. Idrian paused at the fork long enough to drink watered wine from the canteen at his belt and watch the last of the cavalry disappear. His hair was soaked with sweat, his uniform dirty, his armor, sword, and shield packed on the mules with Braileer some fifty yards back. It was getting dark, and he fiddled with the sightglass in his pocket, wondering if Demir had some kind of night raid in mind.

"I'm going to miss them," Mika said, stopping beside him. "There's something reassuring about having a thousand heavy cavalry in front of you."

Idrian could only grunt his agreement. His mental faculties were beginning to crumble without enough rest. For the last mile he'd heard the constant laugh of a child from somewhere in the woods. He knew it wasn't real, but it still made the hair on the back of his neck stand on end.

"Do you have any idea what Demir is up to?" Mika asked. "We've got enough powder in those wagons back there to blow up a whole fort." She paused briefly, her eyes widening. "Shit, he's not going to have us blow up Fort Alameda, is he?"

"Why the piss would he do that?"

"I don't know! To keep Kerite from capturing it?"

Idrian fixed her with a look that he hoped told her just how stupid that was. "Really?"

"Oh, come on. Everyone is whispering about Holikan. Everyone is . . ." Mika paused, glanced around to make sure none of the passing soldiers seemed to be listening in, and continued in a hushed tone, "Everyone is talking about how crazy he is. He told Tadeas he was going to go on the offensive with just those cuirassiers and us."

"I know," Idrian said. Tadeas had been tight-lipped about the actual plan, which meant that it was probably a bit crazy, and that Idrian himself wasn't an integral part of it. "Speaking of which . . ." He nodded back down the column, where he could see Demir and Tadeas coming toward them on horseback. The two reined in beside Idrian and Mika, and Demir stood up in his stirrups and called out to the passing column.

"We'll make camp just up ahead! We have double rations for everyone tonight—no beer, but triple on the meat. Wine will be on me after the attack!"

Hundreds of sets of tired eyes looked back at Demir. There were no cheers, even at the mention of a triple meat ration, and Idrian cringed inwardly. He could hear nearby engineers whispering to each other about what exactly Demir meant by "attack." He could see in their eyes that they were wondering if Demir was going to get them killed first thing in the morning. If Demir noticed, he gave no sign, swinging down from his horse and leading it over to Idrian.

"Tad," he called over his shoulder, "set a triple guard in case Kerite gets wind of our presence, but the glassdancers *should* provide us with a screen against her scouts. Everyone else needs to get some rest—they've earned it. No singing tonight in camp. Keep the noise to a minimum. Mika, can I talk to you for a minute?"

Demir handed the reins of his horse off to one of Valient's infantrymen and came and threw his arm around Mika's shoulders. She gave Idrian a wide-eyed glance as she was led away, Demir whispering in her ear, and Idrian turned to Tadeas.

"You going to tell me what the piss is going on?" he asked.

Tadeas snorted. "Demir will when he's good and ready. Just gotta trust him."

"What's this about a double march and then us just making camp? I thought we were hurrying down here to *do* something." Idrian could hear the irritation in his own tone. The exhaustion was getting to him too, despite the forgeglass in his ear. He clenched his fists and half turned after Demir, but Demir and Mika had already disappeared around a bend in the road.

Tadeas slapped him on the shoulder. "Get to camp. I already gave orders to put up your tent first. Use some dazeglass if you need to, I want you to get some sleep. Demir says he needs you in your armor by ten o'clock."

"So it's a night attack, then?" Idrian asked. "Tad. Tad! Glassdamnit, don't walk away from me."

"Get some sleep!" Tadeas called over his shoulder as he hurried down the column. Idrian swore softly to himself and had no choice but to follow. Might as well do as he was told. Who knew what was coming up tonight?

〉 〉 〉

The few hours of sleep Idrian managed to get were restless and unfulfilling, and he'd spent the last half hour before he was meant to meet with Demir scraping yellow glassrot scales off his arms and legs using his shaving razor. The process was relatively painless, which meant he hadn't done any permanent damage. *This time.* He edged around the few spots of permanent glassrot on his calves and hips, and one on his left arm. They were scaly to the touch, and though they would come off with the straight razor it would be damned painful and they'd just grow right back.

People always assumed glazaliers were immune to glassrot. He wished it were the case. Resistance was not immunity, and glassrot could still be as painful to a glazalier as to anyone else.

A small scuffle brought him out of his tent, and he made his way to the edge of camp where Valient and a couple of his soldiers stood in a circle around Squeaks. It was the first time Idrian had seen her since helping drag her out of that collapsed tenement in Grent, and he walked over to join them, feeling cranky and defensive. "They bothering you, Squeaks?" he asked.

Squeaks sat on a stump in the center of the little group, Valient holding a lantern up to her face and examining her eyes. She turned away from him. "Thank piss. Idrian, can you tell them I'm not crazy?"

"She's not crazy," Idrian told Valient.

"Mmm," Valient answered, grabbing Squeaks by the chin and steadying her to look in her eyes. "She might be."

"She's seeing things," one of the other soldiers explained.

"I am *not* seeing things," Squeaks insisted. She shook like a leaf, her eyes wide, pupils dilated. "There's a glassdamned monster in the woods."

Idrian frowned. He was sympathetic to seeing that which wasn't there, but had spent his whole career judiciously analyzing what was and wasn't real so that it didn't affect his job. Was Squeaks mad as well? Did he need to take her aside and have a talk, away from everyone else? He aimed a boot at the closest infantryman. "Go on, get out of here. Leave her alone." He waited until it was just him, Valient, and Squeaks before he turned back to her. "What did the monster look like?"

Squeaks shuddered. "Like a . . . Piss, I don't know! Like a monster! Maybe five feet tall, thin and wispy with a long neck and beady little eyes." She cast about her, as if looking for the right words, then pointed to her jaw. "It had long jagged teeth sticking out like, uh . . ."

"An underbite?" Valient asked.

"Yeah, that!"

Idrian grimaced. That sounded nothing like the shadows he saw due to his madness. Perhaps she'd injured her head in the rubble of that tenement, or during the defeat in the Copper Hills. He hoped not. The Ministry of the Legion made an exception for his mental state because he was a glazalier and a damned good breacher. They wouldn't for Squeaks. She'd be kicked out no matter what anyone said, and then Fenny would be all alone.

"Probably a deformed dog," Valient suggested.

Squeaks scowled at him. "It wasn't a dog. I've been to the circus, I know what malformed animals look like."

"What happened to the monster?" Idrian asked gently.

"Thing saw me, turned toward me with those little black eyes, and then poof! Disappeared."

"All right," Valient said, standing up. His eyes met Idrian's over her head and Valient gave an irritated shake of his head. "Go see Glory for some dazeglass and then get some sleep. You're off guard duty for the night."

"I'm not trying to get out of it!" she objected. "I really did . . ."

"You didn't see anything," Valient assured her. "Let it go."

Squeaks looked like she wanted to argue. After a few moments her shoulders slumped. "Yes, sir," she replied, slinking away to find the battalion's head surgeon.

Idrian waited until she was out of earshot before turning to Valient, who was staring after her with a scowl. "You okay?"

"Everyone's just . . . not doing well," Valient replied. "That loss to Kerite really shook us."

"Did anyone else see a monster?"

"No. There's no glassdamn monster in the woods, but Squeaks isn't the first soldier to break down today. Morale is low, exhaustion is high." Valient sighed. "I hope Demir genuinely has a plan." *Or they would all die unpleasantly* was the silent implication.

Idrian nodded in agreement. He desperately wanted to believe in the Lightning Prince, but he still couldn't tell which version of Demir had marched them down here, all on their own, while an entire division of crack enemy troops lurked somewhere in the vicinity. "Do you know where we are?"

"Vaguely," Valient replied. "I think Tad has our exact location, but he went off with Mika about an hour ago, along with all that powder Demir brought with us."

Now what the piss were they going to do with all that? Despite being somewhere just west of Ossa, they were in the large "wilderness" that provided hunting grounds for the guild-family elite. There was literally nothing to blow up out here, unless Demir's grand plan was destroying a few hunting lodges. It didn't make sense. Idrian bit his tongue before he could say so.

It was a good thing too, for Demir emerged from the darkness just a few moments later. He had a pistol and smallsword at his belt, and was wearing a piece of sightglass in his left ear. A glassdancer egg hovered over his shoulder in that disconcerting way that some of them liked to keep their glass at the ready. "Did I hear something going on?" he asked Valient.

"Just one of my soldiers having a bit of nerves, sir. I already took care of it."

"Good. Idrian, armor."

"Five minutes," Idrian replied, and returned to his tent. He found Braileer and got help getting into his armor, then told the young armorer to take the rest of the night off, barring further orders. He returned to find Demir standing by himself on the edge of camp, looking out into the forest. With the sightglass in his armor, the world was lit up as if it were early morning, giving Idrian clear vision into the murkiness. Some hundred yards out he saw a fox trot by, pausing to look toward the camp before hurrying on. An owl swooped down, hitting the ground silently and then returning to the trees.

"Ready, sir," Idrian said to Demir.

The younger Grappo did not move for several moments, then gave a sharp nod and a small sigh. He seemed more at ease here than he had been back at Bingham—but then again, this wasn't an active war zone. At least, not yet. "Come with me."

Idrian followed him out of the camp and down a narrow hunting track that forced him to walk behind Demir. Despite wearing sightglass, Demir seemed to be *too* confident with his movements, walking quickly, taking a fork in the path once, and then another fork a few hundred yards later. They came over a hill, down through a gully, and then up again to find themselves walking along the side of a small lake.

"I used to holiday here as a child," Demir suddenly said, breaking the silence for the first time since leaving camp.

"Oh?"

"This is a man-made lake," Demir explained, gesturing across the still water. "You can see a forester's hut off behind those thick reeds if you look closely, and farther downriver is the Kirkovik's ancestral hunting lodge. Which is a damned joke, since it's almost as big as their city estate. My mother and I spent many summers here. Hammish Kirkovik used to take me into the woods and we'd draw up mock battles with sticks and trees. He's the one who suggested that my mother get me a proper tactician as a tutor, even though I was only six."

Idrian had never actually *been* to the Kirkovik's hunting lodge—or any of these lodges for that matter—but he'd seen maps before. "Good place for an ambush?" he asked.

"Better," Demir answered. He did not explain himself further.

They wound their way along the lake for some time. Once, Idrian thought he saw people moving on the far side of the water, but when he brought them to Demir's attention, Demir just shrugged it off. Was that Tadeas and Mika with her engineers? What the piss were they up to? All Idrian could imagine was that they were setting some sort of trap. Not a bad idea, actually, especially if Demir really knew these forests so well. They could draw Kerite away from the river, up into these hills, and do some real damage.

So where had all those cavalry gone? They would be practically useless in these woods.

Demir paused, gesturing him close. "Stay ready for anything."

Idrian held his sword and shield at the ready, his senses keen, watching and listening for movement in the brush. They split from the lake and began a rapid ascent, working their way up the back of a rather steep hill. It was a long, exhausting hike that made Idrian wish he'd had more sleep. His sorcery hummed along, keeping him going, but the faint nausea of glassrot came on faster than usual and he began to hear rustling whispers in the corners of his mind. He hadn't spent nearly enough time away from godglass.

After some time, Demir suddenly gestured for a halt and paused to kneel in the brush. Idrian knelt with him. Several minutes passed before Idrian thought he heard the distant sound of voices. He cast a questioning glance at Demir.

"We're on the back of Kirkovik's Rock," Demir explained in a whisper. "I figured Kerite would send some scouts up here." Another gesture and he began to creep forward. Idrian followed, keeping an eye on their flanks, ready to leap in front of Demir with his shield in case they were spotted. Kirkovik's Rock was a massive, stony hill; a landmark that could be seen from much of the river valley where Ossa and Grent met along the Tien. It was about a mile north of the river, and was famous for its vantage point.

They crept another twenty yards or so, right up to the top of the trail, where the ground suddenly leveled out on top of the Rock. Up ahead, Idrian could see four figures all huddled together, wafting the scent of cigarette and pipe smoke. They wore blue-and-green mercenary uniforms and spoke in Nasuud. Their voices were not loud, but they didn't seem to be trying very hard to stay hidden, either. Why would they? There shouldn't be another soul all the way from here down to the river. At least they didn't have any lights on them.

Idrian reached out to stop Demir. "There's someone sitting next to a tree just about fifty feet to our left," he whispered. "A sentry."

"He's been dead for thirty seconds," Demir replied.

Idrian shuddered. It was good, from time to time, to remember just how terrifying glassdancers could be. As if to accentuate the point, the faintest sliver of movement caught his eye, like a falcon diving at its prey. It took off from just over Demir's shoulder. A moment later a groan issued from the group up ahead and, as if they'd been knocked over by an invisible wind, they all just *fell*.

"Sweet pissing godglass," Idrian swore quietly. "Why did you even bring me?"

"Check the perimeter," Demir replied.

"Prisoners?"

"Not tonight. No tongues to wag about what happened here. I want Kerite to wonder."

Idrian did as he was ordered. He found two more sentries. He managed to jump the first unawares, killing the woman before she could so much as cry out. The second demanded a password in Nasuud, and he received the tip of Idrian's sword in response. A few minutes later Idrian joined Demir at the crest of the hill, where the younger Grappo had already dragged the corpses over and rolled them into some brambles down the slope.

"I brought you," Demir said, finally answering the question, "in case Kerite anticipated me and sent a breacher up here with her scouts."

Idrian nodded in agreement, and walked to the other side of the hill, where the trees opened to bare rock and the world spread out before them. To their right, the glittering lights of the Grent Delta spread out for what seemed like an eternity, the city flowing west to the ocean and south into the far hills. To their left was a bend in the Tien, and a series of hills that prevented a good look at Ossa itself. They could, Idrian suddenly realized, see Fort Alameda. The bastion was mostly dark but for the lights of a handful of sentries on the walls. It was massive and foreboding, its star fortifications looking impossible to breach. Idrian would have been impressed if he'd not heard the report on the state of the Ossan star forts.

"It never occurred to me how good the view was from up here," he said to Demir. "Why isn't there a lookout tower?"

"Because the Kirkovik wouldn't allow it. And besides, there are better lookout towers closer to the river." Demir pointed to locations that eluded Idrian's eyes, but he could only assume were watchtowers. Demir led him farther along the hilltop until it began to slant back down toward the river, then stamped around for several minutes before choosing a spot and settling down. He seemed to relax entirely, his silent caution from the walk up now gone. "This will do for our vigil."

Idrian looked around for a moment. There didn't appear to be any danger; nothing that warranted his armor at all. "Can I remove my helmet, sir?"

"Feel free."

Feeling unsettled, Idrian did so, setting his sword and shield to one side and then taking a spot on the ground beside Demir. They sat in silence for several minutes before Idrian's irritation got the best of him. "Sir," he said, "if that's all, maybe I should return to the Ironhorns. There could be more of Kerite's scouts in these hills and I don't want a breacher to come upon *them* unawares."

Demir set his glassdancer egg on the ground between his knees and spun it around on the dirt. "Stay with me for a time," he said. "Now, if you look over there to our right, you'll see the edge of the lake we passed. The moonlight reflects off it nicely. If you look straight ahead for quite a long way, and then down—you see those lights there?"

Idrian squinted, trying to orient himself. The lights Demir was referencing were on the north side of the river, and they certainly weren't the lights of a city. If he had his bearings right, they were spread out across a series of large floodplains that were left fallow during the spring rains and then farmed during the summer and fall. They'd grown disused over recent years, the crops famously suffering from the muck dumped into the Tien by Ossa's Glasstown just a few miles upriver.

Idrian's breath caught. "Is that the Grent army?" he asked.

"That it is. Both the duke's forces and Kerite's mercenaries, with reinforcements coming up the river by the hundreds every hour. There's an island just off the north bank that represents a blind spot in Fort Alameda's defenses. Kerite can set up her artillery there and fire away without being hit back. I suspect she has already done so, and will begin the bombardment first thing in the morning. It's a position with every advantage: her back is to the river, easily supplied by Grent, on soft ground that would be very difficult for us to hit with cavalry. We don't have the present strength to mount a frontal assault, so she can grind down Fort Alameda and then hit it hard from several sides at her leisure."

Idrian found himself staring at Demir. "How the piss do you know all of this?"

"I've been coordinating with our scouts the last few hours, and I have access to the Inner Assembly's combined spymaster reports. As for the blind spot: I noticed it during one of my military architecture lessons when I was eleven years old. I told my tutor, and he said I was a fool, so I double-checked my work and my mother fired him." Demir paused briefly, chuckling to himself. "I even sent a letter to the Ministry of the Legion to point out the flaw. I never got an answer, and they never made an effort to fix it."

"And you think Kerite knows about it too?"

"As soon as I saw her camped on that floodplain down there, I knew exactly what she was up to."

"It sounds like we would need twice her number just to root her out."

"At least," Demir admitted.

"So we have to play this defensively? We have no choice, right?"

Demir cast him a sidelong, unreadable glance. He did not answer.

"Then why," Idrian continued on, feeling emboldened by the lack of rebuke, "did you tell Tadeas that we were going on the offensive?"

"Because we are."

"When?"

"This very night."

The word "bullshit" very nearly escaped Idrian's lips. That definitely would have crossed a line, and he was glad he held it back. But what the piss was Demir up to? He'd already said that the soft ground Kerite was camped on was impervious to cavalry. So where did he send those thousand cuirassiers? None of it made sense, and Idrian found that it caused his own nerves to come unsettled.

The night wore on. An hour passed, then another. Idrian kept track of time by the movement of the moon and tried to force himself to enjoy the quiet night. Demir was not unpleasant company, and he talked a little about his time out in the provinces, telling stories of fleecing provincial bookies that Idrian did not necessarily believe, but found quite entertaining. Idrian returned the favor, telling Demir about the campaign in which he and Tadeas had become friends in far-off Marn.

He'd almost forgotten their purpose here—or rather, what little purpose Demir had revealed—when he spotted lights bobbing through the hills below them. He tapped Demir on the shoulder and brought them to his attention. Demir stared for several moments before speaking. "Dragoons, by their speed. Maybe fifty of them. Probably sent off to loot the guild-family hunting lodges. Gotta pay for the war, right?"

Idrian reached for his helmet. "Shall we intercept them? The two of us alone should be enough with the element of surprise."

"Hmm." Demir checked his pocket watch. "If they'd arrived a half hour ago, I would say yes. But I think we'll be okay. The road they're following comes up the tributary into the Kirkovik's hunting grounds."

Idrian watched the line of torches continue to move. His whole body itched at the sight of them. "We should warn Tadeas," he finally said.

"No."

"Sir!"

Demir smiled. "Tad has his own sentries down there. He'll see them coming. But they won't be a problem."

Minutes continued to tick by. The dragoons grew perilously close to that sliver of lake that Idrian could see over the treetops. He could hear no alarm, see no movement of the Ironhorns among those trees. Fifty dragoons might not be much compared to a battalion of combat engineers, but the two groups stumbling on each other in the dark *would* cause casualties—and then the dragoons would return swiftly to Kerite and betray the Ironhorns' position. Idrian got to his feet. "Sir, I can't—"

"Wait!" Demir said, cutting him off but standing up next to him. Demir held his pocket watch, his attention fixated on the dragoons. "Wait," he said again, drawing the word out. Even in the darkness his gaze was intense, and after a few more seconds he whispered, "Now!"

There was nothing. Idrian scowled at Demir, then down at the dragoons, then back at Demir. He opened his mouth, only to have the words snatched from his breath by a deep, reverberating *thump* that rattled through the rocky earth and up deep through his bones. The sound came from the direction of the Ironhorns. Down below them, the company of dragoons came to a stop, their torches flickering uncertainly in the night.

"What just happened?" Idrian whispered to Demir.

"Listen!"

Idrian turned his head, straining with all his senses. The whole world seemed to have gone completely still. He could hear nothing. Except . . . He shook his head. It was as if the sound of his own blood rushing through his ears was growing steadily louder. It made no sense. Idrian peered into the darkness, wishing his sightglass was even better, when the torches of that company of dragoons just . . . went out.

Not all at once. The lights disappeared one at a time, in rapid succession, and Idrian found himself staring in horrified fascination as the very earth seemed to swallow them up. He thought he heard a few screams, but they were difficult to make out over the rushing sound in his ears. A slow realization reached him, and he found himself fighting for the right words before finally turning to Demir.

"That man-made lake down there. You just blew up the dam, didn't you?"

Demir didn't answer for a long time. He stood frozen, holding his pocket watch up in front of him like a coach-service conductor noting the time on her arrivals. The seconds ticked by, and then the minutes, before the rushing sound in Idrian's ears finally began to abate slightly.

"If," Demir finally spoke up, "my calculations are correct, the water should arrive any moment."

Idrian turned his attention back to Kerite's camp. One by one in rapid succession, just like the torches of the dragoons, cook fires began to go dark. It was a silent, eerie process, as if a giant were pulling a blanket over the entire camp. Inky black spread along the floodplain, and the distant sound of shouts reached him. "Did you just destroy all of Grent?" Idrian asked, his whole body numb with the realization of what was happening.

"Of course not. I'm not a monster. Grent's flood-control measures are far too good, and the lake Mika just emptied far too small. But those floodplains Kerite is camped on are specifically meant to be flooded."

"And our cavalry?" Idrian asked. As if to answer his question, he suddenly heard the distant cracks of muskets, carbines, and pistols. He thought he saw muzzle flashes on the northwest end of the floodplains. No, he *definitely* saw muzzle flashes there. Battle of some kind had been joined.

"Kerite's forces not swept away asleep in their tents will try to reach high ground on the Grent-Ossan Highway. Those two battalions are sweeping along it at this moment."

"A cavalry attack? At night?"

"I . . . might have confiscated a very large, very valuable shipment of sightglass from a Magna warehouse earlier today, and distributed it to our cuirassiers."

Idrian could do nothing but watch, dumbfounded, the chaos unfolding in front of him. It was difficult to make out in the darkness, even with his sightglass, but he could understand at least some of what was going on. It was devastating and brutal, and for some reason it made him feel sick. Demir could not hope to take Kerite on the battlefield, so he'd unleashed the very forces of nature upon her.

"You wanted me to see this, didn't you?" Idrian asked breathlessly.

Demir was quiet for a moment, his eyes fixed on the distant events. Finally he said, "I know what everyone is saying about me, even among the Ironhorns. I know they think that I've broken, that I'm insane, that I can't be trusted to keep them alive. I *did* want you to see this. Tadeas might be the head of the Ironhorns, but you're the beating heart, and I want you to understand that all of those things might be true—but that there is still a little of the Lightning Prince left in me."

Demir turned suddenly, putting his pocket watch away and heading back the way they'd come. He stopped after a few paces and continued, "More importantly, I wanted you to see that Kerite is not invincible. She can—she will—be beaten. Come, let's get back to camp."

Idrian tore his gaze away from the horizon and set it upon the retreating shoulders of the younger Grappo. All his doubts and worries of the last week were still there, tumbling about in his head and heart, but Demir's words seemed to mute them all.

The Lightning Prince was back, and he would do anything it took to protect Ossa.

39

Kizzie hurried across the yard of a small estate on the outskirts of Ossa. It was about one in the morning and the world was quiet. The silence from Grent—where artillery exchanges had gone on for over a week—was deafening. A day and a half since the defeat and the newspapers tried to spin it as positively as possible, but an undercurrent of dread now hung over Ossa. Everyone knew that the real damage had been censored, and whispers repeated in every corner about how it would take weeks for Ossan reinforcements to trickle in. Everyone wanted to know who would take over command of the Foreign Legion with Stavri dead. Citizens fled to the provinces by the thousands.

Kizzie was not concerned about the Stavri heir. She was interested in his little brother—a member of the Glass Knife, and an apparent blackmailer. In the chaotic jumble, Agrippo Stavri's family seemed to have been forgotten. The house was dark and quiet, most of the family sent away and servants dismissed. There were no bodyguards or enforcers, just a handful of National Guardsmen doing a slow circuit around the outer boundaries of the yard. They were easy enough to avoid. Kizzie reached the patio, crouching briefly beneath the window of the main-floor office. The office windows were made of hammerglass, preventing her from removing the panes with her sorcery.

A military-grade razorglass knife pulled from her boot did the trick.

She cut the window lock with her razorglass and pushed the window open, slipping quickly inside, where she paused to put on a pair of powerful sightglass earrings that she'd borrowed from the Vorcien enforcer armory. Once they were in place, she could see Agrippo's office as if it were bright as day, hear even the quietest squeak of a mouse in the basement, her nostrils filled with a thousand near-dormant scents. It was brilliant, incredibly expensive sorcery. Even her sense of touch was magnificently amplified, to the point where merely stubbing her toe would leave her in agony.

Kizzie stood frozen, listening carefully, trying to sort the sounds of the world out from the beating of her own heart. No footsteps, no talking. Somewhere far away, all the way at the other end of the house, someone wept quietly. Probably the widow.

Satisfied that she would not be interrupted, Kizzie proceeded carefully, trying not to let her senses overwhelm her as she passed through the remnants of days-old perfume or heard the creak of a board magnified a dozen times beneath her own feet. The office was much as she expected of a guild-family member—a large room, decorated with built-in bookshelves, drinks cabinet, glass-fronted gun cases. There were tables laid out with diverse hobbies, and a big desk topped with a globe of the world that she swore every damned elite in Ossa owned.

Kizzie inspected everything. She lifted decorative busts, rooted through drawers, checked behind tapestries and paintings for hidden safes. She was looking for blackmail material of whose nature she was uncertain. It could be incriminating ledgers or letters, and it could be hidden just about anywhere.

She was not optimistic about her prospects, but she had to stay focused and hope that Agrippo was too paranoid to stash the blackmail with a friend or at a bank box.

The desk turned up nothing, nor did the wall decorations. Kizzie crept along the floor on her hands and knees, looking for any sign of peculiar scratches on the wood flooring or discoloration that would indicate a commonly moved rug. Again, nothing.

Hours passed and Kizzie's frustration grew. The weeping from the other end of the house had long since ceased. Footsteps passed the office without stopping, then returned the way they came. She grew more and more nervous. How long until dawn, or Agrippo's restless widow came to the office, or a proper enforcer patrol checked on the house?

It was the bookshelves that finally proved her patience. Kizzie removed books one by one, flipping through each until a copy of Turio's *Sapphic Compendium* betrayed its late owner. A handful of letters were hidden inside, along with what appeared to be a set of military orders. Kizzie compared the letters with the one she'd stolen from Agrippo's corpse. Definitely the same handwriting. She turned them over, searching for proof of the sender.

Only one of them—the first, before the blackmail victim wised up—had a return address on it. Kizzie read the address, almost laughed out loud from pure shock, and then read it again. Her legs felt a little wobbly. Sinking down to the floor, she set the letter to one side and then opened the military missive. It said:

For immediate distribution to all officers: Demir Grappo has ordered the sacking of Holikan. Proceed without delay.

—*Capric Vorcien*

Kizzie ran her hand through her hair. There wasn't much to know about the disaster at Holikan. Nothing ever came from it. The city was sacked, Demir had a mental breakdown, and then Adriana and the Assembly covered up the entire affair. Civilians could barely find anything in the history books and any information to be had was all word-of-mouth. It was one of the biggest cover-ups of the century.

Among people who gossiped about such things it was widely accepted that the Lightning Prince, high on his own power, had ordered the sack of the city, only to be overwhelmed by guilt the next morning.

Kizzie had always tried not to think too much about it. She didn't want to believe that her childhood friend was a butcher. Here, in her hand, was evidence that vindicated that belief. Capric, her own half brother, had given the order. Not Demir. Kizzie tried to swallow, her tongue dry as sand, and looked around for a glass of water before remembering where she was.

She withdrew from the estate, clutching all the evidence of Capric's double guilt, and couldn't think straight again until she was riding safely away in a hired hackney cab. She rubbed the military missive between her fingers, wondering idly how much this thing was worth. How much would Capric pay to get it back? What would the Ministry of the Legion give to know what really happened at Holikan? And Demir . . . what about Demir?

Kizzie opened the letters one at a time, carefully reading through the correspondence between Capric and his blackmailer. There were threats, recriminations, begging, and refusals. Eventually Capric gave in, agreeing to any demand.

What to do with this information? Sell it? Give it to Demir? Give it to Capric? Kizzie felt the hungry pull of her own greed. With these two pieces of information she could get herself well back into Father Vorcien's good graces. He might be involved or he might not, but he would want the whole thing buried for good. Demir, he would tell her, must never know about either betrayal—to protect Capric, and to protect the Vorcien name.

She leaned back in her seat, warring with herself, and thrust her hand into her pocket. She felt something there—a tiny piece of wax paper. It still smelled faintly of toffee, and with that smell came a flood of memories. She could remember playing with Demir and Montego on the floor of Adriana's study, and dozens of times Adriana had shown Kizzie kindness in ways that her own family never would: dinner at the formal table, gifts for her birthday, washing her hair when she fell in the mud.

"I can't serve justice for you," Kizzie whispered. "Not this time. I'm sorry, Adriana." She looked down at the letters in one hand, then the military missive in the other. "Perhaps, though, I can get Demir some closure." She reached up, pounding on the roof of the hackney cab. "To the Vorcien estate," she ordered.

⁊   ⁊   ⁊

Kizzie sat outside Father Vorcien's office, drumming her fingers on her knee. The foyer was mercifully empty this early in the morning, her only companion a young man who smelled like coal dust. She'd been waiting for almost an hour, careful to remove all the emotions from her face but boredom and a bit of impatient consternation. Listening to the ticking of the grandfather clock, she was painfully aware of her precarious position in the guild-family.

The door finally opened and a nod came from Diaguni, granting Kizzie access to her father for however many scant minutes he'd allow her an audience. She strolled inside, stopping in front of his wheeled chair and kneeling to kiss his silic symbol. He stared down at her with a bemused expression.

"Has Demir constructed a working phoenix channel already?" Father Vorcien asked.

"No."

"Then why the urgent request for an audience? I am a busy man, my bastard daughter, and I do not like having my time wasted."

Kizzie ignored the implied threat. He would make time for *this*. She produced the stack of letters from her pocket and tossed them on the little table beside Father Vorcien's chair.

"What are these?" he asked, tapping his finger on them.

"That," she replied, "is a correspondence between Agrippo Stavri and the man he blackmailed into helping murder Adriana Grappo."

"And who was that unfortunate soul?"

"Your fourth child, Capric."

Kizzie had never actually seen her father surprised before. His eyes bugged slightly, his fingers hovering just above the stack of letters. His gaze darted from the letters to Kizzie and then back again, and they remained in silence for an uncomfortably long time before he spoke again. "You're certain?"

"His return address is on the first letter," Kizzie told him, "and the correspondence matches his handwriting."

"Diaguni," Father Vorcien called, "delay my next appointment by twenty minutes." He then began to read each of the letters, just as Kizzie had done earlier in the cab. Kizzie waited in silence, ignoring the drops of sweat rolling down the small of her back. When he finished reading he took the whole stack and shuffled it carefully, lining up the edges of each letter, his gaze distant.

His next words were spoken very carefully. "Have you told Demir?"

"Of course not," Kizzie snorted. "I came directly here."

"Where is the blackmail material?"

Kizzie tried to keep her expression neutral as she shrugged. "I have no idea. The letters reference some kind of important military missive. Capric spent what, seven years as an officer? It could be damned well anything." She tilted her head as she examined her father, her heart skipping every other beat. Had she ever lied to him directly before? Had she ever dared? She went on, "It may be in a bank box somewhere, or it might never have been in Stavri's possession."

"Explain."

"I've uncovered four of the six of Adriana's killers. The Grent agent, Churian Dorlani, Glissandi Magna, and now Capric. Churian was ordered by his grandmother. The Grent agent was sent by the duke's brother. Glissandi killed herself rather than confess under shackleglass. Capric was blackmailed by Agrippo Stavri. The instigators are connected by a single thread: they all belong to the same Fulgurist Society."

"Which one?"

"The Glass Knife."

"I haven't even heard of it," Father Vorcien snorted.

"Well, they seem to be at the center of things," Kizzie said, "and if anyone has that blackmail material, it'll be one of them." She searched her pockets until she found the list Gorian gave her. "A membership roster," she said. "I don't think it's complete, but it has given me some direction in my investigation."

Father Vorcien looked over the list, scowling. "There are too many important people on this list for me not to know the name of the Society."

"They appear to be *very* secretive. The National Guard is keeping tabs on them."

"They keep tabs on every Society. Make me a copy and leave it with Diaguni."

"Of course."

Father Vorcien laced his fingers beneath his chin, staring off at the other side of the room. If he suspected that she was withholding anything he did not show it. He seemed to meditate for a time before stirring once more. "Capric's involvement in Adriana's murder can never be revealed."

"Agreed."

He looked up at her sharply. "You don't want to tell Demir?"

"That my half brother killed his mother? Absolutely not." No lie there. Kizzie had played such a conversation out in her head while waiting to see her father. Even just the mental pantomime was deeply unpleasant.

"And your personal feelings?"

"Adriana was always kind to me. I know it's not my place to say anything as a bastard, but . . . I'm never going to be able to look Capric in the eye again." Another truth.

"He will not be punished. Surely you must know that."

Kizzie flinched. She'd guessed as much. "I know."

Father Vorcien leaned forward, searching her face for some time before finally reclining in his chair. "You so desperately want to tell Demir," he said. "I can see it in your eyes. And yet you came to me instead. You chose well, Kissandra." He rested a hand on the stack of blackmail letters as if to establish that they were now in his possession. "Anything else to report on your investigation?"

"I still have two killers left to discover. Aelia Dorlani and the duke's brother are both beyond our reach, but one of the remaining two *must* be able to give me clearer answers. Someone is orchestrating all of this. I want to find out who it is, and gather evidence against them."

Father Vorcien's eyes became distant, his lips pursed, face taking on that expression she'd always called his "decision-making face" when she was

382 · Brian McClellan

younger. Finally he said, "Find the other two killers and find out why they did it. When you do, come to me first. I'm not going to let Demir start a guild-family war, but leverage over Aelia Dorlani will allow us some measure of justice *and* enrich the Vorcien."

Kizzie swallowed. "Yes, Father."

"This appears to be much deeper than just Adriana, and it may affect the Empire itself. Come back this evening. I'll have my spymaster gather whatever information we have on this Glass Knife Society and make it available to you."

"That's very generous."

"It's not generous, daughter. It's in my interest. Now go."

Daughter. Not *bastard* daughter. Just daughter. She'd pleased him, and she hated how good that felt. Kizzie's heart raced as she followed her father's dismissal. She half expected someone to chase after her and search her as she walked back down the gravel path of the estate, but no one came. She summoned another hackney cab at the end of the drive. As the cab took her out of the Family District and back down into the city, she considered the military missive still in her pocket.

She knew Demir well. The murder of his mother would be met with blood no matter the cost, but Holikan was now distant history. If he found out about Capric's involvement he would respond with the cold calculations of a true Ossan politician. Father Vorcien was wrong—there would be justice, but neither he nor Capric would even see it coming.

Kizzie changed cabs three times to be sure she wasn't followed and then walked the last few blocks to end up at the desk of a postal clerk on the edge of the Slag. "No return needed," she told the clerk, sliding the military missive into an envelope. "Send this to Breenen Alvari at the Hyacinth Hotel."

40

Sweat poured down Thessa's brow as she carefully pushed and turned on a massive hand drill as it bored directly down through the center of the cinderite. The cinderite was clamped in place perfectly perpendicular to the ground, and she stood on a ladder above it for leverage. The drill was from a quarry outside the city, made specially for stone and masonry, and it had been a day-long slog to effectively turn the long piece of cinderite into a pipe that she could run copper cable through.

She dabbed her brow with the corner of her heavy apron, checking all of her clamps before giving the drill another half turn. Behind her, the furnace roared, making the whole workshop uncomfortably hot.

"So that's cinderite?" Pari appeared in the door to the little glassworks, looking distinctly uncomfortable in the purple livery of a Grappo porter. She was framed by a darkened doorway, and Thessa realized that she'd once again lost all track of time. She didn't even remember the sun setting or porters lighting the lamps in and around the glassworks.

"Quickly," Thessa instructed her, "come over and tighten that clamp right there. Just a smidgen, mind you!"

Pari followed her instructions, and Thessa turned her drill just a little bit more. "You've never seen cinderite before?" Thessa asked.

"In the museum once, when I was a child. It was much smaller than that."

"Put your hands here and here. Hold steady, and tell me if you see any sand coming out the bottom of the cinderite." Slowly, carefully, Thessa turned the drill a full rotation.

"Sand!" Pari said. "Definitely sand."

"Good. Almost through." Thessa took the weight of the drill, her arms trembling, so that it wouldn't fall on the cinderite once it was through the bottom. She finished another turn and felt it give. At that moment she carefully pulled upward, bringing the whole drill back up through the center of the cinderite, and handed it to Pari. Looking down from the top, she could see the floor through the tube. "Perfect," she sighed, and climbed down from her ladder. "Did you finish with Breenen?"

Pari shifted uncomfortably and pulled at her purple tunic. "I've never been sworn to secrecy on shackleglass before. He didn't seem to like me very much."

"Breenen is very protective of the hotel, and of Demir's projects. Remember, you're not working for him. You're working for me."

"I thought this was your project."

"It's *our* project." Thessa sat down in a chair beside the cinderite, rubbing the back of her neck. Everything felt stiff and uncomfortable from trying to hold the weight of that drill, and she was grateful that Pari was finally approved to work with her. The extra pair of hands would be invaluable.

Pari fidgeted, looking at the cinderite, then at the big omniglass rings that Thessa had made the day before. "This doesn't look like any godglass work that I've ever seen before."

"That's because it's not." Thessa had thought long and hard about what to tell Pari. To her knowledge, only Demir and Montego actually knew what she was working on. The rest of the staff, including Breenen and Tirana, had been told her work was important and nothing more. But Thessa needed an assistant if she was going to complete the phoenix channel as quickly as she liked, and an assistant couldn't be kept in the dark. "It's a device that will turn energy into sorcery, effectively allowing us to recharge godglass."

It took a moment, but Pari's expression slowly changed from one of dubiousness to one of surprise. "Oh. Oh! *That's* why I was sworn to secrecy."

Thessa chuckled, and turned to look out the window at where a porter was crossing the garden. The young man paused at the door just behind Pari. "Lady Foleer, a shipment has arrived for you from . . ." He paused to consult a card he held. "The Ossan Distributor of Volos Incorporated."

"Ah! My lightning rod. Have it taken to the roof. I'll be up to examine it soon." Thessa hurried around the little glassworks, addressing her notes and thinking out loud. She gave Pari the same quick explanation about the lightning rod that the clerk at the bookstore had given her, then showed off the sketches for her design. "Lightning from the roof will hit this crown here, travel down the copper cable, through the insulated phoenix channel, and then harmlessly into the ground."

Pari stared at her in horror. "You're going to *try* to get hit by lightning? That's madness!"

"It's quite safe if done correctly. It's all explained in that book over there. In fact, you should read that when I don't need your help."

"Um . . ." Pari looked down at the floor. "I can't read."

Thessa paused in her work, a stack of papers in one hand. It had never even occurred to her that Pari might not be able to read. It made sense, though. If you grew up in the Slag, you probably didn't have an education. Thessa had a pang of regret for bringing Pari into her confidence. She pushed through it. Pari had earned some patience and goodwill.

"We'll have to change that. Remind me to hire you a tutor. But not right now. We have too much to do. Now . . . what is it?"

Pari blinked rapidly at her. "You'd teach me to read? *Me?*"

"Why wouldn't I? You're my assistant. An assistant needs to be able to answer correspondence and do sums. *Can* you do sums?"

"A little. Nothing too complicated."

"We'll hire you a tutor for that as well."

"Oh."

"Is that okay? Will you be all right with a tutor?"

Pari seemed particularly subdued, perhaps even overwhelmed, but she nodded. "I think so."

"Good. Now go help the porters take the lightning rod to the roof. Don't unpack it until I know where I'm going to put it."

"Of course."

Thessa clicked her tongue thoughtfully at her notes, thinking over everything, wondering if she truly was mad. A week ago she would have laughed at the very idea of harnessing lightning—of even trying something so foolish—but Professor Volos's book had convinced her it could be done. It was free energy, without having to rely on gas, wood, or coal supply or a dirty, belching furnace.

If it worked.

Thessa finally checked her pocket watch as she headed up the stairs to the hotel roof, squeezing past Pari and the porters as they tried to angle a couple of large crates up the service stairwell. It was almost midnight, a fact that made her laugh at herself. No sense of time indeed. No wonder her back hurt so much, if she'd spent almost the entire day drilling out the cinderite.

She went over to Ekhi's mews first, checking the grub bucket to make sure someone had fed him. She stroked his uninjured wing gently, taking a deep breath, using the moment to decompress from all of her ambitions. She *should* go to bed. She'd been working since early this morning, and she would need rest to finish the phoenix channel without a mistake. But her mind buzzed, her body full of energy. How could she sleep when she was so close?

"I'm going to have to move you somewhere safe," Thessa told Ekhi. "I don't want you up here if I'm going to encourage a lightning strike." The thought gave her some pause and she looked around the roof of the hotel. There were several decent places she could put the rod itself—up on one of the chimneys seemed the most likely, where she could run the cable down her own furnace chimney and then ground it in the garden. But a sense of unease struck her.

What if something went wrong? What if she attracted a lightning strike to the roof of the hotel only to destroy part of it? People could get hurt or killed. Millions of ozzo's worth of property could be damaged.

There was another problem as well, one that she'd been avoiding for the last couple of days. She had absolutely no idea when lightning would next strike. It could be next week. It could be months from now. Would she really be satisfied with setting up her entire project and then simply waiting until something happened? She scowled across the roof, wondering if she should prepare the lightning rod in such a way that she could attach it to the phoenix channel only in the event of a storm. That would let her experiment with other energy methods in the meantime.

Across the roof, the porters finally emerged from the service stairwell with the crates, and Pari directed them to a clear, flat space. Thessa watched them lay out the crates and turn up the gas lamps, then head back into the hotel. Only Pari remained, hovering around the lightning rod, clearly waiting for Thessa to come over and examine it.

Thessa turned up a nearby lamp to examine Ekhi's injured wing, then headed over to join Pari. Something had stalled her—the excitement she felt moments ago had vanished, leaving behind a feeling of uncertainty. What if she was wrong? What if it didn't even work? Could she endanger the entire hotel like this? She ran a hand over her face. Her initial instincts were right. She needed to get some more rest, otherwise she wouldn't be able to think through this.

Pari hefted a crowbar. "Do you want me to open these?"

Thessa made a frustrated noise in the back of her throat. "I'm not sure."

"Second thoughts?"

"Of a sort." Was she moving too quickly? Jumping to too many conclusions, from ordering the lightning rod to hiring Pari? The pressure in Thessa's chest, of knowing that the world would continue to grow more chaotic the closer it came to running out of cindersand, spurred her into a frenzy. But would it be her undoing? Even master siliceers took things slowly, with a lot of careful trial and error. She didn't have room for trial and error. She had only one piece of cinderite and a limited amount of refined cindersand for the omniglass. She had one go at this. Maybe she should stop and step back.

Could she afford to?

Looking out from the top of the roof, Thessa took a moment to admire the view of the city. Gaslights glittered for miles around, lining the street and lighting up the wealthiest tenements and houses. In the distance some dogs barked, and she could hear very faint artillery reports from the north. "They've started back up again," she said to Pari.

"They?"

"The soldiers. Grent and Ossa, shooting at each other."

Pari tilted her head for a few moments. "That's not artillery. That's the Forge."

"It is?" Thessa listened. "So it is. Hah! When the war first started I mistook artillery for the Forge. Now I've done the opposite. I can tell the difference between the resonance of every type of godglass but I can't tell thunder from artillery." Thessa sat down by a chimney stack, unlacing her boots and kicking them off, wiggling her toes to get out some of the ache. "I need," she said out loud, half to herself and half to Pari, "massive amounts of energy to turn into sorcery. I have an original design that funneled heat from a standard glassworking furnace through the phoenix channel and into spent godglass, but the process was imperfect. It took three loads of firewood to charge a single piece."

Pari came to sit next to her. "That's unsustainable, even for a guild-family."

"You see my problem, then? All my thoughts the last week or so, even when I was imprisoned at the Ivory Forest, have been directed toward improving that conversion. I've already incorporated more omniglass to increase the resonance and heavier insulation to reduce heat loss. I latched on to this"—she pointed at the lightning rod—"because it seemed like an elegant solution. This new design needs to charge whole basketfuls of spent godglass. Lightning certainly has that power. But I *am* having doubts now. It's dangerous, but it's also unreliable. How long until the hotel gets struck by lightning? Months? Years?"

"What do you do when you have a problem you can't solve?" Pari asked.

Thessa glanced sidelong at her. "What do you mean?"

"How do you get your brain to start over? My granddad was a philosopher—at least as much as a retired cattle driver living in the Slag can get into philosophy. He used to say that the human mind worked on cycles, and sometimes you need to wait until the next cycle before a solution presents itself."

"Huh. My old master used to say similar things. Back in Grent, I got into the habit of taking Ekhi out to the countryside every two weeks. It kept my creative mind fresh."

"Then do that," Pari suggested with a shrug.

Thessa felt her doubt about Pari waver, dissipating like morning fog. She might not be able to read, but she was damned insightful. "You're sure you never had a formal education?"

"Oh, I'm sure."

"Then we'll get you one. Come on, let's retire. I need to sleep on this."

The hotel was silent as they made their way back to the main floor; the halls empty, all the lamps turned down. The two of them returned to the workshop and cleaned everything up—sorting the notes and schematics, sweeping the floor, and stoking the furnace so it would still be hot in the morning. It was almost one when Thessa finally returned to her suite. Her feet dragged, her head drooping, and she hoped she didn't spend all night lying in bed thinking about a new solution to her energy problem.

Pari was right. She needed to clear her head so she could approach the whole thing with more confidence.

All those thoughts were snuffed away as she opened the door to her suite. The main room was practically destroyed; the table and chairs were overturned, the sofa sliced to pieces. She ran into the bedroom and washroom to find the same. All of her new clothes were strewn about the floor, and the mattress lay against the wall, slashed in several places. Thessa's stomach felt like it had crawled up her throat, and she practically ran down the hall to the night porter's cubby.

The porter inside—the kind young man who'd made her tea on her first night in the hotel—lay slumped over a book, a knife buried in the base of his neck.

Thessa was sick all over the floor, her vision growing cloudy. She stumbled down the hall and pounded on Montego's door. "Montego!" she shouted. "Montego!" When she tried the knob she found it unlocked, and burst inside. What she saw almost made her vomit again.

Montego lay on the floor in his nightclothes, the table and a whole set of tea tipped over on top of him. He didn't move when Thessa threw herself on her knees beside him. It took all her strength to roll him over onto his side and slap at his face. "Come on, wake up! Glassdamnit, you can't be dead." Her hands trembled as a new thought leapt into her brain, and she left Montego to run to his window, which looked down on the hotel garden.

All the lights she and Pari had just extinguished were back on, and Thessa could see several figures in Grappo livery moving about inside her workshop. She didn't recognize any of them, but they were almost certainly packing up her notes and the cinderite.

She had to raise the alarm, and quickly. She tried Montego one more time, slapping his thick cheeks, and was just about to sprint for the door when his hand suddenly twitched, shooting out to grab her by the wrist. The grip was impossibly strong, yanking her down to the floor beside him, where she found herself staring into his foggy gaze. "Montego, you're hurting me."

Moments passed, his grip only growing tighter, before his eyes shot fully open and he gave a great gasp. He let go and rolled over into a sitting position. "Shit and piss," he mumbled, "I'm sorry, I don't know . . ." His words trailed off as he took in the upturned table. "Someone drugged my tea," he said.

"They've killed the night porter and ransacked my room," Thessa explained quickly. "They're in the glassworks as we speak, trying to steal all my work on the phoenix channel."

A great rumbling sound seemed to roll from the center of Montego's chest. He pulled himself to his feet and, though he was still wobbly, produced a massive cudgel from the coat closet of his room. "Whatever they drugged me with," he said, his words growing a little more clear, "they didn't use enough. Don't follow me, and don't look out that window."

Thessa sank down on the floor next to the spilled tea, looking at her trembling hands, trying to get the poor dead porter out of her mind. A few moments later she heard a panicked shout, and then the screaming started.

Thessa wrapped her arms around herself. Minutes passed. The screaming stopped, replaced by the more organized shouts of someone raising a general alarm. She could hear people rushing around the hall for quite some time, and then the door to Montego's suite opened.

It was Pari, looking pale and frightened. She came to Thessa's side and put a hand on her shoulder. "We should go," she said. "Come on, Breenen is getting a new room set up for you while they clean yours."

Thessa allowed Pari to help her up, then shrugged off her hand. "I'm all right," she said, breathing deeply. "I just . . . They killed that night porter, and for a few moments I thought Montego was dead too and that they were going to take all of my work." Thessa looked down at her hands. At least they'd stopped shaking.

"They're not taking anything," Pari said grimly.

"Did Montego . . . ?"

Pari shook her head. "I've seen plenty of violence in my life," she said unsteadily, "but never anything like *that*. You shouldn't look out your window until after they've cleaned up."

"Did they damage anything?"

"No. There's some blood on your notes, though."

Thessa turned her gaze away from the night porter's cubby, where several enforcers were gathered around. She found Tirana in her nightclothes, standing at the end of the hall with her sword in one hand and a pistol in the other, directing the dozens of enforcers that swarmed the halls. Porters went from room to room, quietly telling the guests to stay inside until morning.

Tirana looked absolutely furious, and turned her gaze on Thessa. "That should not have happened. I am so sorry, Lady Foleer."

"I'm fine. I'm more worried about the night porter."

"It was quick. He wouldn't have felt a thing. We'll take care of his family." Tirana peered at Pari. "You, Breenen will want to question you immediately."

"She couldn't have had anything to do with it," Thessa said, stepping in front of Pari. "She's been with me for the last hour, and before that she was with him."

"It's just a formality. He's going to question the entire staff tonight. He'd question the guests if it were up to him. We've sent a messenger to tell Demir that the hotel was attacked."

Thessa felt more secure now, with Grappo enforcers all around, and she felt her confidence returning. "Do we know who it was?" She took another deep breath. She had to look strong—to play her part. She was a Grappo client and partner now, and the staff would look to her as one.

Tirana was shaking her head when Montego appeared. He was a terrifying sight, his nightclothes drenched in blood, his cudgel dripping gore, barefoot and shirtless. Thessa felt her stomach lurch. He padded over to them, surprisingly silent despite his size. He said, "I left one alive for questioning. They were Dorlani. Six of the bastards. One of them snuck in during the dinner rush. Killed Horphel and Faille, drugged my tea, and let the others in. Glassdamnit, I should have realized I didn't recognize the asshole who brought that tea."

"Ah, shit," Tirana grunted. "I liked Horphel. Faille, too. She was a hard worker."

"They know about the . . ." Thessa nearly blurted out *phoenix channel* before remembering how many enforcers and porters were within earshot. ". . . thing?" she finished.

"Not in so many words," Montego replied, "but they had orders to search the siliceer's room and take every scrap of work you'd produced. They were wrapping up your cinderite when I fell upon them. I took care not to break anything."

"Except for them," Pari whispered. She didn't even seem to realize she'd spoken out loud until her eyes widened.

Montego gave her a toothy, mirthless grin. "Except for them," he confirmed.

Thessa returned to her room, where porters were already cleaning up the mess. She found a couple of sets of clothes and her book—Professor Volos's treatise on lightning rods—before following Pari down the hall to an empty room that had been hastily made up for her. She sank down on the edge of the bed while Pari nervously paced the floor.

"Are you all right?" Thessa asked.

"Me? I was already undressed when all this started. It was practically over when I got to the garden." She paused her pacing, turning first to the door, then back to Thessa. "I've heard stories about this kind of thing, but I never believed that the guild-families went through anything as violent as what I've seen in the Slag. But after seeing what Montego did to those intruders, I just . . . I can't even find words for it." She flinched. "I've got to go report to Breenen. I'll hold some glassdamned shackleglass without complaint if it means they don't suspect me."

"You're not going to quit?"

"*Quit?* I've barely been working for you a day and you're the best boss I've ever had. As long as Montego doesn't eat the help around here, I'll be fine." She paused. "Will you?"

"I will," Thessa answered with what she hoped was a confident smile. "I was just shaken up a little at first."

"I'll get you some tea," Pari offered.

Thessa nodded her thanks. She didn't let herself weep until Pari had left the room. The tears rolled down Thessa's cheeks, silent and warm, and she let them go until she managed to get control of herself once more. In all her life she'd never seen a body before a couple of weeks ago. She'd been robbed at knifepoint once, and she'd endured the news of her family's slaughter, but that was the extent of the violence in her life.

Now she'd seen seven bodies. She could double that number just by looking out the window. Piss, she'd *killed* Filur Magna. She'd witnessed murder by both friends and enemies, and been threatened with as much. Demir had warned her this would be dangerous, but she hadn't expected it to strike so close to home.

To calm herself down once more, she picked up Professor Volos's book and began to skim the pages. She read both the text and her own in-margin notes, studying the incomprehensible sketches she'd made on the trip back from the Lampshade Boardwalk. Her tears dried and she felt herself grow more steady. Focus on the work, she reminded herself. Let other people deal with the violence. That was their job, after all.

Pari returned with a pot of tea, setting it on the table and bringing Thessa a cup with sugar and cream. Thessa sipped slowly, feeling the tension seep out of her. "Professor Volos," she said, indicating the book, "describes the location at which she tested her lightning rod as a singular geographic phenomenon—a place where warm air regularly rose up from the sea to meet the mountains, causing frequent lightning storms that allowed her to make good, consistent progress on the lightning rod. I need something like that."

Pari stared at her in confusion. "What are you talking about?"

"A geographic phenomenon is a—" Thessa began to explain.

Pari cut her off gently. "I understood the words you used, but we *have* that. The Forge. It's exactly what you just described. The sound of distant thunder has lulled me to sleep my whole life. You too, I bet."

Thessa felt her eyes widen. "Glassdamn," she breathed, "you're right.

Consistent lightning; a remote location to mitigate the danger; and some-place so out-of-the-way that Dorlani enforcers won't come looking for us." She leapt to her feet, putting her tea aside and snatching Pari up in a hug. They had it now—their first location to test the phoenix channel, and it was less than twenty miles away.

41

Demir made his headquarters at Fort Alameda and watched with bated breath as hundreds of scouting reports poured in over the next day and a half. From the vantage of the fort he could see some of the washed-out remains of Kerite's camp. It looked like a shoreline after a storm, muddy and covered in trash. Thousands of figures picked over the area, removing bodies and recovering equipment.

"What's Kerite going to do next?" Tadeas asked. Uncle Tad sat in the fort commander's chair, feet up on the commander's desk while she was out over-seeing the fresh overhaul of her fort. Demir's maps, messages, and reports lay across every available surface, even covered much of the floor, laid out so he could see them as a whole in one glance.

Demir was not glancing at them now. He was watching the desolate floodplain from the fort commander's office window. "It seems," he said cautiously, "that she and the Grent are on the back foot. Over half their forces were washed down the river. Most of the soldiers seem to have sur-vived, but it'll take her a couple of weeks to bring them back up to fighting strength—they lost so much gear that she can probably only field a fully armed brigade at this moment."

"The Inner Assembly will want you to press the attack," Tadeas said, tap-ping his boot on the desk to whatever tune was playing in his head. It sounded like a funeral march.

"And I'd be a fool if I listened to them," Demir snorted. "The Foreign Legion has had a couple days' rest after that loss in the Copper Hills, but we're still short on cureglass, and morale is low. Our enemy still has more glassdancers, better troops, and they've pulled way back to the coast where they can sit in the Grent suburbs and resupply easily. Any attack on them at this moment would be a fool's errand."

It wasn't just cureglass they were short on. Demir was having a hard time finding enough forgeglass for the soldiers or witglass for the officers. Milk-glass, and the blessed pain relief it offered, was also growing scarce. He didn't tell Tadeas any of this, as it might lead to a more painful conversation. He simply wasn't ready to mention the scarcity of cindersand to anyone yet.

"Is that why you've been ignoring Father Vorcien's demands for an update?" Tad gestured at a neat little stack of messages marked with the Vorcien silic sigil.

"I've been ignoring them because I plan on telling him myself," Demir replied, finally pulling himself away from the window and crossing to the desk, where he pushed his uncle's feet to the floor. He picked up the stack of messages and put them in his uniform jacket pocket. "I've given orders to redouble our scouting efforts, secure lines of communication to Harbortown, and speed up citadel maintenance across every one of our star forts."

"You're going into Ossa?" Tadeas asked with a scowl. "Is that wise?"

"I won't be gone for more than twelve hours," Demir promised. "If Kerite or the Grent so much as twitch from their positions, I'll be back here fast as lightning." He tilted his head at his uncle, whose scowl only deepened. "You don't think I should say a word to the Assembly until I win another victory, do you?"

"It would cement your advantage. That maneuver with the flood was a damned good one, and the cuirassiers did give Kerite a genuine fight, but there's not a lot of glory in either of those things. Ossa responds to glory."

"I seem to remember that you don't care much for glory."

"I don't. But my responsibility is to keep a single battalion of combat engineers alive. You've got to juggle the military, politics, and public perception all at once." Tadeas grinned at him. "There's a reason I gave you my spot on the Assembly all those years ago."

Demir looked back across the stacks of messages, the spy reports, and the maps. He was plagued by a thousand little doubts, bouncing around inside his skull like bullet ricochets, all of them overshadowed by his greatest failure. He didn't want to go back to Ossa. He didn't want to face the Assembly, or see Thessa again, or have the safety of the Empire on his shoulders. He wanted to run away.

But despite everything, glimmers of his old self seemed to have returned. He could see a path to victory. It was a knife's edge, depending on factors outside of his control, but it was still a path. He could defeat Kerite, and in doing so redeem his name in the history books. The cost, however, would be great.

396 · BRIAN MCCLELLAN

Too great.

"I'm not going to fight another battle," he told Tadeas quietly. "I'm going back to Ossa to try and convince Father Vorcien to sue for peace before the Grent can recover."

❦   ❦   ❦

Demir *should* have gone directly to the Assembly, where word had already been sent ahead for Father Vorcien and his Inner Assembly cronies to await Demir's report. But his trip into Ossa was more than just a victory run. As Tadeas so succinctly put it, Demir's position as both a general and guild-family patriarch meant he had to juggle military, political, and public perception all at once. He couldn't afford to let anyone else shape his juggling act.

"I'll be just a moment," he told his carriage driver, then sprinted up the stairs into the Hyacinth. He paused briefly, taking in the quiet lobby and the small lunch rush in the hotel restaurant, before hurrying behind the desk and into Breenen's office. He closed the door behind him, and the hotel concierge looked up in surprise.

"Master Demir! I didn't know you were back."

"Only to make my report," Demir replied quickly. "I have special instructions." He produced several papers from his pocket and handed them to Breenen. "I won a great victory the other day and have been holding back reports from the Assembly. I want this press release in every newspaper for the evening edition, and this press release to go out first thing in the morning."

Breenen glanced at both press releases, a half smile forming on his face. "Ah! Staying one step ahead of the Assembly. Just like your mother."

"Shaping reality is a skill just like any other," Demir responded, "and the advantage always goes to the first person to give the public what they want. The Assembly wants to control information. The public wants that warm fuzzy feeling that everything will be okay."

"Surely the Assembly won't try to suppress a victory?" Breenen said.

"From me? I won't risk it. I have at least two enemies on the Inner Assembly. I have to move quicker than they. I . . ." Demir trailed off, truly looking at Breenen for the first time. Despite that half smile, his brows were knit in worry, his body language that of someone holding uncomfortably to bad news. "What's happened?" Demir asked. "Is it Thessa? Did something go wrong with her project?"

Breenen moved a few piles of papers around on his desk, not meeting Demir's eye. "A couple of things, sir."

"Go on!" Demir checked his pocket watch. He was going to be late for his meeting with the Inner Assembly. "Make it quick."

"Perhaps it should wait, sir."

Demir ground his teeth. It probably *should* wait, but if something bad happened it should slot into his calculations so he couldn't make things worse. "Out with it."

"The Dorlani attempted to burgle the hotel, sir. I sent a runner to let you know, but they might not have been able to make it through the military blockades."

A cold trail of sweat sprang up in the small of Demir's back. His swirling thoughts of powerful arguments and political maneuvering suddenly disappeared, and his focus was now entirely on Breenen. "Thessa's project?"

"It was their target," Breenen confirmed. "They tried to snatch notes, books, and even the project itself. They poisoned Montego's tea and killed a cook and a porter. They might have gotten away with it if Lady Foleer weren't up so late working. She managed to rouse Montego. The intruders were . . . dealt with."

"Piss!" Demir swore. He began to pace around the small office. Their greatest weapon in this silic race for a phoenix channel was that no one actually knew they were participating. That advantage was now gone. "We must have a spy."

"I . . ." Breenen grimaced. "I'm not sure we do, sir. I spent all night interviewing the entire staff with shackleglass. *I* don't even know what she's working on, and none of the staff do either."

"Then how the piss did the Dorlani find out?" Demir demanded. He could feel a rising panic in the pit of his stomach and tried to fight it down. He couldn't defend the Empire *and* his guild-family all at the same time.

"We managed to interrogate one survivor of the attack. Their orders came directly from Aelia Dorlani. She must already know what Lady Foleer is working on."

"But how?" Demir demanded again. His pacing grew more frantic until he forced himself to take a calming breath and sit down in the little chair across from Breenen's desk. "Shit and piss. Well, at least she was already one of our enemies on the Inner Assembly. Does she know her burglars failed?"

"She must by now," Breenen said, "but we've kept it very quiet. She won't know that we pried information out of her lackeys, and she won't know that they're all dead. The bodies are still in our ice cellar. Montego says he's saving them for something special."

"I don't want to know what, but I probably should." Demir considered heading right up to Montego's suite and ordering him to stand down. They couldn't escalate this, not right now. He checked his pocket watch again. He was *definitely* going to be late. "Where's Thessa?"

"She's in the garden, working on her project. Would you like to see her?"

"Not right now." Demir opened the door to make sure no one was standing at the hotel's desk just outside, then closed it again and turned to Breenen.

In a low voice he said, "Thessa is a Holikan orphan."

Breenen's whole face fell. "You're joking, sir."

"No. We almost slept together the other night. We likely would have if I hadn't been called away by the Cinders. I saw her just briefly before heading to the front and that's when she told me."

"Does she know . . . ?"

"No. I don't think she does. She was practically a child when it happened, and wasn't present in the city. My guess is that Master Kastora shielded her from most of the information, but she's going to figure it out eventually. Those press releases have my old nickname all over them. Another victory for the Lightning Prince. If she doesn't make the connection then, the newspapers will make it plain as they dig into my past. Everything Mother buried is going to get brought to light."

"Do you not want me to send the press releases?"

"The Grappo name is more important than my relationship with Thessa," Demir said flatly. He'd been warring with himself about this for days, and it was the only possible conclusion. "I will tell her when I return, and then we'll see how she reacts. I . . . You're giving me that look again."

"What look, sir?"

"Like you have bad news you don't want to have to tell me."

Breenen made a frustrated noise in the back of his throat. "You're very good at reading people, sir."

Demir checked his pocket watch one last time and finally put it away. He should take Breenen's advice and put everything off until later. There was a war on, after all. "Tell me," he ordered.

"Sir," Breenen said, removing something from his inner jacket pocket, "a letter came for you earlier today. It only contained this."

Demir took a yellowed piece of paper from Breenen. He recognized an old military missive right away, from the shape and weight of the paper. It was folded down the middle, and he opened it to find a very short note.

For immediate distribution to all officers: Demir Grappo has ordered the sacking of Holikan. Proceed without delay.

It was signed by Capric Vorcien, and dated the night that Holikan was sacked.

Demir felt nothing for a very long time. He stood next to Breenen's desk, staring at the paper, vaguely aware of the sounds of the hotel outside the little office. He finally licked his lips only to find them parched, both lips and tongue as dry as a mouth full of sand.

"Who sent this?" he asked.

"No idea, sir. Whoever it was didn't want to be found out. They routed the envelope through at least two post offices before it arrived here."

"Is it authentic?"

Breenen hesitated for too long before nodding. "I believe it is, sir."

Demir cast about himself. He still couldn't feel anything. His thoughts and mind were absolutely blank, as if they'd simply been unable to comprehend the crime—the *betrayal*—evidenced before him. He read the missive over several more times. His breath grew short, his eyes having trouble focusing. For half a moment he thought he felt the gentle tickle of his victor's cloak rubbing against his neck. The last time he saw it, it was still wrapped around that poor dead child in Holikan.

"I'm sorry, sir," Breenen said quickly. "It's my fault. I should have waited to show you. I . . ."

"Did you put a tail on Capric?"

"The moment I laid eyes on this note."

"Where is he?"

"Sir, I don't think it's a good idea to respond right now."

"*Where is he?*" Demir couldn't remember a single time—since childhood, perhaps—that he'd raised his voice at Breenen. The words came out as a frantic, furious shout and in that moment it was like a stopper had shot out of a wine bottle and all his emotions suddenly bubbled out bereft of logic or stability. He could feel the cracks forming in his mind, battered by an unstoppable maelstrom of fury. "Where the piss is he, Breenen?"

Breenen flinched away. "At the High Vorcien Club, sir."

"Give me the shackleglass you keep in your desk." Breenen hesitated for just a moment before fetching it and handing it over. Demir slid it into his cork-lined pocket and was out of the office and halfway to the Hyacinth front doors before he realized that he didn't have a plan or any faculty for measured reason. He tried to stop himself—to arrest this idiot course of action—but his feet just kept carrying him forward.

"Sir, the Inner Assembly!" Breenen said, catching up to him and physically pulling on his sleeve.

"Can glassdamned wait." Demir whirled back toward Breenen and took the concierge by both shoulders. "He was my friend," he said softly to Breenen. "He was my friend and he murdered thousands of people and destroyed my life. I want answers and revenge, and I want them *now*."

42

"Block the road," Demir told his driver, leaping down from the running board. The carriage came to a stop at an angle behind him to effectively cut off traffic in front of the High Vorcien Club. The angry shouts and swearing began immediately, starting with the carriage coming toward him from the other end of the road. Demir crossed his arms in front of him, palms facing inward, displaying his twin silic sigils. The opposing driver's mouth snapped shut and he pulled on his reins, parking his own carriage across the street and leaving Demir standing in an empty space perhaps ten yards across.

Pedestrians stopped to look, and riders climbed out of carriages. They were curious at first, craning their heads, shouting questions at Demir and each other, but a wave of frightened silence seemed to pass back along the rows of carriages, leaving helpless consternation in its wake. If a glass-dancer wanted a street blocked, a glassdancer was damned well going to get the street blocked. It would, Demir decided, not take them more than a few minutes before someone sent for the Cinders.

"Tell Capric Vorcien to come out and see me," Demir told the nervous bouncers standing just outside the club. "Tell him to bring his sword. If he slips out the back then I'll come to his house, and I won't be nearly as polite." To emphasize his point, Demir pulled a glassdancer's egg from his pocket and tossed it up into the air, catching it casually. One of the bouncers took off inside the club at a run.

The minutes passed slowly as Demir waited, pacing back and forth in the space between the two carriages, sword in one hand and glassdancer egg in the other. The heat below his collar had begun to cool and he tried to reason with himself—to get back in his carriage and let this thing go until later. He knew that was the smart thing to do, but every time he tried to turn away from this course of action his head began to pound, blinding him with pain and fury.

He thought about Capric while he waited. They'd been friends since childhood. Not the closest of friends, not like him, Montego, and Kizzie, but friends nonetheless. They'd been tutored together, gone on holiday together, even gone through officer training together. Demir had taken Capric on the Holikan campaign because he'd needed an officer he could trust. That was, it turned out, the greatest mistake of his life.

He could sense a hundred sets of eyes on him, the crowd growing as the traffic grew further backed up and more pedestrians stopped to stare. This was a city that ran on guild-family drama, and everyone from the lowest newsie boy to the richest merchant could sense that some juicy drama was in the making.

He slashed his sword occasionally at the empty air, his thoughts tumultuous, his expression a calm lid on the maelstrom of fury battering on his insides.

"Demir!" a familiar voice finally called from the door to the club. Demir turned to find Capric standing just outside, unarmed, staring at Demir with genuine fear as dozens of club clients poured out around him, taking up a position in the streets. The elite of Ossa were no more immune to the draw of guild-family drama than the lowest citizen. Demir let his eyes wander across those faces, recognizing many, before returning to Capric.

Capric opened his mouth to speak again, only to be shoved to one side by his bullish older brother. Demir had never particularly cared for Sibrial Vorcien. He was boorish, loud, consumed by a dozen different appetites, and even by the standards of the guild-family scions considered a bully. The biggest surprise out of the Vorcien these last twenty years was that Father Vorcien hadn't quietly arranged an accident for his heir so that one of the more capable siblings could inherit.

"What is the meaning of this?" Sibrial demanded. He was carrying his sword, and he used it to gesture violently at Demir. "Get this traffic moving! Disperse the crowd!"

"Piss off, Sibrial," Demir called to him calmly. "This isn't your business."

"This is my club! I am the Vorcien heir! I don't care what kind of favor you curry with the Inner Assembly, I won't have some minor guild-family patriarch pissant interrupting the—"

Demir felt his patience crack. Not enough to lose control entirely, but enough to make a point. He tossed his glassdancer egg underhanded toward

Sibrial and put pressure on it mentally. The egg was halfway through its arc when it shattered into six pinkie-sized shards that spread out into a fan shape, their sharp tips all pointed at Sibrial. Sibrial fell silent immediately, his eyes growing wide and his face red. Demir walked across the space between them, the shards of glass moving to hover just over his shoulder like a cannon full of grapeshot waiting to go off.

"I don't let anyone on the Inner Assembly talk down to me, just like my mother didn't," Demir said to Sibrial. "So what makes you think I'll let *you* do it?" He shook his head, barely able to keep his voice calm and measured. "I'm not here for you. Capric, if you don't have your own sword with you, I suggest you borrow your brother's."

Someone else suddenly pushed their way to the front of the crowd. It was Veterixi, the Marnish concierge of the club. She studied Demir's face for a moment, then whispered something in Sibrial's ear before saying loudly, "Whatever is going on, I'm sure we can settle it with cigars and cognac. Master Grappo, please come inside."

Demir admired Veterixi. Like Breenen, she was a common citizen who'd worked her way up to a position of extreme importance and was respected throughout the city. Her intervention almost made him lose his nerve. This was, a little voice in the back of his head reminded him, his last chance. Let it go. None of this was as important as the ongoing war. It could be settled later. But he'd already tipped his hand, and the rage in his breast was too furious to be quelled by the offers of cigars and cognac, even from Veterixi.

"Sorry, Vet," Demir said, giving her a stiff smile. He pointed his sword at Capric. "This is about my friend Capric." He turned his attention back to the fourth Vorcien sibling and took a deep breath, hoping his voice would remain steady. "Here." He dug into his pocket until he found the shackleglass by feel, and then tossed it to Capric. Capric caught it. "Put that on."

"Don't do it," Sibrial hissed. "You have no right!" he shouted at Demir. Veterixi took half a step back. Capric himself held the shackleglass up to the afternoon light, staring at it unblinkingly. His face had gone ghostly pale.

"Put that on," Demir commanded, "or I will kill you and Sibrial where you stand."

"You—" Sibrial began.

"Another word and I will nail your feet to the ground with glass and then laugh while you scream!" Demir could *feel* himself cracking, the seams of his sanity coming apart. The shouting tore up his throat, bringing stinging tears to his eyes. His whole life seemed to march across his mind's eye, showing him all that he had gained in his youth and then all that he had lost at Holikan and in the years following. He had never felt anything like this, not at his lowest or his highest, and all he could do was ride it. "Put it on, Capric," he said in a softer voice.

A collective gasp had gone through the crowd—through the elites from the club, the watching pedestrians, and the stalled traffic. It was followed by deathly silence. Everyone was now asking themselves whether a lone glassdancer had ever publicly called out a powerful guild-family before, and how it had turned out. Demir himself was curious as well. He did not know.

Slowly, Capric threaded the hooked end of the shackleglass into one ear.

"I have in my pocket," Demir said loudly, practically shouting so that everyone watching could hear, "a missive sent to my private secretary from the night of the sacking of Holikan. It is signed by Capric Vorcien, and it orders the sack of the city—a bloody event that has been covered up for nine years, and that was practically—if not legally—blamed on me. Now tell me, Capric. Did you sign those orders?"

Capric stared back at him. He wore no expression, made no sound. His arms hung limply at his sides, the tips of his fingers trembling slightly.

"If this is all a mistake," Demir continued loudly, "if this missive is a forgery, then I will embrace you as a friend and kiss your feet, begging for your forgiveness. I hope that is the case. I *pray* that is the case. So tell me, Capric. Did you order the sack of Holikan and falsely blame me for it?"

No one spoke. No one even seemed to breathe. Demir wondered how many people in the crowd of pedestrians knew what the piss he was talking about. Most of them had probably *heard* of the sack of Holikan. Most wouldn't have associated his name with it. The elites that had poured out with Capric and Sibrial, though? They *definitely* knew, and most were taking Veterixi's cue and shuffling away from Capric. Only his brother remained next to him, glaring at Demir with the kind of arrogance only a guild-family heir would summon in the face of a glassdancer.

Capric lifted one hand, touching the shackleglass at his ear. He looked . . . oddly relieved? He said, "Yes. Yes, I did it."

"Louder," Demir said. Despite expecting this exact answer, he felt his jaw tighten and his eyes begin to cloud.

"Yes!" Capric declared. "I did. Damn you, I did!" He removed the shackleglass and flung it back at Demir.

Demir caught it in one outstretched hand and put it in his pocket. His sword remained half raised, pointing at the ground before Capric. "Borrow your brother's sword, Capric. We duel here. Now." He raised his voice. "My name is Demir Grappo, and two days ago I won a great victory against Grent's mercenary lapdog, the supposedly invincible Devia Kerite. Who will be my second?"

No one from the High Vorcien Club came forward. Why would they? Seconding him would only get them a lifetime ban from the club and the enmity of the Vorcien. Several offers came from the watching pedestrians, however, and soon a well-dressed young woman with a sword at her hip and expensive forgeglass buttons on her travel coat came forward. She introduced herself as Lazza, and gave a brief oath on Demir's shackleglass to serve as his second. Sibrial, of course, seconded his younger brother.

The formalities were quick and cold. The seconds searched their opponents for hidden godglass, checked the dueling swords for the same. "If you live to see tomorrow," Sibrial hissed in his ear as he checked beneath Demir's armpits and groin, "you will regret it."

"I've regretted living for a new sunrise for nine years. Why should tomorrow be any different?" Demir stepped away from Sibrial and gave his sword an experimental swing. Duels were not technically legal within the Empire, but they happened all the time. The rules were simple: Two willing participants. No godglass. No glassdancer sorcery. No interference. Capric certainly didn't *look* willing, but he took up his brother's sword nonetheless. A formal cordon was made by the club bouncers, keeping the onlookers at a distance.

Demir tested his footing on the cobbles. Smooth dirt would be better, but he felt confident in his movement. Capric did the same, the two men staring at each other until their seconds joined them. Sibrial wore a deep scowl, directing it first at Demir and then at Lazza. The young woman didn't seem to notice. She was, if Demir had to guess, cut out of the same cloth as Tirana: a soldier, or soldier of fortune, not easily cowed by guild-family politics. She probably wouldn't even be in Ossa come tomorrow.

"What are the terms of the duel?" Sibrial asked Demir.

Demir nodded at Capric. "What do you think they should be, my old friend?"

"To the death," Capric responded in a monotone. He sniffed. "What point is there in first blood?"

"Do you agree?" Lazza asked.

"I do," Demir answered. He was surprised. He'd expected Capric to take the easy way—to first blood—and live to fight another day. Demir had even hoped it. He didn't necessarily want to kill his onetime friend. He would far rather grind him to dust over many years. Perhaps that was exactly what Capric hoped to avoid. This would be a decisive ending. If Capric won, no one would ever mention Holikan to him again. If Demir won . . . well, it wouldn't matter.

"Then," Sibrial proclaimed, "the duel begins when both fighters are ready!"

"Make your peace with whatever god you wish," Lazza said quietly, and then followed Sibrial to the other side of the cordon.

Demir and Capric faced each other at sword length, smallswords raised. Demir dug inside himself to try and *feel* something. Regret. Anger. There was nothing in the pit of his stomach but cold, dead fury. "You caused the death of tens of thousands of people," Demir said.

Capric shrugged.

"You *destroyed* me."

"I didn't mean to, if it's any consolation," Capric said. "It was just politics. To put you in your place."

"Putting me in my place at the expense of so many lives?" Demir asked, tapping the tip of his sword against Capric's.

Capric shrugged again, and Demir suddenly felt like he was looking at a stranger. They'd known each other since they were children, yet how could he not see the typical guild-family callousness? Capric seemed like he might regret breaking Demir's mind. He did not regret murdering a city. "I had a heavy lunch," he said, tapping Demir's sword back.

"I haven't eaten for days," Demir answered.

"Then this will be interesting." Capric turned, presenting a smaller target to Demir and raising his sword parallel to the ground. Demir mimicked the move, lifting his sword slightly higher and then fending off a sudden lunge from Capric. The duel was then engaged, their swords sliding up and down the lengths of each other's blades. The contact allowed them both to feel the other's movements, and they remained that way, edging back and forth, before Demir felt Capric push slightly on his sword and attempt a thrust.

Demir parried with his open hand, pushing Capric's blade off to one side with a quick movement and coming in with a riposte aimed at Capric's heart. Capric slid to the right and Demir's blade caught his shirt, slicing just below Capric's ear, his sword coming back with blood.

Capric disengaged quickly, and the two were once again at length. Demir watched his opponent carefully, resisting his urges. He *wanted* to be reckless. He *wanted* to attack with the fury of a whole brigade. But a formal duel like this could not be won with fury. Capric might not be the best duelist in the Empire, but he was too well-trained to be overwhelmed in such a manner.

"You're better than you were," Capric said. "I did not expect that. You learn this out in the provinces?"

Demir did not answer. He'd said his piece already. There was nothing more but blood, and he scored it three more times before Capric managed to return the favor, slicing a painful furrow across the outside of Demir's right thigh. Demir took another cut across his left arm using an open-handed parry, and then a nick on his right shoulder. Capric, he realized, was drawing his measure and adjusting after his earlier surprise. It was Demir's turn to disengage.

He could hear little but his own ragged breaths now, his heart beating hard, and he wondered whether he'd be dead in a few moments. It was certainly possible.

They reengaged, and their swords crossed six times before Capric suddenly went for a low lunge, his entire body uncoiling into a long, powerful thrust made even deadlier by his greater height—and range. Demir felt the blade score across his belly and snatched Capric's sword by the guard with his off hand. He followed the grapple smoothly, stabbing downward at an angle for Capric's exposed collarbone.

Capric twisted slightly, and Demir's sword buried itself in the meat of the other man's shoulder. Demir pulled back once more in frustration, twisting his sword as he did, while Capric stumbled to the cobbles.

"He is injured," Sibrial barked, "too injured to continue the fight. You will have to take your satisfaction at a later date!"

Demir shook his head and took a step forward. This was a fight to the death, and respectability meant little. If he allowed it to end, Father Vorcien would never permit another duel to follow. It was either administer justice now, or Demir would watch the whole Vorcien guild-family constrict around Capric, protecting him from personal or legal recourse. "I'll give you ten seconds to get up," he told Capric.

He regretted the promise a moment later, for angry shouts suddenly broke the silence, and the crowd split as brightly clad Cinders converged upon them from all sides. It took Demir only a slight push with his sorcery to feel that the Cinders had multiple glassdancers with them. Within moments he found himself staring down the pink razorglass blade of a Cinder halberd. He let his shoulders fall and dropped his sword to hang from the guard on his forefinger. Every sense crashed upon him as if released from a box where he'd stored them all while he focused.

A Cinder snatched his sword from him, and he sensed his glassdancer egg taken from his pocket by sorcerous force. One of the Cinders—an officer with massive, flowing purple epaulets—pushed his way through his companions and spat at the ground between Demir and Capric. "By the authority of the Inner Assembly, you are both under arrest!"

"That man there is a Vorcien!" Sibrial declared.

"I don't give a shit what he is," the Cinder snapped back. "Both are under arrest."

Demir felt a strong hand grab him by the back of the neck. He was turned away, heavy irons clasped over his wrists. He watched as the driver of his carriage abandoned the vehicle and fled on foot, sprinting back to the Hyacinth to tell Breenen and Montego what had happened. All the feelings that Demir had tried to feel before the duel seemed now to press on the inside of his chest—anger, regret, indignity. He'd come back to Ossa to declare his victory, and now he would have to do so from a cell beneath the Maerhorn.

He was a fool. A damned fool.

43

Every child in the region could talk at length about the Forge. It had a long and storied tradition as a spiritual place—perhaps haunted, perhaps a shelter for ancient gods, perhaps just preternaturally unlucky. It was said to rain almost every other day at the Forge, violent lightning storms causing the thunder that gave it its name happening on a weekly basis. It might be clear and sunny around the entire region, but clouds would cling to the cliffs like otter pups to their mother. Legend spoke of a succession of noblemen who'd tried to build estates, forts, and even a lighthouse on its rocky heights, only for every single project to get destroyed by lightning.

Despite hearing that distant thunder for almost half of her life, Thessa had never actually been to the Forge. She'd sailed past it once on a journey with Master Kastora, noting its towering heights from a long way off, but that view had been nothing compared to actually walking up onto the damned thing.

Standing on its summit, the wind whipping at her hair, Thessa could see from a scattering of old ruins that the stories were at least partially true. People *had* tried to build up here. The only completed building—though it had since been partially destroyed—was the lighthouse. The top floor, including the flame and mirrors, was all but gone, while the main living area was still fully intact, if rotted.

The rest of the stories, of course, were hogwash. The Forge was nothing more than a natural formation, jutting out into the ocean and towering hundreds of feet above the surrounding countryside. Scientists had written about it at length over the last couple of decades, describing a phenomenon much like that Professor Volos spoke of in her book—the shape and massive height of the Forge caused warm air to rise off the ocean and mix with cold air from the nearby Halifax Mountains.

And just like that: lightning storms.

Thessa paced the crown of the Forge, looking in the craggy little nooks among the rock formations and examining the blackened scars across the stone that gave testament to the frequent lightning. She climbed to the highest rocks, trying to remember every detail from Professor Volos's book. Pari and Tirana waited just below, shivering in the frigid wind, still catching their breath from the long, perilous hike up to the heights. Down below—far down below—their carriage waited, loaded down with the crates that contained the lightning rod.

Being this high up, the sun shining in her face, made the darker events of the last couple of weeks feel like a dream. Thessa could barely picture the poor young porter, face down on the book he'd been reading, nor Filur Magna's charred corpse inside his own illegal furnace. They were distant memories. This high place was the future. It was, she decided, where history would be made and change the world forever.

She wondered if Ekhi would like it up here, or if the savage winds would harm his ability to fly. No sense in even trying to bring him here until his wing had healed.

"This will do nicely!" she shouted to Pari and Tirana. Both of them shook their heads, and Thessa was forced to climb back down to where they waited on the trailhead. "This will do," she said again, still having to shout to be heard above the wind. "Come on, this way." She led them up to the very crest of the Forge—a flat piece of rock perhaps twenty yards across. At one end was the foundation of an old ruin, no more than a couple of feet tall and probably hundreds of years old. Sticking right out above the ocean, perched on a perilous drop, were the half remains of the lighthouse.

She turned to her little audience. "According to Professor Volos, lightning strikes are never guaranteed, but they often occur at the highest point in the region. We can either use that rock formation there, or the lighthouse." She tapped her chin thoughtfully. "Let's use the lighthouse. Put a tarp over the partially destroyed roof and we'll have someplace out of the wind to work—and the lightning rod will protect us from actual strikes."

Pari looked around them, clearly nonplussed, but nodded. "I'll get started."

"Are you comfortable setting everything up from my drawings?"

"I am."

"Good. I'll leave you and two enforcers here to get things going. I should have the project itself finished within a couple of days and will return." Thessa paced around the lighthouse one last time before nodding at her own decision. "It's important to remember," she said, more for her own benefit than for Pari's, "that this is just a test. It might not work. We might have to start over. But we won't know until we try."

"All due respect, Lady Foleer," Tirana shouted above the wind, "but this is absolute madness."

"Would you rather I attach the lightning rod to the hotel? Because that's my backup plan."

"I'm not objecting, ma'am. Just stating. I've only been with the Grappo for a few years but I know enough about them to understand that mad ideas have a long and glorious tradition. You're fitting right in."

Thessa felt the corner of her mouth tug upward, and she thought about the kiss she and Demir had shared several nights ago. It was a childish fancy, but an eminently practical one as well. Could there be a matriarchy in her future? "That's the nicest thing anyone has ever said to me."

Tirana shook her head and laughed, then slapped Pari on the shoulder. "We'll be back in a few days. Don't let my enforcers give you any shit. They're here to help." She turned and began walking down the path to their carriage.

Thessa waffled beside Pari for a few moments. "Does this frighten you?" she asked once the master-at-arms was out of earshot.

Pari stiffened, her chin going up, as if the very suggestion was an affront to her honor. She almost instantly deflated. "A little. No one ever asked me to wave a rod in a lightning storm when I was hauling firewood. But the pay is a lot better, and . . ." She looked down at the hand she'd injured. It was good as new, without even a bend. "Well, the benefits are better too. At least I don't have to lick any Magna boots."

Thessa grinned at her. They were so damned close. Just a little more work on constructing the channel and they'd be able to test it. "I'll be back soon. Stay safe. And, uh, if there *is* a lightning storm before I get back, I wouldn't suggest actually touching the rod."

⯈   ⯈   ⯈

Kizzie had spent two days reading the Vorcien spymaster report on the Glass Knife.

Spymaster reports were not, as one might imagine, coherent narratives on a particular person or place, but rather loose collections of information that might or might not have to do with the subject in question. The report provided to Kizzie was no exception. It filled three wooden crates and included everything from newspaper clippings and printed pamphlets to copious handwritten notes from dozens of different sources. Since Kizzie was not allowed to take the report off the estate, she holed up in a spare bedroom in a little-used wing of the house, reading until her eyes grew blurry.

She spent far too much of her time thinking of the way Demir used to consume and digest information. Even as a boy, all he had to do was put a piece of witglass in his ear and his eyes would fly across the page, taking in huge amounts of information at once and—most importantly—*understanding all of it*. It was this last bit that Kizzie was genuinely jealous of, for she spent most of her time with the report just trying to figure out how it all connected.

Kizzie finished her second complete read-through of the file and threw herself down on the bare mattress of the spare bedroom she'd commandeered. It was a damned complicated web. Gorian had only given her a list of names. The Vorcien spymaster report both expanded on that list and tracked the movements and ambitions of every member of the Glass Knife. They were a powerful lot, from a dozen different guild-families and diverse positions within the Ossan government.

It made her wonder why Father Vorcien had never heard of them, if his spymaster kept such good records. But then she remembered that there was likely a file like this on most of the Fulgurist Societies within the city. Still, Gorian's instincts about them were correct: there were dozens of court cases against members or the Society itself—corruption, bribery, assault, murder, mysterious disappearances. Every single case had been buried in some way and then forgotten. Seeing that trail laid out plain in front of her was eerie.

How much had the spymaster missed? How many more members were scattered across the Ossan guild-families, the branches of the military, and the governing apparatus that spanned the entire world? Were they guilty of these myriad crimes? If so, how had they so effectively covered them up?

Most importantly, what did all that have to do with Adriana Grappo? Why kill her? Why use six people to do it in public? Kizzie felt like she could leap to a conclusion on that first question. Adriana must have discovered something the Glass Knife didn't want her to. Something other spymasters had not managed to dig up. A plot of some kind? Another high-profile murder? Had she just dug a little too deep and asked the wrong sorts of questions? Was her public death meant to be a warning to anyone who poked at their members too much? Perhaps the Glass Knife was not daring enough to go after one of the mighty guild-families, but felt confident attacking one of the minor ones.

She was missing something in all of this. Either a piece she had not found, or a piece she had misinterpreted. Her assumptions *felt* right, but she still didn't feel confident taking them to Demir. Piss, she wouldn't feel confident returning to Demir until she had found and questioned those last two killers. Then she could lay out the evidence against the Glass Knife, and Demir could wage his war on *them*.

If Father Vorcien allowed her to tell him.

Her thoughts were interrupted by a gentle knock on the door, after which it immediately opened to reveal Diaguni. The Vorcien majordomo nodded at Kizzie and glanced around the room, taking in the three big crates and all the papers spread out across desks and dressers and the floor. His brow was furrowed, his face pinched as if he was holding in a breath.

Kizzie sat up immediately. "Something wrong?" she asked.

"Kissandra," Diaguni greeted her, closing the door behind him. "How goes your search?"

He had dodged her question. "Do you know about all this?" Kizzie asked, gesturing to the crates. Of course he did. Diaguni probably knew where more bodies were buried than Father Vorcien himself.

"Your father and I discussed the Glass Knife last night," Diaguni replied. "Their operation is not unlike some of the other powerful Fulgurist Societies, but if they truly did kill Adriana then they have gone too far." His voice was soft and calming, but his brow was still furrowed.

"I'm almost certain that they did," Kizzie told him. "Too many of their members were involved for it to be a coincidence. I still don't know why. I have two more killers to track down, and I'm hoping one of them tells me."

"Good, good." Diaguni came to sit on the edge of the bed. His scowl deepened.

"Diaguni," Kizzie prompted, "what's going on?"

"Those letters you brought to your father the other day."

"Capric's blackmailing?" Kizzie felt the bottom of her stomach drop out. Did they know she'd sent the missive to the Hyacinth? How could they possibly, unless they had a spy in the hotel? Had Father Vorcien managed to turn Breenen? Even if he had, she'd been very careful to make the envelope untraceable. Her thoughts raced but she was careful to keep her expression neutral.

"Indeed," Diaguni said. "The military missive Capric was being black-mailed with was evidence that he framed Demir for the sack of Holikan."

Kizzie eyes grew wide. She didn't have to fake surprise. She might already know about the missive, but she was shocked Diaguni would tell her about it at all. "Glassdamn," she whispered.

"Someone—the Glass Knife most likely—sent Demir the missive, and Demir called out Capric in public. They dueled. Both were wounded, but the Cinders arrived and arrested them before the duel could reach its conclusion."

"Oh." Kizzie felt her stomach flip around inside of her. Those two sentences felt horribly understated. She'd expected Demir to find out when he returned from the front in a few weeks. Not *immediately*. She'd expected him to take the whole thing in stride; to destroy Capric slowly over the next decade—not challenge him to a glassdamned duel. She'd miscalculated Demir terribly. Her urge to help her friend find closure might have just started a guild-family war.

More pertinent to her own fortunes, it seemed that Father Vorcien already blamed it on the Glass Knife. At least that was something.

"What do I do?" Kizzie asked. She looked around the room, leaning into her own sudden sense of helplessness. She couldn't let Diaguni have the faintest clue that she was involved with the missive. "Are we at war? Do I stop looking into all this?"

"Your father wants you to remain on task. At the moment, only Capric has been called out and blamed, and so we will pretend that we are all still friends. Proceed in good faith. The answers Demir wants are answers that your father wants as well. Beyond the task he's already given you, Father Vorcien wants you to remain uncompromised in Demir's eyes."

She raised an eyebrow. How could Demir possibly trust her now? If Demir now saw Capric as his enemy, he would see *all* Vorcien as enemies. "How the piss am I supposed to do that?" she asked.

"As I said—proceed in good faith. Do what you can to maintain Demir's trust. Remember what you've been promised." Diaguni stood up suddenly and gave her an almost fatherly smile. "The Glass Knife is attempting to sow discord among the great guild-families. It is even more important that we root them all out. Find answers. Bring your father evidence of their involvement in Adriana's murder." Diaguni left the room, closing the door softly behind him.

Kizzie waited until he'd been gone for some time before letting out a little gasp and checking to make sure she hadn't inadvertently pissed herself. "Damn you, Demir," she whispered. "You weren't supposed to attack Capric directly." Damn Capric, damn Demir, and damn herself.

She paced around the room. Sowing discord indeed. She had done exactly what their enemies would have wanted.

Something prodded at the back of her mind, and she turned her attention back to the spymaster report. Something Diaguni said had grabbed her attention and now she couldn't tell what. She thought back over the conversation carefully, considering every word, until she realized what it was: *discord*.

This whole damned thing was organized chaos. The Grent agent was the thrust of it: a fall guy who was meant to be caught so that the murder was pinned on the Grent. War was declared, destabilizing the entire region. But to what end? War was bad for trade; bad for Grent; bad for Ossa. If Adriana's death was meant to cause all of this, then *why*?

Kizzie paced around the small bedroom, thinking furiously. The Glass Knife had no doubt planned on Demir returning to conduct the investigation directly. They *hadn't* planned on Kizzie. That was their mistake. A mistake that, at some point, they were going to try and rectify. The Tall Man had, she knew, seen her face. She no longer just had to solve this conspiracy to placate Father Vorcien and vindicate Demir. She had to do it to save her own skin before a powerful Ossan Fulgurist Society could put a knife in her back.

A knock on the door nearly made her leap out of her boots, and Kizzie whirled toward the door, stiletto drawn before she even knew what she was doing. She hid the stiletto behind her back and prayed that Diaguni hadn't returned to poke holes in her earlier excuse. "Come!"

To her relief, it was one of the Vorcien maids. She bowed to Kizzie and held out a note. "This just came for you, ma'am."

Kizzie waited until she was gone before opening it. She immediately recognized Gorian's blocky writing.

I've found your Tall Man, it said. *Meet me at the watchhouse at ten in the morning.*

Kizzie pumped her fist victoriously. *Now* she was getting somewhere. Find the Tall Man, confirm that either he or his masters were working for the Glass Knife, and then take them all down. She might damn well get out of this whole thing yet!

44

Idrian stood over a washbasin, splashing cold water onto his face as he stared into his reflection by flickering gaslight in the officers' guest quarters of Fort Alameda. He could see the gray in his hair, and the tiny iridescent splotches of purple and yellow permanent glassrot on his cheeks and neck that were visible only from the right angle. Light reflected off his witglass eye as if from a child's glass bauble, showing the imperfect depths of the glass. Sometimes he fancied he could see through his eye, all the way into his brain, and witness the rot growing within that caused his madness.

He finished shaving and splashed more cold water across his neck and chin, then wiped it all away with a rag. Someone off in the courtyard of the fort was singing along with Braileer's fiddle—the beginning of what everyone hoped would be a long night of hard-earned relaxation. Demir was off in Ossa. Kerite was not an immediate threat. Food and beer had been brought in by the cartload to reward the Ironhorns and their cuirassier counterparts for the maneuver that everyone was calling the Grappo Torrent.

The Grappo Torrent. Idrian chuckled at that and wondered how many commanders over the next hundred years would stupidly try to blow up dams and divert rivers at their enemies without doing the kind of calculations that Demir had carefully prepared.

He pulled on his dress uniform jacket and adjusted the collar in the mirror. He was getting older. Stiffness crept into his skin and bones all over from glassrot. He wasn't far from retirement, and while he yearned for peace, part of him feared having to spend the rest of his life alone on an officer's pension, waiting for glassrot cancers to kill him.

He wanted nothing more than to go out into the courtyard with the enlisted men. Drink beer all night. Maybe spend the night in a cuirassier's arms. Instead he had to attend a formal dinner with the garrison commander, whose name he couldn't even remember.

"Shit and piss," he said to the mirror, pressing on his godglass eye gently, "I'd say getting old is the pits, but every year is a gift for a breacher like me."

He slowly became aware of the sound of feet running in the hallway of the barracks. They came to a stop just outside his door; then came a knock and, without waiting for permission, Squeaks pushed the door open and looked up at him.

He waved her off. "I know, I know. I'm late for dinner, I—"

"Sir!" Squeaks cut him off in a low voice. "It's not about dinner."

Most of the enlisted soldiers called Idrian by his given name. He'd never cared, since he felt more like them than an officer. "Then what's this about?" he asked, turning toward her with a frown.

"There's a problem."

"Then say it quick!"

"I'm a minor talent as a glassdancer."

Idrian peered at Squeaks. "That's your problem?"

"Of course not! It's a secret, not a problem. Only Major Grappo knows and he's been telling me for years not to mention it to anyone. Says it might come in handy one day."

It was an odd thing to keep a secret. Minor talents might have some use in a few occupations, but the military wasn't one of them. If people knew she was a minor talent she might be able to command a few ozzo more per month from her contract, but it made no more difference than that. "So why tell me now?"

"Because *General* Grappo pulled me aside and gave me a task—to be on alert at all times. He didn't want what happened to General Stavri to happen to him."

Idrian was still thinking about having to wear this stiff-collared dress uniform all night. "The general has gone to Ossa. We don't expect him back until late tonight, and assassins aren't going to attack us inside a damned fort. At ease, soldier."

"Uh, sir. I think the assassin might be here."

Idrian looked at the mirror, adjusting his collar once more. Several moments passed before what Squeaks had just said sank in. He whirled back toward her, the hair on his neck standing on end. He looked at her—really *looked*—and could see from the fear in her eyes that this was no joke. Within moments he was striding down the mostly empty barracks hall, every spare piece of godglass threaded through his piercings. Squeaks ran to keep up, talking in a hushed tone as she did.

"There's just one of them," she explained, "perched up there on the roof of the commander's office." Which was, it could be no coincidence, where all the officers were gathering to have dinner as they spoke. Squeaks went on, "I checked around, and not a single glassdancer is unaccounted for. He's definitely not one of ours. I don't even know how he got up there. I didn't sense him coming in. It's like he just appeared out of nowhere."

Idrian looked sidelong at Squeaks. "You're sure it's just the one?"

"Yes, sir."

All the reports Idrian read about Stavri's assassination said that it was carried out by a squad of at least six glassdancers. Any fewer could not have possibly conducted such a precise and immediate slaughter. But there had been a lot more officers and hangers-on at the Bingham Brawlers Club than there were here. "Does he know you've spotted him?"

"My own glassdancer talent is so minor that I'm difficult to sense. That's why I've been able to keep it secret so long. He either doesn't know I'm here or doesn't think I'm paying attention. Glassdancer senses are like any other—you have to have your sorcerous eyes open, so to speak, in order to catch something." She paused and looked worried. "Should I have raised the alarm immediately?"

"No, that would just tip him off. You did well coming to me. How strong is he?"

"Very. He stands out in the empty night like a beacon, sir. If we had any military glassdancers in the fort right now, they'd have sensed him without even having to look."

Idrian vacillated over raising the alarm. A single glassdancer would have a difficult time getting out of the fort alive, but a suicide mission could easily kill Tadeas, Mika, Valient, and all the garrison and cuirassier officers before a proper response could be levied. Idrian needed to turn the tables—to ambush the glassdancer—but that meant doing nothing to tip him off that he'd been discovered. He looked sharply at Squeaks. "Does everyone know that Demir went into Ossa?"

"No, sir. Hardly anyone knows. He wanted it kept quiet in case of spies. I think the garrison commander still thinks he's coming to dinner."

That settled it, then. That glassdancer was likely on a suicide mission, here to kill not a handful of middling officers but Demir himself. He'd probably snuck into the fort hours ago and couldn't sense Demir's absence until he was already in position. That meant he'd either attack anyway, or hope to hide out until he could slip away. Idrian had no intention of letting him do that. He went into Braileer's room, where his equipment was set out for polishing. Idrian picked up his sword and shield.

"All right. I'll deal with him. Go warn Tadeas immediately, but do it *quietly*. I don't want him raising an alarm. A trapped, panicked glassdancer will do more damage than someone who stupidly thinks he has the upper hand."

Squeaks headed out the main door of the barracks while Idrian slipped out the side, keeping himself out of the sight line from the roof of the commander's quarters. He kept his head low, raising a finger to his lips to anyone he passed who gave him a curious glance—and there were quite a few of them. The fort was overflowing with infantry and cavalrymen here for a good military party conducted with the general's blessing. If the glassdancer panicked, he could kill a *lot* of people before they managed to take him down.

Idrian made his way to the far side of the mess hall and found the rusty ladder leading up to the roof. He ascended with his shield on his back, crouching in the darkness for a moment to be sure he hadn't been spotted, before hurrying across the slate tiles. He climbed up two more stories, moving silently on the balls of his feet and keeping his head down so no one shouted to him unawares from the muster yard below.

He'd just crested the roof of the garrison supply depot when he spotted a shadowy figure. The glassdancer was perched a few feet back from the edge of the roof, just above the patio to the garrison commander's quarters. If someone was planning on dropping into the middle of dinner and killing everyone, that was exactly where they'd wait. Idrian was to his right and a little behind, and if the glassdancer noticed Idrian's presence he did not react in any way. Slowly, careful not to let his sword or shield scrape on the slate roof, Idrian worked his way around behind the glassdancer.

He slid his sword and shield off his back and remained in place. The glassdancer was less than thirty paces from him, facing away. He was bigger than Idrian expected, perhaps even bigger than Idrian himself—shoulders hunched, head tilted as if listening, entirely focused on the sound coming out from the open patio door beneath him.

Idrian stared for several moments, unable to shake an unsettled feeling deep in the pit of his stomach. This was odd. *Very* odd. Glassdancer assassins were certainly not unheard of, but since they could be sensed by minor talents they were not widely utilized. A chill went down Idrian's spine as he realized that the glassdancer was waiting for something—likely for all the officers to be present. Idrian himself should have been there. Perhaps the glassdancer still hoped for Demir's return.

Enough worries. It was time for action. Idrian turned the hilt of his sword in his palm until the blunt edge was facing forward. Put a glassdancer in enough pain and they would be as helpless as anyone else. Answers would be very valuable. Break an arm, perhaps? No, a leg. Perhaps both legs with one blow.

Idrian began to sprint, running at full tilt across the slate roof, no longer bothering to hide the sound of his movement. He was wearing enough forgeglass that he could cover the short space in a matter of seconds, and he did just that. He brought his sword out and around in a wide, low swing, his shield held forward. The glassdancer began to turn before Idrian even reached him, but was not fast enough to dodge his sword. The blunt edge came down and across, sweeping at the glassdancer's legs.

This was a maneuver Idrian had done before, and he knew exactly the amount of force to expend. The end of his sword hit right at shin level, but instead of a sweep it felt as if he'd just hit an anvil. The impact nearly wrenched Idrian's arm out of his socket. Both he and the glassdancer grunted in surprise. The glassdancer went down, though not nearly as hard as he should have, while Idrian found himself off balance and careening toward the edge of the roof. He threw himself sideways and rolled across his shield, tumbling loudly across the slate shingles.

He recovered during the roll, returning to his feet with a practiced move, sword and shield positioned between him and his enemy, every muscle of his body coiled and ready to spring forward.

The glassdancer *was* big, over six feet tall and wide enough for two men. A cloak hid most of his body, but Idrian could make out massive arms encased in some kind of matte armor, and a broad helmet decorated with fanciful ridges that reminded him of the spikes on the edges of a crab's shell. They sized each other up for half a second before shouting in the room beneath him caused Idrian to snap out of his brief reverie. It was not an instant too soon. Glass on the windows below them audibly shattered, and he could hear it tinkling against itself as the glassdancer coalesced the glass on all sides. Idrian snapped his sword back around, blade-forward, and lunged.

The glassdancer was surprisingly agile despite his bulk. Steel-shod boots clattered on the roof tiles as he sidestepped Idrian's thrust, ducked a slash, and then rolled out of the way of a second slash. Idrian began to sweat immediately, a fear like nothing he'd ever experienced appearing in his belly and causing his hands to tremble. He didn't have his armor on, but he was wearing enough forgeglass to be about as fast as it was possible to be and this glassdancer was sidestepping everything he could throw at him. He felt something breeze past the back of his neck and realized the glass-dancer was both moving *and* on the offensive—something that took a lot of skill and practice to accomplish.

Idrian caught sight of glittering movement in the corner of his eye and dove to the rooftop, rolling across the shield, followed by the sound of doz-ens of shards of glass slamming into the roof tiles right where he'd been standing. He pulled his shield up to cover his eyes, the feel of a thousand little cuts brushing across his ankles, shredding his uniform pants and the skin underneath it. Against all instincts, Idrian dove forward, forcing the glassdancer to the edge of the roof until the two of them were close enough that he could feel the other's hot, sour breath on his cheeks.

It was the first time he'd gotten a good look at the glassdancer's face, and what he saw made the blood freeze in his veins. That helmet with its crab-like ridges wasn't *right*. The eyes were too far apart, the mouth too low. It wasn't a helmet at all. It was a *face*.

This glassdancer—this *thing*—wasn't human.

The two remained there for a heartbeat, the massive glassdancer just on the other side of Idrian's shield, before Idrian registered the sounds of alarm going up all around them. The glassdancer opened its jaw, unhing-ing it horribly, stretching its long neck over Idrian's shield. Idrian almost didn't respond. This couldn't be real, could it? Another manifestation of his sick mind? At the last moment he dropped his shoulder and shoved, hear-ing the sound of a jaw snapping shut just over his head. The creature reeled back into thin air.

What Idrian had taken for a cloak unfurled into massive wings, beating so hard that they almost drove Idrian to the ground. The light caught the beast for a few moments, showing Idrian that the armor was hard shell, and what he'd taken for steel-shod boots were clawlike feet. The glassdancer shot upward into the night air with impossible speed, quickly getting lost to Idrian's vision. Idrian backed away from the edge of the roof, staring upward, waiting for the glassdancer to return. The whole night was filled with the sound of the garrison and their guests arming for battle. If there was anything to be heard of the glassdancer, Idrian couldn't make it out over the sound of his allies.

He was still staring into the sky when Tadeas joined him on the roof, sword and pistol in hand, Mika on his heels and holding a pair of grenades. They were both wearing heavy cloaks that covered all but their eyes—the best defense against a glassdancer. Idrian looked at them, then back up into the sky, then back at his companions.

"Tadeas," he said, hearing the desperation in his own voice. "I've done it. I've gone mad. I just . . . I just . . . I fought a . . ." He could not make the words come out. Even now, moments after the glassdancer was gone, he was having trouble describing it in any terms that made sense. He must have gone completely insane.

"You're not mad," Tadeas responded grimly. "I saw it from the roof of the barracks. So did Mika. I'm not sure who else, but it glassdamned flew away."

Relief washed through Idrian, a sigh escaping his lips that what he'd seen was actually real. The feeling was quickly followed by terror. That glassdancer wasn't human. It was strong enough to shrug off a disabling blow, and fast enough to dodge those that followed. What kind of a creature was it? Could godglass *do* all that? Was it some Grent monster? Or was it something else?

"Get everyone on high alert in case it comes back," Tadeas ordered Mika. "And Idrian, you've been damn well shredded. Get out of the open and get some cureglass. It's gonna take all night to pick glass out of you."

Idrian could feel the cool air on a thousand little cuts on his legs and his right shoulder. He didn't want to look. He was probably bleeding badly, and the pain would be worse if he weren't wearing milkglass to counter his sightglass. He kept his eyes on the sky, his sword and shield still at the ready. What *was* that thing? Better yet, how could he possibly be prepared to fight it if it returned?

45

Demir's cell deep in the Maerhorn was a small stone room with the luxuries of a fireplace and writing desk. It was lit by gaslight and smelled like the chamber pot in the far corner, its only ventilation coming from a series of tiny holes drilled through the thick stone at the top of one wall. Demir sat on the threadbare bed, his knees pulled up to his chest, still wearing the uniform that he'd rushed back to Ossa in the day before.

He had slept. Pure exhaustion necessitated it. It had been an angry, delirious sleep, and he felt no better for it.

Every attempt to maintain his confidence had failed him. He'd made a mistake, a serious misstep, and now that he'd stumbled, the consequences for his actions and his arrogance would catch up with him. It was a deeply unpleasant thought that rolled around his head like a cannonball on a ship's deck. How to stop it? Was there any way? Or had he pushed himself too hard and managed to break himself all over again?

He didn't *think* he was broken. He knew what that felt like, and the only thing that had ever come anywhere close was fearglass. A misstep. That was all it was. He could get out of this, perhaps even profit from it. But how? He was in a dungeon beneath the Maerhorn. He'd attacked the son of one of the most powerful men in Ossa. He'd done other things too, but had expected to have the time and glory to sweep them under the rug.

He sighed and let his head loll back against the cold stone wall, only to snap forward again at the distant sound of an opening door. He could hear voices, though not make out the words. Another door, closer, opened and then closed again, and Demir peered through the flickering gaslight toward his own door. It was heavy oak, with a small barred window. The tramp of footsteps echoed just outside of it and he saw the flash of passing figures. A couple of Cinders, and Capric's long black hair and sharp profile.

Capric looked toward him for a split second as he walked past, their eyes meeting briefly.

Demir listened to the footsteps retreat. He should have done this whole thing differently. He'd let his broken self, rife with emotional cracks, take over when he should have walked it out with skyglass and witglass, allowing himself to process Capric's betrayal fully before responding to it. Just a few minutes to calm down was all he would have needed, and he would have seen how much better it would be to destroy Capric slowly, bleeding him out from every direction over the course of years. Capric wouldn't have even known they were enemies.

Demir's self-recriminations were brought to a halt by the sound of more footsteps, and the unmistakable rolling of wooden wheels across cut stone. They stopped outside his cell. The door was unlocked, and a lone Cinder pushed Father Vorcien's wheeled chair into the small room and up beside Demir's bed. Demir glanced at Father Vorcien's unreadable face, covered in glassrot scales, eyes traveling up and down Demir as if to strip him naked and read all his secrets.

The door remained open and the Cinder stood just behind Father Vorcien. It was an older woman—a glassdancer, though Demir could sense no glass close enough to affect it—and she kept her hand on the hilt of her forgeglass-studded smallsword.

"I wasn't expecting company," Demir said, licking his palms and drawing them over his head to slick back his hair. "Otherwise I would have cleaned up the place. Please, have a seat."

To his surprise, the corner of Father Vorcien's mouth turned up slightly. He harrumphed, shifting slightly in his wheeled chair, and said, "Whatever else happens, Demir, you should know that I've always liked you."

It was an odd sort of flattery to give someone whose life you held in your hands, and Demir tilted his head to one side and tried to read Father Vorcien. He could get nothing from him. Old and crippled, and yet Father Vee was still the imperturbable statesman. "Then why did you tell Capric to order the sack of Holikan and frame me for it?"

"Right to the point, then?" Father Vorcien asked. "I wish everyone else in this glassdamned city were so forward. But you . . . you don't fear me, not like everyone else. I think that's one of the reasons I like you." He let out a small sigh. "I didn't order Capric to do what he did."

"I don't believe you," Demir shot back immediately. He might not be a fifth as experienced as Father Vorcien, but he was not a fool, either. The old patriarch would say or do anything to maintain whatever he had decided was the truth.

"Believe me or not, I don't particularly care. This is my small kindness to you, and you may do with it what you like. I *did not* give that order. I *did* tell Capric to take you down a rung—to make sure that some humiliation befell you on that campaign. You were cocky and arrogant enough for a dozen guild-family heirs, and you needed to be reined in. Capric overstepped that order by a significant margin."

Demir stared back at Father Vorcien. The coldness he'd felt at seeing the old man was beginning to heat up. He could feel the rage twitching back to life in his belly, and sought to still it. Rage had gotten him into this situation. It would not get him out. "So you're telling me," Demir said flatly, "Capric acted all on his own when he ordered the slaughter of thousands of men, women, and children?"

"Correct."

Demir almost said *I don't believe you* again. But what would be the point? "And how is knowing this a kindness?"

"Because it will, hopefully, prevent you from declaring a guild-family war against the Vorcien."

"And this is for *my* benefit?" Demir asked doubtfully.

"You won't win," Father Vorcien replied simply. "But I don't believe you have changed so much that you would not do some painful damage to my family before we crushed you." Father Vorcien's eyes wandered for the first time, glancing up at the ceiling. "Between you and Montego. Hah! Adriana knew exactly what she was building when raising the pair of you. A lethal combination. You know that he's waiting outside the Maerhorn at this very instant? The Cinders would never admit it"—Father Vorcien glanced over his shoulder at his bodyguard—"but they're pissing terrified of him. Cinders! Terrified of one retired cudgelist! They have four marksmen and two glassdancers watching his carriage."

Demir felt his eyes narrow. Father Vorcien, he realized, had taken him off guard. He glanced down, drawing patterns on his uniform leg with the end of his finger. "How long was your discussion with the Inner Assembly? The one where you figured out what to do with me?"

"Half the glassdamned night," Father Vorcien said with a yawn. "You are a liability. You don't fear any of us. You don't respect any of us. Gregori is furious that you destroyed his ancestral hunting home with your flood. Supi wants those thousand pieces of sightglass returned immediately. And

426 · Brian McClellan

me . . . well, you did force one of my sons into confessing to a war crime in public."

Demir flinched. He did not *think* they would kill him, but he had just noticed the shadows of at least two more Cinders standing in the hall just outside the cell. His life might well depend on this conversation. He should beg, plead, promise. That was what any sane person would do. Then again, Father Vorcien would know it was insincere just by virtue of who Demir was. He spread his arms. "Then what do we do from here?"

"I make you an offer that benefits us both, you accept the offer, and then we move on."

Demir had expected an offer. He did *not* expect it to benefit them both. "Right. The Ossan way." His mind wandered to his soldiers, no doubt getting nervous about his extended absence down at Fort Alameda. How long until Tadeas started asking where Demir had gotten to? How long until Kerite and her Grent allies regrouped and attacked again? Demir's one advantage here was that the Inner Assembly still needed him to command the Foreign Legion. "What's the offer?" he asked.

Father Vorcien looked down at his hands folded in his lap. "Put aside your blood feud with Capric and marry Kissandra."

"Kizzie?" Demir blurted. He'd been caught off guard before; now he felt like the two of them weren't even having the same conversation. "You can't be serious. She's my friend, and she's a bastard."

"She's *my* bastard, and I've been looking for an excuse to legitimize her for years without raising Sibrial's ire."

Demir scoffed. The sound turned into a choked laugh. "I never believed you had a heart."

"Shriveled with glassrot, but it still exists," Father Vorcien replied. His gaze was unwavering; he stared at Demir with the casual intensity of someone who always got what they wanted.

Did he know about the phoenix channel? Demir suddenly wondered. Aelia Dorlani might resort to ham-fisted burglary, but this was far more Father Vorcien's style if he thought that Demir had something he wanted. *And* it was the second such offer, if he included the offer of patronage Capric had brought him the day he found out his mother died. If Father Vorcien *did* know about the phoenix channel, to what lengths would he go to acquire it? Was this the easiest path for both of them?

"If I say no?" Demir asked.

Father Vorcien spread his hands. "If you say no, then I will assume your blood feud continues. First, you'll remain in this dungeon for . . ." He shrugged. ". . . an indeterminate amount of time. I can't keep you here forever since you didn't actually kill Capric, but long enough for my people to destroy what little reputation you have left. Second, I'll blacklist your hotel and every one of your clients and employees. No one will supply them, buy from them, work for them, or hire them ever again. Third, I will order Kizzie to continue her investigation into your mother's death but I will not give you any of the results."

That last one was just adding insult to injury, and they both knew it. Demir scoffed. No threats against his person, but Father Vorcien didn't need to do that. What he'd just described was far more insidious than just killing him and it showed how well Father Vorcien knew Demir: it was more painful to ruin those under his protection than to ruin Demir himself.

"If you accept," Father Vorcien went on, "the Vorcien and Grappo will be tied by blood. You'll be the richest patriarch in your family for generations. You'll marry a friend, which is more than most patriarchs get to do. You'll be a Vorcien in all but name and *that* will be real power. The possibilities will be endless."

"All under the Vorcien thumb."

"You don't think you and I would be able to work together?"

"You *did* destroy me," Demir responded glibly, "and I do have a blood feud against your son. But no, I'm more worried about when you die and Sibrial takes over. You think I'm going to bow and scrape to that ogre?" The very thought turned his stomach, but he tried to ignore it. The old him—the entity that he should have listened to when he first saw that military missive—was fighting for control of his thoughts again. He could feel wheels spinning in the back of his head. Plans created plans created plans.

"I believe," Father Vorcien said slowly, "that you can handle Sibrial."

"You can stomach the thought of me manipulating your heir after you die?"

"I'll be dead, and Sibrial will need a guiding influence outside of his brothers and sisters. I'm not a fool, Demir. I know what Sibrial is. You're getting distracted. I need an answer."

"Now?"

"Now."

Demir settled back on the flea-ridden bed, turning inside himself and listening to those wheels in his head. He didn't like the framing of this at all—Father Vorcien was right about the benefits, but the very idea of marrying Kizzie was too personally complicated. She was almost like a sister to him, and romantically connected to his best friend. Knowing he'd have to sleep with her even just a few times to make an heir of their own made him want to retch. He had no doubt she would feel the same way. Even worse, it further complicated his relationship with Thessa. *Could* that get more complicated?

Demir pictured a mirror in his head. Staring back out of it was his younger self—chubby, confident, arrogant. *Do your duty,* his younger self told him. *This is Ossa, where everything is complicated and there's always a solution. Marry Kizzie as a formality. Take Thessa as a mistress. Take the Vorcien riches and fame. Destroy Capric later, after Father Vorcien is dead. Take everything you'd ever want.*

I'm not you anymore, Demir spat at himself.

You'd be a lot happier if you were.

Would I? No. I'm not you, but I can't be me either. I've got to be something more. Something that takes the best of both of us. Demir looked at those plans that his old self wanted to put into motion. He examined them, plucked at them. They were always moving, like a dozen waterwheels in a massive factory, but they were also always changing. Malleable. His future, he reminded himself, was not set in stone. *You are right,* he said to himself. *Everything is always complicated and there's always a solution. I will do this, but I'm going to do it my way. Not yours.*

Suit yourself, his younger self laughed. *I don't actually exist. I'm just a piece of you that you've never reconciled.*

The image disappeared, vanishing from his mind's eye in a theatrical puff of smoke. He shook his head to clear it and focused back on Father Vorcien. "What do you get out of all of this?" he asked. "Beyond me ending my blood feud and securing Kizzie's future?"

Father Vorcien actually did smile this time. "There. Finally asking the right questions." He leaned forward slightly in his chair. "I *do* get you under my thumb, I won't deny it. More to the point: in exchange for this bounty of riches I'm offering you, you're going right back to the front. Kerite has started to move again, and I need a general to stop her."

So he was right. They still needed him. Demir raised both eyebrows. "The Inner Assembly isn't stripping me of my command?"

"They will if I let them. They want to. But if I assure them you are under my control, they'll hold their peace. For now."

"And if I win, you'll have the hero of the Empire as your new son-in-law."

"Indeed."

Father Vorcien *knew*. Demir was certain of it now. He knew about the phoenix channel and that was the real benefit he gained in all of this. Everything else was a smoke screen. Demir touched his temples, his head hurting from too little rest and too much pressure. He really didn't have a choice. To protect himself, to protect his clients and employees, he had to take the offer. "Is Kizzie going to have any say in this?"

"She wants to be legitimized more than you know," Father Vorcien said dismissively. "She'll find it distasteful, but she will say yes."

"She has to agree," Demir insisted.

"I'll take care of that."

It was an ominous statement that made Demir's stomach lurch. How many lives would Father Vorcien twist to get his hands on the phoenix channel? Any that he needed to, Demir imagined. He took a deep breath, glancing inward one last time. Could he do this without ruining lives? Without hurting the people he loved? "Then it's a deal."

Father Vorcien's glassrot-covered cheeks lifted into a grin. "You will abandon your blood feud against Capric?"

"Yes." *No.*

"You will marry Kissandra?"

"Yes." *Not if I can get out of it.*

"You will bow the Grappo neck to the Vorcien?"

"Yes." *Never.*

"You will return to the front and end this war?"

Demir actually laughed out loud at this last one, but it was a sad laugh. "We should sue for peace. End this without more bloodshed, before the Grent can recover."

"It's not up to us anymore," Father Vorcien replied. "Kerite has already recovered. Her reserves have arrived from the Glass Isles and she's preparing to attack Harbortown as we speak. The Grent still believe they can win. They won't pull back until their pet mercenary army has been destroyed."

"You could have mentioned that earlier." Demir felt a flash of fear. He hadn't faced Kerite directly the first time because he knew he couldn't win. She was just too good a general, and her mercenaries were enough to help the Grent crush the Foreign Legion. How the piss would he beat her on the open field when her reinforcements had already arrived?

"Would it have changed anything?" Father Vorcien asked.

"I suppose not."

"Good." Father Vorcien gestured to the door. "Now go save the Empire, son."

Demir almost laughed at that. *Almost.* Cheeky old bastard. The two Cinders waiting in the hall showed him out in complete silence, and in just a few minutes he was sitting in Montego's carriage, facing the massive cudgelist, his thoughts turning around themselves.

"Well?" Montego demanded. "What happened? Breenen told me about the missive, and the entire city is talking about your duel with Capric. Are you all right? Do I have to kill the Vorcien? Answer the second question first."

Demir snorted. *Kill the Vorcien.* Not just one of them, but the entire guild-family. Only Montego would ask such a bold question. "No, you don't have to kill the Vorcien. I've struck a deal."

"You mean Father Vorcien forced a deal on you," Montego said flatly.

"Correct."

Demir drummed his fingers on the wall of the carriage. He couldn't remember the last time he'd so much as considered lying to Montego. They'd never held anything back from each other, not in twenty-five years of friendship. "Father Vorcien knows about the phoenix channel."

"You're sure?"

"He didn't say as much, but it explains his maneuvering."

Montego leaned forward, peering at Demir sharply. "He offered you a marriage, didn't he?"

"Kizzie," Demir answered.

Montego inhaled sharply. Demir could see the calculations in Montego's eyes, no doubt extrapolating the entirety of the conversation Demir had had with Father Vorcien. Montego took a few shallow breaths and said softly, "She's always wanted legitimization more than anything. This would secure her future."

"Could you handle it?" Demir asked.

"You know that I would not let my personal feelings get in the way of either Kizzie's or the Grappo's future," Montego said slowly. "However, I would . . . not be able to stay in Ossa if you marry Kizzie." No angry outbursts, no demands that Demir recant the deal. Just a simple statement. It was surprisingly gentle from one so known for violence, but it hurt more than if Montego had punched him. If the deal went forward as Father Vorcien wanted, Demir would lose his best friend.

He tried to focus. He had a war to win, and the Grent were already on the move. Every minute he spent here might lose him what little advantage he had. He suddenly felt a great indignation—for himself, for Kizzie, for Montego. Father Vorcien might think everything was just business, but he had no *right* to force any of them into such an arrangement. "This is Ossa. Everything is always complicated, and there's always a solution," he said.

"You have a plan to undermine Father Vorcien?" Montego asked with a frown.

He only had the slightest glimmer of a plan, and he knew that Kizzie's future was in his hands now. Whatever he did to outmaneuver Father Vorcien needed to account for Kizzie. That made it ten times as difficult. "Nothing matters until I return from fighting the Grent," Demir replied. "*If* I return. But Father Vorcien is so worried about the war that he made an amateurish mistake." He grinned at Montego. "He didn't get the deal in writing before I left the Maerhorn."

46

Kizzie was surprised when Gorian intercepted her just outside the watch-house. He was dressed smartly in his National Guard uniform, auraglass buttons polished and jacket brushed. She paused to look him up and down before raising an eyebrow at him. "What are you all decked out for?"

"The glassdamned war," he answered. "They're calling up thousands of National Guardsmen for the front. We've got an inspection with the Ministry of the Legion later today and I want to look and feel my best for it."

"You *want* to get called up to the front?" Kizzie asked in surprise. That was very unlike Gorian. "You know you're not trained for actual combat, right?"

Gorian sniffed indignantly. "I do the requisite military drills every eighth weekend, thank you very much."

"That's not combat."

"Nor do I intend on actually seeing any." He tapped the side of his nose with one finger. "A friend at the Ministry gave me the skinny. This business with the Grent and Kerite—they're only sending useless meat from the National Guard out there to get ground up. Everyone who looks and acts sharp stays in the city to protect the interests of the guild-families." He gave her a self-satisfied grin.

That sounded more like Gorian. "You're a weasel."

"I'm your weasel, Kizzie, and I'm very useful."

"Tell me just *how* useful. Where's the Tall Man?"

Somehow, Gorian's grin grew even more self-satisfied. He breathed on the fingernails of his right hand, polished them on his jacket, then held them out for inspection. "He's just inside."

"You caught him?" she blurted in surprise.

"Not at all. He paid me to set up the meeting."

Kizzie was not proud that her bowels did a backflip inside her, but they did just that. "Are you insane?" she hissed, snatching him by the arm and pulling him over to the side of the street. "Why the piss would you set up a meeting for him?"

"Because he asked," Gorian replied with a shrug. "Come on, Kizzie. It's in a watchhouse. Ten of my best are in there playing cards at this very moment. You wanted to find him and that's the best damned place for a meeting you could possibly imagine."

Kizzie walked to the middle of the street and back again just to try and get out some of her nervous energy. "So he's not inside of a cell?"

"No."

"I'd feel a lot safer if he were."

"What, because you think he's involved in this secret sorcery war?" Gorian's self-satisfaction began to fade. "He's tall, I'll give you that, but he's not even carrying a weapon. No visible godglass. One of my crew is a minor-talent glassdancer, and the Tall Man is not one of them. Perfectly safe."

Kizzie looked one way and then the other to make sure they were alone, then leaned toward Gorian. "You heard about General Stavri's assassination?"

"Yeah."

"He was *there.*"

Gorian's eyes widened. He didn't look so pleased with himself anymore. "But he's not a glassdancer."

"I didn't say he did it, I just said he was there."

"How do you know?"

"Because I was there. I walked into it minutes after it happened to look for Agrippo Stavri. I raised the alarm and don't—*don't*—mention that to anyone."

"Right, right," Gorian said, nodding emphatically. He glanced uncertainly toward the front door of the watchhouse. "He was probably there to make a report to someone and just missed the assassins. Just like you."

"Well then we're both damned lucky," Kizzie said. She swore under her breath. She wasn't ready for this. If Gorian had mentioned that the Tall Man was *here,* she would have come with twenty Vorcien enforcers armed to the teeth.

"You want me to go in there and arrest him?" Gorian asked.

Kizzie considered the offer for a moment, then wondered if she *should* go get twenty Vorcien enforcers. But she couldn't risk spooking the Tall Man. She needed answers out of him. And, it seemed, he needed answers from her. That second thought was far more terrifying. She stopped herself in mid-thought. *Why* was she so terrified of him? She hadn't actually seen him do anything. He might just be an observer or a spy or . . . something else.

It was the way he just watched. When Glissandi died, and after Kizzie raised the alarm at the boxing club. She could still see those calm, cold-fire eyes when she went to sleep. *That* was why she was so terrified.

"Don't try to arrest him," she told Gorian. "I'll go in there and talk to him, but I want you to be ready to act. That asshole screams violence to me."

"Eh. Guys that big don't move so fast."

"Did you ever see Baby Montego fight?" Kizzie snapped.

"Ah. Point taken." Gorian inhaled sharply through his teeth. "It's fine. Twelve of us, one of him. I'll make sure everyone is on alert while you talk to him. If anything goes wrong, just snap your fingers and we'll put the bastard on the floor."

Kizzie shook out both arms and then threaded her braided godglass earrings through each ear, giving herself a moment to grow accustomed to the sorcery now flowing through her. She adjusted her stiletto, switched her blackjack to her left pocket, and nodded at Gorian. "Fine, let's go chat with him."

The Tall Man sat quietly in the corner of the watchhouse, calmly sipping a cup of tea while he read the morning newspaper. Kizzie paused briefly when she saw him there, looking as normal as anything, wondering once again why she was so afraid until he lifted his piercing gaze up to meet her eye. "You gave him tea?" she whispered to Gorian.

"It seemed polite," Gorian responded, heading over to the other National Guardsmen playing cards beside the holding cells. The room was quite crowded with eleven of them, the Tall Man, and her. Gorian and his comrades were not subtle about the way they shifted for their truncheons and knives. Kizzie rolled her eyes and forced herself to walk straight over to the Tall Man, sitting down in the chair with its back to the wall and gazing across the table at him.

"Good morning," he said. His voice was oddly gentle and melodic, as if practiced to be at odds with his height. "You're Kissandra Vorcien."

"I am. And you?"

"My name is not important," he said, glancing down into his tea with a small smile. "I have a message for both you and Father Vorcien."

Kizzie tensed and took a long, slow breath. How would Father Vorcien do it? Piss, how would *Demir* do it? Probably let the guy talk and hope he gave her the answers she was looking for along the way. "I'm all ears," she said, returning his smile.

"The Vorcien will withdraw any inquiry into the murder of Adriana Grappo, and in return we will maintain the peace between us."

Kizzie scoffed. What kind of damned arrogance was *this*? "That's not a message. That's a demand."

"It is what you make of it."

"The Vorcien don't take well to demands."

"And my master doesn't take well to meddling."

Kizzie felt the wan smile slide off her face. "Perhaps your master would like to meet with Father Vorcien himself. Let the two of them work it out."

"Then what would us poor servants have to do with our lives, hmm? No. This is a one-time thing. A warning. A demand. A message. Whatever you want to call it, take it back to Father Vorcien."

"You haven't even told me who you are or who you work for."

"Nor will I."

"Then why should I so much as sniff at you?" she asked. "I may not be a full-blood Vorcien, but I *am* a Vorcien." She laid her right hand flat on the table to show the small silic sigil. "Until I know who you actually are, I can only assume you're a nobody. A spot on the road. Father Vorcien would laugh me out of his estate if I came back to him with such a demand."

"Not all power comes with a famous name."

"Have you been in Ossa long?"

The Tall Man chuckled softly. "You're charming, Kissandra Vorcien. Just the right mix of clever and arrogant to make a good enforcer. But at this moment you're making a mistake. Take the message to your father."

Kizzie couldn't shake the feeling of unease itching between her shoulder blades, like she could sense a marksman on a nearby roof with her head in the crosshairs. There was no marksman, though, and she wasn't even near a window. She thought of what she'd told Gorian earlier about the Tall Man oozing violence. It was the same sort of sense, she suddenly realized, that she used to get from Montego. They both had the same subtle, animal ferocity just underneath the surface, like a spring loaded into a trap.

All her instincts told her to stand up and walk out. If she did, how could she possibly explain that to Father Vorcien? That she let herself—a Vorcien bastard and a prime enforcer—get pushed around by a nobody? It was absolutely out of the question.

"I don't have the patience for this," she finally said, raising her chin. She signaled to Gorian with the roll of one finger. All conversation from the other end of the room ceased. Gorian and his National Guardsmen got up from their card games, spreading out, crossing over to them with weapons in hands. Kizzie said, "I want answers from you, asshole. Why were you at the Brawlers Club?"

The Tall Man gave a long-suffering sigh.

"Answer me," Kizzie demanded. "Who's your master? Is it a member of the Glass Knife? Out with it now!" Moments passed and the Tall Man finished the rest of his tea, then carefully folded his newspaper before making to stand. "Gorian, arrest this piece of shit," Kizzie said.

Gorian stepped forward, putting a hand on his shoulder. "You stay seated until Kizzie says otherwise," he ordered.

The Tall Man sighed. "I see. You really aren't taking this seriously, are you?" he asked Kizzie.

"I will when you do," Kizzie replied, reaching for her knife.

In the time it took her to grasp the hilt of her stiletto, the Tall Man had broken Gorian's arm. It happened in the blink of an eye, so quick that for half a second she thought she'd imagined it. But in the next moment, Gorian was on the ground screaming in pain while chaos erupted around her. Kizzie drew her stiletto, summoning all of the strength granted by her forgeglass to shove the table against the Tall Man.

It was like pushing against a boulder. The Tall Man barely seemed to nudge the table back and Kizzie found herself flung against the wall, stunned by the impact, watching with dizzying horror as the Tall Man seemed to *whirl* around the room. He caught a guardsman by the throat, rammed his fist into the chest of another, snatched the woman's truncheon, and then swung it in a lazy-looking arc that dashed the brains out of two more. The guardsmen, all of them wearing low-resonance forgeglass, looked like they were standing still compared to the Tall Man.

Kizzie fought through her daze and tightened her grip on her stiletto, leaping forward to plant it square in the Tall Man's back. Or at least, that had been her intention. He seemed to sense her movement behind him and stepped out of the way. Her blade barely slid along his side, a deep but not inconveniencing cut that he answered by smashing his elbow against her chest. The blow knocked her back against the wall once more, all the air forced out of her lungs.

By the time she had recovered enough to move, everyone else—eleven glassdamned National Guardsmen—was on the ground. Kizzie sank low, cursing the Tall Man silently as she darted forward. The pisser was fast as anything she'd ever seen, but she was no slouch, and she would not go down without a fight. He spun toward her, smacking aside the blade of her stiletto with the flat of his hand. He did not, however, see her blackjack. She clocked him on the side of the chin with every bit of force she could muster, the blow hard enough to wrench her own wrist around painfully.

He did not go down. He barely even flinched. He batted the blackjack away, punched her in the stomach hard enough to make her see stars, and then snatched her by the throat and lifted her up to his eye level. Kizzie scratched his arms, kicked at his knees and groin, all to no avail.

"This is your one warning," he told her over the sound of her own struggles. "Give it to Father Vorcien. There won't be another."

The next thing Kizzie knew, she was lying flat on her back, staring up at the watchhouse ceiling. Stars circled her vision, and every damned part of her hurt. It felt like she'd fallen off a two-story building directly onto her chest. Her throat felt absolutely crushed, but she found she could both breathe and speak.

"Gorian," she muttered, flailing around, trying to find her knife. She lifted her head enough to see that the Tall Man had disappeared. The room was completely silent, which was a relief for a few moments until she realized just how completely. There wasn't a moan or a curse or even the sound of breathing. Panicking, she scrambled to her hands and knees and flailed over body after body, looking into lifeless faces that she'd bribed and bought drinks for over the years.

Gorian was in the corner. He must have gotten back up after having his arm broken, because he was some distance from the table. He lay with his head propped up against the wall, a surprised look on his face, eyes glassy and chest not moving. Swallowing bile, Kizzie gently shook him and bent to put her cheek in front of his mouth. "Gorian?"

Nothing.

Gorian was dead, and Kizzie had nothing to show for it.

➤   ➤   ➤

Father Vorcien's carriage was halfway down the estate drive, probably heading off to the Assembly District, when Kizzie forced it to stop by standing in the middle of the gravel. The driver pulled up, bodyguards leaping from the running boards and reaching for swords. Men and women that she'd known her entire life looked like strangers to her, the world dark and unfeeling. For half a moment, she thought they were just going to shoot her down right then and there, but a word was exchanged and a hand cracked by glassrot scales reached out of the carriage window and beckoned her forward.

"What has happened?" Father Vorcien demanded, looking her up and down from inside the carriage. His gaze lingered on her neck, and she wondered how red it was. It certainly hurt like a bitch, even with milkglass on.

"The Tall Man I told you about," Kizzie managed. "I cornered him at Watchhouse One-Eight-Seven and he just pissing killed *everyone*. Gorian, Philli, Stalia—glassdamned everyone."

Father Vorcien remained silent for a moment. "Except you."

Kizzie found herself giving him a quick, terrified nod. Glassdamnit, when had she become such a coward? She'd seen death. She'd killed. Friends had died. But this . . . she'd never seen anything like it. "He sent me with a message—that we're to stop looking into Adriana's death, and in return he won't attack us."

"Who is he?"

"I have no idea. He refused to tell me. A lackey of the Glass Knife, perhaps?"

"Ah." Father Vorcien settled back into his carriage seat, his eyes turning to stare at the far wall of the carriage. She could see small tics play out across his face, the corners of his eyes tightening. "So that's how it is."

"Do *you* know who they are?"

He shook his head.

"Father. He killed them all."

To her surprise, Father Vorcien did not rebuke her display of weakness. He gazed at her for a long time before saying, "That is most distressing. Diaguni!"

Kizzie turned to see that the majordomo had hurried from the house to see what the holdup was. He joined Kizzie at the carriage door. "Master Vorcien?"

"Clean up Watchhouse One-Eight-Seven. Those were our clients, no matter how far down the rung. Make sure their survivors are taken care of, and make sure nothing leaks to the papers."

"Yes, sir."

"Take a very thorough description of the assailant from Kissandra. I want everyone watching for him. Follow, but do not engage. I want to know who his master is." He turned back to Kizzie. "And you, daughter. Clean yourself up. You have black gunk all over you. Then get back to the Hyacinth."

"But . . . Demir has a blood feud against Capric."

"It has been ended."

"How?" Kizzie's mind reeled. She knew Demir better than Father Vorcien did, and she could think of nothing in the world that would cause him to let go of a blood feud.

"I'll explain when you've finished. For now, I want you to endear yourself to Demir. Get closer. Finish the puzzle around his mother's death."

"What about the Tall Man?"

"Forget about him."

"He just killed eleven of my friends. How am I supposed to . . ." She choked on her own spittle, the only thing that kept her from raising her voice to her father.

Father Vorcien drummed his fingers on the windowsill of his carriage. "Every Vorcien enforcer and client in the city will be on the lookout for him. We'll take him down or run him to the ground. Either way, he won't get so much as a chance to shadow you. You might be a bastard, Kissandra, but you are *mine*. No one decides your fate but me."

His words were reassuring, in a patronizing way. Kizzie swallowed hard and nodded.

"Good. Continue." He pounded on the roof of his carriage, and suddenly it was off.

Kizzie stared after it for several moments before looking down at herself. Father Vorcien was right, she was covered in black gunk, splashed across her jacket and pants like a blood spatter. There was some on her hands, too. She put it out of her mind and stared off across the estate grounds, thinking of the bodies of all those men and women she'd known for years. Gorian hit her the hardest, but they'd *all* been friends. Drinking together. Card games. Brothels. She was closer to them than she was to most of her fellow enforcers.

"Kissandra," Diaguni said gently. She started, turning to find that the majordomo had taken her by the arm. He went on, "Come inside and give me that description. I'll find a brandy and some better skyglass to calm your nerves."

"Thank you, Diaguni," she said, gesturing for him to lead the way. She desperately tried to stay in her own head, wrestling with the fear and helplessness. A single cut. That was all that she'd managed to get on that asshole with eleven armed companions. She didn't know if anyone else had managed to tag him. She watched Diaguni walking toward the house, willing herself to follow, but still uncertain.

Over the course of a few moments, she felt her terror turn to anger. Everything that *kept* her from acting suddenly seemed so stupidly unimportant. The Tall Man had killed her friends. What were family ties or secret histories or even her own damned pride in the face of that? She was Kizzie Vorcien, damn it. People respected her. People depended on her. If she couldn't protect them, then she would damn well avenge them. To do so she would need help.

It was time to swallow her pride and seek an alliance with the only person in Ossa who terrified her more than the Tall Man.

47

Thessa took Ekhi to a park near the hotel. It wasn't a proper break—just an hour to get away from the hotel and, as Pari had put it, allow her mind to start a new cycle—but she didn't know just how much she needed it until she was standing beneath a gnarled old olive tree with Ekhi perched on her glove, the sun shining through the branches to mottle shadows upon them both. Her carriage driver and a single Grappo bodyguard stood nearby. She was not going to allow a repeat of that assault at the Lampshade Boardwalk.

Ekhi flapped his injured wing experimentally. It was clear that he would need a lot more time before he could fly again, but he seemed pleased to be away from the mews. He screeched, dancing about on her glove, occasionally trying to fly. Thessa watched for his signal and kept a firm grip on his jesses to curtail any attempts.

"You," she told him softly, stroking a finger down his chest, "need to let yourself heal before you get too adventurous."

He screeched back at her and tried to flap.

"I know, I know! It's good to be out. When I return from the Forge I promise I'll take you to the countryside. You might not be able to fly for a long while, but you need fresh air just as much as I do." She wondered if his hunting instincts would flag during his convalescence. Perhaps she could arrange for some injured mice for him to pounce on at their next trip to the park.

She walked around the perimeter of the park, holding her gloved arm high to give Ekhi the best perch, enjoying the way that his eyes seemed to track every little movement. Thessa allowed her mind to wander, wondering if she and Ekhi were now a permanent fixture at the Hyacinth. Was that their home now? She had a partnership and a contract, though only regarding the phoenix channel. She could get rich from the phoenix channel and then break away, starting her own glassworks. She could truly be independent. Or she could romance Demir and secure her future in a different way. It was a decision she would have to make eventually.

Was he even looking for romance? Was *she*? They'd known each other for so little time, perhaps she was getting ahead of herself with fanciful thoughts of being the next Lady Grappo. She snorted. No, she wasn't getting ahead of herself. This was Ossa, where romance was a business transaction. Ending up with someone you genuinely liked was a luxury, so why not consider it seriously?

Which brought her back around to Demir. Was he interested in more than a little fun? Would he reject her outright? He was a guild-family patriarch and a glassdancer. He could have his pick of guild-family heirs or foreign princesses; of women who could benefit him more long-term. Thessa waffled back and forth, feeling at a loss. None of this mattered until he returned from the war. It might not even matter until she'd completed and tested the phoenix channel.

That, she decided, would be a good time to test the waters. After she'd shown him just how useful she could be.

Despite her tumultuous thoughts she had a calm, quiet walk, and by the time she returned to her carriage she wished that she could spend the rest of the day out here.

Just a few hours later, Thessa twisted the nuts on a large wooden clamp, trapping the two halves of one of her omniglass rings around the cinderite. She was absolutely soaked with sweat, her hands caked in sand, dust, and ash. The tiny glassworks was blazing hot, even with a window cracked to let in a small amount of cool winter air. She paused long enough to make a slight adjustment to one of the clamps, then continued turning the nuts. Slowly, the two halves of the omniglass ring pressed tightly against the outside of the cinderite. Each turn gave a slight crunching sound, and she lowered her head right up against the cinderite to make sure that it was maintaining its resonance.

"That's enough," she whispered to herself, and stepped back to take in the device.

The irregularities on the cinderite had been carefully chiseled away, a process that it had shocked Thessa to discover would actually increase the natural resonance. It really did look like a cannon now, albeit a strange one—a long cylinder propped in an iron frame, with seven translucent omniglass rings held in place by massive wood clamps. It practically hummed, and Thessa refused to let anyone but her remain in the workshop for longer than an hour at a time, lest they come down with terrible glassrot.

"Well," she said out loud, "it certainly looks distinct."

Pushed up against one wall was a casing for the phoenix channel that Demir's tinsmith had made to her specifications. It looked like an armored box, stuffed with cork and asbestos. She would need help to lower the phoenix channel inside, but once she did the entire project should be ready to take straight to the Forge. She wondered how long it was since she'd last slept. On the carriage ride back from the Forge yesterday, perhaps? She was pushing herself too hard and she knew it, but there was nothing she could do. She was practically giddy with excitement.

The phoenix channel was complete. All she had to do now was test the damned thing. If it worked, she could use the Forge to charge thousands of pieces of godglass with every lightning strike. It was not a perfect solution to the world's shortage of cindersand, but it was a start.

Thessa walked across the garden and into the hotel, where she caught the arm of the closest porter. "Has Demir returned?" she asked.

"No, ma'am. We're not sure when to expect him."

Everyone had been on edge since the attack by the Dorlani, but something else had happened and Thessa just could not get to the bottom of it. Porters and waiters talked in hushed tones, scattering when she approached, and Breenen had been in and out all day. Montego was nowhere to be found. Even Tirana had disappeared, rushing off in a quiet conference with Breenen the moment she and Thessa returned from the Forge.

"Do you know where he is?" she asked the porter.

"No, ma'am." The porter swallowed hard and hurried away, leaving Thessa with a scowl on her face. Shouldn't he have answered that Demir was still at the front with the army? Very odd. Thessa felt her shoulders slump and wished she'd brought Pari back with her as well. At least then she would have had someone to share this momentous occasion with. Instead, she had nothing to do but walk back into the workshop and stare at the phoenix channel, listening to the quiet hum of its sorcery.

It *had* sorcery, of that there was no doubt. The question to answer next was whether the sorcery worked. Feeling suddenly very alone, Thessa began to clean up the workshop and prepare all her notes and the phoenix channel for shipment to the Forge.

▸   ▸   ▸

Demir returned to the Hyacinth to change uniforms and wash the grime of the Maerhorn dungeon off himself. He didn't know why he bothered. He was heading straight back out to the front again, where he'd soon reek of powder smoke and death. To his consternation, he found the hotel nearly empty and Thessa nowhere to be found. It was a mixed blessing, as his mood swings had taken him from wanting to confess all about Holikan to cold-blooded manipulator and back again several times since his conversation with Father Vorcien.

He felt like he was at a loss for words, and that hadn't happened to him very often. Even after Holikan he'd always been able to make excuses—to charm and wiggle his way out of damn near anything. And yet he owed so many people so many explanations at this moment that he felt as if his head were going to pop. He thought about that kiss he'd shared with Thessa, and the implicit promise regarding his return. It made him sick. Despite the revelation about Capric, he still felt responsible for the slaughter of Thessa's family. And he was now promised to another woman.

And if he was to ultimately outmaneuver Father Vorcien, he would need to *act* like he was promised to another woman. He wouldn't be able to explain himself to Kizzie or Thessa. The lie would have to be complete, like some overcomplicated mummer's farce. He would have to tell the hotel staff and all his clients that they would soon be part of the Vorcien guild-family. They were still their own guild-family, of course, and in theory autonomous, but they would all know what his marrying a Vorcien would mean.

And how to negotiate things with Thessa? There was a distinct possibility that he was developing feelings for her. Did she reciprocate? Was she just looking for a bit of fun, or a stepping-stone as she climbed the rungs of Ossan society? Someone of her talents could make a home with one of the great guild-families, or even as an independent operator. Did any of this matter? It would be all over once he told her about Holikan.

He would have to take this all one step at a time. First, he needed to defeat the Grent.

He was just getting dressed when Breenen entered his rooms after a light knock.

"Master Demir."

"I have to go, Breenen. I'm expected back at the front, and if the latest intelligence is to be trusted I'm going to be late to whatever party Kerite and the Grent have decided to throw for me."

"I assume that's not a real party, sir."

"Figure of speech. Where's Thessa?"

"She's gone to the Forge, sir. She left less than an hour ago. I don't really know the details, but I understand she's going to use lightning to power the device she's been working on."

Demir checked his face in the mirror, realizing he'd forgotten to shave during his bath. Too late for that, he could shave in camp. "Wait, what?" he said, jerking his gaze toward Breenen. "I . . . No, never mind. I don't want to know. I don't have room for it in my head. Have we heard anything from the Dorlani?"

"Not a peep, sir."

"I don't like that they got in the hotel," Demir said, thinking out loud. "Will Thessa be safer or not out in the countryside? The Forge, you say?"

"Yes, sir. For the frequent lightning strikes. I truly hope that makes sense."

"It does, I suppose. It's insane, but it makes sense."

"She had one of those new lightning rods with her, and quite a lot of copper cable."

"That makes even more sense." Demir wanted to pull on that thread, to find out what exactly was going on. Piss, he wanted to go up there himself at this very moment. If Thessa truly thought she could use lightning to power the phoenix channel, that was a spectacle Demir wanted to either talk her out of or see himself. Alas, he did not have moments to spare, let alone the day it would take him to get up there and back again. "I don't want her undefended."

"She has Tirana and a dozen enforcers with her, sir." He paused. "I share your worry. Even when the hotel was burgled, we were able to respond quickly and easily. Master Montego took care of the problem in moments. Out there, however . . ."

"Right. I suppose calling her back is out of the question?"

"It would seem so. She's very set on her experiment."

"Take two dozen more and go join them."

"Is that wise, sir? Leaving the hotel undefended?"

"There will be nothing of consequence here. Besides, it'll hardly be undefended. We have dozens more enforcers and Montego. Go make sure

Thessa is protected. Remember, she's in charge of the project. Don't inter-
fere, and give her what help you can. Leave immediately."

"Yes, sir." Breenen withdrew, leaving Demir to finish dressing. He stared
at his baggy spare uniform in the mirror, wishing he hadn't lost so much
weight since Holikan. "I'm going to have to fight Kerite head-on," he said
out loud. "I might never see this room again." He chuckled and shook his
head. "Not with that attitude, I won't. Come on, Demir. You can do this."

Despite knowing he needed to hurry, Demir went down to the family
mausoleum, where he stood before his parents' ashes for several minutes
of quiet contemplation. His mother's bust still wasn't finished, causing a
flash of annoyance. If he was going to die out there, he would have at least
liked to see her likeness finished before he did. He wondered who would
commission his own bust if he were to die, and took solace in the fact that
Montego would take care of everything.

The Grappo would be dead, but at least the hotel and its employees and
clients would be cared for during Montego's lifetime.

He returned to his office, where several new crates of spy reports had been
delivered. He didn't have time to truly analyze them, or even read everything
there, but he allowed himself to browse the notes, ledgers, and memoran-
dums, looking for anything that might help him in the fight against Kerite.
He was, he eventually realized, dawdling. The fear of facing Kerite on the
open field—the fear of his own death—loomed large in his mind, and he
was trying to think of anything but that.

He opened the top drawer of his desk and stared down at a little cork
box that contained a fresh piece of high-resonance witglass. He knew the
resonance couldn't get through the cork, but he still imagined he could hear
it buzzing away, giving him a terrible headache. Could he really risk something so reckless in the middle of a battle? The other day, when he'd been
planning the Grappo Torrent, was the first time he'd worn high-resonance
witglass in years. Just a few minutes had left his head aching all day. Would
he drive himself mad if he used it more?

He snatched up the box and put it in his pocket, then summoned two
porters. "Load these crates into my carriage," he told them, indicating the
spy reports, "and have the horses ready in fifteen minutes. Has Breenen left
already?"

"About ten minutes ago, sir."

"Good. Until Breenen returns, Montego is downstairs. He's in charge of
the hotel until one of us gets back."

"Of course, sir."

Demir threw himself into the chair behind his desk, trying to clear his head while his carriage was readied and porters moved crates out of his office. This was his last chance to flee—to put on an old tunic, slip out the back, empty his bank accounts, and disappear forever. He would never have to fight another battle, or face Thessa, or explain himself to Kizzie. He could end up in Purnia or Marn or somewhere even farther away, where no one knew anything about him except that he was rich.

It was a powerful compulsion, and he twitched at the thought again and again. Absolute freedom. No responsibilities. No one to hate him or depend upon him. And yet . . . he couldn't do it. He was no longer the child he was back at Holikan. Those responsibilities were *his,* and he would face them head-on. He was a Grappo, and if he was the last, then he would be himself proudly.

There was a gentle knock on his door. "Sir? Your carriage is ready."

"Thank you."

"There's also a missive for you from the Ministry of the Legion. They said it was urgent." The porter crossed the room to give Demir an envelope with the Ministry's sword-flanked silic sigil. He tore it open, standing to head out the door, only to pause in the middle of the room.

General Grappo, it said, *Kerite has regrouped and has deployed her forces to encircle Harbortown. We fear if she is unopposed she will take the district in days. Make haste.*

Demir felt a hard knot form in his stomach. Encircled Harbortown. Not just marching at it from the south, but taking it from all directions. That wouldn't be such a problem, except for the fact that you could see the Forge from Harbortown. The glassdamned Grent and their mercenaries were going to be right on top of Thessa's experiment.

"Shit," Demir spat, and ran for his carriage.

48

Kizzie arrived at the Hyacinth after dark, pausing in the flickering shadows of the gas lamps, searching the streets behind her for any sign that the Tall Man had followed her here. She saw nothing, but couldn't shake that itching sense between her shoulder blades that she was being watched from the darkness. It wasn't just the Tall Man she had to worry about, she reminded herself. What other agents did the Glass Knife have? With so many powerful guild-family members in play, any enforcer or spy or even client was suspect.

To her surprise, there were Grappo enforcers standing watch just outside the hotel. The Grappo had always been circumspect about their use of enforcers, keeping them on hand but out of sight. The fact that six men and women now guarded the front entrance, wearing purple tunics with the cracked silic sigil of the Grappo on their chests, spoke much to how things had escalated in just the last few hours. They were all armed with swords and pistols, and Kizzie thrust her right hand into her pocket as she jogged up the stairs past them. She didn't have to worry about them being with the Glass Knife, but no telling how little goodwill they had for the Vorcien at this moment, regardless of whatever Father Vorcien had done to smooth things over.

Despite the enforcers out front, the hotel lobby was bustling with the normal evening hubbub, guests checking in with the help of dozens of porters. The porters, she noted, were all wearing smallswords at their belts. This was damned serious, and she couldn't help but feel as if she'd entered enemy territory. She swallowed her fear and edged around the side of the lobby, making for Breenen's small office behind the concierge's desk. Breenen, to her surprise, wasn't at the concierge's desk. It was one of the senior porters, someone that Kizzie didn't recognize.

She waited until he was between guests. "Is Breenen here?"

"I'm sorry, ma'am, he's not."

"Demir?"

"Not at the moment."

Kizzie kept her hand in her pocket to hide her silic sigil. She still didn't know if she had already been fired—maybe banned from the Hyacinth for life. She reminded herself she wasn't actually here to see either Breenen or Demir and licked her lips. "Montego?"

"Master Montego is on the premises, but he doesn't want to be disturbed. Can I leave a message?"

Kizzie wanted to punch that ingratiating public-facing smile. She wrestled with her nerves, still uncertain she was taking the right path. She'd feared this moment for years—feared Montego's response. When they were children he was a kind soul, despite his reputation for physicality. He'd been loving and forgiving and gentle. But *that* Montego was still a boy. She didn't know the famous cudgelist with insatiable appetites and unmatched violence.

Making a decision, she put her hand flat on the concierge's desk to show her silic sigil. "You can tell him Kizzie is here to see him."

"Ah." The porter's eyes tightened ever so slightly. "Miss Vorcien. Of course. Master Demir left word to accommodate you in any way."

"He did?" Kizzie asked in surprise. So she hadn't been fired? Father Vorcien really had smoothed things over?

"You can find Master Montego in the hotel gymnasium. I trust you know the way?"

Kizzie almost *did* punch him, though she didn't think he meant it sarcastically. "Thanks." She headed up the main stairs, feeling off-kilter. Demir attacked Capric in the street just two days ago. He had every reason for a blood feud, even a guild-family war, and yet all that bad blood was gone just like that? What the piss could possibly cause them to bury the hatchet so quickly? She tried to shake it off. She should be ecstatic! No one had died, no war had started. She didn't have to feel guilty about sending that missive anymore.

Kizzie navigated to the top floor of the hotel. She paused briefly in the hallway, gazing at the sign in front of the gymnasium door that called it OCCUPIED. Her heart was hammering in her chest, her palms were sweaty; a moment she'd made every arrangement for and yet still avoided was about to come true.

"Whatever you do, Baby," she whispered to herself, "don't send me away."

The Hyacinth gymnasium was a massive room taking up a full quarter of the floor, with high ceilings topped with massive windows to keep it well-lit during the day. At night, it was a dim room lit only by gas lanterns, casting long shadows across the padded floor and tapestries of men and women accomplishing feats of strength in various states of undress.

Kizzie closed the door to the gymnasium slowly behind her, peering around the room until her eyes landed upon the massive figure of Baby Montego. He was even bigger than she remembered, both fat and muscular, light glistening off the mixture of sweat and oil rubbed into his skin, wearing nothing but a cudgeling girdle. She was off to one side of him, though he did not seem to notice her presence as he was focused on something immediately in front of him. Kizzie was raising her hand, his name on her lips, when he suddenly ran forward.

He leapt into the air, snagging a thick rope suspended from one of the massive hooks overhead. He swung on the rope, rocking back and forth, using himself as a counterweight to move his arc higher and higher, until he was almost able to touch the ceiling. Suddenly his right hand darted out, snagging the end of another rope positioned for that purpose. He swung down, up to the top of the next arc, and grabbed another rope. Two more he did, all the way to the other end of the gymnasium, swinging like one of the monkeys in the Ossan zoo.

It was proper aerobatics, of the type one might see in a circus. It felt unreal to watch so much girth accomplish something that required so much agility. She couldn't imagine the dexterity of those fingers to snatch a rope thirty feet up in low light, or the strength needed to hold so much weight aloft. At the bottom of the final swing, Montego threw himself into a roll, tumbling across the padded floor and coming up onto his feet, planting both palms on the opposite wall to stop himself. He heaved and trembled from the effort, stretching his arms out to either side of him.

Kizzie shook her head. She'd read the papers these last few weeks. She knew what they said about him letting himself go, and growing fat and lazy. She hadn't believed them. Not Montego. Not *her* Montego. She now felt vindicated in that belief.

"Bravo," she said, clapping quietly.

Montego leapt nearly a foot into the air, his whole body twisting in the maneuver, and landed with both fists held up in a ready position. Even from across the long room, she could see his eyes go wide. "Kizzie?" Her name echoed.

"Hi, Baby."

Montego's arms fell to his sides. Slowly, he walked in her direction, angling toward the wall, where he fetched a dressing gown big enough for a tent and threw it over his shoulders. The lighting made him appear even more massive—the world champion killer that had grown out of the hulking boy she once knew. Despite herself, Kizzie felt something long forgotten stir in her chest.

Montego pulled his long brown hair back, tying it into a bun behind his head in one smooth motion while he padded silently toward her. His head tilted to one side, his eyes growing small as his whole face seemed to wrinkle as he peered at her.

"You've been avoiding me," he said.

"I wasn't sure I was ready to see you."

"After all this time?" he asked.

She couldn't tell if his furrowed brow was due to anger or confusion. "After all this time," she confirmed. "It still hurts."

"You're not the one whose neck broke Sibrial's cane." Montego pulled away his dressing gown enough to show her a prominent scar just above where his shoulder met his neck. He grunted and hid it again, his eyes looking suddenly downcast as if he was ashamed of it. "I'm sorry for what I did to your brother."

Kizzie stared back at Montego. *Really* stared, her thoughts suddenly fallen into a confused jumble and trying to work themselves out again. Did he think she was mad at him? "Baby," she said, "that's not what hurts. What hurts is the fact that I couldn't look you in the eye. That I never came back for you, or said goodbye, or even sent you a letter. What hurts is that I was so scared of what my family would think if they found out, that I did everything Sibrial told me to do to cover it all up and then never saw you again. *That's* what hurts."

"Oh," Montego responded, his mouth hanging open. The silence between them stretched on, his face rippling and contorting as he seemed to try to find the right words. Finally he said, "I never blamed you for any of that. I was just a glassdamned kid with a good amateur cudgeling record. You did what you had to do. Is that why you've never come to see me again? Once we were both adults, I mean. Because you thought I was angry?"

Kizzie's guts were so tight she thought they were going to suck her whole body into them, twisting her into a little lump of intestine. She nodded.

He continued, "I was never angry. Heartbroken, yes. But not angry. You were my Kiz. I was your Baby. And then one day I broke your brother right in front of your eyes. That must have traumatized you something fierce."

"A little," Kizzie admitted.

"It's me who should apologize. I should never have put you through that. You know, I've heard rumors. About the way Sibrial has treated you over the years. It's taken all my self-control not to crush him into a pulp. I only didn't because I knew you'd want to do it yourself."

Kizzie couldn't stop staring. This was not at all how she'd imagined this meeting. She'd shadowboxed with recriminations and swearing and Montego's quiet but terrifying anger. She had not expected this. She wiped tears out of the corners of her eyes and took a steadying breath. Hesitantly, she ventured a small smile. "You never came to see me, either."

"Because I was a coward. Even after I got famous, even after the *rest* of the world knew me by Baby, I couldn't bear the thought of you rejecting me. Not as a lover, mind, but as a friend. If you'd turned your back on me it would have broken me as surely as Holikan broke Demir." Montego's head was up, his stance tall and powerful as if he was owning his own admission of cowardice. Why wouldn't he? He'd conquered everything else in the world. Why not shame as well?

"Glassdamn, Baby," Kizzie managed. "All these years, scared of each other, like idiot children."

Baby's round face suddenly split into a massive grin, and he lurched forward, pulling her into a hug. She found herself squeezing him back, breathing in that scent of sweat mixed with jasmine oil that brought a thousand memories to the front of her mind. "You even still smell the same."

"Yes, but I can buy jasmine oil by the bargeful now, instead of stealing it from Adriana." They separated, and Kizzie felt some of the fear, shame, anger, and helplessness of the day seem to just melt out of her. She had a thousand questions to ask, sixteen years to catch up on. "You didn't just come to apologize, did you?" Montego asked.

"I need help," she admitted. "Not from Demir, not from my own guild-family. Help from you."

Montego frowned. "Explain."

So she did, running through the entire story from when Demir hired her to the present moment. She left out only the missive and the blackmail, certain that her involvement in those things should never pass her lips again. They moved over to benches in the corner as Kizzie talked. Montego listened through the whole thing without interrupting her, all the way to the end, when she threw her hands up. "And so I'm here, and I'm ashamed it took me the deaths of my friends to come and see you finally."

"You should be a *little* ashamed," Montego said, his tone teasing. "But you did the right thing. This Tall Man, you say he killed eleven armed National Guardsmen in under a minute?"

"Yes."

Montego rubbed his chin. "You've gotten faster. I'm impressed you were able to cut him at all. I would be hard-pressed to kill so many bare-handed in that little time."

"I haven't gotten fast enough. He must have punched Gorian hard enough to stop his heart. I'm only still alive because he wanted me to deliver that message to Father Vorcien. I need help, Baby. This Fulgurist Society—this Glass Knife—I think they killed Adriana and I still don't know why. I want to trust it to Father Vorcien, but I'm one of the best fighters the Vorcien have and I could barely nick the Tall Man. He'll murder his way through every one of my fellow enforcers, and he probably won't break a sweat. I need a breacher to deal with him, or . . ."

"Or me," Montego said.

"I don't want you to think I'm trying to manipulate you. I didn't apologize to get your help. I apologized because I've wanted to for sixteen years." Kizzie tried to smile, but it felt forced. "I will absolutely understand if you're unwilling."

"Why would I be unwilling?" Montego made a fist between them, leaning close. "I came back to Ossa because my adopted mother was murdered. Demir may have a thousand other things on his mind but I do not. I've only been waiting for him to give me the word, but I'll take it from you just as readily. Say the word, Kizzie."

"Please?" Kizzie said. "Is that the right word?"

Montego's grin returned. "You know that Aelia Dorlani is definitely involved?"

"Without a doubt," Kizzie said. She felt a flutter in her belly at the gleam in Montego's eyes. That gleam happened for only two reasons, and one of them was when he was itching for a fight.

"Tell me," he said, "what plans have you made to isolate and question her?"

"I've thought through a few scenarios, but she's on the Inner Assembly. I can't touch her. Not even Father Vorcien would be able to protect me if I did."

454 · BRIAN McCLELLAN

Montego's nostrils flared. "I have the corpses of six Dorlani enforcers on ice in the cellar. I don't give a shit who she is, I will not allow her to go unpunished for her involvement in Adriana's murder or the invasion the other night."

"Invasion?"

"Dorlani enforcers killed a porter and a cook in an attempt to burglarize the hotel. They were after a project of Demir's. They even managed to poison my tea, but they didn't use enough."

Kizzie stiffened. What was Father Vorcien looking for? A phoenix channel? The Dorlani must be after it as well. "That's awfully bold, even for Aelia."

Montego nodded.

Kizzie thought back through a half dozen half-cocked ideas she'd considered for trying to reach Aelia. They all still felt like suicide, but if Montego was willing to take the Dorlani's ire . . . perhaps not so much. "All right," she said. "I think I have something that might work for the two of us."

49

There were few things worse than waiting for the next battle but not knowing when it would happen.

The socket of Idrian's false eye itched horribly, making him want to claw out the eye and scratch back there with a dinner fork. It was almost two days since anyone had seen Demir. Tadeas's messages back to Ossa had gone unanswered, aside from a single missive from the Hyacinth Hotel saying that Demir was imprisoned in the Maerhorn and they were trying to get him out. Only Tadeas and Idrian knew the truth, but the entire camp, from the Ironhorns to the regular infantry to the fort garrison, was wondering whether they still had a commanding officer.

That glassdancer—that *thing*—that attacked the other night had not returned. The rumors about it were spreading too. Only about a dozen people had seen it, but that was far too many to keep a secret. Whispers crisscrossed the camp that the Grappo Torrent was the last gasp to defend Ossa; that they'd all been abandoned, and that Kerite would return with fresh troops and monsters to boot, grinding them into a pulp.

Through all of these doubts and questions, Idrian grappled with his madness. Sometime during the last day or so he'd decided that this was not an aberration manifest from his grief for Kastora. The child's laughter happened so often that he barely noticed it now, but worse specters haunted his waking moments. Shadows flitted in the corners of his vision. Most were nothing more than that—dark splotches, moving about on their own—but on occasion he thought he saw people he knew were long dead.

One of two things was happening: either the eye was degrading faster than it was supposed to, or something had changed within his own mind that made the eye no longer adequate. The former could be solved by Demir's phoenix channel. The latter could not, and the prospect terrified him. If the madness continued to worsen, and he could no longer tell the difference between what was real and what was imaginary, how could he possibly defend the Ironhorns? What happened when that flying glassdancer returned? Could Idrian even trust himself to tell whether it really existed?

Idrian stood on the bastion wall of Fort Alameda, looking out over the fires of the camp. Roughly a third of the Foreign Legion was gathered here. The rest were back up at Fort Bryce, and he wished they were all together. They would need every soldier on hand the next time Grent and their mercenaries came knocking. If that itch in his eye socket was anything to judge by, it would happen soon.

His sword lay before him on the bastion merlons, ready to be snatched up the moment he saw something strange in the sky. He knew it was unnecessary—Tadeas and the garrison commander had agreed to quadruple the watch—but he stood his vigil anyway, remaining on the wall until he was too tired to keep his head up.

Perhaps he was a fool, and all this extra worry and effort only made his madness worse. But what else could he do? Stand down and risk people dying?

"Good evening, sir."

"Good evening, Braileer." Idrian glanced sidelong at the young armorer as he mounted the bastion wall and came to stand beside him. "Dinner was fantastic tonight. Thank you for that."

And it was. Braileer was better than the garrison cook, bringing Idrian half a duck and a loaf of rosemary bread soaked in duck fat, all done over a soldier's cookfire instead of in a proper kitchen. Idrian did not admit that he'd barely tasted any of it.

"My pleasure, sir." Braileer held his fiddle case, and set it down at his feet. "I was hoping I could take your sword for polishing and repairs. There are a few nicks I could work out of the razorglass in the garrison glassworks."

He'd asked the same thing for the last two nights, and Idrian had refused him both times. The very thought of being more than a few feet from his sword caused him to panic. He ran a finger down the flat of the pink razorglass ribbon, then laid his hand on the steel that supported it. "Does Tadeas keep sending you up here hoping to distract me?"

"Major Grappo is very concerned about your well-being, sir."

Idrian snorted, swallowing a sharp retort. Braileer didn't deserve it. "You can rest easy tonight. We'll be back to fighting soon enough. Take what relaxation you can get."

"Thank you, sir." Instead of heading back down into the bastion, Braileer reached down and laid his fiddle case flat, flipping it open and drawing out the instrument. "Do you mind, sir?"

"I . . ." *Want to be alone* was what Idrian wanted to say. To be alone with the specters flitting about, where he could concentrate on telling the difference between what was real and what was not. But he knew that remaining alone just made things worse. The shadows were less common in company. "Go on, then."

Braileer set the fiddle to his neck and plucked at the strings a few times, then produced his bow. He finished tuning and then, slowly, the sound almost imperceptible, he began to play.

Idrian leaned on the merlon beside his sword, his eyes raised to the sky, his thoughts distant. The song played in the back of his head, low and mournful, before it picked up into a steady cadence. He half listened for some time until he realized that he was humming along with it. He turned sharply to Braileer. The young armorer didn't seem to notice the look and kept playing.

Idrian waited until the melody came around again, and then he sang.

"'Bend your back to the work, raise your arm with the flail, for the winter she be coming. Grain for the man, straw for the cattle, for the winter she be coming. It'll blow in hard, it'll blow in cold. If we don't thresh this field, then our bellies will starve and our hearts will freeze, and we shan't plant more in the spring. And we shan't plant more in spring.'"

Braileer repeated the final refrain four more times, then lowered both fiddle and bow.

"That's a Marnish farmer's song," Idrian said, shaking his head. "Depressing as piss."

"It's the only Marnish song I know," Braileer admitted with an embarrassed smile, "but I thought it might cheer you up. Did I . . . misjudge that?"

"No, no." Idrian felt suddenly overwhelmed, his mind leaping forty years and eight thousand miles away. "I haven't heard that since I was a kid." He gave a shudder and pressed on his godglass eye. "Another gift from Tadeas?"

"No, sir. Just me, sir."

Idrian turned to stare back at the horizon. Several minutes passed in silence, during which Braileer plucked at his fiddle, adjusting the strings once more, but did not play again. Something about that song seemed to stab right through Idrian, and he found himself smelling crushed grain and mountain flowers, accompanied by the trickling sound of a high stream. He swallowed a lump in his throat.

"You're a good man, Braileer. Go play for the soldiers again. They need it more than I do."

"Yes, sir."

Idrian waited until the armorer had left, and finally abandoned his vigil to walk down into the bastion, his sword on his shoulder. The Ironhorns had the distinction of camping in the fort courtyard, and it didn't take him long to find Squeaks. She and Fenny were cuddled together in the corner, behind a tent, their hands out of sight and giggling to each other. "Squeaks," Idrian called, averting his eyes. "Just a moment, please."

Squeaks extricated herself from her wife and came over to join Idrian, her cheeks red. "Evening, sir. I never asked, but did those gloves fit?"

"Just as gloves should," Idrian replied, giving her a soft smile. He heard his own voice and realized that the edge that had been in it since that flying glassdancer was now gone. Was Braileer's fiddle—a brief memory of a long-forgotten home—all that he needed? Or would it be back soon? It didn't matter, not right now. "That thing I fought on the roof up there," he said, gesturing to the high window of the garrison commander's quarters, "did you get a good look at it?"

Squeaks seemed to draw into herself a little, her mirth disappearing. "Not any more than anyone else from the ground. But . . . yes, I suppose I could describe it."

"Did it look like the strange creature you saw in the forest the night of the Grappo Torrent?"

From the way Squeaks stiffened, Idrian guessed he was the first person to ask her that—and that she'd been thinking about it a lot. "No. Not a thing like it. As different as you and me."

"Was the thing in the forest a glassdancer?"

"I certainly didn't sense it like a glassdancer. Not like the thing on the roof."

Idrian looked back up into the sky, thinking.

"Is that all, sir?"

"That's all, Squeaks. Give Fenny a kiss for me."

That seemed to break the somber moment, and Squeaks grinned at him. "Right away, sir," she said, and hurried back around behind the tent.

There were, Idrian considered, two possibilities: One was that they were all a little mad, and Squeaks was seeing things in that forest. The other was that there wasn't just one creature. There were two, or three, or a dozen, or a hundred. It was impossible to tell. Were they spies? Assassins? Were they some secret Grent weapon? Had Kerite brought them with her from a distant land?

It did not matter. The next time he saw that flying glassdancer, he was going to kill it.

➤   ➤   ➤

Thessa did not want to admit how relieved she was when Breenen caught up with her and Tirana on the road, trailing several carts full of supplies and another two dozen enforcers. It brought their total number up past forty. Not an army by any means, but if the Dorlani or the Magna or any other guild-family happened to follow them out into the countryside, they weren't going to sneak up and steal the phoenix channel from underneath their noses.

Their convoy didn't arrive at the Forge until almost midnight. It was drizzling and windy, though it had been clear less than a mile back, and Thessa was grateful when she hiked up to the crest of the Forge to find not only that Pari and her helpers had set up a number of tents wherever a windbreak could be found, but that the lighthouse had been secured with canvas and a fire blazed in the hearth of the main floor.

"The lightning rod is in place," Pari reported, clearly pleased with herself. Thessa stood outside long enough to squint up at the copper crown rising a dozen feet above the lighthouse ruins, then went inside and examined Pari's handiwork.

"No problems?"

"I just followed your diagrams."

A thick copper cable came in through the roof, hanging loose just above the ground. Nearby was a shorter length of cable that would thread right though the middle of the phoenix channel. Next to that, a third length was buried in the dirt floor of the lighthouse. Each length ended in a coupling that could be easily fitted to another; the lightning rod would attach to the phoenix channel, which would attach to the grounding element. If Thessa's theory was correct, the lightning would pass through the center of the phoenix channel, providing energy that the phoenix channel would amplify and direct forward into a small basket of spent godglass. The lightning would then bury itself harmlessly in the ground.

The phoenix channel was brought up first, and though the hour was late, Thessa knew she wouldn't be able to sleep until it was installed. She fixed the couplings in place wearing thick leather gloves, though she had no idea if they would actually stop lightning from killing her in the case of a freak strike. Pari helped her, scrambling around, bringing in everything that the Grappo enforcers carried up from the carts.

When they finished, Thessa stood back with a happy sigh to examine her work. It was one thing to examine diagrams and have theories and draw up schematics. It was another entirely to have it all come out to her specifications.

"You really think it's going to work?" Pari asked.

"Either we're going to go down in history," Thessa replied, "or we'll have wasted quite a lot of Demir's money."

"Or both."

"How so?"

"Well, we could end up being famous for getting a bunch of us killed by lightning." Pari raised her eyebrows, and it took Thessa a few moments to realize it was meant to be a joke. Sort of.

"We're not going to get killed by lightning," she said, hoping she sounded confident. Tirana already thought she was a madwoman. Best if that idea not spread around the rest of the enforcers. "As long as these three lengths of cable are attached and the phoenix channel is grounded, there should be no danger."

"What happens if it's not grounded?" Pari asked.

Thessa shook her head. "Then the lightning will jump. That's not going to happen, though. We've followed all of Professor Volos's instructions. The worst that will happen is nothing." That might, she silently admitted to herself, be a fate worse than death. Working so hard, creating so much, only to have to start over from scratch. If this failed, she would have let down herself and Demir, but also Kastora's legacy.

"Funny," Pari said, chuckling to herself, "but my dad has kept every piece of godglass he's ever used over the years. It's in a little hatbox underneath his bed, and my grandma has been begging him to throw it out since I was a little kid. He must have hundreds of pieces of low-resonance forgeglass. Maybe a few others. If this works, and we can actually recharge godglass, we'll never hear the end of it from him."

"My aunt used to do the same," Thessa admitted. She felt her smile falter and worked to keep it in place. Best not to think of the people long gone, but how happy they would be to see her succeed. "Think of it: secondhand godglass will become a thing overnight. First thing I'll do is tell Demir to buy this piece of land. We could have a permanent outpost up here with a dozen lightning rods and phoenix channels and . . ." She was getting ahead of herself now and she forced herself to stop. "It could be grand," she finished.

Their conversation was arrested by a distant scream, followed by a series of shouts. Thessa and Pari exchanged a glance before rushing out into the open. Thessa shielded her eyes from the drizzling rain, peering toward the lanterns on the other end of the Forge. By the time she reached them she found most of the Grappo enforcers milling about near the ledge, Tirana and Breenen among them.

"Did someone fall?" Thessa asked.

Tirana swore, looking around at her enforcers. "Who was it? Who's missing?"

"I think it was Justaci," someone answered. Within a few moments the name was confirmed, and the party grew somber. This was a bad omen at best, to start the phoenix channel with a death, even an accidental one. Thessa briefly wondered whether she was cursed, or if the goddess Renn had finally turned on her for what she did at the Ivory Forest Glassworks, but she pushed the thoughts out of her head. Damned foolish.

"Are we going to try and get him?" someone asked.

Thessa pushed her way into the group, to where Tirana and Breenen were conferring underneath an umbrella. "We could lower a rope," Breenen suggested.

"That's a two-hundred-foot drop onto the rocky coast," Tirana responded, her tone tense. "He didn't survive that, and I'm not sending anyone down there in the dark in inclement weather."

Thessa looked between the two, then around at the concerned faces. Almost all of the supplies and equipment had been brought up, and the enforcers looked exhausted from all the effort. "We should post someone down at the bottom of the trail with sightglass," Thessa said. "It's unlikely anyone survived that fall, but if he did we want to be sure we rescue him."

"Agreed." Both Tirana and Breenen nodded, and within a few minutes a small group of volunteers, including Pari, was heading back down the slippery trail. They would get as close to the bottom of the cliffs as they could, peering into the darkness with sightglass. The rest of the enforcers soon disbanded, heading to their tents, leaving Thessa shivering beside Tirana. The master-at-arms remained close to the ledge, her neck craned, wearing a look of consternation.

Thessa moved to return to the lighthouse, but Tirana took her by the arm. "Thessa, Demir forbade all of us from asking you what's actually happening here. I get it—a secret silic project. He doesn't want to risk a leak to the Dorlani or anyone else. But I have to ask you . . . is this worth people dying over?"

Thessa glanced involuntarily at the ledge. Was there a right answer to this? "Yes," she said, "it is."

"Would you die for it?"

"I'd rather not," she said with a half smile. When Tirana remained serious, Thessa swallowed the lump in her throat. "Yes, I would."

"Good. Because I don't know if that was an accident."

"Why would you say that?" Thessa asked, feeling her stomach tighten. "It's slippery, it's dark."

"No one saw Justaci fall," Tirana replied.

"That's not enough for real suspicion, is it?" Thessa didn't want to scoff at Tirana's instincts, but this seemed to take it too far. "Anyone could have . . ."

Tirana raised a finger. "When we arrived here, Justaci took me aside at the first chance he could get me alone, and he told me that someone left the basement access to the Hyacinth unlocked. Those Dorlani enforcers didn't get in by wile or accident. Someone *let* them in. I don't know who it was. I don't even have any suspicions. But keep your wits about you. We may have a traitor on our hands. One that's willing to kill."

Tirana strode off, calling to a pair of nearby enforcers to post a night guard, leaving Thessa wet, alone, and very frightened. She looked up into the pitch-black sky, raindrops hitting her face, and hugged herself.

So much for leaving the city for safety.

50

Demir returned to command of the Foreign Legion as if nothing had happened—as if rumors about his duel with Capric weren't flying around the capital in every direction, and practically everyone he passed wasn't burning with questions about how he dodged Father Vorcien's fury. Demir ignored it all. He couldn't afford further distractions, not now.

Careful to keep a steady line of communication with his scouts, in case the winds of this war shifted once more, Demir regrouped the Foreign Legion just a few miles northeast of Harbortown. It was not an ideal location—the ground was a little too soft for heavy cavalry, and sight lines were ruined by the windbreaks between the farms that stretched across this northern edge of the Copper Hills—but the location effectively prevented the enemy from trying to turn and encircle Ossa. They would have to either come through him, or retreat back to Grent and the river.

What's more, he could see the Forge in the distance from here. Not close enough that Kerite suspected anything valuable was there, but enough that he could intervene if she made a move in that direction. It was a wildly in-appropriate mismanagement of his priorities as commander of the Foreign Legion, and he didn't give a shit.

It was midday, the weather cold but sunny, and the camp bustled with the activity of some fifteen thousand soldiers and twice that number of sup-port staff. Demir had just arrived, and columns were still marching in from Ossa while a steady stream of scouts reported the enemy's positions on a regular basis. That steady stream, he noted as he stared across at the crate-loads of information gleaned from spymasters, gossipmongers, and the Min-istry of the Legion, seemed to have flagged since this morning. He needed to know why, and soon.

But then again, he needed to know a lot of things.

He sat in his big commander's tent on the only piece of furniture—a folding stool—staring at the cork box balanced on his knee. He imagined he could hear the resonance of the powerful witglass within. He needed that sorcery. He needed his mind to work like it used to; to be the human thinking machine that could carve circles around the next-best strategist. He flipped open the box to reveal a little piece of purple godglass, the same color as his family crest, in a crescent-roll shape with a hook at one end.

He took a deep breath, snatched up the earring, and threaded the hook through one of his piercings.

The pain started immediately—an ache at the base of his skull, creeping up the back of his head and then stabbing inward, like hot lances through his brain and into the backs of his eye sockets. He gritted his teeth, bearing the pain, waiting for it to subside enough for him to actually *think*. But it didn't subside. It intensified, growing with each passing second, a sweet agony that wouldn't let him get a thought in edgewise.

When he finally tore the witglass from his ear and thrust it back into the box, he felt like someone had burned through his soul from the inside. His mouth was parched, every nerve tingling at the memory of suffering. He raised a hand to see that it was trembling.

"Well," he said to himself, "that isn't going to work." And if it didn't work, how could he possibly win the war? His enemy commanders would all have witglass. Even the least of them would be able to think faster and more capably than he—and Kerite was far from the least of them. He was outnumbered and facing the greatest general in the world, and he didn't have the wherewithal to plan.

"General Grappo!" a voice called from outside. "Major Grappo and Captain Sepulki are here to see you."

Demir tossed the little box across the room and folded his hands to keep them from shaking. "Show them in."

Uncle Tadeas and Idrian entered, pausing as one to look across the myriad of reports that covered the ground. "No chairs, huh?" Tadeas asked.

"I can send for some."

Idrian grunted at Tadeas and pulled one of the crates over next to Demir, dropping onto it and popping his jaw. "Don't be prissy, Tad."

"Please, have a seat," Demir said sarcastically. "Is everyone here?"

Tadeas raised an eyebrow. "Who else did you want at this meeting?"

"I meant the glassdamned Ironhorns, and those cuirassiers that were at Fort Alameda."

"Oh, yeah." Tadeas snorted. "Yeah, everyone is here." He peered at Demir. "How are *you* here? Last communiqué I received from Breenen said you were locked up in the Maerhorn."

"It was . . . smoothed over," Demir said.

"Is that it?"

"Long story. I'll tell you sometime. Where's Mika?"

"She's off working over the supply runners from Ossa as we speak, stealing every last ounce of gunpowder that they'll let her get away with." Tadeas tapped a fingernail against one tooth, watching Demir with an expression that said he wanted to know more about the business with the Maerhorn. Well, gossip would filter into camp soon enough.

Demir plowed onward. "Good. I want her engineers making grenades between now and the moment we next join battle." Demir cleared his throat, shifting on the little stool, trying to ignore the little pit of despair that the witglass had left behind with all that pain.

"Do we know when that is?" Idrian asked.

"Within the next three days. No longer. I—" He was cut off by some very creative swearing outside his tent. The flap was thrown back and Colonel Jorfax strode inside, taking all three of them in with her icy stare. She looked just as immaculate as she had on their last meeting, her uniform pressed, not a hair out of place, hands clasped behind her back. Demir started, realizing he hadn't even sensed her approach through his sorcery. He needed to pay better attention, or the assassins that killed General Stavri would get him, too.

"Colonel," he greeted her, "good to see you again. I trust you didn't murder my bodyguards outside?"

"If anyone ever tries to keep me from seeing you again, I will," she snapped. "What are you going to do about this? What actions have you taken?"

"Wait, wait." Demir realized he had stood by pure instinct, his sorcery grasping at the glassdancer egg in his pocket. He forced himself to untense. "What the piss are you talking about? I've been in camp all of twenty minutes."

Jorfax's gaze swept around the tent as if she were examining a concert hall full of her enemies. Her gaze lingered briefly on Idrian before returning to Demir. "That should have been enough. My glassdancers—the sorcerers you appropriated to act as scouts—are dying."

"Oh shit," Demir said, wiping a hand across his face. He glanced at his uncle, who just shook his head. No help there. "I thought the system was working. We blinded the Grent, we washed them out with that flood. Have they countered us already?"

"I told you not to underestimate Kerite."

"I think," Idrian spoke up suddenly, matching Jorfax's stare with a cool one of his own, "that you'd better explain."

Jorfax seemed to genuinely get a grip on herself, and when she spoke next some of the anger had gone out of her words. "It started yesterday. First one, then two—now eight of those scouting parties, each accompanied by one of my glassdancers, have gone missing. We finally found one just a couple of hours ago. Completely eviscerated—torn to pieces, taken completely by surprise. My subordinate's glassdancer egg was still in his pocket."

"And you think the same thing has happened to seven other scouting parties?" Demir asked carefully. This was bad. Very bad. If the Grent, or Kerite, or whoever, had already turned the tables on that little maneuver, then the Foreign Legion might be damned.

"It's the only explanation for their disappearance. I've sent out riders to make contact and warn all the remaining scouts to be on the alert. I don't want anyone to go down without a fight—but you should recall them immediately."

Demir was surprised she hadn't recalled them herself. Was that an oversight on her part, or did she actually respect his command after the Grappo Torrent? It didn't matter. He said, "Keep four of them out there doing circles around the camp—just enough to deal with anyone who tries to get a close look. We'll recall the rest."

For a moment he thought Jorfax would protest, but she gave a sharp nod. "Agreed."

"We should tell them," Idrian suddenly said.

Demir turned toward him. "Eh?"

"Including her?" Tadeas asked.

"Yes. She has a right to know. It's her people out there getting killed."

Demir glanced between his three companions quickly, and could see that Jorfax was just as confused as himself. "What's going on? Tad?"

Tadeas cleared his throat and leaned back on his crate. "We haven't made a full report yet—no reason for the Ministry of the Legion to recall us because they think we're insane—but you're going to start hearing rumors. Both of you. We were attacked at Fort Alameda the night you went back into Ossa."

"Attacked?" Demir said. Every glassdamn word was another piece of bad news. He didn't think he could wind himself any tighter at this point. "Why didn't I hear about this sooner?"

"Because it was a glassdamned monster," Idrian spat. "That's why."

"You're joking," Jorfax scoffed.

"I wish I were," Idrian continued. "Demir, it was your secret glassdancer alarm that saved us all."

"Squeaks?"

"Yeah. She warned me there was a glassdancer on the roof of the officers' quarters of the fort. I have no doubt it was the same assassin that killed General Stavri and his officers. I managed to get the drop on him, but when I engaged it was not human. It was taller than me, built like a breacher with skin like a hard shell. It was faster and stronger than me with my armor on, and when I pressed it, the damned thing flew off. It had wings, Demir."

Demir felt every hair on the back of his neck stand up. In a less serious situation, without Jorfax present, he might have accused Tadeas and Idrian of playing a prank on him. It was the type of thing Tad might do for a laugh. But one glance at both of their faces told him that there was no joke. "Who saw it?"

"I did," Tadeas said, "Idrian, Mika, Squeaks. A dozen engineers and seven soldiers. Whatever it was, it was *there*."

To Demir's surprise, Jorfax paled and sank down on a crate next to Idrian. It was the first time he'd ever seen her lose her composure, and it was almost as shocking as Idrian's revelation. She said, "I thought sentries were just making things up."

"What do you mean?" Demir asked sharply.

"I mean, about eight weeks ago, well before this bullshit war, the garrisons at two of our northern forts sent reports back to the Ministry of the Legion that they'd seen some kind of large animal in the sky at night. It was a strange report, but nothing came of it, so we ignored it. It could have been anything, after all—an albatross, or a trick of the light, or just some sentries bored out of their glassdamned minds."

Demir might have lambasted her if he didn't agree. It was nonsensical, and the Ministry was right to ignore such reports. Until suddenly they weren't. "So what is it?" he asked. He didn't think he could feel any more helpless, not after having his mind so firmly reject that witglass. But here he was, floundering, presented with something so far outside of his experience that not even the old Demir could have planned for it. "A Grent weapon of some kind? The results of godglass experiments?"

"Idrian and I have been talking about it for three days," Tadeas said, "and that's our best guess. Godglass that gives you pissing wings. Think of that."

"There's more," Idrian said. "More of whatever that was." He glanced at Tadeas and then continued, "Right before the Torrent, Squeaks was taken off guard duty because she said she saw a monster in the forest. She said it was short, with a long neck and a delicate face. Oh, and an underbite. Definitely not human. It even disappeared when she looked at it. Valient and I thought she was just exhausted and seeing things, but I'm not so sure anymore. There may be more of them, and we need to be ready."

Demir felt a cold finger move up his spine. That sounded a *lot* like the face he'd seen in the window of his mother's study when he first returned to Ossa. Was he being followed by some otherworldly presence? He tried to shake off a sudden bout of the chills.

"So we have a flying glassdancer," Demir said, "and a disappearing monster with an underbite. Sweet godglass, how the piss do we plan for *monsters*?" He inhaled sharply, part of him wanting to go looking for that piece of witglass again. Maybe if he tried just one more time. Maybe if . . . He stood up, turning his back on his three guests, staring at the wall of his tent. There was a new hole—a gaping one—in his half-constructed plans. He didn't even know how to deal with the problems he had, let alone *this*. Once again he felt the sweet draw of cowardice—of fleeing into the provinces, never to be seen again.

Idrian spoke up. "The winged glassdancer we saw must be what killed those scouting parties. You said your glassdancer didn't even take the glassdancer egg from his pocket?"

"Correct," Jorfax answered.

"Of course he wouldn't. Nobody expects an attack from above. If this winged glassdancer is swooping down on our scouts, it explains why we've only lost eight parties rather than all of them. He can only work so fast, after all. It also gives us an opportunity."

"What kind of opportunity?" Jorfax asked.

"A trap. Send out me, Mika, some engineers and soldiers disguised as scouts, and a single glassdancer. When that thing attacks us, our glassdancer will sense it coming—he'll be paying attention to the sky this time—and then Mika can drive it to the ground with explosives and I can kill it."

"Ooooh," Jorfax said, the word almost sensual. "I like this plan."

Demir did not turn around. The word "disguised" had touched something off in his mind but he couldn't quite grasp what it was. He could feel the frustration building, like an expert marksman who just couldn't quite seem to hit the target before him. He forced himself to take a deep breath. To *focus*.

This wasn't him. It couldn't be him, not if he was going to protect the people he loved. What had he told himself days ago? No more arrogance. No more foolhardiness. No more crippling self-doubt. He had to shed it all like a snake shed its skin and arise anew with what was left behind. He needed to be the best of his old self and his new self.

Did he even know what his "new" self was? A grifter? A con man? Someone who consorted with cudgelists and fixed fights for money and entertainment? Demir frowned, struck by a sudden realization that he had spent so much time separating his life into "before Holikan" and "after Holikan" that he'd never really stopped to consider that maybe he hadn't changed all that much.

He still charmed and blustered and organized. After all, what was a political savant but a formalized con man? He'd just lost the confidence to do it in public.

The line of thought brought him back around to Idrian. *Disguised.* Why was that word tumbling around in his head? Was it because it felt so familiar? All con men needed disguises, but never mind how it was useful to Demir the grifter. How was it useful to Demir the general?

"Demir?" Tadeas prodded. "What do you think of Idrian's plan?"

Demir whirled to face the other three. "This trap is a good idea. Make it happen. Whatever this monster is, we'll lure it out and kill it."

"That's just one tiny aspect of this conflict," Tadeas pointed out. "We haven't even talked about the Grent yet. Or Kerite. I hope you came up with some good battle plans while you were in the city."

Demir waved off his uncle's question, still deep in thought. He could feel pieces falling into place—little bits of information scattered throughout his brain coalescing to form a coherent narrative. "Listen, Jorfax is right. I can't outthink Kerite. She's the best general in the world. But she only has perhaps seven thousand mercenaries, right? The rest of her forces are all Grent."

"What are you thinking?" Tadeas asked, sitting up straight. He seemed to have noticed a change in Demir's countenance. Good. Let him take whatever confidence he could get from it.

Demir said, "When I was out in the provinces, I fixed a lot of cudgeling matches. I couldn't always bribe the judges, but I realized early on that the judges are beholden to the crowd. If a judge thought there was foul play, they would stop the match and investigate. But if the crowd absolutely believed in the fight—if it was just too damned good—no judge would dare to intervene. They went with what the crowd wanted.

"Kerite is the judge. She's the arbiter of the battlefield—someone who will read my every move and respond accordingly. I don't need to play her. I need to play the Grent officers that hired her. How many National Guardsmen do we have on hand?"

"Sixty thousand," Tadeas answered thoughtfully. Idrian and Jorfax both frowned, but Demir could see that his uncle had an inkling of where he was going with this. "But," Tadeas continued, "you said yourself they are worse than useless. They'll only panic against real soldiers, and if they run it'll be worse than not deploying them at all."

"We're not going to deploy them to *this* battle," Demir said. His thoughts were whirring along now, moving so quickly he could barely keep up with them. Not as fast as with witglass, but with more alacrity than he'd ever experienced unaided. It was as if all the different parts of him—grifter, politician, and general—were finally talking to each other. "Send a fast rider back to Ossa. I want them to find every single spare uniform they can get their hands on at the Ministry. I need at least ten thousand, preferably more. We'll stuff each one with a National Guardsman, and then we'll send them into Grent. March them down the street, capture bridges, occupy tenements. No real fighting, mind you. Just bodies on display."

It was Jorfax who seemed to figure it out next, followed quickly by a widening of Idrian's one eye. Jorfax said, "The Grent will panic and pull out all their forces. It won't matter what Kerite says or does—her employers will insist she withdraw from Harbortown at speed in order to protect Grent."

"And when she does," Demir finished, "when her troops are spread out on the road, at their most vulnerable, we'll hit her hard and fast from the flank."

"Glassdamn," Tadeas breathed. "That just might work."

"It pissing better," Demir replied, "because it's the best I've got. Idrian, organize your trap. I want you riding out first thing in the morning. Jorfax, recall most of your glassdancers. We'll need them for the upcoming battle. Tad, I want you running point with all the other officers of the Foreign Legion. They need to understand that if we're going to win this, they have to follow the orders of their disgraced commanding officer."

The others scattered, leaving Demir alone in his tent full of information. He found the little box with the high-resonance witglass and set it on top of one of the crates, staring at it. "You're a crutch," he whispered, "and I can't yearn for you any longer. With or without you, I am still a Grappo. I am still the Lightning Prince."

51

Over the course of the last few weeks, Kizzie had considered a dozen different scenarios that would let her get Aelia Dorlani alone for questioning. She'd discarded all of them because the risks were too damned high—either get herself killed in the process of trying, or earn the direct enmity of one of the most powerful people in Ossa. Montego changed all that. Perhaps his presence made her reckless, or perhaps she just knew that he would attract—and be able to defend against—that enmity himself.

He was all too enthusiastic about her best plan. He even added his own twist on it.

They stood just outside one of the upper-class pubs on the edge of the Assembly District. Kizzie wore a jacket, scarf, and cloak to protect her from both prying eyes and the cold winter air, while Montego wore a richly embroidered green-and-purple tunic that probably cost more than Kizzie made in a year. His round white face was red from the cold, and his very presence seemed to act as a sort of beacon. Passersby stopped and stared, nudging and whispering to each other. Some called his name, but no one dared approach.

It was the first time Kizzie had stood next to someone genuinely famous. Not guild-family famous, surrounded by bodyguards who would whip the insolence out of anyone who got too close, but so famous that his lone presence could command more fear and more attention than any number of guild-family lackeys. The attention made Kizzie feel naked, and she was glad that her hands and face were hidden behind gloves and a scarf.

"Do people stare like this all the time?" she asked in a low voice.

"They do," Montego replied, sipping a beer from the pub, his cane grasped in his off hand, the silver bear pommel wagging occasionally at a passing face, as if he was taking special note of them.

"This is awful," Kizzie said.

"You have no idea."

"How do you get anything done?"

"Well, I don't do my own shopping, if that's what you're asking."

Kizzie looked at Montego sidelong to see that he was smirking at her. "You know what I mean."

"You mean without everyone noticing? I don't often, but my mere presence acts as a very good distraction."

"I'll keep that in mind." Kizzie didn't need a distraction tonight. She needed timing, luck, and a little old-fashioned brutality. "You realize we might start a guild-family war?" she asked, lowing her voice even further.

"Perhaps," Montego responded.

"Should you get Demir's permission?" Kizzie's nerves were starting to act up. Just standing next to Montego was enough to do that—her childhood love, the most celebrated killer in Ossa, talking to her in the flesh after sixteen years. Add in the fact that they were about to attempt something truly reckless, and she allowed herself to dip a trembling hand into her pocket and fix a piece of skyglass to her ear.

Montego stared off above the heads of the passing crowd for a moment before answering. "I may be a Grappo by adoption, but I am still Baby Montego. Demir does not presume to tell me what to do any more than I presume to do the same to him."

Oh, to have such terrible confidence. Kizzie was jealous of it, though she knew she shouldn't be. Montego had earned it. Kizzie checked her pocket watch. "That's settled then. It's time. Meet me at the park?"

"I'll be there. Good luck."

Kizzie broke away, hurrying off into the night, keeping her scarf up around her face in case anyone got too curious about Montego's evening companion. She ducked down a nearby side alley and navigated her way through the labyrinth of alleys, service corridors, and servants' tunnels that connected the dozens of buildings in the Assembly District. She emerged into Assembly Square, just to the right of the main Assembly building, and paused to take stock of her surroundings.

The cold night left the square mostly empty. A line of carriages were parked along the far side of the square, waiting to pick up their important charges and carry them home. It did not take long for Kizzie to spot Aelia Dorlani's carriage. The damned thing was a behemoth, the envy of all of Ossa, with an advanced steel design that was still talked about in the papers a year after Aelia had it delivered from a Marnish craftsman. It was outfitted in Dorlani green, the curtains proudly stitched with their silic sigil. Rumor was that it had a whole bed inside, and that Aelia used her late-night drives to cover for rendezvous with lovers all over the city. It was a bullshit story, but it amused Kizzie all the same.

Kizzie found a deserted brazier, burning low, one of dozens specifically for the bodyguards and pages that had to wait for instructions out in the cold. She warmed her hands in front of it, watching the carriage carefully. Occasionally, she checked her pocket watch.

She had done only a little research for this possible plan before abandoning it weeks ago, and had spent the day scrambling to fill in the cracks. Aelia was at the Assembly almost every day. She stayed until well after dark, and then she drove home, where she would have a late dinner and retire for the night, either working or entertaining personal friends.

The only *reliable* time she wasn't guarded by the Cinders at the Assembly, or by her entire guild-family at her estate, was on that drive home. She always made it a long drive too, because why not? She had the most luxurious carriage in the world. Might as well use it.

Kizzie waited for almost an hour before Aelia's lavish monstrosity of a carriage pulled away from the line, the four white horses clopping across the wide square's cobbles until they reached the main Assembly building. It stopped at the bottom of the massive marble staircase, and within moments Aelia Dorlani swept out of the building and down the stairs, flanked by six bodyguards. Two of them got inside the carriage with her, while the other four leapt onto the running boards. They were off just as quickly as that.

Kizzie waited a few beats, then sprinted down one of the side streets. Her route took her back through a half dozen narrow alleys and turns, but it was a much more direct route than the one Aelia was taking. Kizzie crossed a stone bridge, glancing to her left just long enough to see that Aelia's carriage proceeded along the road as predicted, then heading down a wide stone staircase, past an iron light post. She jumped a railing, slid down a muddy embankment, and leapt a small creek.

The run had taken her about fifteen minutes, and she reached the heavily wooded Waterside Park with her heart pounding. At a quick glance the park seemed deserted, no one present but a few tramps sleeping beneath burlap bags in the underbrush some ways off. Kizzie continued to search, trying to spot Montego without any luck. A worry hit her, that he'd gone to the wrong park or been waylaid somehow. That wasn't like him. He'd always been punctual, even as a kid.

She hurried forward, looking for a massive, tangled-root old oak right next to the road. Way off to her left she could see Aelia's carriage descend carefully from the main road, its oil lamps flickering as it rocked over the uneven cobbles. It would drive slowly through the park, the bodyguards alert for trouble while their master enjoyed the luxury of looking out across the river at the lights of the city.

Kizzie's heart hammered in her ears and she tried to think of everything that could go wrong. What if Montego wasn't here? What if they couldn't stop the carriage? What if . . . what if . . . what if . . . ? She silenced the thoughts as her eyes finally found the big oak she was looking for. She ran to it, fixing her braided earrings into place as she snaked around behind the tree and scurried up the big, thick branches.

To her relief, there was a large form waiting for her about twenty feet up. It wasn't Montego. It was something better—three corpses, lashed together by their legs, their bodies lying carefully across the branch so that a simple shove would send them tumbling off. This was Montego's twist to her plan, one that was devilishly macabre.

Kizzie climbed carefully out onto the thick limb until she could reach the trio of corpses. She was positioned immediately above the road now and all she had to do was wait, listening to the sound of her blood pumping in her ears.

The carriage drew closer and Kizzie peered around in the darkness, still trying to find Montego. The bodies were in place, which meant he was here. Any doubt that he could make such a climb burdened with three bodies had been put to rest watching him on those ropes in the gymnasium last night. But where the piss was he? How bloody hard could he be to spot?

Kizzie clung to the thick limb beneath her, counting down in her head as the carriage approached. She felt too exposed up here, and half of her expected one of the bodyguards to spot her hiding place and halt the carriage. She studied them carefully as they, in turn, studied the forest around them. One of the bodyguards tapped another on the shoulder and pointed off into the darkness. For half a moment, Kizzie feared that they'd spotted Montego.

But the carriage did not stop.

She couldn't help but notice how thick-necked the bodyguards on the running boards were, or the blunderbuss lying beneath the driver's legs, visible only from above. This whole plan, she decided, was very stupid.

She pushed on the corpses.

They slid off their perch, a grisly flailing of stiff limbs that tumbled through the night air and landed squarely on top of Aelia's carriage. One of them clipped the driver on the back of the head, nearly throwing him off his seat. The second knocked two bodyguards off the left side of the carriage, while the third tore directly through the roof and into the middle of the interior.

The startled driver yanked on the reins, bringing the horses to a stop while a series of terrified screams erupted from within. Eight different people shouted at each other all at once. Kizzie found herself enthralled by the sight of six of the most dangerous enforcers in Ossa thrown into a jumbled panic.

Corpses from heaven would do that to anyone, she supposed.

She waited. Not long. The bodyguards tried to pull the corpses free, not seeming to realize they'd been lashed together. Aelia's angry, frantic screams made the chaos even worse. All Kizzie needed was for them to recognize the bodies.

"Wait," one of them suddenly shouted. "This is Bridgette. Glassdamnit, this is Bridgette. And Koren, and Duff. Lady Dorlani, these are our enforcers!"

Not a single one of these idiots had actually looked up yet, and Kizzie wasn't going to give them the chance. She pulled her stiletto, gave a little prayer that Montego was lurking nearby, and dropped down from her branch. She landed on the driver's seat, immediately next to the driver, and buried her stiletto in his neck before he could so much as reach for the blunderbuss under his legs.

On a good day, Kizzie considered herself the equal of any of Aelia's burly bodyguards. She was faster, smarter, and she had just as good godglass. Her attack on the driver was swift but did not go unnoticed. A whole new round of shouts erupted from the carriage as everyone reacted to her presence. One of them leapt for the driver's perch, drawing his sword, but Kizzie's boot caught him in the face before he could take a stab. A second reached for his pistol. Kizzie threw her stiletto hard, catching him just below the heart.

It was a very good start, one that she would have been proud of at any other time. But there were still five living bodyguards. Even with the element of surprise, she would not last against them for long. She needed help. She needed it now.

And she got it.

The specter that swept from the trees moved so quick that it almost fooled her eyes, hitting one of the bodyguards from behind like a charging bull. The bodyguard's body was thrown so hard that it broke one of the carriage's wooden wheels, causing the vehicle to crack and rock violently. Kizzie reached down to steady herself, and in that time Montego's cane whipped around and removed the lower jaw of a second bodyguard.

Montego was like a glassdamned dancer, his massive form moving with astonishing grace as he whirled around the back of the carriage. His arm rose and fell twice, the heavy silver bear on the end of his cane splashing blood across the carriage's brightly colored side. The final bodyguard—the one Kizzie had kicked in the face—was still lying on his back. Montego stepped on his forehead, grinding his heel as if he were stepping on a roach. The poor bastard twitched twice and fell still.

Kizzie stared down at the carnage for a moment, her mouth hanging open, before she remembered to check that her scarf was still hiding her face. She leapt from the driver's perch, landing beside Montego, and reached for the door of the carriage. Montego stopped her with one hand, then used the other to rip the door off its hinges.

Say one thing for Baby Montego—he was a showman at heart.

Aelia Dorlani sat inside, her lips curled back, a pistol pointed at Montego. "How dare you!" she spat. "Do you know who I am? Do you . . ." She trailed off as she seemed to realize exactly who it was she was talking to.

Kizzie took Aelia's moment of shocked realization to reach in and wrench the pistol from her hands, tossing it beneath the carriage. "Aelia Dorlani," she intoned, "you have been named by your grandson Churian as instigator in the murder of Adriana Grappo. Do you want to confess, or am I going to jam a piece of shackleglass down your throat?" Kizzie felt a dangerous thrill go through her. She had always wanted to threaten an Inner Assembly member. She just never thought she would get the chance.

Aelia trembled with rage, but as Kizzie had expected Aelia's eyes weren't even on her. They were glued to Montego. "You common pissant!" she snapped. "You piece of gutter trash! Not even you can get away with this! I will see you sliced to ribbons! I will crush the Grappo into a pulp!"

Montego grasped the carriage doorframe with both hands and *shoved,* the walls crinkling outward as if they were paper. "You killed my adopted mother. You had your goons poison my tea and attack a hotel under my protection. This is not a Grappo matter, Aelia. This is a Baby Montego matter and I would be nothing but the gutter trash you call me if I didn't respond in an appropriate manner."

Kizzie tapped Montego three times under the arm, reminding him that they did not have much time to finish this. There had been no pistol shot, but someone was sure to have heard the commotion. National Guardsmen would be here soon, and if not then Aelia's household up on the hill would get curious once she was late. Montego seemed to get the message and stepped away from the carriage.

"Answer the question," he demanded. "Confess, or we will put you to a shackleglass test."

Kizzie held the small, light green earring up in the palm of her gloved hand. It glittered in the still-burning lights of the carriage's lamps. Aelia stared at the piece of shackleglass in horror, a look of realization crossing her face. "You wouldn't. I am on the Inner Assembly. The secrets I know! If the rest of the Inner Assembly finds out you put me to shackleglass they will *end* you."

Montego shrugged. "Then I will just have to drown you in the river afterward so there are no witnesses."

Aelia stared for a moment longer before Kizzie could see the nerve go out of her eyes like something had died within her. "Yes. Yes, I ordered the death of Adriana Grappo."

"And who else was involved?" Kizzie snapped. "I want names. Who organized this conspiracy?"

"I did it alone," Aelia claimed, recoiling.

"No, you didn't. I have confessions. Dorlani, Magna, Grent, Vorcien. Give me the other two names."

Aelia's lips curled back in a sneer once more. "No."

"We already know the Glass Knife," Montego rumbled. "I will have the answer one way or another. I want the names of your co-conspirators, and I want to know whose idea it was to kill Adriana."

"This is your chance, Aelia," Kizzie said, letting her tone grow soft. "Pass on responsibility. Give us someone more palatable to all of us so we can destroy *them* instead of *you*. Then you can take your—" She counted in her head, including the other three still in a wagon somewhere nearby. "—thirteen corpses and go home. This will all be over for you."

"You think this will ever be over?" Aelia hissed. "Not until you're dead, Montego, and the Grappo are ashes."

Kizzie swallowed hard. She absolutely believed Aelia. The guild-family matriarch had enough manpower and clout to have her revenge. Thankfully, Aelia was still staring at Montego. She'd not even glanced at Kizzie.

"You don't have enough enforcers to kill me," Montego said in disgust. "And I'm not even the dangerous one in the family. Do you think Demir would give you the courtesy of a duel when he finds out you helped kill his mother? He will cut you to ribbons the next time he lays eyes on you. Enforcers can't protect you against a glassdancer. My presence is a kindness that you should be grateful for."

"Two names," Kizzie prodded forcefully. "Who were the other two killers?"

Aelia's face fell, her eyes taking in the carnage that Montego had caused outside the carriage. "I didn't know their names," she said. "They were nobodies. But I do know who planned it."

"Who?" Kizzie asked.

"Aristanes," she replied.

"I have no idea who that is," Kizzie snapped.

"He's a Purnian priest for some god you've never heard of. He's as rich as a guild-family and twice as cruel. He's the real killer—the one who wanted Adriana out of the way."

Montego leaned threateningly against the crumpled exterior of the carriage. "And why did he?"

"I have no idea. I just . . ." The words seemed to stick in Aelia's throat, causing a flicker of emotion to cross her face. ". . . I just follow orders."

Kizzie found her mouth hanging open once more. *Follow orders*? Aelia was on the Inner Assembly! One of the five most powerful people in Ossa. Who could possibly give her orders? A foreign priest? That was insane.

"If you want answers," Aelia finished, "then go find him."

"Where?" Kizzie demanded.

"The Zorlian Mansion, outside the city."

Kizzie had a dozen more questions to ask, worried that Aelia was outthinking them and had just set a trap for them to walk into. But they didn't have any more time. Every moment they remained heightened the risk of being discovered here. If word got out that Montego was behind the attack, Aelia wouldn't have the option of hiding her humiliation like Sibrial had all those years ago. Kizzie tapped Montego under the arm once more.

Montego nodded. "If I discover you have lied to me, I will not do you the kindness of killing just a handful of your enforcers in the dark, Aelia. I will crush your entire extended family. I will do it in the daylight, and then I will happily meet my fate when the other guild-families avenge you." He whirled and strode away.

Kizzie kept her eyes on the frightened old matriarch for half a moment, but any sympathy she might have felt was destroyed by the thought of Adriana being bludgeoned to death on the steps of the Assembly, and Kizzie's idiot brother blackmailed into having to take part. She followed Montego, running to catch up.

They were out of the park within minutes, finding a carriage Montego had left with a loyal Grappo driver and leaving Aelia far behind. Kizzie half expected to hear shouts and alarms, maybe even the sound of pursuit as the scene was discovered. Only silence followed them. They rode for some time, both of them contemplating their inner thoughts, until Kizzie said, "That won't be the last of it. She will try for vengeance."

"We should have killed her," Montego grumbled.

"A dead Inner Assembly member would have the whole city up in arms looking for us," Kizzie replied. "The Dorlani were already our enemies. At least this way we haven't made any more."

Montego sniffed. "I know. It was the right call. But I will not hold back when she comes for me."

"Do you really think you could crush her entire guild-family? She has hundreds of enforcers."

Montego considered the question for a moment and frowned. "I was bluffing, but I'd give a good go of it."

Kizzie shook her head. Her adrenaline was still pumping, riding a high from doing something so damned dangerous and knowing there was a good chance she'd get away with it. Aelia's ire was directed entirely at Montego. Not that Kizzie *wanted* that to be the case—but Montego welcomed it. She wondered if he could truly fight several hundred armed guild-family members single-handedly. It wouldn't be all at once, after all. Montego was too cunning for that.

Perhaps he could.

Montego suddenly took her by the hand. "You're trembling."

"I just helped attack an Inner Assembly member," Kizzie snorted. She moved to pull her hand away, but she found she liked Montego's callused fingers gently holding hers. "The Zorlian Mansion might be a trap," she warned him.

"We'll be ready for it."

Kizzie could taste the end of this damned conspiracy on the tip of her tongue. After weeks of investigation, being beaten and tricked, watching friends die, she would finally come face-to-face with Adriana's real killer.

52

It was late when Idrian finally managed to track down Mika. She was well behind the camp, all the way back with their support staff, who had taken over a little farming village a good three miles to the east of the rest of the army. Dozens of her engineers swarmed all over one building in particular, as well as the massive conical kiln in the garden behind it. Idrian surveyed the workstations covered in clay, then walked over to tap Mika on the shoulder.

"What is it, big man? I'm busy."

"With what?"

She sucked on her teeth loudly. "Thinner walls," she instructed one of her engineers, "thick at the bottom for weight. These things have to *soar,* remember?" She glanced at Idrian. "Glassdamned Demir Grappo told me to design a new grenade. He wanted it small enough to use in our grenade slings, light enough to fly a thousand yards, but packed with enough powder to crack breacher armor."

Idrian scoffed. "And when did he give you this assignment?"

"About eight hours ago."

"And?"

"I had to use a new powder blend I've been experimenting with, but let me tell you: I'm amazing, Idrian. Just the absolute best at what I do. I want you to remember that when some enemy copies my design and flings them at you."

"So you're saying that you're going to someday, indirectly, get me killed?"

"Correct."

"Oh good. Is this whole process well in hand?"

"I suppose. Why?"

"Because Demir said I could borrow you for a few days."

"A few days?" Mika echoed, glancing distractedly at her engineers.

"Squeaks!" she shouted. "You're just playing with that clay now! Get back to work!" To Idrian she continued, "Everyone says Kerite and the Grent will be back for blood soon. What devilry gets you and me away from the army for that long?"

Idrian jerked his head, indicating for Mika to follow him out into the street and away from the flurry of activity that was her impromptu workshop. "You remember back in Marn, when we first met? We were sent to hunt down that glassdancer that was killing all our cattle in the hopes of destroying our meat supply and transportation?"

"Yeah, sure. That was a hairy situation, I tell you. I swear that scar on my ass hurts every time I see a glassdancer."

"Tadeas and I told Demir about the winged glassdancer on the roof of Fort Alameda. We think it's been targeting our scouting parties. He's given me permission to go on the hunt. We'll disguise ourselves as scouts on patrol. When the thing comes for us, we'll kill it."

"Is that a good idea?"

"It's the best idea I have. That thing killed General Stavri's entire staff. It almost killed all of us. I'm not gonna give it a third chance to sneak around murdering people. I want to lure it in and kill it." He paused, waiting for some kind of retort, but Mika just chewed on the inside of her cheek and stared off into the darkness. When the silence continued, he said, "I'll understand if you need to stay here to oversee things, but I will need a couple of your engineers. I want to use grenades to drive it to the ground."

"Idrian," Mika said quietly, "I haven't been able to sleep well since we saw that thing. I don't know what it is—some kind of mythical monster or the results of experimental godglass—but it haunts my dreams. Yeah, of *course* I want the chance to blow it up. When do we leave?"

Idrian felt a stab of relief. He would have taken any engineers, but having Mika herself was better than any three of the others. "Before first light. We'll cover the regular patrol all day, then return to camp. We'll stay close enough that if a battle does start, we can be back to help in no time at all."

"I'll be there." She tilted her head thoughtfully. "I know just which type of grenades to bring."

"Bring Squeaks, too. I've already asked Valient to lend me Fenny and a handful of his best infantry. Jorfax is giving me a glassdancer."

"Done."

"Then I'll see you at my tent before first light." Idrian slapped Mika on the back and began the long walk back to the main camp. It was a solitary walk, despite the constant flood of soldiers, support staff, and camp followers. Idrian spent it in his own head, half wishing he hadn't come up with this damned plan. He preferred to rest before a battle—to drink, play cards, maybe share his sleeping roll with someone. Instead he was heading out to lure in some great winged piece of shit that might well kill him and his companions. It was a dour thought that made the child's laughter come back, distant and following him through the darkness.

He was just walking up the hill to the Ironhorns' camp, passing rows of tents marked with the wolfhead sigil of another battalion, when someone fell in beside him. She walked with a stiff gait, back perfectly straight and head raised as if constantly scanning the horizon for threats. Even though it was after ten o'clock at night, every blond hair was perfectly in place and her uniform was immaculate.

"Colonel Jorfax," Idrian greeted her.

"Don't do that, Idrian."

Idrian glanced around and took a deep breath. "Tilly," he said. Not many people actually knew her given name. It was, even by the standard of military nicknames, a silly one; the fact that she'd been born with it made it worse. He often wondered if her demeanor would be quite so cold, her reputation quite so fierce, if her parents had named her something less diminutive. "How are you?"

"Pissing nervous. We've got Kerite less than six miles away, Grent reinforcements just behind her, and our commanding officer is a volatile, half-broke piece of—"

"Careful," Idrian cut her off. "That's Tad's nephew you're talking about."

"Yeah, well. It's my people who are getting killed because of his plan."

"We're soldiers. Our job is to get killed. And his plan was working until a great winged beast started killing those scouting parties." Idrian took another deep breath. Jorfax's presence wasn't unwelcome, it was just . . . complicated. She was one of the few people who had known him before he was a breacher—and one of even fewer who had known his father. It was a connection to his past life that left him on edge. The madness creeping around in the back of his head responded by causing little shadows to dance around her shoulders. "I still need that glassdancer for *my* plan."

"To use as bait," she said flatly.

"The whole group will be bait, myself included. The glassdancer completes the deception and lets us know when that winged asshole is getting close. Don't push me on this, Tilly. People will die. Maybe me. Maybe the glassdancer. Maybe one of the trusted friends I'm bringing with. And don't try to tell me about how one glassdancer is worth a hundred soldiers. I've killed glassdancers. They're just as gooey on the inside as anyone else, and they die as badly as the most naïve Ossan officer."

They'd known each other for over thirty years and Idrian still had no idea why Jorfax let him talk to her like that. It wasn't because of their shared past. She'd abandoned closer friends to secure her place in the world. It wasn't because he was a breacher. She'd once nailed a breacher's feet to the ground with glass for groping her ass. But she'd never rebuked him, or turned that cold stare on him. He spread his arms, waiting for one of those things to happen.

She just snorted. "I envy you, you know?"

"Don't patronize me," Idrian retorted. His blood was up now, and he just wanted to go to bed. He pressed a palm against his godglass eye, listening to the distant sound of child's laughter. Was it laughter? Or was that child actually saying words now? He tried to ignore both the hallucinated sound and the rising panic that came with it.

Jorfax stopped walking, forcing Idrian to turn around and face her. She shook her head. "I have never been able to separate caring about people from killing. If I care, I can't kill. If I kill, I can't care. You're a superb killer, and yet you have hundreds of friends. You care about your battalion like a father. I respect my people—my glassdancers—and I do my best to keep them alive, but I don't *care* about them. I will spend them like soggy banknotes if need be. But you'll put up that mighty shield of yours, your own life on the line, for people you've never even met."

"And you respect that?" Idrian asked doubtfully.

"I do. I find it weak and demeaning to your entire role as a killer, but I respect it all the same."

"I feel like this conversation isn't reflecting well on either of us."

"I want to know how you do it. How do you look at all these"—she gestured at the camp around them—"insignificant ants and care about them? They aren't strong, not like us. They have no sorcery, no armor, no resistance to glassrot. Just those little godglass baubles that they cling to like it makes them better."

Idrian thought about that for a moment. "Because I don't look for their weaknesses. If that's all you want to find, of course you think of them as ants. But if you find the strength in your friends, and you nurture it, then you will always be surrounded by giants."

Jorfax walked past Idrian, slapping him on his shoulder as she went. "You're an optimistic idiot, Idrian. It's going to get you killed someday. Strangely enough, you'll still die content, which is more than I can say for myself. I'll see you before first light."

"Wait," he turned to call after her. "Does that mean you'll send someone?"

"That means I'm coming myself. Don't worry, you're still in command of the mission. But nobody, not even a monster, spends the lives of my people. That's my job."

Idrian pressed hard on his godglass eye as he watched her go. For the first time in days he thought of the debt marker hanging around his neck. How long did he have left on it? Just a couple of weeks? The time was ticking down in the back of his head, like the pendulum of a grandfather clock. Was it a blessing or a curse? Would he ever even know?

53

Thessa was silently cursing the sky, telling it to send her a proper thunderstorm instead of these damned depressing drizzles, when the messenger arrived. Thessa and Pari sat around the little fire in the lighthouse. They were both still wet and somber from the brief memorial Tirana gave for her fallen enforcer, and Thessa had spent the entire memorial studying each of the enforcers, wondering if one of them was a traitor.

The messenger was a young woman in a black Foreign Legion uniform, a yellow ram stitched on her breast and little ram's-horn forgeglass earrings dangling from her earlobes.

"Private Fenny, ma'am!" the woman said, snapping a salute. "Message for Lady Foleer from General Grappo."

Thessa glanced sidelong at Pari. *General* Grappo. *Lady* Foleer. It seemed so formal for a pair who'd escaped a labor camp not long ago. "Go on, Private."

"General Grappo wishes to inform you that there will be a battle in the vicinity of the Forge sometime in the next few days, and asks that you move your operation behind Ossan lines where you'll be safe until after the battle."

Thessa's stomach fell. "Here? Really? I thought all the fighting was farther south."

"The Grent have encircled Harbortown. General Grappo is trying to lure them back to Grent, but he's still worried about active combat."

Pari spoke up. "Damn. I thought I saw strange lights north of Harbortown last night. Didn't think much of it."

"That would be Kerite's Drakes, the mercenary company," Fenny explained. "Those are the ones General Grappo is worried about."

Thessa leaned close to the fire, still trying to get the cuffs of her jacket dry. The wind howled outside, rain pattering constantly on the tarpaulin secured over holes in the lighthouse roof. "Does that mean Demir is camped nearby?"

"He is, ma'am. We're about three miles from here."

Thessa turned to look at the phoenix channel. It didn't look like much—just a copper cable coming down from the roof and into one side of an insulated box, then out the other and into the ground. She doubted that Fenny had even taken note of it. Did it matter? Demir would send a message only with someone he trusted. Besides, Thessa knew that crest. It belonged to the Ironhorn Rams, the most famous member of which was a longtime client of the Grent Royal Glassworks.

"Is Idrian Sepulki there?" she asked.

"The Ram? Yes ma'am, of course. He's our breacher. Horns ready, hooves steady." Fenny pounded a fist against the ramshead sigil on her uniform.

Thessa considered the flames of the little fire for a few moments, tilting her head to listen to that patter of rain. Still no sound of thunder. "That's not far," she said, considering. "Take me to Demir."

⋗　　⋗　　⋗

The walk to the Ossan camp was dark and miserable, but blessedly not too long. Thessa refused a piece of sightglass—it wouldn't help her anyway—and stumbled along close behind, a hand on Fenny's belt. By the time they reached their destination it was no longer raining, and Thessa was grateful to leave her jacket hanging by the fire outside Demir's tent before heading inside.

Demir sat cross-legged in the middle of a bare floor, hardly any furniture filling his massive tent. Every surface was covered in papers, with crates of more shoved off to one side. Demir looked up from his studies in surprise. "Thessa? I'm glad you got my message."

Thessa remained just inside the flap. "What," she asked, "is the actual danger to us at the Forge?"

"I can't be entirely sure," Demir said, setting aside some report. He stood up, stretching out his legs and pacing around for a moment before offering her the only little stool in the tent. "If the Grent notice you, they may send someone to investigate. Otherwise you're only in danger if we lose the battle and have to flee."

"But you're not going to lose the battle, are you?" Thessa asked, raising her eyebrows.

A small smile flickered across Demir's face. "I'm not one for bravado.

There's a very distinct chance that I will lose. I have a good plan, but Kerite is a sharp one. I wouldn't put it past her to turn my plan against me in some way. I'd rather you and your team at the Forge be safe."

Thessa almost told him about the death of Tirana's enforcer. She should. Demir had a right to know. But she could also see the redness in his eyes and the slump of his shoulders. He was exhausted. Giving him another problem to deal with at this moment would be cruel. "Are you ordering me to withdraw from the Forge?" she asked.

Demir frowned. "I'm not going to order you to do anything. You're my partner, not my client. We made that very explicit."

"Then we're going to stay. The phoenix channel is set up, our camp is in place. We could get a lightning strike literally at any hour. Before I left to come see you I gave orders for all lights to be extinguished and noise kept to a minimum. No one is going to notice us up on the Forge."

"You're certain that's wise?"

Thessa finally walked over and sank down on the stool Demir had offered. "I can't stop thinking about that riot, Demir. Despite your efforts, dozens of people died. Newspapers are reporting riots like that all over the world—not just in the Empire—and they're going to escalate. I'm not a politician but I know how precarious a government can be. We are inches from sliding into chaos, and the phoenix channel might be all that stops it. I understand if you don't want to risk your enforcers, but I tell you now . . . I *will* risk my own life to gain days." She ran a hand through her hair. "And I might need every day. This is just a test—an experiment—and it might not work."

"Then," Demir said, spreading his hands, "I'll respect that decision."

No argument. No scolding. He actually listened, just like that. Kastora used to tell her that people in power *never* listened. They just wanted you to follow orders. Thessa wondered how she could be so lucky. Demir stood over her, his attention turning back to the papers spread out all over the floor, and she remembered her feeling of isolation upon finishing the phoenix channel the other day. No wine, no celebration. She stood up, bringing her face-to-face with him, just inches apart, and ran a finger along the collar of his uniform.

"You have a battle to plan, I know. But can I have an hour?"

Demir swallowed noticeably, taking in a sharp little breath. Was he nervous? If so, that was adorable. "Thessa . . ." he said, taking a half step back.

Thessa didn't let it show on her face, but that half step hurt. Even if he hadn't meant it to be, it was a rejection. "If you don't have time, that's okay."

"It's not the time I'm worried about."

Thessa felt her heart fall. She hadn't *consciously* come out here for a dalliance, but now that she was here she realized how much she needed it. By that look of uncertainty in his eyes, he at least partially needed it too. He gave her a pained look.

"Okay, Master Grappo." What little patience she had was now gone, killed by that pained look. She squared her legs and faced him full on. "Then what is it? What's going on here?"

Demir stiffened visibly. "What do you mean?"

"You and me. I've seen dozens of young siliceer apprentices drive themselves mad with pining and confusion and miscommunication, and I'm not damn well doing that. When you left to face the Grent that first time, you and I were minutes from sleeping together. Now you're being evasive. If it's not the right time just say the word. But if it's something else, I deserve to know." She poked him in the chest with a finger. "What is happening? Did you fall in love with someone while you were at war for three glassdamned days? Did you decide I wasn't good enough for a romp? Did a musketball castrate you?"

"Perhaps we should talk about this later," Demir said, taking another half step back, his eyes darting evasively, as if looking for an exit.

"No," Thessa snapped. "I am exhausted, cold, surrounded by the very soldiers that invaded my adopted country. I'm out there sitting on a rock above the ocean just waiting for glassdamned lightning to strike. Are you going to keep me warm or give me a good reason why you can't?"

The color seemed to drain out of Demir's face. "We're doing this now, aren't we?"

"Yes we are." Thessa gloried in her own emotional momentum. No more dancing around things. Straight to the point.

"Fine," he said. "Did you know they call me the Lightning Prince?"

The reply took her by surprise. She didn't know what she expected, but it hadn't been *that*. "I suppose I heard a few of the porters at the hotel whisper about it. Sure."

"Do you know why?"

"I don't."

"Because nine years ago, I led one of the most stunning campaigns in

Ossan history by putting down a provincial uprising in just seven days. At my command, the Foreign Legion crushed the armies of Holikan. The resulting sack of the city was considered a nightmare and my involvement scrubbed from official records."

Thessa barely heard anything after the word "Holikan." Her own blood suddenly pounded powerful in her ears, as if she had thrown herself off the Forge and was falling toward the sea. "You were there?" she asked, unable to keep the tremble out of her tone.

"I wasn't just there," Demir said gently, "I commanded the campaign."

Thessa suddenly felt dizzy, her senses muted. She stumbled and sat back down on the stool, staring up at him. "That's not possible." He did not respond, and Thessa tried to grapple with this new knowledge. In her mind she played back every conversation they'd ever had, stopping that night he returned from the Inner Assembly. She distinctly remembered the fear that flashed across his eyes when she mentioned Holikan, and the way he'd disappeared coldly from her room. It all made so much sense. "How long have you known I was from Holikan?" she asked.

"Only since you told me."

Just as she thought. She clutched at her stomach, feeling it twist and turn like she was on a ship's deck in bad weather. "You butchered my family," she whispered.

Demir's face grew stricken. "Thessa, I was there. I admit it. I knew I needed to tell you. But I did *not* give the order to sack Holikan. I was betrayed, and I only recently found out by whom. I can't make it right, but I *am* looking for justice."

Thessa was still reeling on the inside. Demir—a man she'd known only a couple of weeks, but who she thought was the kindest, most considerate guild-family member she'd ever met—had conducted the Holikan campaign. Lightning Prince. The words tasted like ash on the tip of her tongue.

"Let me explain," he began.

Thessa cut him off. "No. I don't want to hear it from you." She got to her feet, grabbing on to one of the tent poles for stability. She could hear the coldness in her own voice, and she did not try to temper it. "I can't trust a word you say." She left, lurching and dizzy, hurrying out into the cold winter air, feeling a stab of betrayal—at Demir, at Ossa, even at her very happy intentions being dashed against the ground.

She stopped just outside, gathering her wits. Part of her hoped Demir would rush after her, but when she peeked back inside the tent she found him standing stock-still, staring at the wall. She looked at her hands. Did consorting with him put Holikan's blood on them? Of course not. She didn't know. But it sure felt like it. What could she do now? She was in too deep with the Grappo. She had a contract. She was surrounded by his enforcers. The only person in her world who was beholden to her instead of him was Pari.

Thessa found the messenger nearby, sitting with a young woman by the fire, listening to someone a few fires over play the fiddle. "Private Fenny?"

"Ma'am?"

"Where is Idrian Sepulki?"

"He's out on a mission, ma'am. He was due to report back in half an hour ago. I imagine he'll be along soon. Would you like to wait for him?"

"If it's not too much trouble." Thessa remained standing, warming her hands by the fire, trying not to get sucked into the despair of her own thoughts. The night air helped to cool her head, but her chest hurt with a helpless fury for a crime that had happened over a third of her life ago. She tried to picture her parents and her little sister the last time she saw them as she boarded a coach service for Grent. As seemed to happen more frequently these days, she could not remember their faces.

"Thessa?"

She jumped, not knowing how much time had passed as she stared into the fire, and looked up to see Idrian standing across from her. He looked a little older than when she last saw him—a little more weary with a few more scars, and a chunk missing from one ear. He wore his brightly colored armor, his helmet under his arm and his hair slick with sweat. A young man stood at his elbow carrying his sword and shield. Idrian's presence seemed to ground her thoughts.

"You remember me?"

"Of course I do! You helped Kastora on this the last two times." He tapped his godglass eye. "I see that Demir succeeded in fetching you."

"It's a long story," Thessa said, trying to smile.

"One I'd like to hear."

"Someday. I'm sorry to spring this on you, and I know we haven't seen each other for years, but could I have a word in private?"

"Of course!" Idrian dismissed his assistant and led her to an avenue between the tents, where he gave her an apologetic smile. "This is about as private as it gets in an army camp. What's going on?"

"I'm looking for someone—anyone—who was at Holikan," she said. "I'm hoping you can point me in the right direction."

Idrian's gaze grew far away and he touched his godglass eye. "Did you say Holikan?"

"I did. I need to talk to someone who was there."

Idrian shifted from foot to foot. "Well, no one else was. The Ironhorns were on the campaign, but they never actually got to Holikan. They had orders to blow up bridges fifty miles away."

"You said 'they,'" Thessa said, feeling her stomach tighten once more.

"I did," he admitted. "Because I was there."

"What do you mean?" This man, someone Kastora respected above all others, was at Holikan? And Kastora never told her?

"I fought in the battle just outside the city. It was bloody but quick." His shoulders sagged, his face growing grim at the memory. "So yes, I was there."

"Did you . . . participate?"

A look of horror came over Idrian, so acute that Thessa immediately felt the tension leave her body. "Participate?" he asked in disgust. "In the sack? No. If I'd had it my way, every one of those that did would have been shot."

Thessa had a hundred more questions but she couldn't let herself ask them, not now. She reached out and took him by the arm, looking into his good eye. "Idrian, please. Tell me what happened that night."

"About the sack?"

"About Demir. Did he give the order to destroy the city?"

Some measure of understanding seemed to enter Idrian's expression. "In a word? No. We won the battle, the Holikan armies were put to flight, and the city was open to us. Demir had direct orders from the Assembly to decimate the city—it's an old punishment for rebels, and a brutal one. Demir refused. He spared the mayor's life, and he ordered Holikan to be spared as well. The words were barely out of his mouth when we realized that the army was marching on the city."

Thessa stared, openmouthed, the sound of her heart hammering away almost drowning out Idrian's words. She'd never actually heard a firsthand account. All she knew was that one day her family was still alive, sending her letters at her apprenticeship with Kastora, and then news came of the city rising up against Ossa. Months passed, news was sparse, and then word came that Holikan had been destroyed. That was the end of her old life.

Idrian continued, "Demir galloped off alone in the night, trying to stop them, but someone had given false orders for the army to sack the city. Once that bloodletting is out of the bag, there's no putting it back in again." Idrian shuddered, and Thessa wondered what a man as strong as he must have seen to make the memory so painful. "I didn't find him until the next morning, cradling the corpse of a little girl he tried to save. It broke him. He went from the greatest politician in the Empire—the Lightning Prince—to a mental invalid overnight. He resigned his commission, disappeared into the provinces, and only returned a few weeks ago when his mother was murdered." Idrian passed a hand across his face. "The Assembly buried the entire thing. His involvement was stripped from the official records."

"So he's not a butcher."

"Butcher?" Idrian asked in surprise. "I've never met someone so dangerous who cares so much about other people. I'm not sure if he can talk about Holikan still. How did you even find out about it?"

"He told me," Thessa said softly, trying to digest Idrian's story. She looked around her, then back up at Idrian. "My family was at Holikan when it happened."

Idrian's eyes widened. "Oh."

A thousand emotions warred inside her, all trying to come out on top. She was angry, confused, sad, hurt, relieved, even a little happy. None of it felt *good*. If this was true—and she had no reason to disbelieve Idrian—then Demir was just as much a victim of the sack of Holikan as she was. Someone had undermined him, given false orders, and destroyed his life. The stricken look on his face when she wouldn't let him explain himself was probably the same look she'd worn when she received word of the sack.

She felt her resolve strengthen. All her life, things had been taken from her—her family, her friends, her master, her homes. She could *not* let fate snatch this new life from her. She turned to Idrian. "I'm glad you're safe. I'd like to catch up, but . . ." She squeezed his arm. "Thank you for telling me. I have . . . an apology to make."

54

Demir stared at the wall of his tent for some time. He was, he eventually realized, in shock. Over the years he'd had plenty of women mad at him. Some fairly, some not. Never had one genuinely believed that he was responsible for the massacre of her family. How did he come back from that? Was it even possible to reconcile?

"Well," he said aloud to the empty tent, "she hates me forever now."

It was a painful realization, made no easier by the fact that he'd been trying to prepare for this moment since the word "Holikan" left her lips a week ago. He *wasn't* prepared for it, and his last-ditch effort to put the conversation off had probably just made her angrier.

Something made an audible *crack* nearby, and it took a moment for Demir to realize it was his glassdancer egg, discarded with his uniform jacket on one of the crates. He was clutching at his sorcery without even realizing it, like raising a fist subconsciously in anticipation of a fight. He forced himself to let go of the pieces with his sorcery. Such a lack of control was dangerous for a glassdancer.

He knelt down among all his reports and plans, trying to remember where he was when Thessa had entered. Did it matter? He felt a whirlpool of despair in the back of his mind, trying to suck him down into the dreaded blackness that had taken him after Holikan. He fought it, weakly, wondering if there was a point to his flailing. Even if Kerite fell for his trap, he wasn't going to win this battle. She would turn it on him, slaughter his people, and if he survived he'd return to Ossa in shame. Thessa hated him, and with her hate the phoenix channel project would no doubt die.

He went to his officer's trunk and began rooting around inside for civilian's clothes. He could still run. Slip away. Disappear. The Grappo name would be forever destroyed but at least he'd be free of all his responsibilities.

He clutched at a tunic, staring at it, wondering why it seemed familiar, when he realized it was the last thing he wore before returning from the provinces. One of his porters had packed it for him unknowingly. Demir the friendly grifter. A wanderer. A nobody. This tunic was freedom.

And cowardice.

It took him some time to realize he was weeping, and he used the tunic to wipe the tears from his cheeks. Such weakness. Such cowardice. Perhaps he should be glad his mother was dead, so she couldn't see what he'd become. She'd practically handed him a way to save the world and he couldn't even do that right.

"Demir?"

Demir leapt to his feet and whirled, throwing the tunic back into his trunk like he'd been caught with a stolen bauble. Thessa stood half inside the tent, the flap raised above her head. She seemed more somber, her jaw tight.

"Can I come in?"

He wanted to tell her to piss off; that her dead family was not his concern. He had a war to win, after all. He had responsibilities greater than her feelings. He bit down hard on his tongue until the urge passed. He had, after all, just seriously considered running away. "Please," he said. Once the tent flap had closed behind her, he continued, "Thessa, I'm sorry, I should have told you the moment you mentioned—"

"No," she said firmly, cutting him off. She squared her shoulders and stood up straight, reminding Demir that she was just a bit taller than him. Was she trying to be intimidating? She went on, "*I'm* sorry. I shouldn't have said you butchered my family. I should have let you explain yourself."

Demir felt his mouth hanging open, at a loss for words. "Your anger was justified," he managed.

"Justified but misdirected. I didn't think I could trust anything you said at the moment, so I asked Idrian Sepulki. He told me what happened at Holikan. The whole story. I believe him. I want you to know that."

Demir felt something *change*. It was like a knot he didn't know was there, centered at the base of his neck, suddenly disappeared. A rush of relief flowed through him, his body loosening, his legs turning to jelly for half an instant. "I'm glad," he said.

"Do you know who betrayed you? Who caused the sack?"

"Capric Vorcien," Demir answered.

"What will you do with him?"

"I already tried to duel him. The Cinders intervened, but he won't go unpunished for what he did. I swear it." *How* Demir would punish him, when he'd promised Father Vorcien to drop his blood feud, he still wasn't sure.

Thessa took a deep breath, let it out slowly, and then took another. Her fingers trembled, and on an impulse Demir reached out and took them in his. They were freezing. She did not pull away from him. She looked down at their intertwined fingers, then up at him. "I do not hate you, Demir. I do not blame you for the deaths at Holikan." She seemed to be forcing the words out, each one a painful grating. Demir would, he decided, take it. "I'll reserve my hate for Capric Vorcien."

"And me?" Demir asked. It was a selfish question, but one that he needed the answer to or he wouldn't sleep. "I understand if you'd like to cancel the project. I'll tear up our contract. The phoenix channel is yours. Take it, go back to the hotel and get Ekhi. I'll make sure Breenen gives you some money to get started wherever you go next." He meant every word, too. If this was the end of their partnership, he wanted it to be without guile or reservation. There was already too much of both in his life.

"Shut up, Demir," Thessa said, and wrapped her arms around him. The embrace was the most comforting feeling Demir had had in years. It was warm and pleasant, and Thessa put her head on his shoulder, burying her cold nose into the crook of his neck, causing goose bumps to form all down his arms. When they finally separated, her eyes were red but clear. He could still see the anger written across her face, but it didn't feel directed at him.

"I meant what I said," he told her.

"I'm not going to break the contract." Thessa drew herself up. "I'm a Grappo partner, and I'm proud to be one. As for the rest . . ." She looked away uncertainly. "It's going to take time for me to sort out. I'm not ready to be more than your business partner."

The fact that she would even remain that genuinely surprised him. Demir let out a relieved laugh. "Completely understandable."

Despite her words, she didn't pull away from him. They stood, inches apart, holding each other's arms, neither of them seemingly willing to let go. Was he supposed to kiss her, despite what she'd just said? No, he couldn't kiss her. She'd made herself very clear. She might have forgiven him for his involvement, but it was a complicated matter. Her partnership—her friendship—was a damned gift.

His eyes lingered on hers, the silence between them broken only by the distant roll of thunder. Thessa cocked her head, looking over her shoulder.

"There's a new storm brewing at the Forge. I should get back as quickly as I can."

"I'll have Fenny escort you," Demir told her, relieved at the distraction to remove temptation.

Within minutes she was gone. Demir felt lighter and heavier all at the same time. Some—not all, but some—of the guilt he'd been carrying around with him these nine years seemed to have vanished. In its place was something else. Longing? Did he have genuine feelings for this woman he barely knew? It didn't matter. He couldn't act on them.

He found himself taking deep, measured breaths. "Damn it," he whispered, "I'm getting too involved." He had to tell her about Kizzie and the Vorcien deal. Not tonight. No more drama. But at the next opportunity.

55

"Is there a word," Thessa asked, "for when circumstance keeps you from getting some?"

Though Thessa had rushed back to the Forge and hardly slept, lying awake next to the phoenix channel until the wee hours of the morning, there had been no lightning strike. Thunder seemed to roll past them all night, small flashes of lightning high up in the sky. Not a one had decided to jump down to earth for her test. The dawn came on with a warm updraft blowing off the ocean, taking the chill out of the air, and the wind was picking up once more.

Pari stood next to her, looking out the little window in the stone lighthouse that faced out across the water. "I spent a lot of time with river pigs when I was a teen—you know those insane log drivers who move timber down the river? They used to call it a logjam when something interrupted their, uh, dalliances."

"Logjam," Thessa scoffed. "I don't have a log, but I like it. Look at that storm out there. It's almost black. We're going to get some real proper rain soon. Let's hope it comes with lightning." She tapped her fingers nervously against the stone wall. Did she really regret not sleeping with Demir, even after finding out about Holikan? The very thought seemed twisted, and yet . . . the anger was gone, her fury snuffed out. He was another victim, tortured by culpability that it didn't sound like he even deserved. Their shared experiences had absolutely nothing to do with Holikan.

She'd spent the whole night thinking about him; wondering what would happen after the war and the phoenix channel test. The fact that she still felt a spark with him even while telling him they couldn't be more than business partners made things complicated. She needed to step back. To *think*. They'd known each other for less than two weeks. Once the battle was done—once the test was conducted—she had to promise herself not to rush into anything she would regret later.

She found Pari watching her with a leering smile. "What?"

"Demir Grappo, eh?"

"Don't," Thessa warned her assistant.

Pari threw up her hands. "Fine, fine. What's next, Jailbird?"

"Everything is next. If that incoming storm brings lightning, we need to be ready for it." Thessa hurried over to the phoenix channel, running her hands along the copper cable. She checked that the copper didn't touch the tin casing anywhere, and that the insulation was in place. She checked each coupling for the tenth time in the last hour. The truth was they really didn't have anything to do. The phoenix channel was ready. They even had a neat little basket of spent godglass sitting on a stool on the "exit" side of the phoenix channel.

Satisfied that she'd done everything she could to prepare the test, she headed outside to the camp of Grappo enforcers. Aside from a handful of enforcers on guard duty, everyone else was huddled under tarpaulins or in the shadow of the craggy landscape, trying to stay warm without a fire. She'd offered to let them rotate through the lighthouse last night for a bit of warmth, but not a single one wanted to stand near either the lightning rod or the audibly humming box of sorcery it was attached to.

The first thing she saw when she stepped outside was Tirana. The master-at-arms seemed to be waiting for her, and before Thessa opened her mouth she said, "We need to talk. Alone."

"Of course. Inside? Pari, give us a minute, please."

They were soon inside the lighthouse, where Tirana stayed as close as humanly possible to the door, glancing askance at the phoenix channel. She produced something from inside her jacket and held it out—a strange coil of burnt paper wrappings. "Do you know what this is?"

"It looks like a bigger version of the wrappings soldiers use on gunpowder charges," Thessa said, thinking back to watching the glassworks garrison take inventory in the courtyard when she was younger.

"It's a military signal flare," Tirana answered in a low voice. She pushed the door open just slightly, looking out into the Forge through the crack. "I found it burning underneath a rock half an hour ago. Someone must have set the damn thing early this morning."

"Underneath a rock?" Thessa echoed.

"Out of the rain, hidden from us, but so that the light would reflect out toward the south. Toward Harbortown."

"Ooooh," Thessa said, drawing the word out. She reached out and touched the damp wrappings, then looked up sharply to meet Tirana's eye. "Someone set this deliberately to signal to the Grent besieging the harbor."

"It's the only explanation, and I'd stake my career that it was whoever pushed Justaci off the edge two nights ago." Tirana shoved the burnt wrappings back in her jacket angrily. "I've got all my enforcers on high alert, sleeping four to a tent, keeping an eye on each other without knowing that's what they're doing."

"Did any report anything suspicious?"

"Not one of them."

"Does Breenen know about all of this?"

Tirana hesitated. "I haven't told anyone but you. After what happened at the Hyacinth earlier this week I don't trust anyone but Master Demir and Montego. The only reason I trust you—no offense—is because Demir told me you were in charge of this operation."

So who the piss could it be? Thessa swallowed a lump in her throat, thinking through all the enforcers. There were forty people out there and she knew the names of only half of them. Any could be a spy or a traitor. Even Breenen, though that seemed outlandish. Was it Pari? Was it Tirana herself, trying to throw Thessa off the scent? She wondered if she'd made a mistake refusing Demir's offer to move into the shelter of the nearby army until this battle was over. Perhaps she still should.

But that storm would arrive before they could even pack up. No sense in wasting the opportunity. Besides, her logic was still sound. If there *was* a traitor among them, taking more time would just give that person more opportunities for betrayal.

"How does that flare work?" she asked.

"It's just a cylinder filled with a particular blend of slow-burning gunpowder and some chemicals to add color," Tirana answered. "You pull a cord, it causes a spark inside the flare and starts to burn."

"Will it leave powder residue on the hands? Like when soldiers fire a musket?"

Tirana's face brightened. "It will! That's brilliant."

"Let's check everyone," Thessa said. "Subtly, mind you. So they don't spook." Her fear mixed with righteous indignation. No guild-family traitor was going to ruin this moment, not if she could help it. This test would succeed or fail on *her* merits. "You check," she said, "I'll talk."

"Agreed."

They went back outside, where Thessa carefully glanced at Pari's hands first. A little dirt, but no powder residue. That took a weight off Thessa's shoulders. She was beginning to like Pari a lot. The woman had saved her life, after all. She was glad she wasn't a spy. Thessa continued past, motioning for her to follow, and walked over to the firepit that had been cold since Demir's messenger last night.

"Everyone!" she said, shouting to be heard above the growing wind, "listen up! As you all know, there's going to be a battle nearby sometime in the next few days. I'm hoping we'll all be gone well before the fighting starts. To that end, I want everyone packed and ready to leave at a moment's notice. This incoming storm is promising. All I need is a lightning strike to hit that rod over there, and my test will be complete. We'll wait out the rest of the storm and get out of here as soon as we're able."

As she spoke, Tirana moved surreptitiously around the little camp, whispering in enforcers' ears. She carried a roll of banknotes and slipped a few to each of the enforcers in order to check their hands. Clever woman. Thessa continued, "Thank you all for coming. I know you have your orders, but thank you nonetheless. I hope this becomes an important moment we all remember." It wasn't much of a speech. It certainly felt lackluster for a moment that might change the world. She gave them a confident smile and glanced at Tirana, but the master-at-arms was still working her way quietly through the enforcers.

Breenen joined Thessa wearing a soft smile, and shook her hand. She took the opportunity to check his hands—nothing. He said, "I'm glad you're keeping everyone's safety in mind. This test, whatever it is, has kept Demir afloat since he returned. He seems to think it'll save the Grappo. You have my gratitude for that."

Thessa felt her cheeks flush. "Thank you. I—" They were interrupted by a sudden scuffle, and Thessa turned to find that Tirana had drawn her sword and held it to the neck of an enforcer that Thessa didn't recognize.

"Thessa!" Tirana barked. "Now!"

They both hurried over, a growing sense of alarm passing through the gathered enforcers. It took several moments for things to calm down enough that they could talk over the wind. "What's going on?" Breenen demanded. "Why is your sword out?"

"Because," Tirana said, "his hands have the residue of a military flare—a signal left for our enemies to find us. Explain yourself, Kempt!"

The enforcer tried to draw away from Tirana's sword, his eyes darting everywhere at once. "I don't know what you mean! That's just powder from my pistol."

"Breenen, do you have your shackleglass?" Tirana asked.

"I don't take it out of the hotel," Breenen replied with a growing look of dismay. "Do you mean to say Kempt has betrayed us?"

"He killed Justaci for trying to warn me about a traitor, and now he's signaled to the Grent," Tirana said. "Do you have anything to say? Lie, and I'll cut you apart myself. You'll go under question with the shackleglass as soon as we return to the Hyacinth."

Kempt's jaw snapped shut, and he glared around Tirana defiantly. "Piss off!"

Tirana cuffed him across the forehead with the guard of her sword. "Gell, Yants, bind him and keep him under watch."

Thessa hung back through the whole drama. Even if she was in charge of this test, this felt like something outside of her authority. The enforcers around her muttered and swore, one of them even spitting after Kempt as he was led away. Thessa returned to the lighthouse, feeling a distinct sense of unease. It was one thing for Tirana to suggest they had a traitor. It was a whole other to find evidence and make the accusation.

"I don't like that," Pari said when they were once again alone, scowling at the wall as if she could see through it to the enforcers gathered outside. "Glassdamn. I know that the guild-families spy on each other all the time, but is this whole thing really worth it? Did he really push that enforcer off the cliff the other night?"

Thessa glanced at the phoenix channel, remembering what she'd told Demir—she would risk her life to gain just a few days. "Yes," she answered, "it's worth killing over."

"Well, they're not killing us," Pari declared, drawing her belt knife and checking the blade. "I'll keep watch tonight, here at the door."

Thessa hoped they'd be on their way back to Ossa by then. From what she knew of the storms here at the Forge, they blew through hard and fast. She paced the lighthouse floor, thinking. Who was Kempt signaling to? Did anyone see that flare? If he was working for the Grent then why did he leave the door open for the Dorlani back at the hotel? None of it made sense, and it made the Forge seem even more hostile and cold.

"Lady Foleer!" Tirana suddenly shouted, barging into the lighthouse, the door banging open. She paused, her eyes wild and her hand on her sword.

"We just spotted dragoons in mercenary colors. There's a whole company of them, and they're heading right this way."

Thessa followed her out to the southern edge of the Forge, looking out over the scrubland between here and Harbortown. She couldn't make out much of anything but a little bit of movement off in the olive groves. "You're sure?"

"Positive."

"Do we have time to run?"

"We'll be twice as vulnerable on the open road."

They were joined by Breenen. The old concierge wrung his hands as he stared out toward the south, and Thessa wondered if he regretted leaving the safety of his hotel. "We should barricade the path up to the Forge," he suggested.

Thessa squeezed her hands into fists until it hurt, measuring her breaths until she realized that both Tirana and Breenen were staring at her. Glass-damnit. She was in charge of a phoenix channel test, not *this*. It felt like the attack on the Grent Royal Glassworks all over again and it nearly made her lose her nerve. Gathering what reserves of courage she had left, she said, "Breenen, send one of your enforcers on horseback to Demir. He's on hand for this exact reason. Tirana, barricade the path."

"We only brought twenty rifles," Tirana said in dismay. "We were expecting the Dorlani, not actual cavalry."

"Twenty rifles will have to do." The wind continued to pick up, and Thessa thought she heard the rumble of thunder.

⟩ ⟩ ⟩

To Thessa's surprise, the mercenary dragoons didn't seem to know what to do with this small group of guild-family enforcers camped out on a desolate rock miles from the city. They approached cautiously, riding about the entire area as if checking for spies or reinforcements, before they officially took control of the carriages and horses that the Grappo enforcers had been forced to leave on the mainland. They corralled their own horses and then set up a cordon around the approach to the Forge, effectively cutting Thessa and her companions off from escape.

There was something frightening about the slow, deliberate way in which they worked. It felt very professional and only made it harder to watch them helplessly from atop the Forge, knowing that the phoenix channel expedition was completely trapped. When one of them finally came forward—an officer by his epaulets—he marched up the approach until he was just below the rocks and empty crates Tirana's enforcers had used for their barricade.

"Ossans!" the mercenary officer called. "My name is Captain Hellonian of Kerite's Drakes. I am obliged to inform you that you are inside of an active war zone. If you will hand over your weapons and come down from there peaceably, we can take you into custody and make arrangements for your ransom." It sounded almost gentlemanly, as if this were just a bit of bureaucracy for them all to go through so they could go home.

Thessa knelt behind the barricades with Tirana and Breenen. "What do you think?"

Tirana shook her head. "We have a very defensible position, but they outnumber us four to one. Maybe they'll attack. Maybe they'll take our carriages and horses and leave us here under guard. It's impossible to tell."

"If they take us into custody," Breenen said with a grimace, "it's hard to tell what will happen. If they ransom us to Demir, we could be free in days."

"And if they don't ransom us?" Thessa asked.

Breenen grimaced. "They'll ransom us. We have no value beyond that."

Thessa bit down on her tongue until she tasted blood. Was she even capable of surrendering? "The last time soldiers took me into custody, I wound up in a labor camp. I'm not doing that again. If they find out what we're guarding, they won't give it back. They won't give *me* back." She wrestled with herself, trying to decide on the right course of action. She was surrounded by enforcers, not soldiers. Their lives might rest on whatever she said next.

"Did you get a message off to Demir?" she asked Breenen.

"I did. It should have already arrived."

She turned to Tirana. "You're the only one here with actual military experience. Can we hold out long enough for Demir's people to arrive?"

Tirana squinted down at the officer below them, who tapped his foot impatiently. "I think it's a bluff. I think Kerite saw that flare early this morning and sent someone to investigate. Captain Hellonian isn't going to sacrifice lives just to capture a bunch of trapped enforcers."

Thessa considered her options once more and took a deep breath before she stood up. She addressed the mercenary officer. "This is a scientific expedition. We were here before we knew it was a war zone. I suggest you leave us in peace, and I give my word that we'll be gone by tomorrow."

The captain looked unimpressed. "A scientific expedition is not immune to the rules of war. Surrender immediately so things don't have to get nasty."

"There are no rules of war," Tirana whispered beside Thessa, rolling her eyes. Louder she said, "We're civilians. You've got nothing to gain from forcing our hand."

"You do not surrender, then?" the captain asked.

Thessa and Tirana exchanged one last glance. "No," Thessa declared. "We do not."

The captain pursed his lips and looked along the makeshift barricades for several long moments. He sighed and tugged at his riding glove to remove it, then held up his hand with the back facing them. Tattooed where guild-family members had their silic sigil was a small knife with a pink razorglass blade. "Does this change your mind?"

Thessa exchanged a glance with Tirana. "Why would it?" As the words left her mouth, she saw some movement in the corner of her eye. Several of the Grappo enforcers suddenly turned their pistols, pointing them at their companions. *Traitors.* The word shot through Thessa's head in half a moment. She reached for her own pistol, only to come up short as one was thrust in her face.

On the other end of it stood Breenen, the concierge, his jaw set in a sad line of determination. "Yes," he said loudly, "it does change our mind."

The entire barricade erupted in chaos.

56

"I have good news and bad news."

Demir jerked awake, flailing about himself for a weapon before remembering where he was. He lay on the floor of his tent, his uniform jacket pulled over him for warmth, surrounded by missives and spy reports. The last thing he remembered was giving out a handful of orders to tired messengers in the middle of the night. He rolled over, searching for his pocket watch before giving up and finally turning his attention to Uncle Tadeas sitting on the crate next to his head.

"I like good news," he mumbled.

"The good news is your ruse with the National Guard worked. They moved into Grent yesterday afternoon, and we just got word that the Grent encirclement of Harbortown is broken. They're moving south as quickly as they can."

Demir sat up, rubbing the sleep out of his eyes. "Have you roused the camp? I want the cavalry ready within the hour. If we're going to hit them on the move, we can't waste a single moment."

"You might want to hear the bad news first."

"Shit." Demir stared bleary-eyed at his uncle. "What is it?"

"Kerite's Drakes didn't go with them. They're coming right toward us."

It took a few moments for that to sink into Demir's addled thoughts, and when it did he scrambled for his clothes. He was running out the tent flap a moment later, shouting at the line of messengers that tried to keep up. "You, tell the Third and the Eighth that we're switching to plan C. You, get me Halfwing. I need her artillery up and ready to fire. You, tell Coordinator-Lieutenant Prosotsi that I want all support staff to pull back two miles. Tad, how long do we have?"

Tadeas pushed a messenger out of his way to keep stride with Demir. "If she comes straight at us the way she did in the Copper Hills, three hours. But there's no telling what she's going to do. What's plan C?"

"You didn't read my orders?"

"You gave me sixty pages of orders to read at four in the morning. I didn't get past plan B."

"I hope the rest of our officers are more dedicated to winning this glass-damned battle. Plan C is we fall into a battle formation and present ourselves exactly like General Stavri did in the Copper Hills."

"I really hope that's a trap, and you're not just planning to do the same damned thing over again."

"Of course it's a trap." He stopped, swinging to grab Tadeas by the front of his uniform. For the first time in years his mind felt clear. Plans within plans within plans spread out across his mind's eye, and he wasn't even using witglass to access them. "Remember what I said the other day? About playing the Grent?"

"Yeah, you said you can play the Grent, but you can't play Kerite. We may outnumber her right now, but she's coming at us like a warhorse. She's got better troops, better godglass, and a record of never losing a battle."

"It's her legend. She's good, no doubt, maybe even the best, but it's her legend that keeps her going. It gets inside your head." He made a motion with one finger, like a drill going into his skull. "She's been studying me. She knows my record. She knows that I'm a broken genius, and she's going to expect damned grand things. What's the one thing she doesn't know?"

"That you've gone completely mad?" Tadeas asked lightly.

"She doesn't know what I've been doing for the last nine years. I *can* do this. I was the best grifter in the provinces, and what's a general but a glass-damned gambler trying to fix the fight?"

"Gambling with people's lives," Tadeas reminded him.

"Yeah, I know." Demir began to walk again. "She's going to come over that hill over there"—he pointed to the western horizon a couple of miles away—"and she's going to see us in exactly the same formation as she fought at the Copper Hills."

Understanding dawned on Tadeas's face. "And she'll think you're still broken. That you caved to the pressure of having to save Ossa, and the most creative thing you can think of is using our superior numbers against her rather than actual strategy. She'll think you're no better than General Stavri."

Demir nodded. "I don't want to spend the next four days dancing with her. I want her to come right for my throat so that I can punch her in the face with knuckle-dusters. I've already informed our officer corps that you're my second-in-command, Tadeas."

"I'm just a major."

"You're a blasted Grappo, Uncle, that has refused promotions on seven different occasions because you enjoy crawling through ditches with the Ironhorns more than taking command of large battles. Now find Halfwing. I need our artillery prepped and ready. I have three hours to make sure plan C is actually going to work on this terrain."

           ▸   ▸   ▸

In Demir's mind's eye, the formation of the Foreign Legion looked like an overelaborate rat trap. Seventeen battalions of infantry—almost nine thousand troops—lay spread out in loose rows across the farmland. There were few hills to use as cover, but his lone artillery battery squatted behind a stand of trees to his left, while two thousand dragoons and cuirassiers held back behind the low rise far to the right. It *felt* obvious, but most good traps did to whoever set them up. What mattered was what the enemy saw.

The entire army waited with bated breath. Nobody talked. The only movement came from a steady stream of messengers and short-range scouts, riding to and from the old barrow upon which Demir had planted the purple flag waving the Grappo silic sigil. Just below him, Tadeas kept up a constant dialog with those scouts and messengers. Demir watched the distant storm clouds over the Forge. He wondered if Thessa's test would work, and hoped the storm passed north of the battle.

Out across the countryside, difficult to see because of the wooded windbreaks between farms, Demir caught his first sight of the Drakes. First, a flag with three blue dragons on a field of green. Within minutes he could see columns of infantry marching in lockstep, sweeping down from the distant hill like a wave rolling lazily toward him. He snapped his fingers at the closest messenger.

"Signal to our cavalry to move to position number two."

Flag signals were exchanged, and he could hear—but not see—the rumble of cavalry as they shifted from their first hiding spot to their second.

The Drakes continued to approach, and Demir raised his looking glass to watch. They were an impressive lot. Their step was perfect, their uniforms were immaculate, their shouldered muskets with bayonets already fixed.

Their very presence oozed confidence. A single line of cavalry moved along their left flank. Demir counted in his head, tallying estimates at a glance.

"Signal our wings," he ordered, "tell them we're missing about eight hundred dragoons."

Tadeas finished with one of the scouts and climbed the barrow to stand beside Demir, gazing at the approaching army. "You really think she's going to come straight at us?"

Demir bit back a thousand little doubts. "If I say *of course* will I look like more of a genius if I succeed?"

"And more of a fool if you fail," his uncle responded.

"Yeah, but we'll all be dead. So it won't matter."

"Fair enough."

"Looks like she has two more battalions than our scouts reported," Demir said.

"A thousand infantry is a lot of firepower. Should we shift back our grenadiers?"

Demir glanced to his left and right. He'd placed a battalion of grenadiers— heavy infantry, with cuirassier-like breastplates and sword-bayonets on reinforced muskets—on his two flanks. "No. In fact let's signal for them to spread out just a little more. I want to look loose. Too loose."

His own troops adjusted per the signal, and across the field a trumpet was blown, and Kerite's mercenaries slowly ground to a halt. The two armies stared at each other from a distance of about a mile. Anxious whispering moved up and down the troops. Every experienced officer looking out across the divide could see that the Drakes remained in heavy columns. They looked sturdy and impenetrable compared to the more shallow rows of the Ossan Foreign Legion.

"Right about now," Demir said to Tadeas, "Kerite will figure out that I'm not using the traditional Ossan signal book. She's wondering what that's all about, and whether she should be concerned." He flinched. "I'm not happy about those missing cavalry. They could be glassdamned anywhere." All those doubts that he'd resisted mentioning to Tadeas swirled around in his head like so many annoying flies. He spat at them internally, bidding them to piss off.

"This whole damn thing is just a game," he said. "Kerite and I sitting here like a couple of old men on either side of a board of squares. We might as well drink wine in front of a fire. Hah! Maybe that's how wars should be fought in the future. Then all these poor bastards don't have to die. *Hey*

Kerite," he said, mimicking a politician's ingratiating drawl, "*take the patri-arch from my board and you can have Ossa. If I take yours, I can have Grent.* That sounds so much more civilized."

He was babbling and he knew it. Demir snapped his mouth shut and searched for a calming memory. The first that came to mind was a game, just like he'd been imagining, but it wasn't against some mercenary general—it was against his mother. He felt a smile tug on the corner of his mouth. "Do you remember how much Mother used to love Kings and Pawns?" he asked Tadeas.

His uncle scoffed. "Don't remind me."

"You never could beat her, could you?"

"I won a few games when we were young," Tadeas said, "but she just kept getting better and better and I didn't. Did you ever beat her?"

"Twice," Demir replied thoughtfully. "The first was when I was seventeen. The second was . . ." He trailed off. The second was just a few months ago, the last time they saw each other. She had demanded a game, and they'd made a bet—if she won, he'd return to Ossa with her and restart his career. If *he* won, she would never ask him to do so again. "I wish," he said quietly, "that I only won that once."

"She ever tell you about her other games?" Tadeas asked.

Demir shook his head. "She didn't like to boast."

"She often played against other Assembly members. I think she won four out of every five games against Father Vorcien, and nine out of ten against Aelia Dorlani."

"Glassdamn. I knew she was good, but . . . damn." Demir wondered where his old set was—the crystal pieces and silver board she gave him when he'd won election as governor. "Could anyone beat her?"

"Just one person."

"Who?"

"Your dad," Tadeas chuckled. "About half the time. Before you were born, I used to watch their games. I've never seen two players so evenly matched. They would play for hours and hours, and by the end all three of us would be so drunk that the hotel staff had to carry us to bed."

Demir tilted his head, listening to the nervous whispers of the soldiers lined up in front of him. "You know, nobody ever talks about my dad."

"It was . . ." Tadeas hesitated. ". . . painful for your mom to talk about him, or to listen to others talk."

"I'd like to hear more stories about them both," Demir said.

"I've got a few good ones."

"Then I have something to look forward to after this battle." The nervous whispers got louder, and all up and down Demir's lines soldiers shifted with a palpably anxious energy. No wonder. The last time they'd faced the Drakes they'd been overwhelmed in minutes. "Hold this," Demir said, handing his looking glass to Tadeas. He strode down from the barrow and through the rows of soldiers, slapping them on the back and shaking hands as he did.

"Chin up," he told one. "Legs squared," he said to another. "You look good. Damned good. Is that brooch at your neck for luck? I wish I had one myself." He reached the front of the formation, where he walked another ten yards out and turned back.

Thousands of eyes stared at him expectantly. He felt something inside of him wilt, his bowels shifting. He forced back his demons and threw his arms wide.

"Citizens! Friends! Companions-in-arms!" he shouted. "We are all that stands between our glittering city on the Tien and a pack of mercenary mongrels who wish to grind it to dust for a handful of banknotes and some glory to hang from their belts!" Only the breeze responded. Demir plowed on. "They say they are the best. You've read it in the newspapers, how the Drakes crushed you in the Copper Hills. How they'll do it again. And their commander? Far better than the broken, barely tested Demir Grappo.

"It's bullshit," Demir spat. "You are the Foreign Legion. You are the best of us. You are the Ironhorns, the Desert Rats, the Winged Jackals, the Mighty Lions! These mercenaries," Demir said, flinging his arm toward the enemy army behind him, "have fought on every continent. So have you! They've made themselves some money, but you have built an empire! You are the best soldiers from every corner of the world. You will not be laid low."

Demir felt tears streaming down his cheeks as flashes of a burning city rolled across his mind's eye. He wasn't sure whether it was the specter of Holikan or fears of what would happen to Ossa. Perhaps both. "We have all failed at times, but failure has not kept us down. We rebound stronger than before. My friends, prove yourselves to me and I swear to you that I will prove myself to you."

The silence was so heavy that Demir thought it might crush him. He let his arms fall and began to walk back to the barrow. As he entered the columns, he slowly became aware of a rattling sound. It was a low whisper, like rocks rolling down a distant ravine. Not a word was spoken, not a voice raised, yet all around him infantrymen shook their ammunition bags.

"What are they doing?" Demir asked Tadeas as he regained his commanding position.

Tadeas wore a lopsided smile. "You told them not to cheer or raise any sound of victory."

"Then what are they doing?"

"They're answering your call—this is a deal struck, Demir. We will all prove ourselves together."

Demir didn't bother to wipe the tears from his cheeks. They flowed freely, his whole body trembling. He took his looking glass back and raised it to his eye. "Kerite is watching," he told Tadeas. "Hesitating, looking for the trap. Perhaps she's waiting for her cavalry to get into position."

"There's not as much terrain here as there was at the Copper Hills. There's no position to get into."

Demir didn't answer. "Use a traditional signal to tell our left flank to hold steady." He waited another two minutes, watching that left flank. "Signal again. Make it look desperate." He waited. "One last time." Once the signal was sent, he could see the grenadiers over on that flank start to crumble. They broke ranks, the whole battalion seeming to shiver in fear and pull back.

"Demir," Tadeas warned, "they're breaking ranks."

"As they should."

"You're playing a dangerous game," Tadeas warned. "Layered orders are difficult to keep straight on the battlefield."

"They can do it," Demir assured. He prayed he was right. "I have spent the last week studying our own troops just as much as I have the enemy's. I know their exact capabilities—who can follow orders to a letter, who will buckle, who will rally. I know when to push and when to pull." As he spoke, his entire left flank began to crumble—the grenadiers were only the beginning, and the next battalion followed them, and then the next. He thought back to the cudgeling bets he'd made with Ulina Magna, and then to the note he'd sent to the various battalions on his flanks with the simple instruction that "hold steady" meant to do the exact opposite.

Across the way, the enemy army did not move. Tadeas swore. "She's not taking the bait. Dangling some uncertain troops in front of her isn't going to work. She's not going to bother attacking until we've *all* broken."

"She's not going to wait much longer," Demir answered. "Kerite might be the best, but she's also vain. She loves to be seen to be clever. She loves the glory. Chasing down a fleeing enemy will get her neither of those things. She's going to either take the bait or sense the trap and withdraw. I hope," he added under his breath. "Come on, Kerite. This is your chance to clobber the Foreign Legion *and* the Lightning Prince."

Demir felt all his senses straining, days' worth of plans balanced on a knife's edge. His heart began to fall. She wasn't going to take the bait. She'd sensed the trap, somehow outthought him.

"Sir!" someone shouted. "We have a cavalry charge coming from the south!"

"Perfect," he breathed, and across the way a hundred trumpets suddenly blared. Kerite's thick columns of infantry ground into motion, their heavy tramp stirring the air. Demir was once again struck by the uniform precision of it all; the tidal wave rolled forward. Could he break it?

"Did you know," he said sidelong to Tadeas, "that slingers of old could send a piece of lead shot over twelve hundred feet?"

Tadeas shook his head.

"Mika only got me eight hundred feet. Too much weight in the grenades. Too much wobble from the powder. But eight hundred will do." He snapped his fingers once more at a messenger. "Signal our left flank to restore cohesion." The signal was sent, and within thirty seconds the disorganized rabble of fleeing grenadiers firmed back into a soldier line, returning to their position. Demir half expected another trumpet call; for Kerite to withdraw her troops. It never came. She was committed now.

"Are you going to do anything about those cavalry?" Tadeas asked. "It wasn't in the notes you gave me for Plan C."

"Yes." Demir tilted his head to listen, and it wasn't long until the sudden roar of cannons split the morning. "I'm going to shoot them in the face with grapeshot from Halfwing's cannons hidden behind those trees." As if to accentuate his point, the screams of men and horses soon followed, a far more unsettling sound than the artillery fire that preceded it. Directly in front of them, Kerite's lines suddenly opened up and dozens of breachers raced forward, charging faster than horses, their swords raised.

"Slingers!" Demir shouted. His entire army, two whole brigades of infantry, knelt as one. The only people who remained standing were a few hundred engineers, whirling slings over their heads. "Loose!" he bellowed. Small grenades, looking tiny and fragile and insignificant, soared in a high arc up across the field. He followed them as black specks until they started to land. For a moment, nothing happened.

Then the explosions started, turning much of Kerite's line of breachers into a tangled mess of flesh and godglass.

"Ossa-ha!" someone shouted, their tenor voice carrying clear and steady in the echoing wake of the explosions. The infantry remained on their knees as the engineers spent the rest of their grenades, targeting lone breachers. "Ossa-ha!" the rest answered. "Ossa-ha! Ossa-ha! Ossa-ha!"

Demir turned to his uncle. "Now," he said, "we have a battle."

Kerite's infantry charged.

57

It was the second day of their search when Idrian's team got their first whiff of the flying glassdancer. Colonel Jorfax, riding just a little out front of the group, suddenly reined in her horse and raised a fist to the air. Idrian pulled up, his eyes immediately shooting to the sky, searching the low cloud cover for any sign of their quarry. All around him, pistols and carbines were produced, eyes raised, thirteen riders all tensed and watching, trying to pretend that they *weren't* watching. They were a lousy bunch of actors, and he hoped that the flying glassdancer didn't notice.

"Is he here?" Mika hissed.

Jorfax didn't move. She didn't even seem to breathe for several moments before she gave the tiniest shake of her head. "This way. Fifty yards." She turned and began to ride quickly, forcing the rest of them to catch up. The countryside here was mostly rolling farms butting up against coastal scrubland. Windbreaks—rows of hundred-year-old trees along country lanes— were frequent, and the landscape was dotted with small farmhouses. Jorfax followed one such windbreak, crossing a ditch and heading up a short drive to a country villa.

Idrian ground his teeth and gripped the pommel of his sword. Despite the cool winter air and the chilly weather, he was sweating continuously under the massive cloak that hid his armor. His sword and shield hung from his saddle, wrapped in loose canvas in an attempt to disguise their nature. breacher armor was not designed for horseback riding and every damn part of him chafed.

Bluffing, Tadeas had told him just before they left yesterday morning, requires patience and perseverance. Never break character until *after* the other person has called. You have to stay in their head to the last moment. Idrian wondered if his was the best advice to follow, considering how much he cheated at cards. But Idrian kept riding, and he kept his damn cloak on.

Even before they reached the decorative brick wall that surrounded the villa, Idrian could hear flies. The stench hit him next, and he had a pretty good idea what to expect by the time they came up to the little iron gate. Idrian glanced sidelong at Braileer, noting the stricken look in his eyes, then pointed to him and four of the soldiers accompanying them. "You five, form a perimeter. Eyes on the sky. Squeaks, search the house."

"Yes, sir."

He dismounted and followed Jorfax and Mika through the gate. The sight that greeted them was much as he expected—another damned massacre. Eleven soldiers, a scout guide, and one of Jorfax's glassdancers lay where they had fallen like a bomb had exploded in the middle of the group. They were shredded to pieces, their sticky blood covering practically every surface. At least two civilians had also been caught by the attack. They lay in the doorway, one of them still clutching the basket full of dates he was bringing the resting scouting party.

"Shit," Mika said.

"Do you recognize them?" Idrian asked Jorfax. "Is this one of the three other groups Demir left in his scouting rotation?"

"It is," Jorfax responded. She knelt over the lone glassdancer, studying the body intently. "His name was Lorstel. We called him Lucky because he's survived so many close calls. Not this one, it seems." She traced paths through the air with her fingers in several directions. Idrian walked over to kneel across from her, studying her face as she worked. He thought he could see a crack in that steely visage. Concern? Fear? She finally spoke again. "This winged glassdancer is damned good. He exploded Lucky's glassdancer egg in his pocket. Looks like the initial blast killed . . ." She stood, walking around the perimeter of the massacre, her lips moving as she traced more paths. "He killed Lucky and these four with that first attack, then cut up the rest. They all would have died within ten or fifteen seconds."

"Having second thoughts?" Mika asked.

Jorfax jerked her head toward the engineer. "Are you?" she snapped.

"Not at all," Mika responded. If she was cowed by Jorfax's famous cold stare, she didn't show it. She held one of her ram's-horn grenades, tossing it up and down, and smiled back at Jorfax. "I just see evidence of something that needs to die."

"Then we're agreed."

Idrian stepped between them. Jorfax's prickly nature had clashed with everyone over the last twenty-four hours. She did not play well with others.

At least she'd kept her promise not to pull rank. "We're all agreed," he assured them both. He turned to Jorfax. "Can you keep him from doing that to you? With the egg, I mean."

"She's carrying a grenade in her pocket and someone else has the fuse," Mika said.

Idrian gestured for Mika to shut up, but Jorfax seemed to relax. "No, she's right. That's exactly what's happening here. I told Lucky to keep his sorcerous attention on the sky. Maybe he did. Maybe he didn't. If I keep my glassdancer egg on me and the flying glassdancer is significantly stronger than me, I'll be dead before any of you even notice. You'll follow quickly."

"Should you leave your glassdancer egg behind?" Idrian asked. He was fully aware that it was the equivalent of someone telling him to go into battle naked and unarmed, and he could see a vein throb on Jorfax's forehead.

"No," she finally said. "I'm stronger than Lucky was. I'll sense an attack from farther out."

Mika pulled a face behind Jorfax's back, but Idrian just shook his head. He wasn't going to press the issue. Jorfax was the professional. Much of her terrifying reputation came from the fact that she was so good at what she did.

"Sir," Braileer called. Idrian turned to see the armorer come in through the gate. Braileer paused at the sight, his body rocking from the center like he was holding in a dry heave. A moment passed, his face turning green, before he got a grip on himself. "Their horses are around back. Spooked but untouched." He swallowed hard, averting his eyes from the bodies. "We should send someone to bring them in."

Squeaks emerged from inside the villa, shaking her head. "There are a couple of laborers dead underneath the kitchen table. Seems like they tried to hide. The thing that did this was thorough about witnesses."

"Prudent, too," Idrian mused out loud. "Didn't try to overextend at Fort Alameda, but no compunction against slaughtering people at an isolated farmstead." He gazed across the corpses, studying them clinically. He was no surgeon, but he'd seen a lot of battlefields in his day. "I'd guess this happened about two hours ago. Do we think he's still in the vicinity? Or moved on?"

"He could be anywhere with this low cloud cover," Jorfax responded. "I'll sense him before any of us sees him. We have no idea how fast he travels. Does he glide like a swan or dive like a falcon?"

"Or both," Mika added.

With that pleasant thought fresh in their minds, the group remounted and returned to the road. Idrian barely thought about his sore ass or his chafing armor. He set his helmet on his saddlehorn, covering it with the hem of his cloak, and tried not to look like he was staring at the sky.

"The low cloud cover works both ways," he said over his shoulder. "We can't see him, but he can't see us either."

"You think it's a him?" Braileer asked. The armorer rode up next to Idrian. His head was high, but Idrian could see some red around his eyes. He wondered if he shouldn't have left him behind. This was no mission for a kid. He snorted inwardly. Was any military mission for a kid?

"Smelled like a him," Idrian responded.

"Is it even human?" Mika asked.

"What else would it be?" Jorfax reclaimed her spot at the head of their little column. "Fearglass can twist the mind. Why not godglass that can twist the body? All the guild-families experiment at length with sorcery. The Grent government is no exception."

"But this flying glassdancer only appeared when Kerite's mercenaries entered the war," Squeaks pointed out.

"Then it's Purnian. Or Marnish. Or Nasuud. The Drakes fight all over the world. Who knows what dark glassworks Kerite might have found, filled with experiments?"

Idrian scowled at the thought. Godglass that could completely change how a person looked? How their body worked? "It's intelligent," he said, "but it moved like an animal. Sleek and graceful. I just hope it's not . . ." He trailed off as a distant sound reached his ears, and he tugged slightly on the reins to bring his horse to a stop. "You hear that?"

They all paused, tilting their heads. It was a distant popping sound, one that might easily be mistaken for fireworks. "Those are my new grenades," Mika said, perking up.

Idrian inhaled sharply and looked at Jorfax. "The pissing Grent must have turned toward Demir instead of retreating back to the city. They've joined battle."

"And we're out here riding in circles instead of fighting," Jorfax growled.

Idrian wasn't going to pretend that he was the commanding officer anymore. Jorfax outranked him, and she'd be even more use than himself on the actual battlefield. "Make the call," he told her.

She hesitated, glancing over her shoulder back toward the massacre at the farmstead. She seemed to waffle for several moments, then swore. "We need to ride. That battle is more decisive than one flying glassdancer." She jerked on the reins, turning to their south, and then suddenly stiffened.

Idrian was already turned around when he noticed that her eyes had gone wide, her jaw tight. "Tilly?"

"He's here," she hissed.

The entire group reacted as one, snatching up weapons and casting their eyes to the sky. Idrian's heart skipped a beat and he signaled for them to hunker low in the saddle. Beside him, Mika loaded a grenade into a sling. Idrian asked, "Where?"

"Just above us. He's high, circling."

"Does he know you've spotted him?"

"I am being very careful not to turn my senses directly toward him." Her hand hovered over the pocket that bulged with her glassdancer egg.

"Everyone keep riding," Idrian ordered. "Slowly. Keep those carbines down. Braileer, stay behind me. Make no move unless it goes for my back. Understand?"

"Yes, sir."

Idrian lifted his helmet, wrapping his reins around the saddlehorn, raising his eyes without raising his head. He could see nothing in the gray-white clouds and it infuriated him. Every second seemed to tick by longer than the last. "Is he still there?" he asked Jorfax.

"Still circling. He hasn't tried to use my egg against me. Yet."

"How close will he have to be?"

"Based on his power? Hard to tell."

"As long as he comes below the clouds we should be able to drive him to the ground." He glanced around at his companions. "Do *not* open fire until he dips down to attack. The grenades will keep it down, and I'll finish it on foot. Understood?" A round of nods answered him. He split his attention between the sky and Jorfax, watching for any twitch that might betray that she'd been bested in a contest of sorcerous will. To their south, the report of cannon fire joined the pop of grenades.

Jorfax suddenly relaxed. "He's pulling up," she said. "Glassdamnit. Keep your eyes open, he might . . ." She stiffened again immediately, her hand shooting to her glassdancer egg. She let out a strangled "He's coming!"

Idrian did not wait for more of a signal. With one hand he slammed his helmet on his head. With the other he threw the wrappings from his sword and shield, ripping them from the bindings that held them to the saddle. "Wait for it!" he shouted.

He didn't get out another word before a black arrow seemed to shoot from the clouds—the flying glassdancer, wings tucked back, diving like a bird of prey. It hit Jorfax's horse hard enough to throw both animal and rider, and all three went tumbling off the road and into the field. The flying glass-dancer was up again, leaping for the sky.

"Fire!" Idrian shouted.

A line of carbine fire erupted from the group, tearing through the crea-ture's massive wings. It hissed and howled, spinning in the air and land-ing on its feet. Black blood oozed from bullet wounds. It seemed annoyed rather than truly injured, and it stared at them all for several moments as a dozen trembling hands tried to reload carbines.

Idrian leapt from his horse, half an eye on the creature and half an eye on Jorfax. She lay beneath her dead horse, her teeth bared and her eyes full of fear. "Kill it!" she snapped. "Before it takes my egg! Ahhhhh!" Her scream reached a fever pitch and the glassdancer egg suddenly tore from her jacket, shattering into dozens of pieces as it shot straight for Idrian. He threw his shield up, listening to pieces slam against the hammerglass. Be-hind him, voices cried out in terror and then pain.

He didn't have the time to see who'd been hit. He leapt forward, guard held close, forcing the creature to dodge his blows, hoping that the action threw off its glassdancer timing. Its wings twitched and moved like second limbs, darting forward to slam into Idrian's shield or bash aside a thrust of his sword. Idrian pressed his attack, unwilling to give it even a moment to reorient itself, forcing it back step by step until it suddenly turned and sprinted.

A smattering of carbine fire caught the beast from the side. It rolled, skidded across the furrows of the fallow field, then changed direction once more, leaping for the closest soldier. It reached the poor woman as Idrian turned to follow, its wings hitting her with enough force to shatter her carbine and toss her dozens of feet. Idrian followed the creature's path, adjusting his own, pushing himself to try and reach it before it could get airborne. His eyes widened in horror.

"Braileer, out of the way!"

It was too late. The creature charged through two more soldiers, batted Squeaks to one side, and then snatched Braileer by his hammerglass buck-ler as it leapt into the air. Idrian continued to pursue, watching helplessly as it squeezed Braileer by the neck. A grenade exploded immediately above the creature. The blast drove it down, forcing it to dive. Idrian discarded his shield, taking his sword over his head in both hands, and leapt. The razorglass swept down, cleaving through bone and sinew in a spray of black blood.

The creature screamed and tossed Braileer. The armorer hit the ground at speed, a rolling, limp mess of limbs. The winged glassdancer hit just after him. It skipped across the dirt like a rock across water. Idrian charged, but the thing leapt back into the air, clearly struggling to fly. Another grenade exploded beside it, but it beat hard at the air, shooting up. Within moments it was gone, disappeared into the low clouds.

Idrian stared after it, gasping for breath, sword held at the ready. The seconds ticked by as he waited for it to return, but the next sound he heard was a gasp of pain from Jorfax.

"Bloody thing has fled," Jorfax called. "Now come get this horse off me!"

Idrian lowered his sword, sweeping his gaze across his team. Mika stood nearby with her legs set, her sling at the ready, Squeaks shakily getting to her feet just behind her. Half the soldiers were down. Idrian's eyes landed on Braileer. The armorer was a dirty mess; an unmoving lump.

"Mika," Idrian called, "help Jorfax!" He hurried toward Braileer, cursing at the sky as he did.

58

The Zorlian Mansion was one of the most famous buildings in Ossa. It was once the seat of the Zorlian guild-family, a powerful and respected group that at their height owned almost a quarter of the city. For generations, every new Zorlian matriarch or patriarch had added a new wing to the mansion, building it out across their country estate in an attempt to leave their own mark on a rich, bloated guild-family.

At some point—the history was foggy to Kizzie—the Zorlian splintered and collapsed. Dozens of family members committed suicide, while the rest changed their names or left the country. In less than a generation the guild-family was no more, leaving behind dozens of bankrupt businesses, thousands of acres of empty land, and the mansion itself—a mighty testament to greed and overreach. No one wanted it. No one even cared for the barren hunting grounds upon which it sat.

Kizzie and Montego arrived in the late morning, taking their carriage up the long gravel drive several miles west of the city borders. It was an overcast day, the erratic breeze cold and humid, as if a storm was sweeping in from the north. Montego drove, while Kizzie sat in the carriage, hugging herself against the weather, staring out into the overgrown, tangled forest that surrounded the mansion. She remembered coming here once as a kid, though she couldn't remember with whom—her half sisters, perhaps—and the small group hadn't gotten more than halfway up the drive before getting too spooked and turning back.

Montego did not turn back, and Kizzie watched carefully as they rolled over a hill, down through a gully, and around a massive embankment. The gravel hadn't been replaced in decades and was mostly overgrown with grass, but it was obvious the drive was in use. Wheel ruts were well-worn through the grass, fallen branches were cleared away, and the bridge at the bottom of the gully had been recently repaired.

Someone was using the mansion.

They came around the embankment and Kizzie got her first good look at the mansion: a glimpse across a massive, overgrown field. Someone had once described it to her as so big that its footprint was measured in acres rather than square feet. "Sprawling" was the only word she could use to describe it, and even that seemed inadequate. The crumbling facade, three stories high, stretched so far in either direction that it disappeared into the forest. It was patchwork and ugly, the extensions done in clashing styles that made her eyes hurt, and she'd never had the slightest eye for architecture. The windows, most of them broken, had heavy bars on them.

Her attention was drawn away from the house itself and to the terminus of the drive. A dozen carriages were parked outside the front door. Some of them even had horses already waiting, as if departure was imminent, and a half dozen workers in dirty tunics were attending to them. They all seemed to stop what they were doing and stare toward Kizzie's approaching carriage, and the feeling of disquiet in her belly grew stronger.

They should have come with an army—fifty Vorcien and Grappo enforcers at their backs—but Montego insisted on immediate action so they didn't give Aristanes the chance to flee. Montego's presence did give Kizzie a sense of invincibility, but even so she checked both her stilettos and the sword at her belt, then made certain the pistol she carried was still loaded. They came to a stop and the carriage rocked as Montego leapt down, opening the door with his back to the workers.

She studied them over his shoulder. Four men. Two women. They looked much like the caretakers of any great estate, but it was their unblinking stare that unsettled her. None of them were openly armed, but one of them slowly reached for a cudgel sitting next to a carriage.

With his back still to them, Montego reached into his pocket and produced a piece of forgeglass. "Take this," he said, "and use it in an emergency."

Simply touching it caused Kizzie's heart to skip from the powerful sorcery that emanated from it. It was hot, the sorcery seeming to sizzle if she listened carefully. "That's high-resonance," she said, keeping it out of sight of the workers. "That's worth twice my yearly salary."

"It'll also give you glassrot in roughly fourteen minutes," Montego said. "Shouldn't you have it?"

"It would only slow me down. It triggers my allergy too quickly." Montego nodded for her to put it away. She did, and let her eyes travel over the workers once more. Her gaze settled on the right hand of one of the men.

She expected a silic sigil of some kind, or perhaps some client paint on his little finger. Instead, there was just one tiny tattoo: a knife with a pink razorglass blade.

"Did you see the tattoos they have on their hands?" she asked.

Montego nodded. "The Glass Knife. Seems we came to the right place."

"Oi!" It was the man who'd reached for his cudgel. He smacked it against his palm and then pointed it toward them. "This is private property."

"No sign of soldiers or enforcers," Kizzie whispered. "But this bastard won't be undefended. Stay on guard." Louder she called, "We're here to see Aristanes!" Kizzie climbed out of the carriage to stand next to Montego. They made, she imagined, an odd pair, considering the difference in size and dress. Montego fixed the same pleasant smile onto his face that he'd worn having a drink at that pub last night, watching gawkers pass by. He held his cane in one hand but was carrying nothing else. It was all he'd need, he'd told her earlier.

The worker glanced at his comrades uncertainly. "Do you have an appointment?"

"No."

"Then you'll have to leave and come back when you do. The master doesn't like unknown visitors."

"My name," Montego said, drawing himself up, "is Baby Montego. There, I am not unknown to you anymore. Now tell me where to find your master." Montego began to walk toward the door. Kizzie was more than content to let him take the lead, and she fell back behind him, watching the rest of the workers carefully. They didn't have the army she wanted, but they did have the element of surprise. It would have to be enough.

At a nod from their leader, two of them bolted. One of them ran inside, while the other followed the facade of the house, glancing over her shoulder at them occasionally as she sprinted through the overgrown flower gardens. The other four put themselves firmly in Montego's path.

"You have to wait," the leader said, throwing his arms wide. To his credit, he seemed to know exactly how stupid he was being. His eyes were wide, his face pale. "We'll let the master know you're here. Just . . . wait!"

Montego did not slow, and neither did Kizzie. They'd almost reached the front door when it opened and a figure appeared on the threshold. He was an older man, probably in his mid-fifties, with the olive skin of a native Ossan and short black hair. His black goatee was sharply trimmed, his eyes were piercing brown, and a small smile was on his lips. "It's all right, Joss. I'll take care of our guests. Come in, please."

The workers dispersed, and Kizzie and Montego were beckoned into the foyer. It was a massive hall, bigger than any entry she'd seen in dozens of guild-family estates, with a three-story ceiling and a grand staircase that went up to the left and right. The size was all that was left of the grandeur, however. The marble floors were cracked, the banisters broken, and the once-fabulous chandelier with its gas lines and sparkling hammerglass shards looked like it might fall at any moment.

"I am Aristanes's majordomo," the man introduced himself. "The master does not usually receive guests without an appointment, but I imagine he will make an exception for Baby Montego and Kizzie Vorcien."

Kizzie felt every muscle in her body tense at once. She was wearing gloves to cover her silic sigil, and her face was not well-known enough to be recognized. So much for the element of surprise. "I did not give my name."

The majordomo smiled. "And yet you are known to us. Please, come with me." He began to walk briskly, forcing them to follow or be left behind. Kizzie let one hand rest on the pommel of her sword, the other on her pistol, as she did.

"Us," Montego rumbled. "You mean the Glass Knife."

The majordomo simply replied with a polite little laugh, as if Montego had told him a distasteful joke. Kizzie didn't know how to read that. She said, "Then you know why we are here?"

"I imagine I do."

Kizzie shared a glance with Montego, not bothering to hide her growing alarm. Who *were* these people? If they knew who Montego was, and why they were here, then why was this majordomo leading them to his master? Was she wrong? Was this a trap? Or perhaps the majordomo was leading them *away* while the master escaped? Either way, there was going to be blood at the end of this walk and she didn't want it to be hers. She should have insisted on that army.

Montego gave her a reassuring nod, gripping his cane in one hand and holding his other off to one side, as if ready to grapple with anyone who might assault them.

The majordomo continued to smile as he led them farther into the mansion. Kizzie was, despite paying rather close attention, immediately lost. Within a hundred paces they'd taken six turns and emerged into one long, massive hallway that they followed for another hundred paces. The place was a damned maze, with bridges that passed overhead without connecting the floors, staircases that seemed to lead nowhere. They passed by a glass room with a gymnasium, lit by massive skylights.

Despite there being very little debris—the floors appeared to be swept regularly—everywhere Kizzie looked was touched with decay. Brick crumbled, marble was cracked, plaster had long since yellowed and leaked. Murals on the walls were faded with age, and the few remaining rugs were threadbare.

"I was told Aristanes was a foreign priest," Kizzie said.

"He is a priest of Horuthe," the majordomo said, "a prominent Purnian death god. Do you know of him?"

The name touched a memory, as if Kizzie might have seen it in a shrine in an omnichapel long ago. "I don't."

"Horuthe is a good god," the majordomo said. "A generous god. I suggest you light a candle to him the next time you pray."

"If we do not find Aristanes in the next few minutes," Montego said pleasantly, "you will find out whether your god is generous or not."

"Oh, Master Montego," the majordomo replied, his tone still light and friendly, "it won't be so long. Please be patient."

Kizzie slowly grew aware that they weren't alone. They were being followed, and watched. Faces peeked out from cracked doors, and occasionally the patter of footsteps came to her from the ends of long corridors. Somewhere in the distance, she heard a door slam. Her mouth grew dry, and that feeling that they were being distracted only deepened.

Finally, Kizzie stopped in the middle of a hallway, reaching out to touch Montego's sleeve as she did. He paused with her, glancing between her and the majordomo. It took their guide several steps before he seemed to realize that they were no longer following.

"You're Aristanes," Kizzie accused.

The man grinned at her and opened a door. "Please, step into my office. I imagine you have a lot of questions." He went inside without answering her. Kizzie held out a hand to keep Montego where he was and proceeded forward to the door, where she glanced inside. It was, much to her surprise, a standard guild-family office. It had a vaulted ceiling, expansive bookshelves, a massive oak desk, and behind the desk one of those big fireplaces that you could walk inside without ducking. There was no fire going but the office was definitely in use and had been, it seemed, repaired while the rest of the house remained a ruin.

There was no one waiting to ambush them. She nodded to Montego, and the two entered, leaving the door open behind them. "So you are Aristanes."

"I am."

"You don't seem scared for your life."

Aristanes gave them a patronizing smile and went to stand behind the desk. "Refreshment?" he asked.

Kizzie examined the room more closely, looking for the sorts of traps one might find in a penny novel—poison darts, trapdoors with spikes at the bottom, suspicious candlesticks. Nothing seemed out of the ordinary. Montego stood in the center of the room, gripping his cane in both hands, staring at Aristanes with those beady, violent eyes. Kizzie wondered idly if this clever old priest knew just how close to violence Montego was.

Kizzie gave up her search and went to stand beside Montego. If this bastard thought he was so clever, so be it. It was time for trial, and all parts would be carried out by her and Montego. She reached into her pocket, ready to produce Demir's shackleglass if necessary. "Did you arrange the murder of Adriana Grappo?" she asked.

"I did." The answer was without hesitation or malice.

Kizzie inhaled sharply. "Why?" Beside her, Montego's knuckles grew white on his cane.

"Adriana and I had a deal," Aristanes said, spreading his arms. "She broke that deal, and so she had to be punished. It was nothing personal, I hope you realize."

"What happens next *will* be personal," Montego rumbled, taking a step forward.

Aristanes held up one hand. "Come now. You came all this way for answers and you won't wait for any?"

It did not take a genius to realize that Aristanes was stalling. But what for? Even if he had hundreds of acolytes in this mansion—which he might—they wouldn't save him from Montego's wrath. Kizzie let her curiosity get the better of her. "You said the two of you had a deal?"

"Indeed we did. Our deal was simple: she would not interfere with the Glass Knife, and the Glass Knife would not interfere with the Grappo. It was a good deal, considering how large and powerful the Glass Knife is. Similar to the deal my servant offered you at the watchhouse earlier this week."

The memory of Gorian's dead body surrounded by dead National Guards-men caused Kizzie's anger to flare. "The Glass Knife," she spat. "A criminal organization masquerading as a Fulgurist Society."

"Calling us a criminal organization is a little demeaning," Aristanes re-plied, looking truly hurt. "The Glass Knife is a social club, just like any other. We just have bigger dreams."

"Oh yeah?" Kizzie asked. "What kind of dreams?"

"Fomenting wars. Speeding economic collapse. Bringing down empires." Aristanes gave her what might have seemed a cheeky smile in other circum-stances. In the moment, it was supremely sinister.

"You killed Adriana to start the war with Grent?" Kizzie found breath-ing difficult, her chest tight.

"Oh, we would have started the war anyway. It's the best way to destabi-lize a region, after all. Adriana died because she broke our deal, like I said. I just used her death to further my goals."

"How," Montego rumbled angrily, "did she break your deal?"

Aristanes considered the question for several moments. He still wore that cheeky smile, as if his death wasn't imminent. "She promised not to inter-fere, and then she went looking for monsters."

"What monsters?" Kizzie demanded.

"Monsters like me"—Aristanes grinned—"and monsters like him." He pointed.

Kizzie whirled, and in the doorway behind them stood the Tall Man. He looked much the same as he had days ago in the watchhouse, wearing what might have been the same clothes, and when he stepped into the room he had to duck. Kizzie did not wait for him to take a second step. She drew her pistol and shot him in the face.

Several things happened at once. The blast of the pistol was deafening, immediately filling the room with black smoke. The Tall Man's head jerked back, and in the time it took for Kizzie to turn back to Aristanes, the priest slammed his fist down on his desk and then . . . vanished.

"He dropped through a trapdoor!" Kizzie swore, leaping over his desk just in time to see a hinged piece of marble spring back into place, closing just beneath where Aristanes had been standing. Even having gotten a glimpse of it, she could barely see the outline of the trapdoor. She slammed her fist onto the desk, trying to replicate whatever mechanism had al-lowed him to escape. Nothing happened.

Montego came around and threw himself to his knees, prying around the edges with his fingernails, then slamming his cane against the marble flooring. "Glassdamnit," he swore loudly, "come, he'll be somewhere on the grounds still! We can . . ."

Both of them saw it at the same time. The Tall Man, whom Kizzie had *definitely* just shot in the face, had not fallen. Instead he stood with his hands braced on the doorframe, his head tilted backward. Slowly, his head came forward, to reveal the bullet embedded in his cheek. It had torn away a massive piece of skin, but his blood was black as tar, tinged with yellow bile, oozing from gray flesh.

"We tried to be reasonable," the Tall Man said. With that, he gripped a flap of torn skin and *pulled.* It came away like sunburnt skin, stretching and translucent, gray flesh popping out behind it like a fat man undoing his corset. A tentacle, ribbed and wiggling, flopped out, then another, until half his face had been peeled away to reveal a dozen of the thrashing appendages framed around a gray, beast-like chin like some sort of beard.

Kizzie didn't have the wherewithal to consider the horror of it. She backed into a corner, trying to reload her pistol with trembling fingers. Montego gave a bellow and hurled himself across the desk, swinging his cane with blinding speed.

The Tall Man *caught* it.

Montego's left fist connected with the Tall Man's stomach. The Tall Man gave a grunt, staggered back, and managed to catch Montego's second blow. Arms locked in a contest of impossible strength, Montego pushed him out of the doorway. Kizzie took the opportunity to flee, getting out of the now-claustrophobic office and into the hallway, where she might maneuver. Giving up on reloading her pistol, she drew her sword.

Montego smashed his forehead against the Tall Man's now-tentacled face once, twice, then a third time before the latter finally jerked backward and retreated several feet. He spat and swore, the intent of the words clear despite coming out in some garbled language that Kizzie did not know. The Tall Man looked like a cadaver now, his head oversized and bloated, flaps of skin hanging off. Giving a bestial bellow, he grabbed a flap of skin in each hand and pulled. More gray flesh spilled out, then two more arms, stretching and flailing like they'd been trapped inside their human vessel for too long. Kizzie suppressed the urge to vomit.

Montego backed away from him, holding his cane up like a holy symbol. Kizzie caught his eye.

"Run," she said.

59

Thessa would have thought she'd grown beyond shock. So much had happened in the last few weeks—the attack on the glassworks, the rescue from the labor camp, Kastora's death, Axio's murder, the riot. Even growing intertwined with a guild-family patriarch she hardly knew. It was a lifetime of adventure, one that should have inoculated her against wild reversals of fortune.

And yet it didn't.

She sat next to the fire in the lighthouse, listening to the now-steady rumble of thunder all around them. Her hands were bound behind her back, and Captain Hellonian of Kerite's Drakes stood just above her, warming his hands by the flames. He wore a pleasant smile, chatting amiably to the two other dragoons with them, barely noticing the prisoners at their feet. Pari and Tirana sat similarly bound against the far wall. Tirana's head bled steadily from a wound taken in the scuffle at the barricade, but she glared up at Hellonian with a righteous fury that Thessa tried to draw strength from.

"How did you turn our enforcers?" she demanded. "How did you turn so many? Was it money? Blackmail? Talk, damn it!"

She'd been asking the same questions for the last few hours. No one answered. No one even acknowledged that she was making noise. Thessa stared at her knees, grappling with her own fury. Of the original thirty-six enforcers that had accompanied them, twelve had turned at Breenen's signal. The surprise of their betrayal was more than enough for the brief battle they waged. At least twenty bodies from both sides littered the barricades outside, left where they lay. The rest of the loyal enforcers, most of them badly wounded, sat under guard just outside the lighthouse.

But Thessa's fury wasn't for Tirana's dead friends. It was for her phoenix channel. It sat dormant just a few feet from her, still connected to the copper cables. Thunder seemed to pass on either side of them but there still hadn't been a single lightning strike. Did it matter at this point? The phoenix channel was no longer hers. It belonged to these dragoons and their mercenary master.

And to *him*. Thessa felt her eyes narrow as Breenen entered the lighthouse. Let Tirana rail at the soldier. Thessa wanted to shove Breenen off the side of the Forge and laugh while he fell. The old concierge paused just inside, glancing at them briefly, before moving over beside Captain Hellonian.

"And you!" Tirana barked, turning her attention to Breenen. "How could you do this? You've betrayed your employees, your master, your friends. These people *depended* on you!"

While the tirade seemed to slide off Hellonian like rain off a turtle's shell, Breenen flinched. "I warned you, Tirana. If you want to get out of this alive, you'll shut your mouth."

"You think I *care* about that? You think I trust anything you say? You're a traitor and a . . ." One of the dragoons suddenly broke away from the fire and crossed the room, kicking Tirana hard in the stomach. She doubled over, gasping.

"You didn't have to do that," Breenen snapped at the dragoon.

"*You* didn't do it," the dragoon said casually.

"Keep your soldiers in line," Breenen demanded of Captain Hellonian.

The captain just shrugged. "The sound *was* getting annoying."

"Then let's get out of this place," Breenen said. "We have the phoenix channel, we have the siliceer. Let's take them both. Leave the rest for Demir to find."

"How will he find anything when he's dead?" Hellonian scowled around the room, then searched his pockets. He drew out a pre-rolled cigarette and stuck it in the coals around the base of the fire before puffing it to life. "General Kerite engages him as we speak. She'll turn his army to mincemeat. She can decide what to do with the rest of these tonight." He gestured lazily at Pari and Tirana.

"I have a deal with your masters," Breenen growled. "I hand the phoenix channel over to the Glass Knife, and in return the Grappo remain unmolested. Kerite is bound by the terms of the deal just like the rest of your damned organization."

Hellonian raised his hands in a calming gesture. "I'm not privy to the details. If Kerite has promised to spare Demir, then she'll spare him. I've already sent a messenger to tell her we've captured the mechanism."

Thessa swallowed hard. What did a mercenary general want with her? Or the phoenix channel? And who was the Glass Knife they spoke of? "Shouldn't you be out there helping her win the battle?" she asked.

Hellonian glanced down at her, flashing her what in other circumstances might have been a charming smile. "We were set aside specifically for this purpose," he said. "The Purnian Dragon plans everything out perfectly. If she says she doesn't need an extra hundred dragoons to win the battle, then she doesn't."

"And you think she can beat Demir?"

Hellonian rolled his eyes. "Of course she can. She's faced greater odds against greater foes and always comes out on top. You, my silic friend, will have the pleasure of meeting her before the night is out."

"Why?" Thessa demanded. "Why does she care about any of this?"

"Even Kerite reports to a greater master, and that master has not given me the specifics," Hellonian replied. "I just follow my lady's orders." He turned his gaze back to Breenen. "The Glass Knife would like to know whether the phoenix channel actually works before we proceed. So we stay here until Kerite arrives, or until we conduct a test. Nothing else is needed, correct? We just wait for a lightning strike?" The question was directed at Thessa. She turned her face away from him. Why give him the satisfaction of cooperation? Why say anything at all? She wondered how long she could keep any amount of stubbornness. How long until she was just too tired of all this maneuvering and backstabbing?

As she looked across the room, her eyes fell on the phoenix channel. It was secured by nothing more than the copper cables—lightning rod and grounding cable. How hard would it be to unhook it, drag it outside, and throw it off the Forge? The thought began to percolate, and she turned back to Hellonian. "Give me a cigarette," she said.

He raised his eyebrows. "Is that the price of a little courteousness?" he asked.

"Yes."

"Then I gladly pay it." He drew another cigarette from his pocket, lighting it on the first and then putting it between her lips.

Thessa drew in, tasting the tar on her tongue. She exhaled through her nose. "Yes," she told him out of the corner of her mouth, "nothing else needs to be done to prepare the phoenix channel."

"Do not," Tirana said between clenched teeth, "tell him anything else."

"Oh, come now. We've won, you've lost. It's time to move on." Hellonian grinned at all three of his prisoners. "The Glass Knife is not without mercy. I won't pretend to know the minds of my betters, but I imagine that by the end of the week you'll be working for them. It's really the easiest way." He then patted Thessa patronizingly on the head. "Enjoy that cigarette, Lady Siliceer." Thessa resisted the urge to bite his hand.

The door to the lighthouse opened once more, a drenched dragoon wearing an overcoat sticking his head inside. "Captain! There's a break in the clouds just now over to the southeast. If you bring your looking glass you'll see the battle!"

"How does it look?"

"Impossible to say at this point."

Hellonian flicked his cigarette into the fire. "Keep an eye on them," he told the other two dragoons, then strode out after his underling. Thessa leaned back on her haunches, careful to keep her own cigarette clenched between her lips. The other two dragoons walked to the door and opened it, leaning against the doorframe as they made bets on how many casualties the nearby battle would produce. Breenen sat at the little window overlooking the ocean, staring into the distance.

Thessa caught Pari's eye, jerking her head slightly at Tirana. Pari's eyes narrowed. She elbowed the master-at-arms. Tirana's head came up. Thessa looked at Pari, then at Tirana, then glanced significantly at the two dragoons. She hoped the message got across. "Breenen," Thessa said, shifting around until she could get one foot underneath her.

"Save your breath," Breenen said. "If you plan to rail like Tirana, you can do it later."

Thessa hauled herself up, wobbled, almost lost her cigarette, then turned to face Breenen. "No," she said out of the corner of her mouth. "You have so much to answer for."

He finally glanced toward her. "Sit down, Thessa."

"I won't sit until you talk!" If the dragoons at the door cared that Thessa was on her feet, they didn't show it. Thessa continued, "Look at me! I want you to look me in the eye, face-to-face, and tell me why you betrayed Demir. You were like a father to him. He trusted you more than anyone else. How could you do it?" As she spoke, she edged around the phoenix channel until she was standing between it and Breenen. She reached back, feeling along the tin casing with her bound fingers.

Breenen let out a sigh and stood up. "You're a Grent siliceer," he grunted. "A nobody. I don't have to answer to you."

"Then what about Tirana? Or all those murdered and wounded enforcers out there? What about Adriana?" Breenen flinched. There it was. The nerve Thessa was looking for. "Did you betray her, too? Were you one of those six who bludgeoned her to death on the steps of the Assembly?"

Breenen's calm, tired demeanor turned steely. "Do you remember the conversation we had a few days ago? When you asked me about my legacy?"

"Of course. You said yours would be about survival."

"And I wasn't lying." Breenen glanced sadly toward the door. "I spent years helping Adriana root out the Glass Knife. I even infiltrated them myself for a time. All our plans—all the work we put in—only resulted in getting Adriana killed. You can't fight people as powerful as them. The best you can do is make a deal with them. Handing them you and the phoenix channel is the only way to secure Demir's future. History will forget both you and me, but I've given Demir the chance to make sure it doesn't forget the Grappo."

"Those sound like the words of a coward," Tirana snapped.

"Perhaps. But you haven't seen what I have. You don't know what I know."

"Then tell us," Thessa urged. "Tell Demir. Who is this Glass Knife? Why haven't you mentioned them before, especially if you knew they killed Adriana?"

"I didn't mention them because Demir is a child; fragile, volatile." He turned to Tirana. "You saw what he did when he found out the news about Capric. All his rage would just destroy the Grappo at the hands of enemies that none of us can truly comprehend."

Thessa's fingers found the coupling at the end of the phoenix channel. She fiddled with it as subtly as she could, searching for the clasp until she found it. "How can we trust anything you're saying? You've betrayed us. You've betrayed Demir. Did you betray Adriana too? Was it *you* that got her killed?"

"Careful what you say next." Heat finally entered Breenen's words.

"I bet you *were* one of those conspirators who bludgeoned her to death," Thessa spat, fixing her fingers on the coupling clasp.

The dig had the desired effect: Breenen suddenly leapt across the room, grabbing Thessa tightly by the chin, causing her heart to skip a beat. "I *loved* her," he hissed. "I would never raise a hand against her. Everything I'm doing right now I'm doing for Demir, because of her. You won't understand. You think I've been out in the rain stitching up wounded enforcers because I *wanted* to hurt them? No! I didn't have a choice. I didn't—"

Thessa tightened her grip on the copper coupling. In one movement, she spat the lit cigarette right into Breenen's face and yanked hard on the clasp. He stumbled back, sputtering and coughing. The two dragoons turned toward them but only laughed. Thessa used her foot to move the copper cable away from the phoenix channel.

"Glassdamn you!" Breenen growled, raising his hand. He seemed to wrestle with himself before lowering it, brushing the ash from his face. "You have no idea what I've been through. What Adriana went through. Why do you even care? You're a Holikan orphan. You should rejoice in anything that hurts Demir."

"If that's meant to hurt *me*," Thessa said, proud of how level her voice was, "it won't work. Demir already told me about Holikan." She raised her chin. "I've already forgiven him what little responsibility he held."

"Hah. So you're stronger than I thought. Fine. It doesn't matter. You're not a Grappo. You're going to Kerite and the Glass Knife, to await whatever pleasure they see fit." He paused, suddenly scowling, his gaze falling to the floor. "Why is the phoenix channel no longer grounded?"

Thessa lashed out with one foot, kicking Breenen in the knee as hard as she could. It was no easy feat with her hands tied behind her back, and she stumbled to one side, tripped on the grounding cable, and would have fallen directly into the fire if she hadn't flung herself across it. She landed hard, the wind knocked out of her.

"Hey!" one of the dragoons said. "Cut it out!" He finally turned to insert himself into the argument. He loomed over her briefly before he went bug-eyed, a gasp escaping his lips. Behind him, Tirana stood free of her bonds, a small belt knife in her hand. She stabbed twice more in quick succession, then did a quick hop and skip, burying the knife in the other dragoon's neck as he tried to draw his sword.

Thessa rolled painfully onto her side, trying to get her knees back under her. "Cut my bonds," she told Tirana, "and unhook the other coupling. I will glassdamned throw the phoenix channel in the ocean before giving it to these Glass Knife assholes." She got one leg under her, tried to get up, and fell. When she tried to get up a second time she came up to find that Breenen was holding a pistol, leveled at all three of them.

"I don't want to kill any of you," he said, "but I will. Now hook the phoenix channel back up to the grounding cable. You're not throwing it in the ocean."

"Piss off," Thessa snapped.

Tirana squared herself, looking ready to leap across the room, pistol or not. "You say you do this for Demir, but can you even imagine what he'll do when he finds out?"

"It doesn't matter what he'll do," Breenen answered. "He will already be saved. That's all I want."

Tirana danced from one foot to the other. A rumble of thunder shook the lighthouse, and through the small window Thessa saw a flash. She looked from the grounding cable to the phoenix channel, then at the lightning rod. A second thought suddenly hit her. She rolled onto her back, kicking the phoenix channel with both feet. It scraped along the floor.

"Don't break it!" Breenen shouted.

Thessa kicked it again. The phoenix channel now pointed at the door and the hundred or so dragoons watching the battle outside on the Forge. "Omniglass magnifies sorcery," she told Breenen. "I wonder if it magnifies lightning as well." Another crack of thunder rattled the lighthouse, followed quickly by another. The flashes of lightning were right on top of the sound of thunder now. Right on top of the Forge.

"Stop touching anything!" Breenen knelt down, snatching up a second pistol from a fallen dragoon and aiming it at Tirana. "Put everything back the way it was, or I'll kill you both."

"No," Thessa spat. No more cowering. No more being bullied and captured. "I am no one's slave."

"Fine," Breenen said, raising his chin. He pulled the trigger, and the blast of the pistol filled the room. Thessa felt something tear through her, snatching the breath from her—a dull realization followed by a sharp, screaming pain. Tirana leapt toward Breenen, knife swinging, while Pari threw herself, still bound, toward Thessa. A second pistol shot rang through the lighthouse. Tirana stumbled, dropping her knife.

The door suddenly burst inward. Captain Hellonian stood with his pistol at the ready. "What the *piss* is going on here?"

Thessa met his gaze, still trying to grasp the pain coursing through her. He frowned, shook his head, and opened his mouth. Before he could say anything, Thessa felt every hair on her body stand on end. A rushing sound filled her ears for a brief moment, and then Hellonian disintegrated in a blinding light.

60

Kizzie kept screaming the word "Run!" She wasn't sure if it was for Montego's benefit or to convince herself to act, rather than dwell on the horror she'd just witnessed, but she made good on her own advice by coaxing every bit of strengthening sorcery from her forgeglass just to keep herself moving. They had to escape this massive labyrinth of a building, to get out into the open, to find safety *somewhere*.

Montego's heavy footsteps followed her, and behind him the screaming of that eldritch creature as it thundered after them. She caught a glimpse of it as she rounded a corner, massive limbs tearing off the rest of its human skin as it ran to reveal rippling, constrictor-like bluish-gray sinew. Behind the creature, like a swarm of rats following in its footsteps, were dozens of acolytes armed with knives and cudgels. A cacophony of shouts echoed from the depths of the building; an alarm passing along to Aristanes's followers. Every turn brought more, sprinting toward them from down long hallways, emerging from doors, appearing on balconies as Kizzie desperately tried to find an exit. Windows were barred, doors locked.

"Where the piss did we come in?" she shouted over her shoulder to Montego.

The cudgelist didn't respond. His heavy breathing was almost as loud as the shouting, ripping ragged from his lungs. She thought she recognized a hallway and took a quick turn, giving her another glimpse of the creature behind her. It had stripped away most of the human skin by now and was gaining on them, almost eight feet tall and wider than Montego, a massive, toothy grin stretching across its tentacled face.

She realized too late that she'd made a mistake, and that the hall she'd thought she recognized was only leading them deeper into the mansion. Glimpsing a heavy door that *might* lead somewhere, she threw herself at it, snaking inside and holding it open long enough for Montego to follow her before heaving it shut behind them. Both she and Montego threw their weight against the door. A massive thump impacted on the other side, hard enough that she thought the whole doorframe might come apart. By some miracle it held, and she threw the bolt and backed away.

"Uh, Kizzie," Montego huffed.

She turned to find him looking around the room, her dismay growing as she realized that this *didn't* lead anywhere. It was an office, a little smaller than Aristanes's, with heavy bars on the narrow windows, a few empty, broken bookshelves, and a dusty, rotting desk.

"Oh no," she whispered. She could barely think through her terror, fumbling in her pocket for skyglass before realizing she'd already put it on. There was another heavy thump on the door, rattling the entire room, causing plaster dust to fall from the ceiling. The creature screamed in something that vaguely resembled a language. "What do we do what do we do what do we do?" she found herself repeating like it might possibly help them. She turned to Montego, her hands trembling. "I'm sorry, Baby. I'm so sorry. This isn't how I meant it to . . ." She trailed off. Something about Montego startled her out of her panic.

His face was calm, his eyes thoughtful. Montego examined the room clinically. "You're small enough to slip through the bars here if we break the glass. You can go for help, maybe drive that *thing* out into broad daylight."

"Wha . . . what? I'm not leaving you here alone." She didn't think she could grow *more* terrified, yet the thought of abandoning Montego did just that.

"Suit yourself," Montego replied. He removed his jacket in a graceful, practiced move. His tunic followed, and he folded them both and set them on the floor. He was left in a long pair of pants. He rotated at the waist, then bent and touched his toes.

His absolute stoicism went miles to calm her. "What the piss are you doing?" she asked, flinching as another thump caused more plaster to fall.

"I'm stretching."

"Why?"

"Always stretch before a fight."

"Are you *insane*?" she demanded.

Montego took his cane in one hand and expertly unscrewed the silver bear head, placing it with his shirt and tunic then drawing out something that looked like a croquet ball from his pants pocket. He slotted the end of the cane against it, twisted both, and as quick as that was holding a cudgel.

The doorframe began to splinter. It would not hold more than a few more moments against the onslaught.

"Baby," she whispered. She was absolutely certain she would die now, and was not taking that new realization well. "You can't fight that thing. You didn't see what it did to the watchhouse."

"If you won't leave without me," Montego said calmly, "then I want you to keep those acolytes off my back. This will take all of my attention."

Montego squared himself toward the door, taking a few experimental swings with his cudgel. "I am the greatest killer in the world," he declared, his voice rising as he spoke, his eyes taking on a terrifying fire. "I will not concede that title to a freak from an adventure novel. I am Baby Montego!" He was roaring at the door now, shoulders thrown back, chest thrust out. "You hear that, Tall Man? I am Montego, and I will *end* you!"

The door erupted inward at the last word, the eldritch being having to duck to lunge through the opening, massive taloned fingers reaching out toward Montego's throat with a speed that Kizzie could barely follow. Even faster still, Montego swung his cudgel, bringing it down across the hand like a teacher might use a ruler to reprimand a student. The creature hissed, pulling back in pain. It unhinged its jaw and let out a scream that rattled Kizzie's bones.

Montego charged. He hit the thing full in the chest with one shoulder, sending them both out of the room and into the hallway, where his bulk smashed the Tall Man against the opposite wall. The impact barely seemed to faze the Tall Man, and it snatched Montego by one arm and hurled him down the hallway. Kizzie suddenly found herself feeling very small and alone, staring through the destroyed door at the horrific beast. It righted itself, writhing inhumanly to get its feet back under it. It stared hungrily at Kizzie, strands of frothing spittle dripping from the corners of its mouth.

Montego reappeared and smashed his cudgel across its face with force that would have turned a man's head into paste. His arm was a blur, face crimson with rage, punctuating every word with a blow that drove the thing back to the ground. "Do! Not! Turn! Away! From! Me! When! We! Fight!" The Tall Man's massive arm darted out, grabbing Montego by the wrist to stop the final blow. Montego balled his left fist and slammed it into the thing's jaw, then grabbed it by the other arm. The two grappled and strained, the creature's claws biting into Montego's arms until blood ran down them. It began to *push* Montego back down the hall.

The two left Kizzie's vision, framed as it was by the destroyed doorway, and were almost immediately replaced by a dozen armed acolytes, stalking after, weapons raised, clearly looking for an opening in which to help their monstrous ally. The sight of them seemed to snap Kizzie out of herself, mind clearing of that terrible fog. She was not Montego. She could not hope to fight something like the Tall Man, but she was glassdamned Kizzie Vorcien.

Human acolytes were not her match.

She thrust her hand into her pocket, finding the piece of high-resonance forgeglass within and threading it through a piercing in her right ear in one quick move. The sorcery pounded through her in an instant, more powerful than anything she'd ever felt, coursing in her veins in a way that made her muscles want to explode. She held her sword in one hand, drew a stiletto with the other, and hurled herself out the door, hitting the acolytes from the side.

Hers was not a brute-force attack like Montego's. She ducked and swerved, sword and knife darting, reversing direction a dozen times in as many steps, dancing through the crowd. Thrust, move, slice, thrust, roll, leap. Her own speed astonished her, so much so that the witglass in her braided earrings could barely keep her mind equal to the tasks her body was performing. In moments she was on the other side of the hall, stumbling, catching herself against the wall and staring down at the corpses now littering the floor.

"Holy shit," she breathed. "This stuff is incredible." She spun on the ball of her foot, looking for Montego, only to see him tossed through a wall. He reappeared a moment later, rebounding through the hole he'd just made with his body, cudgel swinging at a blinding speed as he swept out the Tall Man's legs and smashed its shoulder. The Tall Man forced him back with its talons, and the two wrestled each other around the corner of the next hall.

Kizzie looked down at the gore dripping from her blades. She had mere minutes to wear the high-resonance forgeglass before it began to kill her. The odds were overwhelming, too many acolytes racing down the hall toward her. Montego was already torn up bloody by the Tall Man's claws. They were going to die here, she was certain of it.

But they were going to die well.

61

Despite all his careful planning, Demir's flanks began to buckle. Kerite's infantry were just too well-trained, their forgeglass too strong, and it made them inexorable as their charge turned into a bayoneted shoving match between them and the Foreign Legion. Demir snapped off orders, sending signal after signal, messenger after messenger. His cavalry charged from the side, but Kerite's troops managed to turn and face them, firing a volley before presenting bayonets, forcing dragoons and cuirassiers alike to withdraw.

It was a bloody morass, shouted orders above the sound of men and horses screaming in pain, punctuated by the staccato of musket shots from either side. The air was choked with powder smoke, causing Demir's head to spin. From his vantage point he could see his flanks tremble against Kerite's might, and the center begin to crack. Infantry began to look over their shoulders, searching for a way to run.

Every one of them knew that to run was to die, and yet there was no overcoming the base instinct when they caught a whiff of a losing battle.

"Glassdamnit," Demir called, "get those cuirassiers regrouped for another charge! Don't let the dragoons get caught up with the infantry, I want them harassing from horseback. Halfwing, turn your mortars to the west. Give me shelling at two hundred yards!" He swore again, pacing the top of the barrow as the small honor guard of Ironhorn soldiers fidgeted nervously around him.

"They need more hammerglass in their spines," Tadeas growled. "That center is going to fold!"

"I know," Demir snapped at his uncle. He had nothing left. No reserves, no tricks. It was a slog between soldiers now, and it was clear that Kerite was winning. Out across the battlefield he caught sight of her flag, far to the rear of her soldiers, held in the middle of a group of officers on horseback. One of them, he imagined, was Kerite. As he stared at her, aloof and distant, he realized that he did have one trick left. He had himself. "Get the Grappo flag," he told Tadeas, "and draw your sword."

A couple of hundred soldiers. A handful of engineers. That was all he had left. Not nearly enough to turn the tide of a battle. He cursed the self-defeating thought. This was still a knife's edge. All he needed was a breeze to send it in either direction. "Ironhorns!" he shouted. "Horns ready, hooves steady!"

"Horns ready, hooves steady!" his honor guard bellowed back.

Demir drew his sword and did the one thing that good guild-family Ossan officers weren't supposed to do: he entered the melee. They barreled down from the barrow, slamming into the back of their own troops like hammering a brace into place to steady a cracking roof joist. A handful of short-range grenades soared over his head, exploding among the rear ranks of the Drakes. Demir was shoulder-to-shoulder with the soldiers now, the scent of mud and death burning through the powder smoke in his nostrils. He threw his sorcerous senses wide, searching for enemy glassdancers, then tossed his glassdancer egg into the air over his head.

He only shattered it into two pieces, firing them both in the same direction and guiding their path by feel rather than sight. They sped along, occasionally lagging in his mind's eye as they tore through flesh. The sorcerous light on the edges of his senses suddenly winked out. He spun the glass shards, kept them moving. Another glassdancer died.

He was so focused on his glass that he didn't see the enemy bayonet until it was inches from his eye. He jerked to one side and felt it slice down his cheek and snag his ear, tearing a pained scream from him. He let go of the sorcery carrying his egg and stabbed with his smallsword, ramming it through the chest of the mercenary immediately in front of him. He felt hands on his shoulders, pulling him backward, and then Tadeas stood between him and the enemy, sword swinging.

Demir pressed one hand against his face, the cool air biting at the gash. He reached out his senses to find his glassdancer egg shards once more, using them to cut through a swath of enemy troops. Messengers yelled reports from behind him, forcing him to focus on a dozen different things at once.

His response wasn't enough. Even with the Ironhorns, they couldn't quite push back Kerite's troops. One side was going to break at any moment and Demir could sense it would be his. He swore and shoved and stabbed, urging on the infantry around him.

A bright light suddenly blinded him. It was just a flash, there for a split second, but he found himself reeling backward as he tried to blink the memory of it from his vision. A moment later thunder like nothing he'd ever heard split the air, rumbling over every other sound on the battlefield. He gasped, trying to pinpoint the source—and he wasn't the only one. Even Kerite's infantry stumbled from the light and sound, looking over their shoulders.

It took just a few moments for Demir to realize that it came from the Forge. Even from miles away, he could see that the distant rocky headland *glowed* with orange flame, steam shooting up into the storm still raging above it. Demir's stomach twisted. It could only have been Thessa's phoenix channel, and *no one* could survive a blast like that.

Demir swallowed the lump in his throat, looking around at the soldiers from both sides still reeling and confused. It was as if the fight had been snuffed out of all of them at once. He could use this. He thrust his sword in the sky and he bluffed. "Ossa! Our secret weapon is here! To victory!" He turned to the soldier next to him, screaming with every ounce of confidence he could muster until the victorious joy passed to the next man, then the next, then the next.

"To victory! To victory! That weapon is ours! To victory!" The call raced up and down the lines, putting steel into the Ossan soldiers, who finally began to overwhelm Kerite's infantry.

In that moment, mere yards from the closest mercenaries, he could see the confidence die in their eyes, and they broke.

62

Thessa had never felt such pain. It coursed through her, roiling out from her side in great waves that caused her to convulse, only worsening the horrible feeling. Her vision was cloudy, her thoughts were a mess, and it took her some time to understand that someone was shouting in her ear.

"Thessa! Jailbird, listen to me! You have to bite down on this cureglass."

Thessa blinked until her eyes finally began to focus. The voice belonged to Pari. Both she and Tirana crouched over her. They were still in the lighthouse, though half the wall was missing. She could smell smoke and burnt meat, a terrible heat like a Balkani sauna. Tirana held one hand tightly against her own mangled bloody shoulder, but she had both milkglass and cureglass in her ear.

"I'm sorcery-aphasic!" Thessa finally managed, shoving Pari's offering of godglass away. "It's not going to bloody well help me! I need a surgeon." She tried to shift herself, only for the pain to hit her again. Her memories began to fit together preceding the blinding white light that still echoed in her mind's eye. "Did Breenen shoot me?"

"The traitor shot us both," Tirana spat, looking down at her shoulder. "But he didn't shoot to kill. He was too much of a coward to finish the job. Him and his glassdamned traitor enforcers. I'm going to skin every one of them."

"After we save Thessa," Pari snapped.

"Fine. Come on, this is going to hurt."

"Hurt" was an understatement. Thessa nearly fainted twice as they got her to her feet, one of them under each arm. She looked around, trying to get her bearings, before a realization hit her. "The phoenix channel. Where is it?"

"Where do you think? Breenen and his goons took it when they fled. There were just a few of them left. That blast killed everyone else standing in front of the lighthouse. Every single dragoon."

Thessa felt her knees grow even weaker, and when she tumbled she almost took both her companions down with her. She stared at the empty copper cables that had coupled to either side of the phoenix channel. Its absence felt like a dead spot in her heart. All that work. All that pain and suffering. She turned away, averting her eyes, only to look through what had once been the wall of the lighthouse.

The Forge was completely transformed. The untethered phoenix channel had ripped a valley through the center of it, starting from the door of the lighthouse and disappearing out of sight. It sizzled and cracked in the rain, belching steam that filled her nostrils with the scent of charred rock and burnt bodies. "You said the dragoons are gone?" she asked weakly.

"Yeah," Pari said stiffly. "Along with most of Breenen's enforcers, our carriages, and everything else we brought with us. Our own wounded were around the side and it's the only reason they survived."

"Glassdamn," Thessa whispered. She had hoped for a distraction, not a disaster. "Why didn't Breenen take me with him?" she asked.

"He didn't have enough enforcers to carry both you and the channel," Tirana grunted. "Now come on, we should move."

Pulled along by the other two, Thessa began to limp forward, more and more of the unnatural valley coming into sight as she neared the edge of the Forge. It extended for more than a mile, cutting a jagged furrow across the scrubland below the Forge. Down below, a handful of their loyal enforcers picked at what remained, trying to find supplies. "Wait!" She tried to turn back to the lighthouse, nearly falling as she put all her weight back on Tirana. "Did it even work? The phoenix channel?"

Tirana and Pari exchanged a look. "What," Pari said, "do you think I was trying to get you to put between your teeth?" She reached into her pocket and pulled out a whole handful of godglass, holding it out in front of Thessa. Each piece resonated with sorcery, full of color and life. Thessa's breath caught in her throat, and she pushed down her pain using only her rage.

It worked. It worked, and then it was stolen from her.

"We're going to find those traitors," she told Tirana, "and when we do I'll help you skin them."

>   >   >

Kizzie tore the forgeglass earring from her piercing and hurled it away. Her whole body ached, her head pounding, glassrot nausea sweeping through her so powerfully that she thought she'd empty her stomach at any moment. Both arms and hands were covered in yellow scales, skin crackling as she moved them. She lay sprawled on the ground, her head and shoulders propped up by the wall, tunic heavy with blood that was almost entirely not her own.

A single acolyte, the last man she'd come across before her strength finally failed her, lay on the ground just a few feet away, her sword buried to the hilt in his eye. His foot still twitched, though he was certainly dead. She didn't know what had happened to her stiletto. She found her gaze resting on the razorglass blade tattooed on the acolyte's hand.

Where was Aristanes? Where were the rest of these acolytes? The shouts of alarm no longer echoed through the long halls. Somewhere in the distance, as if from the bottom of a well, she could still hear the Tall Man's snarls and inhuman screams, accompanied by the sound of walls and furniture being destroyed. She should get up, go find them, and do what she could to help. Could she even move? Every sinew felt utterly destroyed by the very sorcery that had gotten her this far.

She had often wondered why the very richest and most powerful guild-families didn't employ high-resonance godglass more often. She'd always assumed it was because the costs were prohibitive, but now that she'd felt the firsthand effects of it, she knew it would take days, perhaps weeks to recover. If she'd fought for just a few seconds longer, it might have consumed her entirely.

She closed her eyes, listening to her own frantic, shallow breaths, waiting for more acolytes to appear and finish her off. It wasn't like she could put up a fight.

Some time had passed, though she couldn't be sure how much, when the distant sound of fighting suddenly ceased. She strained her senses, remembering that she still wore the skyglass and her braided earrings, trying to determine which of the two combatants had come out victorious.

Slowly, she grew aware of a scraping sound, like that of an armored body being dragged along marble floors. It was coming toward her, of that she was certain. Shuffle, shuffle, scrape. Shuffle, shuffle, scrape. Her nerves were dead, her body so wrung out that she didn't think it possible to feel terror for her own death anymore. The sound continued to approach, until a shadow darkened the far end of the hall and a monstrous form appeared.

It was the Tall Man. The creature was much reduced, its massive, leathery body bleeding from dozens of wounds. It left a trail of black, tar-like blood. Yellow bile oozed from the one eye that remained open, and dripped from both ears. Several of the tentacles had been ripped off its face. It swung its head back and forth until it spotted Kizzie, then turned toward her, one leg dragging behind it as it limped toward her.

Shuffle, shuffle, scrape.

Kizzie tried to gather the strength to crawl over to that last corpse and extract her sword. She wanted to die with a weapon in her hand, at least, but found that it was too much. She took a few deep breaths and managed to get the blackjack out of her back pocket. It would do hilariously little to such a beast, even wounded as it was, but at least it was *some* kind of weapon. She held it out in front of her like a pistol, waiting for the Tall Man to fall upon her.

The creature came to within a few feet and stopped, hulking over her like a statue, brilliant blue eyes glistening as it stared down at her. It cleared its throat, and what came out next surprised her with its human sound.

"We were going to offer you a place among us," it said softly.

Kizzie scoffed. "What, you can turn me into something like *you*?"

"No, no," the Tall Man replied, its voice full of world-weary exhaustion. "You cannot change *races*. But you can serve us." It looked down at the acolyte with Kizzie's sword buried in his eye.

"Piss off," Kizzie replied. She felt completely dead inside, all of her fear replaced by the pain and nausea of too much godglass sorcery. "I'm not made to be the acolyte of a monster."

The Tall Man made a motion that seemed very much like a shrug, but Kizzie couldn't be sure with its inhuman anatomy and drooping arms. "Then we have arrived at the same conclusion." It reached toward her with one set of talons.

"Montego is dead?" Kizzie asked, letting the hand holding her blackjack fall. What was the point, anyway? Dying with a weapon? Without it? She would still be dead. Just like Baby. She tried to find anything within her but shock. Montego had been killed, and it was her fault.

The Tall Man paused, head tilting slightly, its talons curling inward in a surprisingly gentle gesture. "I didn't know that a human could fight like that. I will craft a song for him, I think. It's been hundreds of years since I did so, but he was worthy. The Yuglid will sing of him for long after humanity is dead."

Yuglid. So this creature had a name for what it was. A race, even. "There's *more* of you?" Kizzie asked in disbelief.

"You have no idea," the Tall Man chuckled. It looked down at itself, and Kizzie could almost see annoyance in that inhuman face. "It will take me months to grow my human skin back. Oh well. You proved yourself, Kissandra Vorcien. I'll make this quick." It began to reach out once more, and Kizzie closed her eyes and waited for the sharp pain of death. A whisper reached her ears, and then a soft grunt, and she waited for several more seconds before opening her eyes again.

The Yuglid had fallen to its knees, eyes wide in panic, arms flailing. Montego stood over its shoulder, face a sheath of blood both crimson and black, teeth bared and one muscular arm braced across the Yuglid's neck. The Yuglid thrashed, slapping backward with its hands, talons scraping deep grooves across Montego's cherub-like cheeks. Montego flinched, hissing in pain, but did not let go. He raised his other arm, and Kizzie could see that he held her missing stiletto, which he buried in the Yuglid's neck.

The Yuglid's thrashing grew more desperate, but it did not die. It gurgled and spat, mouth hanging open, trying to breathe, eyes full of fury.

"Because," Montego said, as if answering an unspoken question through gritted teeth, "you turned your back on the greatest killer in the world without making sure he was dead." He began to saw with the stiletto, ripping a jagged line across the front of the Yuglid's neck, just above the sternum. "I will not be some glassdamned song for your pissing race. I am Baby Montego and I will sing my own song." The Yuglid shook and stirred, nearly bucking Montego from its back, but Montego's braced arm did not release. He paused with the stiletto long enough to drive an elbow down against the Yuglid's neck, the force of which seemed to break the creature's will. The thrashing stopped, and Montego tossed aside the stiletto and grasped the Tall Man's bestial head between his palms.

Twisting and pulling, he ripped its head off.

Black blood fountained from the severed neck. The creature slumped and fell, leaving Montego standing behind it, holding the head, which slowly slipped from his fingers. It was now, without the Yuglid blocking her view, that Kizzie understood why the Tall Man had thought Montego was dead. The big fighter was torn up, torso sliced to absolute ribbons, pieces of fat hanging from his stomach like he'd been worked over by a blind butcher. His pants were so heavy with blood that they were sliding down, and his mighty body heaved and trembled with every breath.

The eerie silence of death fell across the empty mansion. Montego looked down at himself, then up at Kizzie. "I know I look terrible," he said, "but Kizzie Vorcien, would you like to get tea with me sometime?" His eyes went suddenly glassy, and he collapsed on top of the Yuglid's corpse.

Kizzie summoned every ounce of strength she could muster, crawling across the marble floor until she reached him. He was completely still, no sign of life left in his body until she managed to get her cheek right up against his mouth and could still feel the heat of his breath. She raised her head, looking around at the carnage, wondering how she could possibly get them both out of here.

"I'd like that," she said softly, and began to pull herself up onto her feet.

▸   ▸   ▸

Idrian reached the medical tents with Braileer slung across his shield like on a stretcher, balanced on his shoulder. He'd covered miles at a dead run, listening to Braileer's gasping breaths and panicked crying the entire way. Crying was good, he told himself. It meant the young armorer was still alive.

Idrian shoved his way past the Foreign Legion reserves guarding the medical camp and into the biggest of the tents, where a constant stream of wounded soldiers flooded in carried by National Guardsmen recruited for the dirty but necessary work of dealing with casualties. He set Braileer carefully down on one of the hundreds of bloody wooden slabs. "Glory!" he bellowed for the Ironhorns' own surgeon. "Glory, get over here!"

"One moment," came the answer from the other side of the tent. A dozen heads turned, surgeons and medics staring at Idrian briefly before returning to their work. Some of them did nothing more than distribute cure-glass and then move their patients back out of the tent, while others worked with needles, knives, and bone saws to try and save those that needed more than sorcery to stabilize them.

Idrian was soon joined by a hatchet-faced man with dark Marnish skin, wearing a pair of armless spectacles balanced on the tip of his nose. Glory got his nickname from always giving a little more attention to soldiers who were wounded doing something "interesting," no matter how stupid. He had his work cut out for him in a battalion of combat engineers.

"This is the kid with the fiddle, isn't it?" Glory asked, scowling down at Braileer. He leaned over. "I'm going to need you to stop making that stupid sound," he said in Braileer's face. "It's annoying, and it's making it harder for you to breathe."

"It's called crying, Glory," Idrian said. "And you hear it all the time."

"It's still annoying."

"Take it easy on him," Idrian snapped. His chest felt tight. He *knew* the poor kid was going to die, ever since their conversation about death. He was too soft for the army. Too good-hearted. Idrian should never have let him come on that mission. A dozen other recriminations bounced around inside his head, all while the phantoms of his madness laughed in his ears.

Glory moved up and down Braileer's body with clinical precision, first checking his neck and then listening to his breath at the mouth and chest. "What happened?"

"You know that rumor about the thing I fought on top of Fort Alameda?" Idrian asked. He saw Braileer flail weakly with one hand and reached out to take it.

"Yeah."

"It got him. It broke Squeaks's arm and killed two of Valient's soldiers, too. Jorfax won't be that far behind me either. She had a horse fall on her."

"Squeaks *just* broke an arm," Glory sighed. In Idrian's experience, the surgeon had just two emotions: mildly irritated and very irritated. "Glass-damnit, probably the same one."

Idrian rocked back and forth on his heels as Glory continued his examination, biting his tongue so he didn't yell at the surgeon to hurry up. It would only get on his nerves. Idrian looked around the tent and then toward the constant stream of wounded coming around a nearby hill. "How close are we to the battle?"

"Half a mile behind it," Glory said without looking up. "Some of the Drakes' dragoons brushed past us not long ago but they respected the medical sigils we're flying. Thank the glass for that."

"Any idea how the battle is going?" Idrian asked. By all rights he shouldn't linger. He should get to the front line immediately and see what he could do to help.

Glory shook his head and then produced a piece of pain-deadening milkglass, slipping it into one of the piercings in Braileer's ear. He jerked his head for Idrian to follow. Idrian squeezed Braileer's hand once, then followed the surgeon a few feet away. He could feel his heart fall at the look on Glory's face. Glory said, "He has a crushed windpipe and no small amount of internal bleeding, not to mention two broken fingers. Probably cracked ribs as well."

"Can he be saved?" Idrian demanded.

"Can he, or will he? The answer to the second question is no."

Idrian inhaled sharply. "What the piss is that supposed to mean? He's a corporal and my armorer. Whatever needs to be done you better get to it now!"

Glory took Idrian's arm, his expression hardening. "Look, we have a massive deficit of cureglass right now. I've got a single piece of high-resonance, and orders from both the Ministry of the Legion and the Inner Assembly say I can't give it to anyone but glassdancers, high-ranking officers, and breachers."

"Then pretend it's for me."

"I can't. Those provosts over there are watching for exactly that. My hands are tied. Not even General Grappo can overrule those orders."

Idrian's stomach hurt from worry and anger. Another damned kid dead in another damned war thanks to the orders of rich assholes well away from the fighting. "Who *can* authorize it?" he demanded.

"Lieutenant Prosotsi is just over there. She has the tiniest amount of discretion but she's terrified to use it. She's turned down dozens of requests to use high-resonance cureglass on regular soldiers."

Idrian knew the reality of war, and he sympathized with both the officers and the surgeons. Those decisions—especially when they didn't have enough cureglass—had to be made, and it was unpleasant for everyone involved. "What's going to be done?"

"I'm gonna leave that piece of milkglass in his ear and have him carried out back to the Dying Club." Glory grimaced. "It'll take him a couple hours to die, but he's not going to feel much pain while he does it."

The Dying Club was what the soldiers darkly called the spot designated for those who couldn't be saved. "And how," Idrian asked slowly, "would we keep him from dying?"

"Immediate surgery. Puncture his throat to get him air, open him up to drain excess blood and stitch up whatever is torn, then put him back together again. High-resonance cureglass *might* keep him alive during all that, but there's no guarantee."

Idrian looked over at Braileer, then clutched at the little chain he wore around his own neck. What had Jorfax told him? That he was too soft, willing to raise his shield to protect people he didn't even know? Perhaps it made him a less efficient killer, but it *did* let him sleep at night. Idrian could feel the madness clawing at the back of his godglass eye, auditory and visual hallucinations threatening to overwhelm him. He pressed on the godglass eye until they grew quiet, then strode over to Lieutenant Prosotsi. She was a middle-aged woman with short black hair, looking slightly queasy as she gazed across the surgery slabs.

"Ma'am," Idrian said, "I want you to approve the use of high-resonance cureglass for that kid over there." He pointed toward Braileer. "He's my armorer and he can still be saved."

Lieutenant Prosotsi shook her head regretfully. "I can't do it, I'm sorry. Orders from the top."

Idrian rubbed gently at the temple behind his godglass eye, his stomach falling. Suddenly, as if a candle had been smothered, all the noise in his head went quiet. He knew what he needed to do. He reached beneath his uniform collar and unclasped the little silver tag hanging there. "This is my debt marker. It expires in a few days."

The lieutenant's eyes widened. "You get to walk before this war is over."

"Correct. I'll take another year on this debt marker if you authorize the cureglass."

"Are you sure about that?" She shifted her weight, and he could see the decision rolling around inside her head. A good Ossan would accept in a heartbeat. A good officer would turn him down, not letting him put off his retirement for something so stupid. Lieutenant Prosotsi clearly couldn't decide which she was.

"I'm absolutely certain," Idrian said firmly. "Make it happen."

She walked away, briefly consulting with a nearby provost. The conversation lasted just a few seconds, and when she returned she made an affirmative gesture toward Glory. "Done. The Empire now owns another year of your life, Captain Sepulki."

Idrian turned to fetch his sword and shield. They might need him at the battle, and there was nothing more he could do here with Braileer in Glory's capable hands. He considered what he'd done, already missing the little silver debt marker from where it usually lay against his skin. They'd give him another, with the new dates of his service written on it. What would Jorfax say? That he was a disgrace to killers everywhere?

Let her say it. If Braileer lived, then Idrian would have nothing to regret.

Braileer lay on the slab, delirious from a new piece of dazeglass Glory had thrust into his ear. Idrian paused briefly beside him, squeezing his shoulder, then met Glory's eyes. "Horns ready, hooves steady," he said.

Glory nodded back. "Horns ready, hooves steady," he replied as he lifted his scalpel.

❦   ❦   ❦

Demir watched as the last of Kerite's mercenaries fled the battle, his pursuing cuirassiers destroying all pretense of an organized retreat. He gritted his teeth at the slaughter, his eyes unconsciously avoiding the grisly sight of thousands of dead and wounded splayed out across the field. It was a clear victory, no less bold and dramatic than the one he'd won nine years ago outside the suburbs of Holikan, and a little part of him wondered if he had a military artist to capture the moment.

Why, though? There was no need to picture all the gore and the suffering. People would remember his victory—they'd remember when the invincible mercenary general was rebuffed from the gates of Ossa. That was all that mattered.

"Signal our cavalry to pull back," Demir said.

"Are you sure?" Tadeas asked. Demir's uncle was badly wounded, a saber slash cutting a bloody swath across his chest, though he proudly wore cureglass and milkglass and kept his position at Demir's side. "We have them on the run. It's best to press our advantage."

"We've practically destroyed that mercenary company," Demir said. "No more slaughter. If they regroup, we'll crush them. Otherwise let them flee to the coast. They've served their contract and this is no longer their war."

"I'll send the order."

To the northwest, the Forge still glowed and smoldered as the storm finally moved past it. He made a mental note to send his own dragoons to search for Thessa as soon as the battlefield was completely clear.

Demir caught sight of a small group on a distant hill, and searched for a looking glass to point in that direction. It was a dozen or so cuirassiers in shining breastplates, flying the three blue drakes on a green field. In their midst was a middle-aged woman with light skin and long brown hair, a helmet held under one arm. She stared directly at him, and though she had no looking glass of her own, Demir imagined she could see him just as easily as he her.

Devia Kerite. The hero of his youth. The greatest general in the world, brought low by the disgraced patriarch of a small guild-family. Demir paused that thought and amended it. No. That was not how this had gone. History was written today but not by a minor, disgraced patriarch.

"After you've sent that order," Demir said, watching through the looking glass as Kerite and her bodyguards turned to leave the field, "prepare a missive for the Inner Assembly. Tell them that the Lightning Prince met the Purnian Dragon on the field of battle and was victorious."

EPILOGUE

Professor Sumala Volos lifted her head to the northwest, feeling on edge ever since that horrific sound had blasted through the early-afternoon sky. Everyone for hundreds of miles must have heard it. The birds had only just now started to sing again. Was it man-made? Perhaps an exploding ammunition depot? Or was it natural, like a volcano or a shifting of the continental plates?

She would have to search for answers later.

Volos's ox-drawn wagon, packed with books and experiments and spare lightning rods to sell to Ossan architects, pulled up in front of the Zorlian Mansion. She had never liked the mansion back when the Zorlian guild-family practically owned Ossa, and she liked it even less now that it was an overgrown, dilapidated ruin. She paused at that thought, allowing herself a snort of derisive laughter. Actually, it was rather nice to see the Zorlian legacy laid so low. They certainly deserved it.

But she hadn't come here to sightsee or relive bygone memories. She parked her wagon in front of the mansion beside several carriages, noting that two of them were still hitched up to horses. She deduced that one wagon had recently arrived. The other was preparing to leave, and yet there was no one to be seen—no minders, drivers, or servants. The mansion was occupied, that much was obvious by the trodden grass and half-hearted re-pairs to the structure itself. So where was everyone?

She opened her mouth to taste the air. Death. Anger. Decay. She stretched out her tongue, letting the flavors roll around on it before deciding that the decay of the old mansion was hiding something else, something much harder to describe. It was hiding the taste of eons. She had, she decided, come to the right place.

Volos hopped down and checked the two wagons. One was unmarked. The other—the one that had recently arrived—had cushions marked with the Grappo silic sigil. Fascinating. Clasping her hands behind her back, Volos strolled through the open front door and followed the taste of death.

What she found surprised even her. There were dozens of fresh corpses lying where they'd fallen, their warm blood still spreading across the cracked marble floors. They were human bodies of diverse ages, all of them marked with a small tattoo of a razorglass knife on their right hand. It took her only a few moments to determine that they'd died fighting someone much faster than themselves.

The puzzle grew more interesting as she continued. A path of destruction wound through the middle of the mansion—walls destroyed, doors recently ripped from their hinges. There was blood everywhere, both red and black, and it was the latter that caused her to proceed with greater caution. She stepped lightly, her senses stretched to their limits, pausing to listen at every distant sound.

It was a moan of a dying woman that attracted her attention, and Volos cut through a small, collapsing concert hall and into a new hallway to find even more slaughter. There were another nine human bodies as well as a tenth—massive and alien, gray skin covered in black blood. A tentacled head lay a few feet away, sawed off brutally and discarded.

Volos stared at that head dispassionately for a few moments as she got her bearings, deducing everything that had happened. She dismissed the knife-tattooed acolytes and crouched briefly beside the gray-skinned alien body, touching the skin gently. "I warned you that this wasn't going to end well," she said, "but you never did listen to anyone but him." She lifted her gaze to the human that had killed him; a massive man, practically cut to ribbons, lying slumped in a pool of blood.

She peered harder, surprised that she recognized him. No wonder. It was Baby Montego.

Another moan finally brought her around, and Volos picked her way through the pools of blood over to a woman with a Vorcien silic sigil. The woman had tried to walk away from the fight but hadn't gotten more than a dozen paces. Her eyes fluttered open as Volos approached and knelt down next to her.

"I . . ." she rasped, "have to go . . . for help."

Volos looked her over. "You have acute resonance poisoning," she said. Severe glassrot, in layman's terms. The woman must know this, and yet she still clutched a piece of forgeglass in one hand, no doubt trying to get some extra strength to go for that help she wanted. Volos gently knocked the forgeglass away. "You'll recover," she diagnosed, "but you'll want to go at least a week without any contact with godglass whatsoever and perhaps a month or two after that to feel yourself again."

"My name . . . is Kizzie Vorcien. Help me, please. I . . . will repay . . . you."

Volos sat back on her haunches, considering the small silic sigil on Kizzie's hand. "You're one of Stutd's bastards, aren't you?"

"Yes. Please." It seemed to take her a monumental effort to speak, and yet she soldiered on. "Baby needs me."

"Montego?" Volos answered in surprise. "Montego is dead."

Kizzie's eyes closed and she shuddered. "No. He can't be. He was just standing . . . minutes . . . ago."

Volos almost ignored her. The butchered slab of meat that used to be Baby Montego was certainly dead, and yet . . . when Volos turned toward him, tasting the air, *something* rolled across her tongue. Life. Willpower. It was tenuous but definitely still there.

Volos returned to Montego and checked his pulse. Incredible. No wonder he had bested the Angry One. She checked Montego's neck, then under his arms, seeing a mix of both permanent and temporary glassrot scales. The scales were yellow with an orange tinge. "He appears to have an allergy to godglass," she said, glancing at Kizzie. "Giving him cureglass won't be enough. He needs surgery immediately."

"Please," Kizzie said, "anything you can . . . do to help."

Volos sighed. This was not what she'd expected when she followed rumors to this place. She wasn't ready to get involved yet, and certainly not with the Vorcien. She glanced among all the bodies, considering her options, her thoughts distant enough that she only just heard the sound of approaching footsteps.

"Don't bother with them," a voice called. "I intend to dispatch them post-haste."

She turned to look down the hall toward an older human with short black hair and olive skin who had appeared in a nearby doorway. Volos tasted the air. That sensation she'd touched earlier—the taste of eons passing—came from *him*. She tensed. "Hello Schemer," she said.

"Thinking One," he answered, using her formal name. "It's been a long time."

"Not long enough," Volos sniffed. "What name are you going by these days?"

"Aristanes," he said, bowing at the waist. "You?"

"Professor Volos." She returned his bow.

"Ah! I suspected that might have been you. I read your book on lightning rods. Very interesting research. I was not expecting you, otherwise I would have dealt with all this quicker."

Volos glanced over at Kizzie. The Vorcien's eyes were half open, attention shifting quickly from Volos to Aristanes and back again. She trembled, but there was fight in her yet. Volos could taste it. "It wasn't meant to be a formal visit. My publisher asked me to come to Ossa and sign books. I thought I'd search you out and see if you were still trying to kill everyone. I see that hasn't changed, even if your face has."

Aristanes glanced distastefully at all the bodies and then touched his chest. "You wound me. I'm the Schemer, not the Conquering One."

At the mention of another of their kind, Volos felt her eyes narrow. "She's around here somewhere, isn't she? I'm surprised you convinced her to help you. I thought better of her than becoming one of your lackeys."

"She came around." Aristanes grinned. "Many have. I take it by your tone that you, however, have not."

"Your grudges bore me," Volos told him. Even among the Yuglid she was considered distant and dispassionate, and yet Aristanes's presence stirred feelings inside of her—anger, fear, consternation. She was not surprised to find him sitting just outside the capital of the world's greatest empire, but it did cause her trepidation. What plans did he have in motion this time? How many millions would die? "You need a hobby."

"Destroying human civilization isn't a hobby?" he asked in surprise.

"I meant something like stamp collecting."

"Ah. You still think I should be like you. That I should assimilate." A dark gleam touched Aristanes's eyes. "It's me or them, Thinker, and the humans never stood a chance."

Volos nudged Montego with her boot. "This one did. He killed the Angry One in single combat. When's the last time one of us fell in single combat to a human?"

"An aberration. And soon to be dealt with."

Volos cursed herself silently and stepped around Montego to stand between him and Aristanes. The Willow always told her she had a soft heart when it came to humans. "I think not."

Aristanes snorted. "Battle lines have already been drawn. I don't mind if you watch from the arena walls—I'm not a zealot, after all—but if you get involved I won't give you a second chance."

"The Angry One would have wanted his bester spared," Volos reasoned.

"The Angry One is dead. He failed, so he doesn't get any final wishes."

Volos rolled up her sleeves. "I'm taking both of these with me," she said, reaching down for Montego. She moved casually, as if everything was right in the world, but she watched Aristanes carefully for any sudden moves.

"If you save them, they'll know what you are."

"As if we've never revealed ourselves to humans before—either of us," Volos snorted. "They keep secrets better than one might expect."

Aristanes's expression grew genuinely annoyed. "Why aid them?"

"Because I like humans, Schemer. They're infinitely interesting."

"They usurped our world. I only work to take back what is rightfully ours."

"As I said, your grudges bore me," Volos responded. She hovered just over Montego, waiting for Aristanes to either make his move or leave.

"I could kill you now," Aristanes warned.

It wasn't a bluff. Aristanes was much older and more experienced, but Volos shook her head all the same. "How long would it take you to grow back your human disguise after I rip it up? How many centuries will it set back your schemes when my sister comes looking for me? I'm not declaring war. I'm not attacking you. I'm just . . . leaving with a couple of half-dead humans. That's not a killing offense, and we still live by some codes."

They stared at each other for several moments before Aristanes finally huffed. "Fine," he spat. "Take your new pets and get out of my house." He turned and strode away, not even sparing a glance for the Angry One's corpse. It was that tiny insult toward a departed Yuglid that made Volos decide she'd made the right choice. She'd always thought Aristanes too cruel, but if he couldn't even say a few words in passing then he had truly lost his way.

"Schemer," she called after him.

He paused, his back still toward her.

She gestured at the crumbling, dilapidated mansion surrounding them. "You chose your house well. It is an apt metaphor."

"Go sign books," Aristanes replied. "Soon there will be no one to sign them for." He strode away, his footsteps echoing through the massive halls.

Volos sighed once more, gritting her teeth. What a sad, sad thought. Could he make good on that threat? He'd certainly brought down empires before. What about humanity itself? She did not have enough data to calculate his chances. She slid her hands underneath Montego's body, leveraging it onto her shoulder. The weight was little more than an awkward inconvenience to the eldritch body hidden within her human skin, and she whistled quietly to herself as she finally got him situated. She paused briefly beside the Angry One's body.

"Sleep well, poor soul," she said to him, then proceeded on to Kizzie. Volos scooped the Vorcien up with her other hand, ignoring the way Kizzie shuddered with fear.

"What are you?" Kizzie asked in a strained whisper.

Volos smiled down at her. "I," she said, "am a gentlewoman scientist. Now come, let's get your friend to somewhere I can perform surgery."

ACKNOWLEDGMENTS

Another book written, another gaggle of awesome people who have helped me get it to publication. First, thanks to my wonderful wife, Michele McClellan, for being there to bounce ideas and read my first drafts. Thanks to my editor Devi Pillai for taking a chance on a brand-new world; and thanks to all the support staff at Tor who have had a hand in creating, editing, visualizing, and marketing *In the Shadow of Lightning*.

Thanks of course to my wonderful agent, Caitlin Blasdell, and all the people at Liza Dawson Associates for their work selling the series. Thanks to my assistant, Casey Blair, and artists Ben McSweeney and Nigar Taghiyeva.

Huge thank-you to all of my professional consultants and early readers for helping me get everything straight within the text, including Anthony Scala, Ames Grawert, David Wohlreich, Rachel Lance, Nicole Lazar, Jay Dnihil, Mark Lindberg, Logan Moritz, Kris Nied, David Hill, Sam Baskin, Colton Long, Ted Herman, Chris Bailey, Zarin Ficklin, Clint Sheridan, Jon Seiglie, Rushikesh Joshi, Wyatt Nevins, Leticia Lara, Rahul Kanojia, Joshua Ely, Luke Kramarz, Glen Vogelaar, Josh Mulligan, Josh McDonald, Jordan Stiebritz, Colin Schmucker, Jon A. Melbye, Tim Elliott, and Michael Wyatt.

ABOUT THE AUTHOR

BRIAN MCCLELLAN is the author of the bestselling Powder Mage six-book flintlock fantasy series, published by Orbit in the US and UK. It has more than half a million copies in print and has been translated into more than a dozen languages.